MASTER
OF
RESTLESS
SHADOWS

BOOK TWO

GINN HALE

MASTER
OF
RESTLESS
SHADOWS

BOOK TWO

GINN HALE

blindeyebooks.com

MASTER OF RESTLESS SHADOWS
BOOK TWO
by Ginn Hale

Published by: BLIND EYE BOOKS
315 Prospect Street #5393
Bellingham WA 98227
www.blindeyebooks.com

Edited by Nicole Kimberling
Copyedit by Megan Gendell
Ebook Design by Michael DeLuca
Cover Art by Zaya Feli
Cieloalta City Map by Rhys Davies
Book Design and interior by Dawn Kimberling

First Edition February 2022 Copyright © 2022 Ginn Hale
Print ISBN: 978-1-935560-65-4
Ebook ISBN: 978-1-935560-66-1

Printed in the United States of America

Contents

CADELEON &
SURROUNDING NATIONS

Usane

Radulf
Lands

Labara

Rauma

Ceiloalta

CADELEON

Anacleto

Salt Islands

N
S

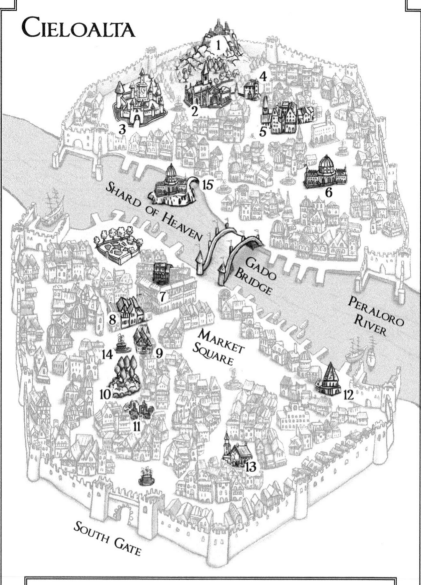

CIELOALTA

1 CROWN HILL
2 LORD QUEMANOR'S MANSION
3 SAGRADA ROYAL PALACE
4 COUNT ODALIS' HOME
5 DUKE OF GAVADO'S HOUSHOLD
6 ROYAL BISHOP'S HOUSEHOLD
7 RED STALLION
8 GREEN DOOR

9 FAT GOOSE
10 CIRCLE OF WISTERIA
11 KNIFE MARKET
12 LORD NUMES' HOUSE
13 SAVIOR'S CHAPEL
14 SHELL FOUNTAIN
15 DASMA BRIDGE

SHARD OF HEAVEN

GADO BRIDGE

PERALORO RIVER

MARKET SQUARE

SOUTH GATE

Ariz turned his short sword over in his hands, inspecting the heavy blade. Hours of sharpening and polishing had eradicated nearly all testimony to the violence of his last three weeks. Now only a single chip lingered to indicate the exact point where vertebrae had ground against the steel edge. No evidence at all remained from his fast, clean thrusts that had plunged between ribs to spear hearts and puncture lungs. At a glance, no one would have noticed anything but a sharp, white line where the setting sun's light caught the length of the blade.

In his youth, Ariz had admired that razor's edge of light and delighted in the thought that the white-hot stroke reflected the ferocity of a master smith's radiant forge. Now, beneath a weeping willow, he shifted his blade to hide its bright, killing edge. A breeze rose from the river and the green boughs swayed around Ariz. He moved with them, as if he were no more than a shadow.

Somewhere beyond this walled garden children laughed and shouted in a game of chase. A lonely nightingale sang out the first notes of an evening serenade. The scent of roses drifted from carefully tended trellises.

Ariz closed his grip on the worn haft of his short sword. The rough sharkskin grip that had once scrubbed his palm and fingers raw now fit his hand like a glove. The sword had calloused his skin and shaped the growing bones of his hands just as his sweat and hard grip had worn the leather. He and the sword were a perfect fit.

But Ariz no longer felt gratified by that thought. He maintained the blade's sharp edge and honed his own swift, sure thrusts not because he took any satisfaction in either anymore, but because it ensured the fastest, most painless end for his victims. That was the only mercy he could offer.

Across the garden grounds, light flared as the gray-haired minister of the navy stepped out from the door of his study. Two of the man's three personal guards hung back in the study. They would entertain and wait upon the minister's pregnant young wife. A single household guard trailed the minister as he ambled toward the decorative stone tower that overlooked the river. Every evening the minister climbed up and, as far as Ariz could tell, simply watched the setting sun light the sails of the ships far below. Perhaps he surveyed the number of Cadeleonian flags flying from masts. Or maybe he noted where foreign ships docked, Ariz couldn't say. What he did know was that the minister came to the tower unarmed and that his single guard's attention very often wandered to the voices of the young women in the scullery. Tonight the minister hummed a melody from a popular opera and the guard smiled in a way that made Ariz suspect that he'd made inroads wooing a scullery maid.

Ariz darted his gaze to the two men standing in the doorway of the study. The minister's wife teased them over their terrible suggestions for baby names and nursery songs.

They all felt so safe in this fragrant, familiar place.

Ariz couldn't shelter any of them from what he must do to fulfill Hierro's mission, but he would grant them what kindness he could. He would kill quickly.

As the minister neared the weeping willow, the scent of pipe smoke grew stronger. The minister ran his hand over the long boughs, inches from where Ariz stood. Leaves fluttered and whispered. Ariz waited, allowing the minister and his guard a few more seconds of peace. Then the minister's hand brushed Ariz's shoulder.

Ariz struck.

The minister's lined face didn't even register alarm before Ariz punched his sword through the swaying green boughs, slashing open the minister's throat. His bleeding body toppled. Ariz sidestepped, lunging for the guard.

The young guard turned at the noise, but he wasn't prepared for any greater threat than a garter snake or loose stone. Ariz drove his sword into the man's chest, then kicked the guard's dying body back off his blade. The guard fell, clutching for his own weapon and offering up a single shout. Ariz silenced him with a second blow, and for a moment burning agony surged through him as he purposefully turned his back on the two remaining guards and the minister's young wife.

Hierro wanted them all dead—slaughtered and gutted—and this peaceful garden transformed into a tableau of violence. He wanted a nightmare brought into the waking world, but Ariz would deny him that. He was no longer an utterly hapless sleepwalker. One day he might wake completely from Hierro's control. Until then, he'd resist as long as he could and endure the pain.

Searing agony shot through the brand in Ariz's chest. One of the guards in the study shouted and the minister's wife screamed. Ariz forced himself to sheath his sword.

He charged up the steps of the stone tower. The river far below shone gold in the sunset. Hundreds of ships plied the waters, looking like apple blossoms scattered across a brook. Ariz hardly noted any of it. He sprinted to the tower's precipice and leapt—heart hammering as his body hurtled through the air. He soared like an arrow loosed from a bow.

Then he plunged down into the dark mass of an aged oak tree.

Leaves swatted his face and his sweat-slick hands slipped across the branches. His shoulder smacked hard against a thick bough as he caught himself. He scrambled through the branches, half falling as he climbed down. Rough bark bit and scraped his fingers and palms. The last ten feet, he simply dropped. He struck the ground, rolled to his feet and launched himself across the cobbled path outside the garden wall. Darting through a back gate, he sprinted up the alley. He raced along four winding blocks, then stopped. In the shadows behind a stable, he drew in a slow, calming breath. He wiped blood and sweat from his face and arms, knocked the leaves from his hair, then pulled off his cloak and rolled it to hide the blood spattered across the left shoulder.

After that, he moved on, but not hurriedly. His arms hung like weights, his expression went slack as sackcloth. He again became an unremarkable man plodding his way home. He passed a few weary fishmongers as he descended to the riverside. There, he let the dark waters take the tattered old cloak. At a waterfront tavern he reclaimed Moteado, his old, dappled stallion.

By the time alarm bells rang out from the minister's grand house, Ariz had reached the Gado Bridge. Naval officers on handsome white stallions and a party of royal guards rode past him shouting murder and calling for the crowds to part. Ariz dismounted and led his aged horse to the side of the bridge. Neither he nor his mount garnered any attention. They presented a dull sight, just two more figures amidst the crowd of commonplace people whose work was done for the day.

CHAPTER TWO

Gold streaks of dawning light glinted across the hill and warmed Fedeles's back as his black warhorse, Firaj, trotted between the breaks of sunlight with the exuberance of a playful foal. Every tree rang with the trills of newly woken songbirds. Fedeles leaned down and patted Firaj's shoulder, thankful for the horse's good temper at being roused to ride the empty city streets so that Fedeles could to work off the anxiety that had kept him from sleep.

Yet another nobleman had been murdered.

And this time it was a gregarious court favorite. Lord Wonena and two of his guards had been found in an alley, gutted like sides of beef. Only the day before Wonena and Fedeles had clashed—as they often did—over the upkeep of roads adjacent to both their lands. It was not a serious matter, but their tempers had flared, as Wonena numbered among the royal bishop's ardent supporters while Fedeles championed Prince Sevanyo. Their exchange had degenerated to the usual trade of petty insults and complaints, none of which Fedeles took seriously.

But now Wonena was dead and every gossip in the city seemed intent upon feeding rumors that Fedeles had ordered the man's killing. If Wonena's death had been the only one attributed to Fedeles, the rumor would likely have died out in a day, but Wonena's murder marked the third death of one of Fedeles's court adversaries. After three killings, even Fedeles's allies had turned suspicious eyes on him. Worse, Fedeles's denials were beginning to sound rehearsed on account of being repeated so often.

He didn't even need Atreau to tell him that.

He was being incriminated, most likely by his brother-in-law, Hierro Fueres, but the knowledge didn't help him know how to combat the growing outrage and gossip at court.

Capturing the true assassin should have been the obvious solution, but there again, Fedeles felt intense uncertainty. As far as Atreau had been able to ascertain, the killings had involved an assassin so silent and fast that the few surviving witnesses swore he'd been unnatural. Courtiers and commoners alike speculated that the killer was some shape-shifting witch loyal to Count Radulf.

As suspicions of Count Radulf and his sister, Hylanya, grew, so did the possibility of another Labaran war. If the conflict escalated into battle, Cadeleonian soldiers would face an army of monstrous creatures, trolls and witches all led by Cadeleon's own champions, Fedeles's cousin Javier Tornesal and classmate Elezar Grunito. The very men who had saved Fedeles from possession by their power-hungry teacher ten years before.

Fedeles couldn't imagine raising his voice, much less a weapon, against Javier or Elezar. Now he found himself forced to contemplate the horror of killing them for Prince Sevanyo's sake—no, for the sake of the nation of Cadeleon itself.

The better option would be to expose the real killer. Except that Fedeles found he couldn't stand the thought of that either. Atreau and Oasia both suspected the brutal killings were the work of Hierro Fueres's deadliest assassin, Ariz Plunado. Fedeles knew they were probably right. The thought of how terribly Ariz suffered when Hierro bent him to his will gnawed at Fedeles's heart. It wasn't merely physical pain but guilt, too, that would torment Ariz, more even than the injuries he must have accumulated fighting so often against so many armed nobles and their guards in such a short time.

No, for now Fedeles would shoulder the suspicions and gossip himself. It wasn't much to endure, and soon enough Hierro and his conspirators would have to make an overt attempt to seize the throne. Then Fedeles would have them. He already knew roughly when they planned to act and where. Hierro was readying his enthralled assassins to strike during Sevanyo's coronation—when all the royal family would be gathered in one place. Atreau's agents and Oasia's informants had provided enough clues to pinpoint when the action would take place, but had not found enough evidence to bring a formal accusation of treason.

"Easy to know, hard to prevent," Fedeles murmured to himself.

Unlike his unhinged brother-in-law, Hierro, Fedeles was constrained by both the law and Prince Sevanyo's forgiving nature. Sevanyo refused to believe that his brother, Nugalo, or any of his sons would carry through with an act of treason. That left Fedeles with no option but to wait until they implicated themselves beyond any doubt.

Fedeles's shadow fluttered as if disturbed by an uneasy wind.

Beneath him, Firaj tensed, pricking up his ears. Fedeles listened too and heard the sound of horses, riding fast and not far from them. He felt the faintest hum pass through the string of red stones he wore beneath his shirt. Like Firaj, the spells of Meztli's shield were sensitive to his agitation.

Up on the small rise ahead of them a flurry of crows suddenly swirled up into the pale sky, shrieking in alarm. Fedeles urged Firaj toward them. He paused a moment, taking in the quiet, shaded grounds of his great house and then the tight formation of armed riders charging from the wide city road toward his home. The riders wore the colors of the royal bishop's guard and numbered at least twenty. At this hour only two sleepy men kept watch over the gates to Fedeles's home. They couldn't hope to repel the small cavalry charging them. Nor could Fedeles; he wore no armor and the only weapon at hand was his hunting knife.

Still, he urged Firaj ahead, and the big warhorse responded at once, breaking into an all-out gallop. Clods of earth and grass flew up in their wake as they tore across the field and raced to intercept the royal bishop's guards. A hedge of boxwood blocked their path. Fedeles leaned forward and Firaj bounded. Fedeles felt his shadow spread out and catch the air like the wings of the crows circling them. He and Firaj soared over the hedge; Fedeles's heart pounded in thunderous unison with his horse's. They took the ground running.

In a flash they reached the pebbled drive that led to the black gates at the front of Fedeles's great house. Fedeles caught sight of his two watchmen's terrified faces as he drew Firaj to a halt in front of the gates. One of the men moved to allow him inside before the royal bishop's guards reached them, but Fedeles shook his head.

"Lock them and keep them locked," he commanded the elder of the two retainers, then to the younger he said, "Call for the house guards and rouse my lady wife."

At once the young man pelted back toward the quiet darkness of the sprawling mansion. Fedeles immediately turned his attention to the riders charging him. They'd narrowed their formation approaching him four abreast, and though they rode fast, Fedeles noted that none of them had yet drawn a weapon. Beneath him Firaj tensed and snorted. He was terrified, and yet he stood ready to charge if commanded to do so.

Fedeles ran his hand along Firaj's glossy neck, trying to reassure the warhorse that he would do all he could to protect him and his household, even if it meant releasing the murderous curse inhabiting his shadow. If he had to kill every last rider facing them, then he would.

But only if he had to.

The royal bishop's men drew near and Fedeles recognized the man at the head of the formation. Blunt-featured, black-haired, and strapping, Captain Yago carried himself with a self-righteous air. Fedeles knew that over the last decade Yago had more than earned his reputation as the royal bishop's butcher. According to Atreau, the captain had even murdered Irsea, an elderly Haldiim woman and the last Bahiim remaining in the city. After that, and while presumably occupied scouring the city for Hylanya Radulf, Yago had found the time to hang an herb girl and a midwife for allegedly practicing witchcraft. His recent authority over the Haldiim District of the city had led to an unprecedented number of Haldiim citizens deserting the capital for far-flung Anacleto.

Now Fedeles watched the man's smug expression shift to annoyance as he discerned Fedeles's presence in the shifting morning light.

Fedeles glowered at Yago in return, holding his gaze and willing him to a halt. Again Fedeles felt a shudder pass from his body and ripple through his shadow. He couldn't be certain, but it seemed to him that Yago blanched. His mount stumbled slightly and tossed its head. Yago stroked the animal's neck, calming it.

Then Yago signaled the men behind him to slow and reined his own gold stallion to a trot. He halted less than a yard from Fedeles and took his time to look Fedeles over disdainfully. His self-assured smile returned.

"You're up early, my lord. Trouble sleeping?" Yago inquired.

Did he imagine that guilt had kept Fedeles from his bed, or was he simply pleased to notice Fedeles's lack of guards and weapons?

"I was enjoying the peace of the dawn chorus," Fedeles replied. "I don't imagine that would mean much of anything to a person such as yourself."

"There you would be correct, my lord." Yago reached into his coat and drew out a rolled sheet of thick paper. He moved as if to hand the paper to Fedeles but paused a moment, casting a wary glare at something just behind Fedeles's shoulder. Fedeles spared a glance back, expecting to see his house guards—he could hear them with their pikes and swords gathering at the gates—but then he noted the crows perched atop the iron finials. Perhaps a hundred of the glossy black birds, and all of them still and silent as statues.

Irsea's familiars—vessels that allowed her soul to remain in the realm of the living even after Yago had murdered her.

Though he'd not known Irsea or her crows long, Fedeles found the sight of them heartening. Particularly since their presence appeared to unnerve Captain Yago.

"I've never had any use for birds except on my plate," Captain Yago snapped.

Fedeles imagined that had he been here, Atreau would have offered some witty rejoinder about the captain eating crow, but as it was, Fedeles simply held his ground and demanded the captain's business.

"I've a summons commanding you to answer before the royal bishop for the murder of Lord Numes, minister of His Highness's navies."

"Lord Numes?" Fedeles didn't have to feign his surprise. He'd not even known the minister of the navy had been killed. "When did this happen?"

"Right now. I'm holding the summons here in my hand!" Yago snapped.

"The murder," Fedeles responded. "I was talking with Numes only yesterday afternoon . . ."

"Arguing with him, his wife says." Yago smiled and Fedeles could see the captain's pleasure in having an advantage over him. "It would seem you were one of the last people to see the minister . . . alive, that is."

Hardly the grounds for an accusation of murder, Fedeles thought, but he couldn't be certain that her testimony was the only evidence against him.

"Your lady wife may have called on him as well," Captain Yago added. "I believe the royal bishop would like to see her also."

"You may believe anything you want, captain." Fedeles straightened in his saddle. "As her husband, it is *my* say whether she answers the summons of any given man, bishop or not."

Yago went very still and his stallion tensed, readying to respond to the slightest of the captain's commands. Fedeles held his gaze. He said nothing but silently assured the captain that he would strike him dead if he attempted to lay a hand upon any member of Fedeles's family.

Yago shrugged.

"If you don't want your lady wife clearing her own name then that's your decision, my lord. It will fall upon you to answer for her actions in any case."

"Indeed," Fedeles replied.

Behind the house gate, he could hear his own guards gathering, forming ranks, and preparing to fight for him. Beyond the clang of weapons rose the alarmed voices of staff and servants: so very many innocent people about to be caught up in the combat. All at once Fedeles felt the living vibrance of each of them.

Oh God, he remembered, his head groom had just taken in his freckled-faced nine-year-old niece. His weathered cook and her husband would celebrate their fortieth year of marriage in two months. There were so many of them. His pages, Oasia's maids, Father Timoteo's flock of orphaned acolytes, as well as Master Narsi and Brother Berto.

No.

No matter how much he feared those undead monstrosities in the Shard of Heaven—no matter what the royal bishop might do to him—he had to shield the people who looked to him for protection.

Fedeles squared his shoulders and lifted his head in haughty disdain as he imagined Oasia would have done. Then he reined Firaj forward at a calm trot.

As he passed Yago, Fedeles caught sight of his own shadow impenetrably black and stretching out far longer than it should have. It coiled beneath Yago's steed and the animal shuddered. Fedeles shook his head. The horse shouldn't suffer just because it was burdened with a hateful man. Fedeles drew his shadow back.

Yago appeared confounded by Fedeles's compliance to the summons. That offered Fedeles a small victory. The captain had expected a fight, perhaps even a slaughter, and Fedeles had denied him that.

"Come then, Captain!" Fedeles called to Yago, as if rebuking an absentminded page. "Let us visit the royal bishop. I have questions of my own to ask."

 CHAPTER
THREE

Atreau knew he was being followed, though he couldn't clearly identify by whom.

Sunrise had yet to dispel the darkness lurking in the narrow, winding alleys of the Knife Market. A damp chill and the smell of decay hung over the multitude of cluttered and cavernous alcoves that pocked the brick walls, rising on either side of him. Patches of bright mosaic tilework glinted here and there, the last testaments to the many Haldiim homes that once stood here. Now Cadeleonian purveyors of indecent and disreputable services sheltered in the gloomy ruins. The deep shadows and high walls provided anonymity for a multitude of sanctimonious customers.

As he regarded the cracked tiles that had once formed a great expanse of gold stars, Atreau thought that the history of this place served as a warning—a reminder that as much as the resplendent capital prospered from easy commerce and noble indulgence, it also thrived upon ages of tragedies and ruthless misfortune. Or perhaps that was simply his own jaded view. He wondered what Narsi would make of the place. Then he pushed the thought from his mind. He couldn't afford the distraction of daydreaming about what Narsi might or might not enjoy.

Atreau skirted a group of ragged streetwalkers sleeping curled together under the shelter of an overhang. Other tired denizens watched him pass as they made their breakfasts of bread crusts and pigeons. Several offered him familiar greetings. Those he knew best shot meaningful glances to the too-well-dressed strangers in their midst. Atreau nodded, having finally picked them out as well.

The six men positioned to watch and follow him.

None wore the armor or insignia of men-at-arms, but the wiry quality of their builds made Atreau think that they were accustomed to hunger and hard labor. To a man, they all sported the waxcloth notch-heeled shoes favored by sailors and butchers. He doubted that a coalition of butchers had banded together to surveil him. These must be navy men, then. But why? And why now?

Atreau stole another glance back and noted that the men studied him with the quiet focus of a hunting party observing deer from a blind.

He would have felt much more secure if he could have brought Sabella along. But with Hierro Fueres plotting to wipe out the entire royal family, her protection of Prince Jacinto took precedence above all other concerns. And Atreau hadn't come entirely alone, in any case.

A grizzled cat stalked alongside Atreau, lashing its tail and growling at everyone. Atreau shared the creature's apprehension. Or perhaps it was Hylanya's uneasiness that coursed through the animal. Certainly if it hadn't numbered among her familiars, the cat would have made itself scarce by now. Even he was sorely tempted to turn around and return to his bed at the Fat Goose Inn. But if he did, he'd be abandoning all hope of finding the pair of spindly siblings who'd served as his informants for five years now.

When they went missing three days prior, Atreau had feared the worst. Then an hour ago he'd received a note declaring that Rinza was alive and in need of him. The brief missive had been penned in a suspiciously elegant script upon a slip of very fine-quality paper. It had been so obviously an invitation to step into a trap that Atreau had nearly thrown the thing away and gone back to sleep.

But he felt a particular loyalty to Rinza and her brother, Riquo. He'd known them for years, and in all that time neither of them had attempted to con or double-cross him, which was more than he could say for most the lovers he took. In any case, who knew when he might need a small, agile thief, and both the siblings fit that description.

And if he managed to play it right, this trap might provide him with the opportunity to confront the man responsible for the recent disappearances of so many of his agents. Counting Riquo and Rinza, Atreau had now lost six of his informants—some of them friends, all of them people whom Atreau had charmed, bribed, and flattered into trusting him. Atreau gripped the hilt of his belt knife. When he caught the man behind his people's deaths, he meant to slit the bastard's throat.

Despite his belief that eloquence and charm could be honed into weapons, there were times when a dagger made its point far more effectively.

Atreau turned slightly to take in the loose formation of the six men stalking behind him in their butchers' shoes. Between their uneasy expressions and their missteps crossing the rutted alleys, he realized that not one of them was familiar with the Knife Market's winding streets, much less the ancient Haldiim tunnels and passages that coiled beneath them. Setting their trap on grounds more familiar to their prey than themselves seemed like a strange mistake to make—amateurish. But if his adversary had lapsed into idiocy—or simply failed to recognize how intimately Atreau knew the Knife Market and its denizens—then Atreau meant to take full advantage.

He turned down a very narrow lane and hurried to where a couple of elderly, white-haired, men wearing blue-stained aprons crouched beside a pot of bubbling ink. The slenderer of the two was dark complexioned and claimed to be a direct descendant of the Haldiim mapmaker who'd planned the entire district some four hundred years ago. His big ra-boned partner boasted the thick beard and pale eyes of a Mirogoth but wore his long white hair in Labaran braids.

The brew of squid offal, rotten snails and madder root that they tended wouldn't perfectly match the rich indigo ink that marked all official church documents, but it came close enough to allow many smugglers to elude the Royal Navy's tax collectors. But forgers' ink wasn't the only service the two old dyers provided.

"Kind sirs." Atreau made a point not to use either of their names when he was being followed. "Would you be so good as to direct me? I seem to have gone astray."

Glancing up, both the dyers offered Atreau knowing smiles.

"Well, let's see what we can do for you, boy." The thinner of the two beckoned Atreau down beside him while his partner continued to stir their large black pot. The rank vapor rising off the ink caught in Atreau's throat, but the warmth of the fire felt good. Hunching down beside the slender man, Atreau handed over four precious silver coins.

"Barrel Alley and Noose Lane," Atreau told him.

The man nodded and closed his eyes in concentration. The fingers of his bony right hand twitched as if tracing an invisible surface. Then he looked back to Atreau.

"Through the snake hole. Five notches on your right hand, then left to the stairs." The man spoke clearly but softly.

The snake hole. Atreau gave a slight shudder, recalling the last time he'd ventured that way. At least it would be quick and close at hand. He edged back toward the shadowed alcove just behind the couple. The smell of decaying fish and rotting weeds drifted off the stacks of weathered pots stored in the space.

The bigger of the two dyers cleared his throat loudly and Atreau looked back to see three of his pursuers tromp into the mouth of the alley.

"They after you, Atreau?" the slender dyer whispered.

"If only they weren't," Atreau answered.

The elderly man smiled. Then he gave a loud shout to the five youths playing dice across the alley. "Come on then you, lag-a-bones. You've deliveries to make!"

The youths snatched up their collection of little jars and ink bottles, then raced over to circle around the dyers' bubbling pot. Their jostling, gangly bodies readily blocked any view of Atreau. He slunk quickly back behind the foul-smelling casks and into a niche in the alcove wall. A gleaming gold patch of Haldiim mosaic marked exactly where Atreau needed to run his hands. One of the tiles slid back and a door hardly bigger than a spice cupboard popped open at the base of the wall. Atreau slithered into the dark, stale space. The cat slunk after him and he heard one of the dyers snap the door shut behind them.

Absolute darkness engulfed him. The walls on either side brushed his shoulders and the ceiling above was too low for him to even rise onto his knees and crawl. Instead he had to inch and drag himself across the dusty floor, stopping every few feet to run his right hand over the bricks of the wall. His fingers quickly found the first notch. A deep gouge that had been polished smooth by generations of refugees and smugglers who had squeezed and dragged themselves through the snake hole before him. Hardly a foot past the notch, the mouth of some other narrow tunnel opened in the right hand wall. Where it led—if it led anywhere—Atreau didn't know.

He kept moving straight ahead. By the time he reached the third notch, the air had grown notably fungal. Atreau briefly wondered what became of the corpses of those people who lost their way down in these dark confines. The tang of rat piss gave him an idea, but he didn't think on it too long. Behind him the cat grumbled. Atreau amused himself by imaging that the creature was arguing with Hylanya about abandoning the venture altogether to chase down some fat rodent.

Just after the fifth notch, Atreau reached out to his left and muscled himself through a gap in the wall. Thankfully the space immediately opened into a tunnel roomy enough for him to crawl through. A little farther and he then he could stand, so long as he hunched slightly. At last he felt the air around him stir. A few streams of dawn light filtered down from cracks in the ceiling above him. Wooden planks creaked over his head and a piglet grunted as he passed beneath the ripe floor of someone's swine shed.

Then, through the gloom he made out a narrow, rough-hewn staircase. Relief washed over him and he loped up the steps with the cat on his heels.

The stair ended in a false but quite sturdy wall. Again the gleam of mosaic tiles showed him where to search for a release. The false wall swung open a crack and Atreau muscled his way out. After the cat stalked past him, Atreau pushed the false wall closed again and surveyed his surroundings. He'd traversed beneath several winding streets and dead-end walls so that now he stood on the far side Noose Lane, well ahead of the men following him and opposite from the direction they would have expected him to approach. Chances were good that he would take anyone waiting for him by surprise.

But just who that would be and how many of them, he couldn't be certain. The narrow lane snaked around a blind corner before it met up with Barrel Alley. That would be the best place to arrange an ambush. Especially at this hour, when Noose Lane stood almost empty. A snoring tramp sprawled beneath a lean-to of half-rotted lumber and a pigeon cooed from a nest up at the top of the high brick wall. Otherwise he and cat were alone.

Atreau glanced to the cat, then crouched down. "Ladies first."

The cat eyed him and made a show of licking its front paw.

"Just stroll around the corner and have a look, will you? See if Rinza is even there, or if there are too many of them waiting. They're hardly going to ambush a cat, so you can take a peek, then pad right back to me," Atreau whispered. He was glad there was no one to witness him cajoling the animal. "Yowl if you want me to follow after you."

The grizzled beast heaved a sigh, then slunk ahead. Atreau edged after it, his hand on the hilt of his belt knife. The cat turned the corner out of sight. Atreau waited.

"Oh, hello, kitty." A man spoke softly but with a tone of affection. "Would you like your tummy rubbed?" A moment later a spitting yowl split the quiet, followed by the man's pained shout.

Atreau bounded around the corner, catching his would-be assailant from behind and jerking him into a choke hold before he could punt the cat off his ankle. The cat leapt away. A few feet ahead of him, Atreau caught sight of Rinza's tiny figure crouched atop a broken wine barrel, a blanket wrapped around her shoulders. No one else seemed to be lying in wait for him, and the man whom he gripped had gone still. He held his arms out in surrender.

The scent of Labaran rose cologne drifted from the man's glossy black hair. Atreau recognized it in an instant. He released his hold and quickly sheathed his belt knife.

His eldest brother, Lliro, gave a cough and then spun to pin him with a censorious stare. Despite himself, Atreau felt an embarrassed flush spreading across his face. For a moment he was once again a seven-year-old child grasping his teenage brother and being chided not to make such a fuss over his big brother being sent to sea. But that had been so very long ago. Since then, both he and Lliro had grown up and taken different sides in the struggle to control Cadeleon.

"Good God." Lliro's words came out rough. "You nearly throttled me."

"I did throttle you," Atreau replied. "What I *nearly* did was slit your throat. What are you doing here?"

"Meeting with you. I believe the note I sent was profoundly clear on that point." Lliro arched one black brow, just as Atreau would have done if their situations had been reversed. Spider shared this trait as well. They'd all picked up the habit from their wastrel father.

"Meeting at dawn in a Knife Market alley seems a bit furtive. Couldn't you have called on me at the Duke of Rauma's residence?"

"Not without being noticed, and I certainly couldn't have smuggled your . . . lady friend out to you." Lliro gestured to Rinza. She remained hunched atop the barrel, looking like a scrawny child, though her mop of shaggy brown hair hid the weathered face of a thirty-year-old. "She was the one who insisted on this location, by the way. And seeing as she's had a rough time of it, I thought it best to take her somewhere familiar."

Atreau noticed that rather than her usual threadbare yellow dress, she now wore a white shift—the costly sort of thing that ministers' pages often sported as underclothes—and a new blue skirt. Her tough feet were bare as always but appeared uncharacteristically clean.

"Are you hurt, Rinza?" Atreau called to her quietly.

She lifted her head to gaze at him with a dull expression. "They tried to drag us down into some hole by the river. I fought hard as I could, took a bite out of one of the bastards. He hurled me into the river. That's the last I saw of Riquo." She dropped her head into her hands as if she might cry, but instead she simply hung there, covering her face. "I don't know where they took him. I don't know if they killed him down in that hole."

Atreau scrutinized his brother.

Lliro had left the family house to serve the minister of the navy at sixteen, and in the twenty-three years since then, Atreau had hardly spent more than a few hours in his company. Lliro's in-laws supported the royal bishop and Hierro Fueres, so he might well have played some role in the abduction of the siblings. Perhaps he'd had Riquo murdered. Though taking in Lliro's neat, understated attire and his concerned expression, Atreau couldn't help but remember how protective he'd been as a boy and how often he'd played the part of the fair-minded judge when Atreau and Espirdro brawled over candies and toys. This entire matter seemed a bit too grubby to be one of his aloof elder brother's undertakings. And yet here they were in a Knife Market alley with the smell of open sewers and rancid lard floating around them.

"What about the six blackguards you had lurking after me?" Atreau demanded.

"My six most trusted lieutenants, you mean?" Again Lliro's brow arched. "They agreed to keep watch and escort you past the riffraff that populate this place."

Atreau almost laughed at that.

"You haven't done anything to them, have you?" Lliro demanded.

"Other than elude them? No. I and the rest of the *riffraff* have left them well enough alone." Atreau stole another glance back to Rinza. "Where is her brother?"

"I don't know. Will you stop glaring at me, as if I've done you some grievous harm?" Tellingly, Lliro abandoned Cadeleonian for the rolling Labaran tongue of their mother. "The ministry has people watching Yago and a number of other men in Lord Fueres's pay—"

"Only Lord Fueres's men?" Atreau too spoke in Labaran, and for just an instant a sense of nostalgia washed over him—almost like they were children again, sharing gossip in a language that only they and their mother could understand.

"Of course not. The navy keeps watch on you and your friends, as well. You all make waves, and our duty is to keep the nation's ships above them. As a rule we don't interfere in the petty rivalries of nobles," Lliro replied. "However, it was dark when one of my men noted Yago taking your little informants, and when my agent witnessed what he thought was a child being hurled into the river, he dived after her and pulled her out. That's how she came to me."

"Her brother?" Atreau asked again, because the spy must have seen something—must have reported something.

"Last seen at the river's edge. I don't know what became of him," Lliro replied. "My agent followed the sister into the water and obviously lost the brother."

"You must have to have some suspicion, if you've been watching Yago. This isn't the first of my people he's taken."

"I serve the navy, not you or your master, Lord Quemanor. And I'm certainly not going to play the role of your skulking informant." Lliro scowled at him. "I shouldn't even be meeting with you, much less returning your . . . friend."

"Then why are you?" Atreau asked.

"Because she was scared and weeping and she reminded me of y—" Lliro cut himself off short. Something like a tremor passed through his composed features, and for just an instant Atreau thought he might be on the verge of tears. "My lord Numes was murdered last night and—"

"What? Who would dare harm Numes?" Even as he asked, Atreau had a sinking feeling that he knew the answer. It was incredibly unlikely that a Labaran agent killed Numes—as far as Atreau knew, neither Hylanya nor Skellan had stooped to employing assassins. Considering the power they wielded, they wouldn't have needed to.

No, Hierro was the one behind it, Atreau felt nearly certain. Though he couldn't understand why Hierro would move against the minister of the navy. The man was as famous for his indifference to the rivalry between Prince Sevanyo and Royal Bishop Nugalo as he was for his dedication to their nation's ships. Killing Numes wouldn't put anyone nearer the throne, but it would ensure that the new ruler would inherit a weakened navy. Numes was no threat to anyone.

Unless he'd discovered something.

Perhaps he'd found some proof that Hierro presented far more of a threat to their nation's stability than did a radical like Fedeles Quemanor or even the heathen Labarans.

Atreau considered trying to pry the information from his brother, but then the deep sorrow in Lliro's expression stopped him. The decades his brother had spent at Numes's side had clearly not been unhappy. He appeared truly heartbroken over the loss.

"I'm sorry," Atreau said belatedly.

"I should have been there with him," Lliro muttered. "But father collapsed two days ago. I was arranging his last rites when my—when Lord Numes was murdered."

Atreau stared at his brother, feeling oddly numb at the news of their father's demise. He would have expected happiness or at least relief, but instead there was only the awareness that his father's death changed nothing of his own past or future. He didn't have it in him to grieve the man, but neither could he summon any sense of joy.

"I suppose congratulations are in order then, Baron Nifayo." Atreau pulled a smile. "I do hope father has left you something more than debts and dead horses."

Lliro studied him with an expression of disappointment.

"I know he wasn't the best of men, but you can't go on blaming him for all the ill that befell our family—"

"Not even when he *was* responsible for it?" Anger flared through Atreau. Lliro had no idea what he was talking about. It wasn't just a matter of reckless bets and drunken binges to forgive. It wasn't just their descent into poverty or the loss of their mother. Lliro hadn't been there—he'd not been pursued through the neglected halls of their decrepit home by soused lechers. He'd not been pinned down or forced to comply with their desires.

"I know that you blamed him for Espirdra's death, but he didn't . . ." Lliro trailed off with a weary sigh. "Would it make a difference if I told you that Espirdra didn't die of bluefever?"

Only years of practice hiding his reactions allowed Atreau not to stare slack-jawed at his brother. How had *he* learned of Espirdro's survival? There were very few people who knew Espirdro's history well enough to have betrayed it, but whoever had, Atreau would need to find them before they endangered—

"I should have told you before now." Lliro's expression turned a little guilty. "Espirdra fled to me here in the capital, and begged me to help . . . *him* reach the Salt Islands." Lliro spoke carefully and Atreau realized that his older brother was attempting to inform him of Espirdro's true identity, in his own tight-lipped manner. Perhaps he thought Atreau had been too young to understand. But even at a mere ten years of age Espirdro was setting gowns alight and donning Atreau's clothes. Espirdro's clashes with their father had been long, graphic and resounding. Atreau would have to have been dead not to understand them.

"It was what mother wanted. In her last letter to me she asked that I help *our brother*." Lliro held Atreau's gaze. Atreau nodded. While she'd lived, their mother had always treated Espirdro as a son. It had infuriated their father.

"I forged papers for him and I saw to it that he reached the Butterfly Temple on the Salt Islands," Lliro went on quietly. "Last I heard he'd been accepted into the temple as an honored member. I should have told you years ago, but considering the crowd you ran with . . . I couldn't risk it becoming common gossip. Then you began publishing those scandalous memoirs and plays. I didn't want Espirdro exposed like that."

"On that we are agreed, at least," Atreau replied. For a moment he considered his brother. "I suppose it's only fair that you know that he and I found each other here in the capital four years past. He owns the majority of an inn called the Fat Goose."

Then it was Lliro's turn to look stunned. Atreau could almost see his brother's thoughts connecting, as realization spread across his tanned face. If the minister's agents had been watching Atreau, then they would have reported on his comings and goings from the Fat Goose.

"The Salt Island Spider?" Lliro asked, then his expression turned alarmed. "No, no. He can't stay here. If the royal bishop and Hierro Fueres have their ways, we'll soon see another purge. You and he both need to leave at once."

Lliro's dark gaze darted over the surrounding walls as if searching for an answer scrawled across the grimy, cracked mosaic tiles. "I can secure you both passage aboard the *Summer Wind*, but we must move fast. The ship will sail—"

"You're damn quick to assume that Hierro Fueres and the royal bishop are going to have their ways, aren't you?" Atreau broke in.

"They are *already* having their way thanks to Numes's wife," Lliro snapped. "She's an extremely devout woman, and she believes that Lord Quemanor is an abomination. When my lord Numes was killed—in the way he was killed—she accused Fedeles Quemanor of the murder and demanded that he be taken before the Hallowed Kings. The royal bishop was more than happy to agree. Captain Yago arrested the duke an hour ago."

"And you did nothing to stop it?" Atreau demanded. "You had to know the Fedeles had nothing to do with Numes's assassination!"

Objectively he recognized that his brother bore no such obligation, but some dark corner of his mind still clung to the image of his older brother as stalwart and ever honest. The sudden rush of fear and anger racing through him had washed away his reasoning and left him feeling like a hapless lad again.

He couldn't lose Fedeles.

He was the only protection Atreau and every one of his agents could rely upon. He was the one soul in the capital powerful enough to shield the entire city. But more than any of that, Fedeles was Atreau's friend, and a better man than most Atreau knew: generous and kind, and he'd suffered far too much in his life already. Atreau's heart ached thinking of how terrified Fedeles would feel, finding himself imprisoned again.

Atreau needed to secure Fedeles's release immediately. His thoughts raced. A passage ran beneath the river and up into the Shard of Heaven. Priests used it to transport luxurious supplies from their warehouses to the Shard without risking encounters with thieves or the base temptations of the city streets. Dressed as priests, he and Sabella might be able to reach Fedeles that way. Could he use the stone of passage to get them all to safety? Or would the spells surrounding the Hallowed Kings stop them?

How much would he have to promise Sabella to convince her to help him? If it came to it—if there was no other way—could he go to Oasia?

"Atreau!" Lliro's voice broke through his racing thoughts.

He met his brother's intent gaze.

"Did he have anything to do with my lord Numes's death?" Lliro asked.

"Of course he didn't!" Atreau snapped.

"What makes you so certain?" Lliro's intent expression lent him an almost feverish look.

"Because I know Fedeles wouldn't—"

"Wouldn't he? There are at least two duelists whom he struck dead less than a month ago. You think I don't know about that hellish shadow of his?" Lliro demanded. "From what my lord's wife and surviving guards described, my Numes and his nearest guard were cut down in an instant. Then the assassin shot away and disappeared, swift and nearly soundless."

Ariz, then. Atreau had suspected as much, but now he felt certain.

"Did the murderer use a weapon?" Atreau asked.

"Of course. A short sword, the guards said," Lliro replied. "Why?"

"Because." Even speaking Labaran, Atreau lowered his voice to a whisper. "I've seen what Fedeles's shadow can do. I've felt its edge. Believe me when I tell you that if Fedeles Quemanor had decided to kill Lord Numes, he wouldn't have any need for a blade. The only thing witnesses would have seen would have been a flicker of darkness fall across Lord Numes, like the shadow of a passing cloud. Then his corpse would have collapsed to the ground in a bloody heap. Fedeles wouldn't have needed to flee because he wouldn't have even been there. He could simply have sent his shadow."

Lliro's eyes widened in horror.

"Believe me. Fedeles did not murder Lord Numes," Atreau insisted.

Lliro nodded slowly. Then his dark brows knit and his mouth turned down in a thoughtful line.

"You can hardly offer that testimony to the royal bishop and expect that it would do Lord Quemanor any good," Lliro muttered.

"No, but I'm telling *you*. It's the truth. That has to mean something to you," Atreau said.

Lliro studied him. Then nodded. "Your lady friend mentioned that you had been asking questions about the assassins who did away with Captain Ciceron."

Both of them glanced to where Rinza sat on the barrel. She lifted a liquor flask stamped with the Cadeleonian naval seal and drank deeply. Then she shuddered and wrapped her bony arms around herself. Her desolate gaze dropped to her feet.

"Should've left years ago," she muttered. "We should've gone somewhere."

"It was a single assassin who murdered Ciceron." Atreau returned his attention to his brother. "And yes, from your description I would say that the same man killed Lord Wonena and your Lord Numes."

"You know who he is?" Lliro asked, but there was certainty in his expression. His brother might not approve of his habits, but he obviously knew Atreau could get results. "Tell me and I swear to God, my men will find him and have a confession from him before this day is done. Your Lord Quemanor will have to be released, then."

If Lliro thought he could torture anything out of Master Ariz, he would be sorely disappointed. Likely Ariz would be as well, considering how desperately the man had struggled to confess anything to Narsi.

Though there was a good chance that exposing Ariz would draw attention to all the time he'd been spending with Narsi. There was danger enough now in just being Haldiim in the city, but a Haldiim who could be connected to assassinations of Cadeleonian noblemen? Narsi would be doomed. Likely Yara and the rest of the growing circle of Haldiim friends who kept Narsi company would fall under suspicion as well.

Pull one thread and the entire tapestry unravels, wasn't that what his mother used to say?

"I can't give you a name. All I know is that he's completely under Hierro Fueres's control." Atreau hadn't expected lying to his brother to feel so bad. He went on quickly. "If you truly wish to avenge *your* Lord Numes, then it's Hierro Fueres who deserves your wrath. And the only man who stands any chance of destroying him is *my* Lord Quemanor."

Lliro's expression grew uneasy.

"The ministry of the navy can't take sides." Lliro spoke the words in Cadeleonian, and Atreau suspected from his tone and expression that he was repeating something told to him. Likely a truism declared by the now deceased Lord Numes. Certainly it didn't sound like advice their father would ever have offered.

"But you aren't the navy, Lliro," Atreau reminded him in Labaran.

"I . . ." Lliro caught himself and returned to speaking Labaran. "Hierro Fueres is not a man to be trifled with."

"He will only grow more dangerous if he and the royal bishop are allowed to destroy Fedeles," Atreau replied. "I understand that you can't openly aid me, but at least help me hire—"

"Atreau!" Lliro broke in. "For one minute, will you stop advocating for Lord Quemanor and consider your own position? *You* are the one I'm afraid for. You aren't safe here any longer. What allies do you have left? Who will help you—defend you? Javier Tornesal is a wanted man living in exile. Elezar Grunito has abdicated and serves a witch in far-off

Labara. And now Fedeles Quemanor, your mad duke, has been arrested. There's *no one* left. No one can shield you now."

Atreau wanted to claim that it made no difference. He wanted to be the sort of man who would risk all to stand up for his friend. Yet there was no denying the cold dread that seized him.

He could almost taste the moldering stale air of the Sorrowlands—the realm of the dead—as he tried to imagine himself marching into the Shard of Heaven. He could all too easily imagine being cut down by guards in an instant. Fedeles would be no better for his death, either. And yet he couldn't abandon Fedeles.

"I can arrange passage for you—" Lliro began, but Atreau refused to hear the tempting words.

"No!" he snapped, and in that moment he remembered Narsi frowning at him from beside Ariz's bloody figure. "There's no reason for me to assume that I can do nothing before I've attempted anything."

Wasn't that what Narsi had told them all that afternoon?

Atreau continued, "There has to be another way. Something that can be done."

Lliro stared at him with a too-familiar expression of anger and frustration, but where their father would have backhanded Atreau's face, his brother simply groaned and then rubbed his hands over his eyes like a man fighting off exhaustion.

"Why won't you see reason?" Lliro asked.

"Because there's more at stake than just my safety. More even than Fedeles Quemanor's freedom." Again he recalled Narsi; how frightened he'd been, and yet he'd refused to flee back to Anacleto. The royal bishop and Hierro Fueres posed too great of a threat to the Haldiim people. And to Spider. Not to mention artists like Inissa or lovers like Sabella and Suelita. Every soul living here in the Knife Market stood to suffer. "They have to be stopped, Lliro. Because if we allow them to abduct, murder and imprison people before they even have power over us, then what do you imagine will hold them back once they've stripped Prince Sevanyo of all his supporters? Allowing the royal bishop and Hierro Fueres to falsely accuse Fedeles isn't maintaining the neutrality of the navy. It's cowardice."

"Atreau—"

"You know that I'm right." Atreau held his brother's gaze. Lliro glared back at him. For a few moments they both stood staring at each other in silence. Then Lliro bowed his head.

"All right. Yes, you're right but . . ." Lliro looked harassed and tired. "What can I do? I can't just order my ships to siege the Shard of Heaven, you know. That would be an act of war. I'm not about to start ordering secret assassinations or . . . God only knows what you're imaging that I ought to do for the sake of your friend."

"You could rouse dissent at court." Atreau spoke as the thoughts came to him. "You could protest that your Lord Numes's murder should not be exploited for political gain. At the very least, you could demand to be present for Lord Quemanor's questioning. Buy me time to . . ."

Atreau didn't know what he would do. Could he manage to break into the Shard of Heaven? Could he get himself and Fedeles out alive?

"All right, I'll do all I can in Lord Quemanor's defense," Lliro said. "But before you race off to attempt some brazenly criminal act on your friend's account, let me point you in a direction that might be more useful. I'm not condoning that you attempt a break-in or robbery, but if something of that nature were to take place . . ."

"What do you mean?" Atreau asked, but Lliro simply gave a shake of his head.

"Just before he was killed . . ." Lliro's expression went entirely bleak for a moment, but then he blinked and regained his composure. "My lord Numes noticed something very odd about one of the royal bishop's ships. No one aboard was clergy, and it was captained by the royal bishop's illegitimate son, Ojoito. Even before it docked yesterday, the royal bishop himself stepped in to ensure that the cargo was not inspected. He paid an unprecedented sum."

"Where did it sail from?" Atreau asked.

"The Salt Islands," Lliro replied. "And one of our agents managed to chat up a crewman and discover that there was absolutely nothing in the ship's hold. Though the sailor thought he saw the royal bishop's son carrying what looked like a small gold box embossed with a hunting scene or some such thing."

"That was all?" Atreau asked. Just a box?

"All I could discover before my lord was taken from me," Lliro replied. "Ojoito and his household have returned to the Slate House at the naval memorial. There might be someone there who knows more. The wet nurse that cares for Ojoito's newborn son and little daughter is a canny woman, I've heard."

Atreau frowned, considering what he should do.

"I don't know if any of that was important, except that Faro—" Lliro caught himself in the midst of using the minister's given name. "My lord Numes spent several hours reading over the agent's report, and the last thing he asked me to do before he was murdered was to place watchmen on Ojoito's home and investigate that gold box. He felt we should sound out the wet nurse in particular."

"And could your men relax their vigil for a day or two? That would certainly make breaking into the place easier."

"They could," Lliro replied. "I don't know that there's anything in all of this that will give you an edge over the royal bishop, much less Hierro Fueres, but if there is . . ."

Atreau nodded. "I'll find it, I promise you."

"We'd best get going then," Lliro said, but he didn't move. Instead he caught Atreau's hand. "Upholding the ministry's business falls to me for the time being. In that capacity I have the power to list you and Espirdro for passage aboard all naval ships. So long as it's in my power, I will do all I can to protect you both, I swear."

Atreau felt truly touched and not a little ashamed of how poorly he'd sometimes thought of Lliro. Still, he couldn't just break down blubbering over a few kind words from his brother. Especially not with Hylanya peering at him through the narrowed eyes of an alley cat and Rinza already on the verge of tears for a far better reason.

"I'll forgo the offer of a month of seasickness, thank you," Atreau replied. "But I'll tell Spider. He might take you up on it."

"Has he kept himself well?" Lliro asked quickly.

"He has. If he suffers from any great woe it's being too much in love with a beautiful woman who returns his affection."

"If only such a tragedy would befall me." Lliro laughed. Atreau hadn't realized how concerned his brother must have felt until just this moment when some of his worry lifted, revealing an unlined brow and the dimples of his relieved smile.

"I would appreciate it to no end if you would speak to him on my behalf. I'll do what I can to call on him in person as soon as I can, but right now—" Lliro said.

"—now, you have dozens of courtiers to rouse from their beds and princes to tear from the arms of their mistresses," Atreau supplied for him.

Lliro nodded and his countenance returned to that of a reserved naval officer.

He straightened and started to turn away, but then he spun back to grasp Atreau in a quick, strong embrace. "Take care of yourself."

"You as well," Atreau told him.

Then Lliro released him and strode away. A moment later Atreau heard him call to his men—they would ride to Prince Sevanyo's palace at once. The rest of Lliro's orders faded away. Atreau took a moment trying to reclaim his normal sense of detachment. So much could go wrong for all of them. Fedeles, his brothers, himself and everyone relying upon them. He couldn't allow himself to think about it or his fear would paralyze him.

He had to have faith that this time they would prevail.

~~~

The gray cat stretched across Atreau's shoulders dug its claws in as he mounted the steps of the Fat Goose. Rinza leaned into him, already staggering drunk. Inside, Spider looked up from the bar and raised his black brows. He shared Lliro's slim build and wiry muscle, as well as their brother's discerning taste in silk doublets. If it hadn't been for his patched trousers and stained apron, he would have cut the figure of a refined gentleman.

Atreau presented no such appearance this morning. It was hard to know whether Spider disapproved more of Atreau bringing Rinza or the cat into his establishment. Atreau guessed it was the cat that inspired his narrow-eyed frown. His brother adored dogs but considered felines "faithless fleabags," and this particular little beast wouldn't have proved him wrong. The feral rat hunter regularly prowled in and around the Candioro Theater, and though a succession of actors and actresses had attempted to domesticate the animal over the years, none ever succeeded. Most recently, Narsi seemed to have fallen for the rangy creature.

"You're gonna buy me wine," Rinza crooned into Atreau's armpit.

"If you'd like." The alcohol would dull some of the aches and bruises Yago's men had inflicted, but largely she seemed intent upon blunting her sorrow over the loss of her brother. The heady perfume of navy liquor already drifted from her hair and clothes.

Spider wrinkled his nose when Rinza leaned up against his polished bar. Atreau requested the wine and a moment later Spider set a small bottle of sweet Labaran wine in front of him.

"Maybe he's just hiding," Rinza murmured to herself. "He's got lots of . . . lots of friends. Maybe in a day or two . . ."

Atreau nodded and didn't comment. If Riquo had been taken by Captain Yago, then the likelihood of him surviving the night was slim, and death might well have come as a relief considering the torture the captain may have inflicted. But sometimes hope and bloody-minded denial was all that kept a person going. Liquor assisted in maintaining both. Atreau didn't have it in him to deny her that.

He handed Rinza the bottle. She clutched it to her thin chest, closed her eyes and swayed on her feet. Gazing down at her matted hair and tiny body, Atreau couldn't help feeling that he presented the disturbing figure of a grown man getting a child drunk.

Fortunately, this early in the day, very few patrons filled the Fat Goose, and those who did appeared far more concerned with their cards and dice than anyone else's vices. Still, Atreau leaned a little closer to Spider as he passed him money for the wine.

"I saw Lliro this morning," Atreau said in Labaran. As innocuous as they seemed, any one of the patrons could all too easily turn informant if there was money enough on offer.

"Oh? How is the navy treating him?" Spider too slipped into Labaran. "Better than that bigoted wife of his, I hope?"

"Couldn't likely do him worse, could it?" Atreau replied, and they shared a brief, sorry smile for their eldest brother. They might have pitied Lliro more, but no doubt his wife's immense dowry afforded him the comfort of any number of sympathetic lovers. "He wanted me to tell you that he's secured you passage aboard any naval vessel that you care to sail away on. He's worried that the royal bishop's recent zealotry might do you harm. He offered me a berth as well. I turned him down."

"Well, I'm certain that we'd both be wiser to leave," Spider responded. "But I have reasons for staying."

Atreau opened his mouth to tease Spider about his sentimentality, but then he caught sight of Inissa dancing up from the wine cellar. Her gray silk dress swirled around her shapely figure. Even in the dim light of the inn, Atreau noticed the radiant flush that lit her face. She sported two combs decorated with butterflies in her thick black hair and carried a willow basket. Atreau wondered if she was fetching cold cuts from the cellar after having spent the night here. Or had she come from farther along the disused Haldiim tunnel that ran below the street?

He knew that Spider numbered among the wary property owners in the Theater and Haldiim Districts who had taken the precaution of ensuring themselves and their loved ones access to passageways leading out of the city.

Though just now, no such grim concern seemed to trouble either Inissa or Spider. In fact, a glow of happiness elevated Inissa from comely to a breathtaking. Atreau smiled just seeing her.

Then he noticed Spider studying him. He quickly returned his attention to his brother.

"You're clearly not staying for my sake, then," Atreau teased.

Oddly, Spider's expression turned momentarily concerned.

"Well, not for you alone, no," Spider said. "You aren't going to claim that you're remaining in the capital for my sake alone, are you?"

"I'd not stay for anyone's sake but my own, would I?" Atreau replied. "If I weren't so afflicted by seasickness, I'd be aboard a ship bound for far away Yuan already. As is, I can just about endure soaking in a bath before I grow too bilious."

Both he and Spider laughed.

"Did Lliro have anything else to say?" Spider asked.

Atreau hesitated a moment but then realized that there was no point in playing careful and caring. "Father died two days ago."

Spider blinked, and for just an instant something not unlike pain flickered across his face—not sorrow, but the reflex of recalling all the hurt that their father's presence had become.

"May the three hells keep his soul for evermore," Spider said. "I have some news for you as well. That friend of mine on the Salt Islands found the physician you were attempting to locate. He gave her warning against the royal bishop's men and is doing what he can to get her story out of her."

"Too much to hope she'd be a forthcoming soul, I suppose," Atreau replied.

"From what my friend has written, it sounds as though the physician feels deeply indebted to a fellow named Timoteo, and it might be his secret that she's keeping. That any use to you?" Spider handed Atreau a page from a weathered-looking letter and Atreau tucked it into his coat pocket.

"It just might be," Atreau replied. It would depend a great deal on how much he could pry out of Father Timoteo. Or perhaps how much he could convince Narsi to get the priest to divulge. "Will you keep looking into it?"

"Of course," Spider began.

"Are you two talking gibberish?" Rinza suddenly demanded. "Or have I gone deaf again?"

"Sorry, my dear, can you understand me now?" Atreau reverted to Cadeleonian. It was for the best anyway, as Inissa sidled up to lean against Spider.

Rinza nodded, but her attention had already wandered from Atreau's face back down to the wine bottle. Spider eyed her for a moment, then he seemed to recall something.

"Oh, before it slips my mind. A man came asking after you yesterday afternoon."

"The Haldiim physician?" Atreau wondered.

"Lord, no! Not nearly so charming as Master Narsi," Inissa broke in. "A sort of bleak, dull creature. Odd how still and quiet he was, though."

Inissa glanced to Spider. "You noticed that too, didn't you?"

"I hardly noticed him at all. I thought he was a fencing dummy until he opened his mouth. What was his name, do you remember?" Spider asked.

Inissa knit her brow as she thought.

Ariz—Atreau already knew that was who it had to have been. But why would he have come here? Unless . . . could he have been ordered to kill Atreau, or perhaps Prince Jacinto?

"Corpse!" Inissa said suddenly and she smiled. "That's what Sabella called him. She knew the fellow from the Red Stallion. They seemed . . . friendly?"

"Comfortable with each other." Spider took up the story while Inissa found a knife and began preparing two plates of cold cuts and steaming-fresh rolls.

Atreau's stomach gnawed at its own emptiness as the aroma of bread and melting butter drifted through the air.

"They had some dull as ditchwater conversation about short swords." Spider rolled his eyes. "But then the Corpse fellow had to go, and Sabella didn't stay much longer either."

"Sabella wanted you to know that she's moved Suelita in with her uncle at the Red Stallion and that she'll be watching over Jacinto at the palace through the night and this morning," Inissa added.

They two of them were already talking like a married couple, completing each other's thoughts, Atreau realized.

"The Corpse fellow left you this." Spider drew a crumpled, twisted wad of paper from beneath the bar. Atreau scowled at the filthy-looking paper. Were those bloodstains spattered on the side? Spider and Inissa both shared his disconcerted expression at the condition of the note. Even Rinza cast the damp wad a dubious look.

"Is that a snot rag?" Rinza queried from her less-than-sober state.

"One hopes not." Atreau reached out and accepted the note. Unfolding it, he quickly he took in a wild mess of crossed-out scrawls that were not dissimilar from the writing in the charm-book that Narsi had been picking over. But then a little sketch caught his eye. A box with what might have been a hunting motif drawn on the lid. At least it looked like a deer.

That couldn't be a coincidence.

Beside the sketch a jittery string of letters looked as if they'd been tossed on top of each other. Atreau studied them closely.

Find it before I do.

"Trouble?" Spider asked.

"No, just poor penmanship. Admirers of my more carnal writings come from many different walks of life; not all are schooled in letters," Atreau replied for the benefit of the few people whose attention had been drawn by Rinza's exclamation. He crushed the note and shoved it into his pocket. Then he lowered his voice. "But nothing from Master Narsi?"

"Not since two days ago when he left you those notes for your play." Spider paused and Atreau thought that his brother was searching his face, but for what he had no idea. Spider's study of him seemed so intent that Atreau nearly lifted his hand to feel for some smudge. Then Spider shook his head. "I don't know that you should hold out too much hope in that regard. From what I've seen he seems to be quite occupied with the company of that actress, Yara. Last time he came she joined him and they were reading lines from the play and laughing themselves into stitches."

"Are we gossiping about Yara and Narsi?" Inissa's expression brightened and she and Spider exchanged another affectionate smile. "They're an adorable couple, aren't they?"

"No, *you're* an . . . an adorable couple," Rinza slurred at Inissa and Spider. Drunk as she was, she wasn't wrong there. Standing side by side, the two of them truly were a handsome couple—both physically attractive and also charming in their obvious happiness simply leaning against each other. Atreau just hoped that word never got back to Jacinto.

"Thank you." Spider paused, considering Rinza, and then cast Atreau another concerned glance, which spoke volumes about his opinion of the pairing Atreau and Rinza made. He added, "Honestly, the master physician seems a little refined for your company."

"Not yourself as well?" Inissa teased Spider.

"Absolutely." Spider grinned at her. "Normally it's quacks and cardsharps that I'm used to chatting up, and here comes Master Narsi making conversation about Salt Island hot springs, medicinal sulfur deposits and mulberry paper used in temple scriptures. That lad is too learned by half."

"Too cultured, too kind and much too striking. A heartbreaker." Inissa spoke as if issuing Atreau some warning. Which was ironic, considering all the times Atreau had voiced his fears of Inissa breaking Spider's heart.

"I couldn't agree more," Atreau replied. "I suspect that the only reason he seeks me out is due to the misapprehension of his calling. The good physician hasn't yet learned that some folks can't be cured of who they are."

"You might be mistaking Master Narsi's bedside manner for devotion, you know." Inissa pushed a lock of her long black hair back from her face and offered Atreau an amused smile. She was definitely teasing him now.

"Of course I am," Atreau replied, and he suspected that he wasn't really lying. "Like most aging degenerates, I indulge myself in the fantasy that it's the complexity of my character that inspires my physician's interest and not my astonishing history of venereal misadventures."

"Now you're just bragging." Inissa rolled her eyes. Then she looked to Rinza and the cat lounging across Atreau's shoulders. She shook her head. "Though perhaps it would be best if you didn't embroil the fellow in your current enterprises. It would be a shame if his shining character became tarnished so soon."

"None of us want that," Atreau agreed.

The fact of the matter was that he couldn't afford to cut Narsi free. He needed Narsi's access to the sacred grove and his ability to both treat and interrogate the murderous bundle of muscle that was Master Ariz. Add to that the fact that Father Timoteo adored him and was most likely to divulge secrets to him—if anyone. No, he truly did need Narsi. At least for as long as he could keep the young man's attention.

Already he suspected that his sway over Narsi waned. Whether that was because Narsi had taken him at his word when he'd claimed to desire only his friendship or because Narsi had discovered other far more alluring companions, Atreau wasn't certain. But the young man certainly could keep himself well occupied in other company.

Between working in Fedeles's household, the Haldiim District and the theater, it sometimes seemed that Master Narsi was busy everywhere else with everyone else. That wasn't even taking into consideration the time Narsi spent deciphering the incomprehensible charm-book he and Atreau had stolen from Hierro's assassin, Dommain. What little free time Narsi possessed, he spent in the Haldiim District—

most likely enjoying Yara's lively company. Atreau guessed that Narsi wouldn't be spending another night with him.

It pained him a little, but he reassured himself that it would be for the best for everyone if Narsi drifted away.

"And speaking of my current endeavor, I'd best get to it." Atreau squeezed Rinza's shoulder, rousing her from her daze. Then he turned and led her up the staircase, leaving his brother and Inissa to enjoy their meal and each other's company.

With a bottle in hand, Rinza tromped alongside Atreau up into the anonymous room that largely served as a decoy for men like Captain Yago to exhaust themselves searching. It wasn't the truly private chamber that he'd once shared with Inissa and that he'd nearly shared with Narsi for a night. But this room served. He'd tidied it a little since Captain Yago had last visited—the mattress was back on the bed frame and the tables stood upright—but between the tattered curtains and the stuffing spilling from one of the chairs, the room hardly looked elegant.

The cat leapt from Atreau's shoulder, landing on the dressing table. There it sat and made a show of licking its paws. Rinza dropped to the edge of the rumpled bed.

"I expected you'd keep nicer house," she mumbled. "Aren't you a lord and all?"

"Alas, a noble upbringing endowed me with little skill in the art of housekeeping," Atreau said. "And even less ambition to improve in the field."

"Me neither," Rinza replied, then she frowned at him. "You weren't hoping I'd play the part of your maid, were you?"

"No, that I am not, my dear. Though I do have a proposition for you." Atreau pulled off his coat and hung it on a brass hook.

Rinza attempted a coy smile, but Atreau could see that her heart wasn't in it. Fear for her brother occupied her remaining cognizant thoughts. Her gaze focused on the bottle of wine in her hands. She flopped back onto the mattress and held the bottle up while Atreau lit one of the lamps on the bedside table and then closed and locked the door. The cat bounded from the dressing table to the bed and stalked to Rinza's side. She paid it no mind, instead turning her head to observe Atreau as he pulled one of the mangled chairs to the bedside.

"Here, let me hold this for you." Atreau reached out and gripped the wine bottle just as the cat lay its paws on Rinza's hip. She opened her mouth to protest, but then her expression went slack and her hands dropped like stones across her chest. Atreau caught the bottle, keeping it from falling onto her head. He set it aside on the bedside table and waited.

In a matter of moments the cat sank down across Rinza's lap, going so limp that it almost looked skinned. It closed its yellow eyes. Rinza opened her brown ones. She blinked at Atreau and then, as she took in a breath, she made a sour face. She glanced down at her own scrawny body and bare feet.

"Now, why is it that you always offer me such foul-smelling creatures to inhabit?" The voice was Rinza's, but Atreau recognized Hylanya's Labaran cadence.

"The sort of people who are unlikely to care that they can't remember hours or days of their lives aren't always the most fastidious members of our population," Atreau replied. It was the truth, though Atreau also tried to pick people whom he knew would benefit from having Hylanya's power course through their ravaged bodies. Rinza, more than many, deserved that small kindness just now.

Hylanya sat up, groaned and closed her eyes. Atreau waited, giving her time to take full possession of the body and heal the worst of Rinza's injuries and ailments. A touch of pink spread across Rinza's sallow cheeks. When Hylanya opened her eyes again, Atreau noticed how very clear the gaze regarding him had grown.

"How much of Lliro's conversation did you follow earlier?" Atreau asked.

"Most of it," Hylanya replied. "And I'd tell you that I'm sorry for your father's passing, but from the sound of things—"

"I appreciate the thought, but there's no need." Atreau shrugged. "It's Fedeles who I'm worried about. Is there anything you can do?"

"Oh, there are many things I could do, but none that I *would* unless I had no other option." Hylanya absently stroked the cat's still body. "The few remaining wards that guard your Hallowed Kings are the very things I would have to destroy to reach him. Then who knows what would be unleashed."

Atreau scowled. Why did Fedeles have to be imprisoned at the Shard of Heaven, of all places? Javier had warned him that the Shard of Heaven housed a world-destroying spell, though Atreau could not fathom why anyone would keep, much less risk unleashing cataclysmic magic. What kingdom would be left to rule once the carnage abated? It made no sense.

"That may be the reason your enemies took Fedeles to the Shard of Heaven in the first place," Hylanya said. "Perhaps they hope that in a panic to break free, he will tear the oldest, toughest spells asunder."

"Could he do that?" Atreau asked.

"His witchflame is strong and wild. He might not mean to destroy the wards, but if he felt trapped . . ." Hylanya shrugged, but her expression turned bleak. "He could do it."

"That can't be their plan." Atreau stared out the small window, taking in the play of bright morning light over the gaudy buildings of the Theater District. Street musicians and jugglers were already staking out their pitches on the narrow streets. The scent of baking bread and brewing kaweh filled the air, as did distant laughter and the first notes of a familiar song. All of this would be lost if the wards were destroyed. "How could it possibly serve Hierro Fueres or the royal bishop to loose destruction on their own city? That can't be their goal."

"If it's not theirs, then it's someone else's," Hylanya replied. "Because it continues every day. Thread by thread, the wards are being picked apart. Another demon lord must not be released."

"You believe it's a demon lord that the Hallowed Kings hold captive?" Atreau glanced to her.

"What else could it be?" Hylanya shrugged again.

Javier had seemed certain that something else, something far worse—a world-destroying Waarihivu spell—lay trapped in the Shard of Heaven. He wondered suddenly if Javier had kept that suspicion secret from the Labarans. Or did Hylanya have reason to think him wrong?

"I'm personally hoping it's an orgy of mythical beasts and wanton Old Gods," Atreau replied. "That or a geyser of wine."

Hylanya laughed.

"As far as you can tell, has Fedeles attempted to break through the wards?" Atreau asked.

Hylanya stared out the window, then closed her eyes for several moments before returning her attention to Atreau.

"No, he hasn't yet," Hylanya replied, but she frowned. "There is something happening there, though. All the lights glinting behind the gold wards. You haven't noticed it?"

"Thankfully, no," Atreau replied. He didn't find the thought of vast, invisible magic whirling and churning all around particularly comforting. "My ignorance may be my greatest source of confidence just now."

Hylanya laughed again but then cast Atreau a reproachful glance. The expression was particularly odd on Rinza's face.

"But that's not wise, Atreau. Cadeleonian sorcery is at work all around you." Hylanya shook her head. "You should practice as our Elezar does. You stare hard where you think there is magic and then close your eyes tight. On the back of your eyelids you will see an impression of the witchflames, or spells. Our Elezar can always find Skellan that way."

"I'll keep it in mind next time I'm playing hide-and-seek with Skellan. Thank you," Atreau replied. No doubt it would be a useful skill to hone, but he'd only been half joking about needing some ignorance to maintain his resolve to stay in the capital. If he could actually see some terrible menace thrashing at the Shard of Heaven and slowly breaking free, he didn't know that he could go on hunting Hierro's agents, much less making conversation and writing scenes for Jacinto's play.

"Do you still want me to attempt to break Fedeles out?" Hylanya asked, and from her tone Atreau knew that she was preparing to refuse his request.

"No. I don't think we'll have to resort to tearing down the Shard of Heaven just yet," Atreau said. "If my brother can't rouse Prince Sevanyo to have Fedeles released, then Oasia will." Atreau had thought the matter over on the walk to the Fat Goose and nearly convinced himself. Oasia wasn't one to meekly wait for powerful men to make decisions for her. She would fight for Fedeles, if for no other reason than the fact that he kept her from being returned to her father's grasp.

Eventually Fedeles would be freed.

He tried not to think of how frightened Fedeles probably felt just now. He reminded himself that Fedeles wasn't a schoolboy anymore but a grown man. He didn't lack courage or other allies.

"Good. The longer the wards hold, the better." Hylanya yawned, then stood and stretched. "We don't want to seize your city, but if another demon lord broke free, we would have no choice."

Atreau felt his frown deepening into a scowl.

"There have been rumors that Radulf County is readying to invade," Atreau said. Unlike Fedeles and Sevanyo, he didn't think the stories were pure conjecture. He'd seen the horror of a demon lord rampage, and he'd witnessed Radulf County make war.

Hylanya didn't deny it.

"It's funny, isn't it," she said at last. "The very people who have been mounting forces all along our borders and daily sailing more troops into the southern Labaran protectorates are the ones who claim to fear that *we* in Radulf County are planning to launch an invasion."

"Certain idiots will always attempt to provoke conflict," Atreau responded. He'd known many such men and they weren't all fools; some were worse: profiteers of misfortune and war. But railing against them wouldn't prevent anything. People like Hylanya were the ones who had to be reasoned with. "You and Skellan are far too intelligent to be drawn in by petty provocations—"

"Neither Skellan nor I wish to wage another war, much less invade Cadeleon. For the sake of peace, we have ignored parades of Cadeleonian soldiers along our borders and your spies creeping through our streets." Hylanya looked as disgusted as if she'd just noticed fleas skipping through her clothes. "But if Cadeleon allows the Hallowed Kings to fail, then our entire world will be imperiled. We are prepared to do all we must to ensure that does not come to pass."

"Even invade?" Atreau asked.

"If we must." Resolve permeated Hylanya's soft voice.

"What does Javier say about that?" Atreau asked, though he suspected that he already knew.

"Much the same. The Bahiim won't allow such a thing either. Still, it would be for the best if none of us were forced to intervene."

"It would indeed," Atreau managed to reply. He'd seen the campaigns that Elezar, Skellan and Javier were capable of waging. For just an instant

Atreau felt sick horror rise in him, as if he were witnessing the Raccroc River again clogged with mangled corpses and the land erupting in geysers of flame.

"If you can discover who is destroying the wards that protect the Shard of Heaven and stop them, then there is hope," Hylanya said. "But it must be done soon. Skellan will not wait much longer, not even for our dear Elezar's sake."

"I'll add that to my list of duties," Atreau replied. "Right alongside exposing Hierro Fueres as a traitor and bringing the royal bishop to heel."

"I'm sorry that I can't give you much help," Hylanya said. "But reaching across so great a distance is tiring and the heavens of Cieloalta are so filled with magic that a single source is difficult to trace. Your Fedeles has set the air ablaze over Crown Hill. Bahiim ghosts rise as storms of crows from the Circle of Wisteria, while spy birds circle the city constantly. And on the streets there are the ever-growing numbers of enthralled assassins."

Atreau scowled. Those would be Hierro Fueres's minions. Their latest assassinations had been so bloody that they threatened to turn popular sympathy entirely away from Fedeles and make the royal bishop seem justified.

"Could the attack on the wards be Hierro Fueres's doing as well?" Atreau wondered aloud. If he was willing to have his own confederates killed simply to throw suspicion on Fedeles and Oasia, would he also risk the destruction of the Hallowed Kings? But what would the advantage be for him? "Who in Cieloalta could possibly benefit from the city's collapse?"

"Who can say, considering how Cadeleonians plot and squabble. It will be the ruin of your nation," Hylanya said. "You have a monstrosity waking in the heart of your city, but all your lords, princes and bishops do is attack one another."

"I recall that Labara had its share of political unrest even in the face of three armies laying siege to it," Atreau responded. He'd been there when Hylanya herself had nearly destroyed the unity of Radulf County.

"We learned to work together in the face of a common enemy," Hylanya said. "Your lords refuse to recognize your enemy. Instead they imagine that we in the north are their greatest threat."

"The fact that you're raising a fleet to invade us doesn't exactly prove them wrong," Atreau retorted. "You just admitted as much yourself, didn't you?"

"You know what they say. Call a monster's name often enough and eventually it will come for you." Hylanya sighed and paced to the small circular mirror that hung on the wall. She raised her hand to the face that stared back at her, lightly touching the bruise that colored Rinza's cheek. Then she pulled back the sleeve of her dress and gazed at Rinza's scraped and bruised arms. "I prefer being a cat."

"Wouldn't we all," Atreau replied offhandedly. Sometimes it was truly evident that Hylanya was still only nineteen. "Look, as soon as Sevanyo is crowned, he'll have the authority to invite you and Skellan to court. Then you should be able to strengthen the wards surrounding the Shard of Heaven. This doesn't have to come to war. None of us want that."

"I don't know. Perhaps someone does," Hylanya said. "Mayhap someone in this city believes a demon lord is as easily enthralled by a Brand of Obedience as a mortal man."

And they were back to Hierro Fueres. Atreau considered the idea. Could Hierro believe that if the Hallowed Kings failed and a demon lord was released, he would be able to make it into his servant? Atreau was forced to admit that Hierro might just be that arrogant.

"Whoever it is, you had best stop them quickly." Hylanya dropped back down onto the bed. "Our ships are ready to sail. If I were you I would keep the stone of passage at hand and be prepared to join Skellan very soon."

"Another week," Atreau said. "Will you ask Skellan to at least wait that long?"

"I'll assure him that you are all doing everything that you can," Hylanya replied. "But you need to understand that this isn't up to Skellan or any of us in Labara. Someone here is destroying the wards and your Hallowed Kings. That is who has set your deadline and ours."

Atreau wanted to argue, but he knew that was no point. Hylanya turned her head to look at him.

"Shall I convey any other messages to your friends back at home?" she asked.

"Tell them that I hope I won't see any of them too soon," Atreau replied.

Hylanya gave a brief laugh, then she closed her eyes and her face went slack.

The cat slowly roused itself and then jumped off the bed and sauntered to the door. Atreau let it out, to go about whatever business Hylanya's familiars engaged in when she had no need of them.

When he turned back to his room, he found that Rinza had sat up and taken possession of the wine bottle again. But she'd not pulled the cork free. Instead she simply studied the pale wine with a desolate expression.

"I need to get out of this city," she said, and she sounded much more sober and certain than she had a mere half hour ago. "This place is doomed. I can feel it in my bones."

Atreau wondered if that idea had been impressed into her by Hylanya's passing presence or if it arose entirely from Rinza's own fear. He reached into his pocket and considered fishing out his coin purse to toss her the funds for passage out of Cadeleon. But then his fingers brushed across the damp note that Ariz had left for him. He recalled his brother's description of the golden box hidden somewhere in the Slate House. There was little chance that Atreau could get inside himself. But perhaps a small, clever thief might.

Atreau leaned back in the chair beside the bed. He offered Rinza his warmest smile. "You'll need money, if you're to start anew."

Rinza looked tired and frightened, but she met Atreau's gaze and nodded, already accepting the bargain that he would proffer. He truly pitied her in that moment, but not enough to set her free.

CHAPTER
FOUR

Narsi crouched low, holding his knife with surgical care. Dim predawn light turned the lush, feathery plants surrounding him into foreign gray masses. With his free hand he traced the bristling, tough stems of squash vines, then a knuckle brushed across the soft, velvety texture of duera leaves. Delicate and dangerously potent flowers hung between these leaves. An involuntary shudder passed through his fingers. Less than a month ago a different poison nearly cost him his right hand. Black scars peppered his fingers and an ache persisted in his knuckles. He felt no desire to endure the experience again. Under other circumstances he would never have harvested these dangerous blossoms in the dark.

But three weeks ago two holy scholars living on the edge of the Haldiim District had been drugged and their lodgings robbed. Both men recovered, but the royal bishop had decreed that until the culprits were found, all drugs would be banned from the Haldiim District. Haldiim pharmacists were not even allowed to purchase medicinal herbs—lest they be used as poisons against their Cadeleonian neighbors.

Narsi had only secured his own plants from the King's Physic Garden by sheer luck. He'd dispatched Father Timoteo's acolyte, Nillo, to deliver his order to the conservators and, faced with a young man dressed in church robes, they accepted the money. The fact that Narsi's employer—Father Timoteo—had been made a bishop and was expected to preside over Prince Sevanyo's coronation had likely been the deciding factor in the conservators' acquiescence to release the potent seedlings into his care. And since the deliveries were made to the Duke of Rauma's household, the conservators could retain some claim of ignorance concerning Narsi's Haldiim heritage if ever they were questioned.

But none of the pharmacists or physicians living in the Haldiim District had his lofty connections. And yet the welfare of thousands of people depended upon them. All at once the contraband plants hidden in Lord Quemanor's kitchen garden became one of the only source of herbs available to the Haldiim District.

Narsi moved his fingertips over each blossom with the hovering flightiness of a honeybee; then he applied his knife. Precise cuts rewarded him with a delicate lilac scent. He added the blossoms to his basket, then crept forward to hunt more of the illicit herbs from where they hid beneath rows of bush beans and squash blossoms. His back ached and his fingers felt stiff from the morning chill.

Querra hunched in the row across from him with her own basket, working her harvest knife quickly and quietly. She paused briefly to roll her shoulders and then returned to work. Narsi suppressed a yawn. It felt like it had been weeks since he'd enjoyed a full night's sleep.

But he wouldn't have been able to respect himself as a person, much less a physician, if he hadn't volunteered to help Querra and Mother Kir-Naham secure medical herbs for the Haldiim District. A few hours of missed sleep wasn't much of a sacrifice, really. Certainly it didn't match the danger that Querra faced when transporting the herbs to Mother Kir-Naham's pharmacy. Thankfully, it hadn't yet occurred to the royal bishop's guardsmen now patrolling the Haldiim District that a Cadeleonian woman like Querra could be the widow of a Haldiim gardener and the mother of a Haldiim pharmacist.

Querra peered between the trellises of climbing beans and offered Narsi a smile through the wan light. He smiled back, but neither of them dared to speak a word.

Many of the people in Lord Quemanor's vast household held tolerant or even radical beliefs, but neither Narsi nor Querra could afford to test just how happily any of them would welcome outright lawbreaking.

Narsi snipped the last blossoms from his row and straightened. Moments later Querra joined him. Despite her age and plump figure, she moved with surprising speed and stealth. The aromatic tang of solanum fruit wafted from her gray hair. The sun had risen enough that Narsi could almost make out the grape-leaf pattern decorating the cloth that she'd spread over her harvest basket to hide the illicit herbs.

"Enough for now, I think," Querra whispered.

Narsi nodded. Milkmaids rose with the sun, as did many grooms, and the roosters out in the chicken coops were already sounding off. Soon the grounds of the duke's household would be bustling with people.

Querra drew back the cloth covering her basket and Narsi emptied his own pickings in with hers. The mounds of tiny violet flowers struck him as dishearteningly small in comparison to the needs of the entire Haldiim District. But it was better than nothing, and he reassured himself that Mother Kir-Naham and Querra's daughter, Esfir, would waste none of it.

"I should be able to deliver this to the pharmacy tonight." Querra flipped the cloth back over the flowers and herbs. "Do you think you'll be free to meet up there for tea and adhil bread tomorrow morning?"

"Absolutely." Narsi had come to cherish his visits to the pharmacy, not only because it offered him an opportunity to discuss medicine in detail but because the visits to the Haldiim District eased the sense of isolation that sometimes seized him living in the duke's household—seeing only Cadeleonian faces.

They started back toward the duke's towering mansion.

"And the Solstice Day Procession?" Querra asked.

"I . . ." Narsi foundered. He wanted to assure her that no matter, what he would be there striding alongside Querra, Esfir, Yara and other Haldiim citizens when they marched from the Circle of Wisteria past the Physic Gardens, even if that route brought them perilously close to defying the royal bishop's edicts.

Over the last month he'd grown close to Querra's family, as well as Yara and her flamboyant friends. He couldn't imagine abandoning them. But he'd also sworn his skill and time to Lord Vediya. And on top of that he'd promised Brother Berto that he would be on hand to look after Father Timoteo—especially now that he'd been made a bishop and carried the burden of officiating the upcoming coronation. Narsi hated the thought of disappointing any of his disparate circles of friends, much less failing one for the sake of another.

There was also the question, if he was hurt or detained, who would care for Master Ariz or be able to extract the vital information he possessed?

Narsi frowned at his herb knife, struggling between his desire to please and fear of failure. So many of the endeavors consuming his time demanded such secrecy that he couldn't even explain his situation to Querra honestly.

Was it so selfish to wish that he wouldn't have to choose between them?

"You mustn't worry that your friend Yara won't be welcomed right alongside us, you know." Querra obviously read his hesitation but misunderstood the reason for it. "Mother Kir-Naham likes to pretend that she's scandalized by the theatrics of the Nur-Aud family, but really it would be a coup if she could introduce so talented a performer as Yara to her associates on the civic council. Esfir loves her company as well."

"I had begun to suspect as much," Narsi replied.

In fact Esfir all but interrogated Narsi over Yara's pursuits and tastes when last they spoke. Since then she and Yara had gone on several outings together. They shared a deep admiration of Bahiim lore and both regularly visited the sacred grove. Though Narsi wasn't certain that Yara's interests were quite as ardent as Esfir's.

"The only trouble is . . ." Narsi groped for any excuse. "I'm not certain that either Yara or I will be free, what with all the rehearsals for Prince Jacinto's play."

"A rehearsal on the Summer Solstice? It's a holy day!"

"Prince Jacinto appears happy to ignore his own Cadeleonian holy days, so I don't know how much sway Haldiim ones hold over him." At least Narsi could speak truthfully about this. "The thing is that he's demanding that his production premiere the first week of his father's reign. But currently the entire thing is a wild shambles. There are roles for swearing parrots and flying nymphs one day, but then the prince will change his mind. New sets are still being built. New battles choreographed, and the dialogue . . ." Narsi shook his head. "Originally I was supposed to be some nobody standing in the wings, and now I have pages and pages of lines to memorize. More every time I attend a rehearsal, and I've begged off from nearly half of them already. Honestly, I have no idea how Yara or any of the actresses with large roles are keeping up."

"Still, it's only a play," Querra commented.

"A play that's being produced by a prince and intended to be performed for the king—" Narsi cut himself off seeing Querra's darkening expression. "But I will do all I possibly can to be at your side for the Summer Solstice, I swear."

Querra looked like she might continue pressing him for a firmer commitment, but then shouts arose from near the front gate. Narsi recognized the voice of one of the night guards. The man bellowed, loud and long.

Captain Yago and his men were at the gates! Immediately Narsi noticed lamps lighting in the windows of the dark mansion. Servants hurried from the kitchen, scullery and their quarters. Armed men dashed from the guards' barracks. The noise and light set the roosters and geese sounding off, and across the vast grounds, even the hunting hounds barked their alarm.

Narsi and Querra exchanged a worried glance.

"I'd best get inside," Querra whispered, and Narsi nodded. Then, glancing down at his own empty basket, he quickly knelt and gathered a fistful of shelling peas.

"To add to the gruel I prescribed for Master Leadro's piles, in case anyone inquires," Narsi said.

"The maids and gardeners know you well enough now not to even bother asking if I gave you leave to gather from the kitchen gardens," Querra assured him. Narsi wanted to believe as much, but he couldn't help fearing that the royal bishop's recent edicts could too easily plant fear and suspicion in the minds of many devout Cadeleonians.

"Tomorrow at the pharmacy," Narsi promised Querra.

She offered him a brief hug, then she dashed away to the scullery building. A moment later she disappeared from sight and Narsi turned toward his own rooms.

"He means to make an arrest!" a pageboy shouted as he darted into the back of the main house. Fear slithered through the pit of Narsi's stomach.

Who had Captain Yago come for? Could Master Ariz's crimes have been traced back to the household? Possibly to Narsi himself? Or was this to do with those secret meetings that Lord Vediya disappeared off to? Narsi stole a glance over his shoulder up to the room that Lord Vediya occupied. The window remained dark, just as it had all the night through. Narsi tried not to acknowledge how aware he was of the other man's comings and goings, but just now it reassured him to know that Captain Yago would not take Lord Vediya by surprise if that had been his reason for coming to the duke's household at so early an hour.

He forced himself to maintain an appearance of calm, though a moment later it occurred to him that looking utterly unconcerned in the midst of so much disturbance was hardly natural.

"Narsi!" Brother Berto's voice rose over the clamor of guards and barking hounds. Narsi looked ahead to see Berto racing from the chapel grounds in the direction of his physic garden. He gripped something dark and oddly shaped in his right hand. Alarm shot through Narsi. Had something happened to Father Timoteo? He'd been looking so much healthier lately, but still.

Narsi sped across the grounds, leaping over mounds of moss roses to intercept Berto. He caught him near the side of the main house, on the white pebble path.

"Berto! What is the matter?" Narsi touched his friend's back. Berto started at the contact and spun around. And his wide-eyed expression turned to relief.

"Narsi. Thank God!" He clapped Narsi on the shoulder with his left hand and Narsi realized that Berto was carrying a pair of weathered black shoes in his right hand. From the size of them Narsi guessed they belonged to Father Timoteo.

"Has something happened to Father Timoteo?" Narsi asked.

"He's fine, though I don't know that I've ever seen him looking so angry before in my life." Berto shook his head. "No, it's you I'm worried about. Captain Yago has just arrested the duke."

"What? Lord Quemanor?" Narsi had heard him clearly enough, but he could hardly believe Berto's words. For a mere captain of the royal bishop's guardsmen to arrest the Duke of Rauma, he would have to be in possession of irrefutable evidence, wouldn't he? A disturbing thought struck Narsi. Could the gossip be true? Had the duke killed Lord Wonena? Lord Vediya had assured him that the rumors were nothing but malicious lies.

Still, Narsi couldn't help but remember that instant when the duke's expression had twisted with fury and the deathly cold blackness of the duke's shadow had swept over Narsi's head.

"What charges have—" Narsi began, but Berto broke in.

"Who cares what noblemen do to each other! Their business doesn't matter. Except that without the duke's protection, his entire household could be in danger. Once the royal bishop's supporters learn what's happened, they'll come after the duchess and the rest of us. But especially you! Narsi, you could be in grave danger." The gloom disguised much of the anguish in Berto's expression but not in his voice. "If they find you—"

"I doubt it's so bad as that." Narsi placed his hands on his friend's shoulders. To his surprise he realized that Berto was trembling, as if genuinely terrified on Narsi's behalf. The argument he had intended to offer—that they couldn't afford to ignore the machinations of noblemen because the conflicts of lords impacted the lives of everyone in the na-tion—died on Narsi's lips. He felt both touched and alarmed at Berto's state of mind, and thought only of reassuring his friend.

"No one is going to come looking for me." Narsi said. "Hardly anyone even knows of me. And I'm certainly not of such importance that the duke's enemies would single me out."

"Narsi, you don't know . . ." Berto shook his head, and he seemed to struggle to find the words he wanted to say. "I . . . it . . . things are getting worse and worse here. You'd be so much safer back in Anacleto. You and Father Timoteo both. If anything happened I'd never—"

Berto was cut off by the sudden, clanging intrusion of armed men charging along the path. Their armor rang like chapel bells and their figures appeared strange and hulking as they pelted from the gloom.

"Out of the way!" one guard shouted.

Narsi and Berto both leapt clear, as did several maids who'd wandered, half dressed, out of the main house. At least a dozen more armed men charged after the first. The rising sun glinted across the tips of their pikes and spears. All of them raced for the front gates of the house. Narsi stared after them as it dawned upon him that the guards moved in formation; they were preparing to do battle.

Narsi touched the strap of his medical satchel.

Should he follow them, in case someone was hurt? Would he only get underfoot and possibly be killed if he followed at such close quarters?

"Master Berto! Master Narsi!" Two of Father Timoteo's young acolytes ran from the chapel. Their unlined black robes fluttered around their nightshirts like sparrow's wings. The taller of the two, Nillo, carried a flickering oil lamp. The smaller, gap-toothed boy was called Reo.

"The Holy Father's gone!" Reo shouted.

"He wouldn't even wait to search for his shoes," Nillo gasped out as he struggled to catch his breath. "I'm sorry. We tried to delay him."

"It's not your fault." Berto gripped the worn shoes and then looked all at once defeated.

"Where has he gone?" Narsi asked of the acolytes.

"To the stables," Reo said.

"He and the duchess plan to rouse Prince Sevanyo, on the duke's behalf," Nillo added. "They're riding to the palace with armed guards!"

"Why does he always have to be this way?" Berto muttered.

Nillo frowned and appeared to consider the question, as if any of them could offer a greater explanation of Father Timoteo's actions than his irrepressibly courageous character. Though it did seem that in the past weeks, as he'd regained his appetite and his strength, Father Timoteo had been more outspoken against the royal bishop and more defiant in his sermons.

Berto groaned and Narsi cast him a sympathetic glance. In his own way, Father Timoteo was as reckless, gallant and fearless as his more famous ancestors and siblings. There would be no point in attempting to keep him from involving himself in the duke's troubles. The only decision left to Berto or Narsi now was whether they should follow Father Timoteo or not.

"Well, he can't ride unaccompanied. Especially not now that he's been made a bishop," Narsi decided, and then he glanced to Berto. "And he needs his shoes."

Berto sighed but then nodded. Together they raced between the camellia hedges toward the towering walls of the duke's stable. There, a flurry of shirtless grooms, irritated horses and flustered servants presented a chaotic scene. A page bellowed for the duchess's charger to be saddled, while guards claimed their own mounts. A horse briefly broke free and ran a little distance into the gardens. Three groundsmen lit after it. They managed to catch the animal's reins and led it back to the stables. One of the duchess's ladies-in-waiting took possession of the animal and it calmed.

Narsi spotted the duchess herself, Oasia Quemanor, amidst the sea of her ladies-in-waiting, maids and guards. Narsi had never before seen her look anything other than perfectly composed, so the disarray of her black hair and her thrown-together, half-laced clothes struck him as truly disturbing. Her ladies-in-waiting and maids looked no better. Among them Delfia Plunado had clearly pulled her dress and knife belt on but forgone the time-consuming task of lacing on her dress sleeves. She wore shoes but no stockings. To Narsi's eye she looked prepared for a fight. She glanced to Narsi and Berto and offered them a brief smile before she returned her attention to her dun mount. She swung into her saddle with consummate ease.

"Narsi! Berto!"

Narsi spun and caught sight of Father Timoteo standing to the right of the stable doors. His short white hair jutted out around his gaunt face. The gold-threaded material of his bishop's robe was too new to spill down his tall, thin frame; instead the stiff fabric seemed to bristle around his body as if the cloth itself was anxious. Mud spattered his stocking feet. Despite the appearance of his hair and clothes, Father Timoteo's demeanor struck Narsi as self-possessed—calm. As agitated maids, grooms and guards looked to him, he offered assured smiles, and when the duchess and he exchanged a glance, Father Timoteo went to her and briefly caught her hand in his.

"We will not allow any harm to befall Fedeles, I promise you that," Father Timoteo said. "Seizing him like this only betrays the level of the royal bishop's delusion. Once Sevanyo is informed, we'll have Fedeles home in no time. Never fear, my lady."

The duchess nodded, then squared her shoulders, and at once her aura of supreme poise seemed to return to her. Narsi wasn't certain how, but even her hair and clothes appeared less tousled than he'd first thought.

Or perhaps that was merely the effect of the sun rising over the household walls and bathing them all in light and warmth.

Father Timoteo turned his attention back to Narsi and Berto. He grinned and he strode to them.

"Ah, Berto! You found my shoes. Wonderful!" Father Timoteo took the shoes from Berto, slipped them on, and then beamed at both Berto and Narsi. "The duchess and I should be back in no time—"

"No. Father, you aren't in good health. You mustn't—" Berto began, but Father Timoteo raised his voice and shouted over his objections, calling to the groom leading his roan stallion from the stables.

"We're coming with you," Narsi informed Father Timoteo. The holy father looked like he might object, but Berto cut him off.

"It's only befitting of your new rank to be attended by at least two servants." Berto crossed his arms over his broad chest. "If you can't be dissuaded from breaking in on Prince Sevanyo's vigil, then you should at least arrive in a manner befitting a bishop."

"I suppose you're right." Father Timoteo smiled indulgently at the two of them. Then he instructed the groom to ready both Berto's and Narsi's mounts. Belatedly Narsi realized that he and Berto had just volunteered to charge into the royal palace and break in upon the royal heir and his father, the king.

CHAPTER
FIVE

The sheer volume of riches scattered throughout the royal palace dumbfounded Narsi. Gilded flowers climbed the lapis-lazuli-inlaid walls and encircled huge ivory-framed portraits of the king. Gold and azurite colored the vaulted ceilings. Pearls and cut crystals encrusted the chandeliers overhead. Even the tiles clattering beneath his boots glittered with veins of gold and opal.

At the top of a huge marble staircase, their party skirted several religious sculptures depicting bravery and sacrifice in the forms of stallions and eagles, but all the precious stones and gold encrusting the figures gave a greater impression of extravagance and luxury.

"Are those rubies?" Berto whispered and pointed to another sculpture. Narsi studied the scene of the king in his youth, wearing gold armor and battling wild beasts. It did appear that several of the dying monsters bled streams of rubies. A piece of polished coral jutted from an enormous wolf's mouth. Narsi couldn't say if it was intended to represent flames or a very peculiar tongue.

All at once, Narsi felt he understood the source of Prince Jacinto's grand, theatrical tastes.

A page boy holding the leashes of two fat lapdogs gave a startled shout. No one paid him any mind. So he simply stood gaping as their large group of men and women—most dressed in Quemanor green and some well armed—stormed through the wide hall. The little dogs cringed behind the pageboy's legs as the duchess and Father Timoteo strode past. Following close behind the holy father, Narsi glanced past Berto and attempted to offer the young page a reassuring smile. The boy nodded and then gawked at the train of ladies-in-waiting, maids and guards who marched on Narsi's heels. After their entire party had passed, the little dogs began to yap.

"Shouldn't we have been challenged by a royal guard?" Narsi whispered to Berto.

Only once had their party been stopped and an explanation demanded of the duchess. That had been at the palace gates and by four men dressed in black-and-violet uniforms of the royal bishop's guardsmen.

"Perhaps they're all standing vigil over the king alongside Prince Sevanyo?" Berto suggested, but he didn't look convinced.

Ahead of them Narsi at last sighted a pair of weary guards wearing blue-and-gold uniforms belonging to the royal guards. They both appeared well past their primes. Narsi wondered if they'd been called back from retirement to fill out ranks. They saluted and then waved the duchess through yet another set of gilded doors.

These opened into an opulent waiting room, where gold and jewels spread from floor to ceiling and silk drapes hung over huge stained glass windows. The ivory handles of the doors at the far end of the chamber had been carved into a white horse. Gold chimes and strings of sapphires dripped from the little stallions' hooves.

Then Narsi realized that he'd been so lost in his wonder at the richness of the huge waiting room that he'd failed to notice three living men lingered beside the doors—their silk clothes hardly stood out from the resplendent surroundings.

Two of the men wore black priest's robes, though the spears that they each held lent them more of the appearance of soldiers. The third man turned as Narsi and the rest of Duchess Quemanor's entourage flooded into the waiting room. For an instant Narsi thought that somehow Lord Vediya had arrived here before them. Then he realized that the other man's face was narrower and more delicate—almost a match to Spider's. He had to be another the Vediya brothers—one commanding a high rank in the Ministry of the Navies, from the emblems decorating his deep-blue jacket.

"What business brings you here at this hour, Lord Vediya?" The duchess strode ahead of her ladies-in-waiting and allowed the nobleman to bow over her extended hand.

"The same trouble that has roused you, I suspect." This other Lord Vediya's voice sounded nearly as rich as Atreau's, though his words came at a more clipped rate—as if he was used to issuing short, quick orders more than engaging in conversations. "Your good husband has been wrongly accused of my lord Numes's murder. I'm here to ensure that there is no miscarriage of justice in the matter."

A faint crease lined the duchess's brow.

"Is it not *your* lady Numes who has accused my husband?"

"I believe that shock and grief inspired Lady Numes's words, rather than actual recognition of the man responsible." The lord glanced back at the rest of the duchess's entourage, then returned his attention to the duchess. "My youngest brother, Atreau, has assured me that you and most of your household can attest to your husband's whereabouts last night."

"Indeed we can. Should I assume that those were Atreau's parting words to you before he sailed off on one of your ships?" The corner of the duchess's mouth twitched, but she didn't manage even a brief smile.

"They were not, my lady," the man replied, and the way he arched one black brow reminded Narsi of his own Lord Vediya so much that he found himself warming to the fellow. "In fact, Atreau assured me that he has no intention of abandoning your good husband's service. But he did entreat me to hasten here to make my opinion known to Prince Sevanyo. However, it seems that the men guarding the prince's door are not inclined to make way for a mere baron such as myself."

The duchess gave a quick nod of her head, then turned on her heel to the priests barring the doors before her.

"We must speak with His Highness Prince Sevanyo. Stand aside."

The younger of the two priests shifted and seemed about to instinctively obey the duchess's commanding tone. But his companion squared his shoulders and slapped his spear between his hands. The younger priest held his ground, emulating his companion's scowl.

"As we informed Lord Vediya already," the older priest stated, "so long as the prince remains in holy vigil, only clergy and our servants are allowed to enter his presence."

Far from appearing cowed by this announcement, the duchess's expression turned hard and she made a gesture of her hands as if flicking used wash water from her fingertips. The older of the two priests shivered. Dread gripped Narsi. The duchess was a proud and imperious woman born of the royal bloodline, but the spears the priests gripped looked deadly sharp. It would take only a single blow to kill her.

In spite of his own fear, he stepped forward. Father Timoteo glanced to him and smiled approvingly. Then the holy father strode forward himself.

"Weapons aside, both of you! I have urgent news for the prince. Open these doors and announce that Bishop Timoteo has arrived." Father Timoteo glanced back to Narsi and Berto. "Along with my attendants."

Both the priests looked momentarily uncertain. But as Timoteo drew near to them, they took in his imposing height as well as the gold threads adorning his black-and-violet robes. Their reluctance collapsed. The younger priest hauled one of the heavy doors open and the elder priest stepped into the dimly lit room beyond and announced that Bishop Timoteo had arrived along with his servants.

Narsi and Berto stood shoulder to shoulder and lifted their chins as they followed Father Timoteo through the door. Neither of them had ever put much value in intimidating those around them, but just this moment as they strode past the two priests, Narsi was glad for his own height and Berto's broad shoulders.

The priests averted their gazes and hurried back to their posts. An instant later they closed the door, shutting out the light. The sharp smell of coinflower distillate saturated the air. It didn't quite cover that sickly tang of bedpans and drying blood. Narsi squinted through the gloom of the immense bedroom. A haze of dawn light drifted from three windows at the far end of the room. One golden-yellow curtain fluttered in the fresh gust of a morning breeze, but the others hung slack. Faint gold light cast the large bed and the group of men surrounding it into silhouette.

As Narsi's eyes adjusted he recognized that five priests knelt in prayer at the foot of the huge bed while four others—all wearing physician's coats like Narsi's over their robes—occupied the far side. Three of the physician-priests worked at a small table, bowed over pestles, grinding coinflower seeds and—from the smell Narsi guessed—duera. The fourth physician-priest stood on the far side of the bed, gazing down at the emaciated, white-haired man propped up on a mound of embroidered cushions.

Clothed in a long gold nightshirt and stretched atop bedding adorned with the brocade crest of the royal Sagradas, the elderly man was obviously King Juleo. But he didn't strike Narsi as imposing or regal so much as sallow and frail. Narsi couldn't help but study him just as he would have assessed any prospective patient.

He lay very still and his eyes were closed, but his breath came too fast and shallow for Narsi to believe that he slept. A worrying bluish tinge colored the king's mouth. Narsi wished the light was brighter so that he could get a better idea of the elderly man's condition.

Then he chided himself for imaging that with four other physicians in the room, his opinion was the one that ought to matter. He'd be wiser to keep his thoughts to himself.

On the near side of the bed, a handsome, silver-haired man of some seventy years sat on a velvet footstool. The golden circlet he wore proclaimed him a prince and Narsi guessed that this was the royal heir, Sevanyo Sagrada. His features reminded Narsi of Fedeles Quemanor's—particularly his large, dark eyes and high cheekbones. He appeared to be on the edge of tears as he clasped his hands in prayer and murmured fervently over his steepled fingers. His stark sorrow and raw voice made the surrounding priests, with their serene expressions and steady intonations of prayers, seem disinterested—almost mechanical.

"Sevanyo!" Father Timoteo called out. The priests at the foot of the bed missed a few of their prayers and glowered at Timoteo. The one nearest hissed for Timoteo to hush.

Timoteo turned his own glare against the priest, and the whole group of them shrank back. Timoteo strode ahead, his expression softening as he drew up beside the prince.

"Sevanyo, I'm sorry for this intrusion, but Fedeles needs you!"

"What?" The prince seemed to take in Timoteo, as well as Berto and Narsi, as if waking from a dream. Narsi wondered how long he'd been here praying for his father.

"The royal bishop has given Captain Yago leave to drag Fedeles before the Hallowed Kings for interrogation," Timoteo stated. "Yago took him before the sun was even up, and now the entire Quemanor household is in turmoil. You must come and make it clear that your brother does not have free rein to arrest whomever he pleases."

"Good God!" The prince started to his feet too quickly after having crouched so long in vigil. He stumbled.

Instinctively, Narsi reached out, caught his hand and steadied him.

"Thank you . . ." The Prince stared at Narsi.

So close, Narsi could see the exhaustion and grief in the man's face.

The prince's lined brow creased and he narrowed his gaze as he took in Narsi's features.

"My personal physician, Master Narsi." Father Timoteo gave the introduction quickly.

"It's my honor to be of assistance, Your Highness." Narsi bowed as he realized how forward he'd been. He released the prince and the other man straightened, but he continued to consider Narsi.

"You are very familiar looking," the prince murmured, then he scowled at the curtained windows. "It's too dark here. Let Papa have some sunlight!"

One of the priests scurried from the foot of the bed and pulled the golden drapes back. The flood of early morning sun instantly lit every thread of gold it fell across, and all at once the aged king and his entire bed turned radiant. The old man's eyes fluttered open and his lips parted as if to speak. The physician-priest at his side looked panicked as the light washed over him. He clutched the king's forearm.

The motion drew Narsi's attention and the wet gleam of blood trickling down the king's wrist alarmed him. But it was the flash of a surgical knife in the physician-priest's right hand that propelled Narsi into action. He leapt onto the bed and lunged across the king to catch the physician-priest's hand before he could slash the king's wrist a second time.

Cries of alarm and outrage rose from the surrounding priests. Their voices almost drowned out Narsi's own shout.

"He's trying to murder the king!" Narsi dug his hands into the physician-priest's wrists as the other man attempted to wrench free of him. The razor edge of the surgical knife gleamed between them. Already extended over the bed—and the frail king's body—Narsi knew he couldn't keep his balance, much less get control of the knife. Instead he shoved the physician-priest back with all his strength and then took hold of the king's bloody wrist and twisted a corner of bedding around the wound to stanch the bleeding.

He half expected to feel the surgical knife slash his back as he bowed over the king. Stealing a glance up, he saw that Berto and two other priests had blocked the wild-eyed physician-priest. He swung his knife at them as they edged nearer.

"Stop me . . . for the love of God, please stop me . . . ," the physician-priest whispered.

At once Narsi remembered Master Ariz's tortured expression as he'd battled against the Brand of Obedience that controlled him.

"Guards! Come at once!" Prince Sevanyo bellowed.

The priests who'd guarded the door dashed in with their spears held low. For a horrifying instant they both turned on Narsi.

"The priest there!" Prince Sevanyo shouted, and he pointed to the wild-eyed physician-priest. Berto and his two companions fell back as the armed priests closed in with their spears. The physician-priest retreated until his back hit a wall.

"Who put you up to this?" Father Timoteo demanded.

The physician-priest's face drained of all color and he shook his head. Then he raised his surgical knife, his arm shaking. With a fast, brutal stroke he slit his own throat. Blood gushed from the wound, but the physician-priest remained standing, staring at all of them with terror in his expression. His mouth moved as is attempting some final words. Blood frothed from between his pale lips. Then he collapsed to the marble floor.

Narsi's stomach lurched. He fought his horror down, focusing on the elderly man whose blood welled up through the cloth beneath his fingers. Here was the life Narsi might still save. He stole a quick glance to the remaining physician-priests. He didn't think any of them were much older than himself, and they'd probably worked closely with the man who now lay dead against the far wall. All three stood gripping their pestles, looking stunned and sick.

"The king's injury needs treatment!" Narsi called to them, then he shifted his gaze to Berto. "We'll need more light."

Berto sprang to the windows and drew back the remaining drapes. With the surge of light, the elderly king's wounds became all the more obvious. Narsi heard Prince Sevanyo gasp, and Father Timoteo attempted to reassure the prince that Narsi and the other physicians would do all they could. Narsi glanced to the other three and found them standing just as they had moments before, foundering in horror.

"One of you prepare alcohol, coinflower and bandages!" Narsi shouted. "I need two of you to help me treat the king. NOW!"

That roused them from their shock. The man standing farthest from Narsi set to work preparing cleansing dishes of coinflower and alcohol. The other two snatched up their medical satchels and raced to the king's bedside. Though as they drew close, Narsi recognized the dread in their expressions. They both stopped short of the bed. Their gazes darted between the aged king's ashen face and Prince Sevanyo.

Neither of them wanted to be the physician treating the king when he died, Narsi realized. Particularly not after one of their own had inflicted these injuries. But doing nothing would only make them all the more responsible for the king's demise.

"Help me, damn it!" Narsi snapped at them. Then he added, "Unless you mean to see your king bleed to death before you."

The threat of that got them moving fast enough.

They immediately assisted Narsi to elevate the king's gashed arm. A brief inspection confirmed Narsi's fear. Two lacerations laid the king's wrist open. The first was small but deep and looked like it had been inflicted several hours earlier. In the darkness it had probably passed for one of the shallow incisions that Cadeleonian physicians regularly employed to bleed patients. But the morning light revealed the depth of the wound, as well as the horrifying volume of blood that had already seeped out into the bed and soaked the mattress. The second gash was a long, shallow stroke that looked terrible, but fortunately missed both the radial and ulnar arteries. Narsi wondered if that small mercy represented the would-be assassin's attempt to resist the spell controlling him. At least it offered some hope of saving the king.

Normally, Narsi would have administered duera to slow the bleeding and ease pain before he attempted to stitch these wounds closed. But even before Narsi could mention the drug, the physician-priest standing nearest him whispered, "He's already taken twelve drams of duera."

"Twelve?" Narsi scowled. A dangerously high dose for a man who appeared so frail and elderly. No wonder the king hardly seemed to note Narsi's presence on his bed beside him. Narsi guessed the large dose had ensured that the king failed to register the injuries he'd sustained. Even now his eyes barely fluttered open. Though it was also possible the potent concentration of the drug had slowed the king's pulse just enough to save him from bleeding out hours earlier.

"Tourniquet, then," Narsi decided. He slid his medical satchel around from his back and handed his windlass cord to the physician-priest gripping the old king's bony elbow. Then he freed his surgical roll and laid it out on the bed. He shot a glance to the medical table. "Cleansing dishes prepared?"

"They're ready," the young physician-priest called back. He raced from the table and brought two cleansing dishes to the bedside.

The other two physician-priests bound the king's arm and twisted the small silver windlass until the bleeding stopped. At last Narsi felt secure enough to release the king's arm and sidle off the royal bed. As he circled around to join his fellow physicians he noted the crowd that had now gathered in the bedroom. Two royal guards and several pages clustered themselves near Father Timoteo and Prince Sevanyo at the bedside. Beyond them, the duchess her entourage and numerous other nobles, including Atreau's brother, edged near the king's bed. Priests, retainers and guards made some effort to keep them at a distance, but more people seemed intent on shoving their way in. Narsi thought he recognized the bruised countenance of Ladislo Bayezar as well as one of the Helio brothers at the edge of the gathering.

Already the gilded room felt confined and too hot.

Someone hissed an outraged complaint at the sight of a Haldiim laying hands upon the king. Father Timoteo told them to shut up.

While the physician-priests washed the king's arm, Narsi cleaned his hands in one dish and then washed his curved needle and suture thread in the second. The strong scent of coinflower drifted up to him. He threaded his needle and fought his growing awareness of all the Cadeleonians now observing his every motion. Narsi suspected that if they hadn't been so shocked by the attempted assassination, many more of them would have voiced objections. Or more likely, they would have hauled Narsi from the room, clapped him in chains and hurled him into a dungeon.

They still might if this went badly.

Narsi could almost feel Prince Sevanyo's stare burning into him. Even exhausted and distraught, the prince presented an imperious figure. What would happen if Narsi couldn't save the king? The elderly man's injuries were so serious, and he'd already lost so much blood. For an instant paralyzing fear gripped Narsi. The suture thread nearly slipped from his needle. He caught it and secured the thread.

This wasn't the place or time to lose focus. He'd preformed far more difficult procedures before throngs of instructors and young medical students. He would face the repercussions of his actions after he'd done all he could to save this elderly man. But right now he narrowed his attention to his patient and fellow physicians.

Narsi worked quickly, first stitching the deeper cut, then the longer, shallower gash. The urgency of the injuries and Narsi's own growing agitation over the responsibility that he'd just assumed set his heart racing. As much as he needed to work fast, he had to remind himself to remain collected. Draw needle and thread through the king's delicate flesh with calm precision, just as he'd been taught.

Thankfully, countless hours spent suturing everything, anything—from banana skins and freshly slaughtered goats all the way to gravely injured civil guards—imbued his hands with a certainty of reflex. The sureness of his fingers gave him something to focus on and something to feel assured of: he'd closed far graver injuries before these. For the briefest of instants he felt a wave of gratitude to all his mentors for the rigors of his training. Then he gave up any concern outside his work.

His knuckles began to ache where the muerate poison had seeped into them. He ignored the pangs and double checked that none of his surgical knots rested directly atop the seams of the closed wounds. Neat rows of salt-washed silk stitches closed both cuts in a ratio of four to one.

Narsi directed the physician-priests to loosen the tourniquet. A faint pink flush slowly colored the king's waxen flesh. Narsi's stitches held nicely. He stepped back as a wave of fatigued relief swept through him.

"I should clean my hands and tools," Narsi said. The three physician-priests nodded. Narsi withdrew to the worktable while they draped loose bandages around the king's forearm and then used pillows to elevate his arm. Narsi observed them almost absently as he cleansed his hands with coinflower distillate. He wanted to look to Berto and Father Timoteo for some reassurance that he'd done the right thing, but they both stood too near Prince Sevanyo and the whispering clots of nobles. Narsi didn't feel quite composed enough to face so many judgmental strangers.

Instead, he found himself stealing a glance to where the dead physician-priest lay crumpled in the corner of the room. Flies buzzed over the open gash in his neck. His bloody hand still gripped his surgical knife.

Someone ought to remove or at least cover his body.

But issuing such an order fell well beyond Narsi's authority and responsibility. He'd already overstepped what little rank he possessed amidst these Cadeleonian nobles. He returned his attention to his needles and tweezers. While he packed his medical satchel, he became aware of people's voices rising around him. A few aimed snide comments at him. Others speculated about the dead physician-priest. Had he been an agent of Count Radulf's? Could he have been enthralled by a witch—by the heathen Haldiim? How many other physician-priests might be compromised?

All the speculation disturbed Narsi but somehow didn't surprise him. He felt relieved hearing Father Timoteo squelch any supposition of Haldiim involvement.

"We must look to our own, where members of the holy orders are concerned," Father Timoteo intoned. "Assassins hardly require spells or thralls to motivate their misdeeds. The man's associates must be questioned closely."

All three physician-priests tending the king blanched, but they continued to attend to the king's comfort. One of them roused the old man long enough to convince him to swallow a few mouthfuls of broth. Narsi respected them for remaining focused on the well-being of their patient despite their shock and the precariousness of their position. Though he knew better than to remain in their company. He made his way around the golden bed and joined Berto, standing just a little behind Father Timoteo. Berto patted his shoulder.

"Thanks to God that you joined us this morning, Narsi," Berto whispered.

Narsi nodded. Though privately he did wonder how much faith anyone ought to place in a god who allowed the situation to go so wrong and then relied on happenstance to save the king's life. Then it belatedly struck Narsi that Berto was one of the few people voicing relief that the king had been saved. Instead the golden chamber seemed to hum with concern about the time.

"Too soon," someone behind Narsi whispered.

"Will he need to be . . . hurried ahead to join the Hallowed Kings before the Masquerade? Or do you think he'll last?" a man murmured.

"Wouldn't it be terribly unlucky to appoint a Hallowed King during Masquerade?" a young woman whispered.

The *timing* of the king's demise rather than the possibility of his death seemed of immense importance. Listening, Narsi soon learned that the royal bishop had not yet initiated the rites that would ensure the king joined his ancestors as a Hallowed King. He'd expected to begin them after Sevanyo's vigil and the fourteen days of Masquerade.

"Nugalo should have been here with me." Prince Sevanyo sounded both aggrieved and a little frantic. "What insanity has possessed him that he imagines harassing Fedeles could possibly excuse his absence now?"

"I'm sure that His Grace would not commit dereliction of his duty, Your Highness," an older priest standing at the foot of the bed responded. He bowed his head when Prince Sevanyo glowered at him but went on. "He couldn't know that this would happen. Your Royal Father was expected to receive his last rites on the final night of Masquerade and take his place among the Hallowed Kings the Sacreday after—"

"Will he survive fifteen more days?" The prince turned on his heel to stare at Narsi.

Narsi met his intense, dark-eyed stare for a moment, then dropped his gaze to where the king lay on his bed. The feeble man drew in quick, shallow breaths and hadn't been able to drink more than a few mouthfuls of liquid before losing consciousness. All of which were very bad signs. There was a slight chance that he might improve if the duera burned out of his system quickly enough to allow him to take in more liquids. But considering the amount of blood he'd lost and the dosage of duera that had been administered to him, Narsi doubted it.

The young physician-priests at the king's bedside swatted several flies away from the drying stain of blood that dulled the golden bedding.

"I can't say, Your Highness." Narsi replied. "Your father lost a great deal of blood, and he's been given a dangerously high dose of duera. If he regains consciousness and can be fed liquids, then he *might* recover. There is always hope. But, in your place I would prepare myself for . . ." Narsi trailed off, seeing the pain in the prince's expression.

He knew all too well how hopeless it was to imagine anyone could be *prepared* for such a loss. Knowing all he had about wasting diseases, Narsi had still wept and pleaded and begged while his mother's life had faded away. And afterward he'd felt almost as if he had died himself. Only the certainty that he would see her again—reborn and full of life and joy—had allowed him to make his peace with parting from her.

Perhaps the promise of paradise could comfort the prince?

Narsi almost said as much, but then he remembered. The king's soul wouldn't be released to enter the Cadeleonian paradise—nor would the prince's soul. They were destined to become Hallowed Kings. Spirits trapped in the mortal realm after their deaths. Uncertainty filled Narsi as he tried to imagine what that actually meant to both the king and prince.

"This isn't how it was supposed to end. Not like—" Prince Sevanyo's voice caught in a strangely childlike manner. He sank down to this father's bedside and briefly touched the old man's waxy cheek. The king's eyes fluttered but didn't open. Prince Sevanyo wiped at the tears trickling down his face. "Oh, Papa."

Then the duchess pushed through the surrounding nobles and strode to the prince. A guard looked as if he might challenge her for just a moment, but she gave him such a commanding glower that he stepped back as if reprimanded.

She reached out and gently placed her hand on Prince Sevanyo's shoulder. Her expression softened very slightly.

"I know you don't feel ready to let him go, Sevanyo. When I lost my mother I thought my heart would tear itself apart. I didn't think I could go on breathing, much less living without her, but I did go on." She spoke softly. "You must as well, because our entire nation looks to you to do what is right—even now in your time of grief. We have no one else."

The prince stared up at her, and despite the fact that he was grayhaired and his face lined with age, it struck Narsi that there was something of a child's countenance in the way he studied the duchess. She wrapped her arms around him, cradling his head in the folds of her gown while he leaned against her waist. For a few moments she simply held him, offering comfort as the prince wept. Then he seemed to calm and the duchess stepped back.

"I know you feel you are at your weakest in this moment," the duchess whispered. "But in truth you stand on the cusp of claiming dominion over all of Cadeleon. You've never been stronger. Fedeles needs you to seize that power *now*. We all do."

For an instant a blue ray of morning sun seemed to radiate from the duchess and illuminate the prince's features. His sorrow smoothed to an expression of resolve. He drew in a sharp breath, squared his shoulders and stood.

"Call my attendants to me and have the grooms make my carriage ready!" the prince commanded. "We will carry the king to the Shard of Heaven while there is still breath in his body. He must join the Hallowed Kings."

"But Your Highness," one of the priests at the foot of the bed objected. "It's weeks too early. The Shard of Heaven hasn't been properly readied. The feast dishes are uncooked and the choir hasn't—"

"Dusting and choir practice hardly matter at this point. We must act quickly or this assassin will succeeded in breaking the line of Hallowed Kings," Prince Sevanyo snapped.

"Thankfully Master Narsi has bought us time to set things right." Father Timoteo offered Narsi a proud smile.

"But . . ." The priest cast an aggrieved look at Narsi then trailed off before voicing any further objection.

Prince Sevanyo had given his orders and they were already in motion. Servants rushed out of the room, and the sound of their racing feet and loud voices resounded. A flurry of disorderly activity followed, as attendants and the remaining physician-priests worked to ready the king to be transported by carriage to the Shard of Heaven.

Onlookers and gossips all dispersed their own pages to summon other nobles or ready their mounts. Narsi joined Berto in drifting back from the frantic hustle. Father Timoteo exchanged a few words with the prince, then he bowed and withdrew from the bedroom. Narsi and Berto followed him. As they found their way down the stairs, streams of servants and guards jostled past them.

The halls of the palace echoed with commands but beneath them rose the soft hiss of speculative whispers. All the finery and gold Narsi had noticed on his way in seemed trite and banal.

"I must accompany Sevanyo to the Shard of Heaven," Father Timoteo told them once they'd stepped outside into one of the verdant gardens. "It might be for the best if the two of you return to the Quemanor house."

"You shouldn't travel alone," Berto objected.

"I'll be fine with Sevanyo," Father Timoteo responded, and then Narsi realized why Timoteo was bringing the subject up at all. Narsi had been blessed in a Cadeleonian chapel, but he wasn't a member of the clergy, nor was he recognized as a noble. He couldn't expect to enter the Shard of Heaven alongside Father Timoteo. Not without causing a scene. He'd already had his fill of that this morning.

"As much as I'd love Berto's company for my ride back to the duke's great house," Narsi said, "I think he should join you, Father. At the very least because I'll want to hear about everything when the two of you return and Berto is a better source of gossip."

Berto smiled, but the fearful expression he'd worn earlier flitted across his face. Narsi found it a little extreme considering the situation. It wasn't as if Berto and Father Timoteo were abandoning Narsi in a dank ally filled with cutthroats or setting him adrift in the open sea.

"I did manage to ride the entire distance from Anacleto to the capital all on my own, you may remember," Narsi said. "And I've navigated the taverns and alleys of the Theater District all this last month."

Berto worried his bottom lip but then nodded. "Promise you'll have a care. Royal court may present a civilized appearance, but it's filled with no fewer cutthroats than is the Knife Market. This place is a snake pit."

"No doubt it is," Narsi allowed. "But I intend to leave all the adders and asps well enough alone. My entire plan is to read a little in one of these gardens while the stable is busy, then after all of you have departed for the Shard of Heaven I'll collect my horse and ride back to the duke's household. After all that excitement, I may just indulge myself in a nap."

That seemed to put both Father Timoteo and Berto more at ease. Though they might well have offered further arguments if three page boys dressed in the Sagrada colors hadn't run them down to inform the Holy Father—now Holy Bishop—that Prince Sevanyo wished him to accompany him in his carriage. Tired-looking guards jogged up behind the pages. They positioned themselves to serve as Father Timoteo and Berto's escort.

Narsi stepped aside as the entire group marched toward the stables. The duchess and Prince Sevanyo joined them while their combined retinues charged behind like a small army. As more parties of nobles and their entourages poured out of the palace, the path to the royal stables became a river of bright silks and brocades. Narsi retreated past ornamental trees and pretty statues to a small stone bench beneath a bower of roses. From his seat he could just see the painted doors of the royal stable.

More courtiers hurried past him to join the growing crowd and Narsi felt pleased that he'd avoided their crush. From where he sat, he overheard occasional bits of chatter and gossip. It seemed that Suelita Estaban had been sighted twice in the company of duelists from the Red Stallion sword house and was now rumored to have turned whore to finance her newfound appetite for poppy smoke and swordsmen. Narsi wondered if Suelita would find such a profound untruth funny or mortifying. He felt a little offended on her behalf, but he hoped that she'd laugh rather than allow petty conjecture to hurt her.

Numerous nobles and their attendants speculated on the recent deaths of the duke's enemies as well as the state of the cursed duke's sanity. And a very few murmured their concern about Prince Remes's unbecoming interest in the widow Clara Odalis.

"His condolences would seem a little more genuine if he wasn't so obvious about ogling her breasts," one courtier whispered. Her companion snickered behind a silk fan.

Then a group of priests appeared, all walking abreast and supporting the weight of a large golden litter. The curtains were drawn, but Narsi guessed that the king lay within. A group of stunned-looking acolytes trailed the litter. The three physician-priests whom Narsi had left behind were nowhere to be seen.

The entire procession passed hardly three feet from where Narsi sat. He half expected one of the priests to spare him a glance, but none of them seemed to take any note of him. The group of courtiers who followed them at a distance even commented on how very much Father Timoteo's physician resembled a Grunito man himself, without seeming to notice him. Then Narsi realized that the angle of the early morning sun cast the lush rose bower arching over him into deep shadows.

At the stables below, the crowds of nobles parted, making way for the king's litter to be loaded onto a royal wagon. Only minutes later the king, Prince Sevanyo, the duchess and Bishop Timoteo, as well as a small army of their guards and attendants—including Berto—rode away. But the stables remained a crush of courtiers, attendants and assorted ministers all vying for the attention of the harried-looking grooms.

Narsi guessed that the better part of an hour would pass before he could hope to secure his mare. He settled back on the bench.

After taking in a few more whispered conversations, Narsi drew the small leather charm-book from his coat pocket and flipped through it, as he often did in his spare time. Many pages remained indecipherable, but every now and then he would see some symbol or series of letters that he'd previously mistaken for unintelligible scribbling. This morning he recognized the null sign that he and Atreau had discussed weeks ago.

A symbol of nothing, silence, emptiness. Or in some cases a placeholder. Narsi sketched the symbol in the dirt with his foot. Could such a mark truly render a man invisible to witches and sorcerers? He frowned at the little circle. Really it could be anything from a mathematic symbol to a sketch of an egg.

Overhead a little cloud of songbirds flitted past, and Narsi watched them wing in circles over the stables and then light off toward the river. He recollected the letters hidden in the charm-book mentioning flocks of freed songbirds, but that would have been years ago.

He sighed and noted that the stables looked quieter now. A groom scowled after someone who must have just ridden inside, while another young man smiled at the coin that had been placed in his hand.

Narsi decided that he ought to go, as he'd promised Father Timoteo and Berto. He searched the pocket of his physician's coat. How large of a tip could he afford to provide to the groom who'd ensured that his mare found a stall?

Then he noted a particularly striking man walking through the garden. He wore tawny colors and the white swan heraldry of the Fueres household. His gold spurs chimed like bells. Someone called a name and the man turned in Narsi's direction. A frown spread across his handsome face and he quickened his pace.

All at once Narsi realized that this imposing, angry man striding toward him was Hierro Fueres.

CHAPTER
SIX

In the early morning, the banks of the Peraloro River already bustled with activity. Fleets of fishing boats plied the waters, and these attracted groups of peddlers who clustered along the wide Gado Bridge ready to serve them hot drinks or to buy their catch. By comparison, the narrow old Dasma Bridge leading to the Shard of Heaven stood nearly abandoned. Four young guardsmen dressed in royal blue stood at each end, looking sleepy. Fedeles hoped these tired boys weren't representative of the majority of Sevanyo's royal guards still remaining in the capital. In the last month, many of the best-trained and most experienced troops had been sent off on absurd and distant missions, such as fetching Nestor Grunito from Anacleto. These boys didn't look ready to stand up to their own mothers, much less armed assassins. Even so, Fedeles expected one of them to at least call out a challenge. Instead they gazed at Captain Yago with expressions that Fedeles felt were altogether too awed.

"Make way, on order of the royal bishop!" Yago roared.

The royal guards darted aside. Yago and Fedeles charged past them and Yago's men followed.

The Shard of Heaven was an island of jewel-blue stone cut through with seams of shining gold that thrust up from the center of the river. The fountains, small gardens and white-walled chapel that sat atop the stone always struck Fedeles as strange conceits of civility. Not unlike the velvet cloths that his grandmother had insisted her personal guards drape over the hindquarters of their stallions, to safeguard the modest sensibilities of any maidens who might have come to observe battle practices and cavalry charges. As if the nudity of the horses was somehow more disturbing than the violence of men and animals training to destroy one another's lives.

To Fedeles's eye, the fountains seemed particularly insignificant. There they stood festooned with trite symbols of holy authority spitting up feeble ribbons of water, while true power of immense grandeur shone all around them. Three giant spears of blazing blue light shot through the gold roof of the chapel and plunged down into the stone heart of the Shard of Heaven. The spears of light crackled and flashed like lightning, while far below golden wards the size of grown men curled and knotted themselves around a furious, pale fire.

Despite all this radiance and magic, the Shard of Heaven fulfilled a very simple purpose. It was a prison. The immense blue stone formed a cell, the golden wards were its bars and the souls of the Hallowed Kings served as its lock. In a way the very grandeur of the Shard of Heaven spoke volumes about the danger posed by the thing imprisoned within it.

Fedeles gazed down through the glassy blue stone beneath him and tried to make out the true form of that captive. He glimpsed a luminous white mist churning between the golden wards that restrained it, and he sensed a simplicity so pure it felt desolate and cold. Neither anger nor outrage colored its struggle against the spells holding it captive. Instead it seemed to tirelessly erode their determination, as if that and only that was its purpose.

It felt like a mechanism—like the mechanical cure that had once held him prisoner—only far, far more immense.

Fedeles suppressed a shudder.

Neither Captain Yago nor any of his men appeared to sense, much less see, anything below the rocky surface they rode across. One rider gazed at the bounty of strawberries ripening between lines of bright marigolds in a flower bed. Another man whistled in response to the little flock of larks gathered atop a fountain.

However, a few of the chapel priests flinched or lifted a hand to their eyes just as Fedeles did when the spells surrounding them flared. One pockmarked young acolyte closed his eyes, clenched his hands in prayer and dropped to his knees. His companions spared him a brief glance but appeared to expect such behavior. Fedeles felt a stab of sympathy for the boy. He nearly drew Firaj to a halt. But then a plump, elderly priest went to the youth's side and crouched down beside him. A moment later they both stood and walked away together smiling.

Fedeles relaxed a little and then silently chided himself for his impulse. These priests and this place were not his allies. This was no time to betray his own abilities—certainly not just for the sake of some anonymous acolyte. Oasia would have called such an action foolish, short-sighted and self-indulgent. Too many people depended upon him for him to risk exposure simply to soothe his own anxiety.

At the chapel doors, a stocky white-haired priest dressed in a black velvet robe stood waiting. Fedeles and Yago dismounted at the steps and, like sparrows flocking to spilled grain, two tanned acolytes wearing muddied, threadbare robes hurried from the stable to take the reins of their horses. Yago escorted Fedeles all the way up the white marble chapel steps before handing his warrant over to the waiting priest. The man offered no greeting or welcome before indicating that Fedeles should follow him. Then he turned and strode through towering gold doors.

Fedeles hadn't entered this chapel since he'd been a boy. But time had done nothing to erase his dread of the place. He braced himself for the disturbing sights to come, then strode inside.

Bright morning light angled in through the high windows, casting deep shadows over the sea of monumental carvings. Mordwolves the size of horses bristled in the coils of a huge serpent. Snow lions arched over swordsmen and web-footed frogwives hefted long spears. All around him, life-size statues filled the chapel nave with the chaos that had been the Battle of Heaven's Shard. In the heat of combat the bodies of beasts, demons and warriors merged into strange, tangled forms.

This sea of violent statuary had been disconcerting enough ages ago when it was first created. But Fedeles found it more disturbing that later, his own ancestors had rendered it even more grotesque by hacking off every single statue's head.

They'd taken the snarling muzzles, merciless faces and even the crushed skulls of the dead and built them into the chapel's high altar. No amount of gilding could disguise the furious, terrified and agonized expressions staring out from the alter at their own bodies. And atop this, on a golden pulpit, sat three reliquary tanks, tall crystal cylinders filled with milky jade water, each containing the still-living remains of one of the three Hallowed Kings.

Most onlookers saw only the vessels, or perhaps a shadow moving in the water.

But to Fedeles the three Hallowed Kings also appeared as ghostly visages: wraiths of once-beautiful men, now stretched and twisted to translucent caricatures. Like tattered kites, their distorted souls floated over their reliquaries, tethered by streams of blue light.

But the worst thing for Fedeles wasn't the sight of the Hallowed Kings; it was that they watched him in return.

The eldest of the Hallowed Kings, Gachello, looked like an apparition summoned from smoke and spider webs. And yet Fedeles couldn't ignore his intense gaze as he opened the chasm of his elongated jaws and mouthed the air, like a landed fish gasping for water. Fedeles lowered his gaze to the floor.

There you are, Fedeles. The ancient king's voice drifted to Fedeles like a chill that only he felt.

As a boy, he'd been terrified by the old king and the way he always searched for him through the crowds of priests and nobles. Back then Fedeles had often felt as if he was choking on his own dank, moldering fear. His heart quickened now just remembering the sensation. But now Fedeles realized that the feeling of trapped dread didn't emanate from himself. It arose from Gachello.

Do you not hear me any longer? Can you not see me? The old king's words seemed so much fainter than he remembered. Fedeles lifted his head and, meeting the ancient king's gaze, he recognized the plea in his drawn expression.

"I hear you," Fedeles whispered. "What would you say to me?"

Gachello opened his mouth, but nothing came out. In the reliquary tank, his toothy jawbones chattered.

Fedeles recognized the old king's helplessness. Fedeles, too, had once found himself trapped and unable to ask anyone around him for aid. He knew the horror of that isolation too well to ignore it now. Instinctively he allowed his shadow to reach out to Gachello's murky tank. He offered his strength into the blue glow of Gachello's soul. And Gachello drew in the slightest gasp. Fedeles strained to catch those faintest of whispers floating like incense through the chapel.

Larks in the morning . . .

Nightingales at twilight . . .

Gachello's voice faded away and his form dimmed. Fedeles frowned, trying to make some sense of the words the Hallowed King had struggled so greatly to convey to him. It had sounded like the beginning of a poem. The water of the king's tank began to bubble and churn. His yellow jawbones worked at the murky foam. A pink tongue lapped the glass and finger bones scraped at the gold lid above them.

Priests hurried from alcoves all across the chapel. The altar became a flurry of black-and-violet robes. Between their anxious expressions and the soothing prayers they crooned to the Hallowed King, Fedeles was reminded of young mothers desperate to quiet their unsettled infants. He'd probably looked the same on those nights he'd rocked Sparanzo's tiny wailing body, singing the newborn back to sleep.

But Gachello wasn't a colicky infant. His ghostly form flared up like a candle flame and he stared intently at Fedeles. Over the priests' murmurs, Fedeles felt Gachello's words more than heard them.

Each day they twist the wards. Piece after piece. They tear away our purpose and we forget . . . we forget . . . Gachello's voice drifted into a meaningless murmur, then rose again over the sea of lulling prayers.

No one sees us. No one hears us. And I no longer hear Irsea. What has become of the Circle of Wisteria? There are only the birdsongs. The larks are too many . . . they are too many for even her crows to keep at bay. We are failing . . . but you have always seen us, always heard.

Then the priest's prayers drowned out Gachello's words. The water in the tank stilled and Gachello's strained expression went slack.

Fedeles frowned at the group of priests who crowded around the tanks. Gachello had clearly spoken of wards being destroyed and his own failing purpose. Didn't any of them see Gachello or hear him? Was he merely some watery reliquary of remains to their eyes? Didn't any of them wonder over the cause of his distress, or was their only concern that of maintaining him in stultifying serenity?

Fedeles was so caught up in his thoughts that for just a moment he failed to recognize the royal bishop kneeling among the other priests, praying to ease Gachello's anxious soul. Then Nugalo rose to his feet and turned to Fedeles. He presented an imperious figure even in his sixties. A little gray diminished the powerful contrast of his black hair and pale face. Smiling, he could appear quite handsome, but glowering as he did now, the sharp angles of his visage took on the harsh features of a snarling mask.

The priest who had escorted Fedeles into the chapel stepped back, as if afraid the royal bishop's disdain might splash across him like boiling oil.

"Your Holiness." Fedeles inclined his head just a little to Nugalo. He hated to bow to the man. "You summoned me and I have come."

"Come to answer for your crimes. That is what you will do, Lord Quemanor," the royal bishop snapped. "This time neither Sevanyo nor any of the Helio lords are here to shield you from justice. After the crimes you've perpetrated, even they must recognize that you are unworthy of their loyalty."

The royal bishop seemed too sincere in his outrage and too certain of the outcome for this to be a bluff. Was it possible that the royal bishop had found evidence to link Fedeles's household to the recent murders? Fedeles felt certain that Oasia or Atreau would have informed him if any such connection existed to be discovered. So either the royal bishop intended to accuse Fedeles of witchcraft and present some proof of Fedeles's work on Crown Hill with Irsea and her crows, or—

The faintest spark seemed to flicker over the royal bishop's brow. Fedeles's shadow stirred in agitation and drew close around Fedeles's body, as if to cloak him. He recognized that magic even in the smallest spark: an air of smug sadism suffused the indigo-blue color. Hierro Fueres had spun another of his spells through the royal bishop's mind.

Fedeles only just stopped himself from reaching out to rip the spell from the royal bishop's flesh. At this point even the slightest sign of violence against the royal bishop could well land him in prison. The entire chapel was full of priests who watched him with suspicion.

As Fedeles noted the long knives and heavy staffs that many of the holy men held, he grew even more uneasy. His shadow coiled around him tightly, like a serpent preparing to strike.

"You will stand before the Hallowed Kings and answer for the murder of Faro Numes," the royal bishop commanded.

"You can't honestly believe that I murdered the minister of the navy?" Fedeles shook his head. "He was alive and well when I left him. His wife and guards saw me take my leave—"

"A nobleman doesn't need to use his own hands to commit murder, Lord Quemanor. But his death is still your bloody work!" The royal bishop trembled with the intensity of his outrage. There would be no reasoning with him, Fedeles realized.

Hierro might have set this suspicion in his thoughts, but clearly it resonated with Nugalo's own prejudice. He wanted Fedeles to be responsible for the murders. And likely he felt pressure mounting the longer Captain Yago and his guardsmen failed to capture the actual culprit. They needed someone to execute to assure the court that Nugalo's chosen men were just as competent as Prince Sevanyo's royal guards. How convenient it would be for the royal bishop if Fedeles could be proved guilty.

But Fedeles had no intention of playing the part of a scapegoat, and though he'd feared the Hallowed Kings as a child, he now found himself pitying them. As he studied them, he thought he could see traces of both his grandmother's features and Sevanyo's in their translucent, distorted faces. Gachello had sought him out—not to declare him an abomination, as he'd once feared, but to confide in. He wasn't alone or without allies, not even here. The thought allowed him to calm his shadow and speak with confidence.

"I have nothing to hide and nothing to fear from the Hallowed Kings." Fedeles stepped forward. "Call them as my witnesses and I will swear that neither I nor anyone in my household played any part in the minister's murder. Nor did I have Lord Wonena killed."

The royal bishop appeared momentarily taken aback. He'd truly expected Fedeles to be cowed by the prospect of being exposed. Then he narrowed his angry gaze.

"You may be able to protest your innocence to me now, but you will not deceive the Hallowed Kings." The royal bishop beckoned Fedeles to the altar. "Step forward to their reliquaries. The light of their souls will burn all deception from your cursed heart."

Fedeles strode up the gilded steps. This close to the Hallowed Kings, their radiance was blinding. The nave of the chapel and all surrounding priests became a haze of blue shadows. The kings themselves towered over him like gauzy veils, or the wind-tossed clouds he'd watched with Ariz. Vaporous, pale forms shifting and turning in the constant grip of some invisible force.

As Fedeles ascended to the royal bishop's side, several lower-ranking priests stationed themselves on the steps. Fedeles recognized the young pockmarked acolyte he'd seen earlier. The youth held a record book and ink bottle for the elderly priest who'd comforted him. The round old fellow dipped a quill pen and began jotting notes of the proceedings.

"Lay your hands against the reliquaries," the royal bishop commanded.

Fedeles placed his right hand on Gachello's tank and pressed his left palm to Leozar's. To his surprise, Leozar seemed to wake at the contact. Like Gachello, he turned his hollow gaze upon Fedeles and then his diaphanous form sank, as if he were attempting to crouch down beside Fedeles. His turbulent features calmed. He looked so much like Sevanyo that it made Fedeles's heart ache a little to remember that he'd died at only fifty years of age.

Have you come to set us free yet? Is it finally over?

Leozar's voice sounded younger and far softer than Gachello's. Faint strips of pale flesh drifted from his bones as the water rolled around his remains.

"If it were in my power, I would do all I could for each of you," Fedeles said. "But I have been summoned before you to prove my innocence against gossip and lies."

A hum passed through Fedeles's fingers as Leozar and Gachello lifted their hand bones up against the glass to meet his own. Several of the priests standing in the nave made noises of surprise, and someone whispered a blessing. The pockmarked acolyte gaped, then leaned close to his elderly companion and whispered something in his ear. The old priest nodded.

"Shall I record that the Hallowed Kings recognize and welcome Lord Quemanor?" the old priest asked.

"No. The water turns without purpose and lifts the bones." The royal bishop scowled at Gachello's reliquary. "It proves nothing."

Then he drew the heavy gold ring of his office from his right ring finger. A violet stone flashed from the clutches of the gold setting. Fedeles could almost hear the spell within it chime like a bell. If it had been one of the blessings up on Crown Hill, Fedeles would have named it *Awaken* and imagined it leaping about like an excited child startling grasshoppers and butterflies before it.

As the royal bishop touched the stone to the gilded lids of each of the three reliquaries, a surge of gold light shot down through the murky water. Bones and decayed flesh shook and slowly congealed into jumbled semblances of hunched corpses. Even as they twisted and shuddered, neither Gachello nor Leozar drew their hands back from Fedeles.

Towering overhead, the three spectral figures seemed to coalesce. Indistinct, soft forms became the singular features of individual figures. Gachello's elongated, twisted body looked all the more ferocious and terrible. Leozar appeared racked with sorrow, and Yusto, with his missing eye and broken nose, gave the impression of a bare-fisted brawler waking after a rough night.

Many of the surrounding priests gasped. The pockmarked acolyte nearly dropped his record book. Fedeles realized that none of them had seen the Hallowed Kings' souls before now. To the surrounding priests, the Hallowed Kings would have seemed to suddenly manifest above them. Even the royal bishop stared up at the Hallowed Kings with an expression of awe. Fedeles realized that it had likely been decades since even he had last seen their distorted spirits watching over them all.

Then he remembered Gachello's words: *No one sees us. No one hears us.*

"My Hallowed ancestors. Grandfather Leozar." The royal bishop bowed his head. "Great-Grandfather Yusto and Great-Great-Grandfather Gachello. I have called you to judge this man's words against the secret deeds, the terrible sins, that are hidden in his heart."

The royal bishop turned his attention back to Fedeles. His dark eyes seemed to gleam with anticipation.

"Now, Lord Quemanor. Confess the part you played in Faro Numes's death." The royal bishop leaned close enough that Fedeles caught the scent of sweat beneath the powerful incense that clung to his robes. "Utter one false word and my ancestors will burn your flesh to ash."

Fedeles felt as much as saw the haze of blue light that rose up from the Hallowed Kings and enfolded him like a fog. The air tasted of damp, warm rot. Was it possible for a soul to molder and mildew, Fedeles wondered, or were these sensations reflections of how the Hallowed Kings felt, trapped in the mortal realm by their own decaying corpses?

"Can't you answer, Lord Quemanor?" The royal bishop grinned.

"Your question hardly deserves a response," Fedeles replied. Then, almost of their own volition, further words drifted from him. "Neither I nor anyone in my household played any role in Faro Numes's murder. In truth, I respected the minister. We might not have agreed on all matters, but he understood that we shared a common goal. We both wanted to safeguard Cadeleon for our children. We wanted it to be a better place for them than it was for us growing up. On occasion he even informed me of where you had Captain Yago searching for Hylanya Radulf. He knew that harming her would have plunged Cadeleon into a war we would not win. The truth is that I will mourn his death."

"Lies!" the royal bishop shouted.

Fedeles found the angry denial almost funny. What was the point of dispatching armed guards to bring him to the Shard of Heaven, then waking the Hallowed Kings and having him stand here in the light of their souls if the royal bishop refused to believe the testimony? It was a joke. Except, of course, that real people were being murdered and the Hallowed Kings themselves were losing their ability to protect the kingdom. Only Gachello seemed to even recall that he had a duty to do so.

Fedeles shook his head.

"There is no end of lies being told to you, Nugalo. But not by me. I have been ever honest about my anger toward you and my resentment of the way you treated Javier. I don't pretend to be your friend and I don't need to lie to you," Fedeles replied. "If you mean to find this assassin, then you should look nearer your own circle. Do you truly imagine that Hierro Fueres is a trustworthy ally? The man means to rule over us all—"

"Your opinion of Lord Fueres is not in question." The royal bishop cut him off, but much of the smug certainty had drained from his expression. "Did you have Faro Numes murdered? Are you responsible for Lord Wonena's assassination? Confess what you've done."

"As God and the Hallowed Kings are my witnesses, I've done *nothing* to either of them!" Fedeles bellowed it out so that even the clusters of priests at the doors could hear him. The old priest on the stairs lifted his pen and jotted his response in the record book.

"I want you to find and punish the man responsible for their deaths," Fedeles went on, "because he knows the blame will be placed at my door. He means to destroy me and my family. So if you truly want to find this murderer, you would be wise to look among *my* enemies, Nugalo. Who among them possesses the cunning and cruelty to murder his own allies in hopes of ruining me and Oasia?"

"You have no proof to support your accusations against Hierro Fures," the royal bishop replied, though Fedeles had not accused the man yet.

"And you have no proof to justify bringing me here to answer your questions. But here I am, telling you the truth, as you demanded. But you are too pigheaded. Too resentful to hear me! What is wrong with your petty mind that you can't—" Further angry words caught in Fedeles's throat as a foreign sense of compassion toward the royal bishop rolled over him.

For just an instant he saw Nugalo not as the condemning, intractable old man before him, but as a terrified child. He wept and stammered pleas as priests dragged him away from his brother and their playmates, stripped him of his royal raiment and locked him in an acolyte's cell to be educated by his dour uncle. A wave of guilt followed the vision, and Fedeles realized that these images and feelings belonged to Leozar. As both the king and Nugalo's grandfather, he could have intervened on the little boy's behalf. Even in death—when he could no longer remember his purpose as a holy guardian—he still regretted that he had not interceded for his grandson.

His compassion tempered Fedeles's outrage a little. He suddenly recognized that the royal bishop was a human being, not simply some icon of zealotry brought to life fully formed. The knowledge didn't make Fedeles like Nugalo, but it did lend him a little understanding of the man's aggrieved and resentful character.

"I'm neither your friend nor your ally, Nugalo," Fedeles said. "But we both love Cadeleon. We both want this nation to flourish and prosper. I am not the threat that you have been led to believe me to be."

"Are you not?" the royal bishop demanded. "Then why did you protect Hylanya Radulf after she began destroying the wards surrounding the Shard of Heaven?"

"Because she wasn't the one destroying them," Fedeles replied. "She was attempting to repair them up until your assassins poisoned her. Now we can only hope that she and her brother don't turn against us and declare war."

"I rightly condemned the countess for practicing witchcraft!" The royal bishop's face flushed with anger, but then Fedeles saw a flicker of doubt in Nugalo's expression. He lowered his voice as he went on. "I never sent an assassin against the countess. I'm not such a fool that I would invite open warfare against Labara. Not before we have purged our nation of the heathens and heretics who would betray us from within."

"You mean our Haldiim citizens?" Fedeles scowled at him.

"They must be expelled or converted, of course," the royal bishop replied with a shrug. Then his expression grew more agitated. He drummed his fingers over the violet stone set in his ring. "However, they are not the greatest threat to the piety of our nation. Haldiim and Irabiim make no pretense of understanding or belonging in the company of devout Cadeleonians. The real traitors are families like the Grunitos." The royal bishop all but spat the name. "A woman leading the household! A Haldiim convert as the heir, another son a bent traitor who champions a foreign power. And a *priest*—a priest, he calls himself—like Timoteo who challenges me with every sermon he preaches, every blessing he dispenses, and every debate that he engages in. He invites *my* followers— my acolytes, priests and nuns to question *me*! He and his entire family are destroying everything my church and this nation stands for! They are a brood of monstrous, unnatural creatures that must be expelled before they can sully the nobility any further."

Nugalo's descent into wild-eyed ranting hardly reassured Fedeles. Though it did reveal an insight into the royal bishop's paranoia that had eluded Fedeles. Previously, he'd imagined that it was Javier and his circle of Hellion friends whom the royal bishop feared. They were defiant and daring. They'd spited his plans in the past. But none of them could challenge Nugalo from within his own clergy. None of them were Timoteo Grunito, who seemed so gentle, so easygoing, but whose sermons could reach multitudes. From common folk to nobles, soldiers to clergy, Timoteo could engage and inspire them all.

"It's not the fact that I protected Hylanya Radulf that makes you hate me," Fedeles realized aloud. "It's the fact that I took in Timoteo and gave him a chapel."

"You dare to imply that the two are not related?" The royal bishop glowered at him as the faintest glint of Hierro's magic flickered over his brow. "If you could have your way, you would have Timoteo unseat me and then invite that witch back into our land to destroy us all!"

"I have no such designs. You—"

The loud clang of sword blades ringing against shields interrupted them both. As a group Fedeles, the royal bishop and all of the surrounding priests turned. The golden chapel doors crashed open and Prince Sevanyo rode in on his white stallion. Silver haired and hollowed as he was, he still looked resplendent to Fedeles. He wore a sapphire-studded crown, and his blue-and-gold cloak billowed behind him. A party of pages and attendants wearing liveries adorned with the royal symbol of a white stallion raced in around him, scattering flowers in his wake. They were followed by a group of priests who shouldered the king's gilded litter between them. Then the remnants of the royal guard surged through the doors. The armed young men pounded their swords against the ceremonial shields they carried.

"What is the meaning of—" Nugalo shouted out, but Sevanyo cut him off.

"Have you no shame?" Sevanyo bellowed, and the fury in his voice drowned out all the sound around them. "An assassin in the grip of some thrall attacked Papa. He's dying! Dying! And you choose this moment to abduct my dearest relation and interrogate him?"

The anger and color drained from Nugalo's face.

"Papa?" he whispered, then he bounded from Fedeles's side to pelt down the altar steps. The moment he drew his ring of office away from the reliquaries, the Hallowed Kings receded back into wisps. The dank taste left Fedeles's mouth, though his skin still felt clammy.

Priests scattered out of the royal bishop's way as he raced through the church to the king's litter. "Let me see him! I must see him!"

Behind the guards, Fedeles noticed nobles pouring into the chapel. He recognized Oasia and Timoteo among them. Then, unexpectedly, he noted that Atreau's eldest brother, Lliro, stood with them as well.

The stocky priests shouldering the king's litter knelt and Nugalo all but tore the gilded door open. He stared into the dark interior and his entire countenance seemed to collapse. Such raw sorrow showed on his angular face that Fedeles half expected him to burst into tears. But the royal bishop regained control of himself. He drew a ring from his left hand. The jade setting held a grasping, sticky little spell.

Seize, Fedeles would have called it.

Nugalo began to chant to it in a low voice and the surrounding priests joined him, invoking the dying king's soul to remain with them.

Nugalo climbed inside the litter and two physician-priests carrying surgical knives followed him.

Atop his stallion, Sevanyo closed his eyes and clenched his hands in prayer.

Battered King Yusto took in the scene, but without the royal bishop's ring rousing him, his expression fell slack and even his spirit faded, becoming a stream of pale filaments in a haze of blue light.

Leozar too diminished and lost the edges that had defined his presence, but despite how faded he appeared, the king clung to some awareness. He stared intently at the royal litter.

My son. That is my son. Leozar's voice drifted over Fedeles, but no one else appeared to hear him. *Yes, bring him to me. Let me see him again. My little boy.*

No! Gachello growled.

From the way the pockmarked acolyte stiffened, Fedeles realized that he too still sensed the Hallowed Kings' presences. But the two of them seemed to be the only ones. Or perhaps Oasia betrayed just the slightest flicker of her lashes. She, like the acolyte, appeared to be doing all she could to feign ignorance.

He must not take my place! I am the only one who remembers. Without me to remind them, they will fail their purpose. Gachello threw his spectral arms wide, lashing them across priests, guards and attendants alike. But it did him no good. His protest might as well have been rays of sunlight filtering through the high windows.

Then he spun and sank down over Fedeles. *Release his soul to paradise before they can capture it. Fedeles, you must do this!*

The pockmarked acolyte stole a quick glance back at them and then immediately returned to staring down at the floor. Fedeles didn't blame the youth. But for all their sakes, Fedeles knew he couldn't ignore Gachello.

"How?" Fedeles whispered.

Break the spell, crack the stone.

Fedeles took a moment to consider how he could manage such a thing without being run through by guards and priests as he attempted to wrest one of the royal bishop's sacred rings from his hand. Even Sevanyo might think him mad if he did such a thing. The pockmarked young acolyte beside him could testify that he too had heard Gachello's command, but only if the royal bishop allowed him to do so.

So Fedeles had to use his shadow to take action. He knew that, and yet he hesitated. He possessed very little control of the power that snarled and rippled through his shadow. What mastery he had achieved largely came down to suppressing and restraining it. But reaching out and grasping a single stone set in a ring on the royal bishop's finger would require both subtlety and precision.

If he made a mess of the attempt—Fedeles stopped himself from considering everything that could go wrong. Instead he remembered something Timoteo had spoken of. A man should hold himself as responsible for the outcome of his inaction as for his actions. Fedeles's own inaction now would render the Hallowed Kings useless and set free the monstrosity they confined.

Fedeles lowered his gaze to his deceptively still shadow. Through it he felt the cold surface of gilded stone at his feet. He willed it to stretch forward, to where the king's litter stood. Slowly, the gray shade slithered past the feet of gathered priests and around pools of sunlight. Never before had he moved his shadow so far without an outside influence, but now under his own control his shadow reached the nave winding between two statues of decapitated boars. Then a sharp resistance jerked at Fedeles's chest, as if the attempt to push his shadow farther would wrench his heart from his body.

A light-headed sensation rushed over him. Spots of light flickered before his eyes and he swayed on his feet. Only his grip on the cool glass of Gachello's reliquary allowed him to steady himself.

He remembered Oasia had described the disturbing sensations of projecting her spirit beyond her body. Decades of practice and discipline now allowed her to stretch her awareness across miles. But when she did so, it left her body stunned and vulnerable. Even a Bahiim as powerful as Irsea rooted her soul in living bodies—either within her crows or the trees of the sacred grove.

Fedeles felt a hand on his forearm. He glanced down to see that the young acolyte had crept up the step to his side.

"Are you unwell, my lord?" the acolyte asked quietly.

"A little overtired," Fedeles replied. He met the young man's nervous gaze and smiled at him, recognizing how much courage it took for him to stand here with him.

"I can stay a few more moments," the acolyte whispered.

"Thank you." Fedeles trailed off as a thought struck him. Could this acolyte's body possibly carry his spirit closer to the royal bishop? Could he take possession of the youth in the way that Bahiim and Labaran witches took over the bodies of their familiars? He remembered the way his shadow had nearly claimed Ciceron's dead body. It might not be all that difficult, Fedeles realized, but what kind of monster would he be if he ripped the self-determination from this youth simply to spare himself a little pain?

"If you would stand with me a little time, I would be most grateful," Fedeles said.

The acolyte nodded.

Fedeles braced himself between the reliquary tanks and the acolyte. He took in a deep breath then plunged his senses down into his shadow. Again he raced for the royal litter, skimming over the stone floor and weaving between statues. This time when he felt his heart jerk and his breath catch, he fought against the taut tether. A sharp, deep pain rocked through him, like the sensation of breaking a bone. His body shuddered and something inside him snapped. Fedeles's senses catapulted from his living flesh. He no longer saw the murky water of the reliquary tanks or felt the acolyte's sweating hand against his back.

Instead, he flew across the chamber to crouch at the glittering door of the litter. He heard the royal bishop struggle to pray as his voice was racked with sobs. He passed through the door like a breeze slipping through a curtain. Inside the dark confines of the litter, the royal bishop held his dying father against his chest and rocked his body. Two other priests hunched across from the royal bishop, waiting for him to secure his father's soul before they applied their surgical knives to the king's already desiccated flesh.

Fedeles felt more than saw the old king's soul drifting from his head like a halo of faint blue light. The jade ring on the royal bishop's left hand tugged at the king's spirit. It would take him in a few moments unless Fedeles could stop it.

He raced ahead of the king's wan soul, curling around the royal bishop's hand. Then all at once he was caught in a grip like that of an undertow. The jade stone seemed to loom large before him and the spell within it threw off tiny rays of silver light, which caught at Fedeles like hooks. Only a few at first, but then dozens, hundreds and thousands of them harpooned into his soul. Each tugged more powerfully, dragging Fedeles nearer the jade stone.

And now he could see the delicate matrix of the jade and how the fine crystalline structure had been etched by the spell within it. Sharp green facets parted like the teeth of a gaping mouth.

Too late Fedeles realized what an idiot he'd been. The ring was meant to capture a soul as it left a body, and that was exactly what he'd made himself into. Now it was taking him in King Juleo's place. He jerked back against the pull of the spell, but it only served to wrench him even closer in toward the jade maw. His every struggle tightened its crushing grip. A sensation like hot breath rolled over him.

Then he remembered a passage he'd read, written in gold on the very walls of this chapel: the words of the Savior before he rode into the amassed armies of the demon lords. *Trapped in the jaws of our enemies, we will plunge even deeper in. We will break their teeth and bloody their throats. We will be a poison in their bellies and their hunger will become our triumph.*

If he couldn't break away, then maybe he could break through.

He concentrated on the shining spell at the very heart of the jade and then hurled himself at it. The hooks and harpoons sped him deeper and faster through clouds of green minerals and glinting crystals. As the shining spell reached out to him, Fedeles poured his strength into it, infusing its shining form with the darkness of his shadow and filling it with his own desire for escape. As it enfolded him, Fedeles reshaped the spell's form and purpose around him. The hooks and harpoons dissipated. Its clutching neediness washed away. What had been *Seize* transformed into the joyous bursting geyser of *Freedom*.

The matrix of stone holding him shattered. Fedeles was hurled through the roof of the litter and up into the rafters of the chapel. *Freedom*, gleaming like obsidian, winged in circles around him and then melted back into him like a breath of fragrant, fresh air.

Fedeles heard the royal bishop cry out and sensed him clutching his hand as his ring fell away in smoldering pieces. Then he saw Prince Sevanyo as well as a multitude of priests rush to the royal litter. Outraged and astonished shouts filled the air and echoed through the vaulted ceiling.

The Hallowed Kings lifted their heads as King Juleo's spirit rose slowly past Fedeles. For an instant Fedeles felt the man's relief wash over him. Then the king's soul dissipated like smoke.

Had he slipped from the living realm into paradise? The journey across the Sorrowlands didn't appear to hold any fear for him.

A hard tug from deep in his chest drew Fedeles's attention. Looking down, he experienced a kind of vertigo and he realized that he gazed at his own bowed head. His body swayed. The acolyte beside him dug his hands into Fedeles's back. He looked terrified.

Immediately, Fedeles gave in to the desperate pull of his physical body. He dropped like a stone back into his own flesh. He gasped and the light flooding his eyes seemed to flare before him. He swayed, nearly toppled, then reclaimed his sense of balance.

"Are you—is it done?" the acolyte asked in a whisper.

"Yes. I'm fine now. Thank you," Fedeles assured him. In truth he felt as if he'd just sprinted miles. Fatigue clouded his thoughts and made his limbs feel like dead weights.

The youth nodded, then scurried back down to join his plump, elderly companion. No one else seemed to have noticed his absence. The chaos surrounding the king's litter held everyone rapt.

In a rare moment of unity Nugalo and Sevanyo both lifted the soulless body of their emaciated father from his litter. Sevanyo wept while Nugalo looked shocked as a man dealt a mortal wound. Blood trickled down his left hand, but he appeared completely unaware of his own injury. Instead he stared desperately at his father's waxy, blank face. The king's attendant priests rushed around them, while gathered nobles whispered and wondered at what had happened inside the golden litter.

Fedeles caught Oasia's gaze and she offered him the briefest of smiles. He didn't know what she'd witnessed of his struggle, but she seemed to accept that his actions had been justified. Perhaps she too had heard Gachello's entreaties.

He wasn't certain why Lliro Vediya stood at her side, but he so resembled Atreau that Fedeles couldn't help but find the pairing amusing. Or maybe his exhaustion edged him near delirium.

Also among Fedeles's allies was Timoteo, looking wild-haired and energetic. Fortunately, he could be depended upon to make peace and offer comfort. Now he gently parted the priests standing before him and knelt beside Sevanyo and Nugalo. He felt for the king's pulse at his throat and then shook his head.

For the first time Fedeles noticed the massive bandage swathing the dead king's forearm. He had no idea what to make of that.

Timoteo reached out, taking both Nugalo's hand and Prince Sevanyo's. He drew them up to their feet. Both of them moved like lost, exhausted children. The king's attendant priests surged past them to tidy the king's somewhat bedraggled corpse and then wrapped him in a shroud. As one, they carried his remains out to be washed and made ready for burial. Nobles, guards and other priests parted before them.

A strange, bewildered kind of silence settled over the entire chapel. Few of the people gathered had ever known of a time without King Juleo. Certainly neither Sevanyo nor Nugalo had.

Fedeles thought of all those romantic tales wherein some warrior commented upon the quiet before a storm. He'd always thought such a sensation was something of a poetic license.

But everyone gathered here seemed united in shock and loss. It couldn't last. Who would want to live in such a peace, so deprived of hope or joy? And yet none of them broke the quiet. Fedeles wondered how many of those gathered understood that from this point on all of

Cadeleon was at stake. No earthly authority remained to restrain Nugalo or Sevanyo.

If either prince willed it, the kingdom could readily descend into war.

Still the silence stretched. Then Timoteo leaned close to Nugalo and whispered something to him. The royal bishop drew in a sharp breath and nodded. Timoteo straightened, though he still resolutely held both prince's hands.

"King Juleo is dead." Timoteo's voice rang like a deep bell. He shot a quick glance to Fedeles.

"Long live King Sevanyo!" Fedeles shouted out in response.

At once, Sevanyo's supporters echoed the words, making them boom like thunder through the chapel. Or, Fedeles thought, as he took in the smoldering anger spreading through Nugalo's expression, the words rang like the first volley of cannon fire.

The battle had begun.

 CHAPTER
SEVEN

At the sight of Hierro Fueres, Narsi froze, gripping Dommian's charm-book. Fear coursed through him like ice water, turning his muscles rigid. A cold sweat rose across the back of his neck.

Hierro Fueres strode past ornate sunvine topiaries and bountiful rose bowers, closing the distance between them.

This was the man who had burned the Brand of Obedience into Dommian and whose cruel commands had tortured the dead guard's every waking moment—the same man who controlled Master Ariz with magic that Narsi's medicines fought every day. At last, Narsi saw the face of his opponent.

With his dark eyes, lean figure and proud features, he bore more than a passing resemblance to both Prince Sevanyo and Lord Quemanor. The golden tones of his resplendent clothes combined with the gold dust adorning his cheekbones and brow to lend him the appearance of a gilded statue brought to life. His spurs chimed with each of his long steps.

He was handsome, but Narsi couldn't appreciate it. He could only think of Master Ariz—bound in ropes, blood pouring from his chest, and welcoming his own death as his only hope of release from Hierro.

This assured, elegant man had pleasured in branding and then mutilating Master Ariz. He'd burned torturous servitude into the flesh of a fourteen-year-old boy placed in his care. He'd ordered the assassinations of complete strangers and plotted the murders of his own son, daughter and nephew. He'd enslaved, abused and degraded the man whose journal Narsi now held in his hands. All that cruelty only represented the people Narsi had encountered personally in less than two months. Hardly drops in a sea when compared to the nobleman's grasp over so very many lives.

Killing Narsi would be nothing to him.

According to Atreau and Countess Radulf, Hierro held a small—but growing—army of the capital's people captive in his sadistic thrall. It could hardly be a coincidence that the man was here when an enthralled physician-priest attempted to take the king's life, could it?

Hierro's eyes narrowed as he closed the distance between them.

Narsi's heart hammered in his chest as his fear intensified to the edge of panic. Forget murdering him. That was the least harm that this man was capable of inflicting upon him. Narsi almost expected to see green leaves wither and flowers die as the man walked past the cascading rose bowers. Instead a cherrylark flitted over his head and then alighted on the shoulder of the slender woman trailing behind him.

Narsi blinked.

He'd been so terrified and angered by the sight of Hierro that he hadn't even noticed the woman. Her sedate gait and gray mourning dress allowed her to nearly melt into the garden shadows. The cherrylark lingered on her shoulder for a moment, as if it had mistaken her for one of the arbors decorating the grounds. Then it flitted away and the woman lifted her wan face to watch it fly. She looked so much like Lady Quemanor that Narsi felt certain that this willowy young woman must be Oasia and Hierro's younger sister, the recently widowed Clara Odalis.

Hierro came to a halt hardly five feet from where Narsi sat.

"What is it you want, Remes?" he demanded.

The man who had shouted Hierro's name marched into Narsi's view as well. He wore a priest's robes and cassock, but the astounding quantity of gold thread decorating his black-and-violet raiment indicated high rank. As Remes approached, Clara Odalis dropped down nearly to the cobblestones in a reverent curtsy. "My prince."

Prince Remes, Narsi thought. The royal bishop's heir and a conspirator in Hierro's plan to usurp the throne, if Master Ariz's disjointed confessions were accurate. Narsi silently willed all three of them to keep walking.

Instead Clara glanced in his direction. Narsi guessed that the flash of sunlight across his shoe might have caught her attention. Or maybe the glittering pebbles flecked with mica drew her eyes. Whatever it was, Narsi felt thankful that it held her focus on the ground at his feet, when she could so very easily have lifted her gaze and spotted him in the shadows.

He tried to assure himself that none of them would recognize him, much less suspect him to be a danger to them. He could pretend to be absorbed in his reading. Maybe they'd ignore him. Except he'd seen no other Haldiim people—or even Labarans—in this place. For that reason alone, he was unlikely to be overlooked.

Clara frowned and narrowed her eyes, in nearly the same way that Hierro had moments before. But where Hierro had lost interest instantly, Clara appeared to concentrate. She stared hard, her dark gaze seeming almost ferocious. Then Narsi noticed faint blue glints of light flickering around the simple null sign that he'd traced through the pebbles and dirt.

However, the longer Clara stared at it, the more it seemed to shine with the radiance of a real spell. The edges took on a sharp definition and flared up across an expanse of stones as well as Narsi's foot. He suppressed the reflex to jerk back from the light. He didn't dare move a muscle.

As he sat rigid, Narsi found that his own gaze now slipped off the null symbol. Even his own feet and legs seemed difficult to focus upon. Something like vertigo washed through Narsi when he tried to pick out the details of his bootlaces.

Was Clara's gaze so potent that it could imbue a simple sign with magic? Or had it been that first glower Hierro had shot at the symbol? Narsi didn't quite know how it had occurred, but obviously the null sign he'd sketched had become a spell. It seemed to avert his and presumably everyone else's vision. He had no idea how long it would last or what other parameters the spell could have, so Narsi sat still and silent, hoping it would continue to shield him.

"Please do rise, my dear." Prince Remes extended his hand to catch Clara's wrist. Her attention snapped to the prince and she straightened at once.

"Forgive me, my prince, I thought I saw . . ." Her gaze slid sidelong toward Narsi again, but then the null sign flared and she shook her head. "How goes your father's vigil? There would appear to be some disturbance."

"More than a disturbance," Prince Remes snapped. His expression turned accusatory as he looked back to Hierro. "*Someone* enthralled one of my grandfather's physician-priests and commanded the man to slash the king's wrist."

"What?" Hierro appeared genuinely taken aback. "Was the assassin stopped in time?"

"You really don't know?" Prince Remes demanded in a whisper.

Hierro arched his brows. He leaned closer to the prince and responded in a low growl.

"How could it possibly profit our plans to have the king die before his appointed time? *We* are not yet prepared." Hierro scowled down at the stables as two carriages and half a dozen riders thundered out, racing for the city streets. He turned back to Prince Remes. "Does the king live?"

Prince Remes considered Hierro, and something about Hierro's agitated expression must have convinced him, because the suspicion faded from the prince's face.

"Some Haldiim physician caught the assassin before he could complete his work," Prince Remes stated. "But even so, grandfather is in a very bad way. They don't know if he'll even survive the ride to the Shard of Heaven."

Narsi scowled. Had he been given any say in the matter, he would not have allowed an injured, shocked elder to be shaken and bounced across uneven roads. The rough treatment was likely to tear the stitches from his fragile skin and start him bleeding again. What the king needed were liquids and natural sleep.

"He damn well better survive," Hierro snapped. The muscles of his jaw clenched so tightly that Narsi could see them flex. And the authenticity of aggrieved rage in Hierro's voice surprised Narsi.

Could it be that Hierro wasn't the man building an enthralled army? Or at least not the only one casting thralls over the people around him? Might there be two different witches at work? Both of them using the same sadistic brand? Narsi and Lord Vediya had discussed the possibility of such a thing, but Lord Vediya had argued very convincingly against it. Now, however, Narsi felt his doubt returning.

"If it wasn't you . . ." Prince Remes again lowered his voice to a whisper, then stole a glance around him. Narsi held his breath, expecting the prince to pick him out in an instant. However, the prince's eyes seemed to slide past the entire bower. He returned his attention to Hierro. "Who is responsible for this? You don't think Fedeles . . ."

"That squeamish half-wit?" Hierro gave a laugh. "He doesn't have the balls to put down a lame horse, much less murder his king."

"Maybe not a horse, but he's suspected of murdering both Lord Numes and Lord Wonena, in case you haven't heard," Remes said. "Numes's wife accused him before my uncle this very morning, and Yago has arrested him."

"Oh yes? Well, let's hope the royal bishop sees justice done." Hierro glanced to his sister and a smile lifted the corners of his mouth. Then his troubled expression returned. "But the attack against your grandfather sounds too manipulative and knowing to have been Fedeles's work. He doesn't possess the intellect to suspect our plans, much less to disrupt them with such skilled witchcraft."

"Perhaps not, but his cousin Javier might," Prince Remes retorted.

Hierro appeared to consider the possibility, then shook his head. "The moment Javier Tornesal sets foot in the capital, he will trigger spells all across the city, and not just mine. We would all know if he'd been here."

"The Labarans, then?" Prince Remes wondered. "Could this be an act of war?"

"It's not impossible," Hierro allowed. "But it seems unlikely that any of their agents would find the opportunity to approach, much less enthrall, one of the king's physicians. And from all that I've heard of Count Radulf and his courtiers, not one of them is clever enough or determined enough to master thralls. No, the Labarans just don't have the brains or the guts."

"Could it be . . ." Clara spoke so softly that Narsi had to strain to hear her. He barely caught himself from leaning forward. He had no idea how little it would take for any one of the three of them to notice him.

"Oh, it's too terrible an idea." Clara shook her head.

"Could it be what?" Hierro prompted his sister.

"You'll think I'm being foolish." Clara bowed her head, looking so bashful and intimidated that she resembled a child more than a grown woman. Narsi felt a pang of sympathy for her.

"A lady as lovely as yourself need not rely upon the merit of her wits to win admiration, my dear." Prince Remes again caught her hand in his. "Gentlemen will always find the whimsies of pretty women pleasant and amusing. Never fear."

Hierro rolled his eyes, then, when his sister remained silent, he snapped, "Just spit it out, Clara."

"I—" Clara kept her head bowed and Narsi guessed that neither of the two men who towered over her could see the secretive smile that briefly flashed over her lips. "It's only that the Haldiim are said to be such a clever race. And it . . . it seems so strange that the only time a Haldiim physician visits the royal palace, he happens to be the only person to notice someone harming the king. Of all the wise, loyal and pious Cadeleonians attending his Highness, I don't understand how only this one Haldiim physician would notice a physician-priest preforming an unimaginable act of treachery . . . unless he knew beforehand."

Prince Remes stared at Clara, his expression shifting from indulgence to horror. Hierro nodded slowly, as if considering some larger matter.

"I could be wrong, of course. My head is so full of silly notions," Clara went on. "But is it possible that the Haldiim physician was part of a greater plot?"

"Whose plot?" Hierro demanded.

"That of the Haldiim race," Clara whispered.

To Narsi's surprise, Hierro scowled at her with obvious exasperation. "You need to get over this obsession. It's already proven troublesome. The Haldiim are a race of simpering girls. We have other enemies."

Clara lifted her head and cast Prince Remes an entreating look.

"It's because they are cowardly and womanish that strong Cadeleonian men like yourself and my brother cannot recognize the true danger they pose. But as a frail woman, I see the treachery of my own weak sex belying their timidity. They disguise their heresies as pretty flowers and wild gardens, all while rooting their poison deep in the hearts of our cities. They sully the wisest men, selling ungodly cures through their pharmacies when prayer is the only true remedy. Their schools instruct children in only lies and their commerce lures women from the rightful paths of humility and obedience. Countless Cadeleonian souls hang on the brink of complete damnation." Clara clenched her hands to her chest as if she were caught by a sudden chill. "For the sake of our godly nation, the Haldiim must be purged from our lands."

Narsi felt a flush of outrage surge through him, and he had to fight to keep from giving himself away with an obscene shout. Even so, he rustled a branch of the bower. All three of the nobles started, turning in Narsi's direction. Horror flooded Narsi. His heart felt like it had lunged into his throat.

Then a cat leapt from a nearby bower, pursuing some tiny prey. As Hierro, Clara and Prince Remes watched, the cat sped across the open path and disappeared into a stand of trees. Narsi waited, his pulse hammering and his muscles straining against the slightest motion. He didn't even dare take a breath.

Remes shook his head. Hierro shrugged.

"I don't dispute the fact that removing the Haldiim from our nation would vastly improve the qualities of our natural Cadeleonian stock," Hierro said after a moment; then he looked to Prince Remes. "But I'm not convinced that any of them would have a reason to attempt to take the king's life. Your grandfather indulged their kind—and any number of their vices. If anything, they'd fight to keep that bent old reprobate alive."

The prince appeared at a loss, but Clara responded.

"They know that nothing will keep the king from death now. Sevanyo will ascend to the throne. They can no longer take royal tolerance for granted. So how better to ingratiate themselves than to stage an assassination where one of their own race plays the hero before Prince Sevanyo?"

Hierro cocked his head to one side and considered his sister.

"If that is the case, how did they manage to enthrall the physician-priest?" Hierro asked in a playful tone, as if he knew she was weaving a wild lie and found it entertaining.

"I cannot know the answer to that." Again Clara bowed her head. "But if I had to guess I would imagine that it took place in or around a Haldiim pharmacy. I'm told that even very pious men of medicine sometimes resort to Haldiim potions in their efforts to undo the holy punishments meted out to the sinful among us."

"Merrypox, you mean? Or are you referring to quim cankers?" Hierro gave a laugh as Clara's face flushed. Prince Remes smiled at her discomfort as well.

"I'm sure I don't know," Clara responded quickly, her expression anguished and embarrassed. Prince Remes responded at once, schooling his countenance to sympathy. He reached out and touched her shoulder, offering her reassurance.

"Your ignorance does you credit, my dear," Prince Remes told her.

Hierro rolled his eyes again, but the prince paid him no heed. His attention remained fixed upon Clara's lowered face.

"All right, your prim little idea isn't completely without merit. I'll give you that." Hierro shifted his attention from Clara to Prince Remes. "But to be certain, I think I should have words with this enthralled physician-priest. I've been practicing a few methods to extract information from even deeply enthralled men. I'd like to put my study to practice."

"You'll have to cross the Sorrowlands and plunge the depths of the Black Hell to do that," Prince Remes replied. "The coward slit his own throat."

"That's vexing." Hierro scowled, then he rested his hand on the hilt of his dagger. "What about the Haldiim physician?"

A shiver of dread slithered down Narsi's spine.

"He arrived as part of Bishop Timoteo's entourage but vanished when the rest of us were busy making grandfather ready for travel."

Narsi didn't recall Prince Remes being busy helping out in any way. Certainly he'd not personally attended his ailing grandfather.

"Now that I think about it, the physician does strike me as suspicious. Uncle Nugalo even mentioned the Grunito family's habit of sheltering dangerous Haldiim. You know it's very possible that they *are* in collusion—the

Haldiim and the Grunitos. Uncle isn't completely deluded on that point." Prince Remes pursed his lips as he trailed off in thought. A moment later he glanced to Clara. "Our lord may well have blessed you with a moment of profound intuition, my dear."

"Oh, thank you, Your Highness. If it weren't for your encouragement I wouldn't have dared to voice my fears aloud. But now that I have, I'm so heartened to know that you believe me and understand how deeply troubling this matter is."

"Rest assured, my dear." Prince Remes squeezed her shoulder again. "I'm not my heathen-loving grandfather, nor am I unmoved by your distress. When the time comes we will address these troublesome people together."

Narsi glowered at them as fury and helplessness churned through his chest like a slurry of mud and ice.

Then for no reason that Narsi could understand, all three of them turned suddenly and stared up at the empty blue sky. Narsi followed their stares but only saw a billowy white cloud. A few doves winged across the sky, and nearby a blue dragonfly whirred past.

"Old King Gachello finally takes his leave." Hierro stopped short and frowned. He narrowed his eyes as if straining to see something. Beside him Prince Remes appeared puzzled; he too squinted but seemed to struggle more than either Hierro or Clara to see clearly.

"Wait . . . no. Oh, Lord, no," Prince Remes murmured.

"King Juleo, I would swear to it." Clara made a holy gesture over her chest, then raised a hand over her mouth as an expression of pretty wonder spread over her features. "Has he been lost to the Hallowed Kings?"

"That can't be possible!" Prince Remes objected. Unlike Clara, he struck Narsi as truly distressed. "I must go at once."

"We'll join you," Hierro offered. "No one of royal blood should travel alone now."

Hierro gave a wave of his hand and at once six strapping guards wearing the royal bishop's colors raced forward from the palace doors. Prince Remes appeared to take their attendance for granted, his attention fixed on the distant sky.

Narsi found it telling that it was Hierro, and not Prince Remes, whose command they'd answered. Then to Narsi's horror, Hierro ordered two of the guards to search the palace grounds for a Haldiim physician and hold him captive when they found him. Prince Remes remarked that the man must be long gone, but Clara suggested that one of the guards watch the stables while the other begin searching in the herb gardens.

"I'm told that it has become common practice among many Haldiim to steal cuttings of medical plants," Clara explained, and Prince Remes gazed at her as if she'd said something terribly witty.

As the party strolled to the stables, Prince Remes favored Clara with his fretful conversation while Hierro followed after them.

Narsi resisted the urge to leap up from the bower. There would be no point in racing out to make his escape from the palace when his horse was stabled in the building that Hierro, Clara and Prince Remes currently occupied. Particularly not when he knew a guardsman would now be waiting there for him. He needed to remain calm and think.

For the moment he seemed safe where he was, so he could afford to wait and see if the guard didn't grow bored. If the guard remained long after Hierro, Clara and the prince rode away, Narsi decided that he would simply walk back to the duke's townhouse. He was loath to leave his mare, but he felt certain that he could convince someone from the duke's household to return and fetch his mount for him.

So he had a plan, for the short term at least. Though how he'd manage in the long run he wasn't sure. If he became a wanted man, then he would be forced to flee the capital. Possibly the nation.

How much support would the prince or Hierro lend to Clara's instigations? Could she convince Prince Sevanyo that Haldiim citizens had plotted to murder King Juleo? Narsi knew next to nothing about these nobles, and yet they held so much power over his life. Over so many lives. Had Narsi signed the death warrant for all his own people simply because he'd taken quick action? Could he warn Mother Kir-Naham and Esfir about Clara's accusations against Haldiim pharmacies? Would foreknowledge only make them appear guilty?

His pulse quickened as anxiety churned through him relentlessly.

A year ago, back in Anacleto, he would have scoffed if someone claimed that leaders and lawmakers would take baseless insinuations seriously. But in the last month, he'd witnessed bigotry and paranoia manifest first in whispered rumors of supposed poisonings—it seemed that nearly every Cadeleonian had heard of a friend who had a relative who knew someone who'd taken ill or died. No bodies were brought forth, no charges laid, nor were testimonies heard. And yet, unfounded as they were, suspicions grew into certainties. Ironically, the very lack of corpses meant there was no evidence to gather to prove the absurdity of the common gossip. So rumors carried on and on like lyrics of a popular song—the words becoming ingrained in people's minds even when they hated the tune.

Then, without ordering an investigation or even convening hearings, the royal bishop had banned the Haldiim people of Cieloalta from accessing medicines they needed. A few Cadeleonians had protested, but they then fell under suspicion as conspirators. As if there had ever been a conspiracy.

Narsi shook his head and then noticed that his hands were shaking. His palms felt clammy. He folded Dommian's charm-book closed and wiped his hands against the cold surface of the stone bench.

Clara's words turned through his mind again and again.

For the sake of our godly nation, the Haldiim must be purged from our lands . . . the Haldiim must be purged from our lands . . . purged . . .

She'd said it so earnestly, and so entreatingly, as if she was pleading for protection—not suggesting mass murder. As if she genuinely believed that innocent Haldiim people simply living their lives somehow presented a mortal threat to a noblewoman like herself. Never mind her entire *godly nation*. It was absurd! And yet there had been such conviction behind her words that it shocked Narsi.

He was used to facing angry, ignorant bigotry—dullards and bullies driven by their own deficiencies to demean and belittle others. But he hadn't before encountered so much hatred disguised as fear. How many Cadeleonian gallants would resist such an entreaty? Evidently Prince Remes had been moved enough to see merit in a story Clara obviously made up on the spot. It hadn't taken anything more than a quavering voice and a frightened, childish tone to convince him.

Narsi shuddered despite the warmth of the rising sun.

All at once those tales of his Haldiim ancestors battling for their lives washed through him with a terrible reality. Thousands of people had died. In this very city he'd seen ruined mosaics standing as testaments to vast Haldiim population that had been wiped out. Was this how it had started back then?

Berto's previous nervousness didn't seem so excessive just now. Haldiim people were already abandoning the city, maybe rightly so. Perhaps he shouldn't have been so hasty in assuring Lord Vediya that he would stay on. Narsi stopped himself even as the idea of fleeing arose in him.

People here depended upon him keeping his word. He couldn't lose his courage.

Narsi drew in a deep, calming breath. Then another. He remembered his mother gripping his hand in hers as they started across the scarlet Ammej Bridge, leaving their Cadeleonian lives behind them. Her fingers had felt like ice.

"Fear is the threshold we must cross every time we find our courage," she'd told him.

He hadn't understood her nervousness then, but later he recognized that as a shunned heram she'd known she would face immense hardship returning to the Haldiim District, but she'd gone anyway—for his sake. She'd refused to let fear confine her.

He couldn't do less. Not knowing that she was now reborn into a new Haldiim family; an infant whose whole future might depend upon him holding to the courage that she'd taught him. Now more than ever, it mattered that he help to keep people like Clara Odalis from working their will.

Narsi took in another deep breath and felt his muscles relax as he released it.

Thinking of his mother, he tried to consider his agitation, rather then simply submit to it. It wasn't only the idea of Clara Odalis's wild accusations that troubled him.

There was also the fact that he'd witnessed an enthralled man slit his own throat and bleed to death in front of him. He flinched from the memory. Not just because of the visceral horror and shock but because in a small way he'd been responsible for the man's death. Narsi took a moment to accept his own feeling of guilt and then to recognize that he couldn't have respected himself if he hadn't acted. He just wished that there had been some other way, another course he could have taken, that might have saved the king and spared the enthralled physician-priest. Had he managed that, then would Clara still have accused him of taking part in a Haldiim plot?

He couldn't know. Even the most harmless and justifiable actions could set off unforeseen repercussions. That didn't make taking action wrong.

In the end, he'd kept the king from bleeding to death in front of him. And as horrifying as it had been to hunch on this stone bench while powerful nobles stood only feet away discussing him and the fate of his people, it had also been revealing. Not only was he forewarned of Clara's persistent goal, but he'd stumbled upon a truly remarkable phenomenon.

He glanced down at the elusive null symbol at his feet. It appeared to have taken its power from Hierro's and Clara's interest. In other words, it had drawn power from them without either of them consenting or even noticing. There had to be a use for a symbol like that, didn't there?

A flutter of motion across the lawn drew Narsi's attention. A man wearing a dull blue cloak sidled out from behind a large sculpture draped with sunvines. He studied the stables briefly, then turned in Narsi's direction, and at once Narsi smiled, recognizing Lord Vediya— *his* Lord Vediya. Atreau.

Lord Vediya squinted at Narsi and tilted his head, as if trying to catch a better angle from which to see him. Then he closed his eyes and turned his head so that he was almost perfectly facing Narsi. Then he opened his eyes, and Narsi raised his hand and waved. Lord Vediya's gaze fixed on Narsi's face and his expression brightened. He glanced quickly around him, then crossed the distance between them in fast strides.

He held Narsi's gaze the entire time and then dropped down onto the stone bench next to him.

"Rough morning all around, it seems," Lord Vediya commented as he surveyed the stable. "Once they're gone, I'll see about getting you out of here."

"There's a guard at the stable and—"

"Yes, I heard them discussing you when they passed me. Don't worry. I have a plan."

"You do?" Narsi couldn't help his dubious tone. Lord Vediya hardly looked like a man in complete control of the situation. The remnant of a cobweb hung in his tousled hair and dirt streaked his breeches and the front of his jerkin, as if he'd been crawling on the ground. Despite his disheveled image, he smelled of soap and rose cologne.

"Perhaps calling it a *plan* is a slight exaggeration. Let's say it's a stratagem," Lord Vediya allowed. "I think that we'd both feel a little more confident if we tried to believe me, so quick now—get your coat off."

Lord Vediya shouldered out of his own jerkin. The front of his shirt hung half open, offering Narsi a glimpse of his naked chest. For a dazed instant Narsi had no idea what Lord Vediya was thinking, disrobing at a time like this, and he considered teasing the man about his so-called stratagem. Then his tired mind bumbled past the impulse of boyish infatuation and he realized that if the guards were searching for a physician, then his gray coat would immediately attract their attention. He removed his coat and accepted Lord Vediya's blue jerkin. The fine leather stretched across his shoulders, but otherwise it fit him.

Lord Vediya shrugged into Narsi's humble coat and then snatched up his medical satchel. Between his rumpled clothes and ruffled hair, he didn't look too different from any number of physicians Narsi had seen roused too early from their beds to tend to emergencies.

Even so, Narsi didn't think that simply exchanging coats was going to disguise him from guardsmen seeking out a Haldiim in the palace.

"Now we go!" Lord Vediya clapped Narsi lightly on the back, his warm fingers brushing the nape of Narsi's neck. Then he sprang to his feet and Narsi followed him.

To Narsi's surprise he didn't make for the stables. Instead they set off at a jaunty pace in the opposite direction. Stunning specimens of flowering trees and artful fountains surrounded them, but Narsi could hardly take them in. His heart raced every time they passed guards or groups of elegant-looking courtiers. Thankfully most of the people out at this early hour were engaged in exchanging rapt gossip about the Duke of Rauma's arrest and King Juleo's assassination.

Seeing their lack of attention to him, Narsi relaxed enough to report everything that he witnessed, from Captain Yago's arrival to his overheard conversation in the bower and the way that the null sign had seemed to take on power after Hierro and Clara noticed it.

"That was mad luck, you realize." Lord Vediya cast Narsi a sidelong glance.

"I do," Narsi said.

"Let's hope your luck holds for a while longer." Lord Vediya dropped his voice as they turned onto a new pathway. A low wall divided the greenery of the open grounds into geometric, distinct plantings.

A medical garden, Narsi realized in shock and horror. Lord Vediya had taken him exactly where he knew the guards had been sent to apprehend him. A sick sense of betrayal slid through Narsi and, seeing the big guardsman striding between the rows of potent herbs, he balked. Lord Vediya caught his arm and pulled him forward.

"Don't look at the guard," Lord Vediya whispered.

Narsi immediately turned his gaze forward to the blue gates ahead of him. A fat peacock sat atop one of the supports, and two dark-complexioned Yuanese men lounged below the creature. Narsi guessed from their beaded uniforms and ornate spears that they were some sort of honor guard.

"Wait! You!" the royal bishop's guard shouted from the medical garden.

"Go straight to the gates and tell them that you've been sent to fetch the costumes for Prince Jacinto's play." Lord Vediya shoved Narsi forward, then he spun on his heel and charged toward the royal bishop's guardsman.

"What do you think you're doing in that garden?" Lord Vediya roared. His voice carried as if it was echoing across the stage of the Candioro Theater. "Only physicians and royal gardeners are permitted in there!"

"I'm here on royal—" the guard began, but Lord Vediya's deep booming voice drowned him out.

"Thief!" Lord Vediya shouted, and the alarm in his tone rang shockingly true. "Guards! Gardeners! Someone! Come take this man at once! Thief!"

Narsi heard the commotion as groundskeepers, gardeners and royal guards came running. Then the air resounded with the crash of bodies and shouts. Narsi didn't dare to look back. He faced ahead and kept walking toward the Yuanese guards, who appeared to be observing the entire debacle with amusement.

"I'm here by order of Prince Re—" the royal bishop's guardsman attempted to call out.

"Pilfering love phlox, no doubt!" Lord Vediya shouted. "Let him try spinning his excuses to the commander of Prince Sevanyo's royal guards!"

Narsi drew to a halt before the two Yuanese guards. Up close he recognized that both looked quite young, certainly not older than himself.

"I—" Narsi was alarmed to hear a quaver in his voice. He cleared his throat. "I'm here to collect costumes for Prince Jacinto—for his play."

One of the Yuanese youths cocked his head and Narsi felt certain that he'd seen through this entire performance. Who in their right mind wouldn't? Narsi's heart hammered in his chest so hard that it felt like it might burst.

"You're very early," the youth said, and he stepped aside. "You'll have to wake him yourself."

The second Yuanese guard moved forward. Narsi tensed, but the young man strode past him for a better view of the swearing guard and the five gardeners who'd pinned him down against the loamy soil of the garden. The Yuanese youth grinned at the sight, then said something in Yuanese to his fellow guard. Narsi thought he recognized the term for fallen fruit. Both the young guards snickered.

Narsi walked through the gate, stunned that such a simple ploy had worked. He had no idea how much longer Lord Vediya could maintain the charade, but he guessed that the farther away he was, the better things would go. So he continued to follow the path before him, though he had no idea where it would lead him or what he should do when he reached his destination. Stands of laburnum and plum trees broke up the vast clover lawn. Bees hummed all around him and butterflies flitted from flowering branches to outcroppings of smoke poppies and moss roses.

As he reached the top of a rolling green hill, he heard voices. Then he caught sight of a large blue silk pavilion standing a little distance from a fountain festooned with golden nymphs. Tangles of human bodies lay across a multitude of bright blankets that spread out around the pavilion like a sea. As he walked closer, Narsi saw that the people were nearly all naked and asleep. Polished silver trays scattered with the remains of fruit, and wine jugs and black poppy pipes lay all around. As did a few musical instruments and heaps of abandoned shoes and clothes.

Narsi studied the face of one of the sleepers and realized that he recognized the woman as well as the two men sprawled across her. They were all performers from the Candioro Theater. He didn't see Inissa, but he thought he recognized Yara and two other Haldiim actresses sleeping on a blue waxed blanket alongside a group of snoring musicians. The few people who were awake appeared bleary-eyed and profoundly hungover. Narsi resisted the urge to race over and rouse Yara. It was enough to realize that despite how isolated he'd felt minutes ago, friends and familiar faces surrounded him now.

He peered inside the pavilion and made out more naked, entwined bodies collapsed together. In the midst of it all Sabella Calies stood, dressed in her dueling clothes and looking bored but also wide awake. Narsi found himself grinning in her direction like an idiot. Sabella offered him a short smile in return and waved him over. Narsi picked his way between people, taking care not to disturb anyone, particularly not a couple engaged in groggy fornication.

Sunlight warmed the pavilion's silk walls and lent a thick heat to the strong smell of costly perfume and sex hanging in the air. As Narsi edged up to Sabella, he noted Prince Jacinto sleeping with his head rested on an actress's stomach and an arm thrown over a stagehand's chest. All three of them looked content and almost sweet in their unguarded slumber. Sabella, with her dark, close-cropped hair, long, angular figure and stern expression, evoked one of those moralistic Cadeleonian etchings of grim death looming over sleeping lovers.

"I've been hearing all hell break loose down on the palace grounds," Sabella said. "What's happening, do you know?"

Narsi apprised her of Lord Quemanor's arrest as well as the assassination of the king. He left out how exactly he hid himself from Hierro, Prince Remes and Clara, but not the fact that he might be a wanted man soon, and that Lord Vediya had sent him here to shield him from arrest.

Sabella raised her brows at the end of Narsi's rushed story, then shook her head.

"Only someone with a screw-worm for a brain would arrange the king's assassination just so he could play hero . . . and in any case, the timing would have been beyond you. How could you arrange for the mad duke to be arrested right when the king was being bled to death, so that you could arrive with the duchess at exactly the right moment to save him?" Sabella's practicality in the face of regicide impressed Narsi. She went on just as easily. "Nah, I'd wager Jacinto's balls that the pretty widow Clara Odalis is up to her neck in the murder. Sounds like quick thinking on her feet, exploiting your presence there to divert attention from the real question of who could have enthralled that priest."

Narsi considered that for a moment. He'd been so horrified and outraged by the sweeping bigotry of Clara's accusations that he'd failed to consider what other motivation could have inspired her charges.

"But I don't understand how it would benefit her or anyone else to kill King Juleo at this point. Wasn't he expected to die soon anyway?" Narsi whispered. In truth, it had sounded like the king's inner circle had actually picked an exact day and time for his demise, which Narsi found a too disturbing to ponder over long.

Sabella shrugged.

"I learned years ago not to expect sense from any noble. The best you can hope for is to turn a profit keeping the harmless ones alive." Then Sabella shifted her attention to Prince Jacinto. She prodded his ribs with the toe of her boot.

"Arise, my prince!" Sabella shouted so loudly that Narsi and several of the people around them startled.

"Nahhhh, Sabs, lemme sleep . . ." Prince Jacinto mumbled several other inarticulate sounds and nuzzled his face into the actress's chest.

"Your Highness, the time has come to rise and shine!" Sabella prodded him again. "We are bereft of your leadership in this, our hour of need! Wake your royal ass up!"

This time the prince and both his sleeping companions woke, though not all at the same speed. The stagehand sat upright, stared ahead as if dazed, and then noticed Narsi and Sabella standing there. His expression turned instantly to alarm. He snatched up a pair of discarded work pants and pulled them on while making his stumbling, hopping retreat to a cluster of women Narsi recognized as costumers.

The actress rolled out from under the prince, shoved thick masses of glossy black hair out of her face and then drew a fallen silk shawl around her body. She picked up a pillow and then leaned back on it, managing to catch a ray of sunlight to perfectly illuminate her pretty face.

Prince Jacinto groaned and heaved himself into a sitting position. His hair resembled a bird's nest and numerous smears of stage makeup streaked his chest and groin. He yawned and slowly turned his red-rimmed, squinting gaze to Sabella. Then, seeing Narsi at her side, the prince offered him a pleased grin.

"Master Narsi! I'd not expected you to join us. It's late but never, I think, too late to welcome good company." The prince yawned but then regained his wide smile. "You must tell me what has brought you here at this monstrous hour and then join me for breakfast . . . and perhaps other entertainments—"

"I'd be honored, Your Highness, but I have news that . . ." Narsi knelt at the prince's side. As carefree and frivolous as the prince seemed, he still deserved care when facing the death of his grandfather. Narsi lowered his voice. "This morning your grandfather was assaulted by one of his physician-priests. We stopped the would-be assassin and treated your grandfather's injuries, but I don't believe that King Juleo survived the journey to the Shard of Heaven."

"What? No, that can't be. I visited the old coot the day before yesterday . . . told him all about the play and . . . and he laughed." The happiness in the prince's expression withered into something mournful and strangely fearful. "What about the assassin?"

"He's dead. By his own hand," Narsi said.

"Was he one of the possessed ones?" Prince Jacinto whispered. "One of the branded madmen Atreau's after?"

"I believe so, Your Highness."

Prince Jacinto's eyes went wide and he looked to Sabella. She nodded. The blood drained from the prince's already pale face. "What hope do any of us have if they couldn't keep the king safe?"

Narsi didn't have an answer for that.

"They're going to murder me." Prince Jacinto's tone rose with his growing agitation. "I don't even want the damn crown but they're still going to murder me—"

"No one is going to lay a hand on you, Highness." Sabella cut the prince off with a sure, cold tone. Her hand rested easily on her sword hilt. "I mean, other than those laundresses you hire for erotic spankings."

The prince managed a wan smile at that. He scanned the groups of people surrounding him in the pavilion, then demanded, "Where's Inissa? Where's Atreau?"

"I don't—" Narsi started to say, but then he caught sight of Lord Vediya tearing across the field in long loping strides. He still wore Narsi's coat and carried his medical satchel. He reached the pavilion in a moment and Jacinto staggered to him. Narsi wasn't certain if the prince's unsteady gait resulted from a shattering hangover or emotional shock. Either way, he and Sabella followed close behind the prince. Lord Vediya caught Prince Jacinto in a supporting embrace, and for a few moments the prince leaned against him, weeping quietly on his shoulder. Narsi overheard only a little of the prince's words, but from them he realized that Prince Jacinto had adored his grandfather and was also deeply afraid for his own life.

"I'm sorry. At least we know that he didn't suffer." Lord Vediya cast Narsi a quick glance as he spoke.

"He'd received a powerful dose of duera. He wouldn't have felt any pain," Narsi added.

Prince Jacinto straightened and turned to study Narsi. "You were there?"

"I came along with Duchess Quemanor and Father Timoteo," Narsi replied.

"And Papa was there with him too?" Jacinto asked.

"Yes." Narsi thought he knew what troubled Jacinto—something that spoke deeply to the prince's own fear and need to surround himself with so many companions at all times. "People who cared for him and loved him were beside him when he passed, I'm sure of that. He was never alone."

The prince seemed to relax slightly. Lord Vediya gave Narsi a brief nod, then he squeezed prince Jacinto's shoulder, drawing the prince's attention back to himself.

"I'm sorry that you're caught up in all these machinations, Jacinto. And I know how overwhelming it feels—"

"Do you?" Prince Jacinto appeared to take offense, but Lord Vediya held his gaze, and all at once the prince's expression softened. "I suppose that you do, actually . . ."

Narsi wondered what had altered the prince's disposition. Did he know how much responsibility Lord Vediya shouldered for the sake of Cadeleon? Or was it something more personal, more private? Narsi stole a glance to Sabella, but her countenance betrayed nothing.

In fact, Narsi wasn't certain that she paid the prince or Lord Vediya any attention at all. She scanned the grounds around them, watching half-dressed people stretching and dressing. Her eyes narrowed and Narsi followed the direction of her interest. A young tousled-looking stagehand, or rather, the semicircular scar on the man's left thigh. An instant later her focus shifted to the dark, round beauty mark on an actress's bare back. Then Narsi realized that she searched Jacinto's companions for the Brand of Obedience.

How much had Lord Vediya told her about the situation? Enough to keep Prince Jacinto safe, obviously, but did she know about Master Ariz? Or even Narsi's role?

Then Lord Vediya gave a flourish of his hand and Narsi's attention returned to him and Prince Jacinto.

"The people here, those in the Theater District and even in the Haldiim District, look to you for their protection, Jacinto. And they will do all they can to protect you," Lord Vediya said—and Narsi realized that he'd missed the question the prince had mumbled. "At this moment you may feel helpless, but the truth is that you are still a royal prince, a nobleman and a Hellion. You still wield great power, and there are many who need you."

The statement reminded Narsi of the assurances Duchess Quemanor had given Prince Sevanyo earlier.

Our entire nation looks to you to do what is right—even now in your time of grief. We have no one else.

"Right now," Lord Vediya went on, "dear Master Narsi could very much use your aid, in fact."

Prince Jacinto and Sabella both looked to Narsi then. From over the prince's shoulder, Lord Vediya offered Narsi a quick smile and a wink.

"Lady Odalis and her brother, Lord Fueres, would like to repay his courage in standing against the king's assassin by having him arrested, just because he's Haldiim," Lord Vediya went on. "I assured Master Narsi that not only would you be delighted to smuggle him past their guardsmen in the palace stable, but that you'd vouch for him with your father."

"I'll talk to Papa, of course." Despite his words, Prince Jacinto's expression struck Narsi as rather hesitant. "But I'm not certain I have any sway with the guards who've been tromping around here lately. They serve my uncle, and not a one of them seems to understand civility, much less the arts. I don't know—"

Lord Vediya leaned into the prince's back so that they were nearly cheek to cheek as they both studied Narsi. "Oh, but think how much fun it would be to fool one of them with something so simple and artistic as a change of costume. And haven't you wanted to see just how fetching a figure Master Narsi might cut in full Yuanese dress?"

"I *have* been wanting to show off the treasures Ambassador Oyoon left with me." The prince's expression brightened, and his smile seemed nearly as delighted as the grin he'd offered Narsi before he'd learned of his grandfather's murder. "Yes, Master Narsi, together we will hoodwink them all. To the three hells with my brother and Hierro Fueres!"

Hardly an hour later, Narsi found himself clothed in the brilliant raiment that a Yuanese dignitary had left behind when he took his leave of Cadeleonian court.

"He traded his wardrobe in exchange for one of my ships and the crew," Jacinto had informed him. Apparently, the two young Yuanese guards, an elderly musician and an imperious valet had also been entrusted to Prince Jacinto's care, and it was this fellow who wound a long band of gold silk from just above Narsi's fourth rib all the way down to his hips. The material was beautiful but Narsi found it a challenge to draw in a deep breath as the valet pinned the sash tight.

"I haven't been able to enjoy sailing since Gael died, so I think we were both happy with the arrangement," Prince Jacinto commented. Though moments later his attention strayed to the dark-haired actress who had woken up with him.

Narsi wondered how the ambassador's servants felt about being left behind and what the ship's crew thought of serving a strange Yuanese master. He took a little reassurance in the fact that the two youthful guards appeared content and the elderly musician seemed comfortable enough with Prince Jacinto to embrace him when she learned of his grandfather's death. The valet, on the other hand, looked vexed. Though his irritation seemed inspired by Narsi's broad bones and his lifelong failure to anoint his elbows with the proper perfumed oils. Narsi struggled not to move as the valet worked gold bands up over his feet and ankles, but the man kept brushing the tender skin at the back of his knees and tickling him. That at least was less awkward than earlier moments when the valet insisted upon manhandling him into an absurdly ornate loincloth.

Yara and three other actresses took a break from costuming themselves with ribbons and masks to observe Narsi's transformation from humble physician to resplendent dignitary. Yara wore a peacock-feather robe over a gown of silk rose petals. Her thick gold curls were festooned with tiny stuffed humming birds.

"I'd say it suits you," Yara commented as she used a hand mirror to arrange another bird in her hair. "Except that you're making a face like a plucked chicken."

"The kamarband belt feels like a python around my waist," Narsi confessed in a whisper. Yara laughed while the valet muttered "skittish child" in Yuanese.

"I did suggest that we do away with costumes altogether, if you recall," Lord Vediya said. Narsi did remember the joke, as well as Lord Vediya's clever machinations that day. They'd outmaneuvered Captain Yago and his men that morning. The memory lent Narsi more confidence. He could put his trust in Lord Vediya.

"I'm not certain that the public is prepared for the unvarnished magnificence of my debut in nude theater," Narsi responded. To his surprise the joke won him a laugh from the valet as well as Yara and Lord Vediya.

Soon after, he was fully dressed and marching back through the garden where he'd hidden from Hierro Fueres. Though now Yara and dozens of other entertainers surrounded him, all of them wearing masquerade costumes. As far as they were concerned, Narsi was simply in a costume as well, practicing his role for Prince Jacinto's play. The two Yuanese guards strode ahead of him while the musician and valet trailed him.

A headdress of iridescent gold feathers cascaded down his bare shoulders, and shockingly heavy gold bands adorned his arms and ankles. The long, heavy panels of the beaded gold loincloth looked like a priceless tapestry and forced Narsi to adopt a careful, stately gait.

He looked and felt anything but inconspicuous.

Though that didn't seem to be the point. Instead, he drew stares and was greeted by passing strangers as if he truly was a Yuanese dignitary of some kind. Following Prince Jacinto's direction, Narsi only acknowledged his well-wishers with a nod of his head. The vibrant feathers all around his face and trailing down his back bounced and swirled with even the slightest motion. He supposed there was a kind of genius to Lord Vediya's plan, though it bordered on mad arrogance as well.

Certainly it wasn't anything like sitting frozen and afraid, praying to go unseen, as Narsi had done in this very garden only an hour before. But there was something more heartening about this bluff and all the people surrounding him.

Not that he felt any less anxious when he strode into the stables, but seeing how easily a voluptuous actress distracted the guard meant to be searching for him, his confidence soared. When Lord Vediya led his mare to him and pretended to explain the finer points of Cadeleonian riding and horses, he played along, and despite his hammering heart and the desire to immediately saddle up and race away, he feigned hesitance to mount. Only after Lord Vediya coaxed him with assurances of the animal's gentleness and excellent training did he deign to mount his mare. Lord Vediya swung into his own saddle. Then the two of them rode from the stable side by side.

   **CHAPTER EIGHT**

Atreau watched Narsi with a sense of awe and also of annoyance. The man waited in the wings of the Candioro Theater, standing between two prop almond trees, politely covering a yawn. Even after the day Narsi had experienced, riding to the royal palace with the duchess and Timoteo, spotting an assassin, tending a king, then being accused of treason, he still remained calm enough that the tedious nature of stage rehearsal could bore him. He had worried that Narsi would lose his nerve. In truth, mortal danger only made him sleepy.

A good sign for Atreau himself, as he could hardly afford to lose another agent. But perhaps not the best thing for Narsi's own welfare. Particularly not now that he'd cost Hierro Fueres one of his best-placed enthralled assassins. Narsi had to be aware that this morning's events would bring him—and possibly all Haldiim physicians—under close scrutiny from the royal bishop, didn't he?

Now would be a wise time for him to flee the city. Perhaps to leave the entire country behind.

The memory of Lliro's offer of passage aboard his ships skimmed across Atreau's thoughts. The temptation to simply run away from all this anxiety and danger was too alluring for him to consider for any length of time. At least not for himself.

But certainly Narsi ought to.

Instead, Narsi patiently waited for his cue to walk on stage and recite his lines, just as he'd been doing for the last quarter of an hour. The three voluptuous black-haired young actresses standing center stage were professionals and quite talented, however the combination of little sleep, hangovers and the shocking news of the king's premature death at the hands of an assassin had thrown them off their strides. Atreau recognized that he hadn't helped matters any by penning absurdly alliterative, tangled dialogue designed to stumble all but the quickest of tongues. The phrase "west coast, wet coats" in particular seemed to trip one or another of them every time.

Still, when Atreau called for another run through, they began the scene yet again with dogged energy.

Jacinto sighed. He and the opulent blue velvet divan he occupied dominated the right side of the stage. Sabella stood guard behind him. A group of extras dressed as rough mercenaries lingered near her, making a study of her stance. Their costumes had been modeled on her russet-and-gray sword-house jacket, though none of the actors' coats bore a champion's emblem from the Red Stallion sword house, nor did they boast the prince's blue-and-gold favor pinned to their chests.

The rest of Jacinto's entourage spread out around him and across the stage. Pretty companions and petty courtiers, most still looking disheveled after their orgy on the palace grounds. Whip-thin and pale as a moonbeam, Enevir Helio balanced atop a wooden stool, rolling his ironwood cane between his hands. Across from him Procopio draped a muscular arm over the slim shoulders of yet another of his sad little cousins whom he no doubt intended to insinuate into Jacinto's bed. His trim black beard disguised the smug smile he turned on Inissa. He nudged his doe-eyed cousin nearer Jacinto, but the girl was far too shy to do more than stand trembling at the prince's elbow.

Inissa knelt at the foot of the velvet divan, looking as beautiful and mournful as a maiden saint from one her own paintings. She clasped her hands into the folds of her gray dress and bowed her head like a penitent.

Jacinto spared her a glance but then returned his attention to Atreau and the actresses standing center stage.

Atreau wished he possessed the means to shield Inissa from Jacinto's displeasure, but he'd already done all he could to conceal her and Spider's romantic assignations. Besides, Inissa's absence this morning hadn't offended Jacinto because he suspected her dalliance. Nor did it matter that she'd neglected the prince's evening indulgences; a kiss and a fondle would have won his forgiveness in that case.

What had cut Jacinto so deeply was the fact that Inissa had been absent when he'd been shocked by tragedy and fear. Regardless of the fact that Inissa couldn't have possibly known the king would be murdered this morning, Jacinto clearly felt betrayed because she'd not miraculously materialized the moment he'd wanted comfort from her.

"How reckless and unreasonable is the heart of a man," Atreau murmured along with the actress reciting the line. "No matter if he's highborn or ill-bred. Flattery and fancy—those winsome twins—grasp his heart, lift his loins and empty his head. Wisdom is ever undone. Passion's already won."

Atreau scowled at his own wordy, wandering phrases. Not his best work by a long stretch, but all he could manage in the little free time left for his writing.

Jacinto heaved another sigh. Being a prince, he hadn't needed to rage or shout his displeasure. Instead he'd simply stood on the stage and snapped out a brief reprimand when Inissa first came racing in to the Candioro Theater.

"Had you been with me this morning in my time of loss, you would already know that I am physically unharmed but my heart is shattered," Jacinto had stated. "I'm not even certain that I will have the spirit to continue sitting for the portrait that you were to paint for me." Then he'd withdrawn and artfully dropped to the velvet cushions of his divan. "Should you deign to join me, there is a place for you at my foot."

In an instant everyone else knew to treat her in the same cold manner. Well, everyone but Narsi, apparently.

"How can people claim to be her friend and then treat her as *heram* in a moment's notice? It's horrible," he'd said.

"No, it's pragmatic for us and her. Jacinto will forgive her sooner if she seems to have no one but him to care for her. He likes to feel magnanimous." Atreau had only dared to offer Inissa a furtive smile. She'd looked away quickly. It wasn't as if she didn't understand the situation or hadn't snubbed anyone herself. Two years ago she'd crossed a street rather than greet Atreau when he'd been in royal disfavor.

Only Narsi had gone out of his way to engage her in conversation. Everyone else knew how to behave appropriately.

Atreau wasn't certain if Narsi did it because he was too kind-hearted to ostracize anyone—even an assassin like Master Ariz—or if he'd acted on moral outrage after witnessing everyone around him accommodate Jacinto's fit of pique. Both were foolish motivations, but in quite different ways. Thankfully, Inissa had assessed the situation quickly and rebuffed Narsi before Jacinto grew further annoyed.

Still, it bothered Atreau a little that he didn't understand Narsi well enough to have anticipated his response. As a rule, Atreau went out of his way to know the agents he entrusted with the most sensitive work. But Narsi, for all his outward amiability, was proving neither predictable nor pliant.

On stage, the actresses at last completed their lines and delivered Narsi's cue. Narsi strode out from behind the prop tree, ducking between sprays of pink paper almond blossoms. The shimmering golden feathers floating around his face caught the faint stage lights and suffused his handsome features in a golden glow. The lithe quality of his bare, toned chest and his long legs made for a mesmerizing sight.

Narsi recited his rejoinder to the actresses and Atreau grinned. The young physician was not a good actor. But there was something about Narsi's stilted delivery that Atreau found oddly charming. His awkwardness on stage lent the pompous astrologer he portrayed a hint of appealing vulnerability. Atreau like the nuance Narsi accidentally added to the character whom he'd originally penned as simple, pretentious buffoon. Since Narsi had begun rehearsals, Atreau hadn't been able to keep himself from rewriting and expanding Narsi's role. Narsi's natural self-awareness in the face of absurdity delighted Atreau.

Of course, Narsi grumbled about the additional dialogue he had to memorize, and Atreau always shrugged, as if the matter was beyond his control—implying that this too was another of Jacinto's demands. All the while he secretly dreamed up another few lines to keep Narsi onstage.

It was foolish, but writing these silly little scenes and seeing Narsi play them out was one of the very few diversions that still lifted Atreau's spirits. And just now Narsi looked so handsome that most everyone watched him despite his ungainly delivery of his lines. Even Jacinto sat up in an attentive manner.

Narsi plowed through a lyrical set of couplets like he was reciting a medical inventory and then frowned at a particularly raunchy innuendo. Nearly everyone looking on laughed, Atreau included, but not unkindly.

"You are so sweet!" the actress nearest Narsi proclaimed. "Atreau is just a dirty old rogue for putting such words in your mouth."

"My words are hardly the worst thing of mine an actor could have in his mouth, my dear," Atreau called back. He waggled his eyebrows and then added, "My cooking is also atrocious."

Narsi and the actresses both laughed at that.

"But you're right, perhaps this dialogue is a bit crude." Atreau considered a less obvious pun. "What if we change it to—" A thunderous crash from the theater doors cut Atreau off. He spun to see a silver-bearded captain dressed in the royal bishop's colors come marching up the aisle. Half a dozen guardsmen followed him.

As they advanced, Atreau edged in front of Narsi and the three actresses surrounding him. He slid his belt knife from its sheath, hiding the blade behind the rolled pages of his script. Across from him, Sabella stepped up to Jacinto's side. She drew her short dagger with her left hand and draped her right hand over the hilt of her dueling sword. The two Yuanese eunuchs whom Jacinto had taken into his entourage both hefted their ornamental spears. Pretty as the weapons were, they could still run a man through.

Atreau doubted that the four of them could overpower all seven of the royal bishop's guardsmen, but their position on the raised stage might offer them enough advantage that they could slow their enemy's approach. It might buy them enough time to get Jacinto out the backstage doors. Silently Atreau cursed himself for not realizing that with the king's death this morning, Hierro might accelerate his plans.

Though if this was an assassination attempt, it seemed like a strangely public one, nothing like the unnervingly swift and silent murders Hierro had previously ordered.

The captain paused short of the narrow wooden steps leading up to center stage. The men behind him studied the stairs and then glanced to Sabella with wary expressions; she possessed a formidable reputation among fighting men throughout the city. Their imperious captain, however, focused his attention on Jacinto.

"I am here by the royal bishop's command." The captain didn't bow; instead he offered Jacinto little more than a dip of his head. "I have been informed that the Haldiim physician Narsi Lif-Tahm is attending your person. He is to be turned over to me at once."

Atreau was glad that he'd positioned himself to block easy view of Narsi. If anything would have given him away instantly it was the way all the color drained from his face and fear lit his eyes at the mention of his name. Atreau brushed his hand with his own.

Narsi drew in a slow, deep breath and seemed to regain his composure. The actress standing farthest from Narsi started to open her mouth,
but then she met Atreau's gaze and pressed her lips closed. Out of the
corner of his eye Atreau noticed Yara edging nearer to them from behind
the line of prop trees. Two slim Haldiim actors followed her. Both of them
looked terrified, but Yara's expression was determined.

Atreau wondered if they could get Narsi out the backstage doors
before the captain could take the stairs.

Not without someone getting hurt, he didn't think. And definitely
not if Jacinto ordered Sabella to turn Narsi over.

Atreau wasn't about to allow that to happen, but publicly overruling
Jacinto could prove dangerous as well. As if sharing his thoughts, Sabella
glanced to Atreau and flicked a quick, questioning hand sign to him.

Wait, Atreau signed back.

Sitting up on his divan, Jacinto glowered at the captain. The captain
placed a foot on the first step leading up onto stage. Atreau recognized fear
as it crept into Jacinto's expression. He was too unnerved by King Juleo's
assassination to stand up to the captain and, by extension, his uncle, the
royal bishop.

Then a blaze of white light flared up at the edge of the stage. The
captain staggered, covering his eyes, and several of his men stumbled as
he fell back into them.

Narsi and the actresses retreated several fast steps toward the
backstage doors. Atreau began to follow them, but the faint image that coalesced within the fiery sphere of white light stopped him.

Floating amidst the white flames like a radiant phantom stood Javier.
His beautiful face appeared hollowed and pale as a skull, while his lean
body seemed nothing more than a diaphanous veil of funerary smoke.
Other ghostly figures moved behind him, but Atreau's attention fixed
upon Javier as he turned slowly, mouthing words. Holy symbols rose
from his lips like vapor. Atreau thought he recognized the symbol for
guardians and another meaning "doom." They burned away in the light
that blazed from Javier's body.

The captain and his men gaped. Numerous actors, actresses and
stagehands made holy symbols over their chests. Sabella drew her sword,
and Jacinto stared as if enraptured. He slowly rose to his feet.

"Grandpa?" Jacinto whispered into the silence.

With the details of his features burned out by searing light, Javier did
resemble the dead king, Atreau realized. Not as he had been in the last
years of his life but how he'd appeared as a young man, immortalized in
so many portraits throughout the palace.

"Don't allow them . . . it's . . . wrong," Javier whispered.

"What's wrong, Grandpa?" Jacinto called. "What should I do? What can I do?"

Javier gave a shake of his head, but Atreau didn't think that he'd heard or even seen any of them in the theater. No, he was still somewhere in the Sorrowlands.

What on earth was he doing?

Or what was being done to him?

Atreau started forward, reaching out to Javier. Then, as suddenly as they'd appeared, the white flames extinguished and Javier was gone. The theater seemed dark in his absence and a faint moldering odor drifted over Atreau. He stood feeling stunned and useless.

God only knew what had happened to Javier or what he'd been trying to convey before he'd been extinguished like a candle flame.

"It's wrong . . . what did you mean? What shouldn't I allow?" Jacinto stared at the empty air, then his gaze dropped to the captain and his men. Jacinto's confused, grieving expression turned to rage.

"You! You and all of my uncle's utter fuckery!" Jacinto snapped. "You can damn well tell him that he has no business harassing *my* Haldiim physician! Or my Haldiim actors, or my friends! In fact, I will not stand for *any* of the fine people in my Theater District to be bothered by his bigotry any longer. You want to take them, you'll have to arrest me first! Then you'll damn well see what wrath my grandfather can bring down upon you from paradise!"

The captain scowled at Jacinto. Then his gaze flickered to where Javier had floated, as if he feared the king's ghost might well swoop down upon him.

"Away with you, I say! Before I set my men upon you!" Jacinto motioned to the dozen extras who happened to be dressed as swordsmen. They stood as if rooted to the boards of the stage, but Sabella advanced. Her murderous expression and the sword-house colors of her leather coat lent authenticity even to the group of men behind her. With the infamous Sabella Calies of the Red Stallion leading them, these had to be her uncle's hardened swordsmen—certainly not a mere assortment of character actors carrying wooden blades in their scabbards.

If they survived this, Atreau decided, he would need to procure some additional real swordsmen.

The captain blanched as Sabella closed the distance between them. His gaze again flicked to the spot where Javier had blazed before him moments ago. He retreated several steps.

"Your uncle will not be pleased, Your Highness," the captain said, but he continued to withdraw. After another three steps backward, he turned and took his men marching up the aisle and out of the theater. Sabella made an obscene gesture after them and then returned to her position at Jacinto's back. She sheathed her sword.

Jacinto stood looking shocked. Then a flush of elation colored his cheeks. Atreau understood the situation at once.

This was the first time Jacinto had openly defied his uncle and won a victory. More than that, he'd defended a truly decent and honorable person—not a reprobate like Atreau or any of his ilk. There was an undeniable pleasure to gallantry that Jacinto was experiencing.

"Narsi," Jacinto called.

Atreau glanced back and saw that Narsi and Yara both lingered beside the black velvet curtains at the back of the stage. All three of the Cadeleonian actresses who'd been with them had fled, as had both the Haldiim actors. Why Narsi hadn't made himself scarce as well, Atreau had no idea. Though his concerned expression when he met Atreau's gaze made Atreau wonder if Narsi hadn't remained out of loyalty to him.

Flattering but much too foolish.

The moment they were alone, he'd have to urge Narsi not to ever delay on his account.

Narsi dropped his gaze from Atreau and turned to Jacinto. He strode out from between the prop trees and crossed the stage to Jacinto's divan. The hesitance of his entrance as an actor had fallen away. Now his bearing seemed to match the striking figure he presented dressed in his resplendent costume. Jacinto watched his approach with obvious and growing delight.

That worried Atreau almost as much as the captain's intrusion had. If Jacinto's interest blossomed into more than a passing curiosity, it could be Narsi's undoing. And right now, Jacinto wore that acquisitive, fascinated expression that Atreau recognized too well. Narsi had sparked some epiphany in Jacinto's heart. Obviously the delusion that his dead grandfather had swept down from paradise to urge Jacinto to defend Narsi played a huge part of that. While Jacinto's misconception might protect numerous Haldiim people—at least in the short term—it could prove a disaster for Narsi himself.

If allowed to, Jacinto would monopolize Narsi for months on end, or even steal him away from Fedeles's household. The last thing Narsi could afford was Jacinto dragging him to court and making a show of their friendship just to spite the royal bishop. Narsi wouldn't live long enough for Jacinto to grow bored with him if that happened.

"Narsi, do you believe in fate?" Jacinto asked.

"I'm not entirely convinced of its nonexistence, Your Highness," Narsi replied.

Jacinto laughed and several of his courtiers followed his example.

"Ah, how clever you are. But you must call me Jacinto," Jacinto stated. "We are all friends here in the theater, after all."

Narsi inclined his head but didn't agree. Atreau smiled, knowing that Narsi didn't for a moment believe them all to be friends, and that he'd find a variety of ways to avoid addressing the prince by his given name—just as he gallingly continued to greet Atreau as Lord Vediya.

"I feel as if fate has brought you to me," Jacinto went on. "No one could deny it now. Not after . . ." Jacinto lifted his hand, indicating the empty spot where Javier had stood.

"Yes, that was an amazing sight, wasn't it?" Narsi replied. He too studied the spot where Javier had floated above the stage, but his expression was more contemplative than awed. "Very different from what I'd expect."

"You've spoken to spirits before this?" Jacinto looked even more excited, but several of his courtiers appeared disturbed. Procopio stroked his black beard as if he was already counting the royal bishop's coins for testifying to Narsi's communion with heathen spirits. Atreau moved quickly to Narsi's side.

But Narsi already began his response, "Not as such. But on occasion I've felt as though my departed mother watched over me. I've remembered her voice when I felt alone. I suppose all of us who have lost someone we dearly love carry memories of them in our hearts."

To Atreau's relief, Procopio looked profoundly disappointed at this response. Enevir, however, smiled with sad understanding, as did a few of the extras dressed in fencing leathers. Even Inissa cast Narsi a sympathetic glance.

"Your grandfather's appearance just now was obviously something different altogether," Narsi went on. "Perhaps the fact that he was a Hallowed King made it possible for him to reach out, or maybe he felt particularly attached to you. As a physician, I'm afraid that my knowledge is limited to living people. It might be more worthwhile to address someone like Fath—er . . . Bishop Timoteo."

"Yes, yes. Timoteo . . . He's well informed in church doctrine, and he has certainly preached loudly on the sacred importance of protecting Haldiim rights," Jacinto allowed. He obviously had no intention of seeking out any clergyman for a conversation. "But he never mentioned that my dear old grandpa would come down and shake a man's bowels loose if he came after you, Narsi! No, Timoteo neither as engaging as you nor as arresting."

"Well, certainly it's better to be arresting than arrested," Narsi responded lightly.

Jacinto gazed at the young master physician as if he was half in love.

Atreau groaned inwardly.

How thrilling to feel like an ardent hero, your blood racing with terror while righteousness pounded through your heart. That euphoria could be as strong as liquor and heady as poppy smoke. Narsi had sparked something greater in Jacinto. He'd certainly never before worried too much over the inequities suffered by Haldiim people. Or the will of any of his hallowed ancestors, for that matter.

"We really must get back to rehearsal," Atreau broke in. "Particularly if you want the production ready in time for your father's coronation."

"I never realized how business minded you were, Atreau." Jacinto scowled at him. "It's not your most charming trait."

"Indeed not," Atreau agreed. "But my patron is a most noble prince, and I have given him my word of honor that this production will amaze and delight his father, the king. And so I must make myself repugnant for my prince's sake."

That at least won a dry laugh from Jacinto. But his gaze remained fixed on Narsi as Atreau led him stage right. Atreau racked his mind for a way to shift Jacinto's interest. Then the obvious means occurred to him. If Jacinto wanted to be a hero to a Haldiim beauty, well, there were plenty of other lovelies to choose from.

Atreau called Yara up onto the stage and watched as she sauntered past Jacinto. The prince's eyes followed every flutter and sway of the peacock feathers that adorned her shimmering cloak.

"I'd like you to run through the new star-charting scene with Narsi," Atreau told her.

"My pleasure." Yara met Atreau's gaze with an amused smile then turned her attention to Narsi. "Our poor astrologer just keeps getting landed with more and more lines to memorize, hmm?"

"And I bungle them all so badly." Narsi hung his head. "I'm sorry if I make a mess of the performance."

"You'll do just fine, and if there's a gaffe here or there, the rest of us can cover it easily enough. Lets just have fun with it." She took Narsi's arm in her own. The two of them exchanged a warm smile that had nothing to do with stagecraft. Atreau felt a strange sort of uneasiness rise in his chest. He refused to think on it. Instead he took relief in noting that his ploy had worked to shift much of Jacinto's interest.

Narsi and Yara practiced their parts. Yara did indeed cover Narsi's gaffes neatly. She had to be one of the best actresses Atreau had ever worked with. Shame it was for such a fiasco of a production. But that was life, wasn't it? Sometimes there was more at stake than artistry or even his own reputation as a writer.

While Narsi and Yara gamely chewed through their unctuous dialogue, Atreau glanced over the notes Spider had passed to him earlier. So much seemed to come back to the Salt Islands and Timoteo. He needed to draw Narsi aside and sound him out on the subject of the holy father and what Grunito secret he could have hidden away. While he was at it, it wouldn't hurt to hear Narsi's thoughts on this sketch that Master Ariz had managed to scribble. There was a chance that Narsi had encountered something like it in Dommian's charm-book. Or Master Ariz may have made some passing mention of it in their earlier meetings.

"Atreau," Jacinto called. "We should add an orgy scene in grandpa's honor."

Atreau repressed the urge to argue. The production was already bloated with scantily dressed girls romping through forests and convents, as well as half-clothed actresses swinging from the catwalks as tempting devils.

"I'll see what I can come up with," Atreau responded.

"And fantastic machines," Jacinto added. "Grandfather adored all those strange mechanisms his Haldiim courtiers created for him."

Did he want clockwork succubi? Atreau wondered how they would even costume that—much less work it into the already bizarre narrative. Then he held his rising temper. Did it truly matter? When the nation and so many lives were at stake, what did his pride matter? He looked again at the paper in his hand and then slipped the pages back into his pocket. In the greater scheme of things, nothing he wrote counted as valuable to anyone's life. He needed to remember that.

"And we ought to make one of our gallant heroes a Haldiim. Grandpa hated the way Uncle Nugalo demonized them." Jacinto glanced to Yara and Narsi. Atreau could almost see the prince actually considering, perhaps for the first time, the threat they lived under.

"Or perhaps one of the heroines?" Enevir beamed at Jacinto. After years of trying to rouse the prince's political interest, this had to be heartening for the fellow. Though Atreau wasn't certain how far beyond the Theater District Jacinto's activism would really stretch. The royal bishop was not easily defied, not even by kings.

"A Haldiim heroine would be more in keeping with the culture and the range of our current cast," Atreau added, and he indicated Yara with a motion. She had the grace not to look horrified at the suggestion that she carry the burden of a wildly expanded role with only two weeks before the likely opening.

"Shall we break for luncheon, while I mull the possibilities over?" Atreau asked.

"I suppose so," Jacinto allowed. He glanced over to Procopio's shy cousin, but then nudged Inissa. "I could sit for my portrait for a little time while someone fetches us something to eat."

"That would be lovely, darling, but . . ." Inissa managed to appear hopeful and contrite at the same time as she twined a lock of her black hair around one of her fingers. "I've nearly exhausted the supply of madder rag I need to make my crimson paint, so . . ."

"Never fear." Jacinto waved Enevir to him and Enevir dropped several of the prince's coins of favor into her palm.

That would be her rent paid for the next two months, Atreau guessed.

"Yara?" Jacinto called. "I do hope you can join us at the Green Door."

"Of course, Your Highness," Yara replied. "You wouldn't mind if I brought along a script of my own that I'm in the midst of writing, would you?"

"Oh! A playwright and an actress, how talented you are, my dear. Yes, you must let me read what you have! Absolutely." Jacinto brightened further.

And maybe Yara would have her rent as well, Atreau thought. But instead of rushing across the stage to fawn on Jacinto, Yara turned back to Narsi.

"You need someplace to stay tonight, I think," she said. "Somewhere that those guardsmen won't know to look for you."

"Mother Kir-Naham has offered to let me stay at the pharmacy in the past." He glanced in Atreau's direction but didn't ask, and Atreau suppressed his urge to offer. Narsi would be safer with Yara than sheltering anywhere near him.

"We'll ask Esfir, shall we?" Yara smiled. "She and a few other friends are coming over for dinner and then we're all going to the sacred grove. If you joined us we could make a little party of it. By the end of the night I'm certain you'll have your choice of invitations to stay the night in good company."

No doubt he would, Atreau thought. A little pain sparked in his chest, but he ignored it. Narsi looked relieved and delighted.

"I'll buy honeycakes then," Narsi agreed.

"Perfect! Come over anytime after fifth bell," Yara said, and then she sauntered to Jacinto. The prince, however, still studied Narsi.

Atreau caught Narsi's hand before he too could be pulled into Jacinto's company. "Master Physician, I'm afraid that I'm in need of your attention. If you can spare me the time."

"Certainly," Narsi replied. "Though first, I do hope you could spare me a change of clothes."

CHAPTER NINE

In the early morning, as bells all across the city rang out the news of King Juleo's death, Ariz led his stallion along the narrow, rocky trail that curved up to the eastern face of Crown Hill. He kept to the shadows cast by overhanging branches, hiding his passage from the spying eyes of songbirds and crows alike. At last he reached the summit, where white marble ruins offered him cover beyond the few stands of saplings. He hitched his amiable old mount to a tree and watched as Moteado helped himself to the wild grass and lush weeds.

Blue wildflowers spilled all across the ground, but as Ariz strode toward the remnants of the temple ruins, hundreds of cerulean butterflies took flight before him, revealing a vast swath of gold and red phlox. The moment seemed magical. He wished Fedeles had been beside him to see it.

Or mayhap he'd already witnessed the sight. Ariz noted the position of one small stone that sat atop the cracked steps. During the past weeks he'd taken to hiding notes to Fedeles in the crevice beneath it. The bas-relief horses carved across its marble face now looked westward, not to the east as Ariz had left them. He rushed to the edge of the temple ruin and lifted the stone. Below it, nestled in the cracked marble, lay several pages of folded notes from Fedeles.

Fedeles first assured him that Delphia and her children were safe and well. He then went on to say that despite nearly a month passing, Sparanzo still complained bitterly of Ariz's absence to everyone in the entire household, including Master Leadro, the music instructor who'd temporarily taken over Ariz's duties. Even Prince Sevanyo had been appraised of the matter on the occasions that he'd visited the children and joined them dancing a ciervaluz.

It heartened Ariz to learn that he was not forgotten and that the people he loved were safe. Fedeles had even gone to the trouble of including a paper charm that Sparanzo, Celina and Marisol had made for him to hang in his room—carefully cut and folded green paper that unfolded to reveal a pattern of ivy radiating out from the center.

Ariz took a moment to admire it before carefully folding it closed again.

Lastly, Fedeles had closed the letter with his own unadorned sentiments.

I didn't realize how much your company lifted my spirits every day until you were gone. I should have recognized how dear you'd become to me sooner. Now each morning I wake delighted and looking forward to seeing you as I have for years, only to remember that you cannot be with me, not even to chastise me for my careless footwork.

How I miss you and long to hold you again in my arms.

Briefly, Ariz forgot about the bells ringing from the Shard of Heaven and how all the chapels across the city echoed the mournful song. He read the few lines over and over, as yearning rolled through him like a great wave. Then he folded the letter and slipped it into the pocket of his dull brown coat. He would have been wiser to destroy the note, but the words moved him so deeply that he couldn't bring himself to do so. Not yet. Maybe after he'd read the letter a few more times.

The note that Ariz placed in the crevice was hardly legible compared to the one he'd taken. Revealing anything that he even suspected Hierro wouldn't want known had been a monumental ordeal. Almost as if possessed, his hands had clenched his pen and scratched out words as he struggled to write them. What remained was a defaced mess of scrawls. Though he'd recently discovered that he could make drawings without having to blot them out. Whether that was because the ineptness of his sketches rendered them nearly unrecognizable in the first place, or because Hierro's thrall didn't affect things he might visualize in the same way it did his word and actions, Ariz didn't know. Perhaps Master Narsi would—if Ariz could ever manage to ask him.

For now he exploited what advantage it offered as best he could. Stick figures and blotchy drawings of little birds represented as much of a warning as he could express about Clara's spying songbirds, while his crude map of the city streets and poor rendering of the brand burned into his own chest signified the place he suspected that Hierro housed a growing number of enthralled assassins.

After that he'd added a few sentences, responding to queries Fedeles had written to him, concerning unimportant matters. He described a happy memory of picking cherries in his uncle's orchard as a youth and the first dance he'd mastered. They were trivial details of a life he'd lost, but recalling them for Fedeles made him feel briefly transported back to a time when his favorite food or song had still possessed any meaning. It had been so long that Ariz, himself, had nearly forgotten everything he'd once enjoyed.

He'd closed the missive with an *A* for his own name and a sentimental scribble of a heart. He couldn't help but feel shame at the ugliness of the note as he lay it down in place of Fedeles's letter, but he'd lost most of his pride in appearances years ago. He only hoped that some of the warnings as well as his affection carried through. He returned the stone and placed it so that the horse faced east again.

Then he stood and indulged himself in a few moments of simply remembering how it had felt to hold Fedeles and dance together. It had been lovely to watch the passing clouds with him and to skip and leap over the ancient, worn stones. Ariz allowed himself to dance the first few steps of a quaressa as the warm, joyful memories washed through his tired, bruised body.

Master Narsi's potions seemed to allow him to steal happy moments here and there—but there was a danger in indulging too much and lingering on an exposed hill alone for hours on end. He might be spied here and his secret notes discovered.

Or worse, he might lose himself in reverie and forget the pressing reason he'd ridden out here today. Ariz stilled. For an agonizing moment his brand flared to life, searing through him with the knowledge that he still hadn't executed Lord Numes's wife and unborn child, as Hierro had wished. Ariz drew out a vial of Master Narsi's potion and drank. For just an instant the fiery pain flared up to a blinding agony. Then it dulled, leaving Ariz with a racing pulse, ringing ears and enough free will to once again suppress Hierro's demands.

He stalked to the edge of the hillside and crouched low, studying the artfully maintained woodlands below. Groundsmen who served both the royal Sagradas and other noble houses maintained large herds of deer and other game for the sake of their masters' dinner tables. Gamekeepers and poachers alike roamed the vast acreages, so it wasn't unusual to see common folk prowling beneath the stands of trees from time to time. Men gathering rabbits and grouse from snares were an ordinary sight.

But not at midday and certainly not armed with only a sword.

Ariz frowned down at his fellow assassin, watching as the man rode toward the Quemanor estate. He didn't seem completely at ease on his mount. Between that, his thick beard and his tanned, wind-beaten complexion, Ariz guessed that the brawny man had lived as a sailor before he'd fallen afoul of Hierro. Now he was a hapless pawn, dispatched to murder three children, most likely.

Ariz hurried back to Moteado. They descended Crown Hill's hidden west trail and rode into the cover of weeping willow stands. He found the spot where the path narrowed and heavy branches hung low. A month ago, when he'd ridden here with Fedeles, he'd surveyed the long cascades of green leaves and deep shadows for the threat of a possible ambush. Now he would be the threat that he'd anticipated.

Ariz led Moteado out of sight and left the stallion to graze on flowers and wild grass. It wasn't a practical decision. Mounted, Ariz could easily have taken the other man, but he didn't want to risk Moteado being injured.

So, Ariz returned to the path and scrambled up into one of the trees. He found an overhanging branch at just the right height and braced himself.

When the assassin reached the scattered shadows of the willows, Ariz swung down, kicking hard against the man's face and chest. The speed of the assassin's mount drove him into Ariz's boots, and the man's inexperience at riding ensured that he lost his seat at once. He fell with a shout and hit the ground like a stone. Ariz dropped down beside him. The stunned man gasped for air and gaped at Ariz in shock. Ariz plunged his short sword into the man's chest, skewering his heart in a fast, clean thrust.

An inarticulate noise rose from the man and he attempted to deliver a clumsy punch. Ariz caught his arm. He met the man's gaze and then knelt beside him, still holding his shaking hand.

"I'm sorry," Ariz told him. "It will be over soon, I promise you."

The man's lips moved fractionally, but if he said anything, Ariz didn't hear it. Strength faded from the man's grip. His eyes stilled. He stared blankly past Ariz into the swaying streams of green willow leaves. Ariz lay the man's hand down. He wondered if he would ever look at a weeping willow and think of it as anything but an emblem of death now.

At least the assassin was free.

Ariz jerked his sword from the corpse and quickly cleaned the blade. Then he rolled the dead body back into the cover of the trees.

That just left the man's horse to deal with. Ariz whistled for Moteado and his stallion galloped to him at once. Ariz swung into his saddle and raced after the riderless horse. In minutes he sighted the young gelding. It had already begun to turn back toward its home stables.

That Ariz couldn't allow. If the horse returned, riderless, then Hierro would realize his plan had been foiled. The longer he remained ignorant the longer it would be before he sent another man after Celina, Marisol and Sparanzo.

Ariz nudged Moteado, and his stallion chased the gelding down. Ariz leaned out from his saddle and grabbed the horse's slack reins. The spooked gelding nipped at his arm, but Ariz hardly felt it. Steadily, he slowed the horse. As it calmed, it naturally fell into Moteado's relaxed gait. Ariz guessed that Moteado's ease soothed the gelding more than his own soft words could. At last they reached the weathered gate that opened onto the rich pastures Fedeles maintained. Other horses roamed across the fields and several napped under apple trees. Ariz led the gelding through the gate. There, he stripped off the animal's saddle, bridle and bit. Then he set the gelding free to romp through the grass and wildflowers.

He closed the gate and Moteado bent his head and took a mouthful of wild oatweed. Ariz scratched the stallion and Moteado sighed contentedly. He loved ambling across these rich pastures.

Ariz was tempted to linger here himself in hopes that Fedeles might ride up to Crown Hill today or come to visit his rescued herd.

Ariz felt the desire to see Fedeles so keenly, it threatened to make him do something truly stupid. He was so very close to the Quemanor household. Riding only a quarter of an hour, he could be back in his old fencing room—or upstairs at the door of Fedeles's private chambers. But then he spied larks winging through the nearby trees.

He couldn't allow Clara or Hierro to discover how close he and Fedeles had become. If they knew, they wouldn't hesitate to use him against Fedeles. That turned the hopeful sentiments humming through Ariz to an icy sludge of dread.

He mounted Moteado and then raced back to Clara Odalis's lands.

CHAPTER
TEN

Later that afternoon, when Atreau entered the Fat Goose with Narsi, he noted that the regular patrons were largely subdued and occupied in speculation about the king's demise. The newest of Spider's serving girls greeted him with just a nod of her head and allowed him back behind the bar without comment. Atreau briefly poked into the back room and found Spider arranging passage to the Salt Islands aboard Lliro's ship *Summer Wind* for one of his other barmaids. The lanky, broad-shouldered maid accepted the forged papers Spider turned over and carefully repeated the directions that would ensure her safe journey to the Butterfly Temple.

If only their mother had lived to see him now, Atreau thought, she would have been so proud of Spider. Not that he would have appreciated Atreau telling him as much. He was by far the least sentimental of all Atreau's brothers.

No new missives had arrived for Atreau, so he made himself a platter of applebread and cheese, filled a jug of barleywater and settled at his favorite table at the foot of the staircase, where he could overlook the various clusters of gamblers and spies coming and going through the door. Narsi dropped into the chair beside him. Yuanese balsam sweetened the astringent scent of coinflower that normally clung to his body.

He accepted the cup of barleywater Atreau offered him. The muerate scars peppering his graceful fingers had faded. Now they nearly matched the bluish birthmark that Atreau remembered on the back of his thigh.

"That wasn't really King Juleo's ghost, was it?" Narsi asked quietly.

"I don't think so," Atreau admitted. "But why do you believe it wasn't?"

"He didn't seem anything like the man I treated this morning. The gestures of his hands looked like Bahiim signs. Actually, he very much resembled"—Narsi dropped his voice to a whisper—"the duke. Fedeles Quemanor."

That possibility took Atreau off guard for an instant. Fedeles and Javier *did* resemble each other more closely than many brothers—and of late Fedeles had even begun to practice magic. Could that have been him?

No. The way that luminous fire had seemed to burn up from the man's features, revealing the hollows of a death's mask, that was unique to Javier and his White Hell.

Belatedly he realized that Narsi had been studying him closely. Now Narsi's gaze narrowed in that quizzical manner that Atreau was growing used to.

"I'm wrong," Narsi asserted without resentment. "Who was it then?"

Atreau considered denying any knowledge, but he was already tired of keeping so many troubling thoughts to himself.

"Javier Tornesal," Atreau whispered. He cut the applebread and helped himself to a little of the soft ripe cheese.

"Really? I'd not imagined him looking quite . . . like that." Narsi took a sip of his barleywater. "What did he mean when he said 'Don't allow them' and 'it's wrong'?"

"I wish I knew," Atreau admitted. Again anxiety closed in around him. Javier had seemed so harrowed. Had he needed help? Atreau swallowed a mouthful of his own drink. The earthy taste of the barleywater reminded him of loam and graves. A weak, worried part of him yearned to find a bottle of wine and pour that down his throat until the anxious churning in his gut drowned. Atreau fought the urge. Easy as that seemed, it would solve nothing and only waste his intellect and time. He simply had to accept that he couldn't know what had befallen Javier and couldn't reach him even if he did know.

"The more pressing matters at hand are these." Atreau slid the notes across the table along with Narsi's serving of applebread and cheese. Narsi scrutinized Master Ariz's sketch and then dug into the deep pocket of his physician's coat and drew out Dommian's charm-book. As he slowly turned through the defaced pages, Atreau noted how much Ariz's missives were growing to resemble Dommian's scratched-out, nearly incoherent scribblings.

Atreau knew from reading over his own diaries and rough drafts that a man's state of mind reflected in both the content and form of his writing. These notes spoke of torment and madness in every stroke and letter. Not for the first time, Atreau wondered if they hadn't gravely erred by allowing Ariz to go on living as a tortured instrument of Hierro's ambition. But what was done was done. Atreau possessed neither the callousness to betray Fedeles's wishes nor the resources to have Ariz murdered. Not unless Narsi could be persuaded to poison the man's medicine, which would never happen.

"Here." Narsi held the book open for Atreau to study. "Do you think it's the same motif?"

Artistic talent obviously was not Dommian's strength and Ariz's drawing could best be described as amateur. Still, the similarities between the two poor renderings were notable. A motif decorating the lid of a box. At the center, an animal—a goat? No, a deer—was depicted in profile, facing left and bounding over something circular. A cratered moon? A skull? A feathery swash spread below the skull like a pair of tattered wings. It was obvious that both men had attempted to capture the same image.

Staring at it, Atreau felt that he'd seen something very like this somewhere else and long ago. He frowned and tried to remember, but the more he attempted to recollect, the more uncertain he became. He wondered suddenly if he wasn't just confusing this box with the golden cask that he'd once searched out in the depths of an ancient chapel in Labara.

"I've been able to use medical lenses to work out a little of the writing here." Narsi tapped the flurry of mangled script crammed around the image in Dommian's charm-book. "It reads: 'Beneath Meztli's shield, Bhadia carried the shroud unseen, Trueno guided the way, but only the Summer Doe's horns could undo them all.'" Narsi frowned. "He's written more, but that's all I've been able to make out. What Master Ariz has written seems more straightforward."

Find it before I do.

"Though what *it* is that he wants found is a good question," Narsi mused as he took a bite of his bread and cheese.

Atreau nodded. A box of some kind brought from the Salt Islands by the royal bishop's bastard son, that was what it appeared to be. At least he guessed as much from what Lliro had told him. But what lay inside?

Across from him, Narsi started to lift his barleywater to his lips but then set it back down. He snatched up the charm-book and turned it to the last page. Then, rather expertly, he teased several tissue-thin pages out from a slit in the back cover.

Letters, Atreau recognized, as Narsi spread them out carefully.

"I should have thought of it earlier. Dommian served the Fueres family before coming to the duke's household," Narsi said, and he tapped single initial used to close the missives. "*C* could stand for Clara, couldn't it? She mentions the Summer Doe's relic and history as if it's a subject they've discussed extensively, and that sketch appears to depict the Summer Doe decorating some kind of cask or reliquary."

"So they're after a relic, you think?" That was consistent with the messages that Suelita had decoded for them. Those, too, had been filled with references to relics from the Battle of Heaven's Shard. Though the very last one had proved much more difficult to decipher, and what Suelita had worked out appeared to be mechanical designs of some kind.

Atreau scanned these delicate letters. The contents proved childish, sad and devout—not unlike Clara Odalis.

Then his attention caught on a single word: Waarihivu. The sect that Javier's teacher had once belonged to and who had crafted spells that destroyed whole worlds. Atreau read Clara's commentary concerning the Summer Doe again, just to be certain he wasn't mistaken.

Is it possible that she stopped Our Savior's Waarihivu invocation from cleansing the world?

"The reliquary could contain the horns of Yah-muur—or the Summer Doe, as you Cadeleonians call her," Narsi clarified. "She's called Yah-muur, the Fawn Goddess, in Haldiim stories."

Atreau nodded, but he was only half listening to Narsi. His thoughts still tangled with the idea that Javier's worst fear was proving true. Had that been what Javier had been attempting to convey when his apparition had floated over the stage? If it was the case, then was this relic a means of stopping the Waarihivu invocation, or unleashing it? Either way, keeping the thing out of the royal bishop's hands would be paramount. Gaining possession of this relic—whatever it was—might even be a way to convince the Labarans not to invade.

If so, then a victory a hundred men-at-arms couldn't hope to win might be delivered by a single thief. Atreau's heartbeat quickened at the thought of the stability and safety of their nation hinging upon Rinza's light fingers. He was tempted to send up a prayer for her safety and success.

"I can try to get more information about the relic from Master Ariz directly," Narsi suggested. That brought Atreau back to the moment.

"No," Ariz snapped. Conversing about forbidden topics with Ariz would put Narsi in too much danger of bloody reprisal. "Just listen to what he has to say, but don't push him. I already have someone looking into our mystery box."

"Oh? Yes?" Narsi asked, but Atreau refused to divulge more. The less any single agent knew, the less they could betray if they were taken by Hierro. Narsi waited a moment and Atreau drank more of his barley-water.

"How do you like the applebread?" Atreau asked.

"The flavor is certainly more subtle than your abrupt change of subject," Narsi replied with an amused smile. "All right, have it your way, my lord. The applebread is quite nice. It matches your choice of cheese very nicely. Though I wouldn't have been disappointed if there'd been a little lemon juice or hot, sweet pepper added to either one. What do you think of it?"

"I like it and then wish that I didn't because it makes me miss my mother," Atreau admitted.

"A family recipe then?" Narsi asked.

Atreau nodded.

"It's hard to lose someone you love," Narsi murmured.

"What surprises me is how much it smarts to lose someone I hate," Atreau replied. "You'd think that the anger and hurt would die along with him, but it doesn't. His passing just brings it all churning back up like a sour stomach."

"Your father, you mean?" Narsi cocked his head, studying Atreau with too much concern.

All at once it struck Atreau how self-absorbed he seemed, whining over a long-past hurt, when here was Narsi with his beloved mother only a year dead, his home hundreds of miles away and his life threatened by no less of a Cadeleonian bigot than the royal bishop.

What in the three hells entitled Atreau to feel so self-pitying? Maybe Lliro was right. Maybe he *did* need to let the past go and move on. He certainly shouldn't be soliciting Narsi for comfort and sympathy.

The trouble was that the young man gave it all so readily. Part of his physician's training, no doubt. However, Atreau didn't particularly want his conversation or company to deteriorate into bedside ministration. He tapped the papers in front of them again.

"What do you think of the second message?" Atreau prompted.

Narsi paused only a moment at yet another change of subject. He turned over Ariz's note and read the letter Spider's friend had sent from the Salt Islands. If Atreau hadn't been watching him so closely, he wouldn't have noticed the stillness that came over Narsi; for only an instant he seemed to freeze. Tellingly, he pushed both notes back to Atreau, distancing himself from them immediately.

"I don't think there's anything I can contribute." Narsi bit off a hunk of applebread and busied his mouth chewing.

"You can't or you won't?" Atreau asked.

Narsi scowled around his mouthful of bread.

"I understand that you're close with Tim. He's like family to you—"

"He *is* family to me," Narsi responded. "He took my mother and me in, despite the fact that he knew what people would whisper behind his back. He had nothing to gain from advocating for us, but he championed us anyway, because he felt it was the right thing to do. He's encouraged me and supported me—"

"I recognize all that." Atreau cut him off before he could go on enumerating the long, long list of Timoteo's virtues. "I'm not implying that Tim isn't a good man. He's as upright and compassionate as they come. I'm also sure that he had good reason for what he did. But whatever his reason for hiding Mistress Kir-Khu—whatever secret he's attempting to bury on the Salt Islands—it's going to come back and bite his ass. The royal bishop's agents are already there and they're already finding things."

"What do you mean? What have they discovered?" Narsi looked almost as uneasy as he had when Atreau had first seen him at the palace this morning.

Narsi knew exactly what Timoteo had hidden away, Atreau suddenly realized.

"If I knew all of what they've uncovered then I wouldn't be asking you, would I?" Atreau met Narsi's troubled gaze and held it. "I certainly wouldn't be wasting time having this conversation if I could get ahead of the matter and make sure that Tim and the rest of the Grunito family are shielded."

Narsi lowered his gaze to his own hands.

"You should tell Father Timoteo what you know and let him decide," Narsi said.

"You're really going to make me waste what little time I have riding Tim down and trying to pry this out of him? All the while your friend

Berto will be shoving me away with a broom and half a dozen acolytes will be glowering at me and pelting me with spitballs?" Atreau responded.

Narsi's mouth quirked up slightly at the absurd scene. Thought Berto going after him with a broom wasn't really much of a stretch.

"What if I assured you that it's nothing to do with any of this going on right now? It's not a matter of reliquaries or spells or assassins." Narsi bowed his head further down so that Atreau could only see the curls of his dark hair. "It's a family matter and not even—nothing is going to come of it."

"The royal bishop's agents aren't acting as if it's nothing," Atreau replied. "They seem to believe that this *family* matter is quite valuable to them. Possibly the key to bringing Timoteo to heel, or even destroying the entire Grunito clan."

"They're wrong," Narsi said, and he at last lifted his face.

"How can you be sure?" Atreau asked.

"Because it's . . ." Narsi sighed, then went on. "It's to do with my mother and my father, the fact that they were legally married."

"*Your* mother and father?" How in the three hells could that be a concern to the royal bishop?

Unless Tim hadn't merely bedded Narsi's mother. Could he have been so foolish as to actually marry her and thereby document the violation of his holy vows? That could cost him his new-won post as bishop and likely get him excommunicated.

"Timoteo legally wed your mother?" Atreau asked in a whisper.

"What?" Narsi looked authentically surprised. Then he rolled his eyes. "Holy Father Timoteo *isn't* my father. He took my mother and me in after my father was killed. To protect us."

That had been Timoteo's claim decades before, but few people had believed him. Elezar certainly hadn't. Atreau had never cared either way, not until now.

"Can't we just leave it at that? For now?" Narsi's expression entreated him to relent. "I swear to you on my honor, this has nothing to do with the threat to the Hallowed Kings or any ancient magical war or the Brand of Obedience. All Timoteo did was to help the physician who witnessed my birth relocate to the Salt Islands."

"*Because* she witnessed your birth?" Atreau asked.

Again Narsi's gaze dropped to his hands. Atreau noted that Narsi was far more used to holding his nerve in the face of a threat than he was practiced at bald-faced lying.

"He says that she wanted to move . . ." Narsi shrugged. "I think he was telling the truth."

Atreau nodded. His concern ran in a different direction. The royal bishop had thrown far too much effort into locating that physician for it to be a matter of mere impulse or whim. He studied Narsi's face—not to read the intent behind his expressions nor to enjoy the pleasing quality of his features—considering only angles and planes. He recalled how when he'd first laid eyes upon him, Narsi had reminded him of Elezar. Narsi's father was obviously a Grunito.

Elezar would have been far too young to father Narsi. If he ruled out Timoteo, then who did that leave? A multitude of candidates in the vast extended family, however very few of the boisterous clan would interest the royal bishop, much less inspire agents to investigate their offspring.

This was a matter of an heir, of an inheritance, likely.

Lord Grunito himself was too old to have secretly wed Narsi's mother before he joyfully took Lady Grunito as his bride. Nestor, too young.

Then Atreau remembered the morning six years ago when Elezar had haltingly confessed the secret of his eldest brother's brutal murder. Isandro Grunito had been tortured and killed by a group of his own school friends. At the time it had sounded like an act of senseless sadism. Atreau had seen enough of such things to accept that, without question. But now he reconsidered. Isandro hadn't been the sort of young man who made for an easy target for bullies.

Quite the opposite; he'd inspired imitators and attracted admirers.

But what if Isandro's classmates hadn't attacked him because they deemed him weak or helpless but because he'd transgressed their values—perhaps he betrayed their belief in what he should have been?

If those worshipful classmates discovered that their ideal Cadeleonian hero had legally wed a Haldiim woman and fathered a son, wouldn't they feel outraged? He would have elevated his Haldiim wife to the status of a noblewoman and passed the entire Grunito earldom to his half-Haldiim son.

Such a revelation would have enraged many of those petty young noblemen just as it would now infuriate the royal bishop. Nugalo would probably shit himself when Narsi claimed his rightful inheritance. And then there were the Grunitos themselves to consider.

As the implications dawned on Atreau, he took in Narsi's expression. His uncertainty and anxiety. This wasn't a secret he was used to keeping. Nor had he been holding on to it to use as blackmail; this was a revelation he could hardly accept himself. As much as the royal bishop or the Grunito family wouldn't welcome the news that Isandro had sired an heir to the earldom, Narsi wasn't happy about it either.

"You didn't come to the capital to claim your inheritance, did you?" Atreau asked.

Narsi seemed surprised by the suggestion, as if it was wildly outlandish. He shook his head. "I had no idea of the truth a month ago. Tim only told me after I was poisoned. He feared that it might have been the reason I was poisoned."

They both knew that wasn't the case, but Atreau could see how Father Timoteo might suspect it was. Why hadn't he instantly sent Narsi away to somewhere safer? Did he hope to protect Narsi's anonymity by keeping him close, just as he'd apparently done decades earlier? Or did he want Narsi within his control to ensure that he never challenged Nestor's claim to the earldom?

"So Tim just told you that you're Isandro's son and left it at that?" Atreau couldn't imagine such a thing, but there had been a lot of what he couldn't imagine going on lately.

"Well, it wasn't . . ." Narsi pulled a face like the entire matter was too embarrassing to retell. "My mother's last letter to him requested that he do right by me or something along those lines. She enclosed proof of my legitimate birth and her own marriage. But it's not so simple a matter as me just tacking the name Grunito onto my signatures. And it's not as if I want to throw the Grunito family into disarray."

Atreau nodded. Narsi was correct. If the truth of his paternity came to light, that would put the Grunito family in nasty position. Either they would need to act quickly to do away with Narsi and eradicate Isandro's only child, or they would have to recognize him as their rightful heir, which would mean handing Anacleto over to a Haldiim stranger, stripping Nestor of his title and placing their entire earldom at odds with the royal bishop.

If it had been any noble family other than the Grunitos, Atreau would have put sure money on Narsi's swift and sudden disappearance.

But Lady Grunito had already defied expectations by accepting a common girl as her daughter-in-law, then refusing to disown Elezar for becoming the champion of a Labaran witch and finally declining to submit Nestor to the Cadeleonian church for trial on charges of heresy. There was just the sliver of a chance that she would make Narsi the first Haldiim to hold a noble Cadeleonian title. That would be a kick in the teeth to the Cadeleonian church and crown alike, wouldn't it?

Still, sacrificing her own son's inheritance as well as endangering the peace of Anacleto just for the sake of a long-lost Haldiim grandson? He didn't know if even Lady Grunito could be that upright or stubborn.

"I assured Tim that I didn't want to take anything away from Nestor," Narsi whispered. "I just wanted to know who my father was. I didn't want . . . it shouldn't change anything."

Unless the royal bishop or, frankly, anyone else found out about it. The potential for blackmail alone would prove far too tempting for many people. The situation was a mess. No wonder Narsi looked so uneasy.

"Knowledge can't be unlearned. This won't simply go away," Atreau said. Narsi looked miserable and Atreau decided against voicing more of his concerns. "Though first and foremost, I feel I should point out that it's a bit rich you going on calling me *Lord* Vediya all the damn time."

Narsi laughed and a little of his natural assurance seemed to return to him.

"You *are* Lord Vediya," Narsi replied.

"I'm the fourth son of a pissant baron and the last in line to inherit a decrepit manor built atop a mountain of debt and dead horses. You, on the other hand . . ." Atreau paused a moment as the enormity of all the prosperity and power Narsi stood to inherit filled his thoughts. Anacleto wasn't just the wealthiest port in the nation, but her earls famously commanded an army strong enough to challenge both a king and his royal bishop.

God's tits, if Atreau found himself the successor to even a fraction of such a fortune, he would have been bellowing his claim through the halls of the palace and dragging witnesses before the king himself.

"*I*, on the other hand, am merely a physician descended from a Haldiim family of papermakers," Narsi stated firmly.

He wasn't *merely* anything, Atreau thought, but for the moment he decided to forgo that argument. Perhaps later, after Sevanyo's rule was secured and Hierro Fueres was dealt with, then they might need to push the matter of Narsi's inheritance a bit further. But now they had more practical matters to consider. He lowered his voice.

"This could go a good way to explaining why the royal bishop sent armed guards to hunt *you* in particular down. If he knows, then it may be wisest if you departed for—"

"But I don't think he does know," Narsi cut in, and he pointed to the date scrawled in the top corner of Spider's letter. "According to this, he's been searching for Mistress Kir-Khu for a month and his agents are still looking. But why would they bother if they already knew who I was? And why wait all this time? That doesn't make sense." Narsi took another slow, purposeful drink of his barleywater. "Considering this morning, I think it's far more likely that the guardsmen came for me because Clara

Odalis has been whispering accusations to the royal bishop. Her insinuations would appeal to him. So he's dispatched men out to find the physician who attended the king."

"Even if you're right—and I'm not convinced that you are—that still puts you in a precarious position," Atreau replied.

Narsi's expression turned momentarily grim. He hid it well, Atreau realized, but he wasn't unafraid. Then Narsi drew in a deep breath and slowly exhaled, and he appeared to relax.

"For now at least, it's worth the risk for me to stay and keep working," Narsi decided. "If you and the duke are right, then Prince—King Sevanyo—is now positioned to curtail the royal bishop's excesses." Narsi's hand absently curled over Dommian's charm-book. "Anyway, I can't abandon Master Ariz."

"You certainly could."

"Not in good conscience," Narsi answered. "And he's not the only one who may need me. Particularly right now."

Atreau nodded, because they both knew that if Hierro Fueres was going to make his move to seize the throne, it would have to be very soon. Certainly before Sevanyo had established himself as king.

"The royal bishop's men will be waiting for you to return to Fedeles's house," Atreau warned him.

"Hopefully in a day or two he will have other matters to concern him, and Clara Odalis's gossip will have been proven to be absurd."

And if none of that comes to pass, Narsi, then what?

Atreau decided not to argue. As wretched as he felt about endangering him, Atreau had no one to replace Narsi. He did need him to stay and continue working.

"Considering Jacinto's influence in this district and his newfound fascination with your shared fate, I suppose you would be best off staying in the capital, near him," Atreau said at last.

"Yes." Narsi frowned. "Though if Father Timoteo doesn't hear from me soon, I fear he might do something fool—"

"Just pen him a note. I'll see to it that he gets it. I can probably manage to pick up a few of your other belongings while I'm at it," Atreau offered. He'd need to return to the Quemanor household anyway to check on Fedeles.

"If you'd spend a little time with my cat, I'd appreciate it. And if you could . . ." Narsi trailed off and Atreau waited, but after several moments he didn't go on.

"And?" Atreau prompted.

"I . . ." Narsi scowled. "I don't want to get you involved in something that might be . . . something that's not completely legal right now."

"You're concerned about involving *me* in something illicit?" Atreau laughed. "I feel I might *just* be able to withstand the pressure of defying the law this once."

"I'm hardly concerned that you couldn't manage it," Narsi replied. "It's that you've taken on so much already."

"Oh, but I live to serve. Particularly pretty young lordlings," Atreau replied.

Narsi cast him an annoyed glance, but Atreau felt he deserved the needling. All these weeks of Narsi calling him lord while he was himself the heir to an earldom. "Come on, I'm dying to know what you've managed to get up to while I've been mucking around the Knife Market and the Docksides."

Narsi considered his plate and stole a glance at the disinterested gamblers scattered at tables through out the inn.

"All right," Narsi said at last. "Can you tell Querra that I'm fine—"

"The woman in charge of the kitchen gardens at Fedeles's house?" Atreau asked. Who knew how many other women Narsi might have befriended, along with Yara and half the Haldiim citizens of the city. Atreau knew for a fact that one of the serving girls at the Green Door had developed a tenderness for him after Narsi had taken a little time to treat a small burn on the back of her hand. He was a charmer, no mistaking that.

"Yes. Mistress Querra Kir-Naham," Narsi clarified, as if it was the lack of formal title that had given Atreau pause. "If you can please assure her that the royal bishop's men aren't looking for me because of . . . ah . . . our recent project. They don't know anything about that."

Recent project? Atreau cocked his head to catch Narsi's lowered gaze. Narsi averted his glance to his applebread.

"What? Have you and Mistress Querra set up shop trading poppy tar secretly grown in the duke's kitchen gardens?" Atreau asked, just to see Narsi's offended reaction. He wasn't disappointed. Though it wasn't exactly disbelief in Narsi's expression, more like guilt.

"Of course we haven't," Narsi muttered. "Smoke poppies would stand out too much from the vegetables, and we couldn't possibly harvest the tar by moonlight. We've been growing duera and a few other medical botanicals in the kitchen gardens and smuggling them to Haldiim pharmacists."

"Smuggling . . ." Atreau swallowed his exasperation along with a mouthful of applebread. God's tits, Narsi truly was a Grunito through and through, wasn't he? Hardly a month in the city and already throwing himself into a multitude of utterly reckless enterprises. Doubtless he felt driven to champion the downtrodden and gave hardly a thought to his

own personal danger. And just as likely, he acted with complete ignorance of the multitude of gangs and corrupt officials who controlled the
city's illicit trades.

Taking in Narsi's handsome, innocent face, he had to suppress a
groan.

"Please tell me that the obscene profit the two of you are turning
makes the risk worth it," Atreau commented.

"Profit?" Narsi's confused response assured Atreau that he and
Querra were no doubt giving their herbs away for free. Probably working at a loss, in fact.

"So has someone in this project of yours at least received the Goat's
blessing?"

"Goat's blessing? Is that a euphemism of some kind?" Narsi laughed,
then when Atreau didn't join him, he sobered. "You're not serious, are
you?" Narsi raised his brows. "There isn't actually some goat . . ."

"There is, and she's the head of an extremely dangerous Haldiim syn-
dicate of cutthroats, extortionists and smugglers." Atreau stole a glance
to the far corner of the inn where one of the Goats's gangly informants
often sat, gathering information and sipping sour beer. Fortunately the
young man didn't keep the early hours of a physician. "I pray you've been
too insignificant so far to catch her attention. That or she's too confused
by your madcap, reckless charity of an operation to want to touch it with
a yardstick."

Atreau shook his head but then went on before Narsi could say anything more alarmingly naïve about his *smuggling* operation. "I'll talk to
Querra for you this afternoon and I'll sound out Spider about the Goat.
If we have to hand over a tribute, then we will. Otherwise she's likely to
have one of her snitches turn you over to the royal bishop's guardsmen."

"I—" Narsi seemed about to protest, but then his expression softened. Something like admiration or perhaps affection seemed to light his
eyes. "Thank you."

Atreau felt the warmth of Narsi's smile as if it were a fire kindling in
his chest. The pleasure of it alarmed him.

"Didn't I say that I lived to serve?" Atreau quipped with a shrug.

"You did indeed, Lord Vediya." Again he flashed that flattering smile.
"But until just this minute, I hadn't realized how often your satirical tone
masks statements of fact rather than underscoring mockery."

"Did you just accuse me of being sincere?" Atreau asked.

"If cloaking honesty in derision could be called sincerity," Narsi said,
laughing. "Then by all means I do accuse you of it, sir."

"Following that reasoning, you may well make an honest man of me
one day, Master Physician." Atreau relaxed back in his chair. "Perhaps

you'll recast me entirely when you pen your own memoir after all this is done."

"I'd much rather read what you'll eventually write." The affection in Narsi's expression touched Atreau. He'd penned nothing but drivel recently and was beginning to fear that it might be all he'd ever be capable of creating from now on. Narsi's confidence suddenly made him feel that he shouldn't give up. It was embarrassing how easily Narsi moved him, really.

"Truly?" Atreau drained the last of his water. "I'd think that you would have lost interest in my writing now that you're trapped delivering my lines on stage."

At the mention of the play, Narsi's smile turned to a grimace.

"It's not your writing that mortifies me so much as my delivery." Narsi looked so grim that Atreau laughed.

"Please promise me that my role isn't going to expand any further."

"Considering Jacinto's current interest and how it's serving to protect you, I'm afraid I can't grant your request." Atreau couldn't help the smug satisfaction in his tone. "You'll have to ask a different favor of me."

"All right. Seeing as you live to serve." Narsi considered for a moment. The way he gazed into Atreau's face made him think that perhaps Narsi would ask for a kiss. Perhaps more. A flutter of excitement raced through Atreau's body, even as he prepared to deliver as gentle a refusal as he could.

"How did you see me?" Narsi asked in a whisper.

"See you?" The question was so far from what Atreau he been prepared to answer that the words hardly seemed to make sense.

"This morning," Narsi clarified. "You picked me out when Hierro Fueres and Clara Odalis and Prince Remes weren't able to see through the null spell. How?"

"Oh, that. It was actually . . ." An unexpectedly deep disappointment wrong-footed him enough that he nearly blurted out Lady Hylanya's name. What was the matter with him? "It's a trick that Elezar picked up in Labara . . ." For just a moment Atreau wondered at all the secrets they each kept for other people. Then he went on explaining the trick that Hylanya had taught him, and Narsi straightened in his chair wearing an excited, thoughtful expression.

"So even though you can't see the spell, its presence is perceptible as a kind of afterimage." Narsi pushed the last of the applebread onto Atreau's plate. "You know, that's very like the most recent theory of how we feel heat."

"With our skin?" Atreau had no other idea of how else anyone would feel temperature.

"Well, yes. I mean more that heat—say from the sun or a fire—is actually a kind of radiance, like light. For example, we can't see if a cook pot is still hot, but we can feel the warmth radiating from the metal," Narsi went on. "So what if the radiance of magic is somewhere between light and heat. Some people have a sensitivity that allows them to see it, but most of us only feel it. What do you think?"

Atreau pondered the idea. It seemed like a good analogy, though it didn't explain how some people could manipulate magic while others, like himself and Narsi, could only wonder about it. Though maybe, if it was a sort of radiance, then some people were ablaze with it while others were faint flickering fireflies.

Though Narsi hadn't needed his own magic to make a spell this morning, had he?

"Or could it be that we all possess some capacity to interact with magic, but that some of us aren't temperamentally inclined?" Narsi went on. "Maybe it's a matter of both capacity and character, like a skill that can be learned but comes more naturally to some."

"Like math?" Atreau asked.

"Yes, just like you suggested earlier." Narsi smiled at him and the appreciation in his expression seemed like its own kind of radiance.

"If Labaran witches are to be believed, it's our souls that are the conduits of magic," Atreau said.

"But what is a soul, really?" Narsi continued his rumination. "How does something spiritual manifest to interact with the physical world we live in, and what are the constraints?"

Before Atreau could comment, the door to the Fat Goose swung open and Jacinto, Yara and a large troupe of actors came pouring in. Atreau pocketed the letters he'd shared with Narsi and then ate the last of the applebread. He frowned as Inissa and Yara briefly broke off from the group to offer Spider a quick greeting. When Jacinto looked in Inissa's direction, Atreau called out a loud greeting to the prince.

Then the entire party charged up to Atreau's table and set about claiming chairs and calling out orders to the barmaid. Atreau exchanged quips and flirtations. He flattered Procopio's niece with a few overlong glances and played smitten when Jacinto introduced yet another orange seller with aspirations for the stage. Now far across from him, Narsi chatted and laughed as a comely Haldiim stagehand fawned over him. Yara indulged them, going so far as to suggest that the stagehand join them this evening.

Atreau's stomach felt sour. Still, he waited a little time and then at last made his apologies to Jacinto. He had work to do and a nest of assassins to track down. But first he needed to report to Fedeles, and that would be best done alone.

He left Narsi to the care and comfort of this new circle of friends.

CHAPTER
ELEVEN

Up in the fencing room on the second floor of the Odalis house, Ariz worked the edge of his sword against the last of his sharpening stones, erasing the scratches and nicks left by the rib bones of the enthralled assassin he'd killed that morning near Crown Hill.

Normally, sharpening his blades felt soothing, almost meditative. He pushed steel across stone, filing away infinitesimal traces of the blade's history. Making it almost innocent again. He could lose himself in the hours of that rhythmic motion and its accompanying low scrape. His mind often drifted into memories of watching ocean waves wash tirelessly over rocky shores.

But this evening he couldn't relax.

From the floor below he could just discern Hierro's commanding voice roll over Clara's soft, entreating tones. He recognized his own name floating on the growls of Hierro's frustration. Clara's voice rose as well, but in echoing pleas. At once Ariz remembered the order that he'd disregarded. Lord Numes's wife, the child she carried and her guards all still lived.

Ariz's brand blazed to life. His sword nearly fell from his hand as he stumbled down to his knees. His sharpening stones and water lay forgotten. Ariz struggled to draw breath as molten agony constricted his lungs and seared through the muscles of his chest.

He ground his teeth and focused all of his will on reaching into the pocket of his vest. His fingers felt like they were on fire and his hands shook so badly that he struggled to grasp the vial hidden in his pocket.

Master Narsi's potion.

The vial slipped from his grip, struck the polished oak floor and rolled. Ariz crawled after it, gasping and trembling. Every motion felt as if it were driving white-hot pokers into his joints. Tears streamed down his face and sweat soaked his back and chest. The vial lay hardly five feet from him, and yet crawling the distance took all of his strength and determination.

At last he grasped the vial and pulled the cork free. He needed both hands to keep it steady as he lifted it to his mouth and drank. He managed to cork the vial again before the wave of blinding white heat rolled over him.

Then the pain faded, torture dulling to grinding pangs. He drew in panting breaths, pushing past the flaring ache of his ribs. He wiped the tears and sweat from his face, then stood and picked up his sword.

He could endure this, he assured himself. He was stronger than he'd been a decade ago. He wouldn't allow Hierro to use him to murder a mother and her unborn child again.

From below he caught the sound of footsteps on the stairs and he froze in dread of Hierro's proximity. But as he strained after the noises of the household, he noted a heartening absence. Those weren't the hard steps and jingle of spurs that announced Hierro's approach. And then he felt the oppressive presence churning in his chest fade; Hierro had withdrawn at least thirty yards from him.

On the stairs the only noise was a soft, sneaking tread. The whisper of heavy skirts. Ariz hid the vial of medicine back away in his vest pocket.

Moments later, the door opened and Clara's slender figure cast a long shadow across the polished oak floor. Ariz bowed his head, pretending to still be occupied cleaning his sword. He studied Clara's approach through the motions of her shadow. He wanted her to believe that he felt relaxed enough in her company to let his guard down; the idea seemed to please her. Behind her a cluster of doting handmaids lingered at the door, like anxious lapdogs hoping to be summoned.

"I'll only be with Master Ariz for a little time, my dears. Then we will get back to making your lovely masquerade costumes. You'll all be just divine in them," Clara said, and Ariz noted how much she sounded like her sister, Oasia, in that moment. Then she pushed the door shut behind her.

The hard soles of her black shoes clicked her advance upon him. She came from the left side and, from the shape of her shadow, Ariz knew she carried the usual envelope in her right hand. He couldn't identify the odd form that draped down from her left arm. Its outline fluttered in a feathery manner. The corpse of another of her beloved larks that Hierro had strangled? Ariz felt a shiver of guilt. Hierro never failed to vent his frustration on the innocent and inoffensive.

"You managed Lord Numes very quickly," Clara said. "Hierro was pleased for the most part, I think. Though . . ."

Ariz waited, head bowed.

"He believes that your mercy toward the wife was my doing," Clara said. "And I've convinced him that the grieving widow has served him better than her corpse could have. He's satisfied, for now."

The last ember of smoldering pain in Ariz's chest faded away. He could save the remainder of his medicine to get him through another day.

"Thank you for that." Ariz raised his head at last.

Clara met his gaze with a wan smile. She looked deceptively young and small. Most people found her very pretty but too pious to easily approach. Few if any nobles noticed that the high collars of her silk gowns often hid her bruised throat in a lacy froth of holy stars. Her widow's veil covered most of her black hair as well as the yellowing remains of an older contusion left by Hierro's hand. She endured terrible abuse, Ariz knew that. But he also recognized that it would be utter idiocy on his part to believe that being victimized defined her. Neither her father nor Hierro could strip her of her cunning, ambition or resourcefulness.

Not to mention her singular drive to scour the Haldiim race from every last acre of Cadeleon.

Despite her facade, she, like Hierro, could be completely merciless.

She'd not wept a single genuine tear after Ariz had murdered either of her husbands. She was fond of her delicate widow's veil and delighted in the opportunity to wear it whenever she could. Clara wasn't one to waste an opportunity or squander a resource. He imagined he represented both to her just now, though she gazed at him with an expression of doe-eyed sympathy.

"I've also persuaded him to keep his distance from you for a little time. It wouldn't do for him to draw attention to his connection to you, after all." She smiled in that hesitant, shy manner that Ariz had come to recognize as a mask imposed on her by Hierro's Brand of Obedience. Just as his expressions remained dull and slack as those of a sleeping man, Clara couldn't range far from the effect of a wide-eyed child.

"Unfortunately, I couldn't keep him from making further demands upon you. I tried, but you know . . ." Clara held Hierro's latest message close to her side. Ariz recognized the fine, flowing script that swept across the snow-white paper.

He looked away before he could read the names of the doomed, sparing himself a few minutes of pain. No matter how often he was bent to Hierro's commands, he couldn't stop himself from resisting and suffering. Inevitably the murderous impulse and burning pain would overwhelm him.

Though his latest defiance buoyed his spirit. It had been a small triumph, parlaying a massacre into only two murders, but it was a start.

"Hierro is growing quite impatient with your progress at the Slate House," Clara commented. "I've convinced him to give you three more days, but I can't win much more for you."

Ariz recognized that it wasn't Hierro alone who wanted him to penetrate the small stronghold at the naval memorial. Clara too desired the deadly treasure that the royal bishop's son had secured. She wanted it so badly that a flush rose in her pale cheeks as she spoke of the Slate House.

"I'm not a thief," Ariz replied.

"You think you're above theft?" Clara demanded.

"No." Ariz shook his head. "I mean that I don't possess the skills of a thief. The Slate House is well made and securely protected. If I force the front door and kill the guards who opposed me, it will raise an ungodly commotion before I can possibly reach the strongroom on the second floor. I can't walk through walls or soar up into the attic . . ." Ariz trailed off in uncertainty at Clara's odd expression.

She looked smug, and he had no idea why. She turned the feathery ruff in her hand in a slow circle and gave an odd little laugh. Then her expression went distant, almost blank, as some faraway thought occupied her.

"Any news of the Quemanor household?" Ariz asked at last. It was as close as he dared come to inquiring after Fedeles. He'd heard whispers among the maids and grooms, but no one truly knew what had happened in the Shard of Heaven except that the king had died there and the royal bishop had been forced by Prince—no, now *King* Sevanyo to release Fedeles.

"You're concerned for the Quemanors?" Clara frowned at him.

"My sister and her children are still in their service," Ariz replied, and he wasn't lying. He feared as much for his family as he did for Fedeles.

"Ah, your sister." Clara smiled, but her gaze was distant. "Sometimes I forget how deeply you people from simple families care for each other. I envy you, even if you live as mere playthings to men like my brother and father."

Ariz bowed his head again. Given the opportunity, Clara would have bent him to her will just as readily as Hierro did. But she liked to believe otherwise.

"Do not trouble yourself," Clara went on. "The household is safe just now. Your sister's children and Sparanzo Quemanor have been shielded from my brother's latest threat . . . as you well know." Her expression turned almost teasing and Ariz realized that she knew what he'd done to Hierro's sailor turned assassin.

Her larks must have seen it all.

"I've already taken steps to ensure that Hierro doesn't discover Xavan's fate," Clara added. "That was his name. The man you cut down under the willow. Xavan. When you pray, you should remember him to paradise."

Ariz nodded. He wished he'd not learned the man's name, or anything about him.

"Will he send more?" Ariz asked. "To kill the children?"

"He may, but I will keep them safe." Clara glanced down at the paper in her hand. "And if we contrive to keep Hierro distracted with the coronation and eliminating his supposed rivals, then he won't have time to fret over Sparanzo. Though that means that he will want to make even more use of you, I'm afraid."

Again, Ariz averted his gaze from the script on the page. Instead he studied the feathery ruff in Clara's other hand. It reminded him a little of one of the bright cloaks that Yuanese ambassadors wore in court—not that any of them were likely to make an appearance these days. The royal bishop had seen to that. The brown feathers were speckled with flecks of gold and tipped in inky black.

"Is he sending me to a costume party this time?" Ariz asked. He'd need more than a little ruff of feathers if that was the case.

"This isn't from him." Clara lowered her soft voice to a whisper so faint that Ariz had to lean close to hear her clearly. She smelled of funerary incense from the chapel, and a new bruise lay beneath the face powder dusting her cheek. No doubt it had cost her some pain to shield him from Hierro.

"This is my gift, to ensure that Hierro doesn't ruin you with all these petty assassinations of his," Clara said. "You need rest, but we both know he won't see reason on that count."

In the last three weeks Hierro had sent him out almost every night to stalk and then assassinate a horrifyingly unprepared assortment of people. Many of them the sad fools who believed themselves to be Hierro's allies.

"We can't allow him to destroy you, Master Ariz," Clara said.

"How did you convince him to agree?" Ariz asked.

"I told him the truth—or some of it," Clara replied. "It would be wisest if you aren't recognized coming and going on his errands. You need a disguise that will turn suspicion toward our enemies in Labara. And by chance this gift will do that. It offers you some respite, as well."

Ariz didn't trust Clara any more than her brother, but he longed so intensely for any reprieve from Hierro's murderous commands that he reached out. His fingers only brushed over the feathers and they rose, fluttering against his palm like living things—like soft, grasping fingers.

Ariz jerked his hand back at once.

"What will it do to me?" Ariz asked.

"It will bestow the wings of a saint upon the talons of an assassin," Clara replied.

Ariz scowled at the cluster of feathers. He'd heard stories of bewitched animal skins that transformed men into beasts. He possessed little enough of his humanity that perhaps Clara imagined he would welcome respite from even the few shreds of conscience and kindness he still retained. But another thing he recalled from the tales of transformed men: those who bewitched them also controlled their actions. He already bore Hierro's Brand of Obedience over his heart; he wouldn't sacrifice the last shreds of his self-determination to Clara.

"I won't be your beast, my lady," Ariz told her.

"Mine? I assure you, I have no desire to make you mine." Clara cocked her head, and Ariz thought she was attempting to offer him a genuine smile. "What little placidity you might have once possessed, my brother's thrall has defiled. Your soul is not a thing I would wish to take possession of, much less hold in the cradle of my own spirit. You are too much his creation now."

"And yet you would have me submit to this." Ariz eyed the fluttering collar.

"This is a holy relic, Ariz, not the work of heathen witchcraft. It's a blessing." Clara leaned slightly closer to Ariz. "Are you among the devout who remember the story of Sainted Trueno?"

"He served Our Savior as a herald and a personal guard. But he was captured, enthralled and ordered to slay Our Savior." Ariz paused a moment to recall the rest of the saint's history. A sculpture of the saint had adorned his family chapel. He'd liked studying the figure during tedious sermons. One night on a dare from his sister he'd even climbed up to the sculpture and left a crown of violets at its feet. "He was enthralled inside the body of an immense eagle, but he refused to strike Our Savior down."

"Yes! His spirit was stronger than those of his captors. He shattered their thralls over him—though his flesh remained transformed. He soared into the sky, and instead of harming Our Savior, he shielded his master from the hundred arrows of the demon hordes with his own body. He died gloriously."

Ariz remembered running his hands over the cold marble where the stone arrow shafts seamlessly pierced the breast and torn wing of the statue. As a child, he'd felt awed by the artistry of the carving but also heartsick that he could not free the majestic eagle from those arrows. They were carved all from one stone, Trueno's suffering becoming as much a part of him as his long, beautiful wings or his wide, pale eyes.

"His is the rise of courage to the heights of bravery," Clara quoted, then she lifted the scrap of leather and feathers into a beam of lamplight. "This is his relic—the blessing of his flesh and spirit. It was long believed lost, and it has taken me years of searching, but I finally found it. I don't offer it to you lightly."

"You want to turn me into one of your birds," Ariz stated.

"I'm offering you the opportunity to become more than the animal that Hierro has made you into," Clara snapped, though even enraged, all she could do was look slightly disappointed. Ariz wondered what little of his own anger showed.

With her simpering expressions and bruised body, Clara was hardly one to call him Hierro's animal. She was no better than he was. Ariz sighed as he recognized the pitiable truth of both their lives.

"I'm touched that you could believe a creature like me merits Trueno's relic," Ariz replied. "Surely if its blessing is so wondrous, it would suit you far better than me."

"Claiming the relic requires physical strength. Bone and muscle to feed the spells. It will not accept my frail, earthly body." Clara shook her head. "Don't think that I haven't attempted it. If it were a matter of will-power alone, then I would be soaring through the sky now."

Ariz believed her.

Not only did Clara seem absorbed by birds and the freedom of their flights, but Ariz had realized that Clara rarely lied. When she practiced deception, it was through silence and omission. Which begged the question: What wasn't she telling him about this blessing? What was her true motive in offering it to him?

"Accept the blessing, Ariz," Clara said. "Trueno's speed and strength can aid you in fulfilling Hierro's errands, and it will ease your injuries. You look as though you are wasting away. Your body is covered in bruises, and I know that you have hardly slept. Hardly eaten. You need respite."

"I am his assassin. A murderer of women and children. I deserve to suffer for what I've done." Ariz glowered down at the dark scabs that dotted his battered hands. He could still see Xavan's terrified expression . . . feel his fingers trembling against his hand.

Clara sighed but said nothing.

They were both silent for a few moments; the noise of the busy household drifted through the room. A gardener sang to himself out on the grounds. Geese honked in reply to the reprimands of a goose girl.

And as always, the bright calls of songbirds filled the air. Clara raised larks, finches and nightingales from tiny chicks and then set many of them free. Some served her, Ariz knew that, but not all of them. Some she released to genuine freedom.

He wondered if he should take heart from that.

Or perhaps he misunderstood the meaning of her actions. Did she offer the fledglings freedom, or was she depriving herself the company of the creatures that she loved the most? Was their absence a penance? Or was she inuring herself to the feeling of loss so that when the time came, she could make far greater sacrifices?

Or did she simply wish to save her favorites from being strangled to death by Hierro?

"Hierro's brand has made monsters of us both," Clara said at last. "I have no doubt that when our souls reach the gates of paradise, we will be consigned to walk the three hells to cleanse Hierro's corruption from us. You and I will suffer enough then, Master Ariz."

Again Ariz thought she was speaking honestly to him. As disparaging as she was of others, she also recognized many of her own failings. She was strangely fair-minded in that way.

Ariz wondered what sort of person she might have become if she'd not grown up under her brother's control. Had she once been as naïve and romantic as Ariz had been before Hierro enslaved him? Had she aspired to kindness? Sometimes Ariz thought that she must have. Certainly, some part of her still longed to love and be loved in return. That showed in her tenderness toward her handmaids and her precious songbirds. Even in the face of Hierro's violence, she never failed to take a stand to protect Sparanzo, and that alone bespoke courage that Ariz couldn't ignore.

Clara straightened her shoulders and held the feathered collar out to him.

"While we are both still alive, neither of us can afford to indulge in self-pity. When the true battle comes, innocent souls will need your strength to shelter them. Just as they will need my courage. We cannot give ourselves up to despair. We must continue to live and to fight for the sakes of those who will have no one else to shield them from Hierro."

"You mean Sparanzo?" Ariz asked.

"Yes, but not him alone. Even in this degenerate city there are hundreds of other innocents." Clara lowered her gaze to the floor. "I admire your sister, and what I've heard about her children makes me like their courage and cleverness. I have thought long and hard on her and those two pretty bastards she bore my brother."

Ariz scowled and Clara lifted her gaze to meet his. He wished could read past her bittersweet expression and gentle voice. She was a treacherous zealot, but she could show great tenderness toward children. And for her own reasons she had gone out of her way to protect Ariz from Hierro's wrath on several occasions now.

"I believe that there is a way to save them," Clara said. "But it would require all of your strength and determination. You must not be worn down or weak when the moment comes."

"If that's true, then just tell me—"

"No. You can't be trusted to keep what I say from Hierro," Clara replied. "Just knowing that you are betraying him will cause you agony—"

"I could say the same for you."

"And you would be right," Clara replied, and she flashed a smile that looked more like a flinch than any kind of happiness. "Hierro's brand burns through me every minute of my life—it has for years now. I live in hell, but I endure because this is the only way to free us all. Do you understand? I am fighting for *all* of us. Not just me or you or Elenna. But for *all* the hundreds of people—men like Xavan and women like my dear handmaids—whom Hierro has enslaved. I can withstand the pain, but it has worn me down. I can't fight him alone. I need your strength, Ariz."

He wanted to believe her, not just because she offered him an opportunity to save all that remained of his family but because he desperately needed to believe that his existence could amount to something more than eviscerated bodies and grieving survivors. He yearned for any relief from the knowledge of what he'd become.

"There's has to be a price," Ariz said. There was always a cost to any gift offered him.

"Pain," Clara said, and a shudder passed through her slender body. "The first transformation is agony—far more than I could endure with Hierro's brand already searing through me. But you are strong. And you said that you deserved to suffer, didn't you?"

"I did." Ariz took the collar from her. The way the feathers twisted and curled around his wrist alarmed him. The hard tips of the quills scratched at the red scars on his forearm.

"You have only one chance," Clara said. "If you refuse the blessing, if you can't withstand the pain, then Trueno's relic returns to being nothing but a collection of feathers awaiting someone worthier of his gift. So you must be strong. Endure it now and it is yours forever."

Ariz forced himself to relax as the collar flexed around his arm like a strange serpent. The hair all across his body rose as if a chill wind rushed over him. The quills scraped and dug at his arm. Pain pricked and grew as one after another, the feathers pierced his skin and continued digging into his flesh. His blood seeped down the shafts, staining the fletching and spattering the fencing room floor.

A deep ache flared through his joints and spread through the marrow of his bones. He noticed the hair of his arms splitting to a delicate gray down. The light and colors of the room flared in his eyes and the notes of the distant gardener's song suddenly sounded like chapel bells, pounding through his skull.

Then waves of hot, sick pain surged through him. His shoulders rolled back with a bone-splitting crack and his lungs seemed to convulse against his ribs. He gasped.

His legs felt as if they were on fire, his spine shuddered and twisted like a worm cut in two. Ariz staggered and fell to his knees. His muscles writhed beneath his skin, ripping apart. A weird moan escaped him as he struggled for breath and choked on a mouthful of his own blood.

For the first time in perhaps years, he felt terrified for his own sake. He couldn't die now, not when he'd come so close to finding a way free of Hierro. Ariz tried to grip his sword hilt, but his arms jerked and snapped behind him. A cascade of gray feathers seared down his chest and spilled over his hip, swallowing his sword and scabbard just as they engulfed his thighs.

Desperately he tried to think on something—anything—to give him strength. Then he remembered Fedeles taking his hand and drawing him close. The sensation of his lips had washed away Ariz's awareness of his injuries and Hierro's brand. Ariz concentrated on that respite, as the marrow of his bones seemed boil. He closed his eyes and drew the cool darkness of Fedeles around him.

"Calm, my beauty." Clara sounded as affectionate as when she spoke to her treasured songbirds. "The worst is done. You're fine now. Oh, and so lovely."

Ariz opened his eyes to see Clara crouched low and leaning over his face. He startled up to his feet. She leaned back from him as a huge gold wing swung past her.

His wing, Ariz realized. No longer an arm but a wing extending almost to the far wall of the fencing room. Splashes of his blood colored the oak floor like spills of ink. Gouges scraped through the wood in a wild pattern.

"It's all right, Ariz. You've passed Trueno's test and proven yourself worthy of his blessing," Clara said. "All is well now. You're fine."

She was right. The raging fire that had seemed to melt the marrow from his bones and char his muscles had turned to comforting warmth.

Ariz cocked his head and caught sight of his faint reflection in the glass of a window.

A huge gold eagle studied him in return. The sight should have alarmed him, he knew that, but his mind no longer felt quite like his own. He was highly aware of tiny figures moving in the trees outside. His feet flexed and massive black talons tore furrows into the polished floor. The faint breezes drifting in from the window seemed to beckon him.

Clara stepped between him and the window.

"You can fly free soon, but first we must both do our duty to Hierro. We would not want him to suspect us. Not yet."

Ariz snapped his beak in frustration, but Clara didn't appear the least bit intimidated. She gave a breathy laugh, then stroked his ruffled neck feathers down. Ariz felt oddly mollified by the action. He settled his wings against his back and waited.

"Trueno's blessing suits you even more than I thought it would. And now you will be able to fly up into the second story of the Slate House," Clara decided. "There is much for you to accomplish there. Many men you may have to do away with. I will tell you their names so that you may pray for each and every one."

She lifted Hierro's letter and began reading not merely names but instructions.

Ariz listened and hoped that Atreau had already acted on the message he'd left for him.

"Leave no man there alive." Clara whispered the order like a prayer.

CHAPTER
TWELVE

Several hours passed before Fedeles was free to leave the Shard of Heaven. Even after that, he didn't immediately return to the Queman-or residence. Instead he escorted Sevanyo back to the palace and stayed with him until his favorite attendants announced the arrival of his sons Xalvadar and Jacinto. Then Fedeles withdrew to allow the Sagrada family to mourn together.

He rode a meandering route on his way home, visiting Crown Hill in the late afternoon. He would have liked to linger there, but he knew Oasia would be waiting for him. Even if she'd understood everything he'd done in freeing King Juleo, she would want to discuss it in detail.

Moreover, the moment he entered the grounds, a flushed page rushed forward to discreetly inform him that Atreau had returned and wished to speak with him about a matter of some urgency.

"He's awaiting you in the library." The page looked uneasy and added, "As is the duchess."

"Both of them together? And the place hasn't erupted in flames?" Fedeles smiled, though he wasn't entirely unconcerned.

He wasted only a few minutes brushing Firaj and gathering his thoughts before entering the house and ascending the stairs to the grand library.

More than any other room in the mansion, the library reminded Fedeles that he was the first Duke of Rauma in history not to bear the Tornesal name.

Ornate carvings of sunflowers and the black sun crest of the Tornesals decorated the towering shelves, festooned the doorways and studded the heavy oak furniture. Fedeles's own Quemanor crest adorned only a few pillows that Oasia's maids had sewn. More than anywhere else in the house, this room made him feel like a poorly prepared actor who had been hastily pushed on stage to improvise the part of "Duke of Rauma" when his cousin, Javier, had been excommunicated for heresy after converting to the Bahiim faith.

Sinking sunlight glinted across the gilded letters that decorated the spines of the countless books he'd neither procured nor read. Though he remembered Javier had often leafed through a number of the old tomes and poked fun at their pompous narratives. He'd even chucked one particularly hateful book into the fireplace to burn.

Fedeles would never have dared to do such a thing himself—not because he revered the bigoted, supercilious men who'd penned works such as *A Glorious History of Cadeleonian War and Conquest*, but because that decision seemed like it still belonged to Javier. Even after holding the title of duke and living in this house for eleven years, Fedeles felt like a mere proxy for his cousin. A placeholder, awaiting the rightful man's return.

So perhaps that was why, for just a moment, he thought he glimpsed Javier floating there in the long shadows of the dark shelves. He seemed both radiant and ghostly. Fedeles almost called his name, but then the vision resolved to a mere shaft of sunlight glowing through the haze of dust.

Even so, Fedeles strode to the shelf and studied the aged leather spines of the books there. Ancient histories. Most of them written in decorative script and brimming with illuminated letters, which rendered them pretty to gaze upon and a slog to read. Then Fedeles noticed a white stone sitting on the shelf and beneath it a slip of aged paper. Possibly a remnant of a page torn from one of the volumes. The handwriting looked so much like Javier's that Fedeles found it unnerving. The ink had faded with time so that Fedeles could only make out one word clearly.

Don't.

And then something that might have been *kill* or *till*, or possibly even *kiss*?

The short *l*'s and long *s*'s common to most noble scripts looked much alike to his eyes. But the faint word that followed looked so much like *Hierro* that it took Fedeles aback.

That couldn't be correct, could it?

Fedeles picked the note up to study the weirdly familiar script. The paper crumbled to pieces and drifted down to his feet like flakes of wood ash. He crouched down, scowling at the tiny yellow fragments. But now he felt certain he couldn't have read the thing correctly.

Even if he hadn't, it couldn't refer to Hierro Fueres. The paper and ink had simply been too old. The note was likely penned a century before he or Hierro were born.

Perhaps too much time spent in the presence of the Hallowed Kings had predisposed him to seeing ghostly forms everywhere this afternoon. And the desire to murder Hierro Fueres was much on his mind as well.

The man's death would solve so much for so many—except that there would be repercussions. Not only could it cost Fedeles everything, but it would endanger his entire household and all those who looked to him for protection. And even if Hierro died, that still left the man's father, the Duke of Gavado, as well as Prince Remes, and the royal bishop to carry on with their treasonous plans.

"Fedeles, is that you?" Oasia's voice drifted from beyond the shelves.

"Yes. I'm coming." He hurried to the reading gallery. There portraits and maps were stored, and rows of long, narrow windows offered the best light.

"Sorry to keep you both waiting," Fedeles added when he reached his companions.

Atreau lounged beside the maps desk in a curule chair. He looked bedraggled and hollow-eyed but still maintained the amused expression that he wore like a mask. Having recently spent several hours in the company of Atreau's older brother, Lliro, Fedeles couldn't help but notice how much harder the years had been on Atreau. He wasn't even thirty and yet silver already streaked his dark hair and lines of both worry and mockery etched his mouth and eyes.

It seemed so obvious to Fedeles that Atreau shouldered more than his share of troubles. How strange it was that so many courtiers deemed him a careless and carefree figure.

Opposite him, Oasia stood near a narrow window, haloed in golden light by the setting sun. She held her smallest set of lace needles. Delicate threads of cerulean spells lit her graceful hands. Her sharp, glinting lace needles caught the strings of spells as she knit them with a silky gold yarn. Her expression appeared distant and beautifully serene. Fedeles recognized that she was neither disinterested nor tranquil. Where Atreau masked his anxiety in a wastrel's smile, Oasia maintained a lovely facade of composure.

More than anything else, the fact that they weren't bickering warned Fedeles that they were both agitated and uneasy.

"How are the children?" Fedeles asked, and a smile flickered at the corners of Oasia's mouth.

"Well, safe and absurdly energetic," she said. "The new boots have given Sparanzo so much more confidence that he's making a fuss over anyone taking his place for the first dance of Masquerade or the coronation. You'll need to talk to him tonight after supper."

Fedeles nodded. He wasn't delighted by the thought of denying his son, but there would be other far safer opportunities for Sparanzo to demonstrate his newfound grace later.

"They pulled the spell-burned corpses of two assassins from the river this afternoon," Oasia remarked. "The pair that Lord Bayezar sent after Hierro, I believe. At this rate the capital won't have any swordsmen left to hire and we'll all have to resort to setting dogs on each other." She shook her head. "News from Crown Hill?"

"Ariz left me this." Fedeles lay the page down on the desktop and gently smoothed its crumpled surface.

Oasia set aside her lacework and Atreau uncoiled from his seat and came to the desk. Both of them studied Ariz's illegible note. Their dubious expressions were strikingly similar.

"I received a missive from him this morning too," Atreau said after a moment.

"Could you decipher it?" Oasia asked.

"What there was of it." Atreau dug into his pocket and drew out several folded scraps of paper. He selected one and hid the rest away before Oasia could more than glance over them. Then Atreau dropped the crumpled message to the tabletop. Fedeles resisted the urge to reach out and smooth it flat as well.

"Find it before I do," Fedeles read aloud.

"We believe *it* refers to a relic the royal bishop may have located on the Salt Islands—" Atreau began.

"We?" Oasia inquired.

Atreau considered her for several moments. Fedeles half expected him to refuse to share the identity of his confederate, but to his surprise, Atreau remained forthcoming.

"Master Narsi and I." Atreau looked just slightly uneasy, though Fedeles couldn't understand why. From what Sevanyo had described, Master Narsi had made a very favorable impression and won the new king's favor. Sevanyo had even gone so far as to chastise the royal bishop for implying that the young physician had anything to do with their father's assassination.

"If you had been there, you would have seen with your own eyes that it was a man in holy colors who betrayed Papa. That half-Haldiim youth fought to save him," Sevanyo had snapped, and after that he'd refused to discuss any further sanctions against the Haldiim population in Cieloalta.

Despite his ghoulish calling, Master Narsi was clearly quite capable.

"He discovered a similar reference in Dommian's charm-book," Atreau added.

"Ah. The physician reveals still more talents. One wonders why the Grunitos didn't keep him closer at hand." Oasia clearly had her own theory on the subject, but she didn't share it. Instead her gaze turned stern. "You've ensured his safety from the royal bishop's guardsmen, yes?"

"He's beyond their reach for the time being," Atreau replied.

"In the Haldiim District? Or the Theater District?" Oasia pressed.

Atreau scowled at her, and it struck Fedeles that Sparanzo often made the same face when he felt harassed. "What business is it of yours?"

"Master Narsi more than proved his worth today," Oasia stated. "I believe that he will soon be offered a position in Sevanyo's court, which would do us and him a world of good. So, I'm hoping that you haven't quartered him in one of your dank holes in the Knife Market or left him stuffed up the chimney of the Green Door."

"He's staying with his Haldiim friends," Atreau snapped. "As far as I know the accommodations are quite comfortable and all of them are perfectly safe and happy."

Something about the way Oasia tilted her head made Fedeles suspect that she enjoyed needling Atreau over the master physician's welfare. Though she wasn't lying about the opportunity for the young physician to rise above the sphere of Atreau's influence and secure a place within the inner circle of the royal court. The transition could offer Master Narsi access to greater power as well as shield him from persecution—as Fedeles had promised Timoteo he would do. But seeing how downtrodden Atreau looked, Fedeles decided to shift the discussion back to the task at hand.

"So then, as for the whereabouts of this relic?" he inquired.

"Likely it's in the Slate House at the Sea Memorial. I have someone working to secure it." Atreau went on quickly, likely to keep Oasia from questioning this agent's identity as well. He tapped the page that Ariz had left for Fedeles. "The larger puzzle is what to make of these . . . what are they? Sketches of birds?"

"Larks," Fedeles clarified. The silhouettes of the birds seemed obvious to him.

"And a heart, if I'm not mistaken," Oasia pointed out.

She smiled knowingly at Fedeles, who returned the expression in a calm, unembarrassed way. It wasn't as if he'd made any attempt to hide his affection for Master Ariz from her or Atreau. Still, he didn't like the thought of either of them making fun of Master Ariz or his struggle to convey all he could to them despite the torture he endured to do so.

Fedeles remember all too well how it felt to be locked inside one's own mind, unable to communicate. As a youth, when he'd spent a year under Scholar Donamillo's thrall, he could hardly jibber out a few horses' names, but here was Ariz battling to keep them informed after decades of complete subjugation.

"The heart's probably not meant for us," Atreau remarked.

"Indeed," Oasia agreed.

All three of them turned their attention to the rest of the lines and letters that made up the latter half of the disfigured missive. Fedeles sighed and glanced up to where shafts of sunset light illuminated a corner of a portrait. Some warrior ancestor smugly displayed the plans for this very mansion, with its plethora of paths and lanes winding throughout the grounds.

He glanced down to Ariz's letter again.

"Might these be city streets?" Fedeles wondered.

"Streets?" Oasia considered the lines anew. "Yes, they could well be. Ah! Here. I recognize this block from my tapestries."

"Yes. The Weavers' Ward, near the dye houses." Atreau's face lit with excitement. "Right. Then this street is Needle Lane. This is the third intersection of Warp and Weft, and this little alley would be Bent Spindle. So the symbol Master Ariz has placed there . . ."

"It's the Brand of Obedience," Fedeles said. "I think Ariz is showing us where Hierro his housing assassins."

"Other than Ariz himself, you mean?" Atreau commented. "Not that he isn't enough on his own."

"He's not responsible for what he's forced to do—" Fedeles began to protest, but Atreau cut him off.

"I know, I know. I just wish he could be a little less capable. We're fucked at both ends if many of these others are as deadly as he has proven to be." Atreau leaned closer to the map of the Weavers' Ward. "There's a warehouse right here. Corrdevo's Wool. The building is large enough to house a good number of men, and I've heard a few secondhand complaints about odd noises coming from inside the place."

All three of them contemplated the fragmented map in silence for several minutes. Fedeles felt certain that the location housed at least some of the men and women now enthralled by Hierro. But what to do with the information? What could they do for those hapless souls?

"We can't just let them be," Atreau said at last. "I know they aren't responsible for what has happened to them. But with King Juleo now dead, there's nothing to hold Hierro back from enacting his plan. He will strike soon. Before Sevanyo gets established."

"Are you suggesting that we kill them?" Oasia asked.

"Do we have the means to free them?" Atreau demanded. He looked first to Oasia, and then he met Fedeles's gaze. His expression seemed as angry as it was exhausted. "At least five of those enthralled people are likely agents of mine. People I know. But if it's a question of losing the entire kingdom to Hierro, then sacrifices have to be made."

"We don't know that Hierro will act at once. There may still be time to save—" Fedeles began.

"You risk losing everyone, by trying to save these few. You understand that, don't you?" Atreau replied.

Fedeles couldn't look at him. Couldn't even think about what Atreau suggested. He knew what it felt like to suffer and rage and struggle against a thrall. He knew the guilt of taking a life against his will. The regret that came in the darkness of night and haunted so many of his dreams. He also knew that a thrall could be broken and what joy there was in being liberated. Every instant of freedom became precious—even small moments felt like celebrations. How could he deny that chance to so many others?

Oasia reached out and took Fedeles's hand in her own. Her fingers felt warm and humming with power. Fedeles's own seemed lifeless in comparison.

"Atreau's fear isn't unfounded, my dear," Oasia said softly. "This may be our only opportunity to act before Hierro unleashes them on the Sagrada family and our own household."

"We have to strike first," Atreau urged. "Hierro isn't fool enough to give us any opportunity to retaliate and you know that."

Fedeles shook his head, hating the thought of an unprovoked attack against the most hapless of combatants.

"They aren't just going to go away because you feel sorry for—" Atreau began.

"So, what do you propose we do?" Fedeles asked bitterly. "Nail the doors shut and burn the building down?"

"Would you really rather see them butcher your family and friends?" Atreau snapped. "For fuck's sake! You think I want to be the one who has to suggest killing my own agents? Do you imagine it doesn't tear me up to think about it? I fucking hate this! But sometimes the only choices any of us have are between bad and worse." Atreau glared at the portraits hanging on the wall, then returned his angry glower to Fedeles. "I adore you, Fedeles, I truly do. But you have no right to make me responsible for this decision. You need to stop waiting for me, or Oasia or goddamned Javier to tell you what needs doing. You're not a child anymore. You have all the damned information you need from me, and I've got a fucking play to write and a cat to look after."

He turned and strode for the doors.

Fedeles started after him, but Oasia held his hand tight and pulled him back.

"Let him go and fume to his cat," Oasia said.

"But—"

"He just learned of his father's death today," Oasia added more softly. "Lliro mentioned it to me."

"He hates his father," Fedeles replied.

"I imagine that's why he's fuming and swearing instead of weeping," Oasia said with a sigh. "Whatever revenge or final scathing words he probably imagined delivering are lost now. He's left with his anger and no one to heap it on."

Fedeles frowned at the chair Atreau had vacated.

"He's right though, isn't he?" Fedeles only managed a whisper, feeling almost afraid to hear the truth. "I have burdened you and him with the responsibility for too many hard decisions."

Oasia surprised him with a genuine laugh.

"I'd say you've employed those best suited to perform necessary work for our nation. Certainly you wouldn't personally slaughter the swine that keep our household fed, would you? Not when there are capable butchers who gladly answer to their vocations. You may hate having blood on your hands." She squeezed his fingers. "But you don't let any of us go hungry."

Was it really the same thing, though? Fedeles wished he could feel more certain, more righteous and sanctified.

"Javier wouldn't have made a mess of all this."

"Fedeles, my dear. Your heretic cousin has done nothing but make messes and leave them for you to clean up," Oasia said. "Atreau isn't wrong where that's concerned. You *do* need to stop waiting for Javier to come back and take over. He's gone."

Fedeles wanted to argue, but really, why was he still clinging to the thought that someday Javier would return and make everything better? Was he so desperate to escape his responsibilities that he now conjured visions of his cousin from shadows and shafts of sunlight?

"I just . . . I don't want to get it wrong," Fedeles whispered, as much to himself as to Oasia.

"But we all get things wrong. Sometimes it's the only way to learn," Oasia said. "And I can tell you from my own experience that doing nothing for fear of making a mistake can be the greatest error of all. We are just as responsible for the results of our inaction as we are for our actions."

Timoteo had said much the same thing to him weeks ago.

Fedeles nodded. He knew she was correct. That didn't make it any easier for him to decide on a course of action.

"You know what Atreau and I both believe, and you have the information that Ariz has given you. Think on it." Oasia released his hand and picked up her lacework. "Tell me when you've reached your own decision."

Again cerulean spells lit around her hands as she looped them into the silk threads on her needles. The charmed lace was so fine and small that Fedeles knew it was meant to be worn by a child. Sparanzo, no doubt. Oasia's expression grew distant. She reminded him a little of the Hallowed Kings, as if she too floated between realms like a sleeper plucking blessings from her dreams.

Then he recalled something that Master Narsi had said about Ariz. That he was a sleepwalker—only it was Hierro who controlled the nightmare he lived in. He glanced down at Ariz's missive.

If only he could wake Ariz and the other would-be assassins. But the brand would burn their hearts to cinders before it would allow them to escape its grasp. Fedeles knew as much from his own years living in its thrall. Resisting the spell only intensified suffering and gave the brand a greater hold. It reminded him of this morning, when the hooks of the royal bishop's ring had dug in deeper the more he fought them.

But when he'd thrown all his strength and will into them, rather than against them, the entire spell had become something new. *Seize* had transformed into *Freedom*. As if, given the power to do so, the spell itself longed to be liberated—to transcend the wretched purpose it had been consigned to fulfill.

Absently, he pressed a hand against the string of rubies that hung around his neck—Meztli's shield—ancient spells remade by his wish to protect his world. They had been roused by affection and valor.

He doubted the same was true for the Brand of Obedience. No amount of good intention would reshape so sadistic a spell into something happy to set its captives free.

He had to think of a different way to place these enthralled souls beyond the brand's power. If attempting to rouse them from their living nightmares only brought them more pain and placed them deeper in Hierro's grasp, then what would free them?

Other than death.

"If one can't wake a sleepwalker, then is it a better course to let him subside into an even deeper slumber?" Fedeles wondered aloud.

"What?" Oasia blinked at him and then stilled her lacemaking.

"Master Narsi said that those suffering under a thrall are like sleepwalkers, do you remember?"

Oasia nodded.

"I thought that if I can't wake them up, then perhaps I could . . . make them sleep so deeply that they won't respond to Hierro's commands."

"Delfia and Master Narsi both feel that it's not so easy as just making them tired," Oasia said. "They have to be nearly dead before they stop feeling the brand. I believe that's why Master Narsi is currently treating Ariz with stimulants."

Fedeles scowled. Despite Master Narsi's declarations, Ariz still suffered under Hierro's control. Now he endured the horrors of a physician's treatments as well. Fedeles shuddered at an unwanted memory of needles and astringent coinflower. There had to be something he could do. Ariz placed so much hope and trust in him.

"Delfia and Narsi are limited to the realm of medications and drugs," Fedeles replied. "But we might be able to create a gentler spell. A magical lullaby."

"You're thinking of only Ariz," Oasia said. "And perhaps your idea could work for a single soul, for a short time. But this lullaby spell would need to be modulated constantly to suit the rhythms of his body and also to mitigate Hierro's presence. Can you imagine doing the same thing for every single soul in Hierro's grasp? I might be able to divide my attention and power between two or three lives and still maintain my wards across the city. With practice, you could manage perhaps five or six. But Hierro has enthralled *hundreds*. And I still don't believe that we could safely sedate them to the degree that they wouldn't suffer when Hierro's demands grew insistent. More likely than not we'd expend a vast amount of time and power just to end up killing them."

Fedeles bowed his head.

"We may have reached a point where we can't concern ourselves with the well-being of the people whom Hierro controls." Oasia spoke in a quiet measured voice. "Though if it's a choice between leaving them living in a nightmare of torment and offering them the release of death . . ."

"If we treat these people as nothing more than Hierro's weapons, then how are we any better than him?" Fedeles asked.

Oasia frowned at him.

"Are we fighting to claim higher principles than Hierro?" Oasia inquired. "Or do we want to destroy him?"

"Both," Fedeles replied. "It has to be both. Because if we win by sinking to the same depth as Hierro, then we won't have destroyed him. We'll only have replaced him—become him. You can't want that."

"Can't I?" Oasia arched her brows.

"I don't think you do, no," Fedeles answered.

Oasia considered him for a few moments, then dropped her gaze to the blessings in her lacework.

"I used to swear that I would do anything to anyone to crush my father and Hierro." Her gaze slid to Ariz's letter. "Since then, I've witnessed vengeance wreck people's lives. It nearly cost me my own. I imagine that the ruthless girl I used to be would think me weak now. I suppose in a way I am."

"Caring for others isn't weakness. It requires true determination and fortitude. And I don't believe that indifference is a strength. It's self-indulgent and childish." Fedeles recalled himself at nineteen. He'd felt so furious and raw that he'd thought nothing of avenging himself against the entire Plunado family. He'd grown so used to imagining himself as a victim that he hadn't recognized how very much power he'd wielded. Now he desperately regretted how selfish his hurt had made him. "It's easy to feel wronged by the world and justified in everything we do. But it requires true courage, real strength, to care for others—to fight for them instead of wallowing in self-pity."

He couldn't stop himself from reaching out and tracing the heart drawn at the bottom of Ariz's letter.

"I suppose you're right," Oasia said. "Besides, I *have* grown rather fond of commanding the moral high ground. I sleep better."

Relief washed through Fedeles, because as certain as he felt in his conviction that shielding the innocent people caught up in Hierro's thrall was the correct course of action, he possessed none of Oasia's skill at weaving the kind of complex spells that could accomplish that goal.

"What are you proposing we do exactly?" Oasia asked.

"I'm not sure of the form the spell ought to take," Fedeles admitted. "But I was thinking of the chants that the priests in the Shard of Heaven use to lull the Hallowed Kings. Could something like that subdue the people enthralled by Hierro?"

"Hmm . . ." Oasia dropped down into the curule chair that Atreau had abandoned. "The trouble with replicating those incantations is that they must be continually invoked by a monastery full of devotees."

"But there must be something." Fedeles racked his memory. "The Mirogoth grimma had spells that turned trolls to stone, but didn't kill them."

"Yes, but according to Atreau's memoir the grimma were Old Gods trapped in human guises. I don't think that either of us is quite that powerful," Oasia countered. "Though there might be something in one of the older holy books that mentions a prayer for calming the heart of a wild beast . . . do you recall?" Oasia gazed at the shelves of books.

Fedeles felt certain that Oasia was correct, but he'd not encountered it. Again, he ran his fingers over the string of spells that made up Meztli's shield.

Fearless in particular seemed to hum like an excited bumblebee as he stroked the surface of the scarlet stones. Fedeles pressed down on it, calming it like he would a skittish horse. As he did this, a thought occurred.

"Is it possible that we could sedate the spells, rather than the people affected by them?"

If it could be done, then he would be able to free Ariz, as he'd promised.

"You mean to sedate the person casting the spell?" Oasia asked.

"No, the spell itself." Fedeles ran his hand again over Meztli's shield and felt courage and resolve radiating up from the stones. "I'm thinking of how all spells up on Crown Hill were so subdued when I first arrived, but they steadily roused. Perhaps we could do something like that but in reverse—"

"Fedeles, my dear." Oasia again raised her dark brows. "Do you truly believe that it was anything other than *you* that animated those incantations?"

"I—" Uncertainty fluttered through him. "They feel alive and individual to me. They're courageous and . . . comforting."

"If they seem that way, it's because *you* are kind and brave, my dear." Oasia's smile was indulgent. "A spell may shift to suit the intentions of the person powering it. It can become more forceful or subtler. It may change color or exude a new perfume. But all of that comes from the person casting it. In itself, a spell is only a tool, an instrument. A pen nib bends to take on the unique angle of a writer's hand. A flute may bellow or whisper depending on the breath that flows through it, but it never draws in air on its own. In just the same way, the characteristics that a spell seems to possess are a reflection of the person giving it power."

Fedeles frowned, though oddly, Oasia's expression lit with a sudden excitement.

"But there could be something in that. Yes . . . Whoever gives the spell power influences it." Oasia jumped up and beamed at Fedeles. "What if, instead of attempting to break Hierro's spells, we focused on usurping them. Imagine how different they would be if you displaced Hierro's hold on the thralls."

"And then broke them, you mean?" Fedeles asked. They'd discussed breaking the brands before, but the likelihood that shredding the spell would also kill the person held in its thrall had been far too great.

"No, I mean, insinuate your will in place of Hierro's. Or at least in addition to his. You couldn't destroy the thrall, but you could diminish Hierro's influence over the spells. Counter his commands—"

"No." Fedeles stepped back from her, feeling almost sick. "I won't enthrall anyone."

"They're already enthralled," Oasia replied.

"Yes, but—"

"But you might be able to soften the thrall's grip. Change the character of the spells. The same way you lent qualities of your character to the spells on Crown Hill." Oasia pressed on. "You might have the power to make the thrall easier to resist. Less hurtful and sadistic. If you could take it over completely, you'd be able to command them to go free and live their lives."

"But I'd have to hold those people in thrall to my will." Fedeles shook his head. "I'd join Hierro in making them my slaves."

"God's teeth, Fedeles! Sabotage isn't a collaboration." A rare noise of exasperation escaped Oasia. "You wouldn't be *joining* Hierro! You'd *undermine* him."

Fedeles recognized the merit in her argument, but he still hated the idea.

"Or," Fedeles suggested. "I could give my strength to you, the way I gave it to Irsea to protect the sacred grove. You could take—"

"Hierro would recognize my presence too quickly. He and I have fought too much and too often for me to go near his spells without him noticing." Oasia shook her head.

"I could distract him," Fedeles suggested. "Irsea and I have been strengthening the bonds between Crown Hill and the sacred grove; we could open the door between—"

"No! You don't give the keys to your wine cellar to a drunkard," Oasia snapped, though her expression seemed almost pleading. "I know myself, and I . . . I don't trust myself to be compassionate to strangers. Not when sacrificing them could save me and mine. The temptation to use them—to turn them on Hierro like a pack of rabid dogs, even at the cost of all their lives—I wouldn't be able to keep the desire out of my mind or out of theirs, and I'm not certain that I'd even try."

Cerulean fires all around her hands crackled to life, burning with a fury that Oasia's cool expression never betrayed. She clenched her hands, smothering the fires in her fists.

"I hate him more than you can probably understand. Believe me."

"I do." Fedeles nodded. He knew Hierro had hurt Oasia in ways that he didn't want to think about—for years. He wished there was anything he could do or say that might diminish her pain. But it was a decade too late for action and she disdained comforting words.

"It's different for you," Oasia went on. "Because *you* know what it's like to be held in thrall. If you despise anything as much as I hate Hierro, it's the thought of enthralling another human being. Presented with the opportunity, you're sickened, not tempted." Oasia gave him an almost pitying smile. "The very fact that I have to argue with you about this is proof that you are the better choice."

Fedeles wanted to refuse, but instead he forced himself to consider Oasia's words—and those that Atreau had growled out at him earlier.

You need to stop waiting for me, or Oasia or goddamned Javier to tell you what needs doing.

"I can try to do it," Fedeles decided. "But I need to go there in person. I have to be sure about the place and feel the wards that Hierro will have raised."

He had to see the people and know that he was indeed helping them.

"Very well." Oasia lifted her right hand and plucked at the empty air. A shining blue thread lit up and shot through the darkness of the library.

"I can light your way, but I think that you'll need to interrupt Atreau's time with that cat to have him guide you to the warehouse."

Fedeles frowned at the idea of intruding upon Atreau further, but Oasia smiled.

"You made a decision as he demanded. After that tantrum, accompanying you is the least the man can do."

ოოო

Fedeles found Atreau fast asleep, sprawled in a chair with a quill pen dangling from one limp hand and Master Narsi's cat lolling across his lap. He waited until the moon had fully risen before rousing Atreau, and even so he felt more than a little guilty for disturbing him. He looked so very tired.

But hearing Fedeles's plan, he'd voiced no complaint, other than grumbling about all the cat hair shed on his new white shirt.

Together they made their way to the dark, cramped lanes of the Weavers' Ward.

Lit from strange angles by the glow of spells and the flickering light of the sacred grove, the whole place looked foreign. Black silhouettes of shabby buildings blotted out vast sections of the sky and cut familiar constellations into ribbons. Gazing up, Fedeles felt that he might be riding through another nation entirely.

Cieloalta as he knew it was a city replete with lush gardens, manicured woodlands and broad promenades. Here, two- and three-story buildings crushed up against each other, forming dense rows. Upper floors jutted out over the streets so far that the lamps from game-house windows licked the shutters of the leather shops across the lane. The noise from busy taverns and inns bounded through the air as if echoing across a canyon, and the smell of wine, stew meat and rank piss seeped out of every dark corner. Even the most modest of shelters in alleys or beneath raised walkways housed populations of ragged people and feral animals.

None of this was new; in fact, he felt certain that he'd passed scenes like this countless times when he'd ridden with Ciceron to opera houses or theaters. But on those evenings he'd been occupied with the pleasure of Ciceron's company, and to a greater degree than he wanted to admit, he'd accepted Ciceron's resigned opinion of the sick, crippled and desperate individuals surrounding them.

There are always people who'd rather beg than take the work offered them. There's nothing to be done about that.

Those nights the gaunt horses, rangy hounds and lanky cats had received more of Fedeles's sympathy. But tonight he felt touched by the humanity of the people around him. In great part because few of them could see his observations. The pale cerulean filaments of Oasia's spells were invisible to them—though for Fedeles they glowed like a dozen full moons, illuminating the features of unsuspecting folk all along the streets.

Drunks and tired peddlers. A young man fingering his nostril and another scratching his balls. None of them performed for the pity of his purse, as Ciceron had called it. Nor were they glowering daggers at him.

Under the cover of night he observed the people around him in repose, and revelry, as well as despair and grief. He considered a wide-eyed man who appeared entirely occupied shouting insults at a rainspout above him. Then his attention shifted to a group of scabbed oldsters sharing a poppy pipe. One of them stroked the shoulder of another, who lay unconscious.

They were ugly and anguished, but also beautiful in their care for one another.

Having spent his whole day in the company of royalty, the disparity of human circumstances seemed suddenly very stark. Was it any wonder that some of these people might resort to picking pockets, mugging and burglary? They possessed so little, while just across the Gado Bridge, people like himself lived in opulence and luxury.

If he had been born to a poor family, would he have fared better than the beggars they passed? When he'd been out of his mind, status and wealth had shielded him, and it had empowered his friends and family with the resources to free him. If Javier had been toiling day and night in a slop-house, neither he nor Fedeles would've attracted Kiram Kir-Zaki's attention. He would never have been saved by the man's knowledge of machinery. Fedeles wouldn't have fared any better than the man now raving at the rooftops.

A figure burst from the shadows.

Fedeles jerked Firaj to a halt as a gangly Cadeleonian girl in a threadbare dress shot across the street. He nearly called out an admonishment to her, but then he saw the Haldiim infant that she snatched up from a heap of rags in the mouth of an alley. She gripped the baby to her chest as three mangy dogs prowled near. They growled, snapping at the girl's legs. She kicked and bellowed obscenities at the animals. Her baby let out a reedy yowl.

Fedeles reined Firaj nearer and the dogs bounded away. The girl shouted after them but didn't seem to notice Fedeles. Tears dribbled down her cheeks and she wiped her face quickly with the back of her hand. Then she began singing in a soft, broken voice as she soothed her child.

Fedeles stared in horrified wonder.

On another occasion, perhaps in different company, he might have sneered at the girl and questioned her quality as a mother for leaving her baby like a heap of offal for stray dogs to feed on.

But tonight he recognized the tenderness in her expression as she sang to the child nursing at her breast. Fedeles took in her battered, bare feet and the chapel star painted across the back of her dress. He saw how painfully young she was, as well as the beggar's cup hanging from a penitent's rope tied around her waist.

All at once he realized that he had no idea about the circumstances of her life. Was she dependent upon a chapel that would have taken her half-Haldiim baby from her if she didn't hide it? Had she been repudiated by her family? Abandoned by the father? He couldn't know and he certainly couldn't judge. The only obvious truth before him was that she adored her child. Just as he loved his. So, how was he any different from this girl, when he too had gone out into the night, leaving his child behind?

He'd inherited a household of maids and guards who ensured his son's safety. But he wasn't on hand to do it himself. This girl couldn't afford sandals to protect her own feet, much less a mansion of servants to coddle her baby. But when her child had needed her most, she'd stood before snarling hounds, placing her own flesh between their teeth and her child.

Fedeles reached into his coat and drew out his coin purse. He swung down from Firaj and dropped the purse into her beggar's cup. The girl's head came up at once and she peered at him through the dark.

"I don't mean to disturb you," Fedeles whispered. "I wish you both well."

"Thank you," she whispered back.

Fedeles gazed at the babe in her arms. "The wisteria of the Haldiim sacred grove could offer you better shelter than this place—"

"Fedeles," Atreau called to him from the road. "God's balls, man. Did you wake me up to do *this*? Because if you did—"

"Sorry." Fedeles left the girl and swung back up into his saddle. He patted Firaj. "Lead on."

"It's not my guidance that's in question. It's you following along that seems less than assured," Atreau muttered.

"There was a girl with a baby. I just wanted to do something for them," Fedeles admitted.

"Keep Hierro from taking over the country and you'll have done her and every other person in this nation a greater good than tossing them a few coins, I promise you that," Atreau replied.

They continued riding along the narrow lane. The pungent odor of tanneries and dyers emanated from dark buildings. Raucous voices roared from winehouses and boomed through the quiet street. A nighthawk swooped down from a tiled roof and snatched a rat from a heap of tanners' refuse.

Atreau scowled at the rodent's brief, shrill squeal. He slowed his horse and peered through the dark. The cerulean glow of Oasia's spells cast a deathly pallor across his face. Fedeles didn't think he'd ever seen Atreau looking so haggard—not even the night he'd bribed the then young Captain Ciceron to release Atreau from the city jail.

Atreau shifted slightly and the distant glow of the sacred grove warmed his features but didn't lift the shadows from beneath his eyes.

"The next street and around the corner. Corrdevo's Wool warehouse will be in the middle of the cul-de-sac." Atreau nudged his gray stallion, and Nube trotted ahead. Fedeles wondered if it was somehow symbolic that he, who could see the city illuminated by charms and spells, had no idea where they were, while Atreau, blind as he was in the dark, knew the way.

"I'll follow right behind you this time," Fedeles replied.

He wanted to say more to Atreau, to somehow engage him in a friendly conversation. Perhaps ask him about the play that he was writing for Jacinto, or inquire after the sales of the Haldiim translation of his latest memoir. But for the first time that Fedeles could recall, Atreau didn't seem in the mood for conversation.

When they rode around a corner, Fedeles's concerns about chitchat vanished. He stared in awestruck silence.

Ahead of them a two-story wooden warehouse sat in the center of a swirling mass of indigo spells. The incantations radiated with such intensity that every crack in the siding of the building—every seam beneath a shuttered window and doorframe—was outlined in spears of brilliant light. The six men guarding the building looked like burned-out shadows as they lounged by the double doors.

"I see it," Fedeles called to Atreau.

Atreau drew his stallion to a halt. He stared straight ahead for a few moments, then squeezed his eyes closed. When he opened them again, his expression was grim.

"The wards defending this place are huge, aren't they?" Atreau asked.

"Yes," Fedeles admitted. "There's a tapestry of indigo spells radiating through the entire warehouse. Some are wards, others thralls, but they look much more complicated than most of Hierro's work. There's something more to them . . ." The spells were far more complex and interwoven than he'd expected. The Circle of Wisteria and the Shard of Heaven were both protected by spells this intricate and vibrant, but those had been crafted by whole communities of clergy and worshipers. Their power had accumulated over generations. These spells couldn't have been more than a few years old. How had Hierro managed to craft them in such a short time, and how on earth could he alone fuel them day in and day out? How much power did the man truly command?

Fedeles found his skin prickling and his hair standing on end as he rode closer. He strained to make out the hundreds of individual symbols that intertwined to weave each of the long, intricate spells. Those, in turn, were overlaid to form a nearly seamless fabric of magic. This was far more complex than the impulsive indigo masses that Hierro had cast at Fedeles and Oasia in the past. Could these be old spells—like the Brand of Obedience itself—preserved in relics or charms and passed down to Hierro?

"Fedeles?" Atreau asked. He peered at Fedeles with a concerned expression. "If this is too much, just tell me. We can find another way."

"No. I—I can do this. But I need to study them more closely," Fedeles decided. "If I can ride around to the west side of the building, the sacred grove will help me discern each of the individual parts of the spells that make up the wards and the thralls . . . I'm wondering how much of this Hierro crafted himself and how much he's seized . . . if that makes sense?"

"You wish to read the individual words from which Hierro has composed his manifesto. Yes?" Atreau cocked his head slightly. "Perhaps some of them are lifted from other sources. Hierro seems the type who'd plagiarize a spell just as readily as he'd claim the work of a forgotten poet as his own, I think."

"He does, doesn't he," Fedeles agreed. It was so easy to forget just how quick and canny Atreau could be. Had he been born a witch, he probably would have mastered magic just as readily as he learned musical instruments and languages.

"Well, you'll need a distraction then." Atreau nodded and gazed at the men guarding the warehouse. "I play a rather engaging drunkard. That should do. But be careful. If this is too much, then . . . just don't get yourself killed for a bunch of strangers, all right. Master Ariz would be heartbroken."

Fedeles felt both flattered and flustered by the sentiment. Before he could think of a response, Atreau swung his leg over his stallion's back and then turned around so that he sat backward in his saddle. He patted Nube gently and the horse gave a relaxed sigh. Nube enjoyed showing off.

Fedeles smiled. When they'd schooled together, Atreau had often amused them all with riding tricks. He'd never been one for the daring charges that Elezar excelled at or the valiant leaps that Javier coaxed from his mount, Lunaluz. But Atreau's clowning and humor had never failed to win him laughs and the attention of numerous delighted ladies. It had been a few years since Fedeles had last seen him perform. Still, he fondly remembered how easy and foolish Atreau managed to make the intricate maneuvers appear.

Atreau caught Nube's tail as if he were gripping reins and then very gently nudged the stallion. Nube trotted backward toward the guards, while Atreau wove and wobbled in his saddle like a drunk about to topple.

As he neared the guards, they came to attention. One hefted a spear and another drew his sword. Fedeles almost called out to Atreau. But then one of the guards laughed and an instant later they all observed Atreau's backward advance with bemused expressions.

"She's left me! Flung me aside like a clipped toenail!" Atreau tilted in his saddle and then flopped forward over Nube's hindquarters. "You lot, come on. Kill me!" Atreau slurred and then let out a long wail. "Cut off my head and rip—rip out my heart! Then give that to her!"

Two of the guards snickered openly at Atreau, but the other four looked more pitying—one even wore the sympathetic expression of a man who'd cried out those same words just recently. None of them spared a glance in Fedeles's direction as he edged Firaj around the west side of the warehouse and swung down from the horse's back.

A dog chained behind the warehouse barked in alarm and Fedeles almost bolted back to Firaj. But then one of Oasia's shining threads hurtled ahead of him and wound around the chained animal. The dog grumbled, snorted and then settled into a deep sleep.

The guards at the front of the building didn't seem to have noticed the barking at all. Instead, one of them assured Atreau that he'd never met, much less seduced, Atreau's wife. Atreau responded with sobs as he begged the man to give her back.

"She farts like the north wind rolling off a refuse heap!" Atreau howled. "But I don't care. Tell her to come back home! Tell her I've written her a poem!"

And then he began reciting:
"How your kisses filled my heart, oh, my ample, breezy love.
But rank wind blew us apart, and drained me limp as a glove.
That stench blown by a hound of hell conjured words I spoke in haste.
Wrongful blame upon you fell, so you fled my choked embrace.
Deprived of comfort and of bliss, I ride in vain pursuit.
I die for a single kiss. Alas you, my love, care not a toot."

Fedeles laughed to himself. Atreau's genius truly was wasted on his perplexed audience. One of the guards commiserated with him while two others seemed to feel Atreau could do better and started dispensing advice about where he could find another woman.

Fedeles turned his own attention back to the warehouse wall. The gold glow from the Circle of Wisteria illuminated more details of Hierro's indigo spells. Here and there the light from the sacred grove seemed to sear the indigo light and give off a faint musky vapor. Irsea was obviously directing the power of the sacred grove to keep Hierro's spells from spreading beyond the Weavers' Ward.

But even as Fedeles watched, the Circle of Wisteria's light dimmed and drifted slightly from the warehouse wall. Irsea's connection to the living realm was fading. Without her, or another Bahiim watching over the sacred grove, its power would be without a direction or a purpose. Ripe for a man like Hierro to steal and twist to his own ends.

Fedeles felt a prick of guilt for secretly hoping that Irsea might come to his aid. She needed to preserve all the strength she possessed just to remain in the living realm until a new Bahiim arrived to protect the sacred grove. That wouldn't be anytime soon, not until the royal bishop was brought to heel.

Fedeles leaned into the wall of the warehouse. Peering through a crack, he spied the interwoven threads of tiny spells that made up the dense thralls that Hierro had cast. Waves of malevolence rolled off the spells and radiated through the wooden walls like heat issuing from an oven. Blue light blazed into his eyes even after he clenched them closed. Up so close, the press of Hierro's presence was pervasive—as if the man's breath filled Fedeles's throat and his fingers pinched and jabbed at Fedeles's body. It revolted him and reminded him of those horrifying years when Scholar Donamillo had slithered into his body and taken possession of him.

Fear set his heart pounding, but Fedeles forced himself to remain where he stood. He let his initial surge of terror fade. Then he focused, studying both the thralls and the protective wards surrounding them. He leaned in, and as his senses adjusted to the onslaught of Hierro's witchflame, he began to discern patterns and structures. Steadily he realized that the bold indigo light of Hierro's power didn't emanate from most of the spells. Instead, it encased them—like a thin skin of gold plating ancient iron.

When Fedeles probed beneath Hierro's indigo aura, he felt momentarily shocked. The intricate spells below looked almost identical to Oasia's work. Fedeles almost felt betrayed by the sight of them. Then he noted that the tight knots and lacy curls turned in the opposite direction to the counterclockwise spells Oasia favored. And as he drew even closer, he caught a scent beneath the brash musk of Hierro's power. Not the subtle lilac that encircled Oasia, but something more complex and rank—like funerary smoke twisting on river breezes.

The power sustaining these spells didn't belong to Hierro alone, Fedeles realized. There was at least one other witch whose soul also fed the brands that Hierro controlled. Or was it that Hierro fed off spells crafted by another far more powerful witch? Was this a partnership, or was Hierro a parasite? As Fedeles studied the way Hierro's presence engulfed and distorted the far more refined spells, he was reminded of the way pincushion galls warped roses, producing fantastical blossoms where a simple leaf would otherwise have grown.

Fedeles had no idea who this other witch could be—except that the resemblance of the spells to those Oasia crafted made him think it was another member of the Fueres family. Perhaps someone who had influenced Oasia's magic. Her mother had died while Oasia was only a child, but her father, Paulino Fueres, remained very much alive. Was it possible that he sustained the ambitions of his son, Hierro, even at a cost to his own soul? As a father, Fedeles understood the impulse. Though he wasn't certain Paulo Fueres was so loving a parent as to sacrifice so much.

Fedeles placed his hands against the rough wooden wall and sent his shadow creeping through the cracks and seams of the building. A few blue wards inside snapped and spit like frying oil struck with water. Fedeles gave no response, holding his shadow like a breath caught in his chest. The wards hissed and twisted, but without direction. Fedeles's lungs began to ache; still he waited. A minute passed, though it felt like an hour. The wards calmed, then settled back into serene tapestries. Fedeles's shadow crept between them like a mere play of light. He reached a thick column where the thralls Hierro controlled were gathered and bundled, like individual fibers spun into a single yarn. Indigo fire encased them all.

Fedeles felt the fire flicker and surge. Again he waited, watching for the moment Hierro's attention fluttered. The instant he spotted an opening, he slipped his shadow beneath the indigo fire. Then he sent his shadow racing along the fibers until he reached the brands, burning within enthralled bodies.

He felt the muscular flesh of young men. Fifty-three of them in this warehouse—laying on canvas cots and clinging to the small respite of sleep. They were bruised and exhausted from training with pikes and swords. The brands gnawed at their hearts. As one, they dreamed a chaos of bloody battle. They killed and were killed as they moaned into their blankets. The air hanging over them stank of stale sweat and a filthy latrine. Dirty food bowls sat heaped on the floor, while roaches crawled over the remnants inside.

Pity and revulsion filled Fedeles. He wouldn't have kept dogs in these conditions, much less men. They had to be freed—now.

Fedeles abandoned his attempt at subterfuge and stealth. He threw all his strength into his shadow, leaving his body to crumple to the ground. His awareness surged from him, along with a gush of bristling darkness. His senses raced over the long string of spells that made up every captive man's Brand of Obedience. The brands glistened like jagged, wet teeth spearing bloody meat. Fedeles shuddered at the idea of touching them. But he knew he had to. These men needed him to find his courage.

He flooded the spells with his power, drowning Hierro's radiant indigo light as his own shadow drenched the knots and hooks that formed complete spells. His will saturated the thralls like a black dye. For the first time he held another life in thrall—many lives. He felt the presence of the sleeping men as if each was a wisp of smoke drifting around his head. Shapes turned and twisted within them. With a breath Fedeles could transform or dissipate any one of them.

Instead he let his strength flow into them. They grew more solid, more human and individual in form. Gashes healed and bruises faded.

Wake up! Fedeles urged them. *You must escape this place.*

The smoky figures before him seemed to rouse, as inside the warehouse the men came awake. They scrabbled through the dark for their clothes and shoes. Then they started for the doors. Fedeles felt his muscles twitching and his heart racing along with theirs. Hope filled him.

Then a furious power surged through the spells, throwing Fedeles's shadow back and slamming each of the men inside the warehouse to the ground. Fedeles gasped as his senses reeled with sick confusion and pain. He gaped up to see Firaj standing over him, protecting his supine body. His chest ached like he'd been kicked by a bull and his nerves felt molten. The taste of blood hung in his mouth.

He didn't let himself think about it. He had to reach those men before Hierro could enslave them again. He couldn't waste time worrying about pain or secrecy.

He sucked in a fast breath of warm night air. Then he threw his shadow back into the warehouse, shattering oak planks and shearing through nails. The wards clawed at him, gashing his arms. Fedeles refuse to care. He drove his shadow through the wards like the blade of a saw, severing spells and leaving trails of blue light spewing from the shredded ends.

Let Hierro feel power pouring from him like blood gushing from an open wound! Fedeles ripped apart the last of the wards.

Then he took in the men he wanted to save. They writhed on the filthy floor, moaning and wide-eyed in agony. Each of them groped at their chests as masses of incandescent spells erupted from their brands, punching through their flesh and diving back in like worms boring through earth.

An almost childlike screech of rage resonated from the brands.

These are MINE! Mine! Mine! Mine!

Fedeles had never witnessed Hierro in the throes of such visceral outrage. Or was this the other presence that he'd felt earlier?

The enthralled men convulsed, their bones and muscles jerking and twisting into huge, grotesque forms. They bristled and howled as their arms and legs bent at wrong angles. Their feet and hands became massive paws. Their skulls thickened and contorted into heavy muzzles. Coarse gray hair enveloped their skins like eruptions of pox sores.

In moments, the men were transformed. Grizzled, panting mord-wolves arose. Each stood nearly the size of a horse. Scarlet tongues lolled and long teeth flashed in grotesque snarls. Fedeles lost any sense of their thoughts and instead found himself confronted with burning whorls of mindless anger—reflections of the rage permeating their brands.

Fedeles reached out, but he couldn't bring himself to rip through these men as he had the wards. He thought of the soothing lullaby that sedated the Hallowed Kings, desperate for anything to help them.

They are MINE! That furious power hurled him away again. This time he could see an incandescent, childlike figure hunching between him and the transformed men. The child's eyes sizzled with a teal light. Its body moved in flashes, like bolts of lightning.

Shall I take what is yours? Destroy your handiworks—your playmates?

The child spun on the transformed men. It threw its arms wide and wild arcs of raw power surged forth in a gushing fountain. The warehouse doors shattered. The enthralled men roared and howled, then as one they charged between the broken doors.

Too late Fedeles considered Atreau and the guards outside.

A guards' alarmed shout turned into a scream. Weapons rang as they fell against cobblestones. Through the chaos of cries and snarls, Fedeles recognized Atreau's stallion give a shriek.

The child turned back to Fedeles and flashed a blazing smile before crackling out of sight.

Fedeles cast his shadow after the transformed men—

No, mordwolves. He couldn't think of them as men, not now.

Flames from shattered lanterns licked up a corner of the warehouse, illuminating five bristling mordwolves as they mauled the remains of disemboweled guards. Fedeles lashed his shadow across them, severing their throats. Another three mordwolves lay in the street strangling in the grip of Oasia's cerulean spells. Where had the rest gone? His senses reeled as he turned through the night, searching in desperation. Then he caught sight of some thirty of the beasts charging west, directly into the golden glow of the sacred grove.

They were going to destroy his handiwork—his playmate. That had to mean Irsea and the sacred grove. What had he done? Guilty horror flooded Fedeles. He had to stop them—

But not before he found Atreau. Where was he? The mutilated human remains beneath the dead mordwolves filled Fedeles with sorrow and dread. The spreading fire lit an outstretched hand. Dark locks lay in a pool of blood. *No. Oh God, no.*

"Fedeles!" Atreau's shout thundered through the darkness. He was alive, Fedeles realized in stunned relief. But where?

"Fedeles!" Atreau's voice sound so very loud, as if he stood only feet from Fedeles. Probably because he did. For the second time, Fedeles plunged back into his sprawled, limp body.

His head throbbed and his muscles ached. He tried to sit up but only rolled onto his side. He pulled his eyelids open but couldn't make sense of the chaos of firelight and jittery shadows before him.

"Fedeles! Wake up, damn it!" Atreau shouted again.

Fedeles's vision resolved. He lay on the ground, staring across dark cobblestones. Firaj stood as he had earlier, guarding Fedeles's helpless body. Smoke and flames plumed up from the wall of the warehouse. Atreau sat atop Nube, gripping one of the guard's pikes as a mordwolf stalked toward them both.

The beast's head was bowed low, its gaze boring into Fedeles's. It snarled, baring its long teeth. Then the mordwolf bounded forward. His heart lurched as he attempted desperately to move.

Atreau reined Nube forward and slashed open the side of the mordwolf's face. The beast bounded back but didn't flee. It paced at the edge of Atreau's reach, its gaze intent upon Fedeles.

"For the love of God, Fedeles," Atreau called over his shoulder. "Get up!"

Fedeles gripped Firaj's leg and pulled himself upright. His hands were sticky with blood from the shallow cuts tracing his forearms. His legs shuddered beneath him. Still, he managed to pull himself into his saddle.

The mordwolf lifted its head and, seeing him, a teal glint lit its eyes. It charged. Atreau thrust the pike, but the creature pivoted. Atreau's pike speared its shoulder. The mordwolf swung its head, jaws gaping wide, to rip through Nube's throat.

Fedeles heaved his shadow forward, nearly falling from Firaj's back. He struck the mordwolf with the grace of a cannon shot, throwing it back to the ground and crushing most of its skull. Still its eyes continued to blaze.

A second blow split it in two.

Fedeles felt like he might vomit. He collapsed against Firaj's neck. For an instant the world seemed to sway around him. Firaj snorted quietly.

Atreau wheeled Nube around. Blood spattered his clothes and dotted his cheek. His eyes were wide and wild, but he held the pike with a steady grip.

"How badly are you hurt?" Atreau demanded.

"I'm fine. You?" Fedeles asked.

"Scratches but nothing more," Atreau said quickly. "Can you ride the distance back to the house—"

"I have to stop them," Fedeles cut him off.

"There are too many." Atreau shook his head. "We need more men. City guards. Even the bishop's guardsmen at this point. I'll raise the alarm. You get back to your house before anyone suspects that you were—"

"There's no time." Fedeles dragged in a deep breath of the night air. "I did this, and I have to stop it before anyone else is killed."

"You couldn't have known they were keeping fucking mordwolves in there. No one—"

"They weren't mordwolves," Fedeles snapped. "Not before I tried to free them." Fedeles groped for his reins with fingers that felt like numbed stumps. At last he caught the leather.

"Those things were Hierro's assassins?" Atreau turned back to where the remains lay on the ground. Animal flesh dissipated like mist rising off a lake. What had been a hulking mordwolf was now a battered and crushed human corpse. Flames licking up the wall of the warehouse illuminated the remains all too clearly now. Hierro's power over the man had been lost, along with his life.

Atreau looked sick.

"They're being driven against the Haldiim District. I have to stop them." Fedeles urged Firaj ahead and the warhorse responded at once. Fedeles clenched his rein, feeling stiff as a scarecrow. He pulled his shadow around himself and Firaj like a cloak.

"This is fucking maddness," Atreau groaned from behind him.

He didn't expect Atreau to follow him, but to his surprise, a moment later he heard the rhythm of Nube's hooves pounding the cobbles behind him.

"Clear the streets! Get inside!" Atreau bellowed out to the shadowed figures of beggars, streetwalkers and drunkards. The blazing warehouse cast a hot orange glow across their backs. Fire bells and shouts of alarm rang across the Weavers' Ward.

Oasia's cerulean spells lit up the street ahead of them as well as the pack of mordwolves racing toward the sacred grove.

People caught out on the open street sprinted for the cover of doorways and scurried up the steps of raised walkways. Shrieks filled the air when a few of the mordwolves peeled off from the pack to give chase.

Oasia's spells split, sending threads chasing the mordwolves and tangling around their legs and necks. The mordwolves fought, and Fedeles could feel Oasia struggling to keep her hold on every one of them. The cerulean light bathing Fedeles grew wan.

One couple of bystanders in canvas coats dashed from a doorway just as Fedeles charged past. Two mordwolves turned back after them. Fedeles crushed the nearest mordwolf beneath his shadow, though he felt as if he was hurling a lead weight. And he nearly toppled from his saddle when his shadow flew from him.

The second mordwolf veered clear of his reach.

"I've got him—you stop the rest," Atreau shouted, and he turned Nube after the animal. Fedeles didn't dare to look back after him. Instead he pressed all his desperation and guilt into closing the distance between himself and the pack.

He and Oasia killed nearly a dozen at the back of the pack. The rest took no notice. Their eyes rolled and foam spilled from their jaws. Hungry teal spells flickered up from their backs, ferocious power driving them on.

Fedeles felt the golden glow of the sacred grove radiating from the grassy knoll ahead of him. The mordwolves raced straight for the ancient circle of magnificent wisteria trees. Irsea's crows swooped down, raking the mordwolves with so much power that their hides caught fire. The burned as they charged ahead.

They raced straight at a figure standing at the top of the rise, among the trees. A young Haldiim woman. She didn't wear the clothes of a holy Bahiim, but spells at the roots of the trees lit and flickered around her feet like faint embers. Fedeles knew the spells: protect, defend, courage. The girl poured her strength into them as she hefted a small herb basket and a pair of shears like they were weapons. Untrained as she was, she'd stepped into the role of Bahiim for the sacred grove.

"Run!" Atreau's voice sounded from far behind Fedeles. "For fuck's sake. Run!"

The girl shook her head, though Fedeles could see terror in her face. Her arms trembled. Irsea's crows whirled around her. Then Fedeles caught sight of the other figures gathered in the sacred grove. Clusters of Haldiim men and women stood farther back among the trees. None were armed with more than garden knives, but they all stood their ground. A tall figure raced to the woman at the head of the group. His curling hair was unusually dark, and his handsome young features were quite familiar. Master Narsi, Fedeles realized in horror.

What was *he* doing here? What were any of them doing here? Were they preparing for their solstice celebrations, or was this a Haldiim holy night? Fedeles's couldn't help his frustrated thoughts, even as he recognized the perversity of them. The Haldiim people gathered in their own sacred grove were not to blame for the danger they now faced. He was.

The teal spells in the midst of the mordwolves converged into that gleeful child's form. It meant to ride this murderous pack into the very heart of the sacred grove. Any worshipers or aspiring guardians would be killed. And if Irsea couldn't drive the pack away, the grove's wards and ages of accumulated power would fall into Hierro's hands.

Irsea's crows dived, consuming the first dozen mordwolves in golden flames. But they were themselves seared to smoke by teal spells. That left less than six of the birds to drive back the remaining mordwolves. And the mordwolves were fanning out, to encircle the grove. Frantic horror lit Fedeles's chest.

What had he done?

Save them, Irsea's voice whispered to Fedeles. *If you can do nothing else . . . save my people.*

How? He was just a clumsy fool. What could he do?

Anything, he realized. Anything but watch the mordwolves he'd released take another life. Anything but feel so guilty and helpless, ever again in his life. Anything but allow himself to be used to hurt the very people he strove to protect. Fedeles felt as if he was choking on frustration and anger. He witnessed so many wrongs and was so utterly helpless—utterly worthless. He couldn't bear it. Couldn't go on like this.

Something inside Fedeles seemed to crack apart. The Old Rage—that seething curse that Donamillo had tortured him with in his youth—shattered through Fedeles's years of suppression and self-control. A glory of power and purpose rushed through him, like elation. Fury as sharp, gleaming and black as obsidian severed his horror and fear. It suffused his shadow and enfolded him and Firaj.

In a soaring leap, Firaj carried Fedeles into the thick of the mord-wolves. Together they crushed the creature they fell upon. Fedeles threw his arms wide, releasing no mere shadow but an immense banner of anni-hilation. The curse streamed out from him, tearing through everything it touched. Blood gushed from slashed throats. Steaming organs spilled from split bellies. Howls and screams sounded, but Fedeles hardly heard them. They were as distant as his insecurity and hesitance. He and Firaj resonat-ed with the curse's righteous purpose. They were vengeance; death and ruin to a corrupt and cruel world.

Cobblestones shattered and wildflowers blackened to ash. Earth crumbled. Golden flames of Bahiim wards burned at him, but Fedeles suffocated them beneath his shadow as he rode over them.

Then he felt that teal flickering presence give a laugh in delight.

And all at once he realized that in killing the mordwolves, he'd encir-cled the sacred grove in his darkness. Now he held Irsea's people in the midst of a murderous curse. Only the sacred grove's wards and Irsea's re-maining crows shielded them from his blind rage. Even as Fedeles fought to suppress the fury coursing through him, three more of Irsea's crows burned away.

Something hard struck Fedeles's back. He wheeled Firaj around, drawing the curse with him.

Atreau sat atop Nube, spattered in blood and gripping the shaft of a broken pike. He aimed the blunt end at Fedeles's chest.

"Stop this now!" Atreau shouted at him. "It's gone far enough. Get ahold of yourself."

All at once Fedeles's senses returned to him; the curse recoiled into his body and fell back into a mere shadow.

Cold exhaustion flooded him. Firaj shuddered.

What had he done?

He looked again to the sacred grove and felt relieved to see that the trees still stood. Though a trench of scorched gore now ringed the hillock below the wisteria. The girl up on the hill fled back into the trees, and two crows winged after her. Master Narsi remained staring down into the burnt, bloody trench. The mutilated bodies of dozens and dozens of men lay there. Narsi gripped his medical satchel but didn't move. He peered into the darkness with such an expression of horror that Fedeles felt sick with himself.

"We have to go. Before the city guards arrive to see you." Atreau threw the splintered pike to the ground. He nudged Nube to Firaj's side and then caught Fedeles's reins. The light of Oasia's wards drifted almost hesitantly to his side.

Fedeles felt like he might be sick or weep. Everything he'd feared of his own weakness had come true.

"I didn't mean to . . . I wanted to save them," he whispered.

"You can't save everyone, Fedeles." Atreau replied. "You'll only get us all killed if you keep trying."

Fedeles bowed his head into his hands and let Atreau lead Firaj away. He knew Atreau was right. If they stayed, then they would be discovered, and then both he and Atreau would face charges of witchcraft—at the very least. But leaving the sacred grove stripped down to a few faint wards and two plaintive crows, that felt so wrong. He'd done more harm to the sacred grove than either Hierro or the royal bishop had managed in years of assaults. He had to put things right.

Fedeles lifted his head and took in Atreau's exhausted figure.

He couldn't drag Atreau back to the sacred grove and risk his arrest.

He scrubbed at his scarred wrists, feeling old guilt and new.

Atreau looked to him, and despite the darkness of the night, he easily perceived Fedeles's thoughts, because he whispered, "We can't go back there."

"I know." Fedeles lifted his gaze to the dark sky. Clouds of smoke and shafts of moonlight created strange forms. Fedeles made out something like the immense wings of an eagle wheeling overhead. Then the wind changed and the clouds rolled into other forms. He thought suddenly of the afternoon he and Ariz had shared on Crown Hill, picking shapes out from the afternoon clouds.

And then he realized what he had to do, where he had to go. Not back but ahead. He caught up his own reins. There was no time to be lost.

 **CHAPTER THIRTEEN**

After Atreau left the Fat Goose, Narsi and Yara describing the upcoming Solstice Day Procession to Prince Jacinto, and he agreed to suspend rehearsals. He even voiced interest in joining them, which delighted Enevir Helio as much as it did Yara. When Sabella pointed out that the prince would likely still be staggering drunk from the Masquerade festivities the night before, Jacinto laughed.

"You can flop me over your shoulder, Sabs," Jacinto decided. "That would be in keeping with Haldiim traditions of women being in charge, anyway."

City bells rang and Narsi and Yara took their leave. At their backs, Procopio and a Yuanese musician struck up a bouncy lute duet for Jacinto's amusement. Striding through the theater district, Narsi hummed the melody to himself as a distraction from the anxiety he felt each time he glimpsed a royal bishop's guardsman on patrol.

He hadn't been aware of how very tense he'd become until they reached the Haldiim District and met Esfir and a group of her friends. Surrounded by Haldiim faces and voices, he relaxed into the crowd. The knots pinching the muscles between his shoulders seemed to melt. He breathed easily and gave himself over to following the crowd and listening to various discussions drift around him.

Though when the subject of Lord Vediya's writing came up, Narsi pounced into the conversation. He and a charming silversmith debated the beauty of passages describing Cadeleonian battle, while agreeing that Kiram Kir-Zaki's depiction as an unprecedented genius was quite astute. Narsi promised to lend the man his copy of Lord Vediya's second volume of memoirs after he returned to the Quemanor estate.

Yara laughed and teased him about his obvious crush on Lord Vediya, though not unkindly. Esfir patted his hand and quickly changed the subject to a book of botanical medicine she'd found.

"Several of the herbs mentions are ones I'm certain I've seen growing in the sacred grove," Esfir said. "I'd like to collect them, if you all wouldn't mind."

So, their party ambled to the Circle of Wisteria. As with the Circle of the Red Oak in Anacleto, the sacred grove was a popular summer picnic spot, especially for the young and unmarried. Because of this, food sellers set up their carts on the peripheral streets, hawking adhil bread, skewered lamb and lemons from Anacleto. In the midst of the Haldiim delights a few vendors also offered sweets made from cow's cream and crisp cheese-covered chips called casocres.

Yara proclaimed casocres "the best thing ever invented by the Cadeleonians."

The sun set and the moon rose.

After a pleasant meal the group of them climbed the rise of the sacred grove and entered the Circle of Wisteria. While Narsi and Esfir shared a lantern and hunted through the wildflowers and weeds for medicinal plants, Yara and the others chatted and sang. Here and there the group of them encountered homeless people—not all of them Haldiim—sheltering beneath the trees. A few engaged Yara or her friends in brief conversation, but mostly they left each other in peace.

Twice the young silversmith brought flowers to Narsi. Afterward he and two of the stagehands offered to put Narsi up for the night if he needed a place to stay. Yara sidled up to hand him a twig of redbells, then teased him about having to make rounds to climb in every bed on offer.

Narsi laughed. The lingering warmth of spiced wine allowed him to ignore the circumstances that deprived him of his own rooms and simply find all the attention flattering and funny.

An instant later the laughter died on his lips.

He forgot the bundles of fragrant herbs collected from the undergrowth, as well as after dinner discussions of literature and where he'd make his bed. Even the gnawing anxiety that he'd carried all day after being singled out by the royal bishop evaporated entirely from his awareness.

Wolves. Wolves in the middle of the city, standing impossibly tall—dwarfing mastiffs and even cart horses. Terror shot through his body. He stood as if rooted in place, clenching a fistful of widow's weed. His horror grew as the glow of the wards protecting the sacred grove further illuminated the dozens and dozens of huge wolves charging up the street straight for the Circle of Wisteria.

They flooded the road and walkways, like a river of bristling hides and gleaming teeth. They scraped against the walls of buildings and bounded over carts. Their speed, their snarls and the flashes of their eyes ignited a primal terror deep through Narsi's body. And the dank smell of them—so very many of them—it caught in his throat. The beasts seemed to grow as they charged nearer. Creatures from nightmares brought alive into his waking world.

All at once the paralyzing fear gripping Narsi shattered before the desperate impulse to escape. Run. Climb up into one of the trees. Anything to elude those jaws and teeth.

Then he heard the alarmed cries from people hiding among the trees behind him. A woman sobbed and the baby in her arms wailed. Haldiim voices shouted out prayers and entreaties, while a drunken Cadeleonian vagrant howled for the mercy of his savior.

The wolves reached the foot of the grove and spread out, encircling the hillock, the way they might surround a wounded deer. Narsi realized that there was nowhere to run, not for him or anyone gathered in the sacred grove. They had to fight. As if she too came to the same realization, Esfir gripped her belt knife and started forward. Yara leaned into the trunk of a tree, whispering prayers into the glowing gold symbols that slowly illuminated the branches and ground below.

Narsi drew his own belt knife and raced to Esfir's side. His legs shook and his heart pounded.

The shining wards rising from the surrounding trees only seemed to draw the wolves closer, faster. Narsi almost wished that he couldn't see the animals so clearly. Their eyes flashed like mirrors and foam dribbled from their gaping mouths.

One massive silvery wolf broke from the pack and charged straight at Narsi. A flock of crows burst from the wisteria branches as the wolf bounded up the hillock. Narsi lashed out at it with his pitiful knife, barely scraping the side of the animal's wet nose.

A crow's wing whipped past Narsi's cheek and the bird hurtled into the charging wolf. Golden flames engulfed them both. Narsi staggered back as heat and smoke rolled over him. More crows launched themselves. A second wolf burned and fell, then a third and a forth.

Esfir lifted her voice and joined Yara's prayers, calling on the ancient trees and the spirits of their ancestors to protect them and the grove. Even a drunk Cadeleonian vagrant shouted, "You shining trees, save me! I swear I'll convert. I'll forswear dice and loose madams." He went on making garbled promises.

"We can win this," Yara stated. "I know we can."

Narsi nodded. But even at a glance he saw that the crows numbered far fewer than the wolves. Perhaps a dozen crows to battle a sea of immense wolves. They rushed up the hillock from all sides now, advancing like a relentless army.

Then a black rider seemed to materialize from the fabric of the night sky. He soared over the street, and an immense banner of hissing, writhing shadows followed him. The wolves turned, snarling and baring huge fangs. Then they and the rider were swallowed, as the glinting shadows crashed down upon them. Gleaming black waves rippled and crested around the hillside of the sacred grove. Where the shadows touched them, stones and earth sheared aside. Furious voices hissed and swore at Narsi from within the roiling shadows, and sudden stabbing pain rolled off it like heat radiating from an oven.

Yara gasped and doubled over, clutching her stomach. Narsi staggered to her, tried to grasp his medical satchel from where it hung across his back. Agony punched through his chest. His legs buckled. He fought to draw in his breath; every inhalation felt like a knife blade plunging into his lungs. He lurched, grasping the trunk of a tree and clinging to it for support. A foot from him, Esfir moaned but continued to pray. Some one behind them sobbed.

In the shadows below them, the wolves' growls turn to screams, whimpers and then silence. Tears blurred Narsi's vision as he watched the sea of shadows crest over the hilltop and continue rising overhead. It blotted out the silhouettes of surrounding buildings. The branches of the wisteria trees threw out golden blessings. But the shadows engulfed them like tar enveloping crumbs. Stars disappeared behind the darkness. The moon was lost. All Narsi saw were flickers of oily iridescence churning within blackness. All he felt was agony.

It meant to devour them all, Narsi thought. He had to do something, but he could hardly move for the pain stabbing through his body. Frustration ignited inside him. He refused to die like this—bowed down and cowering. Narsi gripped the tree trunk and forced himself onto his feet. He glared into the oncoming darkness.

Then the wall of shadows collapsed. Night sky and radiant stars filled Narsi's view.

Then the thick odor of fresh-spilled blood washed over him. On the ground below the sacred grove, tangled, mutilated bodies encircled the hillock in a moat of gore. Narsi stared at the terrible forms as his mind slowly identified one after another. Even through the darkness he recognized the shapes of limbs. Heads. A shoulder. A torso and hip. Bodies. Scattered remains, but none of them belonged to animals. They were all human.

The silhouette of a mounted man rose from the chaos of corpses. Narsi recognized him as well. The Duke of Rauma, Fedeles Quemanor, mounted on a black warhorse. Lord Vediya rode from behind him, bellowing at him to stop, his face ashen.

Narsi stared at the duke's profile, slowly absorbing the grace of his bearing alongside the absolute horror of what he'd wrought. Narsi recalled how that wall of murderous shadow had threatened him once before. Then, just as now, Lord Vediya had intervened to bring the duke to his senses.

Narsi shivered, despite the warmth of the summer evening.

This was all somehow disturbingly familiar. Monstrous wolves—mordwolves—waging a battle against an almost inhumanly powerful witch while hapless people all around were caught up in helpless terror. Enthralled beasts returning to their human forms when death released them from the spells holding them captive. Even the weird red light blazing from across the city. This could have been a scene he'd happily described from Lord Vediya's memoirs only hours ago.

Nothing about the books struck him as amusing or abstract now.

Narsi gazed down at Lord Vediya. But if the man noticed him, he gave no sign of it. Instead, he caught up the duke's reins and led him quickly away.

Somewhere across the city, fire bells clanged wild discordant notes. Narsi wondered if that could have anything to do with the massacre below him. He peered after Lord Vediya and the duke but could no longer distinguish them from the night. The clatter of their horses' hooves already sounded distant. It was hard to imagine that they'd ever even been here.

Except for the dead men and the moat of blood they'd left behind.

How like Cadeleonian nobles to engage in some fantastic battle, then leave the remains and wreckage for others to clean up, Narsi thought in a daze. *Someday someone ought to write an epic poem about the efforts of that.*

The he caught sight of something moving down below him. He couldn't be certain, but he thought something—someone—down in that heap of gore shifted. Could there be a survivor?

"I need light," Narsi called. He gripped his medical satchel and clambered down the now battered and ragged incline of the hill. His boots slipped through blood-soaked mud and he grasped a stone to balance himself. The surface felt hot and smooth, like steel just lifted from a grindstone.

Yara followed him down, carrying a lamp. Esfir climbed behind her, as did a young Haldiim man. Narsi recollected that the man was an aspiring author, but he wasn't certain of his name; that light, jovial dinner they'd all shared seemed days past. The man froze in his steps as Yara's lamp illuminated the bisected carcass of a Mirogoth youth. The author dashed back up the hill. Narsi heard him vomiting.

"We may be on our own for a little time yet," Esfir commented.

Narsi dragged the Mirogoth's remains aside. Another body—or the majority of a body—lay beneath. A gasping moan rose from below. Someone lay buried beneath the weight of the dead.

"I'll need help to reach them." Narsi caught hold of a section of someone's back. A rib jutted from a gaping wound and scraped against his palm. Narsi heaved the deadweight. His fingers slipped through sweat, blood and exposed organs. Then he found a grip and heaved. Esfir found purchase on a leg and dragged off a quarter of some man's corpse. Another body lay under that. The two of them hauled it aside, while Yara lifted the lamp high for them. They rolled another half of a body aside.

Suddenly exposed, a battered, gasping wolf snarled at them. Narsi and Esfir both leapt back, tripping on limbs. Yara screamed and jumped.

Her lamp slipped from her grip and tumbled into a crevice of twisted legs. Its flame cast long shadows across the wolf's exposed head. The beast gasped and thrashed its head, but couldn't fight free of the bodies still pinning it down. A sickly choking sound escaped its gaping jaws as it struggled to draw breath.

Narsi scrambled to his feet, then caught Esfir's hand and pulled her up. Yara snatched the lamp up before its oil spilled. She lifted it high again, illuminating the figure before them.

As they looked on, the wolf's visage began to melt away like burning wax. Huge paws revealed thin fingers and trembling hands. The long muzzle of jagged teeth evaporated, leaving an emaciated, pallid man struggling for breath. Narsi dropped to the man's side. His hands shook with fear, but he felt for the man's pulse. The weakest kick met his fingertips.

As the Cadeleonian man's life faded, his gaunt features grew more distinct. He was dark haired and surprisingly small, hardly larger than a boy, but his face bore the wrinkles and lines of a man in his forties. The burn scar of a fresh brand stood out a bright red against the deathly pallor of his bare chest.

Tears tracked through the blood and dirt on the man's face.

"She safe? My sister?" he whispered, but nothing more escaped him. His half-lidded stare became fixed and dull. The red brand on his chest faded to a faint impression.

Narsi suddenly remembered the enthralled physician-priest he'd watched slit his own throat this morning. He thought of Master Ariz's desolate gaze. Dommian's desperate writing and violent death. Heartsickness and frustration flooded him. These wolves had all been enthralled men rampaging at the behest of Hierro Fueres. That's why the duke and Lord Vediya had slaughtered them.

What kind of monster did this to their fellow human beings? What kind of person seized lives and destroyed them like they were playthings—like they were nothing? No one should be allowed to do that.

"Is he dead?" Yara asked quietly.

He was. The fact that he'd been released from the slavering form of a wolf proved as much.

"Yes," Narsi said.

Only death will break the brand, Dommian had written.

Since then, both Father Timoteo and Master Ariz had told him the same. Narsi saw it for himself now. But he didn't want to accept it. Freedom shouldn't come at so terrible of a cost, not for anyone.

After everything he'd seen and endured today, he couldn't allow the sadist who'd destroyed so many lives to win. He hadn't saved the physician-priest or King Juleo this morning, but he was damn well going to fight to save this man. He refused to simply give up.

He wrenched the immense weight of another corpse off the small man. His leg looked broken and superficial gashes marred his flanks, but Narsi found no mortal wound. Perhaps his heart had failed in the grip of that murderous shadow? Narsi set his hands down against the man's sternum and began to compress his rib cage and heart.

"What are you doing?" Yara demanded.

"Waking a sleeping heart." He continued compressing the man's cool chest in a steady rhythm. "It's a Yuanese technique that one of my mentors taught."

Even at the time, the physician had warned that the technique was a last resort and failed more often than it succeeded. But when the man was already dead, what greater failure could there be?

"Are you sure that's a good idea?" Esfir crouched down beside them.

"I have to try." Narsi kept pumping, willing the man's heart to remember this living rhythm and rouse. "Do you remember the enthralled people from Lord Vediya's memoirs? Witches transformed them and forced them into battle. These men are the same. Look at them all. There are brands on all their bodies, symbols of the thrall that held them captive. They didn't choose to become monsters and attack the sacred grove. They were forced."

Yara lifted the lamp. She and Esfir gazed over the bloody ruin of dead men. Then Esfir reached out and used the tattered edge of a shirt to wipe gore from the chest of a decapitated corpse.

"Is that the Brand of Obedience?" Esfir asked in a whisper.

Narsi nodded and Yara shot him a questioning look.

"Mother mentioned it to us last time she visited." Esfir said quietly. "It's a spell that makes slaves of people. It was borne by an assassin in the Duke of Rauma's household. She said that you tried to save that man as well."

That would have been Dommian. He supposed he shouldn't have been surprised that Querra had worked out much of the man's history. She was clever and paid attention to the people around her.

"He wasn't a willing assassin." Sweat began to bead Narsi's back as he continued to compress the man's cold chest. He fought a mounting agitation, resisting the urge to push too hard, too fast. "None of these people chose to be transformed into monstrosities. They are victims."

"But what if . . ." Esfir trailed off as she studied the man's slack face. Narsi understood her fear—if he was wrong about the thrall being broken, then he was reviving a murderous beast, not a man.

"I suppose it's a chance we must take," Esfir said. Like himself, Esfir had sworn an oath to safeguard the well-being of all people. She shoved a loose plait of her pale hair back from her face. "We need help. I'll have Mouruhd fetch physicians from the Panajha Hospital dormitory. Then, Yara, would you help me search for other survivors?"

Narsi stole a glance to Yara. She looked queasy and grim but nodded. She left her lamp balanced on a cracked stone and then hurried up the hill with Esfir, as if she truly was one of the heroines she played on stage.

Narsi heard the two of them calling out directives to their companions and relations. Then he returned his focus to the body lying beneath his hands. The man looked underfed and worn down. Whether he'd made his living by honest work or as a cutthroat or a con man, Narsi couldn't possibly know. But his last word, his last concern, had been for a sister.

"Come on," Narsi murmured to him, or perhaps to his spirit. "Reclaim your life. Come back for your sister. Come back and reclaim your life, your freedom. You can do this." Narsi spoke more encouragements in an almost mindless stream of words, all while he kept working, willing the man to take a breath, to fight for his life. He didn't know how much time passed.

He heard crow's wings flutter through the darkness. A bird alit directly in front of him, on the man's head. Lamplight caught the black gloss of the crow's feathers. The glinting iridescence reminded him of that darkness he'd witnessed unfurling from the duke's figure. The bird's yellow eyes flickered over Narsi, then it angled its gaze down at his patient's half-lidded, unblinking eyes.

Even the crows that Bahiim kept were infamous for picking out the eyes of the dead. Horror rose through Narsi. He didn't think he'd be able to keep himself from lashing out if the bird began to scavenge the corpse.

But all would be lost if he halted his compressions.

"Don't you dare!" Narsi shouted at the bird. "Leave him! Go!"

The crow shifted its head and seemed to consider Narsi. The angle of the lamplight lent a curved shadow to the bird's beak, making it appear to smirk at his attempt to scare it away. Then, to his relief, the crow spread its wings and leapt into the air. As it rose, the faintest sparks of gold light drifted down to the dead man and Narsi both. Warmth spread across Narsi's hand where one of the sparks landed. Then it died away. Narsi continued to work, but he stole a glance after the crow.

It soared over Yara and Esfir as they dragged a lanky boy from out from beneath a heap of butchered remains. The boy's mouth looked blue even in the yellow lamplight. Likely he'd suffocated beneath the mass of other bodies. The boy's limbs appeared to slump from a tight animal posture as Narsi watched. Paws unfolded into hands and feet.

"We have another!" Esfir shouted, and at once an older Haldiim woman in a gray physician's coat pelted to her. She beckoned and two young students raced behind her with their medical satchels. Past them, Narsi spied other shadowed figures. Most searched among the dead, but three physicians appeared to be working, just as Narsi did, to revive dead men. From behind him he could just pick out the voices of several women discussing in Haldiim how they would shelter any survivors, if there were any.

How long had he been working over this one man's body?

"What about the royal bishop's guardsmen?" a girl asked.

"Occupied by a fire in the Weavers' Ward. With any luck it will keep them busy for a little time yet," a woman answered, then she spoke more softly. "There won't be many survivors here. We'll be done and gone before the next bell."

Narsi looked up to the sky and for the first time realized that it wasn't just lamplight or the glow of distant burning buildings that lent an orange glow to his surroundings.

The trees of the sacred grove blazed with such intensity that they appeared to burn away the clouds of smoke rolling over the stars. Beneath them Narsi glimpsed a figure outlined by the light, and he could have sworn it was Lord Vediya.

But that was impossible, and yet Narsi felt certain he heard him ask, "What have you done?"

What answer Lord Vediya received, Narsi didn't hear over calls of crows. Dozens of them now circled the sacred grove. When Narsi looked back, the figure was gone. Several birds dropped down to feed on unguarded remains, but here and there Narsi sighted a few more of those faint golden blessings raining down from passing wings. Whether they were lending strength to would-be rescuers or simply blessing the souls of the dead, Narsi didn't know.

He muttered his thanks for the warmth that eased the ache of his fingers. Then he returned his attention to his compressions and the cold body beneath his hands. It felt like he'd been at this for hours. His back ached and the scent of blood filled his mouth with a rank taste.

"No, those two are past hope," a physician instructed from somewhere across the sacred grove.

Ahead of Narsi, the older woman kneeling beside the lanky boy shook her head and Esfir looked like she might weep. Yara hung her head. But the student compressing the boy's chest refused to stop her work. For an instant she glanced to Narsi, and he recognized the ferocious determination in her expression. He felt the same drive.

And yet he knew that neither resolve nor willpower could sway the reality of death. If they couldn't rouse the men they worked over, then at some point their efforts amounted to wasted strength that should be used to tend the living.

Not to mention the need to evacuate before the royal bishop's guardsmen arrived. At some point, they would have to give up.

Just not yet.

Not yet.

Then Narsi felt the kick of a heartbeat hammer back against his palm. He nearly missed the weak pulse, almost went on pumping the man's chest. But then as he drew back to prepare for another compression he felt the man's ribs rise under his fingers. He heard the intake of a shaky breath. Narsi sat, stunned between hope and disbelief. A faint, living heat kindled up from the man's chest, spreading across Narsi's palms. The man drew in a deeper breath and then another.

"He's revived!" Narsi shouted.

"Here too!" the medical student called. An instant later a third man revived. Such exhilaration filled Narsi that he threw his hands in the air and shouted a cheer. They'd won in the face of death.

After that, three medical students hurried to Narsi's side. The young women congratulated him as they carefully lifted Narsi's revived patient onto a canvas litter. The man moaned as they shifted his broken leg.

Then he blinked up at Narsi.

"My sister . . ."

"If she's here, we'll find her," Narsi assured him, though so far they hadn't discovered any women among the enthralled dead. "Can you tell me your name?"

"Riquo . . . you find her." The man's eyes fluttered and then fell back closed. The medical students lifted his litter and Riquo again jolted awake. Panic filled his face as he stared around himself. "Where... you taking me?"

"To Panajha Hospital," Narsi assured him. "Your leg needs to be set and your wounds will be cleaned. We'll talk after you've rested—" Narsi cut himself off when he realized that the spindly man had again lapsed into unconsciousness. He let the students take Riquo away and turned his remaining energy to saving other lives.

However, the next hour tempered some of Narsi's triumph. Of the thirty or more men who'd been enthralled and then cut down, only those first three revived. There were no other bodies whole enough to even attempt to bring back. Once the three survivors had been moved to Panajha Hospital, there was little for any of the physicians or their students to do. Narsi gathered up the herbs he'd collected—though his hands were so bloody that he had to wipe them on the wild grasses to get them clean enough that he wouldn't spoil the herbs by touching them.

When he descended the hill, he found Yara, Esfir as well as the physicians and their students all gathered on the road. They all looked terrible. Hands, clothes, faces and hair spattered with blood, their expressions strained. The oldest of the physicians leaned on a cane. Her students ringed her.

The Cadeleonians who had taken shelter in the sacred grove were nowhere to be seen. Taking in the surroundings, Narsi couldn't fault them for fleeing. The smell alone was sickening. Flies and other insects gathered in swarms. It was a charnel house of dismembered men—nearly all of them Cadeleonian—laid out at the foot of the Circle of Wisteria. The scene could have been lifted directly from any number of bigoted Cadeleonian stories of Haldiim curses, sorcery and sacrifices.

"The royal bishop and his guardsmen will blame us for this," the elderly physician remarked. One young medical student standing at her side appeared surprised by the thought. But no one else showed any doubt. The Haldiim population was already blamed for conspiring with Labarans and poisoning holy men. Who knew what horrors might be attributed to them now that so many mutilated corpses ringed the sacred grove.

The author—Narsi still couldn't recall his name—suggested that they bury the bodies to hide them from the royal bishop's guardsmen.

"It would take days to dig a grave deep enough that every cur on the street wouldn't come dig up hands and feet." Yara stared at the mounds of bodies with a grim expression. "It will be worse for us if we try to hide this."

"There's no time, in any case." Esfir pointed, and as a group they all turned to see a Haldiim boy in a courier's uniform come pelting up the road. He ran so hard that he nearly careened into Esfir.

"The fire's nearly quenched, but word's spreading—" The boy paused midsentence, gasping. He bent over and drew in several deep breaths, then went on quickly. "They're saying the wolves and the fire are our doing. A Bahiim curse or a Labaran spell! Captain Yago's been sent for, and a battalion of the royal bishop's guardsmen are on their way here."

"We'd best go. Though we must take care not to lead them directly to the hospital," the elderly physician pronounced. She turned her attention to Narsi. "I don't recall your mother's name, young man. Is there someone looking after you?"

"He's called Narsi Lif-Tahm, he's staying with my aunt and me," Esfir supplied. "But are you certain that we shouldn't remain here to guard the sacred grove?"

"The holy grove exists to protect the Haldiim people, not the other way around," Yara replied. She took Esfir's arm in hers. "And I can assure you that standing in direct opposition to Cadeleonian soldiers will only stoke their violence. It's wiser to present them with nothing to fight, no one to kill. Let them wear themselves out beating at tree trunks and dirt. The roots down deep and the crows on high will be laughing. Isn't that so, Narsi?"

"Absolutely," he agreed. Honestly, he might have agreed with anything if it meant that all of them could leave this place immediately.

Though to his surprise, they didn't make directly for the Haldiim District. Instead they flitted between shadows and edged along walls, working their way to the Shell Fountain. There, they took turns keeping watch for the royal bishop's guardsmen as each of them rinsed the blood from their hands, faces, feet and shoes.

"Wet tracks will be hard to see in the dark and will dry quickly enough," the elderly physician explained. "But bloody ones linger. They could lead Captain Yago right after us."

Narsi scrubbed his boots as well as his hands and face. The entire time he felt certain that he could hear hoofbeats drumming through the cobblestones of the street. Then a door across from the Shell Fountain swung open and light poured out. Narsi flattened himself into the spray of the fountain. Ahead of him a big Cadeleonian man staggered out from the doorway. He swayed on his feet and crooned a drunken melody about the moon. Then he pissed into the gutter, turned back inside and slammed his door closed behind him. The instant he was gone, Narsi raced back to join Esfir and Yara as well as the would-be author, a stagehand and the courier boy against the brick wall of a print shop.

Despite the balmy summer evening, Narsi was still shivering. He thought he could hear Yara's teeth chattering. Finally, the last of the medical students had washed. They agreed to take slightly different routes away from the fountain into the Haldiim District.

Alone on the streets and dripping wet, Narsi shuddered and started at every noise. For nearly half an hour he crouched beside a broken cart after guardsmen rode past him shouting murder. They raced from the sacred grove to the nearest church barrack. When at last the street seemed quiet, he sprinted to the cover of a tavern. There the crowds of stumbling costumed drunks disguised his height. And when he vomited in the gutter, he hardly stood out.

Narsi closed his eyes, willing himself away from the horror he'd witnessed and the terror that smoldered in his guts like an ember.

Fear is the threshold we must cross every time we find our courage. He tried to remind himself. But it didn't feel like a mere threshold now. No, this day had been like walking into an entire palace of terror. But what could he do about it?

Flee? Leave people he cared about to face all this? Near him an inebriated Cadeleonian wearing a dog mask called a cheer for the new king's health and others took up the cry. Someone inside the tavern began singing a lewd song about the royal bishop. Things were going to change, he had to believe that.

Narsi got back up to his feet. If fear was a threshold, then he had to cross it—had to keep crossing it, because retreating wouldn't alter anything. The things that scared him would still be there.

"No going back," Narsi whispered to himself. "Keep pushing ahead."

He sprinted to the alley behind the Kir-Naham pharmacy and scaled the garden wall so that no one would see him enter from the street. His relief when Esfir and Yara welcomed him inside nearly overwhelmed him. For a startled moment he found Esfir leaning against his shoulder and weeping as she tried to express some of her shock. Yara joined him in hugging her. Yara didn't look much better. All three of them jumped like startled cats when Querra came through the door.

Narsi calmed considerably when he learned that she'd brought fresh clothes and other necessities for him at Lord Vediya's request.

"Did he send a note for me or any message?" Narsi attempted to sound unconcerned as he hunched beside the kitchen fire, drying his hair.

The smile Querra turned on him was both knowing and pitying. "Only that I should wish you a good night and sweet dreams."

CHAPTER
FOURTEEN

Ariz rolled his shoulders forward and soared over the burning city. His wings sliced the night air as if sweeping long strokes through dark water. Sweltering plumes of woodsmoke climbed after him. Ariz skimmed the hot, rising currents, soaring so effortlessly he nearly floated. When the

smoke disturbed the animal body enfolding him, he instinctively flicked a
wing tip and banked away from the choking clouds.

To his dark-adapted eyes, the city streets below blazed with torches and lamplight. Flames leapt across rooftops. Shouts and alarm bells
sounded. Guardsmen poured from barracks like ants streaming from
their hill. They meant nothing to the brand smoldering in his chest or
the molten hunting instinct coursing through his blood.

But then he felt a spark of recognition. His attention fixed on a small,
dark form, and for the first time he acknowledged the strangeness of the
scene beneath him. Warehouses burned in the Weavers' Ward, while a
jet-black rider pursued a pack of wolves through the city. The animals
were so large and so numerous that they filled the street like a living
river. The wolves and rider raced toward the growing golden glow that
emanated from the trees of the Haldiim sacred grove.

From this height, the rider and his mount appeared as little more
than slivers of darkness in a vast expanse of the city. But Ariz felt Fedeles's presence radiating from that distant form, like a sweet, soothing
note calling him.

His indifference to the drama beneath him waned.

Ariz banked again, turning from the direction of the Slate House and
swinging into the glow of the sacred grove. He heard crows calling in
clear, sharp voices. Wolves turned on Fedeles. Heedless, Fedeles charged
into the midst of bared teeth and snapping jaws. One wolf sprang up and
Fedeles threw his arms wide. A swath of darkness enveloped them all
and swirled around the sacred grove like a cyclone.

Ariz skirted the edge of the whirling dark turbulence. It buffeted his
wingtips. Flashes of opalescent color shot through the black walls, like
tongues of lightning. Despite the violence within, Ariz felt no fear, and
when the dark masses clipped his side, he sensed only the force of Fedeles's
determination. But others down on the ground screamed in agony. Ariz
dipped low enough to pick out individual voices cutting through the clam-
or of fire bells and animal shrieks. He barely recognized Atreau. The man
looked ghastly and harrowed in the wan light as golden blessings burst to
life around him. He gripped the shaft of a broken pike with one hand and
his reins with the other. His mount shied from the whirling shadows and
tossed its head in terror as Atreau forced the stallion after Fedeles.

"There are people in the grove!" Atreau roared. "You have to stop
this now!" He hefted his pike.

All at once Ariz realized that he aimed it at Fedeles's back.

Rage surged through Ariz. He dived, extending his huge talons for a
killing strike.

Atreau smashed the pike into a crouching wolf, then spun the blunt end up to bat Fedeles's shoulder. The wood splintered, and black shadows rose over Atreau.

"Stop this now!" Atreau shouted. "It's gone far enough. Get ahold of yourself."

And all at once the walls of glittering darkness fell away, leaving Fedeles and his warhorse standing amidst a mass of carnage. Atreau clutched his reins and stared intently at Fedeles.

Ariz twisted in midair, hurling his body aside. His massive talons raked the air above Atreau's head and the pulse of his wings whipped through the man's dark hair, but neither Atreau nor Fedeles noticed his retreat back up into the darkness above them.

The two of them stared at each other. They appeared frozen at the precipice of battle. Both seemed as intent and fierce as the statues that filled the Shard of Heaven. Then the fury in Fedeles's expression dissolved to sorrow, and relief replaced Atreau's horrified alarm.

"You have to get away from here before the royal guardsmen can recognize you." Atreau said more, but Ariz only perceived the fact that neither of them needed him here with them. Certainly not as the creature he'd become.

Ariz's wings hurled the night air aside as he launched himself up the cool heights of the sky. Here, he could reclaim the sense of singular purpose that flooded his eagle's body. The sky, his flight, his hunt—it was all one. All an extension of his being.

But even as he rose, his attention splintered. He continued to observe the scene beneath him. Atreau caught Fedeles's slack reins, while Fedeles hunched in his saddle. He allowed Atreau to lead him away from the multitude of corpses that littered the sacred grove. A shudder of uneasy emotion moved through Ariz as he noticed that the dead men had reclaimed their natural bodies. Death had released them from the thrall that enslaved them.

Fedeles looked as stricken and sick as he had when he'd received news of Captain Ciceron's murder. A part of Ariz longed to go to him and reassure him that anyone living under Hierro's control would welcome the release of a quick death. But he doubted that any words he could offer would be as comforting or potent as the assurances Atreau voiced.

The brand in Ariz's chest smoldered and the Slate House seemed to beckon him across the distance. But he continued to soar over Fedeles and Atreau. They rode past the Shell Fountain and then into the Theater District. There, despite the late hour and the fire bells, people still wandered the streets. Men and women in leather, fur and feathered costumes clustered outside taverns, and the noise of raucous music rose from opera houses along with plumes of woodsmoke.

Moments after Fedeles passed them, three mounted figures broke away from the shadows of a gaming house. When Atreau and Fedeles turned up a lane, the men did as well. When the three passed under the torches illuminating the doors of a gaming hall, Ariz took in the details of their clothes. Royal bishop's guardsmen.

Pain kindled in his chest, but Ariz ignored it. He turned and swooped after Fedeles and Atreau. Gliding between buildings, he observed the three guardsmen. In the darkness they took no note of his shadow hanging over them. However, bats veered out of his way and feral dogs fled. The three guardsmen rode hard, closing in on Fedeles and Atreau. As they approached the Gado Bridge, one of the guardsmen drew his sword and urged his mount into a charge. Ariz folded his wings and plunged down.

He struck the nape of the guardsman's neck with brutal force, feeling the man's bones crack. His talons sliced through leather and flesh like saber blades. As Ariz kicked off, he tore the guardsman's head away. The horse stumbled, then fled as the guardsman's body fell to the cobblestones.

Ariz wheeled in the air.

He took the second guardsman straight on, plowing his claws into the man's chest and throwing him from his mount. Armor cracked, flesh tore like steaming fresh bread. Ribs shattered. His claws sank in deep. Then Ariz bounded into the air, wrenching away meat and bones as he laid the man open.

The third guardsman recognized that Ariz's attack came from above, but in the dark, he could do little more than clip one of Ariz's feathers before Ariz toppled him from his mount. He struck the cobblestones and flopped like a wad of rags. His horse fled and the guardsman limped to his feet and then backed to the wall of a tavern. The faint noise of people laughing rolled from the thick brick wall. Wan lamplight lit the guardsman's bloodied face and shredded jerkin. He gripped his sword, but his eyes were wide and terrified. Ariz circled him, taking in his injured leg and shaking hands.

A hot, predatory exaltation flooded Ariz's chest with unfamiliar pride. He could kill this cowering rabbit of a man in any way he liked. He could be done with him in seconds or play him out for hours. Take his head, gut him. Tear him apart slowly, by nips and strips.

Then Ariz caught himself. What was he thinking?

Fedeles and Atreau were both well away by now, likely already across the Gado Bridge. This unhorsed, injured guardsman no longer presented a threat to them. He could hardly stand. Killing him was unnecessary and cruel.

Taking his life just to feel the easy power of murder—that was something Hierro would do.

The mere idea would have disgusted Fedeles. Less than an hour ago it would have repulsed Ariz too. But now he fought to reclaim the empathy that so often burdened him. His wings beat the night air into a whirlwind as he curbed the instinct of a deadly strike and hovered before the man. Ariz forced himself to look at the man's face and remember the feelings of desperation and fear that he saw there. He noted the humble charm pinned to the guardsman's collar. This man was loved, likely by a family as well as the sweetheart who had embroidered that ribbon. If Ariz killed this man, then so many more lives would be filled with grief. Mourning consuming bright hopes and happiness.

"I . . . choose mercy," Ariz declared. The words sounded strange and sharp even to him. The guardsman gaped at him and continued to stare as Ariz launched himself into the air, seeking out the cold, high currents. The turmoil in him quieted to the instinct of flight. He hovered as winds rolled under his wings.

He felt the smolder of Hierro's brand and the animal anticipation for the fight to come at the Slate House.

"Leave no man there alive." Clara had given him Hierro's order in a clear, even tone. There was no question that it would be a massacre. But the thought hadn't disturbed Ariz as it should have. Only slowly did it penetrate his transformed being.

When it did, Ariz was again alarmed by his own indifference. For more than a decade he'd resisted and struggled against Hierro's thrall. He'd suffered agony for his defiance, but only now did he realize how repulsive it was to be at ease in compliance. His anguish and even his self-loathing were assurances the he still held a shred of humanity. He could still feel guilt and reproach. He knew with absolute certainty what actions arose from his own will and which were born of Hierro's cruelty. For all the years he'd hated his suffering and sleepless nights, he now realized that the torment had been an assurance of the divide between himself and Hierro.

Had Clara known this when she'd given him Trueno's relic? Was this the respite she'd intended to preserve his strength and secure him nights of restful sleep?

A frustrated cry escaped him and he wheeled in the air, refusing to fly straight for the Slate House.

He couldn't allow the animal body he inhabited to smother his compassion. No matter how relieving and easy it felt, he must not embrace that comfort. Not at the cost of his soul. He needed to concentrate on those things that kept him whole and human. Something beyond the exhaustion of hurt and self-hate. Something to give him strength and hope.

From his great height he again caught sight of Fedeles and Atreau. They rode through the wide streets on the north side of the city. Fedeles had taken up his own reins and Atreau appeared to be following him now. Ariz trailed them from above. Breezes fluttered through the long feathers of his wingtips. Ariz angled into a gust and let it carry him over the sprawling Quemanor household. He circled as Fedeles rode through the gates and Atreau came up behind him.

Ariz expected them both to disappear into the stable, and Atreau turned his mount in that direction, but then stopped. Fedeles shook his head, then lit across the grounds, riding westward. Atreau shouted after him. Then he snatched a lamp from a groom and gave chase. Ariz flew above them, taking in the fields and oak trees. He realized what destination drew Fedeles: Crown Hill.

A longing like homesickness filled Ariz. He too yearned to return to the haven where they'd first held one another. He'd felt like his own man there, at least for a short time.

He overtook Fedeles, sweeping over the narrow trail and searching the dark of the wilderness for any threat. A family of foxes prowled near the stream and an owl watched Ariz with wide yellow eyes. But no would-be assassin awaited under the willow or beneath the oaks.

Ariz swooped up in a sharp arc, rising above the scattered ruins and littered grounds on the hill. Rabbits flushed from the cover of flowering brush. Ariz glided down, dropping to the hard earth near a stand of saplings. This body did not feel at ease crouched on the ground. It craved the security of heights. Ariz folded his wings and preened at several of his feathers as anxiety jittered through him.

He heard the sound of horses approaching. The faint glow of a distant lamp lit the wild grasses and brambles growing on the edge of the hill. A grouse startled into the sky.

What would Fedeles make of him? Ariz suddenly wondered. Could he even recognize him like this? If only he could reclaim his true body. He thought of that moment when he'd managed words. It hadn't been the idea of fighting the flesh imprisoning him that had allowed him that small triumph; it had been his concentration on his own capacity for caring, for kindness.

He thought again of the afternoon he spent on this hill with Fedeles. He remembered the joy of dancing with Fedeles. He lifted his arms, spreading huge wings and battering wildflowers. Awkwardly, Ariz stepped into the first position of a quaressa. His massive talons raked the ground. No doubt he presented a ludicrous sight.

He closed his eyes and concentrated, stepping and swirling around. Memories of music and joyous motion filled his mind. How he loved to dance. Even as a small child he'd adored the grace of the motions. The flow of one step into another as melodies and rhythms filled the air. He recalled standing on his uncle's feet and later partnering his sister as they both giggled through their lessons. Passing that experience on to his nieces and Sparanzo filled him with joy. No doubt all three children would have laughed seeing him scratch and flap around now. The idea of clowning for them inspired a rough laugh. Ariz felt the strange sensation of something like a smile curving at the corners of his mouth.

He performed another turn and thought of Fedeles. A different pleasure kindled in him. Holding a partner and being held. The two of them united, and sharing their strength like communion. The heat sparking between their bodies.

Ariz leapt and in midair his legs extended into their natural form. His feet glided into the next step as he landed. The small kick came easily now, as did a simple heel turn. It was an improvisation that Fedeles had seemed to enjoy, he remembered.

Ariz extended his right arm and felt his fingers push out past a fringe of silky feathers. He lifted his left hand and it too slid from the confines of wings. He spun twice more and then touched his face. His calloused fingers rubbed over skin and stubble. He poked his nose and then ran a hand through his short hair. Feeling that stubborn cowlick of hair at the back of his head came as a relief.

His clothes were damp and reeked of a mews. The blood that spattered them was not his own. He resisted the urge to pull off his jerkin and hide the evidence of his violence from Fedeles. He would only do Fedeles a disservice by disguising the real danger he represented. Even so, he stepped back as the light of a lamp crested the hill, outlining two mounted figures.

Fedeles swung down from Firaj, pausing a moment to stroke the warhorse's jaw. Then he strode toward the ruins of the ancient temple.

Behind him, Atreau held the traveling lamp high and muttered, "if this can't wait, you could at least enlighten me as to what it is that requires such an urgent flight to this forsaken place?"

"I must make it right." Fedeles bounded up the cracked steps and lifted a string of scarlet stones from beneath the collar of his shirt. Symbols seemed to glint and spark as his fingers traced them. Then Fedeles lifted his face to the dark sky. "I don't deserve these if I just leave them like that."

"Leave who?" Atreau asked.

But Fedeles didn't seem to hear him. Instead he turned in a circle, reaching out around him as if tracing constellations in the heavens. Glints of gold light jumped from his hands. More and more luminous flecks floated up from him as he strode past the stonework of the temple. And Ariz suddenly imagined him placing stars in the air around them.

Drawn by an almost hapless admiration, Ariz took a step nearer to Fedeles.

"Fedeles, are you even listening to—" Atreau cut himself off short. His attention snapped to Ariz. At once, he urged his mount forward, blocking Ariz's path to Fedeles.

"Show yourself!" Atreau demanded.

Ariz stepped into the lamplight.

Atreau's expression remained wary. Behind him, Fedeles appeared unaware of either of them. The light swirled around him as he continued to pull golden symbols from his necklace. Their radiant light seemed to burn through even the stones of the temple now, opening to a view of gnarled trees and a sky lit by plumes of firelight. The smell of woodsmoke and wet blood drifted to Ariz.

"What are *you* doing here?" Atreau demanded.

Ariz wasn't sure of that himself. He had no way of putting all the inarticulate longing and pain driving him into words.

"I need . . . want to see Fedeles. To be sure he's safe," Ariz managed.

"Whose blood is it that's spilled all across your cloak?" Atreau asked. He made no move to allow Ariz any nearer to Fedeles. Ariz respected him for his loyalty to Fedeles. At the same time, he reflexively calculated the man's quick demise. Atreau held that lamp out too far; Ariz could easily to catch hold of it and hurl the blazing oil on both Atreau and his mount. The horse would panic and throw Atreau. The moment he hit the ground Ariz would run him through. Five seconds at most and the man would be out of his way.

Ariz folded his hands together.

"The blood comes from royal bishop's guardsmen who pursued you and Fedeles when you fled from the sacred grove," Ariz belatedly answered.

Atreau seemed to consider him for a moment, then he sighed heavily and swung down from his horse.

"I could hardly stop you if you'd come here to murder us in any case, could I?" Atreau sounded rueful and looked tired. He handed Ariz the heavy traveling lamp, then hitched his stallion near a sapling. The horse knelt down to sleep and Firaj joined it.

As Atreau returned to Ariz's side, they both stared at Fedeles and the strange landscape behind him. He gestured and more radiant blessings lifted from his hands, circled him and then flew into the surrounding trees. Strings of violet wisteria blossoms swung in a breeze and Haldiim voices called out. Through the incomprehensible whispers and gasps, Ariz recognized a voice speaking Cadeleonian with a gentle urgency.

"Reclaim your life, your freedom. You can do this!" Master Narsi's words seemed to float through the temple ruins.

"Narsi?" Atreau strode toward the temple. He took the steps and Ariz followed close behind him. A branch of wisteria flowers brushed across Ariz's shoulder.

Golden blessings swirled in the air like fireflies, circling Fedeles. He clenched his eyes closed and stretched his arms wide.

"Take this power from me, I beg you," Fedeles whispered. "Take this shield, and all my strength—everything. Protect your people and mine. Let me make things right." Fedeles dropped to his knees and slammed his hands down into the soil. His entire body jerked. A light as brilliant as a lightning bolt burst from his chest and the ground beneath him lit with dazzling gold symbols. At the same time, shimmering black forms ripped up from his shoulders and back.

Crows.

Dozens and dozens of them erupted from Fedeles and swept through the temple to soar over the wisteria trees. Fedeles gasped and shook.

"What have you done?" Atreau demanded. The blessings of the surrounding trees seemed to momentarily light him like sunbeams. Ariz stepped into the shadow of a tree and shielded his eyes with his hand.

Fedeles shook and gasped.

"Protect them. Save them." He bowed his head against the ground. "Please let me make this right. For once, let me make it right."

The light crackling from his chest dimmed, flickered and then went out. All at once the glowing blessings, wisteria trees and furtive Haldiim voices were gone. The walls of the temple stood lit by only the faint flame of the lamp in Ariz's hand.

Fedeles crumpled sideways.

Ariz dropped the lamp, lunged forward and caught him before he struck the flagstones. In his arms, Fedeles's body felt disturbingly cold and limp. Too much like a corpse.

"Fedeles?" Ariz touched the long line of his throat, feeling for a pulse. Fedeles drew a slow breath. Relief flooded Ariz.

"Is he—" Atreau asked.

"Fainted, I think." Ariz drew his cloak around Fedeles and held him close. If only he could share the heat of this own pounding pulse. He rubbed Fedeles's arms with his rough hands.

Atreau crushed out the small spill of burning oil, then righted the lamp with the toe of his boot. He crouched beside them, studying Fedeles. The concern in his expression was obvious, as was his frustration.

"Do you have any idea of what he's done to himself?" Atreau asked.

Ariz shook his head. He, too, studied Fedeles's face, then he noted the slight flicker beneath his eyelids. He felt living warmth slowly seep up from Fedeles's back to spread over his own chest. Fedeles opened his eyes. He gazed up at Ariz with an expression so full of affection and wonder that Ariz felt his face flushing.

"You came for me," Fedeles whispered.

Ariz nodded. They gazed at one another. Ariz knew he ought to look away, but Fedeles's dark eyes and warm expression seemed to hold him captive.

"Wouldn't now be a lovely time to inform Atreau of what's going on? Perhaps reassure him that you aren't dying . . . unless you are?" Atreau asked.

Fedeles shifted his dark gaze to Atreau. His smile was amused.

"I'm just tired," Fedeles murmured softly. He straightened but didn't withdraw from Ariz's arms. "Irsea—the sacred grove's guardian—is gone—"

"I don't know, she seems a great deal more robust than most dead women I can think of," Atreau quipped.

Fedeles gave a tired shake of his head. His hair brushed Ariz's cheek like threads of silk.

"Hierro used me to attack the sacred grove. To exhaust Irsea." Fedeles sounded wrung out and only half awake. "The Circle of Wisteria threatens him . . . or . . . or maybe it's the other power, the one he's hiding. Maybe the sacred grove threatens it . . . I don't know. But I had to undo the damage I wrought to the wards protecting the sacred grove."

"At what cost to yourself?" Atreau asked.

"I don't care." Fedeles hardly whispered the words, then more distinctly he replied, "The Haldiim people *need* the sacred grove. I had to give it to them." He leaned back into Ariz. His eyes dropped closed again. "I had to."

"Just like you *had to* give your entire coin purse to the beggar girl, no doubt." Atreau shook his head. "There's a point where generosity of spirit becomes self-abasement."

Fedeles only sighed and bowed his head against Ariz's chest. His breath came slow and deep, as if he was dozing. Atreau made a soft, irritated sound, then stood and purposefully stamped at the faint wisps of smoke where he'd already put out the spill of lamp oil. He looked back at Ariz.

"I might as well be talking to myself," Atreau muttered. Then his gaze settled on Ariz. "In the Weavers' Ward. Did you know what they'd do—what those men would become when we tried to rescue them?"

Ariz shook his head.

"I didn't know he could do that. Perhaps this offers a glimpse of what he plans—" Ariz struggled for a moment to find words that wouldn't result in a surge of pain. His brand already smoldered in his chest. He couldn't think about Hierro or his plans and continue to speak. "I only hoped that the others could be . . . when men are quartered together they can be . . . handled as a whole in certain ways."

"So, you meant us to nail the place up and set it alight?"

"No." Ariz scowled at the idea of burning anyone alive, let alone men whose only mistake had been to catch Hierro's attention. "I thought poisoning their food or water. Duera can kill painlessly. There's no reason to be cruel. Not if you have a choice."

"I suppose there's something to be said for being so familiar with murder that you can consider a variety of methods and their results." Atreau sat down on the temple steps. He pulled his cloak close as a breeze rolled over the hill. "So, is it a mere chance that you're here? Or has Hierro realized he can use you as a spy?"

The suggestion of Ariz as a charming, smooth spy capable of insinuating himself into Atreau and Fedeles's circle would have inspired roars of laughter from Hierro.

"Hierro has one purpose for me and that is all," Ariz replied.

"But if he asks you about what you witnessed with us tonight?" Atreau asked.

"He isn't so imaginative as to think that I could be in your company if he had ordered me elsewhere. More than that, he'd never credit a creature such as myself with having—" Words to describe all he felt holding Fedeles so relaxed and trusting in his arms eluded Ariz.

Even Atreau, despite his glowers, inspired a kind of respect. Almost affection. How many other courtiers would have ridden at Fedeles's side tonight? What other man would have braved the killing shadows to bring Fedeles away unharmed?

"He wouldn't credit me with friends of any kind," Ariz said softly.

Atreau looked away from him and scowled at his singed boot heel.

"I'm not your friend, Ariz." Atreau didn't lift his gaze. "I mean no offense, but let us be honest. I can't—"

"I know." Ariz cut him off before he caused himself any more turmoil. Long ago he'd learned not to expect friendship from the people around him, but that didn't mean that he couldn't still care for them.

"You're right not to forget what I truly am. What I could become." Ariz paused a moment, fighting his own fear of that possibility. He drew in a deep breath, catching the scents of soap and straw that clung to Fedeles. His body was growing warm now. How rare it was to be able to give comfort and offer protection.

"If a time comes when I'm no longer . . . myself . . ." Ariz wondered if the time wasn't already upon them. He made himself go on. "A lethal dose of duera added to one of Master Narsi's vials would ensure my . . . I would drink and be done."

"Narsi takes his oaths quite seriously." Atreau did meet Ariz's gaze then. "He would never poison you or anyone in his care. Never."

"But you could. He'd trust you with his medical satchel and *you* haven't taken a physician's oath. You aren't my sister. You don't even like me." Ariz brushed a lock of hair back from Fedeles's face. "You could ensure that it's done."

If he ever became a danger to Fedeles, he could depend upon Atreau to remove him. That was part of what made Ariz like him, though he wouldn't say as much aloud. Atreau wasn't his friend, but if he could, Ariz thought he would have liked to have been a friend to Atreau.

"Well, don't cast me as a ruthless villain just yet," Atreau commented. "It's been a damned long night—a damned long day before that. But I don't think we've lost all hope."

"True," Ariz agreed. After all, he'd managed to get a warning to Atreau, and though it hadn't ended as he'd have wanted, Fedeles had freed a battalion of Hierro's enthralled assassins. None of them could threaten the kingdom again.

Another cool breeze whipped through the long grasses. Somewhere in the oaks below them, an owlet called out to be fed. Atreau traced some symbol over one of the stone steps as he absently hummed a piece of song. His voice was lovely. So calm and soothing.

Fedeles shifted in Ariz's arms and Ariz indulged himself for a moment, bowing his face into Fedeles's thick hair and drawing in the scent of him. He closed his eyes and soaked in the heat and weight of every point where their two bodies touched. A slow pulse of desire throbbed through Ariz.

Atreau cleared his throat and Ariz opened his eyes at once. Mortification flooded him, but Atreau simply looked amused.

"You describe Hierro as straightforward. Brutal. Sadistic. But not complex. And from my own encounters I'd say you're correct. If he wants something, he takes it. When he accosted me at the royal fountains last month, he made almost no attempt to hide the attack, even in broad daylight." Atreau sounded like he was thinking aloud as much as addressing Ariz. "And yet his machinations to usurp the throne seem strangely convoluted and complex. Secret messages hidden within secret messages. Undermining the Hallowed Kings. Attacking the Circle of Wisteria. The murder of his own allies as a ploy to throw suspicion on Fedeles. Those aren't the kind of plots that an unabashed bully conceives of."

"No, they aren't," Ariz agreed. He had to be careful here, he knew. Clara's plans interwove with Hierro's so closely and completely that they almost seemed like one and the same. He could easily send himself into convulsions of pain if he revealed too much. But he had to try. "It's as you describe it—a plot hidden within another plot. Like a smile disguised by the lacework of a widow's veil."

"Interesting choice of metaphor."

"I'm not a poet. I simply meant—" But Ariz couldn't explain, not without suffering agony, and he wasn't certain how well he would be able to hang on to his human form if that happened. He didn't want to find out here and now, while Fedeles dozed against his chest and Atreau spoke to him in this nearly relaxed manner.

"Not to worry. I think I take your meaning." Atreau straightened. "More to the point, I think that you understand exactly what it is that I want to know. You have the answers. If only I can find a way to ask you the right question, hmm?" Atreau moved closer, crouching down on the other side of Fedeles. He was attractive, and that expression of intent interest was oddly flattering. Few people bothered to take any note of Ariz, much less to study him as if he was somehow fascinating.

Out of habit Ariz bowed his head, hiding his dull face in shadow. They were both quiet for several moments. Atreau shifted and resettled with his cloak drawn even more closely around his shoulders.

"Our Master Narsi had the chance to observe Clara Odalis early today, and he made some rather interesting observations about your smiling widow," Atreau commented.

Ariz glanced to Atreau, noted the keen edge to his gaze and suddenly wondered how he had ever mistaken the man for a mere hedonist. How did anyone spend time in his company and fail to recognize the cold assessment lying beneath his relaxed smiles?

"He thought that she knew in advance about the plan to assassinate the king," Atreau went on in an easy tone. "But neither Prince Remes nor even Hierro were aware of it. In fact, Remes seemed to completely believe her assertion that a ring of Haldiim conspirators masterminded the assassination."

He was on the right track. A nervous tremor, half hope, half dread, fluttered through Ariz's chest.

"When you face two very strong opponents, directing their might and ire against each other is a wise tactic to employ," Ariz responded carefully. "My sister taught me that."

"Your sister? Oh, *sister*. Yes, I see." Atreau considered. "But how can both the *strong opponents* fail to notice?"

"It often pleases powerful men to view those under their command as devoid of their own great ambitions." Again Ariz picked his words slowly, carefully. Then he remembered something he'd read—from one of Atreau's works, in fact. "'How lulling is our arrogance, how all-consuming our lust, allowing us to fuck and fall asleep never caring for the hungry schemes of lice swarming in our sheets.'"

Atreau lifted a brow and then laughed. "Where ever did you encounter a copy of that old doggerel?"

"Your writing is quite popular at the Red Stallion sword house. A fair number of young duelists there would gladly take on the royal bishop's guardsmen for the sake of their precious copies of your banned works," Ariz replied. To his surprise, he thought he saw a flush color Atreau's cheeks.

"There are moments when you do make it difficult not to like you, Ariz," Atreau commented, then he shook his head. "Best we keep the subject of our conversation centered on your mistress and the lice scheming in her brother's bed, yes?"

Ariz nodded.

"I don't know much and I can say less," Ariz admitted. "But I do know that she looks to the past to find her salvation—her freedom."

"Freedom?" Atreau lifted his brows.

"She bears the same *burden* that I do," Ariz managed to get out, though a sharp pang shot through his chest.

"The same . . ." Atreau looked suddenly disgusted. "He did that to his own sister?"

Hierro had done worse to both his sisters, but Ariz had no desire to expose either of the women in such a manner.

"So . . . there might be a way to turn her against him?" Atreau asked quietly.

"I don't . . ." Ariz trailed off as the pain in his chest spread and his lungs began to burn. He simply shook his head. Not only was the brand unbreakable, but if Clara were freed, he wasn't certain that she wouldn't be just as tyrannical and ambitious as Hierro. There was another matter that Ariz wanted to discuss with Atreau, as well. The reliquary and Slate House. Had Atreau already secured that gold box? Ariz merely pondered the question when a white-hot brand seared through his chest. He felt his skin char and exposed muscle sizzled. He shook in agony. All thought of sharing further information with Atreau burned from his mind.

His shudder seemed to rouse Fedeles.

He cracked his eyes and, as he met Ariz's gaze, he again gave him that welcoming smile. Ariz took in a deep cooling breath of the night air. His pain seemed to ease as he met Fedeles' gaze. Then Fedeles's attention flicked to Atreau. He straightened against Ariz, drawing away. The night air felt chilling in his absence.

"How long was I asleep?" Fedeles asked.

"A thousand years and a day," Atreau replied. "Kingdoms have fallen and arisen while we two watched over you."

Fedeles laughed, then looked to Ariz.

"Perhaps a quarter of an hour," Ariz supplied. "Do you feel better now? Well enough to ride?"

"Give me a moment more," Fedeles replied, and he curled his long fingers around Ariz's hand. His grip was gentle but undeniably strong. So very much like Fedeles himself.

"I'll be here as long as you need," Ariz answered. Fedeles met his gaze and held it. Ariz felt as if he was lifted out of himself, stripped of pain and exhaustion and bathed in a shining adoration. Fedeles drew him a little closer.

"Even if I need you all the night through?" Fedeles asked in a sweet, teasing whisper.

A strangely pleasant heat surged through Ariz.

"I—" Ariz's throat felt too tight. His face felt flushed. He nodded.

"Gentlemen, don't let my presence inhibit you in any way. Think of me as nothing more than a stuffed owl looking on as you tear off your clothes and engage in tireless bouts of passionate lovemaking," Atreau stated dryly.

Ariz had no idea how to respond to the suggestion. Fedeles laughed. His breath was warm and his lips just grazed Ariz's ear.

"I'll just busy myself taking notes for some scene or other in Jacinto's ridiculous production," Atreau went on.

Again Fedeles laughed, then he rubbed his eyes. He wasn't really all awake yet, Ariz realized.

"How is that going, by the way?" Fedeles asked Atreau. "I feel as if it's been months since we just talked about books or plays or music. I've missed it."

"Well, we have all been rather preoccupied," Atreau responded. Then he added, "The play is a shambles. Jacinto wants spectacle after spectacle, but he doesn't understand that narrative and pacing are essential to building drama." Atreau turned his attention to Ariz. "You've probably noticed as much while lurking around in the box seats."

Lurking? He'd simply been waiting quietly, in the dark.

Perhaps that *was* lurking.

"I'm not a good judge of theater," Ariz replied belatedly. "But the play does seem a little . . ."

"Like a disaster?" Atreau suggested.

"Disordered, I was going to say," Ariz supplied.

Atreau laughed and Fedeles smiled.

"Tell me about it, will you?" Fedeles asked. The question seemed addressed to them both. Meeting Fedeles's gaze again, Ariz realized that he wanted to be distracted. He needed a little time to forget everything that had happened and the dread of all that was bound to come.

He wished suddenly that he was more practiced at telling stories or even making jokes. Fortunately, Atreau excelled at both. He amused them, describing the magnificent madness of Prince Jacinto's many requests and demands. Slowly, Ariz found himself drawn out to add his own observations and thoughts. His wit couldn't compare to Atreau's, but he still won laughs from both Fedeles and Atreau when he described his attempts to work out the plot of the production.

"Wasn't it an opera when it began?" Fedeles inquired.

Atreau made a pained sound.

"That was back when Jacinto was fixated on a shapely Labaran singer, who as it turns out is married to a rather infamous duelist. Happily, they both returned to Labara before Jacinto could get himself a case of cock cankers or sword-through-the-heart. That cost me a penny, let me tell you." Atreau grimaced. "Then he stumbled across one of those Yuanese shadow-puppet performers and commissioned a set of giant phoenix puppets. Never mind that they didn't appear anywhere in the original story. I worked them in. But now our sleek puppeteer has packed himself off with a Yuanese ambassador and Jacinto's become fixated on our Haldiim performers."

"Is that why Master Narsi's part keeps expanding?" Ariz had wondered about that. Not that the physician wasn't a striking figure up on stage, but he seemed hardly able to keep from wincing at his own dialogue and delivery.

"More or less. Yes." Atreau sounded oddly self-conscious. Ariz wondered if it didn't irk him seeing Master Narsi pull such pained faces at his script. Ariz found it rather funny but wouldn't have admitted as much to Atreau.

He did however confess to having memorized several of Master Narsi's lines after hearing them repeated again and again as the young physician nervously whispered them to himself in the wings.

"The worse the writing, the less he wants to recall it, I think," Atreau laughed. Then he proved himself to be quite the mimic, delivering several lines in Master Narsi's unmistakably self-conscious manner, even going so far as to roll his eyes and then grimace at himself. "What radiant figure stands before my door? And at this hour, when only stars shine so bright. But *they* are fixed in their appointed courses. Never could one wander so near to my chambers."

All of them laughed. Though Ariz was aware that his own chuckle came out more like a dry rasp.

"He's not a natural actor, then?" Fedeles asked.

Ariz shook his head.

"No, but it's to his credit, I think. He's neither attention-seeking nor deceptive by nature," Atreau said. "And in all fairness, he's not had much reason to practice either until now. That said, he does possess a certain . . . He stays with you and sort of . . . I mean, there's just something about him." For once Atreau seemed to struggle to find words. He trailed off, gazing back at the ruins. Fedeles too looked to the darkness of the temple.

"He'll be safe tonight," Fedeles said. "I made certain of that."

"He shouldn't have been dragged into any of this in the first place," Atreau said.

Fedeles bowed his head. "I tried to stop them before they reached the sacred grove."

"I didn't mean it like that!" Atreau cut him off. "I was just bemoaning how many people are always caught up in the machinations of powerful men. Though honestly, Fedeles. I'm glad that you chose to act. Even if it resulted in a street full of mordwolves. At least we're now forewarned and Hierro has been deprived of a warehouse full of assassins."

Fedeles looked to Ariz, his expression strangely drawn, almost apologetic.

"I wanted to save them," Fedeles said. "Not cost their lives."

For a moment Ariz didn't understand why Fedeles's attention settled upon him with such sorrow. Then he realized that Fedeles must have attempted to break Hierro's thrall over the assassins, and he'd failed, which meant that in all likelihood there would be no way to free Ariz either. Fedeles probably couldn't bring himself to say as much.

"You are not to blame," Ariz replied firmly. He held Fedeles's gaze. "You didn't enthrall anyone. You did what was necessary—what was right."

Atreau nodded. "Ariz is correct."

"I wanted—tried—to free them," Fedeles said again.

"You have," Ariz assured him.

Fedeles scowled at his hands.

"Followers of the sacred grove would say that you've sent them on to find new and better lives," Atreau said.

Fedeles just shook his head. Ariz squeezed Fedeles's cold fingers and he held his gaze.

"There was no other recourse," Ariz stated. "Tonight you killed fifty men to protect the sacred grove and this entire city. You made the right choice. As for the men who died, who among them could have wanted to live as a slavering, mad animal? What you did was mercy. Don't think for one moment that any of us who are—" Ariz couldn't managed the words. Instead he slammed his hand against his chest where the brand smoldered over his heart. "Believe me when I tell you that death would be better than living like that. You know as well as I do what it's like."

Fedeles absently ran a hand over the scars on his own wrists as he studied Ariz's face.

"Yes. You're right," Fedeles said at last.

"Don't forget that," Ariz said. "No matter what might happen, don't forget. And don't blame yourself."

Fedeles nodded. They were all of them silent. Breezes whipped through the grass and wildflowers all around them. Ariz realized that the fire bells no longer rang out over the city.

Atreau stretched out his arms and yawned.

"As refreshing as this getaway is . . . ," Atreau said as he stood. His attention focused on Fedeles. "Our lamp oil isn't going to last us much longer, and we need to return to the house. I still have a play to rewrite, and you have a son and wife awaiting your return."

Fedeles made a soft noise of protest but then sighed and stood. Ariz didn't rise with him or make any move to follow after the two of them as they roused their sleeping horses.

"Keep safe and well," Ariz wished after them when they gave him their goodbyes.

Without their company, his awareness of the brand burning in his chest grew. He resisted it, remaining on the hill, watching the tiny flame of their traveling lamp traverse the meadows and pastures that led back to the Quemanor household. He only stood after he'd seen them disappear into the house.

Then he strode to the south side of the hill where the edge fell away to a sharp cliff. Jagged stones lay far below. Not an easy way to die, but likely it would be quick. Ariz drew in a deep breath and threw himself off. His heart lurched in terror as he fell.

Then powerful wings unfurled and lifted him into the dark sky.

 **CHAPTER FIFTEEN**

Narsi wasn't certain what woke him. A shudder slithered down his back like a droplet of cold sweat. Phantoms and monstrous wolves rippled through his groggy mind, but he refused to focus on them. Instead, he concentrated of the solid reality of where he was now.

He lay still in the darkness of a guest room, feeling the unfamiliar shape of the carved pallet beneath him. With each breath, he drew in the fragrance of medical herbs. Shafts of moonlight filtered in through a small circular window. An alley cat crooned like a drunk singing an off-key love song. Across the room, Narsi could just discern the pallet where Yara slept under the silk blankets Esfir had given her.

He closed his eyes.

Then, in the still of the night, he heard voices. Furtive whispers rasping down the hall. Narsi's eyes sprang open. A door creaked and the cool rush of night air fluttered into the pharmacy. He felt it seep under the door. Then came the patter of soft footsteps. All of which could be normal business, he reminded himself. And yet his heart pounded in his chest.

Maybe Mother Kir-Naham was receiving a friend or some delivery. Possibly some exchange that couldn't be made in the day, when Cadeleonians might be watching. None of his concern, he tried to reassure himself. Nothing to feel alarmed about.

And yet, his agitation persisted. There were too many voices, all trying to speak low and soft. The tones of secrets and conspiracy gnawed at his calm. At last Narsi sat up and pushed aside his blanket. He crept from the pallet to the door and then slowly eased it open a crack. The hall before him lay in darkness, but at the far end, near the back door of the building, a lamp burned. Mother Kir-Naham stood there along with numerous other Haldiim women. Many of them seemed to be wealthy businesswomen or elegantly dressed members of the Haldiim Civic Council. Three of the women wore silver-gray coats adorned with red physician's stars. Others appeared completely out of place in the sedate, tasteful surroundings. Noting the dark kohl that outlined their pale eyes and the weathered quality of their clothes Narsi wondered if they weren't Irabiim nomads. Several of them were armed with short bows and wore fighting knives in their belts. One lanky, white-haired woman carried a Cadeleonian-style sword and sported a short jacket embroidered so boldly that even Prince Jacinto would have been impressed.

Mother Kir-Naham opened the door and Querra entered, drawing back her hood as she did. She respectfully inclined her head to the women waiting inside.

"He has agreed to come," Querra whispered. Then she beckoned someone from the back courtyard.

A moment later a slim Cadeleonian man wearing a black coat stepped into the doorway. His figure and face were so like Lord Vediya's that Narsi's heart lifted in an absurd and boyish manner. Then the man turned toward the lamplight and Narsi recognized Spider.

Several of the refined-looking women standing near Mother Kir-Naham studied Spider with suspicion. One lifted a sachet embroidered with silk flowers, as if warding off a foul smell. Narsi scowled at the response. Spider had a sinister reputation, but in Narsi's experience the man had always treated him with genial indulgence, though that might also be because whenever Spider saw him it was always in the company of his younger brother, Atreau.

"What an honor to at long last meet so many esteemed mothers from the Haldiim Civic Council. I do hope you all forgive my informality, given the late hour." Spider offered a tight smile very like the expression Lord Vediya wore when disguising his distrust behind deference.

"I apologize. We would not normally have imposed upon you so rudely, but the matter is of the utmost importance." Mother Kir-Naham pronounced the Cadeleonian words with great care. She rarely spoke the language and was clearly doing so for Spider's sake.

"Yes. From what I gather, Captain Yago would dearly like to lay hands on someone to blame for that warehouse fire and all the dead men laid out like sacrifices around your sacred trees." Spider arched a dark brow in the manner that Narsi had come to recognize as a Vediya family trait. "There's even talk that you've made a pact with Labaran witches."

"No one in the Haldiim District played any part in that, I assure you, Master Spider," Querra said. "Nor have we had any contact with Count Radulf or any members of the Labaran—"

"I wouldn't give a shit if you women torched every Cadeleonian lord's property in this entire city. As for conspiring with Count Radulf to destroy the *holy* fucking Cadeleonian Church." Spider glanced meaningfully to the white-haired woman wearing the boldly embroidered jacket. He grinned. "I wish you only the best of luck."

To Narsi's surprise, the woman inclined her head and smiled in return.

"But that's not why you called me to you, is it?" Spider returned his attention to Mother Kir-Naham. "No, I imagine you want me to stymy Captain Yago, yes?"

"It is as you say," Querra replied.

"Good. I owe the captain some trouble and more than a little pain." Spider grinned. "So, why don't you all have me in for a sit-down and a drink. Then we'll see how little I'll charge to ensure Yago's frustration."

"Yes, please do come in. You are most welcome in my house," Mother Kir-Naham supplied automatically. She turned and beckoned Spider and the rest of the party after her. All at once the lamplight spread up the hall. They advanced in Narsi's direction.

He stepped back so as not to be caught spying. He watched Mother Kir-Naham lead them into the room next to the one he and Yara occupied. Some fifteen women followed Spider and Mother Kir-Naham. He took special note of the white-haired woman whom Spider had singled out. Deep lines etched her sun-beaten face and she wore a single gold circlet in her left ear, like some sort of pirate. Embroidered goats frolicked across the brilliant silk flowers adorning her jacket. Could this be the Goat, who Lord Vediya had mentioned earlier? Querra went in last and closed the door firmly behind her.

Narsi leaned against the wall, straining to pick out anything of their conversation. He heard murmurs. Were they haggling over the price? Or was it a distance that needed to be traveled? A number of people who could be accommodated? He couldn't pick out enough distinct words to be sure it wasn't something else entirely, or perhaps all three subjects. It sounded like every person in the room was taking a turn talking. Their voices melted into each other and the minutes seemed to drag on and on. Narsi closed his eyes.

The timbre of Spider's voice reminded him so much of Lord Vediya's. When he laughed, Narsi could almost see Lord Vediya smiling at him. His concentration was drifting, he realized. What was it that had just been said? Something about supplies? Lemons, bread and apples? The voices seemed to grow fainted and fainter as he strained to follow the conversation. He yawned and listened for that rich, deep laugh again. His eyelids drooped, then fell closed.

"How do you like the applebread?" Lord Vediya's voice sounded softly against his ear.

To Narsi's delight, he realized that somehow Lord Vediya had arrived at the pharmacy and now knelt beside him, smiling.

"I would need a sample to judge," Narsi replied.

"Perhaps you can taste it on my lips, then." Lord Vediya leaned into him. The kiss felt hot and sweet. Narsi forgot about the people in the other room and about his terrifying evening. Lord Vediya drew him into his arms as their kiss deepened.

"You should call me Atreau," Lord Vediya whispered. "All of my other lovers do."

"But I don't want to be like all the others," Narsi murmured.

For some reason his voice sounded slurred. His limbs felt sluggish. He leaned into Lord Vediya's chest. He'd not noticed how very hard and broad the man's chest was. So very, very hard . . .

Narsi cracked his eyes open to see a stretch of polished floorboards. Faint first light seeped through the far window. His mouth felt dry and his limbs ached. All at once he realized that he sprawled on the floor with his nightshirt tangled around his waist and his head wedged against a door jamb. He must have drifted into a dream while eavesdropping.

He wasn't certain what was more annoying, that he'd fallen asleep in the midst of gathering information, or that his dreams so blatantly betrayed all his efforts to put his romantic ideas about Lord Vediya behind him.

How many times would he have to remind himself that Lord Vediya had rebuffed him—that at the most all he could ever be to Lord Vediya was an accomplice? Still, he couldn't seem to stop caring for the man and yearning for him to return his caring.

It was so childish.

Narsi pulled himself to his feet and stumbled back to his cot. He sank into the sharp scents of the herb-filled pillow and closed his eyes. A moment later, a knock sounded at the door. Narsi sat up.

On the pallet across from his, Yara groaned. "It can't be morning already."

The door cracked open and Esfir leaned in, looking far better dressed and more awake than Narsi could imagine being at this hour.

"There's adhil bread and pepper mackerel on the table. Tea is brewing. And Mother heard some news while she was out—" She quieted as she met Narsi's obviously groggy stare. Yara snatched up her pillow and pulled it over her head, though Narsi wasn't sure if that was to blot out the light or Esfir's cheery voice.

"A number of people have come to the pharmacy looking for medicines. Some of them could really use a physician's care as well," Esfir said. "Though most just need to be assured that they will be fine."

Narsi stifled the childish desire to whine about being tired. Esfir had endured the same harrowing night as he had, but she wasn't sulking or muttering peevish remarks about sleep deprivation, was she?

"I'll be down in a few moments." Narsi sat up. "I think we can let Yara sleep in."

"Yes, please," Yara moaned from beneath her pillow.

Narsi spent the next hour treating the scrapes, bruises, split lips and sprains that the royal bishop's guardsmen had inflicted on the general population of the Haldiim District throughout the night. Esfir and Mother Kir-Naham prepared salves, poultices and other medicines behind the pharmacy table. Querra helped to bottle and label.

During the lulls, the four of them chatted. Querra shared what news and gossip she'd gleaned from merchants and the royal bishop's guardsmen while she'd been out purchasing their morning fish.

"The royal bishop's guardsmen are still patrolling, but none of them are sure of who they should be watching for. Captain Yago has been recalled to the palace, as has the Duke of Rauma." Querra paused to sip her tea and cast a glance to Narsi. "I think you'd better plan to sleep here for the next few days."

Narsi nodded. How badly would things go for him—for everyone associated with the Quemanor household, for that matter—if the duke was blamed for last night's attack? Narsi picked up his own cup of spiced tea and drank to cover his uneasiness. He didn't actually know why the duke had come to the sacred grove last night, but Lord Vediya's presence beside him made Narsi want to believe that they'd arrived to protect the Circle of Wisteria and the people gathered within.

"It's just as well that you stay with us," Esfir said. "We'll all be going to the sacred grove tomorrow morning to celebrate Solstice Day. We might as well travel together."

Again Narsi nodded. Though he couldn't help studying Mother Kir-Naham and then Querra. His memory of their quiet late-night meeting with Spider played through his mind. Had they been planning for an emergency flight from the city? Or had there been something more behind that secret gathering?

Spider's amused words returned to him. *As for conspiring with Count Radulf to destroy the holy fucking Cadeleonian Church. I wish you only the best of luck.*

"I'm not certain of how safe it will be to gather in the sacred grove just now." Mother Kir-Naham massaged drops of oil into her palms before she returned to sorting through the sundry herbs and weeds that Narsi and Esfir had gathered last night.

"What?" Esfir looked up from the aged botanical tome she'd been poring over. "We absolutely must go!"

"Who knows if the king will allow anyone to even enter the sacred grove right now." Mother Kir-Naham frowned. "Nearly fifty men were slaughtered there, and no one knows what actually happened, much less who is to blame. I'm not sure that we should risk more lives for the sake of a ceremony. Keeping the faith in our hearts is what truly matters."

Narsi was inclined to agree with Mother Kir-Naham on this point. In truth, the thought of returning to the Circle of Wisteria right now frightened him, more than he wanted to admit. The memory of all those wolves and then that agonizing darkness sent a shudder down Narsi's spine. He pushed his dish of mackerel and spiced adhil bread away as the scents and sensations of wading through those mutilated remains seeped over him.

"On the good side." Querra's voice broke through Narsi's terrible reverie. "Bishop Timoteo rode to Savior's Chapel at first light this morning and denounced last night's attack on the sacred grove. He's called for all Cadeleonians to stand in support of their Haldiim neighbors."

Narsi felt so proud of his uncle, but then he wondered how well the sermon had been received by the masses.

"If a Cadeleonian bishop is standing up for the sacred grove, how can we do any less?" Esfir stated. "I am going."

"I didn't say that we wouldn't go, only that we might not be allowed," Mother Kir-Naham responded. "And if we are permitted to celebrate, it might be wise to be prepared to leave promptly."

"I don't—" Esfir began, but bells hanging from the door jingled.

Three groups of customers walked in between the fly screens. Esfir left off whatever response she'd been about to make. She rose and politely greeted the older Haldiim woman being carried in on the linked arms of two men who looked to be her sons. They were trailed by an elderly man and a bored-looking girl. Glancing at the elegant matron's extended foot, Narsi suspected that she suffered from gout.

"Mother's toe is bothering her again," one of the men informed Esfir. She nodded and Narsi guessed that she was already quite familiar with the family.

Then a party of four pregnant women marched directly past him and Querra to address Mother Kir-Naham on the subject of morning sickness. Other customers wandered in and out.

Querra offered a warm smile to everyone gathered within, though several people regarded her with unfriendly expressions. Initially Narsi couldn't understand why any of them would view Querra with such hostility. Then he realized that none of them would have guessed that she was a convert. To a stranger she was indistinguishable from any of the humble, middle-aged Cadeleonian women who believed devoutly in their church and condemned Haldiim people as heathens.

Querra excused herself to brew fresh tea.

That left Narsi to look after the two rangy-looking Haldiim men who'd just entered. Both men appeared to be in their late twenties and wore patched traveling clothes. They both looked to Esfir when they first ducked into the pharmacy and then seemed pleasantly surprised when Narsi stepped up beside them. Something about way both men studied him and Esfir aroused his apprehension. Might they be informants for the royal bishop, hunting down the people who had been in the sacred grove last night?

Then the shorter of the two offered Narsi a warm smile and clapped him on the shoulder. Maybe they'd mistaken him for someone else they knew. Perhaps another of Esfir's acquaintances?

"Can I help you with anything?" Narsi asked.

"These are for Esfir Kir-Naham." The shorter of the two men handed Narsi a packet of waxed leather. The contents felt light, like dried herbs. All at once Narsi recalled the smugglers that Lord Vediya had been concerned about.

"Thank you. I'll see that she gets them." Narsi responded with his best professional smile despite his racing heart.

Then the taller of the two men bowed his head and kissed his companion's cheek. They made a rather handsome couple, Narsi thought. As suddenly as it had roused, Narsi's uneasiness with the two of them dispelled. He couldn't imagine the royal bishop or Captain Yago employing Haldiim people as spies, much less hiring adari lovers.

Then Narsi's gaze was drawn to the odd movement coming from the leather pouch hanging from the taller man's hip. A large, yellow rat poked its head out and stared at Narsi. To his shock, it reached out and stroked his hand. Reflexively he jerked back.

"Your—ah—pet is so friendly. It startled me," Narsi said in an attempt to cover his revulsion.

Both men glanced down at the rat and then laughed.

"Queenie is much too forward. And spoiled." The taller man gently stroked the rat's head. Narsi caught a very slight accent to the man's words. Not too different from the Labaran lilt that occasionally sounded in Lord Vediya's voice when he was tired.

"She's not ours. We're only looking after her for our mutual friend," the shorter man said. Then he offered Narsi another particularly meaningful look. "We hope to reunite them come Solstice Day, and so far everything is still going to plan." He spoke as if his words contained a secret code. Could these two be Lord Vediya's informants? But then why would they seek out Esfir?

At a loss, Narsi simply nodded and smiled.

"We must be going, but thank you for your time." The taller man inclined his head in respect. "Good day, Master Lif-Tahm."

"Yes. Good day to you as well." Narsi now felt certain that if they knew his name, they must have seen him in Lord Vediya's company. But he couldn't remember when they'd encountered each other. Were they actors? Had some version of Prince Jacinto's production called for a preforming rat?

"You travel so far and fast," the shorter man said as he turned away. "No doubt we will meet again very soon."

Then the two of them departed.

Belatedly Narsi realized that he'd failed to get either of their names. After the other customers made their purchases and left, Narsi handed the packet over to Esfir. All he could describe of the two men were their basic appearances and the fact that they'd brought a large, yellow rat with them.

"You mean Queenie?" Esfir nodded as she unwrapped the packet. The contents weren't dried herbs, as Narsi had expected, but several aged and fragile-looking pieces of parchment. The writing was faded, but Narsi recognized it as a Haldiim script. Though he wasn't sure of the meanings of all the Bahiim symbols that covered the margins.

"The missing pages!" Esfir's expression lit up as she scanned the weathered parchment.

"Missing pages?" Narsi asked.

"The botanical text I discovered." Esfir dashed to her worktable and carefully withdrew the battered tome from a drawer. Then Narsi remembered. This would be the book that she'd been poring over for the last few weeks. It was filled with as much Bahiim philosophical rumination as medicine.

Esfir smiled fondly as she opened the volume. Previously she'd quoted several lines of amusingly dubious medical advice from the book. Narsi wasn't inclined to offhandedly dismiss anything as foolish superstition, but even he held deep skepticism toward any tome that called for rinsing one's eyes with aged horse urine to reveal wethra steads in storm clouds.

"There was a crumbling letter hidden inside it, obviously penned by an ancient Bahiim." Esfir paused and Narsi saw that the newly delivered pages closely resembled those tucked inside the botanical volume. "Full of prophesies and visions of the world consumed in flames. I've been waiting until now to find out how it all ends." Esfir smiled, but there was a trace of uneasiness in her expression as well.

"Considering the age of the book," Narsi replied, "the prophesized times may be long past."

"Probably." Esfir laughed, but she still folded the pages away reverently.

She turned her attention to grinding more sunvine seeds in her mortar. Behind her, Mother Kir-Naham settled in her favorite chair and continued filling orders from what remained of her herbs and medicines. Querra brought the fresh tea for them.

"One odd thing about the letter is the Bahiim author's name," Esfir went on, and she decanted the sunvine into a bottle. "It sounded so Cadeleonian. It's hard to imagine anyone Haldiim, much less a Bahiim, named Javier."

"People of mixed heritage have always existed. Historians just don't like to remember as much." Querra joined Esfir at the mortars. They both dipped their fingers in warm oil and wax before engaging with the duera blossoms that Narsi and Querra had harvested the day before.

The name Javier seemed so familiar to Narsi. He stood pondering it for a moment. Then, to his chagrin, he realized that he was recalling Lord Vediya's exiled schoolmate, not some ancient mystic. He shook his head and joined Querra and Esfir.

Their conversation continued, lighting upon notable figures of mixed heritage. The astronomer Yassin Lif-Harun numbered among the more celebrated, while the Goat was among the most infamous. Curiosity piqued, Narsi encouraged both Querra and Mother Kir-Naham to tell him more about the infamous Goat. They were both rather hesitant. Happily Esfir launched into a cheery description of tales surrounding the elusive Goat—her real name was Vanji—and her ring of cutthroats and smugglers. The criminal mastermind and her compatriots were apparently famous in the Knife Market and loved for duping wealthy merchants and eluding Cadeleonian law. The escapades won laughs even from Mother Kir-Naham. Narsi warmed to the Goat—or at least, Esfir's version of the woman.

Their conversation dissipated as another group of customers parted the fly screens hanging in the doorframe and wandered into the pharmacy. These were mostly physicians hoping to replenish their supplies of duera. After that, Yara strolled down the staircase.

"Morning, all!" Despite her wrinkled clothes and loose hair, she remained a captivating figure, standing there posed in a golden ray of morning light.

"I promised Prince Jacinto that I'd fetch some leaflets he had Mother Owhar print," she told Narsi. "I should be back shortly. We can walk to the theater together after that, if you'd like."

Narsi nodded. He'd been so preoccupied that he'd nearly forgotten about today's rehearsal.

"Couldn't the prince send one of his servants to fetch and carry for him?" Esfir asked.

"I'm sure he could," Yara replied. "But I'm of a mind to capture the man's attention."

Mother Kir-Naham scowled and two older physicians who'd joined her shook their heads, but Yara just shrugged and sauntered out the door. Esfir gazed after Yara, crestfallen. Narsi felt for her. Unrequited longing was painful enough, but somehow it felt even more agonizing when the person you adored enjoyed your company so much that you constantly endured those moments of hope and rejection.

The next half hour, he went out of his way to cheer her while he treated injuries and gathered ingredients for Master Ariz's medicine.

As morning bells rang across the city, Narsi noticed the perfume of roasting sheep fat drifting in from the road. Vendors called out the beauty of their wares. He was surprised that so many people in the Haldiim District were out on the street. But people had to make their livings, and likely a portion of the population felt that the massacre at the sacred grove wasn't related to them. Or maybe they were like himself, hanging on to normalcy and routine to keep from sinking into terror after seeing such horror unfold around them.

Could this be how Lord Vediya felt every day, as he smiled and flirted all while struggling to keep monsters and sadists from seizing control of the country? How did he manage to bear it year after year? Narsi thought that the next time they spoke, he would have to tell Lord Vediya how much he respected his ability—how deeply he appreciated his efforts to keep them all safe.

All at once Narsi noticed the soft sounds of conversation all around him stop. He looked up and noted a hooded silhouette darkening the woven fly screen. The figure stood as if listening. Inside, they were all silent.

Then Yara swept into the pharmacy and everyone's relief was almost palpable. Yara grinned at them all and twirled around, displaying the new gray silk cloak she'd donned. Her hair shone like spun gold against the black lining of the hood. In her arms she carried a stack of freshly printed broadsheets. Narsi couldn't make out what they said, but they looked like political lampoons of some kind.

"I've come to carry your handsome physician away with me," Yara announced. Then she looked to Esfir with a teasing grin. "Not that you'll have time to miss him. I just passed that Suelita girl on the way here. I believe she'll be calling on you soon."

"Really?" A faint flush seemed to color Esfir's cheeks. She brushed her hair back from her face. Then she added, "You shouldn't make it sound like that, Yara. She's already seeing someone. I'm just helping her translate some passages of archaic Haldiim. And she's been interested in the letter I found."

Yara looked like she was considering a salacious rejoinder when the city bells rang out a new hour. If they didn't leave at once, they'd be late for rehearsal.

Narsi snatched up his medicines and belongings, said a quick good-bye, and then he and Yara raced through the streets on their way toward the Candioro Theater. Neither of them noticed the figures who watched them go.

 CHAPTER
SIXTEEN

Although the Masquerade had officially begun, few people in the Haldiim District sported masks or costumes. Most who did were children. But in the Theater District, where gaudily dressed entertainers normally outnumbered sedate merchants, the first day of the festival transformed the entire population into strange and fanciful beings. Even bakers and brewers sported wigs and ribbons. Passing gamblers donned masks, horns and antlers. A company of silk-winged acrobats practiced their stilt routine while across the way a troupe of dancers dressed in frothy white feathers stretched and gossiped.

The three royal bishop's guardsmen across the street hadn't indulged in any such whimsy. No adornment softened the striking black and violet of their uniforms. Nor did perfunctory half masks disguise their hard expressions. Yara drew her hood up over her blond hair and Narsi bowed his head. As they passed the group, a breeze whipped through the street. Yara gripped her hood and a single broadsheet from the bundle she carried wafted up on the wind.

Horror bloomed across Yara's lovely face as the broadsheet sailed across the street and slapped into the chest of one of the patrolling guardsmen. The bearded guard lifted the page and uttered an enraged obscenity. Then he looked across the street and locked eyes with Narsi. His expression turned murderous. Before the guardsman could call out, both Narsi and Yara dashed through the surrounding bystanders, racing for their lives.

They sprinted several blocks, then both plunged into a crowd gathered outside a bakery. Narsi's heart hammered as he dodged between two plump men dressed in yellow stag costumes. He sidestepped a heap of horse droppings and then ducked into the mouth of a narrow alley.

Yara followed him and they both flattened themselves against the bakery's warm brick wall. Narsi gasped in deep breaths of warm yeast-scented air and concentrated on slowing his ragged breathing. He imagined himself melting into the shadows as he strained to hear the men pursuing them, imagining that null sign in his mind—the one that had made him invisible to Hierro, Remes and Clara.

Not that the same magic would work on common guardsmen. But the sign gave him something to focus on while he stayed still.

Shouts, laughter, music and the barks of a few dogs rolled from the busy street, but to Narsi it was the clatter of heavy boots that sounded like thunderous drums, growing ever louder as three of the royal bishop's guards drew closer. Narsi fought the urge to steal a glance out from the alley. Sticking his face out into the sunlight and staring like a terrified rabbit would give Yara and him away immediately.

Master Ariz would have warned him of that. Thinking on the advice Ariz had shared helped him to suppress his anxiety. A week ago, Master Ariz had spoken of shadows, street noise and the flights of pigeons betraying the position of a man trailing him; the spy had not survived Master Ariz's notice, Narsi feared. But the story itself had made Narsi aware that even the smallest disturbance could prove the difference between exposure and going unnoticed. Narsi focused his attention on the patch of the street view before him. He made out a donkey cart and the two adolescent boys busily loading it with beer casks. Three herb girls stood a little distance away, helping each other twine sprigs of flowers into their braids. All of which told Narsi absolutely nothing.

After all, years serving as an assassin had honed Master Ariz's awareness of his surroundings to a keen edge. Narsi hardly possessed a month's experience of subterfuge and spying. But at least he'd learned to keep still and quiet.

Beside him, Yara drew a silver-cased hand mirror from the pocket of her vest. Her hands trembled, but she managed to angle the mirror to reflect the street. She and Narsi both bent to study the reflected view it offered.

Out on the crowded street the three muscular guardsmen shouldered through a cluster of costumed men gathered around a pretty orange seller. Then the guards' figures darkened the mouth of the alley. They jostled two delivery boys back up against the wheels of their donkey cart before slowing to scan the crowded street.

Narsi caught his breath. Beside him, Yara went very still. They waited, rooted in place, as the guards continued to search.

The tallest of the three bishop's guards swore a long string of obscenities against heathen Haldiim and the perverse actors who kept their company. The second, more squat guard appeared far more concerned by the mass of horseshit he'd stepped in. The third, bearded guard scowled at the tattered broadsheet in his fist.

Narsi squinted at the cartoon printed across the crisp paper. Earlier he hadn't seen it clearly.

Now Narsi studied the page fluttering from the guard's hand: yet another lampoon of dark-haired, blunt-faced Captain Yago and his brutish troops. He noted that the royal bishop's person had been added to the common depictions of giant, bare-assed buffoons defecating all over a miniature of the city.

"You lads lost your way?" A tall, spare figure dressed in gray leather called to the guards from across the street. As she strode nearer, Narsi recognized Sabella's angular face. He didn't know either of the young Cadeleonian swordsmen accompanying her, but the way they moved and the dueling leathers they wore assured him that they hailed from the Red Stallion.

"We're looking for the two pieces of Haldiim filth that are distributing this muck." The bearded guard held up the broadsheet. The younger of his two companions appeared more interested in exchanging apologetic smiles with the pretty orange seller behind them, while the third guardsman scraped the sole of his boot against the sidewalk cobblestones.

"A very tall man and a slim woman wearing a black hood?" Sabella asked.

"That's them." The guard grinned.

"Didn't we see that pair of Haldiim turn and head back toward Pepper Street?" Sabella asked. Her companions nodded, and both of them moved their hands to their sword belts.

"No." The guardsman gripping the broadsheet frowned at Sabella. "We'd have seen them if they'd—"

Sabella stepped closer to the man, and Narsi realized that she shoved something up against his gut as she leaned over him and said, "Now, if I tell you that they turned back, lads, that means they turned back. And you had best take yourselves after them."

The two young swordsmen also advanced on the guardsmen, who very belatedly seemed to recognize the threat they faced. All three of the royal bishop's guardsmen blanched. The youngest glanced to the pretty orange seller, only to have her offer him a pitying shake of her head.

"We serve the royal bishop," the bearded guardsman warned Sabella.

"Yes?" Sabella's smile wasn't friendly. "Tell him Prince Jacinto sends his regards."

Narsi thought he could see the confidence draining from all three of the guardsmen, but they attempted to maintain their dignity. The taller guard straightened to his full height.

"Turn around and search Pepper Street, " Sabella stated. "Your day will be much more pleasant if you do."

Narsi feared that the guardsmen might not heed Sabella's warning. Though she was famed for the number of men she'd slain in dueling rings, Cadeleonian men were not in the practice of obeying women, much less admitting to fear of them. The guardsmen might well feel their pride required them to fight.

Narsi's heart raced as he considered how best to aid Sabella and her companions without getting run through. If he burst from the alley, he might be able to draw the guardsmen away, but after that, where would he run to? Yara snatched a stone from the ground. Narsi admired her bravery while also feeling certain that she might get them both killed if she entered the fray.

Even out on the street, performers and merchants seemed to take note of the tension. A quiet fell over them and they drew away from the potential combatants, opening a wide ring in the crowd. The guardsman gripping the broadsheet glowered at Sabella, and she leveled an unimpressed stare back down at him. His eyes darted to her companions and then to the gold-and-blue pendant pinned to the breast of her jerkin: Prince Jacinto's favor.

"Mayhap we did miss them in the crowd," the younger guardsman suggested to his elder. The third guard nodded.

"Perhaps we did." The bearded guard very deliberately folded the broadsheet and shoved it into his jerkin. He took two slow steps back from Sabella and then turned to stride back the way he came. His two fellow guardsmen fell in behind him. As he went, he made a show of jostling two Cadeleonian merchants out of his way. The younger guardsman muttered something that sounded to Narsi like an apology.

The moment the guardsmen were beyond earshot, Sabella muttered, "Those louts couldn't catch merrypox in a whorehouse." Both of the swordsmen with her laughed.

"Come on, you two." Sabella looked to Yara and then Narsi. "You're late for rehearsal, and Jacinto's anxious to see how his broadsheets turned out."

Narsi stepped from the shadows first. Yara tightened her grip around the bundle of freshly printed pages and followed him.

"Thank you all so much for coming to our aid." Narsi bowed to Sabella and her two companions. Yara inclined her head in respect. The two swordsmen grinned, but Sabella's expression remained grim.

"As sweet as your gratitude is, my lovelies," Sabella said, "it's best you understand this rescue wasn't personal. Jacinto grew anxious for his broadsheets and sent us to secure them."

"Oh." Narsi tried not to feel disappointed. It would have been childishly naïve to expect that a mercenary like Sabella would step in on behalf of himself or Yara without being paid to intercede. "Well, we were very lucky then, I suppose."

Sabella scowled at that.

"Atreau also mentioned that we should look out for the two of you," she admitted. "But if I were either of you, I would not count on hired ruffians like us coming to your aid in the future. You understand?"

Narsi nodded, but Yara heaved an exasperated sigh.

"In the future," Yara stated, "Prince Jacinto can run and fetch his own broadsheets from the print shop." She shoved her hood back and the morning light lit her hair and face to a strikingly lovely effect. Sabella certainly wasn't unaffected. Her expression softened.

"Now that is expecting courage to sprout where no seed has been planted, Mistress Yara," Sabella commented. "Next time, please leave his broadsheets for me or another of my ilk to deliver to him." She held out her scarred hands and Yara passed the bundle of printed pages over to Sabella. Then Sabella turned and started toward the Candioro Theater. The rest of them followed her.

Yara made light conversation about costumes for this evening's First Masquerade. She planned to dress as a paradise bird. Narsi had procured a cat mask, but it remained in his lodgings at the duke's residence. Yara assured him that he could use his costume from the play. The two brawny swordsmen who walked alongside them smiled indulgently, but their attention was clearly focused on the surrounding crowd and the few royal guards whom they passed as they made their way farther into the Theater District.

Narsi tried not to think about how close he and Yara had come to disappearing into some dungeon. He glanced to Yara and noticed that despite the bright tone of her voice, her hands still shook a little. For the sake of his own pride, Narsi made an effort to stand tall and emulate the assured strides of the two swordsmen.

They wound their way through the narrow streets and quickly reached the gaudy, sprawling blue edifice of the Candioro Theater. While the rest of the group tromped through the painted gold front doors, Narsi peeled away to slip around to the backstage entry. Yara teased him for so constantly visiting the cat that regularly hunted in the back alley. Narsi feigned embarrassment at being found out. Sabella and her swordsmen laughed good-humoredly.

In truth he was expecting a visit from Master Ariz and wanted to make certain that the man wasn't lurking, bloodied, among the heaps of discarded trash, in need of medical attention. Master Ariz's disregard for his own pain led him to ignore gravely dangerous injuries. His disastrous physical condition had inspired a series of nightmares in which Narsi found him gutted like a fish and, somehow, still staggering forward with his sword drawn and a murderous gleam in his dull gray eyes.

Thankfully only the grizzled cat awaited him in the narrow back alley. Narsi stroked the rangy creature's chin. Then, feeling relieved, he strode through the back doors.

The scent of fresh paint filled the air. On the far wall, shelves brimmed with gleaming props, stage knives and a small treasure of glass jewels. In the catwalks overhead, pulley ropes and sandbags creaked, holding huge canvas backdrops aloft. When he was feeling whimsical, Narsi liked to look up and imagine that he peered into the dark rigging of some fantastic ship—a rare vessel, crewed companionably by both Haldiim and Cadeleonians alike.

This afternoon a fat rat studied him in return.

All around him dozens of costumers, painters, prop makers and stagehands chatted, while actors and actresses practiced their lines. Narsi passed a thin, one-eyed woman with a large birdcage gripped in her bony arms. The smell of sour beer drifted off her.

"I've brought the trained parrot," she stated. "But no one's told me where I'm to go with him."

One of the pale twin prop masters assured her that he would find out. She and her caged bird joined the gathering backstage.

Narsi continued to wend his way through the crowd.

Gossip flowed freely all around him. An auburn-haired actress, costumed as a novice nun, showed off the glittering bracelet that a wealthy clergyman had bestowed upon her, and she laughed about the fellow's lurid taste for paddling his lovers. Narsi noted the man's name as he passed by. It might prove useful. Three weeks ago, he'd been surprised at just how very much a man could learn simply by listening to the musicians and actors who entertained such a wide variety of Cieloalta's society—from the paupers in their own families all the way up to princes and bishops. It had been here that Narsi had been amused to hear the scandal of Prince Sevanyo's eldest son, Xalvadar, being so estranged from his wife that he'd failed to recognize her twice at parties they'd both attended.

Narsi had won a rare, relaxed laugh from Lord Vediya when he'd shared that.

Of course, most the gossip amounted to nothing at all. Rumors were rampant. This morning everyone had a theory about the king's assassination, as well as the warehouse fires and the attack on the sacred grove. They ranged from a Grunito alliance with wealthy Haldiim mothers to the machinations of Labaran witches, and even speculations that the royal bishop had engineered all three to deny his father a place among the Hallowed Kings.

Narsi took a kind of comfort in how popular the last rumor seemed to be.

"Narsi, dear! You have new lines posted," a spindly Haldiim costumer called. "Atreau must have been up the entire night penning them all."

"What? How much more could he have written?"

She gave a short laugh at Narsi's horrified expression.

It wasn't that Narsi couldn't memorize a few thousand words—far from it. But his acting was abysmal. The larger his role grew, the more apparent that fact became. He had no idea how he'd gone from an unnamed—and somewhat mature—catamite to carrying the speaking role of a scheming court astrologer. He half suspected that Lord Vediya was having some kind of private joke and planned to call in an understudy for the actual performance. But now with Prince Jacinto believing he and Narsi shared some fate, Narsi couldn't see how he was going to get out of the role. Yara and the rest of the cast were already burdened with covering for his stilted, self-conscious deliveries. How much more could they manage when his role expanded once more?

Narsi hurried to the timber where dozens of tattered pages of rag were pinned. Several other actors stood nearby, reviewing their own parts. Narsi's name fluttered on page after page of script. He plucked the papers up and frowned at the dialogue, dashed out in Lord Vediya's quick, fluid script.

Three more scenes. And poor Yara appeared to be performing opposite him in all of them. How on earth was she supposed to keep from laughing herself to tears as he stumbled around looking as wooden as the floorboards of the stage?

And what was this? He was reciting poems now?

ASTROLOGER

How your kisses filled my heart, oh, my ample, breezy love.
But rank wind blew us apart, and drained me limp as a glove.
That stench blown by a hound of hell conjured words I spoke in haste.
Wrongful blame upon you fell, so you fled my choked embrace.
Deprived of comfort and of bliss, I ride in vain pursuit.
I die for a single kiss. Alas you, my love, care not a toot.

Narsi read the lines again and suddenly wondered if he'd actually been cast in a comedy and hadn't realized it until just now. Could Lord Vediya be penning the entire play as some sort of satirical farce? Was it a satire, and Narsi had just been too distracted to notice?

For a moment, the unreality of the last day hit him heavily. How could he be here performing in a play when last night he'd slept on the floor of a pharmacy after being attacked by mordwolves? How could he be expected to take any of this seriously? And yet Yara, who had been there in the sacred grove with him, paced and practiced her new lines as though she'd spent the night in total safety in a beautiful palace.

Even he had somehow distanced himself from the mortal peril of yesterday, as if everything that had taken place had transpired in a fading dream.

Was this what it was to be an actor—or, in his own case, the operative of a spymaster working to make sure Sevanyo was crowned king? Could they all really go on this way, learning new lines as they were written and trying to perform on and off the stage?

He heard Prince Jacinto and Lord Vediya arguing amiably, as they so often did. Narsi slipped past the back curtain, ducked under the branches of prop trees and walked upstage.

On the left wing, a young Haldiim actress ran lines alongside a heavyset Cadeleonian actor. Narsi thought she'd been cast as the Cadeleonian actor's lover—though perhaps she was now his sister. If that was the case, they probably shouldn't still be exchanging a kiss.

Four Haldiim puppeteers up on the catwalk called directions to the Cadeleonian stagehands. Narsi knew they were trying to assemble a firebird from Yuanese lore. Just now it looked more like a heap of black string, yellow ribbons and red feathers. Narsi skirted them and then drew to a halt near two burly, bearded woodcarvers. A few feet ahead of him, Lord Vediya paced boards strewn with wood shavings.

A flush of intense longing surged through Narsi. Even as his heart seemed to flutter in his chest, he felt embarrassed. By now he ought to have shed his childish preoccupation, or at least learned to temper the rush of excitement at the sight of Lord Vediya. Shafts of sunlight glinted across the few white streaks in his black hair and burned away the creases that lined his expressive, dark eyes and the corners of his full mouth. Only a shadow remained of the bruise that had marked his right cheek, though his ink-stained clothes looked like they'd been slept in.

Trying to suppress his romantic impulse, Narsi reminded himself that Lord Vediya was hardly the most striking man in the city, or even on this stage. Many of the actors offered younger, more muscular physiques. Two of the Haldiim puppeteers were beyond winsome, with their lean builds, bright eyes and rich complexions.

Prince Jacinto, stretched across a blue divan only a few feet away, possessed both the strong build and coloring of a Cadeleonian ideal: dark hair and eyes set off by a face as pale as whey. His easy smile betrayed none of the concern that marked so many of the people around him.

Yet Narsi found all of them only passingly interesting, certainly not as fascinating as Lord Vediya even at his most disheveled. The other men surrounding Narsi reminded him of perfectly baked cakes when what Narsi craved was smoky, hot peppers.

He turned his attention from Lord Vediya before someone noticed him staring.

Sabella stood behind the prince, watching the dim shadows of the theater seats. Her two fellow swordsmen lurked in the shadows of the curtain.

"Don't you think it would be more dramatic if it were a sea battle?" the prince called to Lord Vediya. "I haven't seen a sea battle staged before. Not with actual water and boats."

The two grizzled carvers standing near Narsi exchanged the strained smiles Narsi now recognized as particular to artists burdened with a rich but inconsistent patron. Both stopped the work they'd been doing on the thirty life-size wooden horses that the prince had demanded ten days ago. At that time, Prince Jacinto had decided that the duel Lord Vediya originally penned needed to expand into a cavalry charge—a cavalry charge through a burning forest, at first. But Lord Vediya had managed to dissuade Prince Jacinto to forgo his vision of horses lit only by a flaming forest when he'd pointed out that the scene would most likely burn down the entire theater before the production even reached its third act.

"Are you suggesting we flood the entire city block for the season, or just this building?" Lord Vediya asked. He paused a moment to glance in Narsi's direction and offer him a quick nod of acknowledgment.

"You don't like the idea, I can tell," Prince Jacinto responded, and Narsi could hear the grin in his voice. Lord Vediya, too, appeared amused. Narsi wondered if this wasn't how the two of them had behaved with each other during Atreau's second year of school, when he'd served as Prince Jacinto's underclassman.

"I've already purchased the naval costumes. And Sabella would make a brilliant pirate captain," Prince Jacinto announced. "I can so easily picture her swinging from the rigging of a ship to run a man through."

Sabella scowled at the back of the prince's head, as if imagining exactly where she'd strike to knock some sense into him. Lord Vediya glanced at her and gave a shake of his head, and Sabella sighed.

"It's Yara who's taking the role now," Lord Vediya pointed out. "But more importantly, why would she be in the *rigging* during a sea battle?"

"I don't know . . . you think she wouldn't be?"

"From what Morisio has written to me about fighting pirates, they seem to board the decks of ships and murder people there."

"Oh, well, that's dull. Forget the pirates, then." Prince Jacinto sat up and, catching sight of Narsi, offered him a broad smile. "I suppose we'll just keep the cavalry scene as it is, then."

The carvers picked up their chisels and returned to refining the pine warhorses to fit between the branches of prop trees. Narsi admired their work for a few minutes before Lord Vediya called him over.

"Sabella said that you and Yara were pursued by the bishop's men coming from the Haldiim District," Lord Vediya asked, under his breath.

Knowing how voices carried on the stage and down into the trapdoors below, Narsi simply nodded.

"Were *you* being targeted in particular, or—"

"They didn't know me or Yara from anyone else, I don't think." Narsi remembered the bearded guardsman meeting his gaze. But how could he have known Narsi? "Just more random harassment of Haldiim citizens."

"I'm sorry," Lord Vediya said, and he did look sympathetic. "If it's any consolation, Jacinto told Sevanyo about his vision, and it seems that Sevanyo took the entire thing seriously and has blocked the royal bishop from pursuing you. But it's still probably best that you stay with Yara.

Your cat, Brother Berto and Father Timoteo are doing fine, by the way."

He'd only been away a single night, but he couldn't help wishing that he could see his cat and his friends sooner. Strange how easy it was to grow attached.

"Last night," Lord Vediya whispered. "You were there, yes?"

Narsi nodded. "You as well?"

"Yes. We should discuss it in detail later. But right now I need to know if you have any idea what it is that they were after in the sacred grove."

"Are you sure that they weren't just making the capital more unlivable for Haldiim citizens?" The aggrieved tone of his own words surprised Narsi. As a rule, he tried not to let his anger flare up in conversations with Cadeleonians—not even those closest to him—but the terror of being chased through the city streets and then feeling as if he ought to somehow treat that as a normal occurrence—just something he and all his fellow Haldiim would have to plan for now and in the future—sparked a feeling of outrage.

Lord Vediya raised a sharp black brow and gazed at Narsi with an expression of genuine concern. His fingers grazed the back of Narsi's hand.

"If this is too much, I can get you on a ship for the Salt Islands or Anacleto—"

"No. I'm just . . . frustrated." Not that he was wrong to feel angered, but Lord Vediya hardly deserved to bear the brunt of it. He numbered among the few Cadeleonians actively conspiring to curb the royal bishop's power over them all. "I'm tired of feeling scared."

"I know." Lord Vediya looked almost sick. He shook his head. "If they'd breached the sacred grove while it is still without a guardian, it could have been much worse."

"Was it . . . *his* doing, do you know?" Narsi asked.

Lord Vediya nodded. "Hierro Fueres. Fedeles is certain."

"Is he just trying to ensure that the Circle of Wisteria remains devoid of a guardian?" Narsi asked. "Or that the Haldiim and Labarans suspect one another while the Cadeleonians hate us both?"

"I'd say both those motives are at play, but not the whole of his plan. There is something about the place itself that he . . ." Lord Vediya trailed off as two musicians strolled past them.

Narsi glanced back to where Yara sat on the edge of the stage. "Yara's father comes from a Bahiim family. She might know something."

"She has enough trouble already, what with keeping this production going and occupying Jacinto's interest. I want as few people caught up in this as possible." Lord Vediya gave a shake of his head and Narsi caught a faint scent of woodsmoke.

"There's something more . . ." For a moment, Narsi hesitated to tell Lord Vediya what he'd seen and heard at the Kir-Naham pharmacy, partially because he did not want to be the bearer of bad news, and partially because divulging what he'd seen seemed disloyal to Querra and Mother Kir-Naham. But Lord Vediya's own brother Spider had been involved in the meeting. So, as quickly as he could, Narsi whispered what he'd seen the previous night.

As he listened, Lord Vediya's expression stilled, frozen as a stone statue, then he said, "Thank you for telling me."

"I suppose I'll keep poking around there then?" Narsi inquired. "I can't go home anyway?"

Lord Vediya didn't answer right away; instead he frowned at the half-finished carvings of horses. Several disembodied heads lay on the floor and legs reared up from rough wooden blocks.

"Yes," Lord Vediya said at last. He sounded so very tired just now. "Find out what you can . . . but it's not as important as . . . just be careful, all right."

Narsi nodded then held out the pages with his lines of dialogue written across them. "Tell me honestly, Lord Vediya, I'm not actually supposed to recite this fart poem, am I?"

Genuine laughter exploded from Lord Vediya, and he looked so much happier that Narsi felt certain that he really was writing this entire play as a kind of farce.

"Whatever do you mean?" Playfulness sounded in Lord Vediya's tone. "I rather think it marks a turning point for the astrologer. His first realization that the lover he so idolized is as awkward and human as everyone else—"

"Because she farts like a hound of hell?" Narsi had to point out the absurdity.

"I imagined that you, as a physician, would appreciate the demystification of natural bodily functions." Lord Vediya barely suppressed his grin. "If this production does nothing else, I pray that it encourages more women to let loose the gases that cramp and peeve them in resounding trumpets of liberty."

"Oh, I see. It's for the sake of public health." Narsi laughed. "Perhaps your heroine should let loose a deafening wind and so defeat her enemies and win the day, then."

"Beware what you suggest." Lord Vediya waggled a finger at him. "I'm grasping at straws for the final battle. Anyway, Jacinto is excited to see more of you on stage . . . and probably off as well."

"That's just what I don't need," Narsi responded before he could help himself, and Lord Vediya smiled, though it looked strained.

"You could do worse. He's rich and happy to pay generously for the privilege of keeping interesting company. Under different circumstances I might encourage his fascination." Lord Vediya sounded unperturbed, but Narsi recognized the troubled way his gaze briefly shifted. As a boy, Lord Vediya been the object of rich men's interest, and though he made light of those days if he mentioned them at all, Narsi knew that a deep, old pain remained with him even now.

Not that his Cadeleonian pride allowed him to voice as much.

"Mother Kir-Naham would not approve," Narsi commented.

"Oh, yes. We must ensure your beloved pharmacist's blessings." Lord Vediya smiled, but not unkindly.

"At the very least," Narsi said dryly, "I'd want to secure a promise of widespread reforms before I offered myself up."

Lord Vediya cocked his head.

"I can't actually tell if you're joking or serious," he said.

"Joking." Narsi couldn't imagine how Lord Vediya could think he took any of this seriously. Then he noticed the dark shadows beneath Lord Vediya's eyes and the uneven stubble coloring his jaw. "Have you slept at all since I saw you yesterday?"

"What's sleep compared to the sweet balm of seeing this majestic production brought to life?" Lord Vediya attempted a game smile, but the strain of it showed. Then he added, "We truly need to talk more, but not here. My rooms at the Goose, after sixth bell?"

Narsi gave a nod but didn't move. He frowned out at the vast chamber of empty seats surrounding the stage. A feeling almost like futility swept over him. With war looming and the Haldiim District on the verge of abandonment, he found it almost impossible to care about a play—an absurd play, at that. What was the point of them rehearsing and waiting until sixth bell?

"Does this play really matter to you?" Narsi whispered. "Or is it just a means to meet with agents and informants?"

Lord Vediya met his gaze with a smile, but there was no joy in it, only profound weariness:, his amber eyes dull and the seductive curve of his lips fixed as a death rictus.

"That depends, I suppose," Lord Vediya replied. "If we fail in protecting Cadeleon, if the Labarans really do invade, or the Fueres family manages to usurp the throne, or a demon lord murders us all? Then, no. This production doesn't matter a jot. But if we succeed . . ."

Lord Vediya paused, gazing past Narsi to the assortment of performers, artisans and stagehands engaged in their own work and conversations.

"If we succeed in protecting this nation and these people," Lord Vediya went on, "then this production is a source of income for many.

It's an opportunity for men and women of different classes and races to meet and create something together. Even if it's just a bawdy comedy, its connection with the prince will ensure that Cadeleonians will come in droves, and they will see a Haldiim heroine prevailing over all the absurd and arrogant obstacles that men place before her. They may laugh, but it will be *with* her, not at her expense."

Lord Vediya sighed and rubbed his eyes. "I don't know . . . I suppose I want to think that this fantastical piece of fiction matters because I need to believe that there will be a day when this is behind us and the worst threats any of us face are wine bills and petty theater critics. I'm not certain that I could keep going otherwise."

"I—" Narsi hadn't considered any of that. Nor had he realized, until just this moment, how idealistic Lord Vediya truly was beneath all his overtures and subterfuges. Clearly, he'd put time and far more thought into the script than Narsi had even considered before dismissing it so offhandedly. "I didn't mean—"

"It's fine." Lord Vediya shook his head. "You're not wrong to disdain a sprawling work of farts and farce."

Narsi wanted to say something more, to make amends, but two actors called out to Lord Vediya.

"We'll talk more, later," Lord Vediya promised, then he strode to the actors and set about explaining the new blocking for their battle scene. Narsi retreated to sit beside Yara.

She smiled at the sight of him and fought valiantly not to laugh when he delivered his new lines to her. When she did laugh, the delight in her voice made Narsi smile as well. The next time he delivered the lines, he put more effort into sounding awkward and clownish, and this time he was rewarded with not only Yara's charming grin but the laughter of the puppeteers in the wings. Prince Jacinto chuckled as well.

After that, he felt an uneasy awareness of Prince Jacinto observing him and Yara from his divan. Yara shifted just slightly so that a beam of light illuminated her face. She angled her shoulders subtly toward the prince, and Narsi realized that he was probably the only person in the entire theater who hadn't given much thought to the prince's presence and wandering attentions all this time.

"Put your hands on my arms as if you're going to pull me in to a kiss," Yara instructed him.

"If you think so." Narsi obliged and Yara cast a quick, sidelong glance back at the prince.

"I'm not certain which of us he's eyeing. Maybe it's both of us and he wants a more explicit show, if you know what I mean."

Narsi's hands went cold and he felt his face flushing.

Yara laughed.

"That terrified expression is priceless!" Yara grinned at him. "I don't actually plan on seducing you."

"I'm crushed," Narsi replied.

"Hardly. That's what makes it so safe for me to pose and flirt with you," Yara said. "Anyway, we may as well get all we can from the prince's attention while it lasts. I could certainly endure a few lively dinners and a little flirtation if it convinces him to produce my play, what about you?"

"I can hardly afford to buy my own dinner, much less bankroll your play," Narsi replied.

Yara laughed again and the halo of her hair seemed to ripple with her mirth. Narsi grinned; it felt so comfortable and easy just chatting with her.

"I suppose we have to save *this* play first, in any case." She handed the twelve pages inked with her lines to Narsi. He prompted and followed along as she recited. Then she coached him through his own agonizing deliveries. After an hour, both of them had the dialogue memorized. Though Narsi noted that where he simply repeated the words, Yara imbued them with passion and intention. She brought them to life, somehow transforming even the most absurd situation into a compelling moment.

Narsi, on the other hand, couldn't care all that much about the astrologer he was supposed to embody.

Instead he stole glances out into the auditorium. More of the prince's usual entourage arrived, including Procopio. Narsi knew little about the bearded man other than that he numbered among the dozen minor nobles in Jacinto's retinue who specialized in procuring various contraband goods for the prince's pleasure. Sabella hated him. Lord Vediya appeared to feel nothing. Though there had been a few moments when Narsi thought he'd seen revulsion flicker across Lord Vediya's face when Procopio's back was turned.

Then Narsi picked out the shadow of a figure far back beneath the box seats moving closer. He wondered if this could be Master Ariz finally coming for his treatment. That strange mixture of compassion and dread filled him. Ariz suffered immensely, possibly more than anyone Narsi had ever encountered before, but that didn't make him any less terrifying.

But studying the slouched posture and thin limbs of the figure, he decided it couldn't belong to the muscular assassin. Before he or Yara called out a greeting, Lord Vediya strode past them, jumped down from the stage and hurried to the stranger. Lord Vediya and the stranger exchanged a brief embrace and then stood talking together for a few minutes. Narsi thought he overheard the Weavers' Ward being discussed, but not much else. Narsi felt certain that Lord Vediya handed several coins over to the slim figure and was given a sheet of pages. Then the stranger departed and Lord Vediya returned to the stage. Narsi peered at the pages as Atreau tucked them away, but all that appeared to be written on them was a musical score.

"Not going to introduce your friend?" Procopio called from the black velvet drapes at the back of the stage.

"Hoping to work your way down in the world by charming my laundress's son, are you?" Lord Vediya replied lightly.

"No, but I could certainly use some distraction from the tedium of this production. Aren't you ever going to have the script completed?" Procopio replied.

"A masterpiece of this scope takes time." Lord Vediya actually laughed at his own words, and for just an instant he caught Narsi's eye and Narsi couldn't help but smile in response. Then Lord Vediya returned his attention to Procopio. "In the meantime, you might occupy yourself by fetching food and drink for our prince. I think Jacinto is nearly famished from working so hard."

"I'm about to faint," Jacinto declared. "In fact, I may *die* without a bowl of cherries and a bottle of that lovely green wine from Usane. What was it called?"

"M'vin mogo." Procopio's petulant expression lifted. "I still have four bottles at my Bower Street garret."

"God's blood! Four bottles. Bring them at once. They may be all that stands between me and death." Jacinto's grin broadened and Narsi decided that the man did have a rather charming smile. Procopio seemed to think so as well. He certainly appeared amused as the prince went on. "You must do it for all our sakes. If I die now, who could possibly rein Atreau in and get this production on schedule?"

"In that case, it would be an honor, my prince." Procopio doffed his hat and bowed, before turning to stride from the theater. One of the swordsmen who'd escorted Narsi and Yara followed him. Narsi wondered if Procopio had hired him as an escort or if Sabella sent him to keep track of Procopio.

It might be both, Narsi realized a moment later.

After they departed, Lord Vediya pulled Sabella aside and, while discussing the blocking for a battle scene, he passed a coin purse to her. Payment to Sabella's lover, Suelita, for her efforts to deciphering letters? Narsi wondered. He frowned down at the floorboards, thinking that Esfir truly had bad luck when it came to her infatuations.

Bells rang from a distant chapel, and then more sounded all across the city. Master Ariz should have been here by now. Narsi glanced up into the box seats on the far left side of the stage, where he often met with Ariz. He started to turn away, but then something near the ornate carved balustrade caught his attention.

As he stared, the dark silhouette seemed to coalesce from the surrounding shadows. Absurdly broad shoulders and a powerful chest supported long arms that hung in a strangely slack manner. The head remained hidden by a deeper shadow, but Narsi had no doubt that this was Master Ariz. When or even how the man had entered the theater and ascended to the box seats, Narsi had no idea. No one else seemed to notice his passage or presence at all.

Quiet as a ghost. So dull his nickname at the Red Stallion sword house was Corpse.

Narsi forgot about the play, his performance and even the secrets and subterfuges all around him. He returned to himself—a physician whose greatest obligation was to his patient. Of all the actions he'd taken in the last month, advocating for Master Ariz's life was the only one he'd undertaken purely of his own volition and against the advice of everyone, including Lord Vediya, because it was the right thing to do.

Narsi slipped up the back stairs and entered the box seats.

Master Ariz looked beyond unkempt: unshaven, his hair lank with grease, his eyes red-rimmed. Scrapes and bruises covered his big hands, and Narsi knew from their most recent meeting that beneath his drab, sweat-stained clothes, a profusion of ugly bruises mottled his ribs and stomach.

Narsi wondered what had caused the latest ring of bruises around Master Ariz's muscular throat, but all Ariz managed to tell him was that Hierro Fueres had not been happy about the Duke of Rauma's antics in the Weavers' Ward. Master Ariz managed something like a smile at the mention of angering Hierro, and Narsi wondered just how much Master Ariz hated the man that he'd welcome such abuse if it ensured Hierro's displeasure.

Narsi settled into one of the velvet seats. From the glinting embroidery on the arms of the chair, he imagined that he occupied the place normally reserved for some Cadeleonian noble. As always, Master Ariz did not sit until Narsi beckoned him to join him. Even when he did drop down, he remained balanced on the edge of the velvet chair, prepared to bound to his feet at any moment.

"How have you been?" Narsi considered the hollows beneath Master Ariz's eyes as he contemplated the tincture that he'd mixed for him this morning. Nightleaf made up a major proportion of the solution, as did Yuanese chay leaves and feda drops from Usane. The three created a potent combination, one Narsi wouldn't have normally prescribed for any protracted period of time. "Have you noticed the medicine making much difference for you?"

Master Ariz seemed to struggle for words, then he simply shrugged.

"More restless than usual?" Narsi asked. From the look of him, he guessed that Master Ariz hadn't slept much or very well. Master Ariz nodded.

"The pain here?" Narsi lightly tapped Master Ariz's chest where the brand lay beneath his jerkin.

"It's still present, but I've been able to resist more and longer." Master Ariz leaned close and the sharp smell of sweat and blood caught in Narsi's throat. "Maybe with a stronger mix it might fade even more?"

"Perhaps." Narsi reached out very slowly—not wishing to startle the other man—and placed his wrist against Master Ariz's brow. His skin felt damp and too hot. When he gently pinched the skin on the back of Master Ariz's hand, he found it lacking turgor, which meant the man was dehydrated on top of everything else.

Narsi scowled. Clearly, the nightleaf needed to be decreased or abandoned entirely. Yuanese chay wasn't as infamous for suppressing the appetite, but at higher doses it had a well-known laxative effect that could dehydrate his patient even further. Narsi needed to speak more with Mother Kir-Naham. She might know of another medical stimulant with fewer side effects. Though how they would get possession of it, he had no idea.

"Are you sleeping at all?" Narsi asked as he inspected the three new scrapes that marred the chiseled muscles of Ariz's chest. He could feel Ariz's body tremble beneath his fingers and he knew that Ariz was fighting against some violent impulse.

"I can't after I've—" Ariz sucked in a breath between his clenched teeth. "It doesn't matter. *I* don't matter. What's important is that you reach—" He gasped and Narsi could see sweat beginning to rise on his brow.

"Take your time," Narsi said softly. "Think of something else for a little while."

While Master Ariz stared out at the actors on the stage and drew in slow deep breaths, Narsi applied coinflower distillate to his dozens of cuts and gashes. The back of his scalp was matted with dried blood. He also sported three completely healed scars on the back of his neck, which Narsi didn't recall seeing before.

He'd clearly been involved in many very violent altercations since last they'd met. Narsi wondered how many people he'd injured in just this last week. Two of the royal bishop's most ardent supporters had been slain—along with several members of their households—as well as the minister of the navy. Master Ariz could have been responsible.

There had also been several disappearances from the Haldiim community. As the suspicion occurred to Narsi, he realized that he couldn't ponder it and still continue to treat Master Ariz with any compassion at all.

"The Slate House," Master Ariz almost choked on the words as he forced them out. "There might be time . . . if you go—" He clenched his fists in frustration and several scabs broke open.

Narsi quickly stanched the blood with a cloth. Master Ariz sucked in breaths through clenched teeth. Narsi wondered if he ought to ask a distracting question but paused midthought as his gaze fell on the deep indentations of a bite mark on Ariz's forearm. One left by very small teeth.

"A child?" Narsi whispered in horror.

Ariz drew his arm from Narsi's grip and shoved the sleeve of his shirt back down.

"The thing I've become—" Ariz lifted his gaze to Narsi's face, and for just an instant Narsi could have sworn that an odd yellow tone flared through his gray eyes. He arched his neck and cocked his head to one side, angling his gaze at Narsi like some disturbed bird of prey. "Let no man there live—"

Master Ariz sprang forward and Narsi flinched back out of reflex, then he realized that Master Ariz hadn't lashed out at him. Instead he swayed on his feet and slowly began dancing the steps of a quaressa. His hands rose as if gently holding a partner and he closed his eyes.

Even in the grip of intense apprehension, Narsi marveled at both the grace and the silence of his movements. Physically, Master Ariz possessed astounding control. But mentally . . . Narsi had to wonder if the man was losing the last of his sanity right before his eyes?

But steadily, Master Ariz seemed to calm himself as he danced. The tension drained from his face, and for an instant Narsi thought that Master Ariz smiled. Then he stopped and opened his gray eyes.

"Better?" Narsi asked.

Ariz nodded.

"Then tell me about the child. You said there might still be time."

"She wasn't supposed to be there. He was strangling her." Again Master Ariz shuddered. "I hid her. Locked her in. But he won't want witnesses. He could send me back. I took what he ordered but empty. I made sure.... You must find her and find it first—" Ariz jerked like he'd been stabbed through the back, and his voice scraped to a strangled rasp. "Deer—Box—"

He doubled over, gasping and wheezing.

The information Ariz wanted to convey was obviously too important to Hierro for Ariz to even contemplate it without suffering. From experience, Narsi knew that all he could do was offer a distraction.

"Ariz!" Narsi resorted to the commanding tone of an instructor. "Tell me the Cadeleonian dueling postures."

Ariz sucked in a breath and immediately rattled off the eight positions as well as the purpose of each and how they varied in practice from a dueling ring to a street brawls. His expression and tone of voice dulled as he spoke. By the time he described how to entangle an opponent's thrust with a cloak, he looked and sounded like a bored student giving a rote recital.

"Thank you," Narsi said.

"You would be better served to flee." Ariz cocked his head slightly, his slack face shifted, and again Narsi had the impression of some flat-eyed bird of prey contemplating a sparrow. "Though you *are* a physician, so perhaps if you were cornered, you could land a fatal blow. Strike me here. Here or here." Ariz lifted his hand and lightly touched his own chest, just under his fourth rib, then drew his finger across his throat. He then reached up and touched his own left eye, as if it were unfeeling glass. "I would thank you for your accuracy."

"Good to know," Narsi managed to reply. The thought of killing another human being was not one he wished to consider, and the prospect of even attempting to fight a man like Master Ariz terrified him. Narsi focused instead upon the child that Master Ariz had mentioned. How long had she been locked up and where? He'd mentioned her being strangled, so was she even alive? If so, how badly injured? Obviously she was in danger of being discovered by the wrong people. The question was, how best to get Master Ariz to tell him where she was without overtly asking for the address? Doing that would only see Master Ariz shaking in agony and fighting to breathe.

"You know, I've only been in the capital a short time," Narsi said. "Where would you advise me to go for a walk today if I wished to explore and make some interesting discoveries?"

Master Ariz studied him for just a moment, then he seemed to grasp Narsi's intent.

"East Docksides, there's a memorial for those lost at sea. On the east corner of it stands a stone house with yellow doors. Two stories. The roof is slate and a window on the second floor is broken in now." Ariz spoke quickly, as if trying to race against his own awareness of how much he was betraying. "It belongs to the royal bishop's bastard son. He's just returned from the Salt Islands on his father's business. Go there."

"Could you take me?" Narsi asked.

"I can't be trusted. Not there," Ariz replied. "No man there . . ."

He stood suddenly and Narsi thought he might simply leave, as he'd done previously. But Master Ariz paused. "Will you give me another tincture?"

Narsi felt extremely hesitant, but at the same time, the medicine did seem to offer Master Ariz a little more ability to resist Hierro's control. It might have been the only thing that saved a child's life or allowed Master Ariz to tell him about her. Narsi opened his medical satchel and handed over the green vial.

"Take it as sparingly as you can. No more than three drams in a day. I'll see if I can't develop something else a little more suitable before we meet again."

"Thank you." Master Ariz's hand felt feverishly hot as he took the vial from Narsi. He turned and stepped silently back from the velvet seats.

Down on the stage Lord Vediya struck a chord on a lute and sang out a sweet melody. Yara joined him, learning the tune along with much of the rest of the cast. Narsi wondered if he ought to be paying attention as well. It hardly seemed important in comparison to reaching this child Ariz spoke of.

As if sensing his agitation, Lord Vediya glanced up to where Narsi stood watching from the box seats. He frowned at something just past Narsi. Likely Master Ariz's shadow. He gave a slight nod to Narsi.

Then he turned to the actors and actresses surrounding him.

"Very well done!" Lord Vediya clapped. "I'd say you've all earned a drink of that green wine that Procopio appears to be hauling up through the front doors. Wouldn't you agree, Jacinto?"

"What?" The prince appeared to have drifted off, staring at the scarlet puppet now swinging over the stage. He smiled. "Yes! Absolutely, just as you say, Atreau. Drinks all around."

As Procopio and the swordsman came into view below Narsi, Lord Vediya dropped back to the right wing of the stage and then slipped away to the stairs. Seconds later he joined Narsi in the raised box.

"Something's amiss?" Lord Vediya asked.

"Yes, Master Ariz here has just told me—" Narsi turned to indicate Master Ariz, only to realize that the man had already gone. "Did you see him leave?"

"No, I wasn't even sure that he was up here with you." Lord Vediya scowled at the empty seats. "What is it that he said?"

"Last night a child was caught in the midst of Master Ariz's . . ." Narsi wasn't sure why, but he struggled to find the right word to describe exactly what Master Ariz did under Hierro's command. ". . . fight."

"So now we're allowing him to roam the city murdering children, are we?" Lord Vediya muttered.

"He didn't kill the child." Narsi couldn't quite hide the defensiveness in his own voice. He'd prevailed over Lord Vediya's argument for killing the man. Now Narsi felt partly responsible for the murders Ariz continued to commit. He feared that Lord Vediya blamed him as well.

"The child is alive and Master Ariz is concerned that Hierro wouldn't want a witness to be able to describe him. Or at least that's what I assume. He can't say exactly what he thinks. But it's clearly a threat to Hierro."

"When did this take place?" An expression very like worry suddenly flickered across Lord Vediya's handsome face.

Narsi remembered the fresh bite mark.

"Late in the night or near dawn, I'd guess," Narsi replied. "Master Ariz said that no one had yet noticed the killings—"

"Where was it?"

"Some stone house with yellow doors and a slate roof. He said it lay east of—"

"The Slate House in the Sea Memorial? Damn him!" A rare flare of anger showed in Lord Vediya's voice. His attention snapped to Narsi. "You said that she's alive?"

"Yes." Narsi returned Lord Vediya's gaze. There was something telling in the fact that he'd known the place and that the child was a girl.

"I have to go." Lord Vediya turned.

"You may need a physician," Narsi said.

Lord Vediya stilled for only a moment, but Narsi was very aware that in that instant he was caught between impulses. Whether he hesitated because he didn't completely trust Narsi or because he feared Narsi was too naïve to manage what might need to be done, there was no way to know. But then he looked back over his shoulder and smiled.

"You'll have to add the services rendered to my tab, but come along."

CHAPTER
SEVENTEEN

As Atreau and Narsi hurried across the sedate grounds of the Sea Memorial, distant harbor bells rang. Dense corridors of hull oaks and yew trees blotted out all view of the crowded docks and obscured the sight of any ships bobbing on the river. Sheltered from bustling trade and the lively shouts of street hawkers and stevedores, the memorial grounds formed a somber island of dark trees and clover lawns. Row upon row of pale grave markers spread across those lawns. Multitudes of lives lost to the remorseless sea.

And now Rinza might be dying here as well.

Atreau had to resist the impulse to sprint ahead. He couldn't afford to draw undue attention. Particularly not with Narsi alongside him.

They came over a small rise and found a large fountain displaying a bronze tableau of four half-submerged stallions fighting against a ceaseless cascade of turbulent water. The animals' eyes were wide with terror, their ears pinned back. Two bared rusting teeth, as if enraged by the futility of their struggle.

"Are the horses meant to represent the four virtues?" Narsi studied the fountain with a dubious gaze. "They look like they're in nearly over their heads, don't they?"

"I suspect they're intended to evoke the valor of our Cadeleonian sailors." Atreau scowled at the grim display. The reminder that being swallowed by the sea was the fate his brother Lliro likely faced someday did nothing to lift his spirits.

Did this place have to be so utterly disheartening? Wasn't there enough tragedy in all those white stones breaking through the sedate lawn like countless wave caps? Why not at least plant a few flowers or fruit trees as a respite for the heart and eye?

Two larks flitted past. They, at least, appeared pleasantly carefree.

"That must be the place." Narsi pointed across the distance to the gray line of a high garden wall. Just beyond, Atreau made out a dark slate roof. The absence of smoke drifting from the chimney filled Atreau with dread. Not even a cooking fire burned within the building.

Despite the apparent absence of guards—or even a single one of Lliro's agents—patrolling the memorial, Atreau knelt beside a sailor's grave. He pretended to say a prayer as he surveyed their surroundings. No one appeared to be keeping watch.

He and Narsi hurried ahead and slipped past a stand of dwarf apple trees that lined the back garden wall. Bees buzzed through the branches, but their busy wings didn't disguise the hum of the disturbing number of carrion flies that winged past. At the garden gate, no one challenged them, nor could Atreau make out the faintest noise of work or chatter from behind the wall. This time of day someone should have been out hanging laundry, cutting wood or harvesting herbs from the garden beds. Gossip, laughter and grumbling ought to have broken the silence of the surrounding graveyard.

As he pushed open the heavy doors of the back gate, Atreau noticed a bloody handprint on the astragal and vomit on the flagstones beneath. Trails of red ants streamed from both. Narsi frowned at the sight—or perhaps it was the smells already drifting on the afternoon air.

Vomit, blood and the first hints of sickly sweet decay. Atreau eyed the bloody handprint on the gate. The position made him think that someone had steadied themselves just outside the garden wall while they were sick. Too dainty a palm to belong to Master Ariz, too tall for Rinza. A cook? A maid? A mistress? They hadn't seen a corpse among the apple trees, so had she survived Master Ariz's visit? If so, then in all likelihood she would have gone for help—she could be raising an alarm at this very moment.

"I think it might be best if you stayed out here," Atreau whispered to Narsi. "To keep watch."

"If your agent, Rinza, is injured then I should be on hand to treat her at once. And to assist you in carrying her if she can't walk on her own," Narsi replied.

Atreau scowled. He was right, of course. That had been the reason for bringing him along in the first place.

"Inside it may be—"

"Lord Vediya, are you worried for my delicate sensibilities?" Narsi whispered the question with a teasing expression. "You needn't be. As a physician, I've seen death in many unlovely forms."

Had it been that obvious? Atreau supposed so.

He didn't doubt that Narsi had previously encountered both horrific injuries as well as repulsive corpses. But it was one thing to understand death in the professional capacity of a physician, and another matter entirely to walk into the aftermath of a massacre and know the part you had played in the brutal loss of lives.

Then, like an image from a half-forgotten nightmare, he remembered Crown Hill last night. He'd seen Narsi kneeling among bloody remains of mutilated bodies working feverishly in flickering lamplight. While others had gaped and gasped, Narsi betrayed nothing of his own shock. He'd looked so valiant and so determined. Heroic in a way that Atreau couldn't have imagined himself being at the same age.

Atreau shook his head at himself. Who was he attempting to fool?

"I've every confidence in your steady character, Master Narsi," Atreau replied. "I only meant to shield my own vanity. The truth is that no matter how many corpses I encounter, murder still sickens me."

"Do *you* want to stay while I—"

"No." Atreau cut him off. "I need to be there for Rinza. She knows me."

He slipped inside and Narsi followed him. The two guard dogs lay long dead, as did a young man with a pike still gripped in his hand. Atreau didn't look back to see Narsi's reaction. The handle of the kitchen door was bloodstained and also unlocked. Inside it was dark. Atreau drew open a curtain to allow in enough light for the two of them to make their way through the cluttered space. A stocky cook slumped over a small table of costly spices. He gripped a cleaver in one hand and a meat hook in the other. His head lay on the floor at his feet.

Atreau moved on, but when he noticed that Narsi hadn't followed him, he turned back. Narsi stood too still, his expression almost fixed in placid composure. He'd looked the same way the night he'd been poisoned and last night as well. Perhaps this countenance was the mask he wore to hide his shock.

"There's nothing you can do for him, but Rinza was left alive, we know that." Atreau caught Narsi's hand in his own and drew him out of the kitchen into a gloomy hallway.

Several silver mirrors and a few paintings leaned against the walls, having been unpacked but not yet hung. The lower half of a man's body jutted out from an open door. Inside the room—it looked like it would have served as a library, from the assortment of splintered book crates and fallen shelves—four more men sprawled out, displaying horrific mortal wounds. All five men had been armed and likely fought for their lives. Wide swashes of blood smeared across the floorboards and spattered over the walls, even on the ceiling.

How in the three hells had Ariz managed to survive, much less prevail, against so many men?

"Has Master Ariz ever mentioned working alongside other enthralled assassins?" Atreau asked.

When Narsi didn't respond, Atreau glanced back to see him kneeling beside the one man whose head was still attached to his body. Narsi lifted his bloodied fingers away from the dead man's neck and Atreau guessed that he'd tried to feel for a pulse. When he met Atreau's gaze, he looked embarrassed. All the men had obviously been dead for several hours.

"He's never mentioned working with anyone else." Narsi's gaze drifted to a cracked shelf and the weird spattering of blood on the wall. The stain looked almost like a sweep of bleeding wings. "But how he could he have done all this alone?"

"Let's hope we never find out," Atreau replied.

He scanned the room but didn't see any sign of Rinza or the mysterious box he'd sent her to procure. The sound of flies and the smell in the room was oppressive. Atreau withdrew and Narsi followed. Between them they searched most of the first floor of the building quickly. There were no more dead to discover in the storerooms, bath or dining room. But neither was Rinza hidden away in any of the cupboards, closets or chests.

Atreau stilled as he opened the door to the final unexplored room on the ground floor. Utter horror washed through him as he caught sight of a cradle. He remembered Lliro mentioning an infant son and a very young daughter, as well as a young wet nurse, joining the household.

He didn't want to step foot into this nursery.

"What—" Narsi asked from behind him.

"Don't." Atreau cut him off short. "Just stay where you are and wait, will you?"

This time Narsi didn't argue.

Atreau steeled himself and then strode into the airy room, with its cerulean-blue carpet and child-sized furniture. He turned in a slow circle, preparing to see blood and remains. The wet nurse's neat cot stood next to a narrow slit window. A bright yellow rocking horse lay on its side near a large open wardrobe. But other than that, nothing in the room looked amiss. Atreau searched the room with a growing sense of relief and then puzzlement.

Had the wet nurse been away with the children? Considering the hour of the assault, that seemed improbable. Neither the child's bed, the crib nor the wet nurse's cot were neatly made. Instead blankets lay crumpled, as if thrown aside in a rush. Had she somehow slipped past Ariz with an infant and a toddler? That, too, struck him as unlikely. Ariz was nothing if not swift and observant. He wouldn't have overlooked an entire room full of people.

"Are they . . ." Narsi stepped into the room, wearing a harrowed expression. Then, as Atreau had, he stared around the chamber in confusion. "He spared them?"

"Anything is possible," Atreau admitted. "I'm not so certain that it's probable."

"Master Ariz resists as much as he can," Narsi said. "He's not an unfeeling monster."

Atreau wondered if Narsi made the statement to reassure himself or to offer an argument. Atreau shook his head and didn't bother to point out that no amount of feeling on Master Ariz's part made any of this massacre less monstrous. His suffering and guilt didn't bring back any of the lives he took, nor would it stop him from going on to destroy more.

Ironically, Master Ariz would probably be the first person to agree with him. Atreau didn't want to, but for an instant he remembered how accepting, almost relieved, Ariz had sounded last night when he spoke of his own demise.

"I wonder," Narsi said softly. "Master Ariz said something about not allowing any *man* here to survive. Perhaps he used the exact wording of the command to save the children and women. Is that possible?"

"Maybe," Atreau allowed. "Though there's a vast difference between saving someone and not killing them outright."

Ariz certainly hadn't just set Rinza free. And just because they hadn't found the remains of the wet nurse and children, that didn't mean that Master Ariz had left them unharmed. Atreau remembered the bloody handprint on the garden gate. But seeing the guilt in Narsi's expression, he remained quiet and applied himself to searching the large storage closet that adjoined the nursery.

Atreau's gaze fell on the collection of shipping crates and luggage in the far corner of the closet. Baskets. A toy chest. A battered traveling trunk with a key hanging in its brass lock caught his eye. Someone had thrown a blanket over it and left a streak of blood on the edge. It was far too small for a grown man like Atreau or Narsi to fit inside. But a child, or a small woman, might.

Atreau rushed to the trunk and threw open the lid.

Rinza's body lay curled up inside, perfectly motionless. Dried blood stained her mouth and a ring of dark bruises stood out against the pale skin of her thin neck. Had she already been dead when Ariz hid her in the trunk? Or had she died confined and alone?

Atreau's heart sank. He'd endangered Narsi's life for nothing.

Then Rinza cracked one eye open. She offered Atreau a feeble smile as she uncoiled her twisted limbs.

"I smelled your roses," Rinza whispered. Atreau reached out and helped her straighten upright. Rinza flexed her hands and feet. Most of her body was probably numb from lying so still and cramped so long.

"Did you find what I asked for?" Atreau whispered to her.

"I found it. But the master of the house, Ojoito, caught me and went for my throat." Rinza touched her neck and winced.

"I'm sorry," Atreau told her.

"You don't understand. When Ojoito came upon me making off with his pretty box and started throttling me, I thought I was beyond hope. I gave my fate to Our Savior." Rinza's expression struck Atreau as disturbingly serene. "And then, Trueno flew in through the window. He . . . he saved me even though I bit him till I tasted his blood. He just hid me away and said he'd send help." Rinza peered around the room, as if she expected to see the saint standing there.

Atreau wondered just how drunk she'd been when Master Ariz had attacked the household. Or maybe she'd been hit too hard when Ojoito had assaulted her.

"Trueno?" Narsi asked. Though as he drew nearer Rinza, his curious expression turned to surprise. "You look so familiar—have we met before?"

"No, but I know that you're the physician. He said he'd send you to save me." Rinza's smile faltered. "I was waiting so long in the dark and I couldn't get out . . . but he promised and I had faith. Just like the chapel stories."

Atreau didn't like the strange tone creeping into her voice. She'd been through two hells of hardship already, so he could see why, but it wouldn't do any of them any good if she lost her grip right now. Fortunately, Narsi didn't question her explanation. He simply nodded and looked Rinza over with a flatteringly attentive expression. He opened a jar of some astringently scented balm and applied it gingerly to her scraped hands and then her neck.

"By chance do you have a brother called Riquo?" Narsi asked. Rinza stared at him and so did Atreau.

"You know Riquo?" Rinza asked.

"I treated him last night. The two of you look so much alike." Narsi glanced to Atreau. "I found him at the foot of the sacred grove."

Atreau felt a stab of sorrow. So, Riquo had numbered among those Hierro transformed into mindless mordwolves. Until just this moment, Atreau hadn't recognized how strongly he'd clung to the possibility that somehow the canny thief had escaped Hierro.

But no. Of course he hadn't.

There hadn't ever been any real hope for him. Atreau had simply indulged in self-delusion born of guilt. Now he could only comfort himself in the knowledge that Riquo's death would have been quick. Fedeles's shadow was as fast as it was merciless.

"Is he . . ." Rinza didn't seem able to even ask.

"Very weak but alive," Narsi assured her. "He's recovering at the Haldiim hospital. He asked for you directly after I revived him. I think he'll be overjoyed to see you."

Rinza beamed and folded her hands as if sending up thanks to the heavens. A hint of happy pride filled Narsi's benevolent expression. At the same time, Atreau's heart filled with dread.

So long as he was in Hierro's thrall, Riquo could be transformed and used against them all. How many of Hierro's assassins could they afford to keep alive? Then something struck Atreau.

"Did you say you revived Riquo?" Atreau asked Narsi.

"Yes. His injuries were . . ." Narsi gave a quick glance to Rinza. "I employed a Yuanese technique that can revive a heart after it's stilled. And I believe because of that the thrall was broken."

"His heart stopped?" Rinza asked.

"For only an instant." Narsi said it like it was nothing more than a hiccup. "But his soul refused to abandon this world. He's a very determined fellow, I think."

"He is." Rinza wiped at her eyes and nodded. "I should go to him."

"You should both go," Atreau decided. Then he added before Narsi could object, "You can show Rinza the way."

Narsi frowned but didn't argue. Rinza started for the door.

"The pretty box?" Atreau called after her. "What of it?"

"I dropped it when Ojoito grabbed me. I didn't see what fell out." Rinza glanced back to him. "Upstairs in his study. It could still be there."

"Why don't we help you search—" Narsi began, but Rinza was already out the door.

Narsi looked between her receding figure and Atreau, clearly torn.

"Go," Atreau told him. "She may need your care."

More importantly, she and Narsi both needed to get out of this slaughterhouse before anyone discovered them. Neither of them possessed a noble title to exploit if they were captured. Atreau wasn't even certain his own petty claim would shield him if he was blamed for this massacre.

"I'll meet you at the Goose as we agreed," Atreau told Narsi. "You'd best get going."

Narsi seemed frustrated, but he went, calling over his shoulder, "Keep safe."

"You as well." Atreau left the nursery and made for the stairs. There he encountered three more corpses, their remains smeared down the steps like toppled slop buckets. Atreau guessed that they'd been running up in response to a disturbance from the second floor. From the lethal look of their weapons, both had been professional soldiers. And now they lay like discarded scarecrows, with their stiff limbs jutting out at weird angles and their stuffing spilled out around them.

A severed hand waited on the top step. The stiff fingers clutched a golden feather. Atreau plucked the plume. An eagle feather? He frowned again at the mutilated bodies on the stairs. Last night, he'd witnessed men transformed into slavering wolves and set loose, but it was hard to imagine a bird serving the same purpose, much less a flock of them accompanying Ariz on his murderous campaign.

Though eagles the size of those the grimma had commanded would be another matter altogether. Those creatures could tear a man's head from his body with their huge talons. A shudder slithered up Atreau's spine at the memory. The thick stench of blood drifted from a rust-red spatter on the feather and Atreau dropped it.

He wanted out of this place. He turned back, took a step down, but the shame of his own cowardice stopped him. Was he so weak that he couldn't step over another corpse? Not even to save his friends and country? He clenched the banister and then bolted up the stairs. Then raced across the landing and into the wreck of a study.

There he discovered numerous broken casks, fallen crates and a pair of dead guardsmen. Near an oak writing table in the center of the room, the royal bishop's bastard son slumped in a gory heap. Atreau recognized Ojoito by the costly rings on his fingers. His head and chest looked as if they'd been ripped apart in hunks. Flies carpeted the open cavity of the body and a revolting stench rose from him like steam from a fumarole. A naked dagger lay at the foot of the table not far from a matted heap of human scalp. The stench of soiled meat and rancid blood seemed to thicken in afternoon warmth. Sickness rose and Atreau fought to keep control of himself.

Thankfully a breeze of fresh air drifted in through a broken window. He turned away from the corpse and fought back his own reaction. He stared at the writing desk, taking in the ink bottle and packing straw without thought—just fighting to control the horror and sickness lurching through his body. His pulse felt as if it were hammering against his throat. Clammy sweat beaded his brow and slid down his ribs like rivulets of ice.

He'd seen bodies mutilated and mauled like this before—in Labara, when the grimma had unleashed mordwolves and snowlions upon the defenders of Radulf County. He'd seen men and women burned alive as fire rained from the sky, and he'd held screaming, bloody children in his arms as they died. These few corpses shouldn't have affected him so powerfully after all that. But somehow this room—the smell of it and the hum of the flies—seemed to bring all his past horror washing over him again.

Tremors shook through his fingers, as though he once more held a terrified young soldier down while a mother-physician sawed away the spasming gristle and shattered bone of his half-eaten leg. He clenched his eyes closed as if that could blot out the memories.

No one was dying—no one screaming. In fact, it was very quiet. He could hear his own intake of rapid breaths. He forced himself to hold a breath to the steady count of ten. Then another. The pounding of his heart slowed.

As he calmed, he became aware of a strange little bright spot behind his eyelids.

He focused on the distraction to pull himself free of his memories. He looked again to the white oak writing desk. An ink bottle, a pen and paper. There was also a small packing box—not larger than a pen case. Otherwise the desk was unremarkable.

Except that when he closed his eyes, that small square afterimage burned to life again.

Atreau opened his eyes and peered at the desktop.

Now that he looked closely, he realized that a faint rectangular shadow sat on the surface, like a faded stain. Atreau sidestepped the dead body at his feet. He reached out. Where his eyes took in nothing but afternoon light, his fingers brushed over a cold surface. Then a metal hinge. He felt a corner and then a carved lid. A small box. Though he still could not see it, he lifted it up.

As he did so, he exposed a scrap of paper hidden beneath.

Your Holiness,

I hope you will be pleased to learn that I have acquired the relic you desired. The Hor—

What more the paper had said had been torn away. Atreau couldn't see any remnant of the rest of the message on the desk. Then he glimpsed a stained corner of paper peeking out from beneath Ojoito's thigh. He steeled himself turn over the corpse and search.

Then he heard the sound of boots striking the stairs in a fast charge. He straightened and stepped behind the door, gripping his dagger.

A moment later Narsi raced into the study.

"Lord Vediya?" he whispered.

"Here." Atreau too kept his voice low.

Narsi spun around. He looked truly frightened—his eyes wide, his face ashen. Though the moment he met Atreau's gaze, his expression relaxed a little.

"What's wrong?" Atreau stepped forward.

"There are men—bishop's guardsmen—advancing on the house," Narsi whispered. "I counted twenty. There could be more. They're coming toward the front of the house."

"Where's Rinza?" Atreau asked.

"She was already past them and halfway across the memorial grounds when I turned back for you."

"Why in the three hells did you come back?" Atreau demanded.

Narsi frowned at him like he was an idiot. He'd returned for Atreau's sake, obviously. Atreau just wished that he hadn't. Or that he'd followed his own callow instinct earlier and fled this damn place.

"Did they see you?" Atreau whispered.

"I don't think so."

Atreau stepped nearer to the shattered window and peered out. He noted several dwarf apple trees in the stone courtyard below. Odd shadows moved beneath the fluttering leaves of the apples trees. He glimpsed a black cloak and a violet sash. Then he picked out another man in armor, and another. At least fifteen that he could see from where he stood. Narsi's count of twenty was most likely correct. And all of them already on the grounds.

His heart sank.

Narsi edged next to him. "It looked like they were surrounding the building."

Atreau nodded. Should he and Narsi attempt to climb down from here? Atreau couldn't see the faintest crack in the wall that would offer even a toehold. They'd be lucky if they didn't break their legs falling from this height. And even if they could manage that, they'd have to make it out the gates without being detected. In broad daylight, they'd probably be spotted at once.

Would they have a better chance if they hid inside the house? Atreau scowled. Neither of them was so slight that he could curl up in a tiny trunk or slither under the floorboards. Crouching in some cupboard would only delay the inevitable, unless the guardsmen could be distracted or drawn away.

A resounding boom sounded from downstairs. The heavy timbers of the front doors creaked and groaned, and then another barrage of violent thuds pounded through the air. Typical guardsmen, they hadn't bothered to try the unlocked kitchen door. Or, Atreau realized, they'd not noticed it yet. In their hurry, they'd overlooked the garden entry. A flicker of hope lit in Atreau's chest.

If the guardsmen could be drawn inside the house and up the stairs, then there was a chance that someone could escape from the kitchen and slip out the garden gate without being seen. But how to immediately draw them all upstairs? The obvious and terrible solution came to Atreau. One of them positioned at the top of the staircase could provide distraction and lure the guardsmen up to the study while the other fled. Better that one of them live than they both die.

He turned to Narsi, met his gaze and knew at once that if he asked, Narsi would make the sacrifice. He was too courageous and too genuinely noble to refuse.

"I need you to—" The words caught in Atreau's throat.

Narsi cocked his head in question when Atreau didn't go on.

"Just tell me," Narsi said, and Atreau realized that after this he would never know Narsi's trust again. He'd never meet his gaze and feel affection or admiration.

"I need you to . . . take this for safekeeping in your satchel." Atreau caught Narsi's hand and carefully placed the invisible box in his grip. "Fedeles and Oasia should see it."

"Is this another null spell?" Narsi stared down at his hand. Then he quickly closed it up in his satchel.

"A relic, I believe. Oasia is likely to know more about it." Atreau strode from the study with Narsi on his heels. They reached the stairs. Atreau stopped and ran his hand over the banister, then he moved aside to allow Narsi past.

"Go to the kitchen and wait until you hear me shout. Then get the hell out of here." He felt absurd drawing his sword, but he would need it if he was going to keep the guardsmen occupied for any length of time.

Alarm lit Narsi's face.

"Wait. You want me to run away while you—" He shook his head. "You can't be serious. There are at least twenty—"

"It's just a ruse." Atreau took a little pride in how calm his voice sounded. Almost natural. "As soon as they've lumbered up here, I'll go out the window. The same way that Ariz came in. We'll meet up again after you've delivered the box to Fedeles."

There was more he would have liked to have said, more he would have wanted to do. But he could hear the beams of the entry doors giving way. He didn't have any more time. He had to act while his courage held.

"Just go—"

All at once a wave of darkness loomed up before him, standing like an impossible gateway in the open air. A moldering, deathly scent washed over his face.

He heard the doors crash apart. The royal bishop's guardsmen flooded in, swords drawn. There was no time to think.

"Change of plan." Atreau caught Narsi's arm in a desperate grip and plunged into the seeping wall of darkness. The Sorrowlands swallowed them.

CHAPTER EIGHTEEN

Fedeles entered the palace in the midmorning, already exhausted.

The day had begun with news of the massacre at the foot of the sacred grove. Then, before that could be fully investigated, there came word from the Slate House that the royal bishop's bastard son, Ojoito, and all the men in his household had been slaughtered. Despite that, servants throughout the gardens tossed perfume and orange blossoms into the fountains and hurried to heap feasting tables with flowers and delicacies. Groups of musicians loitered near hedges, practicing festive songs.

The holy Masquerade and great Cadeleonian victories that it celebrated would not be abandoned. Not even in the wake of horror and tragedy.

Fedeles swayed, then forced himself ahead. Riding to the palace, he had nearly fallen unconscious. Oasia had caught his arm, steadying him, and sent a quick stream of cerulean light surging over him like a splash of scalding water. He'd jolted upright and remained alert the rest of the way.

But as that rush of alarm faded, exhaustion crept back over him like frost. Icy sweat beaded his chest. He shuddered. Despite the summer heat, the many layers of his silk clothes and his cloak, he felt chilled to the very core. He couldn't seem to retain any warmth since he'd reignited the wards of the sacred grove the previous night.

He was empty.

But he didn't regret his decision. Nor did he regret battling the mordwolves on the open streets of the city, especially since it was his interference that had roused the creatures in the first place. He only wished he'd been slyer about it. If only he'd thought to wear a disguise, a mask at the very least, he might not be facing charges for the second day in a row. This time there might even be witnesses to speak against him, accusing him of witchcraft.

A grim air pervaded the throne room. As Fedeles entered, the assembled courtiers parted, leaving a path that he walked like a gauntlet straight to Sevanyo. As he passed by, the sea of beautifully costumed nobles and courtiers resumed their normal positions. Anxiety fluttered through their whispered gossip, eroding the majesty of their presentations. Fedeles understood their fear.

Survivors of the attack on the Slate House had described a monstrous eagle with sabers for talons and wings like knife blades. Men transformed into slavering mordwolves filled all accounts of the massacre at the sacred grove. Both evoked voracious beasts commanded by Labaran witchcraft.

Now the sea of men and women all costumed as whimsical incarnations of those mythic beasts seem ominous. Even treacherous. The unfortunate few courtiers who'd dressed as birds appeared particularly uneasy as Fedeles brushed past them on his way to Sevanyo and the royal bishop. One young girl crumpled a mask between her hands.

Fedeles took the marble steps up to the throne in swift strides, hoping his speed would hide his exhaustion from onlookers. Momentum more than strength propelled his aching legs. His arms swung like slack ropes, and his fingers felt numb as weights dangling from his limp hands. Even his normally willful shadow hung listlessly beneath his feet.

He halted on the tenth marble step. He felt as if he'd climbed a mountain; tremors fluttered down the muscles of his back and thighs. Cold sweat dribbled down the back of his neck.

A few feet from him Nugalo swayed with one hand pressed over his eyes. His shoulders trembled and the choked noise that escaped him made Fedeles think that he was fighting not to weep aloud. Fedeles averted his gaze. He despised Nugalo, but knowing the man had just learned of his son's violent death, Fedeles couldn't help but feel sympathy. If Sparanzo had been murdered, Fedeles would have been roaring with tears and fury. Even imagining the possibility filled him with sickened horror. He had no idea how Nugalo summoned the restraint to stand so quietly before the king's court.

"I'm sorry for your loss," Fedeles whispered.

Nugalo dragged his hand back from his red-streaked face and glowered at Fedeles.

"The king's passing is a loss for our entire nation," Nugalo bit out.

Fedeles sighed. It was too much to hope that the royal bishop would put the dignity of his title aside even to mourn his child.

"May he have peace in paradise," Fedeles replied. The royal bishop didn't meet his gaze but scowled down at the nobles gathered below them with a bleak expression.

"Fedeles," Sevanyo called softly from the steps above. Fedeles lifted his gaze.

Sevanyo leaned forward on his marble throne, looking wan and worn, as if he'd aged a decade in a day. His eyes were bloodshot hollows, his mouth a pallid gash. His formal gold robe seemed a little too small, while the gold crown weighing on his brow appeared heavy and antiquated. Fedeles recognized that both had belonged to King Juleo. Sevanyo's own crowns and royal raiment were still being finished, since no one had expected him to have to take the throne so soon.

The flock of white-robed physician-priests who once clustered around King Juleo were all gone—either to their executions or a royal dungeon to face interrogators. In their places, Sevanyo retained two attendant youths dressed in gold-and-blue uniforms as well as four well-armed royal guards.

When Sevanyo met Fedeles's gaze, a flicker of a smile lifted the corners of his pale lips.

"Come to me, my boy." Sevanyo waved him forward.

"It would be my honor, Your Majesty." Fedeles held himself straight as he took the last steps to the foot of the towering marble throne. A wave of dizziness washed over him and for an instant he thought he might collapse as he had on Crown Hill. Instead he managed to merely drop to his knees. One of Sevanyo's youthful attendants slunk forward and offered him a silk pillow to rest on, but Fedeles waved him away. Discomfort was one of the only things keeping him awake right now.

"You've heard about the murders last night?" Sevanyo asked. "Fifty men killed in the Haldiim District and another dozen slaughtered in the Slate House."

"I have." Fedeles prepared himself to argue his innocence. But he was so tired that he could hardly think, never mind interweaving the truth with enough lies to protect himself and his household. People had to have seen him, perhaps not clearly in the dark streets, but when the sacred grove had lit up with blessings, he'd been illuminated as if standing on a stage. So he knew he couldn't deny any involvement with the mordwolves.

He glanced down at the throng of gathered courtiers and briefly met Oasia's intent gaze. The fanciful styling of her green dress and black tresses lent her the appearance of a summer queen. Her ladies and maid surrounded her like a retinue woodland nymphs. Several older noblemen drifted near her. All of them were supporters of Sevanyo's—if not direct allies to Fedeles.

The instant she noted Fedeles's attention, she flicked her fan and a cerulean spark flew to a corner near the servants' doors in the back of the room. The height of the throne allowed Fedeles to look beyond the vast crowd of costumed nobles and recognize Captain Yago's blunt face. Two of his soldiers stood behind him, guarding a slender Cadeleonian girl. She no longer wore a threadbare shift painted with a chapel star. Instead she'd been clothed in a modest ochre dress. A blue braided belt hung around her hips instead of the penitent's rope that had previously held her beggar's cup.

The half-Haldiim infant she cradled was swaddled in a dark brown blanket, which closely matched the kerchief that held back the beggar girl's dark hair. Clearly Yago had gone to some trouble to clean the girl up and make her appear presentable to court.

Fedeles's heart sank. Not only had this girl heard his named called out near the warehouse, but she'd seen him at the sacred grove.

A wisp of Oasia's cerulean spell curled around the beggar girl's throat.

Fedeles frowned. He remembered how desperate the girl had been last night, and then how hopeful she'd appeared when he'd given her his coin purse. He didn't want to take that hope from her or her child, not if he didn't have to.

Fedeles looked to Oasia and gave the slightest shake of his head. She scowled in response but then released the cerulean spell.

"They are saying that Count Radulf is seeking revenge." Sevanyo's words drew Fedeles's attention back. "Nugalo condemned his sister, and so he sent an enchanted eagle to kill Nugalo's son."

On the steps below them, the royal bishop grimaced. But what did he expect? That they would all pretend to be unaware of the child he'd fathered, even when it came to investigating the slaughter of some sixty people? The entire court could be so absurd in its hypocrisy. Why did they all insist on claiming so much ignorance and clinging to so many lies? Was there any advantage to disgracing an innocent child as illegitimate while celebrating and acknowledging others? What did such laws do but foster resentment, envy and shame?

Church edicts forbidding magic were just as injurious, Fedeles thought as he took in the faint light of old and new spells hanging throughout the throne room. What good did it do anyone to force people like himself and Oasia to pretend not to notice the magical powers that were so clearly at work all around them? Instead of speaking frankly, they were forced to prevaricate and manipulate everyone around them. Who knew how many other people throughout the throne room also feigned ignorance? Fedeles was certain that Sevanyo wasn't completely oblivious. And yet the very laws he upheld cornered them into this awkward conversation.

The entire predicament would have been laughable, except that so many lives stood to be lost—not to mention the ones that had already been sacrificed.

"I do not believe that Count Radulf is to blame," Fedeles replied. "Such a claim is, at best, an ill informed, war-mongering provocation."

Fedeles didn't miss the surprise on the royal bishop's face, but he had no time to enjoy it. Instead he searched the crowd for Hierro Fueres. The man stood farther back than normal and looked uncharacteristically withdrawn, his shoulders slumped and his expression sulky. Fedeles was relieved to see that their battle last night hadn't been without cost for Hierro. His sister Clara hung at his elbow, her features hidden behind her translucent widow's veil. Then Fedeles's attention caught on the austere figure standing amidst Clara's attendant maids.

Master Ariz.

Even across the vast throne room Fedeles noticed the bandage wrapped around his hand and the dark ring of bruises coloring his throat. Fedeles felt his heart lurch in his chest. What had Hierro done to him in the hours since Fedeles had last seen him? How much more would he have to endure?

"What makes you think this has nothing to do with the count?" Sevanyo pitched his voice to carry over the whispering courtiers.

Fedeles dragged his attention away from Ariz, suppressing his fear for the other man. Right now he needed to keep their entire nation from going to war against Count Radulf. And he needed to do so without incriminating Oasia, Atreau or himself.

"First, because I've met Count Radulf and it's not in his character to attack his enemies in a sly manner and leave it to them to work his motivation." Fedeles addressed himself to the simplest matter first. "If these killings were his doing, he would have declared himself and his intention to make the royal bishop suffer."

"Indeed, the count is well known for his brash character." Sevanyo nodded and a little color returned to his pale cheeks. Almost absently he reached out and patted Fedeles's head. A rush of heat soaked through Fedeles's scalp. "And why else?"

"Secondly," Fedeles went on, "the larger attack wasn't related to the royal bishop in any way. Quite the opposite, it was aimed at the Haldiim sacred grove, which the royal bishop is known to despise."

"You can't possibly know the direction of the assault, Lord Quemanor," a man dressed as a velvet lion shouted from beside Hierro. "Not unless the rumors are true and you were there among those monsters."

Fedeles hardly spared the man a glance; instead he looked to Oasia. If he denied having been there, then he couldn't testify to the truth he'd seen with his own eyes. If he admitted to being present, he opened himself up to accusations of practicing sorcery and witchcraft. He could protect himself, but only at a cost to their entire nation.

They had both agreed that Hierro would never expect him to admit to having been on hand at the warehouse or the sacred grove last night; the possibility of Fedeles being exposed as a witch was far too dangerous. Hierro would take Fedeles's fear and silence for granted. The faint crease of a frown flickered over Oasia's serene face. She nodded for him to go ahead with his confession. Behind her Delfia and Elenna quietly slipped away to prepare the children in case it became necessary to flee.

"In fact, I was there," Fedeles admitted. He wasn't surprised to hear gasps and see wide eyes staring at him. He went on before anyone could interrupt him with accusations. "I witnessed men imprisoned in the Corrdevo's Wool warehouse transform into mordwolves. Their attack on the men guarding the warehouse started the fire there. I then saw them attack the sacred grove."

"What a coincidence that you just happened to be there, Lord Quemanor." A lady-in-waiting dressed as a dove and poised beside Clara

Odalis spoke up first. "Almost beyond believing."

"I too doubt it could have been a coincidence," Fedeles answered. "I believe that the sorcerer who was holding those men prisoner chose to use them when he realized that I had stumbled upon his machinations and was about to expose him."

"So, you just happened upon this warehouse in the middle of the night?" the royal bishop demanded. And, though his tone was sharp, his expression struck Fedeles as unusually curious.

"No, I sought the place out to investigate rumors of animals being held and mistreated there. People throughout the Weavers' Ward have gossiped for weeks about pitiful noises coming from inside the warehouse. When news reached me, I went with the hope of rescuing the creatures," Fedeles stated, and the brief look of indignation on Hierro's face offered him a small reward. "Of course, I'd thought those creatures were lamed horses left to starve."

Had another man made the same claim, it likely would have been met with skepticism, but for the first time in his life, Fedeles found that his reputation as an eccentric lunatic with an obsession for rescuing elderly and lame horses actually served him. The royal bishop and most other courtiers appeared to accept his explanation. Even Hierro frowned, as if he wasn't quite certain that Fedeles hadn't stumbled upon his assassins by chance while searching out pitiful horses.

"Instead of animals, I discovered men being held captive. Before I could find a way to free them, they transformed into monstrous wolves." Fedeles shuddered at the memory of their contorted bodies and agonized cries. "The fires started when they broke out of the warehouse. As a group they charged onto the open street, attacking anyone in their path. I did what I could to stop them, but they were intent—driven—to assault the sacred grove in the Haldiim District."

"If not you, then what did stop them?" Sevanyo's hand stilled on the top of Fedeles's head.

"The Bahiim blessings that protect the sacred grove ultimately destroyed them. The men's bodies returned to their original forms when they died," Fedeles said. "I myself was exhausted after the ordeal and collapsed as soon as I reached my home. I'm ashamed to admit that I only woke an hour ago, when I was summoned by Your Highness."

For a few moments the entire throne room was so quiet that the distorted notes of some musician out in the garden tuning his lute could be heard clearly.

"And you're certain Count Radulf had nothing to do with it?" Sevanyo asked.

"I am."

"But you have no proof of any of this! Can you offer anything more than mere words, Lord Quemanor?" the royal bishop asked.

Fedeles straightened and stood to glower down at the royal bishop.

"I have already proven my loyalty and honesty before the Hallowed Kings, your Holiness," Fedeles snapped. "Can any of the gossips, sycophants and pickthanks who slander me make the same claim?"

All around them, furtive and excited whispers rose in waves. If anyone had been ignorant of the fact that Fedeles had stood before the Hallowed Kings and been found innocent, they were informed now.

The royal bishop's gaze darted from Fedeles to Hierro's direction. Fedeles followed his stare and realized that the old man now studied his heir, Prince Remes. Unaware of his uncle's scrutiny, the prince bowed his head, whispering into the veils hiding Clara Odalis's face. Hierro, however, appeared to notice the royal bishop's aggrieved glower. He drew himself up straight.

"I understand that Captain Yago, of the royal bishop's guardsmen, wished to present a witness as well." Hierro raised his deep voice over the rumbles of exuberant speculation. "A second testimony will perhaps clarify Lord Quemanor's recollections."

"Perhaps," the royal bishop agreed, then he looked askance to Sevanyo.

"I'll hear this witness out," Sevanyo allowed. "But it should be clear to everyone that I place my faith in Fedeles Quemanor's word. His integrity has indeed been extolled in the Shard of Heaven by the Hallowed Kings themselves."

Captain Yago already shouldered his way through the crowd, though he took trouble not to jostle high-ranking nobles and instead pushed aside maids and minor attendants as he brought the beggar girl and her child up to the foot of Sevanyo's throne.

"Who is this witness?" Sevanyo asked.

"Chispa Kir-Madi," Captain Yago answered. "Widow of a cartographer who served aboard Prince Gael's vessel and was lost with the prince."

Sevanyo went still at the mention of Gael, and Fedeles frowned. Sevanyo cherished Gael above all his relations; just the mention of the prince's name never failed to affect him, not even now.

It would have been an astounding coincidence if this beggar girl truly was connected with the prince in any way. However, providing her with this false identity was certainly a clever ploy to tug at Sevanyo's heart. Gael had been famous for favoring Haldiim cartographers and navigators. Not only had he learned the Haldiim language to facilitate conversations with them, but he'd championed several of their marriages to Cadeleonian women. So, this cleaned-up waif with her half-Haldiim child did indeed look the part.

"Chispa Kir-Madi." Sevanyo repeated the Haldiim surname with particular care. "Did your departed husband ever speak of my son?"

The girl stood stock-still for several seconds, then slowly nodded.

"Everyone loved Prince Gael," she said. "He is always in my prayers."

Sevanyo smiled, then beckoned to the girl. "Come, child, let me look at you and hear what you have to say."

The girl curled her arms around her swaddled baby and started up the large marble steps. She kept her head bowed. As she came forward, Captain Yago continued to address Sevanyo and by extension the court.

"The widow was on hand last night when a group of Haldiim gathered at their grove to practice magic," Yago stated. "They clearly summoned the wolves with the intent to release them against the city. After hearing the good widow's testimony, I request that His Majesty give me leave to take control over the Haldiim District and all Haldiim citizens in the city to fully investigate and discover the culprits responsible."

The girl reached the eleventh step as Yago concluded his statement. She stopped short of Fedeles and averted her gaze when he looked at her.

"This is a very different testimony from Lord Quemanor's." Sevanyo cocked his head to the side and considered the girl. The warmth drained from his expression as he went on. "One could almost imagine that the two of you were in completely different places last night. Or that someone is lying."

This close, Fedeles could see tremors of fear shaking the girl's body. Sweat beaded her brow. She had to recognize how precarious her situation was, and yet, what power did she have to protect herself or her child from the nobles all around her? He felt a sudden sympathy for her.

"The good widow isn't lying." Fedeles took the initiative to show her a little mercy; he hoped that she would return the kindness. "She was at the sacred grove last night. I saw her there."

The girl looked to Fedeles. Her dark eyes went wide with surprise, and he offered her a brief smile. Perhaps they could find a way through this together.

She bowed to him.

Suddenly a whip of indigo light lashed up from Hierro's hand, streaking toward the beggar girl's back. Fedeles didn't have the strength to break the spell. Instead he pulled the girl upright, turning her to face Sevanyo and placing his own body between her and Hierro.

Hierro's attack slammed across his shoulders. Fedeles suppressed a gasp of pain. Stinging curses punched into his shoulders and spine.

You will obey me, bitch. Hierro's threat crawled into Fedeles's ears like a slick worm. The curses bit into him again and again like a storm of wasps. Fedeles shuddered, but this was far from the worst pain he'd endured.

Then as Hierro's spell sank into him, Fedeles felt a strange burst of heat and a flush of power seep into his muscles. The icy numb lifted from his fingers and his shadow flexed against the marble step at his feet.

Fedeles stood, stunned for a moment.

There was no way that Hierro had intended to lend him this strength. Was it possible that Fedeles had so depleted his body that it had reflexively drained the power from within Hierro's curse, like a parched animal gulping down filthy water regardless of muck and scum?

He tensed, expecting Hierro's curse to intensify to a brutal agony. But sapped of energy, the punishing intent of the spell seemed to shrivel. Fedeles felt only a hum and prick, hardly more than the bite of a horsefly. Then it was done.

Below him, Oasia stared with an expression of amazed relief, while Hierro looked like he might vomit. Fedeles felt as shocked as the two of them. Never would he have imagined that his very desolation could be used as a kind of shield.

Still he smirked down at Hierro. Let Hierro think that he'd mastered the ability to devour curses and drink poison. Then Fedeles schooled his expression to a more somber countenance and returned his attention to Sevanyo and the beggar girl. He stepped to the side so that the girl could see his face.

"It was dark last night and confusing, so I believe that though this good woman is honest, she may have been mistaken on several points in her testimony," Fedeles added, holding her gaze.

"It *was* very confusing. Very frightening," the girl agreed.

"But you're safe now," Fedeles assured her. "So, if you think back, could you try and remember what direction the wolves came from?"

"From the Weavers' Ward," she whispered.

"Speak up, my dear," Sevanyo told her. "I'm not a young man, and my hearing is not so good."

Sevanyo's hearing, like his sight, was quite keen, in fact, but Fedeles understood that he wanted the girl's testimony to carry to the royal bishop as well as all the surrounding courtiers.

The girl straightened and drew her sleeping baby close to her chest.

"The wolves came from the Weavers' Ward. I remember because the fire bells were ringing in that direction, and I could see flames rising behind them. And then I saw him . . ." She gestured to Fedeles.

"Lord Quemanor?" Sevanyo supplied gently.

"Yes. Lord Quemanor came riding after them, and I heard him shouting warnings to the revelers out on the street. He killed several of the wolves—"

"And how did he manage such a daring feat?" Hierro demanded from below them.

Fedeles tensed. He'd killed the mordwolves with his shadow and his rage. For an instant he read the uncertainty in the girl's face. Then she offered Fedeles the faintest of smiles.

"A pike, I think," she said.

It had been Atreau who'd fought using the pike, but in the dark and through the chaos, Fedeles felt certain most facts surrounding the event would be confused. At least this detail would match other pieces of gossip already circulating on the city streets.

The girl went on. "There wasn't much light until the blessings in the sacred grove all lit up. Then it was almost too blinding to see anything other than those beasts being wiped away."

"And the Haldiim who had gathered in the grove, what of them?" It was Ladislo Bayezar, standing not too far from Oasia, who called out the question. Fedeles wasn't certain of his intention until he added, "I take it that they did not summon these wolves. Nor were they the witches Captain Yago has claimed them to be?"

"From what I saw of them—" The beggar girl paused briefly, but it seemed like an eternity to Fedeles. So many innocent lives depended upon her words. "I think they were courting couples who'd gone to the grove to . . . um . . . I dare not say words that might offend His Holiness or His Highness. My departed husband always called it 'making magic under the moonlight.' That was what I told the captain." She trailed off, looking embarrassed.

Half-suppressed laughter and open snickers sounded from many of those below them, and Sevanyo gave the beggar girl an amused smile. She kept her head bowed.

Fedeles resisted the urge to grin at her. How exceptionally clever. By claiming that modesty led her to employ a euphemism in her testimony to Captain Yago, she'd devised a means to retract the earlier statement without admitting to perjury. This even allowed Captain Yago to withdraw his accusations as a mere misunderstanding.

"So, you witnessed those people engaged in activities that a young lady can't easily describe. Particularly not to an imposing and unrelated man like Captain Yago. Yes?" Fedeles decided to make the matter explicit and be done with this.

"Yes, my lord," she replied. "I didn't know how to say it. I didn't mean to mislead anyone, but I didn't know how else to say . . . that."

"Your modesty is nothing to be ashamed of," Sevanyo assured her, but his attention turned to the royal bishop. "Don't you agree, Nugalo?"

"Of course," the royal bishop ground out, though oddly, Fedeles thought that it wasn't the beggar girl or even himself who inspired the royal bishop's ire. He cast another glower down at Remes and then scowled at Yago.

"Corrdevo's warehouse, its owners, as well as all movements surrounding it in the past months will be investigated by my city guards. The commander will make his reports directly to me. As for the Haldiim District and our Haldiim citizens . . ." Sevanyo steepled his fingers in thought.

Fedeles fought the impulse to urge him to recall the royal bishop's guardsmen from the district. Sevanyo had already made a show of favoritism toward him. If he went too far, it would only inspire resentment and retaliation from the other noblemen. That in turn would require Sevanyo to make some show of reproaching him. Fedeles clenched his mouth shut.

"The royal bishop has been quite generous in lending Captain Yago and his men to help patrol while my royal guards escort Lord Grunito from Anacleto," Sevanyo went on. "However, I feel that we can only take advantage of His Holiness for so long. Beginning tomorrow, responsibility for the patrols should be returned to the city guard."

"But Your Highness," Captain Yago objected. "It's widely rumored that dissidents among the Haldiim community are planning to throw the city into chaos on the Solstice. The city guards as well as your own royal guards have heard news of this!"

Sevanyo scowled at Yago but then glanced down to the commander of his royal guard. The gray-haired man nodded in response and Sevanyo sighed heavily.

"Very well, you will coordinate your patrols with the royal guards on the Solstice Day to ensure the safety of all our citizens."

Fedeles opened his mouth to object, but Sevanyo went on before he could speak.

"However, since Solstice is a holy day for our Haldiim citizens, I wish to make it clear that they are to be allowed to gather and celebrate. Their sacred grove shall not be denied to them in any way." Sevanyo waited until Captain Yago acknowledged him with a bow. "As the second day of the Masquerades falls on the Solstice this year, I also urge all the city guards to show restraint while maintaining order. A certain amount of mischief is expected, after all."

"Very well, Your Majesty." Captain Yago looked none too happy as he again bowed and then withdrew from the foot of the throne steps. The commander of the royal guard sent an underling to meet with him in the crowd of courtiers. Sevanyo returned his attention to Fedeles and the beggar girl in front of him.

"I'd like to see this young widow and her child settled comfortably," Sevanyo said. "Can I entrust the matter to you, Fedeles?"

"I and my household are at your disposal, Your Highness," Fedeles replied, then he took the girl's rough hand in his own and turned her to look down to where Oasia stood in the midst of her ladies and maids. "That beautiful woman in green is my wife, Lady Quemanor. Join her and ask that she arrange an escort to take you to my household and into Bishop Timoteo's care. You and your child will be safe, I promise you."

The girl nodded and quickly descended the steps. Four of Oasia's maids met her at the bottom and escorted her back to Oasia's side.

A few minutes later Sevanyo dismissed the gathered nobles and courtiers, bidding them to put their worries aside and enjoy themselves in his gardens while they celebrated the first day of Masquerade. Fedeles turned to leave, but Sevanyo caught his hand and drew him back to the side of his throne.

"First Papa's murder, then all of these transformed beasts," Sevanyo spoke in a whisper. "Is this truly nothing to do with Count Radulf?"

"He makes an easy scapegoat, but I promise you it wasn't the count who enthralled the physician-priests or the men kept in that warehouse." Fedeles bowed his head to whisper close to Sevanyo's ear, so that even Sevanyo's personal attendants and guards couldn't hear them. "I would've recognized his magic if it had been. Count Radulf's witchflame is brilliant scarlet, and it feels warm and floral—like summer wind. The spells last night were indigo and teal and rippling with sour rage."

"You recognized them?" Sevanyo asked.

"I'm certain Hierro Fueres imprisoned the men, but I'm not sure of his role in the attack on the sacred grove." Fedeles frowned at the memory of that strange childlike presence that had driven the mordwolves. "I suspect that one of his conspirators exploited my discovery of the enthralled men at the warehouse to force Hierro to assault the sacred grove. But that wasn't what he intended to do with them originally—at least not so soon."

"What do you mean?"

"From what I witnessed of the place before the fire, I think he meant to use those men as assassins. But once they were exposed, he had to dispose of them and destroy the warehouse to erase as much incriminating evidence as possible. To that end, he spread the fire and threw those men against the wards of the sacred grove. But I don't think that was his original plan for them and if we're lucky he hasn't had time yet to completely erase all traces of his connection to the warehouse," Fedeles said. "The investigation into the warehouse could also turn up other names and provide us with evidence that even the royal bishop can not dispute."

Sevanyo nodded but his gaze drifted out over the statues and paintings that decorated the throne room.

"Why kill Ojoito?" Sevanyo asked.

"I don't know how his death could serve Hierro or the royal bishop," Fedeles admitted. "He's always been steadfast in supporting Nugalo. Recently, he even procured a relic from the Salt Islands at the royal bishop's behest, so he clearly hadn't shifted his allegiance. It doesn't make sense as far as I can see."

Then Fedeles recalled the glower Nugalo had aimed at Remes, and he considered the men who had been assassinated in the last month. While they could have been counted as Hierro's allies, they were all far more loyal to the church and the royal bishop.

"Unless there's been a schism between Hierro and the royal bishop. That would mean Remes would have to take a side." Fedeles didn't dare speculate further out loud. Sevanyo already appeared far too alarmed, and one of the attendants looked a little too interested.

"Remes would never . . ." Sevanyo shook his head and ran a hand over his red-rimmed eyes. "Ojoito adored him and spoiled him like a little brother. Remes wouldn't play any part in harming him."

Remes had allied himself with Hierro with the intention of seizing the throne; such ambition went far beyond having a bastard cousin murdered. But Fedeles kept his silence. Sevanyo was by nature sentimental and could only bear so much heartbreak at once. As much as he favored Fedeles, he likely felt even deeper affections for his sons and perhaps his brother as well. It made him a humane prince but also blinded him to the avarice and treachery of those closest to him.

Fedeles wondered if Oasia and Atreau saw him in the same way.

"If they mean to remove every possible Sagrada heir—" Fedeles began softly, but Sevanyo shook his head.

"There's no use in speculating without proof of some kind," Sevanyo said, though he was the one who'd brought the subject up in the first place.

Fedeles sighed but nodded. In his heart, Sevanyo still clung to the belief that he could win Remes back to his side, maybe Nugalo as well. The matter couldn't be forced.

Sevanyo's attention drifted past him to the line of gold-framed paintings decorating the far wall. Fedeles followed his gaze. One painting depicted a majestic seascape and the resplendent ships that Gael had commanded.

"It's so heartbreaking to lose a child," Sevanyo murmured at last. "As much as Nugalo infuriates me, I wouldn't wish this pain on him."

"I know." Fedeles shared Sevanyo's sympathy but wondered if sparing compassion for a man who had wantonly destroyed so many other lives—devastated so many other families—wasn't misplaced.

"Tomorrow morning Nugalo and I are holding a private ceremony to lay Ojoito's soul to rest. Very close friends and our family only. Though who knows if my wayward Jacinto will rouse himself to attend." Sevanyo gave a heavy sigh. "I want you and Oasia to join us. Bring the children. It will do all our spirits good to see their sweet little faces and watch them play. And I have gifts for them."

"I'm not sure Nugalo would want me, or my family, on hand," Fedeles objected.

"Perhaps not. But *I* want you there." Sevanyo gripped his hand. "And I want him to see you at my side and understand that you mean as much to me as his son meant to him."

Fedeles felt so touched that he couldn't argue.

"It would be my honor to stand with you," Fedeles assured him. In truth Sevanyo meant more to him than his own father ever had.

Sevanyo smiled and then slowly released Fedeles's hand.

"But enough of these maudlin thoughts. It's the first day of the Masquerades. I expect to see you costumed and making merry in my gardens tonight." Sevanyo glanced back to his two attendants, and the youths' expressions brightened with excitement. "My own costume may confound the entire court. I plan to astonish everyone when I reveal my identity at midnight. And I've written a little song and dance as well."

Even Sevanyo's guards smiled at that. Clearly Sevanyo's creative work had been a subject that buoyed all their moods.

"I'll look forward to it," Fedeles said.

In previous years Fedeles had enjoyed the games and frivolity of the Masquerades. Last year he'd turned over armloads of old and foreign coins for Sparanzo and the Plunado twins to make themselves mock chain mail.

But these past weeks, Fedeles had been so distressed and distracted that he hardly gave the holiday a thought. Now he had to hope that his valet had arranged some fitting costume for him, otherwise he feared he'd end up dressed as one of Oasia's woodland nymphs.

A few minutes later, Fedeles withdrew, leaving Sevanyo to the care of his eager attendants and guards as well as the pretty maids who waited at the bottom of the steps with tempting morsels and his poppy pipe.

Crossing through the royal gardens, Fedeles noted nobles, courtiers and their favored subjects playing games and chasing each other between flowering hedges and around the gushing fountains. Laughter sounded as did the strains of music. Three men clothed in little more than antlers and velvet capes fled as a group of women wearing paper wings pelted them with flowers and pursued them through the maze of rose arbors.

Watching them, he felt almost as if he were wandering through a dream, wherein only he knew of last night's horrors. Everyone else lived in a colorful, carefree ignorance, like brilliant butterflies fluttering through flower beds. Their revels were alluring, and Fedeles yearned to leave all his worries behind and simply enjoy himself. But who would protect their happy existences if he didn't? And who would he burden with his safety if he decided to shirk his responsibilities? Oasia? Atreau? The already overworked royal guards? This playground of blissful amusements could only exist because others stood sentry outside the comfort, indulgence and frivolity.

He wondered suddenly if Ariz ever felt this way. Then he wondered where Ariz was now and how badly he'd been injured. Again he remembered the bandage he'd glimpsed, as well as Ariz's bruises. Fedeles rubbed his forehead, trying to massage away the tension building in his mind.

Just then, a man moved from the shadows of a vine-draped statue. Fedeles stilled, taking in the man's naval uniform and not-quite-familiar features. Lliro Vediya held a half mask in one hand as a concession to the holy day but clearly had not come to frolic through the palace gardens.

"Lord Quemanor, I would have a word." Lliro wore an uneasy expression and spoke quietly. He'd never numbered among Fedeles's allies, but since the death of his master, Lord Numes, he'd made overtures of support for Fedeles's politics, if not his person. Fedeles waited for Lliro to speak and then, noting the other man's nervousness, moved nearer to him, so that their conversation wouldn't carry.

"I'd be delighted to hear what you have to say, Lord Vediya." Fedeles recalled that Atreau's father had died and so Lliro now held the family title. "Or should I address you as Baron Nifayo now?"

Lliro frowned. Maybe he didn't like the thought of delighting Fedeles with his conversation, or perhaps his new title weighed upon him.

"Vediya is fine," Lliro replied. He stole a wary glance to the archways of rose arbors that sheltered many of the white pebble paths from the afternoon sun. Fedeles looked too, but saw no one. Instead the old blessings flickering from the statue behind Lliro played over his senses like fluttering firelight. Fedeles had to resist the urge to lift his cold hands to the statue to warm them.

"Did my brother enter the Slate House at your behest?" Lliro asked in a whisper.

"No," Fedeles replied, but then the implications of the question filled him with alarm. Had Atreau numbered among the men at the Slate House? "He was there? Is he hurt? Was he—"

"He and a tall Haldiim man arrived after the killer fled but before any alarms were raised. Such precise timing seems a little suspicious." Lliro studied Fedeles intently as he spoke.

"I didn't send him to the Slate House," Fedeles stated. Then another thought occurred to him. So many rumors of his involvement in murders abounded that even after he'd proven his innocence in the Shard of Heaven, suspicions were bound to persist. "Nor did I play any part in the massacre that took place there. I didn't dispatch Atreau to clean up, or whatever else you suspect me of."

"You expect me to believe it was just a coincidence?" Lliro demanded. His flat expression and masterful tone bespoke the years he'd spent commanding warships at sea. But on land Lliro was only a baron. and Fedeles wasn't about to lower himself to providing an obsequious explanation.

"I've told you the truth," Fedeles snapped. "You can believe me or you can fuck off. I don't care which you choose."

Lliro arched a sharp black brow at Fedeles's childish flash of temper. His sardonic expression reminded Fedeles forcefully of Atreau, as did the grim smile that curved the corners of his mouth. His gaze remained cold and assessing.

The heat of an embarrassed flush crept across Fedeles's cheeks. He really had been too childish just now.

"My lord Numes always jested that you were incapable of lying." Lliro nodded. "I see what he meant now."

Fedeles wasn't sure if that was a compliment or not. He let it go.

"Is Atreau safe?" Fedeles asked.

"I don't know. The royal bishop's guardsmen stormed the Slate House before my agent could approach Atreau or his companion—"

Horror bolted through Fedeles's chest.

"The royal bishop's guards captured them?" He had to free Atreau right away.

"The bishop's guardsmen didn't capture anyone. They barely caught a glimpse of them." Lliro's soft voice brought his racing thoughts to an abrupt halt.

"Then is he with your agent?" Fedeles asked.

Lliro shook his head.

"I have no idea where he is now," Lliro said. "But I know it's not safe for him to remain in the capital any longer. That's why I approached you. I have a ship sailing to Anacleto tomorrow morning. I want him aboard it."

"This is a matter you need to discuss with him, don't you think?" Fedeles said.

"No. Obviously, I don't." Lliro glowered at Fedeles. "He is too loyal to his friends, too ready to let all of you use him as you need and then abandon him once you've achieved your goals. He's already dragged himself through thieves' warrens, snake holes and the Knife Market on your behalf. He won't leave on his own, but you owe it to him to send him away."

Fedeles opened his mouth to object, but Lliro went on.

"I'm entreating you to do right by him for once. Take his well-being into account. When next you see him, no matter what you have to tell him, get him aboard that ship. I'll make certain he's safe from there on out."

"I—" Fedeles struggled with the thought of banishing Atreau from his side. He relied on him so much. Then Fedeles remembered Atreau's drawn face last night as the mordwolves charged him and he fought to rouse Fedeles from the grip of his own rage. Only later, when Atreau had briefly spoken about his play and Master Narsi's performance, had the weariness seemed to lift from him. At the time Fedeles had found it startling, but now he realized how wrong it was that he'd allowed himself to grow used to Atreau's despair as the price for Sevanyo's well-being.

Lliro wasn't wrong in saying that he owed Atreau better. Especially now, when they all knew Hierro was preparing some violent attack.

"What's the name of the ship?" Fedeles asked at last.

"The *Summer Wind*," Lliro stated.

"I'll do what I can to send him to you," Fedeles decided.

Perhaps Lliro hadn't expected Fedeles to agree; he appeared momentarily startled, then he smiled. The expression lent his stern face a boyish charm—though both his surprise and his smile proved fleeting. An instant later he, schooled his expression back to cool regard and offered Fedeles a deep bow.

"Thank you, Lord Quemanor," he said, then he turned and strode away.

Fedeles watched him go, then he too turned and continued along the pebble pathway under the rose arbor. It would be better to give up Atreau's company for a few months than to risk losing him forever. Perhaps he ought to send Sparanzo away with him. He pondered what Oasia would say about the prospect. Nothing very complimentary, he didn't expect.

He stepped through a flowering archway. The perfume of summer roses filled the cool shadows. The deep-green leaves caught the afternoon sun, casting emerald shadows all around. Tiny pink blessings hummed like honeybees from the arbor overhead. Fedeles basked in the calm for a while, then stepped out into the sunlight.

A man, all dressed in white, charged him.

Fedeles registered the gleam of a naked sword blade before he recognized Hierro Fueres's sneering face. Fedeles leapt back as his shadow lurched up from his body, tearing through brambles and flowers. It struck the spells surrounding Hierro like a wave hammering the hull of a ship. Hierro snarled an obscenity and skidded back across the pebbled path. Fedeles gasped for breath beneath the bower. His shadow curled around him. He'd burned through the little strength he'd stolen earlier. Now his head spun and his body trembled as if he'd plunged into ice water.

Hierro charged again, swinging his sword high overhead and grinning. Fedeles grasped the hilt of his own sword. Rose thorns clutched at his arm and shirt sleeve as he pulled it free. He was too slow, too clumsy. Hierro's blade descended like a bolt of lightning.

A dark figure lunged between them, blocking Hierro's blade with a sheathed short sword. The man shoved Hierro back two strides, then stole a glance to Fedeles.

Fedeles recognized Ariz even before he saw his stern face.

Fedeles released his sword. He couldn't fight Hierro with Ariz trapped between them. Instead he reach up and caught the honeybee blessings in his hands. For a moment his mind filled with tiny pink symbols and the scent of roses. He peeled aside the gentle designs enclosing the magic at the core of the blessings and drew in their power.

Ahead of him, Hierro hammered his sword down again and Ariz again parried the thrust.

"You dare oppose me?" Hierro bellowed.

A visible shudder passed through Ariz's body. Fedeles threw his shadow over Ariz's back, pressing the strength of the small blessings into Ariz. Ariz straightened and again drove Hierro back with his sheathed sword.

"You piece of shit—" Hierro spat.

"My lord, the royal bishop forbade bare blades in the presence of the royal family." Ariz spoke over Hierro in a flat tone. "On pain of death."

Hierro stilled, then cast an unconcerned glance to his right. Fedeles glimpsed a man and a veiled woman standing near a fountain. Prince Remes and Clara Odalis looked on. Fedeles noted that the prince held Clara back from reaching out to Ariz. Courtiers dressed as silk and velvet beasts surrounded them, but most turned away when Fedeles looked at them. They weren't so bold as to join Hierro in ambushing him, but neither were any of them so upright as to interfere.

"I do beg the prince's indulgence," Hierro called lightly to Remes.

"Let us agree that I wasn't here and have seen nothing." Remes gave a laugh and beamed at Clara. Fedeles wasn't certain if it was the wind blowing through her widow's veils or if Clara shook her head.

"But Prince Remes is not the only royal son on hand, my lord," Ariz stated. He gestured to the crest of a grassy hill on the left.

Jacinto and what appeared to be an entire theater troupe in bright costumes cleared the rise and came ambling toward them. Musicians struck up a melody of lutes, flutes and drums, while several boys and girls dressed in ribbons danced around them. Jacinto himself held hands with a striking Haldiim woman. Both of them wore golden silk costumes, festooned with ribbons and bright paper flowers. A silver moon crowned the woman's blond curls, while Jacinto sported a diadem adorned with gold stars.

Hierro's lip curled at the sight. However, when the dozen royal guards skirting Jacinto's party came into full view, he sheathed his sword and withdrew several feet nearer to Remes. Ariz's tensed shoulders sagged and he returned his own weapon to his sword belt. Only then did he move away from the rose bower. Fedeles stepped out of the shadows, brushing roses and fallen leaves from his clothes.

As he started toward Jacinto's party, he stole a glance back at Ariz. Last night they'd been in each other's arms, but Fedeles had hardly been conscious and the darkness had disguised them both. Now he realized how deeply the strain of the last weeks had carved Ariz down to taut muscles, protruding bones and dark bruises. He looked haggard. His knuckles were scabbed and a distinct scent of dry blood drifted from him. Even the defiant curl of hair at the back of his head appeared limp.

Fedeles wanted to touch him, to offer him some reassurance and protection. He started to extend his hand, then noticed Hierro studying the two of them with an intent, narrowed gaze. Fedeles dropped his hand back to his side, but he feared it was too late. Hierro's earlier frustration and rage seemed to have melted into a smirk.

"It would seem that Lord Quemanor harbors sympathies for mongrel dogs as well as lame geldings," Hierro stated.

Fedeles's heart lurched in his chest, but he gave no response. He didn't even dare spare Ariz another glance. Not when a word from Hierro could cost Ariz his life.

"My prince," Hierro called to Remes, but his attention remained fixed on Fedeles. "Tonight, let me offer this servant, Ariz, to entertain you with fool's dances and the clowning he provided for me at school."

Remes nodded offhandedly before returning his attention to Clara Odalis and her circle of maids.

"Perhaps Lord Quemanor will even deign to join us for the unmasking at midnight." Hierro grabbed Ariz's ear and hauled him close to him. "I'm certain we can arrange something that will entertain everyone, hmm, Ariz?"

Ariz said nothing. His expression remained impassive, his gaze lowered, as Hierro smirked at him. Fedeles couldn't watch and continue to restrain his anger. Instead he pointedly turned his attention to the fountain where Clara and Remes stood surrounded by maids and noblemen. Clara pulled her hand from Remes's grasp and drifted away through the fold of her maids. Remes and his entourage followed after.

Fedeles thought again of Ojoito's murder and the assassins that Hierro had lost in the assault on the sacred grove. Neither action seemed to advance Hierro's personal interests, but they'd served someone, just as King Juleo's assassination had.

Hierro had to suspect who it was, if not how they'd outmaneuvered him.

"It would seem that Lord Fueres is so preoccupied with my amusements that he's lost track of his little sister," Fedeles pointed out.

Hierro looked to the fountain, then scowled at Clara's retreating back.

"Come, you." Hierro slapped the side of Ariz's head, then turned on his heel. Over his shoulder, he called, "We are not done, Lord Quemanor."

Fury shook Fedeles's body and he had to ball his hands into fists, digging his fingernails into his palms to keep from launching himself after Hierro. As it was, he couldn't keep from pacing a few steps after Ariz.

He reached the edge of the fountain when a wave of exhaustion washed the last of his strength from his body. He dropped down to the fountain's edge. A fine spray of water misted his face and neck. He hardly noticed it.

Staring ahead, Fedeles watched Ariz trail Hierro and his companions without sparing a glance back. Soon they disappeared into a maze of flowering hedges. He didn't have the strength to follow, much less to free Ariz. He bowed his head in shame.

He closed his eyes and let his arms fall lax. His left hand dropped into the fountain. All at once the soft hum of tiny spells rippled over his arm. Charms, long ago tossed into the water, glinted through his mind. Fedeles drew them in, stripping away the symbols of their original creators as if he was unwrapping candies from foil and devouring them.

Slowly he regained a little strength. Fedeles lifted his face and for the first time today the sun's warmth seemed to reach his cool skin.

He heard Jacinto and his sprawling party slowly descend the hillock. None of them seemed in a hurry. Fedeles waited, taking what rest he could, as Jacinto strolled to him. Bells and music filled the air, as did subdued laughter and companionable conversations.

Belatedly, Fedeles realized why Jacinto had been so lackadaisical in advancing on Hierro and his party. Up close, it became obvious that the dozen royal guards escorting Jacinto were merely actors wearing well-made costumes. Fedeles suspected that at least half of them weren't even armed with real swords.

If Hierro had realized the truth, would he have retreated? The man's recklessness was certainly approaching the point that Fedeles might be justified in killing him as an act of self-defense.

Was that because Hierro couldn't contain his frustration after losing fifty assassins all at once? Or was it that Hierro's plots were so near fruition that he believed there would be no one to condemn him in the near future?

Jacinto grinned at him, but in a wide-eyed, nervous manner. The Haldiim woman beside him appeared to offer him a reassurance, patting his hand. Knowing how unsafe the palace was for anyone of Haldiim heritage right now, Fedeles was impressed with her courage in accompanying Jacinto. As she drew nearer, she met Fedeles's gaze with recognition. He studied her as well, and then recalled that she'd been one of the two women who'd stood to protect the sacred grove last night. She turned her hands to sign a Haldiim blessing. Fedeles stared at her for a stunned moment, then returned the gesture.

"Yara Nur-Aud," she introduced herself and gamely extended her hand to Fedeles.

"I'm honored to meet you, Mistress Nur-Aud." He took her long fingers and bowed over them. "Do you perhaps hold the title of a Bahiim?"

Jacinto laughed, but Yara didn't.

"When I was a little girl I studied with our Bahiim at the Circle of Wisteria, but my family's business is in the theater, so I never took vows."

"Truly?" Jacinto frowned. "I had no idea."

"People are full of surprises," Yara replied, and Fedeles wasn't sure, but he thought she shot him a rather conspiratorial smile.

"That is so true," Jacinto responded, but his attention focused on the distant flowering hedge that Hierro and his party had disappeared behind.

"Lord Fueres made a quick retreat, didn't he?" Jacinto sounded relieved. "Always better to see the back of him than the front."

Fedeles nodded. Really, it would be best to see Hierro dead in a grave.

"What was all the business with that slumping servant about just now?" Jacinto murmured. "Did he really think that he could lure you to your demise with the promise of some plain-faced nobody?"

"A bluff, nothing more." Fedeles had to believe that right now. He didn't want to discuss the possibility that it could have been anything else, particularly not with Jacinto. Instead he scanned the lively costumed crowd surrounding them.

"Where is Atreau?" Fedeles asked.

"I thought he'd be with you." Jacinto's expression grew all the more concerned. "He's not at the Green Door or the Fat Goose. He hasn't delivered the pages I need for my play, and now his mistress, young Suelita, has run me to the ground to find you in his stead." Jacinto wiped his brow and then gestured to a couple behind him. Two figures approached. One was petite and curvaceous, the other lanky and surprisingly tall for a woman. Jacinto continued, "He'd better not have run off to Yuan with your comely physician."

Fedeles nodded absently, keeping his attention on the two women. He knew Suelita Estaban from dances and dinner parties. Previously she'd struck him as a gloomy girl, always hunched into her gauzy silk gowns and hiding her face behind a fan or book. Now, despite her sloppy-looking braids and the humble quality of her faun costume, she impressed him as more straight backed and assured than he remembered. She easily met his gaze.

The broad-shouldered, short-haired woman wearing dueling leathers who walked alongside Suelita was a stranger. But from Atreau's descriptions, Fedeles guessed she was Sabella Calies. Her tanned face and hands were nearly as scarred as Elezar's. The cold confidence of her expression reminded him of Elezar as well.

"Lord Quemanor." Suelita greeted him with a curtsy.

"Lady Estaban." Fedeles leaned forward in a half bow. "Your family would be reassured to see you looking so very well."

She paused, clearly unable to say the same to Fedeles.

He felt certain he appeared pallid and ghastly. His shirt hung damp against his skin, while his hair and clothes were scattered with rose leaves, thorns and petals. He felt half dead.

His left hand draped back into the fountain. A frog dived through the rippling water to lurk beneath a lily pad. The sensation of its heartbeat fluttered over Fedeles's fingertips like a tiny red incantation enfolding a bright spark of magic.

Suelita cleared her throat and Fedeles pulled back from his reverie.

"I was remiss in allowing Atreau to shoulder so much blame on my behalf. I know it caused strife for him and the Quemanor household as well. I'm sorry." She cast a guilty look back to Sabella and a little flush colored her face. "I have since written to apprise my family and Ladislo Bayezar of my safety and my circumstances. By now they should all be aware that Atreau played no part in the matter."

"Thank you for that." It had been good of her, though probably not all that easy, Fedeles thought. Then he wondered if her correspondences might have inspired Ladislo and Lord Estaban to set aside their animosity toward him and take Fedeles's side today in the throne room.

"Atreau was supposed to come collect these." Suelita slid a small pack down from her shoulder. She withdrew a sheaf of papers and handed them to him. He took them in his right hand, while his left remained in the fountain catching the blessings that swirled there.

"The archaic symbols involved threw me for a curve," Suelita began. "But after visiting the Haldiim District, I realized my earlier errors and was able to decipher the text surrounding the symbols. However, once I realized what I had, I knew it couldn't wait. So, I'm afraid I took advantage of His Highness to bring them to you directly . . ."

Suelita offered Jacinto a quick smile.

Jacinto nodded before returning to his nervous surveillance of the surrounding hedges. His eyes darted to the papers in Fedeles's hands, but then he turned away, as if afraid to see more. He walked to a dark-haired woman wearing a gown that shimmered like snakeskin and threw his arms around her. Another of his companions handed him a wine bottle and Jacinto drank, while two pretty girls dressed a cats struck up a boisterous song.

"You are mentioned by name on the second page," Suelita whispered to Fedeles.

Fedeles returned his attention to the sheaf of papers. He quickly realized that he held a collection of excerpts taken from Genimo Plunado's journals and correspondences. They described the spells that Genimo and Scholar Donamillo had used to take possession of Fedeles's body and make him the vessel of a shadow curse. He and Oasia had theorized about the existence of such a collection, but the reality of it still stunned Fedeles.

Horror and sick memories flooded him as he took in the words. For years he'd burned in agony, nearly drowning in the grip of madness. His stomach clenched and the deep scars that marked both his wrists seemed to flare, as if he was again slitting open his flesh.

Fedeles wanted to rip the pages to shreds—destroy every remnant of those years. Deep humiliation welled up just knowing that Suelita had read these letters—knew all the details about what had been done to him.

His fingers tightened, crumpling the paper.

He heard Suelita gasp. He glanced up.

Suelita and Sabella both glared at him as if they feared he'd gone mad, and he stopped. Atreau had described how difficult it had been to intercept these missives and the difficulty in deciphering them. This collection of spells hadn't been collected, encrypted and then smuggled across the country simply to embarrass and degrade him, but because they were of value to his enemies. Other people had fought, killed and died for this information.

Fedeles smoothed the pages against his thigh. Then he forced himself to read through it all again and think rationally.

Why would anyone dredge up the master plan for this old crime?

Was there something unique about this array of spells in particular?

After all, Hierro and his conspirators were already capable of enthralling hundreds of people. Hierro could torture them, transform them or kill them as he wished. With the Brand of Obedience, he manipulated and suppressed others in both mind and body. So what more could the spells in Genimo's letters allow him to achieve?

The frog at the edge of Fedeles's awareness hurtled itself from the water to snap after a dragonfly. For a light-headed instant Fedeles felt as if he too shot up into the strange atmosphere of dry air—his heart hammering, his body soaring. Then he returned to his senses and it suddenly occurred to him.

Only these spells could separate a soul from its body without destroying either. His old teacher Scholar Donamillo had used them to move his own spirit into Fedeles's body, in an effort to claim Fedeles's identity and become the Duke of Rauma. And even beyond that, this exact collection of spells held the secret to constraining sorcery as powerful as a shadow curse within the frail cage of a living person.

The only other array of spells that came close to achieving anything similar were those in the Shard of Heaven. But both the bodies and souls of the Hallowed Kings had been ruined by the force of restraining the malevolent magic within the Shard of Heaven. Fedeles, on the other hand, had not only carried the shadow curse within his body but also held Donamillo's soul as well as his own.

It was as if the spells had carved a hollow in him where his shadow coiled, ready to encompass any force it encountered. Briefly, Fedeles thought of the way his ravenous body had devoured Hierro's curse earlier today. A feeling of disgust crawled through him. Was there anything his soul couldn't tolerate, nothing it wouldn't accommodate?

But other than making a monster of him, what was the use of any of that? Could Hierro mean to contain some immense magic within a living body? Was he tearing apart the wards of the Shard of Heaven and attacking the Hallowed Kings so that he could take control of the monstrous spell they restrained? It struck Fedeles as a foolhardy tactic. Why would Hierro risk such devastation in the very place he wanted to rule? Why unleash something just to have to struggle to contain it? None of that trouble would advance Hierro's ambitions to take the throne.

Fedeles sat thinking about that for a few minutes, while whirlpools swirled around his fingers. A faint blessing—more of a wish than anything else—winked from a coin, tickling the pad of Fedeles's thumb. He drew it in without thinking, feeling a momentary warmth like a ray of sunlight passing over his fingers.

Was it possible that Hierro planned to transfer his soul into someone else's body?

If he stole Sevanyo's body, then he would become king in an instant—an aged king, but a king nonetheless. However, if that was Hierro's intention, then why had he wasted so much time and so many resources on assassinations? Why weaken the Shard of Heaven? Why bother killing Clara's husband or forming an alliance with Remes?

Fedeles scowled.

In addition to everything else, he simply couldn't imagine a man as conceited as Hierro abandoning the power, beauty and privilege that his current body provided for him. Likely even commanding the supple flesh of forty-eight-year-old Crown Prince Xalvadar wouldn't tempt Hierro.

But what if these letters weren't part of Hierro's designs? He wasn't the only one capable of commanding forbidden magic or scheming to rule the nation.

Fedeles looked to Sabella. Atreau had mentioned that she'd been the one who secured most these correspondences.

"These are copies of letters that were intercepted?" Fedeles asked.

"That's right, my lord," Sabella said.

"And the originals were delivered to the royal bishop?" Fedeles asked. He couldn't imagine Nugalo wanting or even understanding these spells. He remembered finding it strange even when Atreau had first informed him that the royal bishop was connected to the letters.

"They were actually received by a renounced nun who serves the royal bishop's son, Ojoito," Sabella said.

"At the Slate House?" Fedeles asked. What were the chances?

"Indeed. The woman works there as a nurse to Ojoito's children. But the letters didn't remain in the Slate House even a day," Sabella said. "She turned them over to an herb girl, who carried them to the Odalis household. Both Hierro Fueres and Prince Remes visited the house that evening, so I can't say where the letters were taken beyond that."

Fedeles nodded thoughtfully.

Remes, like Hierro, commanded far too much status, wealth and power—not to mention youth and health—to bother inhabiting another body. In addition, he was already a suitable heir to the throne. Hierro's assassins could much more reliably make him king than this massive assembly of complex invocations.

Combinations of spells this intricate easily turned volatile. They weren't something to be invoked on a whim, nor were they easily endured. Fedeles had suffered successive bouts of suicidal madness while in the grip of them.

So, who among Hierro's conspirators would risk so much?

Out of all the people who could have procured the letters, only Clara truly stood to gain from these spells. Her branded body enslaved her to Hierro's will. Escaping his control might be worth the risk of ripping apart her spirit. If the transfer worked, then not only would she be free in a new body, but she would retain the power of her soul and her command over magic.

Fedeles nodded to himself, stirring the water around his fingers as he absently sought other abandoned spells to feed him. Dragonflies hummed past. Briefly, Fedeles felt their living warmth and it seemed hardly different from the heat he'd drained from spells. His shadow fluttered, but he let the dragonflies go. Instead he dug a decayed silver ring from the muddy bottom of the fountain. Rusted, forgotten affections flitted through him.

Spells on the magnitude of the ones in these letters required power far beyond the witchflame of a single soul. When Donamillo had turned the spells against Fedeles, he'd sustained them with steam-powered machinery.

Clara too would need a means to power these spells. But she was neither a master mechanist nor had any spy reported her constructing a huge machine on any of her holdings. She would need to find another way—a magical entity with enough sustained power to transport her entire blazing soul from one body to another. Of these, Fedeles could think of three: the ruins at Crown Hill, the Circle of Wisteria and the Shard of Heaven.

Fedeles held Crown Hill, so that couldn't be used.

Could it be that the motivation behind Irsea's murder and the persistent attacks against the Haldiim sacred grove had been part of an effort by Clara to seize control of the Circle of Wisteria? Except that those assaults had been so violent, so malevolent. There was a clear intention to destroy the sacred grove rather than carefully secure it.

That left the Shard of Heaven—the place that Lady Hylanya had come from Labara to investigate because the spells that held it together were beginning to fail.

King Gachello had told him that he no longer heard Irsea or felt the Circle of Wisteria, which meant that Irsea must have been communicating with him and using the sacred grove to help him shore up the failing wards in the Shard of Heaven. So killing her and destroying the Circle of Wisteria would be necessary if a person wished to seize the Shard of Heaven for her own use.

Previously Fedeles had assumed that the only reason anyone would want control over that place was for access to the monstrous threat it restrained. But now he thought again of the Hallowed Kings and the reliquary spells that held their souls captive but still alive.

Entire pages of the correspondence that Fedeles held looked like they could have been copied directly from those reliquary spells. Though many additional symbols filled the letters, the Shard of Heaven itself was replete with other spells, as well as worshipers who'd fed their prayers into them for generations.

And Fedeles knew himself how easy it was to reshape the name and purpose of a magical symbol. Given enough time and intent, couldn't entire arrays of spells be altered? Was it possible that instead of attacking the Shard of Heaven to unleash some ancient horror, Clara had been secretly but steadily reshaping its purpose to her own ends?

This was all pure conjecture, Fedeles knew, but at the same time it explained so much of what had seemed convoluted and contradictory about Hierro's actions. Previously, both Atreau and Oasia had commented on how out-of-character and incongruent many of his machinations seemed. Fedeles himself had noted how authentic Hierro's displeasure at King Juleo's assassination had appeared. Now he realized Hierro might not have played any part in the old king's demise. He hadn't been prepared yet to seize the throne at that point.

But Juleo had been meant to replace Gachello as a Hallowed King. Therefore Juleo's assassination must have been Clara's attempt to eliminate Gachello from the Hallowed Kings and remove the last soul that still recollected their original purpose. Without Gachello present, she would have been free to finally reshape the entire Shard of Heaven to serve her.

"How driven she must be?" Fedeles murmured.

"Lord Quemanor? Are you all right?" Suelita's voice drifted to him, and he realized that he'd been silent with his eyes closed too long.

"Just thinking," Fedeles assured her. He folded the letters and slid them into the inner pocket of his coat. "Thank you for all this."

"It's no more than what you've paid me to do." Suelita smiled. "I can't think of another nobleman who would have entrusted me or supported me as you have."

He supposed she was right, though in truth Atreau had been the one to recognize the young woman's genius and make use of it.

"Then other noblemen are fools," Fedeles told her, and it heartened him to see how she beamed in response.

"Fedeles," Jacinto called from the far side of the fountain. "Shall we fetch you some little delights from father's tables? Or are you returning to your own house?"

"I'm off to see my lovely lady wife." Fedeles rose to his feet. "You?"

"I do love to gaze upon Oasia, thank you for the invitation." Jacinto grinned and then offered the dark-haired woman next to him a teasing wink. "But I mustn't make the beauty at my side now too jealous. We'll stay to descend upon father's bounty like locusts."

"Send word if you encounter Atreau." Fedeles glanced from Jacinto to Sabella and then Yara as well.

"You'll spend the first night of Masquerade at your house then?" Jacinto asked.

That would be the safe thing to do. The wise choice to make. But Fedeles couldn't forget Hierro's taunt. The thought of him striking Ariz burned in Fedeles's chest, and he felt his shadow bristle.

"I plan to return to the gardens tonight," Fedeles decided. "Hierro and I have unfinished business here."

CHAPTER
NINETEEN

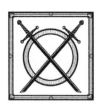

Ariz jerked his head out from the hot water and wiped his face. Clouds of perfumed steam drifted through the room. One attendant clutched a fistful of his hair. A second groped in the tub to grasp his foot.

Both men set to work scrubbing him, while Hierro leaned back in his luxuriant gold seat wearing a smug smile.

Late afternoon sun reflected across the ivory-tiled floor and gleamed along the curves of the gilded tub. Servants in white Gavado liveries hurried in and out of the chamber. Page boys proffered refreshments to Hierro and Prince Remes as well as the twenty brash young noblemen who made up Hierro's entourage. Older servants hovered around the nobles like grooms ministering to prize studs: buffing their fingernails, shining their boots and refreshing the fine powders of gold dust that adorned many of their faces. One young man crouched at Hierro's feet, carefully polishing his gold spurs. Wearing an almost playful smile, Hierro kicked the man's ribs and dismissed him.

Ariz didn't fight the ministrations of the bath attendants washing him. It would only entertain Hierro to witness him injure two hapless servants. Though the younger of the two attendants was none too gentle as he dragged his scrub brush over the bruises and scrapes that peppered Ariz's legs. The older man shoved Ariz's head back under the bathwater to rinse the last trace of the dull stain from his hair. Ariz stared up through the water, watching the attendant out of habit.

But what was the point? If the old man decided to drown him, would it really be so bad of a thing? The soap stung Ariz's eyes and at last he closed them.

He remained beneath the surface, holding his breath and willing his heartbeat to slow to silence. Floating beneath the water wasn't so different from drifting through the sky. The currents felt warmer and gentler. It wouldn't be so bad to just slip into unconsciousness under the water. It couldn't be worse than whatever Hierro planned to do with him this evening.

Then he remembered holding Fedeles in his arms the previous night. The desire to survive, to find a way free of Hierro and to reclaim his life as his own surged through him.

Again Ariz pushed himself up from the water and into the cool air. A reflexive breath filled Ariz's lungs. The bath attendant looked Ariz over with a cold expression, as if Ariz was a dirty shirt in need of tough scouring. Who in the Gavado household could afford to feel sympathy for him? Definitely no one who served Hierro directly; Ariz understood that well enough not to expect any kindness.

"Don't let them drown the man," Remes directed from behind Hierro. He snatched up a cherry from the silver dish on Hierro's dressing table. "It would sadden Clara. She rather pities the poor fellow."

"She *pities* him?" Hierro's smirk gave way to a rich laugh. "Have you actually looked at Ariz, my prince? I assure you, there's not an inch of him that's pitiful."

Remes and a number of other nobles turned their attention to Ariz, studying his naked his body with the expressions of buyers appraising a horse at auction. Ariz lifted his dull gaze to meet the prince's amused stare. Remes's expression turned uneasy, as if he'd just noticed a spider amidst his cherries. Ariz immediately bowed his head in deference. Hierro laughed again.

"You see? Master Ariz is a deceptive one, isn't he?" Hierro went on in amusement. "At first glance, he's the plainest clod you could imagine. A bland, slack-faced nobody. But wash him up, dress him properly and have him hold his head up. Then all at once you have an auburn-haired heartbreaker on your hands."

If he'd heard those words as an infatuated fourteen-year-old boy, Ariz would have been overwhelmed with joy. Now the appraisal filled him with revulsion and dread. Nothing good ever came of Hierro's appreciation, nor were his intentions ever so benevolent that he'd actually bother to "make the servant attending my dear sister look a little more presentable for the Masquerade," as he'd earlier claimed.

Clara had recognized as much as well, though her surprise at seeing Ariz in human form had obviously delayed her response. Belatedly she'd tried to stop Hierro from dragging Ariz away, but in the end she only succeeded in dispatching Remes to ensure that nothing too "ridiculous" befell Ariz.

"I'd call Ariz a lady-killer, but I'd hate to limit his scope." Hierro winked at Ariz as if they were sharing a joke. "Especially not when we're going to see Lord Quemanor again so soon. Imagine how surprised he'll be at the transformation."

Ariz felt sick and tried to assure himself that Fedeles would know better than to seek him out, particularly tonight.

The younger attendant cast him a worried glance and Ariz wondered if his disgust had somehow shown, but then he realized that one of the deeper scrapes on his thigh had opened. A ribbon of scarlet blood swirled in the bathwater. It was pretty, in a way, so vivid. Ariz hardly felt the pain of it.

"You think Fedeles will really bother showing up?" Remes ate another cherry and spat the pit into a cup held by a page boy.

"I'd bet his life on it," Hierro responded lightly. He bowed his head and returned to folding the freshly penned notes on his dressing table.

Several young men in the crowd snickered. Ariz wondered how many of them understood Hierro's true intentions. How many of them mistook his cruelty for sardonic humor? How many assumed that he possessed even a shred of compassion? Did any of them recall that once Ariz, too, had stood alongside Hierro laughing and misunderstanding the avarice in his smile?

The tangles of old scars disfiguring Ariz's chest and back ached as he shifted in the water. Dark bruises and fading ones mottled his skin. So much blood had dried under his nails that a rust-red stain remained as if he'd painted them. Ariz wondered if even one of the noblemen surrounding him recognized his ruined state as a warning.

Assessing their cheerful expressions from shadows of his lowered lashes, Ariz thought that none of them did. Not even Remes, who *knew* that Hierro used him as an assassin and who had spent all this morning raging over Ojoito's murder. Not even he made the simple connection between that brutal attack and the multitude of injuries that marred Ariz's body.

Ariz gazed down at his hands and the deep bite mark on his forearm. Up in the dim box seat of a theater, Master Narsi had taken one glance and been horrified. But here, lit by sunlight and blazing lamps, thronged by a veritable crowd, not a single person revealed the slightest concern. They merely chuckled at Hierro's insinuations while the man penned orders for assassinations and abductions in front of them.

In his youth Ariz had assumed that Hierro was such a consummate actor that he fooled everyone. But as he'd grown older Ariz recognized that Hierro hardly bothered with any pretense at all. Instead the people surrounding him obligingly deceived themselves and each other. Some simply didn't want to know the truth while others couldn't afford to know.

Remes was likely a little of both. He'd already become a conspirator in treason alongside Hierro. He'd feasted on veal with Captain Ciceron's head serving as a centerpiece on the table, he plotted murders and turned over purses of gold to buy the properties that housed Hierro's enthralled assassins. He was years beyond repentance or regret and far too entangled with Hierro to consider the danger of their alliance.

Remes picked up another bright red cherry, then frowned at Ariz.

"I can see why Clara might feel concerned for him," Remes mused. "For a *master* swordsman, he really does look rather battered. Generally one expects a bit more poise and swagger from their sort."

That inspired another round of snickers.

Ariz lifted his head and caught Remes's gaze with his own dead-eyed stare.

"Oh, but Your Highness hasn't seen the state of my opponents." Ariz spoke softly, without inflection. "Their blood washed the floors, and their bodies—"

"A gentleman doesn't brag about his conquests, Ariz." Hierro spoke and Ariz's throat tightened, almost choking him. Hierro wrote out a few more missives, then looked to the bath attendants. "Get him out of the water. Bandage those scrapes and dress him. We shouldn't keep the duke waiting too long."

The bath attendants dragged Ariz from the water more than they assisted him out of the tub. Two valets and a boot boy joined them, escorting him to a dressing table hidden behind a silk screen. Ariz dried himself and saw to his own injuries. Hierro's servants laid out a black silk-and-leather raven costume as well as Ariz's boots, belt and weapons. From the folds of his discarded brown cloak, Ariz dug out the vial of elixir that Narsi had given him, as well as the crumpled paper charm his nieces had made for him. Then he turned his attention to the glossy dark costume. The silky shirt felt too thin and looked far tighter than anything Ariz would normally wear. The black leather breeches weren't much better. Ariz caught sight of himself in one of the silver-backed mirrors.

He looked like a stranger—the sharp angles and hard planes of his body seemed too brazen, his hair too glossy and clean. Meeting his own stare, he found his exposed features strangely imposing. He brushed a lock of his hair down over his brow to shadow his hard gray eyes. That was a little better.

He frowned at the tight, dark costume clinging to his body. A slashed pattern of indigo played along the length of his thighs and glittering silver buttons studded his chest. Ariz opened his mouth to demand a pot of liver-of-sulfur to blacken the buttons, but then he caught himself.

If it meant giving Fedeles advance warning, then he didn't want to go unnoticed through the night. Even if it was only the flash of torchlight across a few buttons. It might make all the difference. Thinking of it that way, he allowed the valets to comb gold dust through his hair and trim his boots with silver laces. As he drew the showy blue-black cloak over his shoulders, a commotion sounded at the door of the dressing room. Ariz's hand went instantly to his sword hilt. The valets with him behind the screen edged away, but none of them made a sound. Like Ariz, they all stood alert and silent, peering at the shadowy figures beyond the patterns of painted silk.

A burly man in a dark uniform barged into the dressing room. Drafts of cool, dry air swept over Ariz's damp skin. Several footmen followed the man, protesting. None of them dared lay hands on him, however.

Hierro made the slightest gesture of his hand and Ariz knew that if the intruder drew too near, he'd find himself convulsing within an agony of spells. In fact, it seemed a wonder that he'd gotten this far into the Gavado household—unless it was Hierro's will that he be allowed to play out some scene.

"I beg Your Highness's forgiveness, but I must speak with you!" the man shouted. Ariz recognized Captain Yago's voice. "The matter is urgent."

"If you must, then I suppose you must," Remes allowed.

"Privately, if you would be so kind, Your Highness," Yago muttered.

Remes tilted his head in Hierro's direction and Hierro leaned back to whisper something in Remes's ear. Ariz couldn't hear the exchange, but he understood that Hierro was indulging Remes in the pretense of making a decision. Ariz wondered if Remes himself recognized the shift of power between them.

"Gentlemen!" Of course it was Hierro who raised his voice to address the surrounding nobles. "His Highness and I will join you in the garden shortly. In the meantime, please do feel free to take full advantage of the Gavado household's amenities." He waved a hand, and in a matter of moments the noblemen and all the attending servants withdrew.

Only Ariz remained behind the screen.

So long as Hierro didn't call him out, he intended to remain and glean what he could.

Maybe it amused Hierro to have him overhear Yago, or perhaps he thought so little of Ariz that his presence was negligible. Either way, neither Hierro nor Remes ordered him to leave with the others.

"All right, Captain," Remes said. "What is it that you want to tell me?"

"Your Highness." Captain Yago went down on one knee. "I'm truly troubled by the rumors of a Haldiim uprising planned for the Solstice. Your uncle is too distraught to counter your father's orders, but the situation isn't one that can be ignored."

"So what is it that you want from me exactly?" Remes asked.

"When Haldiim gathered at the sacred grove rebel, I and my men must not delay in suppressing them. But if we must seek out the king's permission it could waste hours." Yago paused a moment. "But if you gave us leave . . ."

"Rest assured, you have my permission to suppress them if they stir up any sort of trouble. That should be obvious," Remes replied. "Not even my father would argue that point."

"Yes, thank you for clarifying that, Your Highness," Yago replied. "I'm only hesitant because several informants have mentioned that your younger brother, Prince Jacinto, has recently involved himself with

Haldiim malcontents and firebrands. There is a chance that he might be mixed in with them at the sacred grove. This being masquerade, I and my men might not easily distinguish the prince or his noble associates from the rabble . . . if Your Highness understands what I mean."

Ariz certainly understood even if Remes didn't.

Captain Yago needed a royal authority to take responsibility for the injuries—small or mortal—that he planned to inflict upon Prince Jacinto and his circle of noble friends.

Remes was quiet for much longer than Ariz expected. Ariz wondered if he was aware of the numerous clashes that had occurred between Yago's men and Jacinto's friends. Did Remes know that Jacinto had publicly humbled Yago before a crowd gathered at the Green Door when the captain had been searching for Countess Radulf?

Yago was not a forgiving man. Doubtless he wanted this excuse to vent his rage against Jacinto and his friends. Atreau Vediya and Master Narsi could well number among them.

Fear for them shot through Ariz, setting his heart racing. But there was nothing he could do for either of them right now.

Though the longer Remes remained silent, the more Ariz began to hope.

Remes could refuse. After all, it was easy to talk about killing, particularly when you'd never borne the effort of it or endured the guilt afterward. Even acts of treason, mused upon while sipping wine and ogling a lovely conspirator, might seem abstract and romantic. But when it came down to the real brutality of murdering his own brother, could Remes carelessly carry through with it? Might the loss he felt over Ojoito's death temper his enthusiasm to wipe out his entire family?

"Clara has been so troubled by that sacred grove," Hierro murmured. "Ever since those Haldiim miscreants assassinated your grandfather. Do you think they might be behind Ojoito's demise as well?"

"Fine," Remes snapped. "Do what you must to keep the peace of our nation, Captain. I will take responsibility. If my brother or any of his degenerate friends associate with heretics and dissidents, then . . . then they deserve what happens to them. They only have themselves to blame."

"Very good, Your Highness." Yago bowed so low his head nearly touched the floor. Then he stood and withdrew.

For a few moments the room was quiet. Ariz stood observing, while Remes stared at the ceiling and Hierro put away his pen and ink.

"He won't be there anyway," Remes muttered, as if reassuring himself. "Our family is holding a private memorial for Ojoito tomorrow morning."

"Really?" Hierro sounded genuinely surprised. "A memorial for a bastard?"

"Ojoito's mother served as my wet nurse. He grew up in the palace with the rest of us. . . ." Remes trailed off and Ariz wondered if his expression conveyed melancholy or merely nostalgia. "You wouldn't understand."

"True," Hierro admitted. Then he raised his voice and called out, "What about you, Ariz? Weren't you fond of bastards back in our school days?"

Ariz noticed Remes startle slightly. He guessed that the prince hadn't been paying much attention to the people around him. He'd missed the fact that Ariz had stayed behind when everyone else left the room.

"Far worse than a bastard," Ariz said as he stepped out from behind the screen. "I made the mistake of idolizing a monster."

Remes shot him an affronted look, but Hierro smiled.

"And lucky you," Hierro said. "You get to destroy a monster tonight."

 CHAPTER
TWENTY

The moment he stepped through the entrance to the Sorrowlands, a geyser of red flame tore through the air. Atreau leapt away and collided with Narsi. They fell, entangled. The ground felt strangely soft and giving when Atreau hit it. Narsi's hand grazed his cheek, but otherwise his weight hardly impacted Atreau. Narsi sprawled against his chest, one hand lightly curled against Atreau's hip. The living warmth of Narsi's body felt so comforting after all the corpses and death that had filled the Slate House. Atreau had to stop himself from simply closing his eyes and resting his arms against Narsi's back.

"What is this place?" Narsi's breath fluttered over Atreau's ear.

"The Sorrowlands. Bahiim call it the Old Road," Atreau replied. As much as he dreaded the visions that he would see in this dank, haunted place, he forced himself to look around. Atreau already knew what specters of memory would torment him as they traversed this road. But who knew what grief the devils here would conjure in their attempts to ensnare Narsi?

However, something was terribly wrong with the Sorrowlands— more wrong than the normal horror of the place. Instead of desolate, endless gray expanses haunted by luminous blue vapors, an apocalypse of fiery geysers and crumbling city streets surrounded them. Translucent phantoms howled as collapsing stonework crushed them, black rifts swallowed them and fires consumed them. But the most alarming thing was that he could not see Javier anywhere.

Surely he must be present. Who else could have opened the doorway and allowed them inside? What in the three hells was going on?

They definitely shouldn't be lying on the ground like this. At the same time, he didn't want to alarm Narsi—the Sorrowlands themselves would do that and feed off Narsi's fear.

"My shoulder is going numb," Atreau announced.

"Sorry." Narsi rose to his knees. He stared through the chaos surrounding them. Whirling flames cast golden light across the sharp angles of his face. "Is that the Fat Goose burning?"

Atreau surveyed the scene. He thought he recognized faces in the chaotic crowd of people fleeing before splintering beams and falling buildings. Spider and Inissa gripped each other's hands as they struggled over smoldering rubble. Sabella swore as she ripped a spear of splintered timber from her bloody chest. A wall of black smoke swallowed them all.

"This place isn't quite as I imagined it from the description in your memoir." Narsi spoke so quietly that Atreau nearly missed the tremor in his voice. "Is this . . . part of your escape plan?"

Atreau shook his head and sat upright.

Far in the distance, an immense tower glowed as flames surged up it. Walls of masonry blackened and tumbled down. Out of the corner of his eyes he glimpsed a man's towering silhouette—it could only be Elezar—fall to his knees over another man's body, and then both of them seared away like vapor. Atreau's heart lurched in his chest.

It didn't make sense. The creatures of the Sorrowlands plucked images from the memories of their victims and recreated them as apparitions.

But as horrifying as the sight was, Atreau knew it didn't arise from his memories. Nor did he imagine that any sorrow in Narsi's past had conjured up this horrific landscape. There was only one other possibility left.

"Javier!" Atreau shouted. His voice hardly carried over the pandemonium of human cries and roaring fires.

Atreau remembered Javier's ghostly visage floating over the theater stage with a growing dread.

God's blood, what has happened to him? Atreau scrambled to his feet, snatched up his sword and sheathed it.

"Javier!" Atreau bellowed again.

Staring past Atreau's shoulder, Narsi's eyes went wide. Perhaps he gazed on the aspect of a lost loved one conjured from the mists of the Sorrowlands. His mother had died a little more than a year ago. And there was his father's murder as well. Either one might haunt him here.

"Don't look too closely," Atreau warned him. "They aren't who you think they are. This place feeds on regret and . . ." Words died on his lips as he turned.

Walking through whirlpools of fire, dressed in smoldering gold robes, a skeletal figure approached them. Atreau gripped the hilt of his sword. But as the deathly form drew closer, Atreau glimpsed pale wisps of living features clothing the sharp bones. A countenance like smoke hanging over embers. Javier gazed at him from the black chasms of his white skull.

"We cannot linger." Javier's words sounded distant and hollow. "Stay close."

He strode ahead. Atreau caught Narsi's hand and hurried to follow.

"Are we dead?" Narsi asked in a whisper.

"No, we're—"

"You die on the staircase of the Slate House, Atreau." Javier's voice was rough. "Fedeles falls in the Royal Star Garden. The Shroud of Stone unfurls across the lands. The seas, the wind, the very earth stills. Skellan destroys himself and Elezar tearing it away. Those who survive face fires and ruin under the rule of the child tyrant, Sparanzo."

Javier stilled and lifted his skeletal hands to the chaos surrounding them. "We lose everyone," he said.

Atreau stared at him, feeling too stunned by Javier's first revelation to even attempt to understand the rest.

"I'm—I've died?" Atreau asked.

Javier turned back. For a brief instant, his face was again that of a handsome youth. Tender sorrow filled his expression. Then the blazing skull burned his features to shadows and white flames erupted around him, scorching his robes and filling Atreau's mouth with smoke.

"No! We do not accept it!" Vapor rose from between Javier's teeth. "I—I will break with fate. Shatter the stones of this vei. We forge another way. He lives—you live . . . because we—I—*I* command the roads of death and they reach all places and all times. I . . . will not accept it!"

Atreau frowned at Javier's raving tone and strange, disjointed words. He sounded half mad and looked like a walking nightmare.

"Javier, what are you doing?" Atreau reached out, despite the flames and smoldering cloth. What did fire matter if he was indeed already dead? He gripped his friend's shoulder. Ice couldn't have felt colder. Then the frigid white fire surrounding Javier died back. Javier's radiant bones dimmed, allowing Atreau to once more glimpse the veil of his living features. Javier's lips curved in a boyish smile. His dark eyes gleamed.

"I'm doing what we Hellions always do." Javier's voice sounded almost normal. "Breaking rules. Refusing to lose."

"What rules?" Atreau asked.

"The same rules that my master, Alizadeh, broke. It got him exiled from the Eastern Kingdom and inspired the Bahiim of Cieloalta to ward the city against him and me both," Javier replied. "Fuck them. We'll unmake history if we have to. But Atreau, we—we must be quick. The wheels are grinding apart. The spells are breaking. We must not linger past the toll of the noon bells." Then he drew back from Atreau's grasp. White flames engulfed him once again. "Come back with us. Fast as you can!"

Javier ran.

Atreau gripped Narsi's hand and followed. The moldering air of the Sorrowlands caught in Atreau's throat. He spat and kept running. Narsi matched his pace in long, fast strides.

The landscape surrounding them continued to burn and crumble. Atreau kept his attention focused on Javier's back, averting his gaze from the parade of violent deaths surrounding them as best he could while keeping a firm grip on Narsi's hand. Narsi seemed to not be able to keep himself from assessing the scene around him.

"Do you think these are visions of events that will come to pass?" Narsi's words came between gasps for breath. "Or just senseless nightmares?"

"I don't know," Atreau replied. In his own experience, the Sorrowlands only preyed upon his memories—taking on the form of his guilt, grief and regret. "Keep moving!"

"Memories. Our—*my* memories. Your future," Javier called back to them as he waved at the screaming, dying populace. Flames swirled around his bony fingers. "I've scoured the roads of death and seized the forbidden spells of the Issusha. With them I will shatter time and murder fate. And who can stop me? Who would dare? We will find the way and I will slit the future's fucking throat!"

"Does he normally . . . talk like this?" Narsi asked in a breathy whisper.

As fast as they both sprinted, they couldn't seem to ever catch up to Javier. Atreau's legs were beginning to ache. A cramp bit into his side.

"Not really," Atreau replied. Though he did vaguely recall back in their Hellion youths that when he'd been roaring drunk on white ruin,

Javier could rant about blazing visions and issue grandiose declarations with some frequency.

God's teeth, he hoped Javier wasn't drunk now. Though that would be better than him going mad.

"Is this Issusha a Labaran magic?" Narsi gasped. "Or some kind of vei?"

"Not one I've ever heard of." Atreau shook his head. Then, seeing Narsi's expression, he added, "This is Javier's domain, and you can trust that he'll take us wherever we need to go. But as for everything else, I have no idea of what it is we're seeing or what he's talking about, so don't waste your breath interrogating me. Just run!"

Cracks splintered the ground beneath them, and they had to leap across gaping pits in pursuit of Javier. They charged up a hill as houses on either side of them caught fire. Atreau stole a glance back to see a huge wave surge over the banks of the Peraloro River. Walls of black water hurled ships aside and flooded through the wreckage of the smoldering city. Atreau saw the massive timbers of the Red Stallion sword house shatter and sink beneath fetid roiling water. He watched an immense gush of fire consume the Fat Goose, the Green Door and every other building on the busy street. When he turned his head away, he witnessed countless strikes of lightning tear through the towers of the royal palace. Fires and floods surrounded him. As they descended after Javier, packs of feral dogs appeared. They scavenged scattered corpses.

"That's the Circle of Wisteria." Narsi squinted at a smoking rise of dead trees. Then his eyes went wide. "Atreau . . . is that us?"

Atreau looked in time to catch sight of two very distant figures running in the opposite direction as monstrous amalgamations of men and animals bounded after them. They could have been the mirror image of himself and Narsi. Then a plume a smoke swallowed them.

And then much nearer, Atreau glimpsed Narsi kneeling over him in a gutter. He looked terrified as he struggled to slow the stream of blood gushing from Atreau's leg. Snarling mordwolves bounded toward them. The nearest took Narsi by the throat.

Atreau looked away at once.

Beside him, Narsi stumbled, looking waxen and nauseated. Ahead of them Javier briefly paused, swaying.

"Noon to the east or to the west?" he muttered. "Remember. Remember."

Javier started to turn left but then veered right and broke into another sprint. Atreau and Narsi pelted after him. When Atreau stole a glimpse at Narsi, he was relieved to see that Narsi had reclaimed a semblance of calm—though he gripped the strap of his medical satchel so tightly that his knuckles stood out.

"I think that's the third time I've seen myself killed," Narsi murmured.

"It won't do you any good looking at any of this," Atreau replied. He was reminding himself as much as Narsi.

"But they've all been different. Earlier I was at the Circle of Wisteria with Yara and Esfir. Before that I was outside the Slate House. And they were dragging your body away." Narsi looked ill again.

"Don't think on it," Atreau told him. He certainly didn't want to.

"But how can this be a memory? How can I die in different ways and places?"

Atreau blinked at Narsi. "Are you actually attempting to apply logic to this fever dream we're running through?"

"I . . . what else can I do?" Narsi looked very briefly scared and Atreau suddenly felt like a bastard for challenging him, when he clearly needed some way to deal with all of this.

"Ignore me," Atreau told him. "I'm acting like an ass because I just found out that I'm dead."

"You are not dead! Not yet," Javier shouted. "We stole you away."

We?

Atreau narrowed his gaze at Javier's back.

Who exactly does he mean by we?

"I appreciate the intervention with all my heart," Atreau called to Javier's back. "But where in the three hells are you stealing us away to?"

"When," Javier replied, and he sounded oddly amused.

"What?" Both Atreau and Narsi asked in the same breath.

A strained, dry laugh escaped Javier in a plume of white vapor. Then he stopped and turned to face them. They barely avoided falling over him.

"The answer is always here." Javier lifted his hands and the white flames wreathing his finger bones leapt up. He traced a scorching arch in the air over them. "And here is always now. But where we step out—what was, or what will be. That's the difference."

"For fuck's sake, what does any of that mean?" Atreau doubled over, gasping for breath.

Javier seized Atreau's and Narsi's hands in his blazing-cold grip and jerked them through the flames with him. Atreau felt the atmosphere change and the light shift as they broke out of the Sorrowlands.

They stood in a large chamber surrounded by twelve huge silver-and-glass mechanisms. The roar of the giant machines thundered around them. Steam billowed across Atreau's face like damp, fevered breath. Massive pistons hammered up and down, driving rings of steel ribs in fast circles. Arcs of light jumped between the machines and danced across the webs of copper wires hanging over them. Swirling above everything, a sphere of white and gold symbols blazed like a sun. It had to be a spell—some immense sorcery, powered not just by Javier and the White Hell but by the raging fires of a dozen sweltering steam engines.

Directly beneath the blazing symbols, Kiram Kir-Zaki sat dressed in the worn leather garb of a smithy. Water droplets beaded his dark skin and condensation hung in the curls of his blond hair like rain drops. He didn't lift his gaze from the supine man whose head rested on his lap. Atreau gaped at the man laying in repose. White Haldiim prayer clothes draped his lean, youthful body. His long black hair fell across Kiram's lap like spilled ink. Even with his dark eyes closed and his expressions lost in the tranquility of sleep, Atreau knew him immediately.

Despite the fact that Atreau could feel Javier's hard grip around his hand, there was no denying that it was also Javier who rested with Kiram.

"How could there be two of them?" Narsi whispered.

"We're here." Javier released him and Narsi.

We, Atreau thought. Did Javier mean all of them, or was he talking about the two of himself?

Javier strode to where his body lay with Kiram. Though as he neared he seemed to grow fainter, almost translucent. He knelt and then stretched out across his own sleeping body. His bones sank into the flesh of the body lying on Kiram's lap like mist soaking into parched ground. A spark of white light flashed up from Javier's brow and Kiram caught it in one hand. He held the shining sphere, contemplating it, and then he flung it up into the swirling white and gold mass of spells circling over his head.

Behind them the machinery screeched. Wisps of black smoke rose from between growling gears.

"Kiram, what—" Atreau began.

"No!" Kiram didn't look away from Javier. "Not yet."

Atreau shut his mouth. He waited in silence beside Narsi.

A few feet from them a gray archway appeared, and another skeletal vision of Javier stumbled out. His hand bones looked burned and blood stained the side of his skull. He staggered to Kiram and collapsed down into his own body. Again a light sparked up from Javier's brow to Kiram's hand. Kiram turned it over, and then it too joined the others in the whirling spell.

The third time Javier appeared, his bones were chipped and filthy with sludge and seaweed. The forth time he dragged his blackened, charred remains across the stone floor. Narsi started toward him. Atreau held him back.

Whatever this was that Javier and Kiram were doing, it couldn't be interrupted. That was obvious to him. Though it was horrific to watch Javier claw his way to Kiram. Seeing his charred remains melt away came as a kind of relief.

Another shining sphere joined the rest, and then all at once the spells fell to the floor, burning into the stone like acid. Curls of smoke rose, then dissipated, leaving rings of tangled black script smoldering around Kiram and Javier.

Very faintly, Atreau heard a city bell ring. Then another and another sounded out in bright, distant peals—the distinctive sound of all the city clocks in Milmuraille tolling the noon hour. Atreau had suspected as much when he saw Kiram, but now he was certain that the Old Road had taken them to Labara.

Kiram extended his left hand and slammed a large silver locket closed.

At once a shudder seemed to pass through the floor under Atreau's feet. Behind him, pipes howled. He startled at the sound of cracking glass.

Billows of steam hissed as they filled the air with hot clouds of water vapor. The huge mechanisms surrounding them snarled and wailed. Pistons sheared apart and gears crumbled. The spinning silver ribs ground to a jerky halt. Then one entire mechanism collapsed into a smoldering heap hardly five feet from Kiram and Javier. Both Atreau and Narsi jumped, but neither Javier nor Kiram made the slightest move.

A single screw rolled across the floor. Kiram stopped it with a flick of his index finger. For the first time Atreau noticed that a gold chain hung between his right wrist and Javier's. The red symbols etched into the links looked as if they were stained with blood.

At last Kiram looked up from Javier's motionless face. His pale blue eyes were red-rimmed. He scrubbed a track of tears from his cheek with his left hand, then clapped his fingers over his own mouth as a sound like a ragged sob escaped him.

In all the years he'd known Kiram, Atreau had never seen him so undone—racked with raw emotion and utterly incapable of hiding it. Atreau glanced away, giving him time to regain his normal air of intellectual dignity. Narsi gripped the strap of his medical satchel and started forward. Again Atreau held him back.

"Let him compose himself," Atreau whispered.

That drew Kiram's attention to them. He stared as if they'd just manifested from the air. Could he have forgotten shouting at them minutes ago?

Kiram wiped his face again and reclaimed that expression of cool, intellectual interest that was so familiar to Atreau.

"You . . . you're *really* here," Kiram said.

"Javier brought us from Cieloalta." Atreau finally let go of Narsi's hand and took a step forward. Javier's skin seemed too pale, almost luminous, and a blue tinge colored his lips. He looked dead. But then his chest rose with a slow breath. A blush of color appeared to return to his cheeks. Relief flooded Atreau.

"When?" Kiram demanded.

"Are you serious? Just now." Atreau frowned at Kiram. Had he truly been so overwrought that he'd forgotten their arrival? "You saw—"

"It's the first day of Masquerade and tomorrow will be the Summer Solstice!" Narsi called out as if he'd suddenly solved a difficult puzzle in a mathematics class. "Thirteen Sixty-Two."

Atreau lifted a brow at the addition of the year. Then he recalled Javier's ramblings about hours and ages. About defying fate and changing the future.

"What's the . . . year here, now?" Atreau asked.

"The same year," Kiram supplied. "But two weeks earlier. Twenty days before the world falls to ruin."

"How is that possible?" Atreau understood that the Sorrowlands reached across the entire world and that time didn't pass quite normally within them, but this was far more than stealing across miles in mere minutes.

"Has he ever mentioned anything about Alizadeh or the Waarihivu before?" Kiram stroked Javier's brow, brushing aside a long, damp lock of his black hair.

"He told me that his master, Alizadeh, belonged to an order of demon hunters called the Waarihivu before he converted to become a Bahiim. To battle demons, the Waarihivu crafted spells that could destroy an entire world at once. Javier suspects that the Shard of Heaven and the wards around it restrain one of those spells," Atreau said.

"Yes, the Shroud of Stone. But there's more. The Waarihivu were the first to access the Old Road or, as the northern witches call it, the Paths of the Dead." Kiram absently stroked Javier's hair, then he went on. "The Waarihivu used the Old Road to cross between worlds in pursuit of demons. But in the course of traveling between worlds, they realized that the paths of death touch everything in existence across all of time. So, in theory, the Old Road intersects with infinite destinations in both place and time. Do you understand?"

"Not at all, but seeing as Narsi and I have just been ushered back two weeks in time, I'm willing to take your word for it." Atreau shrugged.

"I think I can follow in concept, but I still have a lot of questions," Narsi spoke up.

Kiram blinked at Narsi, looking him up and down. "I don't believe we've been introduced—"

"This is Master Physician Narsi Lif-Tahm," Atreau supplied. "And this is Master Mechanist Kiram Kir-Zaki. The sleeping youth is Javier Tornesal."

"It's an honor to meet you. I've read so much about you both." Narsi gave Kiram a short bow. "As a physician, is there anything I can do to help your husband?"

"No, he'll wake when he's ready." Kiram managed a half smile. Then for the first time he seemed to actually take in Narsi's appearance. "Have we met before?"

"Narsi served in the chapel of the Grunito house. You probably saw him before Nestor's wedding," Atreau said.

Kiram regarded Narsi with the same curious recognition that Atreau supposed everyone familiar with the Grunito family did, upon first seeing his obvious resemblance to them.

If the scrutiny bothered Narsi, he hid it well.

Narsi nodded. "So then, back to my question—how can all times exist at once?"

"I can't claim to fully grasp the entire matter. But from what Javier has been able to describe, it sounds as if the passage of time on the Old Road has come undone from the physical world that we live in. There, it's as if all of the past is an ocean depth that we in the present float across. The most difficult part is finding your way once you dive in," Kiram said. "Apparently as a member of the Waarihivu, Alizadeh helped designed a huge array of spells called Issusha to navigate the entirety of the Sorrowlands. It would have allowed them to move precisely through time as well as across space. But their own queens condemned the Issusha and executed most of those who'd designed it. The surviving Waarihivu dispersed and fled to other realms. Alizadeh hid himself here."

Atreau nodded. His mind still reeled from everything he'd witnessed in the Sorrowlands. He clung to any line of reasoning or logic. At least this explained Javier's strange pronouncement about changing fate and claiming forbidden spells.

Kiram went on. "In twenty days, the Hallowed Kings fail and the Shroud of Stone escapes. Nearly every magical being in this world is wiped out within a day. Skellan and many others die to stop the Shroud of Stone from consuming everything. But after that, almost no one is left to defend us . . . The child tyrant Sparanzo takes power over Cadeleon. He leads a vast enthralled army on a crusade, slaughtering and enslaving nation after nation. Five years from now he will butcher the last of the Old Gods and burn the single remaining sacred grove. I and the few remaining Haldiim die in that battle. Then Javier's master, Alizadeh, breaks his vows and reveals the forbidden Issusha spell to Javier. Alizadeh sacrifices his own soul to send Javier back into the past to find me so that we can build the Issusha and change the future."

Narsi opened his mouth as if he was going to argue, then after a moment he said nothing and closed his mouth again. Atreau too struggled with all the implications of that revelation.

The Shroud of Stone wipes out nearly every magical being. Sparanzo—Sparanzo?—leads an enthralled army. Entire nations slaughtered and enslaved. Kiram and every Haldiim person killed . . .

Atreau glanced to Narsi, but he couldn't bear to think of that. He closed his eyes, seeking momentary calm in the darkness. God's tits, Javier traveling through time didn't seem nearly so shocking as the thought of so much loss and devastation.

"So," Narsi asked at last, "then at some point in the past this Javier from the future contacted you and the Javier from now?"

"Yes." Kiram nodded. "Though we met on the Old Road, outside the normal passage of time."

"Then are there *two* of him here now?" Narsi glanced meaningfully to Javier. Atreau frowned at the thought.

"Not anymore, no. Our living realm doesn't seem to tolerate paradoxes easily or for long," Kiram replied. "We met and planned our strategy on the Old Road, but when the Elder Javier stepped out into this living world, he and my Javier immediately merged into one man. You saw the same thing happening earlier. The moment they touch, they merge."

Atreau nodded. Though now he wondered just how many versions of Javier resided in that single body. Burned, broken, crushed—how many of those experiences could he carry with him?

"I spent the last year constructing these spell engines to power the Issusha spell that allows my Javier to travel back in time." Kiram's pale eyes flickered over the steaming, broken heaps of metal surrounding them. Then he again stroked Javier's brow. "Since then, Javier has traveled back to hundreds of points in history attempting to prevent the events that led to—or will lead to—the Shroud of Stone being released."

"Hundreds?" Narsi whispered softly.

Kiram didn't seem to hear him. He continued to gaze down at Javier.

"But the engines can't sustain the Issusha spell for long." Kiram's expression was bleak, his voice dull. "So, after they collapse, we live through history. Watch events play out and record them, until the time comes again that Alizadeh sends Javier back to me . . . and we try again."

Kiram's hand dropped down to touch the multitude of dark symbols etched into the stone floor. Their successive circles reminded Atreau of growth rings of a tree.

What would it feel like to be torn asunder hundreds of times? What was it like to reunite with aspects of himself that had experienced entirely different histories? Was it any wonder Javier had sounded half mad in the Sorrowlands?

"So, it's like a loop that circles back on itself endlessly?" Narsi asked. Atreau had no idea how he managed to gamely continue asking questions as if all of this was merely educational. Then he realized that Narsi probably needed to treat the matter as academic to keep from falling apart. It seemed to be a trait he shared with Kiram. In their company, Atreau could only try to suppress his own anguish and attempt to follow the conversation.

"I hope not endlessly," Kiram replied. He lifted his head, making an effort to look collected. "I prefer to think of what we are performing an experiment where we try new variables each time. Javier brings me the results of the previous test and then we attempt a new theory. We change something new and refine the results as best we can."

"How does he remember it all?" Narsi asked.

"He doesn't have to remember everything." Kiram lifted up the golden locket that had linked his and Javier's hands. "This ghost locket records all the events that we burn into the stones surrounding me. At the end of the five years, Javier brings me the locket."

Atreau studied the tiny symbols etched into the stones but couldn't read them.

"It's hellscript. The full extent of each symbol can only be seen in the light of the shajdi, Javier's White Hell. Because the script exists in the shajdi, it's shielded from the changes we make to history and remains the same," Kiram supplied.

For a few moments none of them seemed to know what to say. Kiram stared at Javier and Atreau stared at the mangled machinery surrounding them. Some pipe still whistled like a distant teakettle, then slowly quieted.

"This is amazing. I only understand half of what you explained, but still . . ." Narsi smiled at Kiram. "You truly are an unsurpassed genius, Master Kir-Zaki."

If the circumstances had not been so dire, Atreau would have teased Narsi about the level of reverence in his voice—though he supposed constructing a hybrid of magic and machinery that could hurtle a man back in time truly was astounding. Atreau just had difficulty appreciating that in the face of all the ruin and death Kiram foretold.

"If Javier can travel back in time," Atreau asked, "what's stopped him from keeping the Shroud of Stone from being released?"

"Altering history isn't so simple as it first seems. For one thing, he's restricted by wards and other spells that were made specifically to bar Waarihivu magic, like the Issusha spell. There are places he simply cannot go. On top of that it's difficult to make a change without setting off numerous unforeseen consequences." Kiram frowned. "But the greatest problem we've encountered is that some events never seem to change. A religious man might say they were fated. For example, my spell engines always collapse as the noon bells sound. Every time, it's always the same."

Kiram touched a small series of dots, then traced the same symbol where it appeared again in another ring of hellscript. He sighed.

"You truly believe that this is fate?" Narsi too studied the markings.

If this is fated, Atreau thought, *then fuck fate.* All at once he remembered Javier's rambling that he would murder fate.

"I prefer to believe that certain events are simply highly probable to occur." Kiram set the locket down and then carefully freed his and Javier's right wrist from the gold chain that had bound them together.

Kiram met Atreau's gaze, and he managed a smile. "Though it's encouraging that Javier's brought you back with him this time. Perhaps we've discovered that highly improbable sequence of events that we need. Maybe there's still time before it all falls to ruin once again."

That thought sparked hope in Atreau. There was still time.

"How *exactly* does Cieloalta fall? What's happened—or is happening?" Atreau's head throbbed just trying to think about all this.

"What will happen, perhaps?" Narsi offered.

"Didn't you see it for yourself in the Sorrowlands?" Kiram's gaze remained focused on Javier. "In twenty days the Hallowed Kings fail, the Shard of Heaven breaks and the Shroud of Stone—"

"That can't happen now. Fedeles holds Crown Hill, and he's lent his strength to the Circle of Wisteria. He'll keep the Hallowed Kings from failing," Atreau objected.

"Fedeles won't be alive when the Hallowed Kings are destroyed. He's killed on the same day as you." Kiram met Atreau's gaze, then looked back down to Javier. "You have no idea how many times Javier has tried to save him. But Fedeles always dies. Hierro Fueres does as well. Directly after

Hierro Fueres's death, the wards surrounding the Shard of Heaven and the Hallowed Kings are torn asunder. Oasia Quemanor and the young Bahiim in the Circle of Wisteria restrain the Shroud of Stone's advance for a time—long enough for Skellan and Elezar to reach the Shard of Heaven. Then they all die. Only the child tyrant survives."

"That can't be. If Hierro is killed, then how is the spell released?" Atreau demanded.

How could everything they'd done—everything they'd sacrificed— have been for nothing? Atreau felt sick and light-headed at once. The idea horrified him more than contemplating his own demise. What in the three hells was the point of all these fucking murders and lies, if they changed nothing? Anger and loss roiled in his chest. He wanted to shout the walls down or rip something apart.

"Maybe . . . maybe it's never been Hierro Fueres . . ." Narsi murmured. "What if his attempt to usurp the throne isn't related to the destruction of the Hallowed Kings? What if that's a different person. What if someone is using Hierro Fueres's plot to usurp the throne as a distraction?"

"Who?" Atreau snapped. "Sparanzo? He's five years old, for fuck's sake. How does he end up a child tyrant? Is he enthralled? Is he possessed?"

"I . . . I don't know," Narsi whispered.

Narsi's quiet suddenly dampened the frustration churning through Atreau. A month before, Atreau wouldn't have noticed the fixed quality of his calm expression. He might have even marveled at how composed the young man remained. But now he'd seen Narsi in states of shock, fear and embarrassment. Only intense distress inspired Narsi to take on such an air of silent dignity.

The last thing Atreau wanted was to lash out at him, of all people.

"Sorry," Atreau murmured.

He glanced between the desolate Kiram and the terrified Narsi and realized that he needed to stop grousing and rally. Self-pity and sniping wasn't going to help anyone or change anything.

"All right, then we'll add that to our list of things we need to work out." Atreau purposely lightened his voice and then looked to Kiram. "Who else knows what you're attempting?" He suspected he already knew the answer.

"No one," Kiram said. "It's only been Javier and me. Always."

"Well, with Narsi and me, you've doubled your numbers. And we have twenty days still, don't we?" Atreau ran his hand over his face and shoved his loose hair back from his eyes. Narsi gazed at him with such hope that Atreau even managed to pull his usual cocky smile. "What can we do right here, right now, to help?"

"My apprentices will be arriving in a few minutes. They don't know what these mechanisms were built for but they'll be more than able to clear the wreckage away." Kiram's attention returned to Javier. "Elezar and Skellan come thundering over a few minutes after that. Javier won't want them to see him like this."

"Then may we assist you in making Bahiim Javier more comfortable somewhere else?" Narsi rallied and went to kneel beside Javier. "I think that between the three of us we should be able to carry him away."

Atreau joined him. Together they improvised a sling from Javier's cloak and easily carried Javier in it. Kiram led them out of the huge machine workshop and through a verdant courtyard. Unique scents and tastes of Milmuraille drifted on the summer breeze: sea salt, beer and frying butter. From beyond the stone wall of the courtyard, Atreau heard street vendors calling out in Labaran. They carried Javier into the back of a rather stately timber-framed house and up to a second-story bedroom that overlooked the courtyard.

Atreau fetched water and then towels and bedclothes, while Narsi assisted Kiram in undressing Javier and washing the sweat, dirt and traces of blood from his body. Narsi assured Kiram that Javier wasn't suffering from a fever or any deep injuries—though to Atreau's eye he looked far too gaunt and nearly as pale as a corpse.

Twice Javier called out in inarticulate horror and Kiram whispered assurances to him until he quieted. The third time Javier stirred from his pillows, it was only to glance up to Kiram and then Atreau.

"We did it. We got you out," Javier whispered.

"You did," Atreau assured him.

Javier fell back into the pillows, grinning as if he was once again that irrepressible youth who'd stood before a cheering crowd to receive the golden circlet of a Grand Champion. Then Javier's expression slackened into the languor of sleep.

Atreau wondered how petty it was to envy him even a little.

CHAPTER TWENTY-ONE

An hour later, Atreau leaned against the windowsill, enjoying the feeling of fresh air rolling over him. In the courtyard below, Kiram, his apprentices and a team of burly half-dressed workmen hauled melted gears and ruptured pipes out to heavy carts. Two of the young women chatted with Kiram about the process of melting down the parts and recasting them. The other four gossiped and flirted with the workmen. Kiram's Haldiim accent lent a lilting quality to the Labaran language. Atreau wondered if Narsi would also sound so musical speaking Labaran.

He stole a glance to Narsi. The young man lounged in a wooden chair at Javier's bedside with his head leaned back and his eyes half lidded. A shaft of sunlight fell across his face and he stretched, reminding Atreau more than a little of that sleek, languid cat that shared his rooms.

Javier shifted amidst his pillows and then sat up. Narsi came to his side right away. Javier offered an easy smile in response to his concerned expression and made a few flattering comments about how well Narsi had grown up since the days he'd been a skinny chapel boy. Narsi flushed. He stepped aside to fill a cup of lemon water for Javier with a smile.

"As kind as you are handsome," Javier said, and he accepted the cup.

Javier's playful flirting annoyed Atreau, but he didn't want to consider the reason. Javier met Atreau's irritated gaze with a smug expression. As if he knew paying attention to Narsi bothered Atreau and so, like the ass he was, he would continue for the sake of his own amusement.

"Have Skellan and Elezar arrived yet?" Javier asked.

"Come and gone." Atreau had pointed them out to Narsi as they strode through the courtyard to greet Kiram amidst his heaps of wreckage. Hard-featured, wearing a white bearskin cloak and carrying a long sword, Elezar towered over everyone else in stony silence, while Skellan swayed and danced barefoot between the steaming machines. His dogskin cloak and dusty pants lent him the look of a beggar, but there was no mistaking the power that whirled around him, lifting his long scarlet hair like a summer wind.

Atreau had overheard a little of their conversation. Most of it had amounted to Skellan informing Kiram that his machines had sensibly fallen apart rather than enter the revolting Bahiim paths of the dead.

Narsi had grinned at the sight of Skellan and informed him that he'd described the man perfectly in his books. But watching him, Atreau had seen that it was Elezar who Narsi studied with a wistful expression.

That had been nearly half an hour ago; since then a jolly housekeeper had brought them a pitcher of lemon water as well as buttered black bread, rabbit stew and a steaming pot of frog tea.

Atreau took a sip from his enameled iron cup. Strong herbal flavors rolled over his tongue, reminding him of the tea his mother had loved. He set the cup on the windowsill.

"So, why don't you want them to know about all of this?" Atreau asked.

"Because . . ." Javier scowled up at the blue sky, pinning a passing cloud with a particularly pained glare. Atreau waited, but Javier offered him nothing more. He continued to stare out the window. Several birds winged overhead.

Crows, Atreau thought.

"Because?" Atreau prompted.

"Because saving some is better than none." At last Javier looked Atreau in the eyes. "If Elezar learns that Skellan dies in Cieloalta, he'll stop him from going. He will fight me, Alizadeh, you—anyone to protect Skellan. And if Skellan knows that Elezar will die along with him, then he'll break the bond between them to save him. But I've seen how that ends. Skellan needs every shred of strength and power—his and Elezar's—to contain the Shroud and save this world from oblivion. They must both die, or everything will be lost."

"I thought you were going to murder fate. Shatter time. Slit the fucking future's throat?" Atreau easily recalled Javier's words.

"I am. I will. But—" Javier looked momentarily lost. Atreau didn't know that he'd ever seen Javier like this, so unsure and harrowed. "Some events have been unfolding for centuries. Their fates—the path of their vei has been building for ages. The way canyons are carved by the wind and rain. Countless individual impacts creating something inevitable. How do I stop just the right raindrop to turn aside a river?"

"You saved me," Atreau pointed out. "You saved Narsi."

"Yes, but that was only a matter of altering a single instant, and one very close to the time I traveled from. But the Shard of Heaven, the Hallowed Kings and the Shroud of Stone, those are ancient and complex. That's not even considering the fact that Crown Hill and the Circle of Wisteria guard against me setting foot in the city for most of Cieloalta's history."

"Forgive me, but I'm still not certain why that is," Narsi said.

"Because the Shroud of Stone is a Waarihivu spell that is contained by the Shard of Heaven. Crown Hill and the Circle of Wisteria also guard against it. But because my master and I use Waarihivu magic as well, all three of those sites will assault us if we enter Cieloalta." Javier drained the last of his water. "I've had to wander deep into the Sorrowlands to reach an age before they barred my teacher and me. Little of what I've done then seems to have survived." Javier scowled. "I can only go so far and change so much. The altered histories start to cloud my mind and break us—me—"

Atreau frowned at the thought. In the Sorrowlands Javier had seemed to be going mad. Kiram also clearly feared for him.

"Are you all right?" Atreau asked.

"Now? Yes. But I don't know how many more times I can break into the past before I'm unable to come back together again. If that happens, then I must still ensure that there will be someone who stops the Shroud of Stone from consuming this entire world."

"So Skellan's and Elezar's deaths are your insurance in case you're unable to return," Atreau realized. God's blood, but what a grim thought that was.

Javier closed his eyes and fell back into his pillows. "At least some people would survive that way. I've seen the other option . . ."

Narsi reached out and rested two of his fingers against Javier's wrist, taking his pulse and likely checking for a fever as well.

"If I understood what Master Kir-Zaki told us, it will be another five years before you invoke this Issusha spell to travel back in time, correct?" Narsi asked.

"Yes, however the Shroud will be unfurled twenty days from now." Javier said.

"Then you should try to eat something to regain your strength up," Narsi told him. He brought Javier a bowl of stew as well as several slices of buttered bread. Javier ate, listlessly at first, but then like he was famished.

Atreau handed over his own nearly full bowl. He didn't really have a stomach for anything right now—though a part of him craved a bottle of white ruin and some dark corner where he could drink himself into thoughtless oblivion. But that wouldn't solve any of their problems. To do that he would need answers to painful questions.

Javier finished his second bowl and looked better for it.

"How exactly is Fedeles killed?" Atreau felt like an ass asking, but he had to know.

Javier's expression turned hurt and almost angry, then he closed his eyes.

"The first night of the Masquerade, in the Royal Star Garden. There's a man in attendance who—" Javier scowled. "He's difficult to describe. Always half in shadows with his head bowed, but he moves so, so quickly—"

"Master Ariz," Narsi said.

Atreau nodded and a cold dread filled him. What other assassin could get close enough to murder Fedeles? They should have put Ariz down when they had the chance.

"Ariz Plunado," Atreau told Javier. "He's the same man who beheaded Ciceron. And Ojoito. And Lord Numes. Just to name a few of his victims. Hierro Fueres holds him in a thrall."

"I guessed that he was one of Hierro's assassins. But I can't work out what is going on." Javier sounded oddly puzzled but then went on. "Just before midnight, this Ariz receives a note from Hierro. He reads it and goes to where Fedeles is talking with Jacinto. He steps out but then turns and retreats. For no reason that I can discern, Fedeles leaves Jacinto and his friends and follows Ariz. As they near Hierro, Ariz draws a short sword and plunges it into his own chest—"

"He does what?" Atreau had braced his nerves for a description of Ariz murdering Fedeles. This turn of events dumbfounded him.

"Oh no," Narsi whispered.

"He kills himself." Javier's expression darkened. "And then Fedeles kills Hierro."

Atreau could all too easily imagine it. Fedeles would be heartbroken and furious at once.

"When I say that Fedeles kills Hierro, I don't mean that he merely runs the man through or strangles the life out of him," Javier went on. "I mean that he loses all composure. He tears Hierro to pieces and rips the hedges, statues, stonework and fountains asunder. He doesn't even attempt to hide his shadow, and half the surrounding court sees him. I can't hear much from inside the Sorrowlands. But I see it. Again and again." Javier closed his eyes. "His rage is endless."

Atreau waited but Javier remained silent.

"And then?" Atreau prompted at last.

"Then Prince Sevanyo orders his royal guards to stop Fedeles." Javier lowered his face into his hands. "It's not always exactly the same after that. Sometimes Fedeles kills dozens of them, sometimes only a few. But he always dies weeping, with the man—Ariz—in his arms."

Across from Atreau, Narsi looked gray with sorrow. Atreau felt sick and angry at his own helplessness. However, he had to remember that none of these things had happened yet. And if this was the first time he and Narsi had been saved, then perhaps this too could be altered.

"What was written on the note, do you know?" Atreau asked.

Javier nodded, but slowly, as if he didn't want to admit as much.

"I thought that if I knew, I might be able to stop it all from happening." Javier rose from the bed. He swayed as if dizzy, but then he walked in sure, even steps to a writing desk. He opened a drawer and drew out a small envelope. He gazed at it with a troubled expression.

Atreau too studied the envelope, but it seemed unremarkable. He stole a glance to Narsi. The young physician was still frowning at some thought of his own. Most likely wondering if he'd made the right decision by saving Ariz.

"The power of the shajdi is immense and sacred. As the guardian of that power, I am given the Old Road. Death is my kingdom. But it's sacrilege to tamper with the other half of the shajdi. The power of creation."

Atreau frowned at Javier. He had no idea what had prompted this speech. Javier met his gaze and gave a rueful smile.

"You don't understand anything I'm saying, do you?" Javier asked.

"No, but feel free to explain," Atreau replied.

"Hierro hasn't written this note yet. Not in this time." Javier turned the envelope over.

"So how do you have it, then?" Atreau asked

"Did you bring it with you when you came back from five years from now?" Narsi asked.

"In a way. I remembered it and wanted to see it. To study it in hope that I might somehow save Fedeles. I wanted it so, so very badly." Javier continued to eye the envelope with an uneasy expression. "And then there it was in my hand when I walked out of the shajdi one afternoon."

"You summoned it across time?" Narsi asked.

"I manifested it from another time. Brought it into being here." Javier said it very quietly, almost to himself. "My desperation is beginning to creep into the shajdi's power of creation. I am corrupting it."

"But this is just a note," Atreau pointed out.

Javier gave a quick shake of his head.

"So far. But I'm not certain of what more I might make real if I continue going back and living through the same years again and again. I don't know how much longer I can do this. How many more times I can see all of you die." Javier shook his head and then held the envelope out as if he couldn't stand holding it any longer.

Narsi took it from him and slid a small piece of plain white paper out. His brow furrowed as he read aloud, "Kiss Fedeles Quemanor?"

"Kill," Javier corrected.

Atreau almost laughed at the misreading. Under other circumstances it would have been hilarious. Narsi handed the note and envelope to Atreau.

"All the flourishes in some noblemen's script often defeat the point of writing anything at all," Atreau said

"It's too bad it doesn't say 'kiss.' Can you imagine if it did?" Narsi commented.

"Well, given his feelings for Ariz, I think that Fedeles would be delight—" Then it struck Atreau. Why couldn't it say kiss? How difficult could it be to make a forgery with the curling *l*'s traded out for *s*'s? Atreau studied the note more intently. No watermark on the paper, nothing remarkable about the ink. It wouldn't be easy to switch out Hierro's original for a forgery but compared to the other challenges that they now faced.... At least Atreau knew how to accomplish something like this. He grinned. "Narsi, don't take this the wrong way, but I think I love you."

Narsi's face colored just slightly at that, but then he gave Atreau a skeptical glance.

"And what would be the *right* way to take that statement, Lord Vediya?" Narsi inquired. Javier actually laughed. Atreau smiled, but he knew that Narsi wouldn't like what he would suggest next.

"Since we know exactly when and where all this will take place, I say we pass the wrong message to Ariz and before Hierro can discover the exchange, we . . . remove Ariz."

Narsi scowled at him, but Javier appeared relieved.

"It won't be without risk," Javier said. "But the fact that this all takes place during the Masquerade and at night will work in your favor, I think."

"Why *remove* Ariz and not Hierro?" Narsi asked.

Atreau opened his mouth to explain how difficult it would be to kill Hierro—how many would-be assassins Hierro had already destroyed—but then he wondered if it wouldn't be possible to use a forged note to turn Ariz against Hierro. Before he could even make the suggestion, Javier cut him off.

"Because Hierro's death is the catalyst that destroys the Hallowed Kings and the surrounding wards," Javier said. "The longer he lives, the more time we have to discover a way to deal with the Shroud of Stone. A way that doesn't leave the world devastated and at the mercy of a tyrant."

"You're sure that it is Hierro's death that destroys the wards?" Atreau demanded. Could Narsi have been right earlier? That another opponent lay behind Hierro?

"Yes." Javier looked tired. "Because so long as Hierro is alive, the wards hold. As soon as he's killed, they begin falling apart at an astounding rate."

"You know that for certain?" Atreau asked.

"Yes. I've seen it and I've triggered it, more than once, myself," Javier admitted. "I've tried saving Fedeles by killing Hierro. The wards fall with him. Sometimes within moments, sometimes within the day, but they always begin collapsing as soon as he dies."

"Then Ariz will have to go," Atreau said. "Just not in front of Fedeles or anywhere near Hierro."

Narsi looked none too happy, but the fact of the matter was that Ariz had already cost too many innocent people their lives. Narsi had to know that; he'd seen the dead at the Slate House for himself. Narsi frowned in silence, leaning against the wall while Atreau and Javier worked out the details.

"Ariz won't fight us. He knows that he could destroy the very people he loves the most." Atreau made the comment as much for Narsi's benefit as to inform Javier. "Last night on Crown Hill he asked me to have him killed if he became a threat to Fedeles. He has already agreed to this decision."

Atreau met Narsi's stubborn glower.

"But I don't agree," Narsi snapped. "Master Ariz has already suffered so much and had so much taken from him. His life is all that's left to him. It's defeatist and just so . . . cruel."

Javier cocked his head in Narsi's direction, studying him.

"Even if we do nothing, he dies in any case," Javier stated. "He falls on his own short sword and drives the blade through his heart."

"Javier is right." Atreau said it as calmly he could. "The only thing we have a say in is how much he suffers and how many other people die because of him."

Narsi opened his mouth but only exhaled a long breath and then nodded. "I'll make a mixture of duera and black poppy for you to give to him. He won't suffer."

"Thank you." Genuine gratitude shone in Javier's expression. "You're saving Fedeles's life."

Narsi inclined his head but then rose and went to the window. He gazed out onto the courtyard, face dark with resentment. Atreau decided against attempting any kind of consolation. No doubt Narsi knew he was making the right decision, but arranging a person's death wasn't easy, not even for a man as practiced as Atreau at strategic sacrifice. For a young physician, who had hoped to cure Ariz, it had to feel like he'd swallowed pitch. Narsi would have to find a way to come to terms with this on his own.

Javier closed his eyes and sank back into his bed. His breathing came slow and deep, but Atreau didn't think he was quite asleep. He traced signs into his sheets with his fingers.

Atreau took the chair Narsi had abandoned. He leaned back and stared up at the carved ceiling beams. An overhead spray of the wooden blossoms reminded him of the flowers he'd seen up on Crown Hill last night, listening to Fedeles's exhausted rambling words after the attack on the Circle of Wisteria.

. . . or maybe it's the other power, the one he's hiding . . .

The other power. Who was it? Could Hierro have enthralled some witch or—

Atreau sat upright. Damn it! Ariz had all but told him, hadn't he?

A plot hidden within another plot. Like a smile disguised by the lacework of a widow's veil.

Wasn't that what he'd said? He'd been describing Clara Odalis's part in Hierro's machinations, and according to Ariz, she bore his same *burden*. The same Brand of Obedience. God's blood, he should have realized all this sooner. But he'd been so tired and distracted by trying to rewrite Jacinto's play.

"Narsi, do you still have Dommian's charm-book with you?" Atreau asked.

"Yes." Narsi cast him a sullen look. Then he drew the small book out from the inner pocket of his coat. "Why?"

Atreau bounded up and joined Narsi at the window, where the light was strong and bright. Javier's eyes cracked open, but his expression remained distant, on the edge of sleep. His hands continued to shake and twitch against his chest.

"I think we need to look again at those letters that Dommian kept." Atreau edged closer, hoping Narsi would allow it, given his current opinion of him and his decisions.

"Clara Odalis may be the one attacking the Hallowed Kings. Her letters might tell us what she's trying to achieve."

"Apart from the elimination of the Haldiim race?" Narsi's tone was sarcastic, but he still opened the book and slid the letters out from the incision in the cover.

Atreau took the fragile papers and scanned each until he found the passages he had recollected. "This passage addresses the subject of some unknown man's books; now I believe this must be Hierro."

Thank you for telling me where he hid the books. I have read them and copied as many pages as I could. I think that you are right. He doesn't understand the importance of history. He only sees things that are of use to him. I will try to be wiser than that.

Atreau tapped the second paper. "As to the contents of these hidden volumes, I feel certain that at least one must concern the mythical figure of the Summer Doe and her part in the Battle of Heaven's Shard, because it's here in Clara's second letter."

Is it possible that she stopped Our Savior's Waarihivu invocation from cleansing the world? Did she betray Our Savior? Or are we still awaiting the final battle of that war?

Previously the word Waarihivu had so captured Atreau's attention that he'd dismissed the rest as the casual ruminations of a zealot. But now he absorbed all that those brief sentences implied.

"Not only does Clara regard the release of the Waarihivu spell, the Shroud of Stone, as a cleansing act to the world, but she has reason to suspect that the Summer Doe had possessed the means to stop the spell," Atreau said.

"Which interests her because if the Shroud of Stone has been stopped once, that means it can be stopped again," Narsi said. "Which Lady Odalis would not want . . . unless she intended to unleash the Shroud in the first place. Perhaps as a display of power?"

"Or to wipe out any witches who could challenge her when she en- thralls Sparanzo and begins her crusades. But either way, she would certainly want a means to stop the Shroud." Just considering this, Atreau felt his heart begin to race. They needed to find out as much as possible as quickly as possible about the Summer Doe—Yah-muur— and her relic.

"Clara must have been plotting and manipulating events behind Hierro's back for years," Atreau said. "Ariz told me as much, but I didn't understand the magnitude of her ambition. Likely it has only been the impediment of Hierro's control of her that has kept her from unleash- ing the Shroud of Stone years ago. She must be the one who sent Ariz to retrieve the relic box decorated with the Summer Doe's image from the Slate House. He told me to find it before he did. But the fact that he could warn me about it, or that he could leave it behind, would imply that he had some choice in the matter. Securing the relic might not have been Hierro's order, but Clara's."

"So Ariz was sent to the Slate House with two different missions from two different masters?" Narsi asked.

"Exactly," Atreau said. "For Hierro, Ariz was killing Ojoito, a potential Sagrada heir. But I'm guessing that unbeknownst to Hierro, Clara charged Ariz with retrieving the prize Ojoito had acquired for the royal bishop, which was the relic box. If nothing else, we managed to keep that out of her hands."

Atreau flipped through the pages of the charm-book to again study Dommian's poorly rendered image of the relic box in question. Some- thing about that hunting motif nagged at him. Just like the last time he'd studied the image, he found it vexingly familiar. Somewhere, years ago, he'd seen an image very like it.

"Why don't we open it and find out?" Narsi asked.

Atreau shook his head no, but it was Javier who answered. "Casks and boxes of that nature contain magical items of incalculable power. Opening it without knowing what it contains could be considered willful self-destruction."

Narsi nodded. Then after moment he said, "Sparanzo's part in this. Do you think Clara Odalis could enthrall him without anyone noticing?"

"If Fedeles and Oasia are both dead, Clara would become Sparanzo's legal guardian. She'd certainly have the opportunity." Atreau frowned at the idea of his son suffering such a fate. Fuck fate, he thought again, and felt better for it.

The door opened and Kiram entered. He offered Atreau and Narsi a nod of recognition but went to Javier's side. Javier started to sit up, but Kiram pushed him back into his pillows.

"You must sleep." Kiram caught Javier's twitching fingers in his own hands and gently massaged them. "Elezar will come fetch you tomorrow to assist the city coven with the invasion fleet. It's going to be tiring work."

The words "invasion fleet" sent a thrill of fear down Atreau's spine.

"Yes. Yes, I know. I need to rest. But Atreau and young Narsi have come up with a plan to save Fedeles." Javier beamed at the two of them, then returned his attention to Kiram. "It may work this time."

Kiram glanced questioningly to where the two of them stood by the window. Atreau nodded in answer to his silent question.

A little of the worry in Kiram's expression seemed to lift. "That's wonderful. And all the more reason that you should finally be able to sleep easy."

"We still have to dismantle the Shroud," Javier muttered. "For Skellan and Elezar's sakes, we have to get it right."

"You will. There's still time. But for now, you need to let Atreau and Narsi rest too. They're not used to traveling the Old Road. They're likely exhausted." Again Kiram looked to him and Narsi, then directly at the door.

Atreau got the message. "Truth to tell, I could do with a nap. I was up most of the night. As was Narsi."

"Oh. Yes. I was, actually." Narsi gathered up the letters, closed the charm-book and pocketed it again.

"The two rooms at the end of the hall have been prepared for you. Have a good rest." As nicely as he put it, Atreau understood at once that Kiram wanted them out.

Oddly, Narsi seemed to have missed much of the exchange as he continued to gaze out the window with an expression of intense concentration. Atreau nudged him with his toe.

Belatedly Narsi said, "Ah, yes. Thank you."

He followed Atreau out of the room, but after they'd reached the end of the hall, he stopped.

"I think I know where you remember it from," Narsi said.

"Remember what from?" Atreau arched a questioning brow at the sudden non sequitur. Maybe Narsi truly did need some sleep.

"The symbols on the relic box. It was Bishop Palo's chapel," Narsi said. "In your memoir you described descending into an ancient catacomb where the priests were copying spells from a pillar to recreate golden casks."

"Yes. But that—" Atreau cut himself off. At the time he'd been focused on evading the notice of both priests and armed guards in his pursuit of one of those casks that had trapped a demon lord.

The catacomb had contained eight immense stone pillars that supported the underground chamber. There had been one in particular that he'd lurked behind for nearly two hours. Holy men had come and gone while Atreau had absorbed the carved image of a deer bounding over the circle of a moon, while an eagle soared below.

When he'd written about the experience, he'd mentioned the designs and surrounding symbols only to point out that, contrary to Bishop Palo's belief, the chapel could not have been the final resting place of Our Savior's bones. It had clearly been erected much later in history and built atop the foundations of some far more ancient heathen temple. Just like the ruins atop Crown Hill in Cieloalta.

Now Atreau realized that Narsi was correct. Those images and inscriptions had indeed been similar to the ones Ariz and Dommian sketched. Not exactly the same, but too much alike not to bear some relation.

"You wrote—" Narsi began again.

"Yes. I remember now." Atreau shook his head. "Though how you did, I've no idea. You've an amazing mind, you know that?"

"Not as amazing as Master Kir-Zaki." Narsi smiled in his usual self-deprecating manner. The man was far too unaccustomed to receiving the appreciation he deserved. It made Atreau want to heap so much praise on him that he couldn't disregard it all. Or at least not shrug it off as if Atreau's admiration meant nothing.

"Should we go there?" Narsi asked.

Atreau frowned, thinking it over. He wasn't certain how warm a welcome he would receive there.

After Bishop Palo's murder, the man's niece, Abea, had inherited the property. She and Atreau had been quite intimate for a time. He'd gone to some trouble to keep her from being executed for conspiracy, and she'd expressed her gratitude with delightful musical compositions and several hours of pleasant dalliance. However, recalling the way she'd wept and cursed him when he'd left her, he wasn't certain that much love remained.

Still, Narsi was correct, they needed to see that chapel and glean all they could from the ancient pillars beneath it. Too many lives and nations were at stake not to go.

"At least I'll have a physician at my side if the lady of the house decides to carve my heart out," Atreau muttered, then he laughed at Narsi's alarmed expression and added, "Well, come along."

CHAPTER
TWENTY-TWO

Being a native of the vibrant and diverse port city of Anacleto, Narsi took pride in comporting himself with a certain unflappable, urbane demeanor. So as he strode down the streets of Milmuraille, he managed, for the most part, not to gawk like a bumpkin at his surroundings. But when several long-tentacled, bat-like creatures winged past his head, he couldn't help but stare after them. They darted through the air, chasing a fishmonger's heavily laden cart.

He truly had been transported to the magical city he'd read about only in books.

Despite all the earlier shock of this day, and his sorrow over Master Ariz's fate, Narsi could not help but be filled with a sense of wonder. He smiled as he traversed the maze of brilliantly painted wood-timbered buildings, colorful signs advertising curious services and a wonderfully diverse populace. Novel sensations washed over him from every direction.

The air tasted of beer hops, shellfish and sweet butter. Painted banners and statues of bizarre animals stood guard outside doorways and on street corners. And all around him people bartered and conversed in blends of Labaran and Mirogothic. What Cadeleonian phrases and Haldiim words he overheard sounded strongly accented and fascinatingly new. Even the woodsmoke smelled different here.

"Those are cloud imps, aren't they?" Narsi asked. The white curls of their fuzzy hides and the springing quality of their quick tentacles were exactly as Lord Vediya had described them in his memoir. Though their calls reminded Narsi more of excited hens than doves.

Lord Vediya glanced to where the flock of white creatures fluttered above the slow-moving cart. He nodded, but his expression remained distant, distracted. None of this was startling or new to him.

The cart driver gave a shout as two of the cloud imps dived past his head. A lanky, moss-haired girl crouching in the back of the wagon looked up. Narsi felt the breath catch in his chest as he took in the round eyes and wide mouth of her frog-like features. She swatted the grasping tentacles away from the baskets she guarded with her broad, webbed fingers. The cloud imps squealed like excited children as they darted away.

"Is that girl a frogwife—" Narsi began, but then he realized that Lord Vediya had moved on. Narsi raced through the crowded street. He caught sight of Lord Vediya's figure just as the man stopped and looked back at him with an annoyed expression. Narsi hurried to his side.

"I'll give you a proper tour of the city when—if—I manage to get through this visit in one piece," Lord Vediya said. "But for now, try not to wander off."

"Technically I stood still and you wandered," Narsi pointed out, but, catching Lord Vediya's narrowed gaze, he added, "I'll keep up with you."

Considering the pace Lord Vediya set, it was no easy feat. Quite soon they reached a section of the city that resembled Cieloalta more than the previous streets. Here sedate, symmetrical buildings stood in measured rows and the roads appeared to be laid out along grid lines, like an army encampment. None of the houses or grounds were as vast as Lord Quemanor's residence, but many clearly aspired to noble grandeur. Servants in silk liveries stood guard at iron gates, and Narsi noted glossy carriages coming and going from the grounds.

Lord Vediya drew to a halt outside a particularly new-looking set of entry gates that stood before a hulking white residence. Numerous servants dressed in cream uniforms dotted the grounds and surrounding hills. Teams of gardeners busily trimmed shrubs and harvested huge sprays of cut flowers, while house servants unloaded barrels and crates from delivery wagons.

Narsi wondered if they were preparing for a celebration of some kind. Then he caught sight of the gold spire of a Cadeleonian chapel rising just beyond a stand of filbert trees. That must be the ancient chapel Lord Vediya had described in his memoir. He fought down the urge to race straight there. The house guards wouldn't take his trespass kindly, he didn't think.

At the entry gates two blond guards watched as delivery wagons rolled passed them on the way up to the house. After a brief pause, Lord Vediya straightened and seemed to steel himself, then he walked through the gates with his head held high. Narsi ambled alongside him.

"Your business, good sirs?" the shorter of the two guards inquired. But the second, taller guard's face lit with recognition.

"Your lordship!" The taller guard smiled at Lord Vediya. Then his expression turned apprehensive. "Her wedding is tomorrow, sir."

"Never fear, Ayer. I've only come to wish her and her lucky husband a happy future," Lord Vediya answered. "If she's not home I can wait in the chap—"

"She's here, my lord. I think that she may be expecting you." The guard inclined his head respectfully to Lord Vediya and made no attempt to stop him or Narsi from entering.

Once they were out of hearing, Narsi stepped a little closer to Lord Vediya's side and whispered, "Do you know why that guard seem so concerned?"

"Because half the world seems to believe I possess both the time and inclination to carry off every pretty woman who finds herself engaged to another man." Lord Vediya stopped briefly beside a rose bower. "I've yet to be suspected of whisking away some comely groom, but I suppose that can't be too long off as well."

Narsi frowned. Not that he doubted Lord Vediya's capacity to charm any susceptible man or woman, but it brought up the question of why anyone in Labara should expect him to be here to do so. Beyond the two of them, only Kiram and Javier could have known that they'd arrived today.

"But you live in Cieloalta," Narsi commented. "Why would anyone think you'd be here?"

"I'd guess that most of the household knows that Abea sent me a message some three months back." Lord Vediya studied the bounty of white blossoms, then felt through his coat pockets and drew out a folded page. Musical notation covered the paper. "The Labaran ship carrying it was delayed and the letter only reached me today—or what was 'today' when we left Cieloalta. Which will be two weeks from now."

"What did she write?" Narsi asked in a whisper.

Atreau handed him the paper. Narsi wasn't so musically gifted that he could read the melody, but the name of the song and the lyrics seemed clear enough. *No Longer Will I Await Your Faithless Love.*

Why would a woman send a man such a song? Was it a rejection? A validation? A challenge?

From the reaction of the older guard, Narsi suspected the latter and cringed a little anticipating the scene about to unfold when the lady discovered that they'd come here on business. Was Lord Vediya considering making good on her challenge, since he had miraculously now arrived in time? The thought pained Narsi.

Lord Vediya continued to contemplate the roses. He lifted his hand as if to pluck one of the blossoms but only brushed his fingers over the petals before turning on his heel and striding ahead. Narsi jogged after him.

At the gilded front doors of the grand house, Lord Vediya was again recognized—this time by several dumbfounded footmen as well as a pair of passing maids. The maids appeared thrilled and scandalized, but the footmen, like the guard at the gate, looked uneasy. None took much note of Narsi, nor did they ask why he and Lord Vediya had come calling. Lord Vediya's affair with the lady of the house appeared to be well known and, Narsi guessed, a source of turbulence.

A month ago, Narsi would have been surprised not to have read some hint of this infamous affair in Lord Vediya's memoirs, but now he understood how much the author had left out of his supposedly unexpurgated confessions.

A stout, dark-haired footman escorted them back to a spacious study. Several dulcimers occupied the shelves standing on either side of a large window. Sheet music lay across a harpsichord, and a lute leaned at a rakish angle in a nearby chair. At the far end of the study, a black-haired Cadeleonian woman with a heart-shaped face looked up from her desk. Her dark eyes went wide and the pen slipped from her hand.

"Abea!" Lord Vediya offered the shocked woman a handsome smile. "I pray I'm not too late to wish you and your lucky bridegroom the happiest of futures together."

The woman's face trembled as if dozens of conflicting expressions warred within her. For an instant Narsi could have sworn that she gazed at Lord Vediya with open adoration, then something like grief flitted across her face. At last her eyes narrowed and her lips curled into a sneer.

For himself, Narsi felt the tiniest bit of relief, while simultaneously wishing Lord Vediya had left him outside the door.

The footman bowed very low and fled.

Narsi stuffed the musical score he still held into his pocket. Fortunately, Abea didn't appear to take any note of his movement or even of his existence. She pinned Lord Vediya with an imperious glower. Indifference settled over her countenance like a frigid snowfall.

"What are you doing here?" Abea demanded.

"Aside from wishing you well?" Lord Vediya asked. "I had hoped to take a small tour of the grounds."

"Well wishes and a tour?" Abea's brows rose. "You expect me to believe that *you* sailed all this distance just to walk through my garden and then personally hand me over to another man?"

"I swear." Lord Vediya held up his empty hands. "I've no intention of disrupting your wedding. Nor do I wish to embroil you or your future spouse in any trouble."

"Do you think I'm an idiot?" Abea appeared rightly skeptical. If he hadn't known better, Narsi wouldn't have believed Lord Vediya himself. But the fact was that Lord Vediya's presence here was due to Narsi's own speculations. Clearly he hadn't wanted to come or to cause this woman such distress. Narsi felt like he ought to say something in his defense, but he had no idea what.

Abea stared unblinking at Lord Vediya and traced the gem dangling from a gold chain around her neck.

"I admit that there's more, but it's nothing to do with you or your marriage." Lord Vediya's expression turned sheepish. "I've come at the behest of Lord Quemanor, to study your chapel. It seems that the chambers—"

"What kind of fool do you take me for?" Abea bounded to her feet, icy demeanor shattered. "You come here, to me today—of all days! And you claim it's to see that moldering wreck of a chapel?"

"Time is short and I didn't know if you would be holding the ceremony there tomorrow," Lord Vediya replied.

"You expect me to believe that?"

"What would be the point of lying?" Lord Vediya asked.

"What is the point of anything you do, but to satisfy that chasm of insecurity in your soul?" Abea snapped. "You toy with people just to prove to yourself that you have any kind of power! I know all too well how badly you crave love. How desperately you need to be wanted and desired."

"Abea, I know I haven't been—" Lord Vediya began, but she cut him off.

"This is low even for you, Atreau. Arriving here just to tell me that you *don't* wish to see me? That my wedding to another man means *nothing* to you?" Abea shook her head. "Are you really so pathetic that you had to come here just to try and break my heart one last time?"

"No." Lord Vediya spoke softly. "I truly didn't want to hurt you."

"And yet here you are," Abea replied. "Saying you wish one thing while doing just the opposite."

Lord Vediya dragged his hand through his loose hair, shoving it back from his face. Narsi recognized his frustration and genuine distress, but Abea had reached the point of total rage.

"If this weren't a matter of vital importance, I swear, I wouldn't have disturbed you," Lord Vediya said. "But—"

"Don't you dare try to claim that this is anything to do with politics or spies or assassins. Or—or anyone but you, Atreau! You have other agents who you could employ, if you wanted to. No, this is about what you desire." Abea stepped around her desk. She gripped her necklace so tightly that Narsi feared she might tear it apart.

"This is *not* what I want—" Lord Vediya began.

"Listen to how earnest you sound." Abea gave a hard laugh. "My God, are you lying to yourself as well as the rest of us? Do you even know what designs truly lurk in that lying heart of yours?"

Abea relaxed her grip on the necklace enough that Narsi could see the bright red jewel in the center. It seemed to glow in Abea's grasp. Lord Vediya noticed it for the first time too. His expression turned tense and he took a step back.

"I see that you recognize this candor stone. Lady Hylanya gifted it to me as a wedding present." Abea smiled, but not kindly. "I wonder, Atreau, are you even capable of telling the truth? Would it kill you to speak an honest word?"

Candor stones were enchanted jewels that witches used to extract confessions. An appropriate gift to give a woman about to be married, Narsi supposed, but the worst kind of threat to a spymaster whose mind held countless secrets.

"Don't." Atreau backed up another step, his shoulder bumping up against Narsi's. "Abea, please don't—" His words seemed to catch in his throat.

"Reveal to me what you truly desire," Abea ordered.

Lord Vediya spun away from Abea and the radiant stone that she held. Narsi stepped forward to shield him. Lord Vediya glanced up at Narsi. His expression was so tense that he looked almost angry—his amber eyes seemed to bore into Narsi, and a flush colored his cheeks. He caught Narsi's hand and Narsi thought he meant to flee the room.

Instead he jerked Narsi into his arms. He gripped Narsi tight against his own body and he kissed him.

At first, Narsi was too stunned to react at all. Then a surge of heat flooded from Lord Vediya and rolled over him, rousing a desperate pleasure. He opened his lips and tasted Lord Vediya's insistent tongue. He dug his hands into the muscle of Lord Vediya's back, drawing their bodies closer.

Lord Vediya's blazing fingers slipped past the folds of Narsi's coat and shirt, tracing his naked belly and the muscles of his chest. One of Lord Vediya's fingers scraped over a nipple, while his right hand slipped downward to Narsi's groin.

"Stop!" Abea's shout barely penetrated Narsi's dazed mind.

Lord Vediya released him at once and stepped away, doubled over, hands on his knees, breathing hard.

Deprived of the heat of Lord Vediya's body, Narsi's skin felt cold and exposed. His pulse hammered, throbbing through his loins and pounding in his chest. Belatedly Narsi realized that in the brief time they'd kissed, Lord Vediya had not only unbuttoned his coat and shirt, but he'd unbuckled Narsi's belt.

For his part, Narsi had only managed to rumple Lord Vediya's clothes, but the other man still looked flushed, wild and breathless.

"Narsi, I'm so sorry," Lord Vediya whispered. He straightened and started to reach out to him. Perhaps to straighten his clothes. Then he pulled his hands back as if he couldn't trust them. He turned back to Abea.

The flush of rage had drained from her face and she now stared on in stunned astonishment.

"Happy?" Lord Vediya demanded. He looked both angry and miserable at once.

Abea ignored him, regarding Narsi as if he'd just stepped out of thin air before her.

Narsi hurriedly buckled his belt and began buttoning up his shirt. He had no idea of what he should do or say. He wasn't even certain of what exactly had happened to the two of them except that it must have been witchcraft. Waves of heat still rolled in his chest and a very faint ringing sounded in his ears—as if he was recovering from the aftermath of an intense fever.

"Who in the three hells are *you*?" Abea asked.

Narsi wanted to tell her it was none of her damn business. But he suppressed his anger. They needed her permission to get into that chapel. Countless lives could be at stake. Narsi drew in a slow breath and released it. The buzzing in his head faded away.

"Narsi Lif-Tahm. Master physician to Father Timoteo Grunito, acting in service to the Duke of Rauma," Narsi replied with as much dignity as he could manage.

"The duke. You actually serve Fedeles Quemanor?" Abea's gaze darted to Atreau but then flitted back to Narsi. He straightened and decided, in true Cadeleonian style, to push on as if none of this had happened.

"Indeed, my lady." Narsi couldn't quite bring himself to meet Lord Vediya's gaze yet, but he managed to give Abea a curt smile. "Lord Vediya didn't want to disturb you or your household. He came here at my request so that I could see the chapel. It truly is a matter of great importance for both our nations."

"You call him Lord Vediya?" Abea cocked her head. "How formal you are, Master Physician. Surely your lover allows you—"

"Abea!" Lord Vediya snapped. "I don't care what you say to me, but leave Master Narsi out of it. He's done you no wrong, and he's already endured more than enough shame for no greater sin than suffering my company."

"*Suffering* your company? Isn't he . . ." Abea glanced to Lord Vediya. He held her gaze for a moment, then looked away, and for some reason Abea suddenly dissolved in a riot of laughter. "Well, that's just . . . hilarious."

Narsi knew he'd missed something but couldn't even hazard a guess at what it could be.

When Abea had finally composed herself, she continued, "So then, what is it exactly that you need from me, Master Physician?"

"Would you be willing to allow us to examine your chapel?" Narsi asked. "What we find there could be the difference between life and death for—"

"Just go. Take whatever you can use from the rotten old heap." Abea sighed and then walked back to her desk.

"Thank you, my lady," Narsi said.

Abea held up her hand to stop him speaking. "All the thanks I want is to never lay eyes on you or this degenerate dog again, Master Physician."

Narsi bristled at her denigration of Lord Vediya, but managed to incline his head in acknowledgment. He turned to take his leave and Lord Vediya fell in just behind him.

"I hope he breaks your heart," Abea called after them.

Narsi didn't suppose it mattered which of them she meant.

ꞔꞔꞔ

Narsi hardly registered their walk through the gardens. He couldn't stop thinking of Lord Vediya's tongue sliding between his lips. The taste of him, the heat of him. Everywhere Lord Vediya had touched and caressed felt tender and aroused, as if his skin couldn't stop reliving the sensations.

He stole a glance to Lord Vediya's face but was disappointed by the other man's apparent composure. Only the distance that he put between the two of them as they walked and his abnormal quiet betrayed any lingering turmoil. He still smiled and offered friendly greetings to the gardeners and groundsmen as they passed them. Though he looked away when he noticed Narsi studying him.

When they reached an isolated stand of filbert trees, Lord Vediya drew to an abrupt halt. Narsi noted the chapel steeple just beyond the rise of the hill, and he wondered if they needed to discuss their search of the place. A weathered stone bench stood amidst a riot of lavender and ivy a few feet away, but Lord Vediya didn't move toward it.

"I brought you into Abea's study because I thought that she'd show greater restraint with a stranger present." Lord Vediya spoke without meeting Narsi's gaze. "I miscalculated at your expense. I shouldn't have allowed you to be humiliated like that, much less played party to it. I'm truly sorry."

"Were you any less humiliated?" Narsi didn't see the point in either of them apologizing. It wasn't as if they'd chosen to be enchanted. Their entangled kiss and wild embrace had been embarrassing, but no hardship. It in no way compared to the agony that Master Ariz endured or even the desolation that Bahiim Javier put himself through. Yet, observing Lord Vediya's tense figure, Narsi recognized that the man seemed to think he'd done something profoundly wrong.

"It was hardly your fault," Narsi replied. "And it's not as if we haven't kissed before."

"Before, we were in private and you were a willing participant. But just now I nearly betrayed everything I hold true." Lord Vediya shook his head. "If Abea hadn't released us when she did, I don't know . . ."

Narsi frowned at Lord Vediya's troubled expression. What might he have betrayed? A cloud of little gold bees buzzed past them and dived into the lavender flowers.

A disquieting thought occurred to Narsi. Could Lord Vediya have employed that outrageous kiss simply to shock Abea and make her break the spell before vital secrets could be exposed? Was that what Lord Vediya felt guilty about? Exploiting Narsi's willingness to be drawn into his arms simply to horrify the lady's Cadeleonian sensibilities?

The possibility stung Narsi's pride and filled him with hurt. Would Lord Vediya so misuse their friendship? Then he caught himself.

Firstly, this was pure speculation on his part.

Secondly, what would he have expected Lord Vediya to do? Allow a furious woman to interrogate him at her leisure and risk blurting out anything and everything? Narsi tried to imagine what he would do in the same position. What better solution was there to choose? In any case, Narsi knew he shouldn't leave these suspicions to silently grow in his mind.

"You safeguard secrets that protect so many lives." Narsi approached the subject carefully, since Lord Vediya clearly already felt guilty. "How can I blame you for using a small display of affection to shield them?"

For the first time Lord Vediya met his gaze. His expression no longer betrayed guilt but instead appeared profoundly dismayed.

"What are you talking about?" Lord Vediya asked.

"You kissed me to shock Abea and keep her from using the candor stone to reveal your real secrets, didn't you?"

To Narsi's surprise, Lord Vediya looked momentarily repulsed.

"Didn't you?" Narsi felt a growing unease.

"All right. If it makes you feel better, then I can claim that's the case." Lord Vediya flashed him a hard, superficial smile. Then he turned away to the rise of the hill. Narsi again noted the mass of a stone chapel there. Rusted scaffolding ringed it like a cage. But it hardly held Narsi's attention right now. He couldn't fathom how having his admiration and longing exploited ought to make him feel better. Better than what? What was Lord Vediya thinking to even suggest such a thing?

Unless Narsi had gotten it all wrong.

"Didn't you start stripping off my clothes as a ploy?" Narsi asked.

"You attribute such cunning to me, Master Narsi. And no small amount of cruelty, as well. Though I suppose I am cruel, aren't I?" Lord Vediya's tight smile faltered and he shook his head. "Little wonder you moved on in your affections."

"You aren't cruel. It's just the circumstances," Narsi began to protest, but he wasn't certain that he was clarifying the most important matter.

Lord Vediya appeared to have lost all patience with the conversation. He strode away up the hill so quickly that Narsi almost missed his last words.

"Someday you may forgive me."

"I—wait! What are you—" Narsi stared after Lord Vediya.

Who said I've moved on in my affections? What is there to forgive if you didn't kiss me as a diversion?

He rushed after Lord Vediya, but when he cleared the rise of the hill, he discovered the man already engaged in a conversation with a pair of youthful Cadeleonian priests. The eldest looked to be in his early twenties and the younger couldn't have been much past sixteen. Narsi guessed that only the scarcity of Cadeleonian clergy in Northern Labara allowed men hardly older than acolytes to be entrusted with a chapel—even a dilapidated one.

Lord Vediya turned as Narsi approached and again offered him that bright, artificial smile. He introduced Narsi to the black-robed priests who tended the building. In just a few words he managed to make it sound as if Narsi had been dispatched by Father Timoteo to investigate the history of this holy site. Lord Vediya presented himself as little more than a companionable guide. Then he withdrew from the three of them to gaze at the chapel doors.

Narsi wanted to draw him aside and clear up their conversation, but the priests eagerly engaged him. He politely provided them with news of Cadeleon and Father Timoteo in particular. They beamed when Narsi informed them that the holy father had at last been anointed as a bishop. Lord Vediya shot him a sidelong glance. Belatedly Narsi remembered the date and realized that these two were likely receiving the news only days after Timoteo had—far too soon for word to have spread throughout Cieloalto, much less reached Labara.

"Bishop Timoteo is right to be interested in this place. There's a huge pagan temple down there, full of weird carvings and witch signs." The younger priest grinned as if he were sharing salacious gossip. "Some nights you can see the stones of the support pillars give off this faint glow. And you can even hear whispering voices."

"Don't embellish. Starlight filters down through the holes in the ceiling and the wind makes noise. It's nothing more than that." The elder of the two rolled his eyes, though Narsi wondered if the younger priest might not be one of those few people able to sense magic. If so, there truly might be something of use to him and Lord Vediya here.

The elder priest continued, "I should warn you that the entire upper story was left open when the renovation was abandoned, and much of the floor is rotted through."

The younger priest nodded. "Be particularly careful exploring below the apse. The whole sanctuary above is only hanging on by a few boards and nails, and the floors are covered with engravings, so mind your step."

Neither of them appeared terribly distressed by the thought of the chapel's collapse. Narsi guessed that it hadn't been a comfortable place to live or pray for the past four years. They'd likely be relieved to move on.

Then Narsi noticed that Lord Vediya no longer lingered in the doorway. He'd gone in without him.

"Thanks again." Narsi raced into the chapel after Lord Vediya.

Shafts of sun streamed through cracks in the chapel roof, illuminating random sections of the vast interior but leaving most of the space in gloom. Narsi frowned at the gaping hole in the floor where a pulpit should have stood. An entire carriage could have fallen down it. On the walls, a single stained glass window depicting a Cadeleonian saint on a rampant stallion remained—the rest had been boarded over. More rusted scaffolding appeared to support the pockmarked south wall, as well as a large number of birds' nests. Some creature—perhaps a fox—fled into the shadows of the moldering pews.

Narsi didn't see Lord Vediya anywhere.

He wandered farther inside. The boards beneath his feet creaked and squealed.

As he studied the figure in the stained glass window, his toe caught on a loose board. He tripped forward and nearly tumbled into a gaping hole. He lurched aside, landing hard on one knee. A pang shot up his leg. But at least he'd struck a solid board. He regained his feet quickly, heart still hammering in his chest.

He'd been so distracted by thoughts of their shared kiss that he'd nearly been defeated by mere flooring. He felt ridiculous. What a foolish way to go, but also so near of a thing. He wondered if Lord Vediya would appreciate the irony of that.

He scanned the long nave but still didn't see any sign of the man.

"Lord Vediya!" Narsi called.

His voice echoed through the building and faded to silence. Narsi waited. As seconds stretched into minutes, Narsi's uneasiness grew. Could Lord Vediya have fallen, the way Narsi nearly had? Was he lying somewhere unconscious or dying?

"Lord Vediya!" Narsi roared his name in alarm.

"Would it kill you to call me by my given name just once?" Lord Vediya's voice drifted up from Narsi's left. He sounded irritated but not injured. Giddy relief flooded Narsi.

"It would pain me unto the point of collapse, my lord," Narsi replied. The happiness in his tone lent his words a teasing quality.

"As I've no time to waste reviving you," Lord Vediya answered, "I suppose I must endure it for now."

Narsi searched through the gloom, then noticed a faint glow shining up from yet another black chasm in the chapel floor. As he drew closer, he discerned the mouth of a narrow staircase that descended far down beneath the nave of the chapel. He took the stairs cautiously. The wooden steps felt worryingly soft beneath him.

"You are kind to indulge me," Narsi commented. The lamplight grew bright enough for him to make out Lord Vediya's figure ahead of him.

"Yes, how very kind I am. You capture my character in a single word." Lord Vediya awaited him, leaning against a stone wall with an oil lamp held up in one hand. The warm light turned the gray streaks in his hair gold and softened the exhaustion in his face. Despite his vexed expression, Narsi thought he looked handsome. He couldn't stop himself from grinning at the other man.

Lord Vediya arched a brow in response.

"Annoying me makes you so happy?" Lord Vediya inquired.

It's better than being ignored by you, Narsi thought, but instead of the glib response he answered truthfully. "I feared you'd fallen through the floor, so now I'm simply pleased to see you alive and well. Even if you are still in a bad temper for reasons I cannot comprehend."

Lord Vediya gave an exasperated snort.

"There's no point in staying irritated with you, is there?" Lord Vediya shook his head, but a smile curved his lips. He turned and beckoned Narsi to follow him. "Stay close and watch your step. The passage gets tight and pitch-black before it opens into the chamber where the pillars stand."

He wasn't exaggerating. The farther Narsi followed, the more he felt the walls closing in on him and shutting out all light and air. Cool, dank stone brushed his shoulders and condensation pooled on the floor, creating slick wet puddles. Rodents skittered over his boots and whiskers flicked past his hand when he touched the wall. A sticky, fine veil swept into the side of his face and Narsi gave a startled yelp. Lord Vediya spun back with the lamp just as Narsi realized that he'd merely walked into a mass of cobwebs. He slapped the spider webs from his face and hair.

Amusement lit Lord Vediya's face.

"Now who's happy?" Narsi commented to him.

"Just pleased to see that you are still alive and well, Master Narsi." Lord Vediya grinned.

"I feel like I made a mess of our earlier conversation," Narsi said.

"It doesn't matter." Lord Vediya's terse tone belied his words.

"Perhaps not to you, but it does to me," Narsi replied.

Lord Vediya's shoulders rose, perhaps in a shrug. Narsi decided to take it as an invitation to go on.

"I didn't understand why you felt the need to apologize to me, since we were both caught up in the spell of the candor stones. So, I made an outlandish guess about what troubled you. Clearly, I guessed wrong, but I didn't mean it as an accusation."

"No?" Lord Vediya asked.

"No. And thinking it over, I realized that no one could have instantaneously conceived of and implemented such a convoluted plan. It was like something from an adventure novel. I'm simply too used to imagining you like that. A daring figure from my favorite book."

"The reality is a little disappointing, I suppose," Lord Vediya commented.

"Are you joking?" Narsi demanded then he added in a light tone. "It was a thousand times better to kiss you than any one of your books."

Lord Vediya laughed dryly.

If it was not a ruse, Narsi wondered, *then does that mean you do want to be with me?* Narsi couldn't bring himself to ask aloud, but the possibility filled him with hope.

Lord Vediya gave a soft sigh. "So have you forgiven me for making you party to Ariz's end?"

"There's nothing to forgive." Reminded of Master Ariz, Narsi's excitement dulled. "I know your reasoning is correct and I'll comply if I have to, but until then I won't give up trying to find another way."

"As expected," Lord Vediya remarked.

Despite the feeling of descending deeper below the earth, the passageway grew steadily brighter. Fresh air washed over Narsi and he heard the distinct sounds of chirping birds.

Lord Vediya turned around a corner and called back to Narsi, "Here we are at last."

When he stepped out into a vast circular chamber, Narsi saw that they stood some three stories directly below the collapsed apse of the chapel. Only a few timbers blocked the overhead view of the bright blue sky. At the center of the chamber, weeds and a few small saplings had taken root. Flowers and leaves reached up to the afternoon sun.

"It's quite beautiful, like a hidden garden," Narsi said.

Lord Vediya extinguished the lamp and balanced it atop of a pile of rubble.

"When I was last here the ceiling was still closed off and the room was crawling with spiders and a good number of men who'd gladly have seen me dead."

"A great improvement then," Narsi replied.

Together they strolled around the eight pillars that encircled them and reached all the way to the rotting trusses of the chapel floor. The tops of the pillars branched out like the limbs of trees. Their carven bases spread over the stone floor just like roots.

Narsi couldn't keep from running his fingers over the carved trunks of the pillars, feeling the patterns of rough bark and knotholes. He paused as he noted that the sculptors had gone to the trouble of hiding a little owl in one of the tree hollows, and carving several moths resting on an outcropping of moss.

This was too much detail to be believed, Narsi thought, unless . . . could these truly be living creatures who had been turned to stone? A pang of sadness and pity moved through him at the thought.

"The inscriptions are carved on the eastern and western faces of the pillars." Lord Vediya stopped and ran a finger down the pillar's trunk. Narsi turned his attention back to the purpose of their exploration. He could wonder how the place had been created later.

Narsi circled around to the west side, opposite Lord Vediya, and studied the corresponding series of carvings. At a glance they gave the impression of narrow strips of exposed wood, with rough bark peeled back to expose delicate carvings of both images and numerous letters.

A deer appeared, bounding over other figures and symbols, just as Lord Vediya had described in his memoir. But what caught Narsi's attention were the thin rows of words carved alongside the images.

He couldn't read them or even recognize the alphabet, though a few of the symbols reminded him of Yuanese script. He went to the next pillar and circled it. There, he immediately picked out Haldiim words and phrases he knew at a glance. He'd encountered similar antiquated forms of Haldiim script in many old medical texts.

"This is an archaic form of Haldiim. I can read a fair bit of it," Narsi called.

"Excellent. I've found some old Labaran here. What does yours say?" Lord Vediya strode around another of the pillars.

"Mine starts with a list of names. Then it says, 'In this place we bind ourselves in alliance. We unite against the demons who would conquer us. We unite against the Waa . . . hahra . . .'" Narsi scowled as he tried sounding out the unfamiliar word. He suspected that it wasn't native Haldiim but a foreign term written out phonetically.

"Waarihivu?" Lord Vediya asked.

"Most likely." Narsi smiled at him, then returned to reading. "'We unite against the demons who would conquer us. We unite against the Waarihivu who would extinguish life from this world. Together, we steal the profane weapons of our enemies and fashion them as our own. With the flame that devours light . . .'"

"Over here the passage says, 'We reshaped our enemies' weapons into our people's salvation,'" Lord Vediya supplied from the opposite side of the pillar. "It goes on to say, 'The Black Fire may devour the greatest of . . .' Then it's worn away. Does your inscription have anything about the Black Fire?"

"Let me see . . . yes. 'A Black Fire will devour demon lords. The Stone Veil will smother the Flame. And we shatter it into pebbles. We make it naught.'" Narsi traced his finger over the worn carving, trying to pick out the shapes of the following letters. "Do you think that the Stone Veil mentioned here could be the Haldiim name for the Shroud of Stone?"

"In the Labaran passages here it's called the Stone Shroud, so yes. They should be the same thing." Lord Vediya crouched down, running his hands slowly over the inscriptions in the pillar. "It says Bahiim and northern witches created the Old Gods and pitted them against the demon lords and the Waarihivu as well. After their enemies were defeated, the witches constructed sanctums to restrain the Old Gods that they'd created."

It was all fascinating, but Narsi wasn't sure what it told them about their present situation with the Shard of Heaven and Yah-muur—or the

Summer Doe, as she was also known.

Narsi scanned the script for her alone. "'Yah-muur runs in all directions, bringing life to the wind and waters. Even the stones wake and breathe at the touch of her horns . . .'" Another section had been worn away, but the inscription then went on, "'The corrupt weapons are wiped away and unmade. The Fire smothered by the Stone Veil. The Stone Veil torn asunder by the Horns. The Horns consumed by the Fire.'"

"Read that last bit again, will you?" Lord Vediya called.

"'The Fire shattered by the Stone Veil. The Stone Veil torn asunder by the Horns. The Horns consumed by the Fire,'" Narsi repeated, then he wondered, "If both the Black Fire and the Stone Veil, or Shroud of Stone, are Waarihivu spells, do you think that the Horns of Yah-muur are also?"

"I don't think so." Atreau answered. "The Black Fire and the Shroud of Stone both seem to be spells. Probably Waarihivu spells. But Yah-muur and her horns sounds like a living being."

He was right. In fact, as Narsi looked, he could see that the old Haldiim script even added the honorifics of a goddess to Yah-muur, while the Shroud of Stone and the Black Fire were described as weapons.

"There's another thing about that passage." Lord Vediya's eyes went wide and he suddenly circled two other pillars, searching them as if his life depended upon what he read there. He stopped at a third and grinned.

"What does it say?" Narsi asked.

"Exactly what you just read aloud," Lord Vediya replied. "It's like a game of stone, paper, blade."

"The children's game?" Narsi asked.

"Exactly. Stone breaks the blade. Blade slices paper. Paper enfolds stone." Lord Vediya made each of the familiar hand signs as he spoke. "The Black Fire consumes the Horns of Yah-muur. The Shroud of Stone smothers the Black Fire. Horns of Yah-muur tear apart the Shroud of Stone."

Narsi stared at him. He was right. It did sound like a game of stone, paper, blade—a trio of powers that balanced each other.

"The chapel priests mentioned that there were more inscriptions on the floor." Narsi toed a broken board aside. He and Lord Vediya both regarded the masses of rotting debris surrounding them. Clearing it would be a monumental labor. But how could they walk away when the answers they needed might be right here under their feet?

"No point in trying to stay above the muck." Lord Vediya sighed.

He stripped off his coat and then very carefully removed his snow-white shirt and folded it inside the faded coat. Watching him, Narsi was reminded of the evening Lord Vediya had lamented his bloodied ribs, not because of the pain they caused him but because the bloodstains ruined his clothes and he could ill afford to purchase more.

"Someday I'll forswear shirts altogether," Lord Vediya remarked.

"I wouldn't complain if you did," Narsi replied.

Lord Vediya just smirked at him and hefted up a slimy beam. Narsi had glimpsed his naked body before, but only in a dim room at night. Stripped to his trousers in the full sunlight, Lord Vediya presented a figure of solid strength—a Cadeleonian man in his prime and at ease with his own prowess. Narsi admired the muscular curves of his shoulders and back as well as the tapered line of his waist. Speckles of ink stained his right wrist; his belly and chest appeared pale compared to the deeply tanned skin of his face, neck and forearms. He didn't rival Master Ariz's murderously sculptural physique, but Narsi found the imperfection and humanity of him both pleasing and touching by comparison.

His ease, grace and muscularity made Narsi feel self-conscious of his own stringy body. He'd inherited his father's height but none of his bulk. When he was feeling confident, Narsi like to think of himself—as one lover had once described him—as lithe. But gripped with self-consciousness, he too often felt that he was more like the scrawny rooster that his aunt had regularly likened him to. So, despite the muggy heat, Narsi kept his shirt and coat on. He didn't even bother to remove his satchel from his back.

Together the two of them dragged aside boards and nails, fallen leaves and animal nests for nearly an hour. The summer sun beat down on them and Narsi wiped sweat from his brow as he tossed aside the colorfully stained remnants of what must have been a scribe's desk. Beneath that, Narsi discovered mounds of white mushrooms flecked with remains of gold leaf growing through discarded piles of vellum.

"They let the place go to ruin once Bishop Palo died," Lord Vediya commented. He dragged aside a mass of moss and weeds, which had taken root in a decaying rug, exposing several feet of flowing inscriptions carved in the floor. "Looking at it now, you'd never suspect this chamber once housed a workshop full of acolytes, would you?"

Steadily they exposed more and more of the floor and the detailed carvings that formed concentric circles all across its rough surface. The figures of the bounding deer appeared dozens of times, but so too did images of crows, wolves, eagles and horses. Not to mention people in unfamiliar garb. Inexplicably, the name Yah-muur seemed to appear beneath many different figures, not just those of deer.

Lord Vediya crouched down beside Narsi. His hands and shoulders were spattered with dry mud.

"Is it possible that Yah-muur isn't the name of a single person, or deity, but a title?" Narsi wondered.

"I was thinking along the same line," Lord Vediya replied. "The sections that I can read on the floor make it seem as though there are different people fulfilling the role of Yah-muur."

"Yes!" It delighted Narsi that they'd both independently formed the same opinion. If he and Lord Vediya both noticed the pattern, then it was unlikely to have arisen from Narsi's imagination alone. They might be on to something. "It could have been a position, like judge or captain. So, one explanation for why there are at least three different versions of Yah-muur in myths could be because there have been at least three different individuals who held the title."

Lord Vediya nodded.

"That would explain why so many writings describe Yah-muur as dying and then still being alive an instant later. It could be a case of people writing something like 'The king is dead, long live the king' to indicate the transition from one ruler to another." Lord Vediya dug at one of the etched lines with his finger, wiping away the mud. "Though I do wonder if wielding her horns and then perhaps shedding them might indicate that the role is transitory. A very short-term job, if you will."

"Fatal, you mean?" Narsi asked.

Lord Vediya nodded. And Narsi considered the possibility.

"You could be right. Shedding her horns and then leaping into another life is described again and again in the Haldiim passages I've been able to read," Narsi said. "But I'm still not clear on how exactly a person uses the horns to stop the Shroud of Stone, or how the horns are acquired."

"Nor am I," Lord Vediya said. "By the way, did you notice that a term like 'strongbox of spells' kept appearing before Yah-muur manifests?"

"Yes. It's called a 'golden cask filled with life' in the Haldiim writing. But I'm not sure what that really is." Narsi scratched a flake of mud off the back of his hand, then resisted the urge to brush a patch of mud off Lord Vediya's bare chest.

Narsi stared at the dirty symbols and words that littered the floor all around him, willing himself to have some further insight, but nothing came to him. The more he stared, the more it all started to seem like meaningless scratches.

He lifted his face to feel the sunlight and was surprised to realize how low the sun had sunk in the time he and Lord Vediya had spent hauling aside all the refuse of the collapsed chapel. It must have been three hours or more, and then perhaps another hour just trying to read all they could from the concentric circles they uncovered. No wonder his mind felt foggy.

"I'm too tired to think about all this right now. We need a rest." Narsi sat back.

"Do we?" Lord Vediya smiled down at him. Narsi wasn't certain if it was the dim light or his own imagination, but Lord Vediya's gaze seemed deeply appreciative.

"Yes," Narsi replied. Then, despite the dirty floor, he sprawled out on his back. His medical satchel dug into his shoulder. He slipped it off and set it aside.

Lord Vediya moved to kneel down beside him. He touched Narsi's shoulder gently, but then his brow furrowed and alarm lit his amber eyes.

"On your feet!" He caught Narsi's hand and jerked him up. Narsi scrambled to get his feet under himself. As he rose, he saw what alarmed Lord Vediya.

Seams of golden light streamed up from the carvings in the center of the floor. They brightened and spread, illuminating more and more rings of inscriptions. Narsi and Lord Vediya both stepped back as the light advanced, but it surged out too quickly for them to escape. They were surrounded by walls of brilliant light in an instant.

"What happ—" Narsi began, but then the familiarity of this golden light within a circle of trees struck him. The night he'd carried Lady Hylanya's necklace into the Circle of Wisteria, the entire ground had been illuminated by golden blessings. Then he suddenly realized that the extraordinary unseeable object Lord Vediya had given him in the Slate House was still stashed away in his satchel. It had to be a testament to the strangeness of this entire day that something so bizarre could completely slip his mind.

Narsi leaned down and pulled open his bag. It was as if he'd released a geyser of sunlight. Brilliant golden beams exploded out and Narsi stumbled back, shielding his eyes. Lord Vediya caught him and held him close.

"Are you all right?" Lord Vediya's voice was calm, but Narsi's hand rested against his bare chest and he felt Lord Vediya's heart pounding.

"I'm fine." Patterns of gold light blazed behind Narsi's eyelids and warmed his face. "I think that thing you gave me back at the Slate House set off some spell here. The same thing occurred when I carried Lady Hylanya's necklace into the Circle of Wisteria."

"But why would a Cadeleonian relic box rouse anything in this place? Unless . . . God's blood!" Lord Vediya said it quietly, as if thinking aloud, but then he raised his voice. "Narsi, it's nearly the same as the golden cask that imprisoned the demon lord Zi'sai. Golden but invisible. We may have returned it to the place where they were both created."

The burning radiance behind Narsi's eyes faded; now the air filled with rustling noises and a faintly woody scent. Narsi cracked his eyes open. The etched lines of script at his feet gleamed like streams of molten gold, but all around them the stones appeared to have turned to dark soil and mounds of green moss. Beside him Lord Vediya cocked his head.

Both of them glanced to the tattered leather of Narsi's medical satchel. His cracked, burned medical supplies lay scattered around a bright gold box. The lid hung open on its hinges. Narsi started toward it, but Lord Vediya caught his arm and glanced upward.

What had been eight stone pillars were now towering trees. The ground under his feet appeared to be covered in clumps of moss and dwarf heather. Moths fluttered up from a branch. The owl he'd seen before briefly peered at him, then winged up into the sky. As Narsi followed its flight up past tangled branches, he saw that the dark green leaves hid hundreds of glossy black crows.

"I haven't seen this many Bahiim crows since the war," Lord Vediya whispered.

One after another the birds took flight, circling high over the golden box. So many of them filled the air that they looked like a black cloud, and a breeze rose from beneath their beating wings. They dived down through the branches of the trees. A gust of wind rushed over Narsi and Lord Vediya. Leaves shook, then lit up with Bahiim blessings. Soft light like that of a setting sun filtered through the branches.

"We have heard you. You search for Yah-muur's Horns. What is your purpose?" Whispering voices rose like a warm breeze. The words were accented but still clearly Haldiim.

Narsi glanced to Lord Vediya, uncertain of how much of the language he understood.

"I got most of that. But you'd best speak for us." Lord Vediya snatched up his coat and pulled it on.

"We urgently need to learn all we can about the Horns of Yah-muur in hopes of using them to stop the Shroud—the Stone Veil." Narsi raised his voice to carry over the rising wind. Lord Vediya's loose hair whipped around his face.

"You children presume that you can defeat a profane weapon of the Waarihivu?" Disbelief sounded in many of the whispering voices, mockery in others. *"Do you even know what the Stone Veil is?"*

In the Circle of Wisteria, Narsi had bristled after being addressed as a child, but just now he felt that even grandmothers would seem young in comparison to these Bahiim souls who had been locked away in stone so long that an entire chapel could be built on top of them.

"We know that the Stone Veil is a spell that threatens our entire world. It must be destroyed," Narsi replied. In truth, his conception of the spell was vague. The name made him think it was a paralyzing, suffocating sort of curse. But on the Old Road with Javier, they had seen buildings collapse, fires rage and floods swallow city streets. It had seemed like an endless onslaught of every sort of disaster. A complete apocalypse.

"It is an unbearable blessing. The infinite peace of complete death. Quietude entombing all that is sacred, silencing all magic, stopping all life." The voices turned mournfully solemn. "It first consumes those who could defeat it: those who possess powerful souls and holy spirits. Then it spreads across all life until it has silenced even the air, earth and sea. It is the blessing of a dead world."

Narsi glanced to Lord Vediya.

"So the only people who could get close to it are those who aren't magical?" Lord Vediya asked. "It sounds a little like a sanctum, capturing and turning the most magical beings to stone. Using that power to enthrall everyone else."

Narsi nodded in agreement.

"The Stone Veil is a wildfire compared to a sanctum's candlelight! After hundreds of years a soul can still wake from the thrall of a sanctum. After only a day it would be destroyed beneath the Stone Veil." The Bahiim souls inhabiting these crow's bodies had clearly understood Lord Vediya's words and bridled at them.

"But the Stone Veil has been stopped before," Narsi said. Hadn't he and Lord Vediya read as much in the inscriptions? Lord Vediya gave him an encouraging nod and Narsi went on. "It can be done."

"To battle the Stone Veil is to sacrifice all hope and join the holy dead. You think yourselves truly worthy of such a legacy?"

From the way Lord Vediya's eyes narrowed at the question, Narsi suspected that he too understood the exchange perfectly.

"Worthy or not, we are the ones who are here to do it," Lord Vediya responded. "So are you going to help us or just perch up there squawking?"

The crows were silent for a moment. A few preened, then they peered down at Narsi.

"To tear the Stone Veil asunder is to walk through flames, to bathe in muerate poison and sacrifice your life. Do you claim such courage?"

"No," Lord Vediya snapped. "Do any of you?"

The crows fluttered their wings and the golden glow of the trees seemed to dim around them. Narsi wasn't certain how, but he thought that the Bahiim crows were receding from them, withdrawing in the face of Lord Vediya's insolent response.

"*To tear the Stone Veil asunder is to walk through flames, to bathe in muerate poison and sacrifice your life. Do you claim such courage?*" This time the crows' voices sounded softer and farther away. More like a distant whisper that Narsi strained to discern.

Then it occurred to him that their questing wasn't rhetorical, nor was it a mere taunt.

"*To tear the Stone Veil asunder is to walk through flames, to bathe in muerate poison and sacrifice your life. Do you claim such courage?*" The third time, their words sounded faint as a last breath. The trees dulled and the crows sat motionless.

A thrill of fear washed over Narsi.

"I—" Narsi's throat tightened. He truly didn't want to endure flames or the agony of poison, but he forced himself to go on. "I have endured muerate poisoning. I'd do it again to stop the Stone Veil."

Narsi lifted his right arm, displaying the blue-black scars marring his fingers.

Lord Vediya scowled at him like he thought he'd gone mad. The crows all turned their heads to watch him.

"*Do you claim the courage to battle the Stone Veil, child?*"

Narsi drew in a slow breath and hardened his resolve.

"Yes," Narsi whispered.

"No! Damn it, you fool." Lord Vediya jerked Narsi's raised arm down and gripped his hand in his own. "What in the three hells are you thinking?"

"If the Stone Veil destroys all life, then our only choice is between risking death to stop it, or simply dying along with everyone else." Narsi spoke directly to Lord Vediya as he freed his hand from the other man's hard grip. "There's nothing to lose by fighting it."

"There's everything for *you* to lose," Lord Vediya growled, and he glared up at the crows. Narsi couldn't tell if Lord Vediya was too angry to bear looking at him or if his fury was aimed at the birds. "Let the fuckers up above us take that risk. I don't believe for one moment that Bahiim, who can escape death to take the bodies of birds, couldn't contrive a way to survive the Stone Veil."

To Narsi's shock, a soft sound almost like laughter rose from the crows and echoed around them.

"*Our time of sacrifice has already passed. And the child has already chosen his fate. Now, come receive your legacy.*"

As one, the crows rose from the tree branches, blotting out the sunlight in a mass of gleaming black wings. They dived and a violent wind swept over Narsi and lifted him off his feet. He felt Lord Vediya grasp his hand and heard him swearing. But the brutal wind tore them apart and engulfed them in darkness.

Narsi touched ground again, but it felt soft and strange. He stumbled forward and turned in a slow circle, trying to discern solid black shadows from the deep gloom. His ears rang and his mind seemed weirdly muddled, as if he'd just been caught in a wave of drunkenness. He took a few more staggering steps.

A wilderness of bushes and other trees seemed to have risen up around the eight encircling him. On the ground before him, a small gold cask lay open. The interior looked like it was lined with polished topaz and emanated the faintest warm glow, like a pool of water reflecting moonlight.

Something ahead of him moved through the black thickets, sending hares running and flushing flocks of songbirds up into the dark sky. At last Narsi recognized the silhouette of a huge deer walking between the trees. It stood so tall that its massive antlers resembled oak branches.

The creature pinned him with a gaze like dancing candle flames. Narsi froze where he stood as the deer paced closer to him. The ground shuddered beneath him. A strong, musky scent rose around it. The light of its eyes illuminated the verdant moss and grass that made up its hide as well as small flowers growing across its head and back like a mane. The deer angled its head to gaze down on Narsi with one blazing eye.

"Yah-muur?" Narsi felt strange, as if he was in some dream, and at the same time he knew that he couldn't be.

"*I will answer to that name. But it is not mine alone.*"

Narsi took in the huge antlers crowning the creature's head. They gleamed with the luster of obsidian. Tangles of ivy and rose vines hung from them, as did wild grapes and fragrant hops.

"Are you an Old God?" Narsi whispered.

"*That too is a name I claim.*" The voice sounded amused but not unkind. "*However you wish to call me, I have come. But the Bahiim cannot summon me into flesh for long. We must be quick if you wish to claim my gift and complete the Battle of the Peraloro River.*"

In her letter, Clara had asked: Did she betray our Savior? Or are we still awaiting the final battle of the war?

Could Yah-muur have been killed before she could use her horns to tear the Shroud of Stone asunder? Or had something else stopped her?

"Are you . . . dead? A ghost?" Narsi suddenly wondered if he'd again been drawn onto the Old Road. But this place felt different, lush and saturated with life. The grass and flowers beneath his feet seemed to grow in the glow of Yah-muur's gold gaze, and all around her head, bees and butterflies whirled. Birdsong sounded from the trees, as did the chirp of crickets.

"I am the will to exist that burns in every living thing. So long as there is life in this world, I am undying. I am the desire that inspires a seed to sprout and the spark that ignites with the first beat of a heart. This body you see before you is merely a fleeting conduit. But outside of this place and moment, I blaze within countless creatures. I am life itself. The Stone Veil is my opposite, forever dead. An endless desolate stillness. I exist to tear such stillness apart and fill the silence with glory and chaos. I am its defeat."

Narsi felt the heat of her breath blowing over him like a humid wind. His pulse quickened just drawing in her exhalations. His skin tingled.

"If that's true, then why couldn't you destroy the Stone Veil during the Battle of Heaven's Shard?"

"Because I am too vast to be confined to a single body in the mortal realm. Even here, I can only be summoned for moments. To do battle, a mortal champion must carry my blessing and wield my relic against the Stone Veil. But my last champion was betrayed before she could strike down the Stone Veil. Instead, she sacrificed her soul to imprison the Stone Veil, and she bound her bloodline to restrain it. But the strength of her descendants is failing now."

She meant the Hallowed Kings. Did that mean that the last person to carry Yah-muur's horns had been a Sagrada?

"How was she betrayed?" Narsi asked.

Yah-muur blinked and for an instant total darkness and silence fell over Narsi. Then the twilight surroundings reasserted themselves.

"Strength fails even the bravest body. Even the strongest of hearts cannot keep beating with a knife blade driven through it. But that hardly matters now. Those souls have been absolved by death. They are reborn and redeem their pasts."

Yah-muur shook her head and a cloud of bees, moths and flies rose up off her. She seemed utterly indifferent to the past.

"The relic I entrusted to the mortal realm was lost for a time, but now you have returned with the cask. The Bahiim retain enough strength to summon me once more to bestow my blessing and my horn. It may not assure our triumph, but if you are willing to endure, then there is still hope. Will you accept it?"

"I . . . yes," Narsi replied—there was nothing else to say but yes. "What should I do?"

"To carry it from this place into your mortal realm, you must place it inside the cask. The Bahiim will seal it with the remains of their lives. It will open for you in the light of another sacred grove. Do you understand?"

"The Circle of Wisteria?"

Yah-muur nodded.

"But what do I do with it after that?" Narsi asked. "How do I use it against the Stone Veil?"

Tear it asunder. Unmake its meaning. Scrape away the silence and fill it with the joy and agony of life.

"But how exactly—"

Carry my blessing into the heart of Stone Veil and there make battle against its peace. The Stone Veil is lifeless perfection: inert, silent, immobile. Use your rage and joy, your agony and lust, to carve riots into its incantations. Crack its faultless grasp and fill the quiet with your screams and laughter. It will be undone. When the time comes you will understand. There is nothing more I can tell you. The Bahiim cannot hold me here much longer. Be brave, endure and seize the victory you so desire.

Yah-muur bowed her head. The flames of her eyes burned like twin suns and Narsi lowered his gaze.

Grasp my horn and take it if you can.

Narsi reached out and grabbed one of the thick tines of the glossy horns. The glassy edge sliced into his palm, and rose thorns bit into the back of his hands. Yah-muur bucked up, pulling him off his feet, and Narsi gasped in pain, but he held on. Yah-muur threw her head, jerking Narsi to the side.

Agony flared through his shoulders. He fought to catch his footing. At last he jammed his boots into the roots of a tree and jerked against Yah-muur with all his strength. His arms felt like they were being pulled from their sockets. A loud snap rocked through his hands. The horn splintered, shards biting into his palms. A blazing-hot fluid poured over Narsi's arms and seared down his shoulders. He gasped and his entire body shook, but he hung on with both hands.

He couldn't afford to fail. Too much depended on this one chance.

Yah-muur bucked up again, and Narsi wrenched against her heaving body. The piece of antler tore away with a thunderous crack. Narsi fell to his knees and Yah-muur loomed over him with her hooves high in the air as fountains of shining gold light gushed from her broken horn.

Narsi's blood covered the shard in his hands, but it still gave off a radiant light and seared his fingers. Narsi shoved it into the golden box in front of him and slammed the lid closed. At the same moment Yah-muur crashed back down to the ground. Her impact shattered the earth and stone. Narsi clutched the box to his chest as the world fell out from under him and he plummeted down into absolute darkness.

CHAPTER
TWENTY-THREE

A bolt of blinding white light exploded across the chamber, tearing apart tree trunks, stone supports and wooden beams. In the afterglow, Atreau sighted Narsi's swaying figure. Rafters above him cracked like thunder. Atreau bolted forward, jerking Narsi aside. Narsi crumpled into his arms.

"I got it. Yah-muur's horn." Narsi clutched a golden box to his chest with a deathly grip. Blood and inexplicable streaks of gold caked his arms and hung through his hair. He'd only disappeared from Atreau's sight for an instant, but whatever he'd endured, it had left him battered, gleaming and hardly conscious.

"We can save every—" Narsi sagged again.

Atreau caught his slim, blood-spattered body and dragged him up the dark, narrow passage toward the doorway.

Of course, the fucking crows were nowhere to be seen now.

The trees they had perched in screeched and snapped as they reverted to brittle stone. The chapel above heaved as the pillars surrounding Atreau and Narsi burst apart. Spears of wood plummeted down from the chapel roof, crashing into the stone floor.

Narsi's eyes hardly fluttered in response to the noise and chaos. Another section of the roof crashed down, bringing branches of carved stone, rubble and dust after it.

"Fuck." Terror flooded him with a wild strength. Atreau swung Narsi up over his shoulder, grabbed his lamp and sprinted up the stairs.

The roar of collapsing supports and shattering stones hammered at his back like a physical blow. He stumbled, swore and kept running. The ground rocked under his feet as if he was racing across a ship's deck in the midst of a storm. Clouds of dust billowed over him. He coughed but didn't slow.

He hefted Narsi's limp body as if it weighed nothing and kept sprinting. At the top of the steps he faced the cratered expanse of the chapel floor. Atreau pushed on, balancing on splintering supports before lunging over one gaping hole after another. Sweat poured down his back and face, stinging his eyes. When he reached the chapel doors, he kicked them wide and bounded out down the crumbling stairs. He kept running.

Some hundred yards from the chapel, Atreau's legs gave out and he dropped down to his knees on the lawn. Behind him violent crashes boomed like thunder or cannon fire. Atreau looked back over his shoulder. A huge cloud of dust rose in his wake. All he could make out through it was the chapel spire jutting at a sharp angle from a vast chasm.

He couldn't see the sunset sky, or the rising moon. The dust hurled up from the chapel obscured them, as if he once again knelt in the desolate gray expanse of the Sorrowlands.

A profound quiet filled the air, as if the rest of the world had been startled into silence by the building's sudden and complete destruction. His own heartbeat came like a wild drum hammering away in his chest. His back ached and his arms trembled. He lay Narsi down on the grass and then fell to his side, gasping for breath. Belatedly, he realized that countless bits of falling debris must have grazed him; dozens of small scratches mottled his hands. The wet heat of blood threaded down his scalp and dribbled past his left ear as well.

And he'd lost the last of his good shirts.

A quiet laugh escaped him. Twice today he and Narsi had evaded death by mere seconds. Now simply surviving felt like a triumph in the face of ruthless fate. He closed his eyes, allowing relief to wash over him.

Through the quiet he listened to Narsi draw in slow, deep breaths. It felt natural to reach out and touch him. A wave of comfort rolled through Atreau when Narsi slid his warm fingers between Atreau's.

They lay together holding hands.

Evening breezes fluttered through the grass and carried the perfume of lavender to him. Stars peeked through the dust cloud overhead. The moon appeared like a ghostly haze. Atreau thought he heard concerned voices coming from Abea's household and the chapel. Lamps flashed, but the people carrying them were still distant. None of them called for Atreau or Narsi.

"Where are we?" Narsi whispered at last.

"Labara," Atreau replied, then added, "Bishop Palo's chapel just collapsed."

Atreau turned his head to study Narsi's profile. The flecks of gold scattered through his dark hair and streaking his face reminded Atreau of the first time he'd caught sight of him outside the gates of Fedeles's house. Marigold petals had hung in his hair then, and even hours later Atreau had found himself unable to forget him.

At the time, he'd attempted to pin his fascination to distinct features; perhaps Narsi's shy glances and long lashes drew him, or maybe his tall, slender frame and flattering smile. Through the passing weeks the list had grown: his courage, his composure, those skilled hands, his loyalty, his optimism, his laughter, his bright eyes, and his hot, inviting mouth.

Atreau could have filled pages in an attempt to dissect the other man's hold over him. But he could never seem to parse the exact allure. Atreau had bedded other men and women who surpassed Narsi in one attribute or another, and yet none of them seemed to compare. Not one of them possessed the wholeness of character and quality that pierced into Atreau's very heart and held him. It was only Narsi himself—his courage and resilience, his compassion and wit as much as his physical beauty—who fascinated and delighted Atreau. The man filled him with admiration and such intense longing.

And then alarm.

How much of a fool could he be? Allowing himself to fall for someone whose heroism would inevitably lead to an early grave. Narsi had raised his hand like a schoolboy hoping to be called on when the fucking crows described the agony that the person battling the Shroud of Stone would endure. Now Narsi held the golden cask against his chest with one battered hand, cradling his prize as if it would guide him anywhere but his doom.

Atreau pressed his eyes closed.

Despite his frustration, he squeezed Narsi's free hand. He didn't want to admit it even to himself, but he feared that the traits he admired and adored in Narsi were the same ones that doomed him.

I'm an idiot, Atreau thought to himself.

"How did we escape? I could hardly stand." Narsi looked at him. Then realization lit his face. "You carried me out?"

If anyone else had asked, Atreau wouldn't have hesitated to play off his desperate, blind scramble as an act of ludicrous romance.

With such a lovely companion in my arms, my heart had already taken flight; my legs simply followed.

But in Narsi's company the glib rejoinders failed him. He didn't want to spit out the sort of pap of flattery and lies that he served up to everyone else. They might joke about all this later, but right now the terror of those minutes in the chapel were still too fresh.

"Thank you," Narsi whispered.

The warmth of his expression lit a spark in Atreau's chest and filled him with absurd happiness. His cheeks flushed. How ridiculous to feel so touched. He was no longer that nineteen-year-old youth who had yearned to be loved despite his weakness and failings. He didn't know why he was acting so hapless and smitten now. At least dusk and dust served to hide his embarrassment.

Narsi continued to regard him with open affection, but then his expression turned a little melancholy and he shifted his gaze away to the dusty sky.

Atreau felt his withdrawal like the cool breeze rising between them, chilling his sweat-drenched body. He suddenly hated it, despite the fact that he had been the one who had originally instigated it—insisted on it even in the face of his own desire. At the time, he'd thought up so many justifications for distancing Narsi from himself. But now they all struck him as facile. The truth was that he was afraid of harming Narsi and terrified of how badly Narsi might hurt him.

But how pointless was it to languish, filled with desire and longing for a man who wanted him in return? What pain was he saving himself from by wasting the little time that remained to them? If he lost Narsi— and that golden box glinting against Narsi's chest assured him that he would indeed lose him—then what consolation could he take in a cold bed and memories of abstinence?

"You make it very difficult not to fall for you, Lord Vediya," Narsi commented.

"Then perhaps you should," Atreau whispered. "I've been assured that I'm a more pleasurable entertainment than even my books."

Narsi looked to him again. "You shouldn't tease me, my lord."

"I'm quite serious," Atreau replied. Narsi's eyes widened, his expression wavering between hope and disbelief.

"Earlier, you insisted—" Narsi paused and Atreau thought that the memory must have hurt him a little. He regretted that. "That you only wanted my friendship. We shouldn't—"

"I lied. By character, necessity and profession, I am a liar." Atreau cut the excuse short, forcing himself to speak the truth. "Years ago, I attempted an affair with another man, but it cost him his life. I feared I would do the same to you. So I lied to you and myself. But the truth is that I don't only want your friendship. I desire far more. All of you. And I hope that you still want me, as well."

"I . . ." Narsi glanced away, and all at once Atreau felt very uncertain.

Had his confession come too late?

Narsi obviously attracted other lovers. Atreau had witnessed the open affection between him and Yara firsthand. Women and men throughout the Theater and Haldiim Districts flirted with him and sought him out. Narsi had no need of the desire of the gutless man who'd rejected him.

Perhaps not even for one night.

Then Narsi met his gaze again. "Of course I do."

They reached for each other in the same moment. Narsi's long fingers curled around the nape of his neck, drawing him close. Atreau took his mouth, kissing him deeply. Narsi responded with the slick flick of his tongue, inspiring Atreau to work open the buttons and buckles that kept him from exploring more of Narsi's body. Arousal surged through him as quiet sounds of pleasure escaped Narsi. He arched into Atreau's hands.

Atreau broke their kiss to sweep off his own coat and set the golden box aside in its folds. Then he gently pushed Narsi back into the soft grass and leaned over him, admiring his exposed chest and loins amidst the disarray of his rumpled clothes. He traced the tender lines of Narsi's body. Narsi gasped and trembled in response to his strokes.

"Ticklish?" Atreau teased.

Narsi laughed, then deftly ran his hands over Atreau's chest and down to his groin. Atreau's breath caught. God's blood, but his touch was skilled.

"It seems I'm not the only one who is," Narsi replied.

They kissed again—Atreau catching Narsi's lip between his teeth for a teasing instant—then Narsi rolled Atreau onto his side. Though slim and lean, Narsi possessed a very pleasing strength. Atreau played at re-claiming his position, but the moment Narsi relented, Atreau found he didn't want to loom over him. Instead Atreau stretched out beside him. They touched and explored one another with caresses and then more knowing kisses.

"You're so very"—Narsi paused, catching his breath—"very skilled, my lor—"

"Don't." Atreau cut him off, pressing one finger lightly to Narsi's lips. "Please. Can't you just say my name?"

Even through the darkness Atreau saw the hesitance in Narsi's expression. He didn't understand it. Unless . . .

"Do you want me to act as a commanding lord to you right now?" Atreau asked carefully. He'd encountered both men and women who'd desired dominating and even cruel lovers, but personally he'd endured too much of the reality to find such games appealing. Though perhaps for Narsi he could attempt it. The idea made him uneasy.

Narsi's soft laugh surprised him.

"I'd like to see you try," Narsi said.

He brushed a lock of Atreau's hair back from his face and Atreau realized that to a great extent he'd mistaken Narsi's humility and deference for uncertainty and inexperience. But feeling Narsi's caress and meeting his bright, honest gaze, it was clear that he felt far more confident in this moment than Atreau did.

"Why won't you call me by my name?" Atreau asked.

"I don't want to take anything away from you," Narsi replied. "Your noble rank seemed so important to you when we first met, and all your books declare your full title. I find it hard to believe that it's meaningless to you."

It surprised Atreau that Narsi took his dignity so seriously. He hadn't thought that anyone would still attribute any self-respect to him to be lost. He felt absurdly moved and hid it by kissing Narsi's stomach. Then he looked up at him.

"When we first met, I was a boy, still terrified of what could be done to me if I was stripped of my title. And it has served to shield me to a degree. I doubt most commoners could publish the works that I have without being jailed or even hanged. So yes, there's a value to calling myself Lord Vediya," Atreau admitted. "But the truth is that I hate carrying my father's name. If I could scrape every last trace of the man off myself, I would." Atreau sighed and shook his head. He hadn't meant to stray so far from the sweet, meaningless chatter of lovers.

Now Narsi considered him with a serious, thoughtful gaze. Atreau suspected that Narsi wanted to give in, but just needed a little push.

"Come on, everyone calls me Atreau."

"Everyone." Narsi scowled disdainfully. "I don't want to be lumped in with all the clodpots and prats who call you Atreau, as if they know the slightest thing about you. I don't want to be like everyone else."

Atreau almost laughed at the idea of that. It was likely shallow of him, but he felt rather flattered realizing that all this time Narsi had been vexing him by using his lordly title largely to stand out from Atreau's past lovers.

"Narsi, I schooled with a damned duke, a mechanist who has constructed a spell to turn back time, a world explorer and a warlord. I know infamous duelists, decadent princes, witches who commune with entire plagues of rats. I've bedded men and women from dozens of nations and rubbed shoulders with saints and rogues. But you are still one of the most singular and fascinating men I have ever met. How on earth can you imagine that I would ever mistake you for anything less?" Atreau shook his head. "Clearly, you've not had enough attention given to you. Please allow me to remedy that neglect at once."

"How do you propose to—"

There might come a time for further confessions and more earnest words between them, but this was not it.

Atreau nudged Narsi back and slid down his tense body, until he came to his taut groin. With a smile, he applied his indecent mouth and cunning tongue to display all the skill that a life of debauchery had imparted to him. Narsi gasped and twined his hands through Atreau's hair, his body responding with gratifying drive. Glorious thrills shuddered up Atreau's body when Narsi whispered his name again and again as he trembled and bucked beneath him in the last moments of ecstasy. Then Narsi collapsed, his entire body limp and sweat soaked as he drew in deep breaths.

Gazing at Narsi, Atreau thought he understood a little of the satisfaction, wonder and exhaustion artists felt having completed masterpieces. Atreau wiped his mouth with the back of his hand.

Narsi reached for him and Atreau stretched beside him, kissed him with swollen lips and let Narsi hold him tight. His straining erection pushed against the spent heat of Narsi's body. The contact was tantalizing and frustrating at once. To Atreau's relief, Narsi took him with his deft hands. It had been more than a year since he'd trusted anyone to touch him like this. Now the sensation felt startlingly intense. The contact of Narsi's hands, the friction of his fingers, seemed to thrill through his entire body, like notes resounding through a bell. Narsi stroked and worked him from gentle elation to a gasping, frenzied release.

Then they lay entwined and spent.

Atreau wanted to say something, but no words seemed to capture the delicate, strange feelings churning within him. In the end he simply bowed his head next to Narsi's and held his damp hand in his own.

CHAPTER
TWENTY-FOUR

Narsi studied Atreau's sleeping face. His thick lashes lay like bold strokes of ink beneath his sweeping brows, and his long mouth curled in a smile. Relieved by sleep from his worldly burdens, he looked young, tender and contented: an ideal image of a dashing man in the prime of his life, resting in his lover's arms. Narsi resisted the desire to trace the curve of his soft lips.

Atreau's chest rose and fell with soothing steadiness. The hot weight of his legs and hips against Narsi's bare skin felt new and thrilling. One of Atreau's hands curled against Narsi's arm. Narsi caressed Atreau's fingers, feeling old calluses and fresh scrapes.

The scent of lavender flowers and rock dust surrounded them. A breeze raised goose bumps across Atreau's shoulder. Narsi rubbed his cool skin, feeling warmth kindle between them.

He stared at Atreau, wishing that he could somehow preserve every detail of this time, when they were together, safe and at peace. Surrounded by so much turmoil and death, the respite felt precious and fragile.

You can't know how much you matter to me. How badly I want to take you away and keep you safe.

Narsi felt ridiculous even as he acknowledged the thoughts. If he confided his feelings for Atreau to Yara, she would have laughed at him. Esfir would've offered him a sad, sympathetic smile and a cup of tea. As for Atreau himself, he'd probably be horrified if he even suspected how much Narsi cared for him.

The knowledge was like a bitter medicine. He flinched from it but knew that he shouldn't. For his own good, he couldn't afford to indulge in romantic fantasies. He wasn't a twelve-year-old boy anymore. As tempting as it was to imagine that true love inspired Atreau's coaxing words and passionate kisses, Narsi had seen where that delusion led. Meeting Abea today and witnessing the rage, longing and anguish that tortured her through so many years, he'd realized what an immense blunder it was to mistake Atreau's passing affection for commitment of any sort. The man gave no promises nor asked for any. If Narsi hoped to retain a shred of dignity in the future, when faced with any number of Atreau's other lovers, then he needed to temper his infatuation.

At the same time, it was so hard to resist the temptation. Atreau was a skilled and generous lover. How could Narsi completely suppress all the happiness and wonder of feeling admired and adored?

He brushed powdery dust from Atreau's temple and wondered again at how much strength and drive it must have required for Atreau to carry him out of the crumbling chapel.

Narsi studied their surroundings.

Collapsed ruins behind them, a dusty gray sky overhead. He gazed up into the haze. How many stones, now pulverized to specks, drifted above them, he wondered.

A flare of red light caught Narsi's attention, rousing him from his languor. He sat up as a second scarlet flame blazed in the heavens. The light reflected through the floating dust and turned the drifting clouds a murky red.

Narsi shifted. Small aches played through his shoulders and back where the ground had dug in, but he was surprised to find that his encounter with Yah-muur hadn't left him in far worse condition. At the time he'd been in agony, but now he only felt a slight pinching sensation in his palms. He glanced down at his hands and noticed two thin streaks of glossy scar tissue. They looked metallic in the strange light, like streaks of gold.

Narsi shook Atreau's shoulder.

"Lord Ve—" Narsi caught himself. "Atreau. Wake up. Something's happening. The sky has turned red."

Atreau's eyes snapped open. In an instant all languor drained from his face. He jerked upright and scowled at the hill behind them.

Dark silhouettes moved through the veils of dust, backlit by the fiery red glow. They darted in and out of sight, merging with the ragged shapes of the collapsed chapel. The stocky figures and shadowy spears certainly didn't belong to the groundsmen, nor either of the priests they'd spoken to earlier.

"Garrison soldiers. The spells in the old temple probably triggered witches' wards all across the city," Atreau said. He touched Narsi's shoulder.

Above them, the twin scarlet flames swirled through the dust clouds like a powerful wind sweeping aside a curtain. Patches of twilight-blue sky and scattered stars appeared in their wake. Narsi squinted up at the bright red orbs.

"Those can't be torches," he murmured.

"It's a witch's aura. One powerful enough that even we can see it. We'd best make ourselves presentable, I think." Atreau snatched up his coat and handed Narsi the golden box. Narsi quickly straightened his own clothes and did what he could to clean himself up. He reached out for his medical satchel, but then he remembered that it had been destroyed in the chapel. He folded his hands around the golden box. Only then did he notice the streaks of gold leaf clinging to his hands and arms.

Tiny flecks of gold also glinted on Atreau's skin and through his hair, particularly where Narsi had gripped and stroked him. He considered brushing some of it from Atreau's hair but was distracted by another flare of the red lights.

The flames descended, clearing swaths of haze surrounding the chapel grounds. For the first time Narsi caught a clear view of the grounds he and Atreau had fled. The sight astonished him.

Wreathed in red flames and suspended in the air, hundreds of stone slabs, pillars and entire archways floated as if weightless. Some thirty feet up, the chapel steeple turned in lazy circles like a lost compass needle. A lanky silhouette danced beneath the suspended wreckage.

"That will be Skellan," Atreau said.

For a shocked moment Narsi remembered the wreckage he'd seen on the Old Road. Taverns, houses, entire palaces all torn asunder and scattered like dice. At the time he'd assumed that the Shroud of Stone had laid waste to the city, crushing, burning and then flooding everything.

But now, recalling Yah-muur's description of the Shroud of Stone as deathly peaceful, unbearably quiet and perfectly still, he grew doubtful.

A new, anxious possibility flitted through his mind. Javier had said that Skellan would battle the Shroud of Stone and destroy it at the cost of his own life. But how long might that battle last and what forces would it unleash? Just how much destruction would Cieloalta suffer before its conclusion? Witnessing massive blocks of granite bob and drift like leaves in a stream, it didn't seem at all unreasonable to imagine that Skellan could wreck a city.

And if it was the price for saving a world, then who could argue that he shouldn't? Having seen his own death and Atreau's in that future, Narsi felt sickened. He gripped the small gold box in his hand so hard that it bit into his palm. Now that he possessed Yah-muur's horns that battle wouldn't occur, he assured himself. He and Atreau would destroy the Shroud of Stone. They would stop the Javier's visions from ever coming to fruition.

"And wheresoever Skellan wanders, Elezar is never far away," Atreau murmured as he peered up the hillside.

Beneath the vast array of red light and suspended rubble, armed soldiers searched the remaining wreckage. Then, as if to prove Atreau right, a towering figure appeared amidst the ruins. Earlier, Narsi had observed Elezar from Javier's bedroom window, feeling stunned by how the striking youth he recalled from years ago had grown into such an imposing man. Even through the gloom and at a distance, he remained an intimidating presence.

"Atreau!" Anguish boomed through Elezar's voice. Narsi's impressions of him as some unassailable stranger shattered. Elezar tore through the ruined chapel, hurling aside timbers as he and his soldiers searched. "Atreau! Can you hear me? Atreau!"

"We're here!" Atreau shouted. "Unharmed!"

Elezar spun back and raced down the hill like a charging bull. A dozen soldiers stormed after him. Behind them, the scarlet flames dimmed and the stones that had made up the chapel walls settled to the ground as gently as if they were dishes being laid out on a table.

Narsi's attention returned to Elezar—his *uncle*, Elezar. Merely naming their relationship in his own thoughts, Narsi felt anxious. The desire for warmth and familiarity keened through him and he felt stupid and childish for it. Elezar couldn't know who he was, much less think of him fondly.

The flickering torches carried by surrounding soldiers accentuated the harsh shadows of Elezar's angular, imposing stature. His heavy brows and thick, dark beard only emphasized the severe quality of his face.

Narsi shared very few connections with this uncle of his, other than the fact that as a child Elezar had been ambushed and nearly killed when Narsi's father was murdered. That was hardly something for the two of them to recount fondly. Most of what Narsi knew about Elezar's character and history actually came from Atreau's memoirs.

It was also Atreau who inspired Elezar's concern now. Elezar's cruel appearance changed immediately when he sighted his friend. His relief and joy were laid bare in a wide grin. He caught Atreau in a fierce hug.

A startled, slightly pained gasp escaped Atreau.

Narsi bowed his head to hide the weird expressions he felt quivering across his own face. He studied Elezar and Atreau, both admiring and envying their reunion. They looked relieved and pleased—though Atreau's arms were caught in a slightly awkward position.

"The priests said you'd gone into the chapel before it collapsed." Elezar didn't go on but simply clapped Atreau's shoulder a few times before releasing him. "But you're safe. Good."

"I certainly was until you decided to crush my ribs just now," Atreau replied.

Elezar laughed. Then he shifted his attention to Narsi. His brows rose in curiosity, but the smile remained on his face.

"This is Master Physician Na—" Atreau began.

"Narsi Lif-Tahm. How could I not remember Tim's boy?" Elezar stepped closer to Narsi. "God's blood, but you've grown up so much. Last I'd heard your mother took you to the Haldiim District to attend medical school."

Narsi nodded, embarrassed by how happy Elezar's words made him feel. He supposed he shouldn't have been surprised that Elezar recalled his name. Even as a youth Elezar had gone out of his way to know the servants and staff in the Grunito household. On top of that, he'd often needled Father Timoteo to acknowledge Narsi and his mother as family.

"How have the two of you fared since then?" Elezar asked.

"I've been well, but mother—" A pang of sorrow welled up in Narsi. His throat tightened on his response. "She passed away last year."

Elezar looked taken aback and then mournful.

"I'm sorry." Elezar lifted one of his hands, perhaps to pat Narsi's shoulder, but then stopped. He appeared at a loss, perhaps even nervous.

Both of them stood in awkward silence, too much strangers to each other to know how to proceed, but too intimately related not to care.

"I hope you'll both forgive the intrusion"—Atreau stepped in—"but there seems to be something of a crowd gathering on the hill, and it really would be best if I could be whisked away from here before the lady of the house can see any more of me."

Narsi glanced to the hill to see that, indeed, a growing crowd of people gathered to gawk. Some wore the garb of household staff, but many others appeared to be curious neighbors and passersby.

Most stared at Skellan. He circled around the ruins in dancing strides, with the wind whirling through his long red hair and fiery lights sparking from his fingers. Glowing crimson streamers hung behind him as he moved, leaving traces of the symbols he sketched in the air. A shape like a tree branch floated before burning out. Then another that Narsi thought might be antlers. Wings and scarlet eyes.

"She's to marry tomorrow." Elezar's quiet words drew Narsi's attention back.

A dry laugh escaped Atreau. He cast Narsi a sidelong look, as if they were sharing a joke, before returning his regard to Elezar.

"That's not why you're here?" Elezar asked.

Atreau held up his hands. "I swear, my presence here is all down to Javier's delivering Narsi and me through the Sorrowlands."

Hearing him admit as much, Narsi was startled, but then he realized that *how* they had been transported to Labara wasn't a secret—only *when* they'd come from was.

"Then Narsi surmised that a weapon to combat the Shroud of Stone was hidden away under this chapel." Atreau went on with a gesture to Narsi. "Left to my own devices I'd still be in Cieloalta, scrawling out drivel for Jacinto's theater production."

"What weapon?" Elezar asked.

Narsi lifted up the golden box into the torchlight. Elezar stepped back, eyeing the box as if he half expected the thing to explode.

"Another golden cask?" Elezar asked, and Narsi realized why he'd responded with such horror. A previous golden cask had released a demon lord on Milmuraille.

"This one holds Yah-muur's horn, which—"

"Which Narsi and I can explain somewhere more private." Atreau gestured to the crowd of onlookers on the hill.

"Right. We'll get you away from here." Elezar turned back to the brawny soldiers standing behind him and issued two orders in Labaran. Narsi didn't recognize all of his words but caught the gist of his commands. Elezar would personally attend to Count Radulf's safety. The guards were to escort and protect Atreau and Narsi. He didn't miss the fact that Elezar specifically referred to him as his nephew. After that, it seemed that several of the guards regarded him with warm expressions.

While Narsi and Atreau withdrew, Elezar went to Skellan and stood whispering into his ear. Then the group of them slowly made their way past the chapel and the main house, marching by household staff, wide-eyed priests and curious neighbors..

Narsi attempted to surreptitiously study Skellan. His long, red hair whirled in the evening breeze and the scant clothing he wore hardly befit a stable hand, much less the ruler of all Radulf County. His exposed chest and bare feet lent him the look of a beggar boy. But his skin appeared luminous in the dark, as if the immense power churning through him was lighting him up from within. Then Skellan's attention swung directly to Narsi. His green eyes all but glowed through the evening gloom and a cold wind gripped Narsi, curling around his hands and throat. Narsi froze in place just as he had when Hierro Fueres had stared at him at the palace.

The scars on Narsi's palms tingled and seemed to turn almost feverish.

"Come. If you stand gazing at the count any longer you'll wound my delicate vanity," Atreau said. He caught Narsi's elbow and drew him away.

Narsi rolled his eyes at Atreau's teasing words, but their exchange appeared to distract the count. Skellan's interest swept back to the chapel ruins, and the uneasy sensations in Narsi's hands faded.

When he and Atreau reached the street, Narsi half expected to simply be sent on his way, as so often happened to him in his capacity as a common physician among nobles. Instead, the guards escorted them to a glossy red carriage. Atreau exchanged a few Labaran words with two of the guards and then informed Narsi, "We're being treated to baths at the garrison."

Elezar and the soldiers escorted them on warhorses. But the thing that stunned Narsi was seeing Skellan flip the hood of his crimson fur cloak up over his head and then, in a single leap, transform into a long-legged red dog. He raced alongside Elezar, keeping apace with the horses. Narsi stared at him, struggling to accept what he'd seen. Even after all the strangeness, horror and wonder of this day, witnessing a man's body so effortlessly melt into the shape of a hound astounded him. At last he released the curtain of the carriage window, allowing it to fall closed.

"He's agitated," Atreau said.

"The count?" Narsi asked.

Atreau nodded, then offered a commiserating smile in the face of Narsi's further confusion. He'd seen people express anxiety in nervous tics, repetitive motions and even bouts of hiccups and yawns. But what sort of person turned into a dog to race across the city?

"Witches take some getting used to," Atreau said.

Narsi laughed and leaned back into the padded leather seat. Atreau shifted next to him, resting his hand in Narsi's. It was a small gesture, but somehow it made Narsi feel immensely better. He relaxed, allowing himself to lean against Atreau for the remainder of their journey.

The garrison was blessedly mundane. With its gray stone walls, open grounds and simple, clean barracks, it reminded Narsi of the Haldiim fields and halls where he'd trained in archery for his year of civic duty. Elezar offered them use of a private bath in the infirmary. While there, Narsi requested coinflower distillate and other medical supplies. A red-robed, elderly sister-physician delivered them along with a fine leather medical satchel. She and Atreau greeted each other with great enthusiasm. She turned the medical supplies over to Narsi and then seated herself on a stool beside the large soaking tub.

Narsi applied the distillate to the few scrapes and cuts that marred Atreau's arms and hands. He was relieved to note that none of the gashes required stitches—though he did wonder if it been by sheer luck that they'd both escaped unharmed, or had some lingering spell sheltered them?

"Where did all these flakes of gold leaf come from?" Atreau brushed his hand through the curls of Narsi's hair, sending a dust of gold drifting through the air.

"I think it was the fluid that poured from Yah-muur's antler when I tore the horn free," Narsi told him.

The white-haired sister-physician nodded, as if this was a common subject of everyday conversations.

"Old Gods and wild spirits bleed gold and magic. It didn't burn you, so it must be a blessing." The elderly sister-physician pronounced the Cadeleonian words precisely but with an unusual, almost musical cadence. She collected several of the larger pieces of gold, rolled them between her fingers and then popped them into her mouth "Gilded in good luck by a goddess. That's the line from a poem, isn't it?"

"Yes, but it's not the best part," Atreau replied, then he went on, but in Labaran. Narsi understood a few phrases, enough to assure him that the poem was one of the sensual works that made Labaran literature infamous.

Absently he gazed down at his own hands, studying the thin gold scars that bisected his palms. Then, belatedly, he saw that the aching, blue-black stains left from his muerate poisoning had vanished. He flexed his fingers and for the first time in a month felt absolutely no pain.

The sister-physician laughed and clapped Atreau on the back, complimenting his recital.

The fact that he and Atreau were only half dressed and preparing to share a steaming bath didn't appear to bother the elderly sister-physician at all. She chatted while Atreau stripped off the last of his clothes and then soaped and rinsed his naked body. She and Atreau shared news of affairs and scandals that Narsi knew nothing about.

However, when they lit on the subject of transporting medical supplies, Narsi was drawn in. As the three of them discussed spoilage of medicines and shipboard hospitals, Narsi realized that several Labaran warships must have already set sail and more would be launching in the next few days.

Then it struck him. Ships sailing from Labaran ports *now* could have easily reached Cieloalta in two weeks. When he and Atreau had been searching the Slate House, Labaran ships would have already been hiding along the Peraloro River. Labaran forces might be ready to attack when they returned. He cast a glance to Atreau, but the man appeared unsurprised. Narsi realized that he had already known.

At last Atreau eased himself down into the steaming water in the soaking tub and sighed.

"You should join me while it's still hot," Atreau told Narsi.

Narsi hesitated with his hands on his belt. He wasn't particularly shy, but just now Atreau's naked body and inviting gaze was so affecting. He had to avert his stare to keep from reacting too strongly. Opening up the front of his breeches seemed far too revealing, particularly with a stranger just sitting there watching.

The elderly sister-physician glanced from Atreau to Narsi, then cracked a gap-toothed grin.

"Oh! I see. Some privacy for the two of you wouldn't go amiss, would it?" She hopped up from the stool and skedaddled.

"Well, that's half of Milmuraille informed of our affair," Atreau commented, but he didn't appear worried. "Mother Solei will present us in a better light than Abea would if we left the gossip for her and her handmaids to spread on their own."

Narsi hadn't even thought of who might be spreading word about their . . . had it even been an affair? It had hardly been an hour. But clearly Atreau had already considered how to manipulate the story.

"How did she guess?" Narsi wondered what could have given him away.

"Do you really think I stare at just anyone the way I've been looking at you?" Atreau asked, and Narsi thought he might be teasing him, but he wasn't certain.

"Come here." Atreau beckoned him. "Join me while the water's hot."

Narsi stripped and lowered himself into the bath alongside Atreau. His long legs tangled with Atreau's. At first Narsi found the close contact in the confines of the tub awkward. He felt like a scarecrow stuffed in a wine barrel with a wet mink. But Atreau offered to massage his back, and soon he caressed and coaxed away Narsi's self-consciousness. Narsi returned the favor, working the knots out from Atreau's shoulders and lean back. Then he ran his hands over Atreau's chest and stroked him even lower.

Their closeness grew truly pleasant. They spent far more time admiring, kissing and exploring each other's bodies than they did relaxing in the tub. If they hadn't both been so tired, Narsi thought they probably would have splashed the entire contents of their bath onto the floor.

But eventually the water cooled and they remembered that they still needed to discuss matters with Elezar and Skellan. They withdrew and toweled off.

Earlier, Elezar had left clean garments for the two of them to wear while their own clothes were laundered. At the time Narsi had been preoccupied with the medical supplies he might need and then distracted watching Atreau empty a variety of notes and letters from a surprising number of hidden pockets in his dusty coat. So Narsi had only noted that the neatly folded new clothes lay alongside a set of fresh towels. He'd assumed the garments would be assembled from the garrison's spare uniforms. Studying the clothes now, both the quality of the cloth and brilliant colors of them surprised him.

He couldn't help but admire the fit of the green-and-gold wardrobe that Atreau donned. The cut of the silk shirt displayed Atreau's chest nicely. The breeches fit his legs and hips so well that it was hard to believe they hadn't been tailored for him, and the stockings clung perfectly to his calves. All together the cost of the attire was far beyond anything Narsi had ever seen Atreau wearing in Cieloalta or Anacleto. These were clothes fit for a prince. Or, Narsi realized with a smile, fit for the Duke of Rauma.

"Are these clothes from six years ago when you came to Labara to impersonate the duke?' Narsi asked.

"Indeed they are." Atreau appeared pleased as he straightened the cuff of his shirt and fastened it closed with a gold link. Then he looked to Narsi. "But did you notice that your attire befits a man planning on impersonating Count Radulf?"

"Hardly." Narsi smiled at the idea of anyone mistaking him for Skellan. Then he noted the embroidered design of golden wolves bounding across the red silk of his breeches. These did look like they belonged to a man far above Narsi's position. The thought made him uneasy, and he wondered it he ought to attempt to find different, more humble attire. "Will the count take offense?"

"Skellan? He'll be gleefully pleased that someone else has been gulled into wearing lavish formal attire in his stead," Atreau replied. Then he seemed to read something more from Narsi's expression, because he added. "Truly, you needn't worry. The populace of Radulf County is far too irreverent and diverse to enact sumptuary laws or sartorial codes. Skellan himself doesn't give a fart if anyone is better dressed than himself. Half the time the man doesn't wear much more than a dog collar. Anyway, silk and scarlet both suit you. The colors of the Grunito crest would be a perfect match."

Narsi had no idea why Atreau would mention it now. He decided to take it as a joke.

"I'll keep that in mind, in case I don't find impersonating Count Radulf daring enough. Perhaps I might parade around Anacleto as the earl," Narsi replied.

"If you declared yourself to Elezar, I'd vouch for you and I think he'd believe you." Atreau toweled his hair and then pulled it back from his face with a ribbon. Several strands fell loose against the column of his neck, but he didn't seem to notice or care.

"What would the point of that be?" Narsi asked.

"Securing the support of several members of the Grunito family will place you a step nearer being acknowledged as a rightful heir. While Elezar isn't recognized as a Cadeleonian noble any longer, his importance as a Labaran warlord may soon carry a great deal of weight."

That was all far too much for Narsi to think about at this moment. Attempting to protect his fellow Haldiim citizens from the royal bishop while also stopping the Shroud of Stone before it triggered a war—not to mention his longings and heartache—already occupied all his thoughts and energy. As much as being recognized and acknowledged by the Grunitos would have meant to him even a few days ago, it now seemed trivial and selfish. He knew who his father was and that he and his mother had been dearly loved; it didn't matter if anyone else knew it.

Narsi just shook his head. Atreau frowned.

"It's not as though you *aren't* a legitimate heir. You are Isandro's son and have every right to be recognized as one of the Lords Grunito, if not the Earl of Anacleto." Atreau paused and Narsi attempted to appear disinterested.

"If none of that matters to you," Atreau went on, "then at least consider that while you're living here in Labara, the connection to Elezar and Skellan would offer you a leg up as a foreign physician competing against guilds of sister-physicians."

"Living in Labara?" Narsi stared at him in disbelief. He didn't understand how this had even become a subject of conversation. Was Atreau really so eager to be rid of him already? "I've hardly unpacked my belongings in Cieloalta and you're already relocating me to Labara?"

Atreau scowled at him, then turned and jammed his collection of notes back into the pockets of his ermine-trimmed coat. Narsi just watched him, trying to work out Atreau's true intent and subdue his own feeling of being rejected yet again.

"Why are you suggesting all this?" Narsi asked at last.

Atreau stilled and stood with his head bowed and his eyes closed.

"No matter what happens in the coming months, Cieloalta will be in turmoil. Everyone living there could be in danger," Atreau whispered. "You've already risked so much and come so close to dying. You've done enough. You deserve a respite. If you remain here in Labara, you'll be safer."

"So would you," Narsi replied glibly.

"You think I don't know that?" Atreau gave a wry laugh and shook his head. "I'm too involved to get myself out. I don't even know what I would do if I ever did. But you, Narsi, you have so much potential. You deserve so much better."

Atreau's expression was so bleak that it startled Narsi. All at once he wanted to win back some of Atreau's hope and happiness.

"We've accomplished so much in a single day." Narsi lifted the golden box for Atreau to see. "We've secured Yah-muur's horn and we have a plan in place to save the duke—to save everything. I know that we can do it, and I intend to be right beside you when we do."

"You truly believe that?" Atreau asked.

Narsi nodded. To his surprise, Atreau suddenly drew him into a passionate kiss. The two of them stood holding each other until Narsi drew back before this became as distracting as their efforts at bathing.

"Very well, I suppose I must abandon my plan of moving you to Labara to secure a lovely little cottage where I might someday foist myself upon you." Atreau's hands slipped from around his waist.

Narsi smiled at the thought of the two of them living such a charming, simple life, then shook his head. He took up the gold box and secured it in his new satchel. Then he slung the satchel over his shoulder. The weight against his back felt reassuring, reminding him of exactly who he was, regardless of his parentage.

He and Atreau reached the door together, but when Narsi gripped the pull, Atreau stopped him, placing his hand on Narsi's.

"I still think that you ought to confide in Elezar," Atreau said. "Even if it isn't for your own sake. It would mean so much to him if he knew that Isandro left a child in this world."

Narsi frowned. Part of him wanted to tell Atreau that none of this was any of his concern. At the same time, he recognized that Atreau meant well and wanted the best for both Elezar and himself. It was just that the truth might not be so welcome as he imagined.

"My legitimate birth was the motive behind Isandro's murder. It was the reason Elezar was tortured and nearly crippled. How could he help but feel resentment toward me, if he found out? He lost a brother he adored only to gain a nephew who is a stranger. It's a poor trade, by any standard," Narsi said. "But if he believes that I'm Father Timoteo's bastard, then there could be a chance for us to grow closer. Our relationship doesn't have to begin with a tragedy."

"No, it will begin with a lie," Atreau replied.

Narsi met Atreau's warm gaze but couldn't hold it. He bowed his head.

"I know it's selfish. Maybe it's even wrong, but just for now I'd rather enjoy the simple comfort of a lie than have to struggle through a painful truth. I don't know that I could bear for him to blame me for my father's death. Can you understand that?"

"I can," Atreau replied. He released Narsi's hand. "Rest assured, I won't say a word about it unless you want me to. Just know that when you *do* decide to tell him, I'll support you."

Narsi didn't know why, but Atreau's assurance touched him deeply. On an impulse he leaned forward and kissed him lightly on the cheek.

"Thank you," Narsi said. He opened the door, stepped out, and slammed into Elezar's broad chest.

He'd been waiting for them, Narsi realized.

How long had he been there? How much had he overheard?

Narsi felt afraid to look him in the face, and yet he couldn't stop himself.

The tension in Elezar's expression startled him. If Atreau hadn't been directly behind him, Narsi would have jumped back from the weight of Elezar's dark gaze.

"Now that you're older," Elezar said, "you really do look like him."

Waves of anxiety, guilt and hope swept through Narsi, choking his attempt at any response to an inarticulate murmur. This wasn't how he'd wanted this conversation to go—not that he'd wanted to ever have it.

"I'm so sorry," Narsi choked out at last. He wasn't certain of what he was apologizing for. Standing here at such a loss? Attempting to keep the truth from him? Or for all of that as well as costing him his brother?

"Narsi, you have nothing to apologize for. Certainly not to me," Elezar told him. "You must never think that Isandro's death was your fault. The only people to blame were the men who killed him. Not you or your mother or me."

The last admission startled Narsi out of his stunned shock.

"You? How could you be to blame?" Narsi asked.

Elezar's brows furrowed as if he was in pain. A glint of light flickered in his dark eyes.

"I was the one who asked him to come out hunting that day and led him to the cave where he was trapped." Elezar fell silent, his expression bleak. "He didn't escape because I was wounded. He refused to abandon me, and it cost him his life. Knowing that, you could also say I was to blame for Isandro's murder."

"You were barely eleven years old," Narsi said.

"And you would have been, what? Four?" Elezar asked with a melancholy smile. "How could I ever blame you?"

"I . . ." Narsi didn't know what to say or do.

To Narsi's surprise, Elezar wrapped him in his powerful arms and pulled him into his chest. The embrace was incredibly relieving but also somewhat overwhelming. Elezar was so large and so strong that Narsi almost felt as if he was a little child. There had been so many nights when he'd been a boy that he'd wanted to be held and reassured like this.

"Elezar," Atreau called. "I think you're smothering him."

"Sorry." Elezar released Narsi and offered him an apologetic smile. "Javier, Kiram and Hylanya have already arrived, so if you're not too exhausted, Skellan is hoping that we can all discuss this Horn of Yah-muur and the spell beneath the Shard of Heaven."

"Certainly," Narsi replied. Beside him, Atreau simply nodded.

Elezar escorted them across the grounds and past the barracks, returning greetings to the soldiers keeping watch on the garrison walls. Inside the headquarters of the bustling garrison they passed groups of Irabiim archers, Mirogothic pikemen and frogwives armed with harpoons. All of them wore gray uniforms decorated with the scarlet wolf of Radulf County.

Briefly Narsi feared that they were all being gathered to discuss Yahmuur's Horn, but then he realized that the majority of the soldiers were bound for the massive dining hall that occupied most of the ground floor of the building. Just in passing Narsi caught a cacophony of different languages echoing through the hall. The scents of brine, yeast and butter suffused the air. Someone played a bright melody on a bone flute and several voices rose to sing along.

The sheer number of men and women housed in the garrison stunned Narsi. The previous night, at the foot of the sacred grove, he'd struggled when faced with fewer than fifty casualties. Now the enormity of the impending war penetrated his consciousness. So many lives in both nations were at stake.

Narsi took in a slow, deep breath and curled his hand around the strap of his satchel. He felt the weight of the golden box shift against his back and reminded himself of what he'd just told Atreau—they would succeed.

Ascending a wide stone staircase, they passed fewer people. Even so, several men and women wearing the badges of captains stopped Elezar to hand over written accounts, offer him quick reports and receive orders. Despite the brevity of the interactions, Narsi steadily absorbed the fact that not only was a fleet of Labaran warships sailing under the cover of frogwives' spells, but on the northern border, several skirmishes had already been fought between the Duke of Gavado and Radulf County's troll allies. Elezar flashed a grim smile when a delighted Irabiim captain informed him that many in the Cadeleonian vanguard had suffered a literally crushing defeat before their infantry withdrew back to the borders of the Gavado dukedom.

"Our friends are willing to push farther south if you wish them to do so, sir," the Irabiim captain proposed.

Narsi noticed Atreau tense at the suggestion, but he seemed to relax when Elezar shook his head.

"The Gavados are famous for feigning retreat to lure their enemies into ambushes," Elezar said. "Advise them to hold the border and make the Cadeleonian forces march through marshes and forests to get their noses bloodied."

The Irabiim captain laughed and all at once Narsi felt that there was something very familiar about the man. The captain saluted and started down the stairs. Narsi studied him as another taller Irabiim man joined the captain. Seeing them together, Narsi remembered where he'd seen them. This morning at the pharmacy, they'd come in and had already known his face and name.

After that, Elezar led them across the second story of the garrison to a large room that Narsi took for a library. The familiar leathery smell of aged vellum and tanning lime instantly recalled the hours he'd spent poring over medical tomes back in Anacleto. Fortunately, the evening breeze drifting through a single open window saved the place from feeling too stuffy. Taking in the shelves that lined the stone walls, Narsi noted that that scroll cases and maps, rather than books, appeared to make up most of the collection stored here. Several large maps lay on the large oak table in the middle of the room—though none of the people sitting in the chairs around the table appeared absorbed in the maps. They all looked to Atreau and Narsi.

Slumped in a seat near the cold fireplace, Javier appeared the least attentive to their arrival. Considering how deathly ill he appeared, Narsi was surprised that he'd even left his bed.

Beside him, Kiram spared Narsi, Atreau and Elezar a rather appraising glance before returning to his task of drawing a fox-fur cloak closed over Javier's chest.

Lady Hylanya wore her red hair up in a thick braid and was clothed in a light suit of red silk that greatly resembled Narsi's current wardrobe. She offered Narsi a passing smile but considered Atreau with a far more curious expression.

"I didn't expect to see you here quite so soon," Lady Hylanya murmured.

Atreau only shrugged.

Skellan, on the other hand, stared directly at Narsi. His green eyes flared like candle flames. Narsi thought he could feel the count's gaze strike his face. Narsi was reminded of the Yuanese tales of deities who disguised themselves as tramps to wander among mortals. Even his bare, dusty feet seemed to glow with a pearly luster.

"Count Radulf, it's an honor to—" Narsi began to bow, but Skellan bounced up to his feet, shaking his head.

"You're my man's nephew, and he and I are close as cock and foreskin. Separating our kin and friends cuts at our shared skin." Skellan's bright, melodic tone softened his crude language a little. "Call me Skellan, and if you don't mind I'll call you my nephew, Narsi. Yes?"

"I—yes, of course, Skellan," Narsi managed to reply. He stole a glance to Elezar just in time to see the look of open affection he gave Skellan.

"Then the same goes for me, as well." Lady Hylanya's expression was almost smug, and Narsi guessed that she found it amusing to claim a man older than herself as her nephew. "Not only are you kin, but you came to my aid. And I can tell just by looking at our Narsi that we share tastes. Partial to adventure novels, Labaran roses and cats."

Narsi wasn't certain what that had to do with anything, though she wasn't wrong.

"Good. Then that's formalities done away with." Skellan grinned and Narsi noticed how sharp his teeth were. "Come sit your asses down and let us all have a good chat about what you found in that church you pulled down."

While Narsi and Atreau seated themselves at the table across from Skellan, Elezar settled into the high-backed chair on Skellan's right. Narsi had been so occupied studying the people gathered in the map room that he hadn't really taken in the papers or graphite styluses and maps on the table. Now that he did, he nearly startled back to his feet. A large golden rat crouched only inches from his hand. The rat flicked its whiskers across Narsi's finger then scampered to Skellan's elbow.

At the same moment, a glossy black crow winged from the window-sill to perch on the back of Javier's chair. The way it angled its head gave Narsi the uneasy feeling of being closely considered.

"The rat is called Queenie. She's the witch Cire's familiar," Javier spoke up. "This crow is my master's. If there's trouble in Anacleto, he'll inform us. For now he's assisting Nestor Grunito to delay his arrival in Cieloalta until after we're certain it's safe."

Narsi nodded and stole a glance at Atreau's profile. He, like everyone else in the room, appeared at ease with the company of enchanted animals.

Narsi did his best not to stare. The two Haldiim men who had come to the pharmacy this morning had a rat called Queenie. Only it wouldn't have been *this* morning but rather a morning two weeks from now. The contradiction made Narsi feel dazed, and all he could do was watch the plump rodent while realizing that the two men must have been Labaran spies after all.

The rat, Queenie, hefted up a graphite stylus and started making the map of Cieloalta and the Peraloro River with it. Then she dropped the stylus and scampered to a small dish of grain near Skellan's elbow. She ate and then curled up on top of the remaining grain.

"So, now, what is all this about the Yah-muur's Horn?" Hylanya directed the question to Atreau.

"I'm not sure I'm the most informed on the subject." Atreau spared Javier and Kiram a questioning glance. Javier shrugged beneath his cloak, his dark eyes hanging half closed.

"Don't worry," Kiram spoke up, "Javier will feel free to interrupt you if he thinks you've gotten anything wrong. Go ahead."

"Too kind," Atreau replied dryly, then he shifted his attention back to Hylanya, Skellan and Elezar. "I assume that Javier already informed you that he and Alizadeh discovered an ancient spell trapped within the Shard of Heaven."

"The Shroud of Stone," Kiram specified. "Also called the Stone Veil in some writings."

No one appeared surprised by any of this. Narsi himself had guessed as much weeks ago after reading over Cadeleonian holy books. But until he and Atreau had ventured down into the chapel ruins, he hadn't known anything of its nature.

"We know its name, but as to what it actually does, do we know any-thing yet?" Hylanya directed her query to Skellan—not Atreau. Elezar, too, looked to Count Radulf.

"It suffocates the soul—destroying the very essence of magic—and entombs the body in stone. The more powerful and exposed the soul is, the more quickly the Shroud of Stone engulfs and kills it. But given time, the Shroud of Stone will spread across lands and seas, through the wind and earth, smothering even the tiny spirits of flowers and fleas, until the deepest buried magic at the heart of the world is dead." Skellan scowled up at the ceiling. His hands twitched and a faint breeze stirred in the air. The map of Cieloalta fluttered.

"What?" Hylanya looked horrified.

At the same time, Javier straightened and stared at Skellan. His red-rimmed eyes appeared bloody against the pallor of his face.

"When did you learn this?" Javier demanded.

"An hour ago. I heard the whispered secrets rising from the broken stones beneath the chapel," Skellan answered.

Narsi gazed at him in wonder. He had seen Skellan dancing through the dust and ruins, but he would never have guessed that Skellan could pull information from the very air.

"Though I've sensed the Shroud of Stone's presence since the Hallowed Kings began wasting away," Skellan went on. "But even in my dreams I couldn't grasp its essence. Every time I attempted to drive it back from invading my body and soul, I didn't meet any resistance. Instead my witchflame was enveloped in silence and stillness. My heart calmed and I quietly died."

Skellan fell silent. Narsi dropped his gaze to the tabletop. Guilt gnawed at him, but he resisted the urge to blurt out all he knew of Skel-lan's possible death. Atreau, Javier and Kiram all remained silent, and they knew far more about the situation then he did. He put his trust in them and tried to repress his agitation, but it felt awful.

Some of his uneasiness must have shown, because Atreau dropped his hand and rather slyly patted his thigh.

"It was strange," Skellan went on. "Most spells are half alive, whis-pering with intention and radiant purpose. They resonate like notes, full of color, and even smell different: sweet, or sweaty, even sickly. But the Shroud of Stone is just . . . inanimate. More of a poison than a spell. As if someone refined tranquility into a weapon."

Narsi furrowed his brow at Skellan's description.

"Do you mean to say that you've been fighting it already?" Narsi asked.

"Only in my dreams. Or nightmares, really. I've deprived our Elezar of a dozen nights of good sleep with all my howling and kicking." Skellan gave a self-conscious laugh. "Ever since Hylanya brought back stones from the shattered wards surrounding the Shard of Heaven, all of us in Radulf County realized that the Shroud of Stone is a far greater threat then even a demon lord. It has to be stopped—destroyed. But to battle it in reality . . ." Skellan trailed off as he gazed down at the map of Cieloalta.

He extended his hand and a crimson glow lit the icon marking the Shard of Heaven. Steadily the red light spread out across the rest of the city.

"I'd have to strip the power from every stone in the city and devour the sky and river to claim enough strength to destroy the spell before it killed me." Skellan's fingers trembled.

"It won't come to that." Elezar caught Skellan's hand and drew it back from the map. "Hylanya and Cire are using their familiars to build wards around the Shard of Heaven. Fedeles has claimed Crown Hill and made an alliance with the Circle of Wisteria. You won't face this alone."

"We'll all be with you," Hylanya agreed. To Narsi's surprise, the rat roused itself to nuzzle Skellan's wrist. Skellan appeared moved.

Narsi tried to ease his own sense of guilt. Maybe they could fight the Shroud of Stone as a group? Perhaps this time Skellan's death could be avoided?

Then out of the corner of his eye, Narsi noted Javier bow his head and slump back in his seat leaning into Kiram. A very soft sigh escaped Atreau. He patted Narsi's thigh again, then drew his hand back.

"In addition to that," Atreau spoke up, "Narsi here has secured a weapon that we believe was specifically made to destroy the Shroud of Stone." Atreau beamed with flattering confidence. "A horn from the goddess Yah-muur."

Narsi drew the gold box from his new satchel and placed it on the table.

Kiram studied the box with keen interest, while Skellan, Hylanya and Elezar seemed lit with excitement. Queenie, the rat, sniffed the air around the box, and even the crow perched on Javier's chair eyed it in fascination. Only Javier remained withdrawn and grim-faced. Narsi hoped exhaustion was to blame for his demeanor rather than any greater knowledge of future failure.

"You did far more to discover and secure the horn than me," Narsi insisted. Then, hoping Atreau would take the lead in offering explanations and answers, he added, "I wouldn't have known where to begin, left to my own devices and resources."

"You're too humble," Atreau commented, and Narsi felt almost certain that he was teasing him. Thankfully, Atreau still took on the burden.

He quickly summed up what they'd learned of Clara's and Hierro's plans, as well as their interest in the Horns of Yah-muur and the discovery that the golden box was created to house and transport the horn.

He made no mention of the Waarihivu or traveling back in time. And all Atreau said about crossing the Old Road was that he hoped laundering would lift the dismal smell of the place out of his clothes.

"After we arrived here, Narsi connected the images engraved on the golden box to a passage in my latest memoir describing the pillars below Bishop Palo's old chapel. He's terribly well read." Atreau cast him a brief but flattering glance before going on. "We investigated and discovered that there was a trinity of spells used to combat demons, and that each one of them can be employed to destroy one of the others."

Again Atreau glanced to Narsi.

"The Black Fire consumes the Horns of Yah-muur. The Shroud of Stone smothers the Black Fire. The Horns of Yah-muur tear apart the Shroud of Stone," Narsi supplied from memory.

"The Horns of Yah-muur tear apart the Shroud of Stone," Hylanya echoed as she gazed down at the gold box. A bright smile lit her angular face. "Can it truly be that simple? That easy?"

"Well, it wasn't exactly easy," Atreau muttered. "We had to argue with a flock of demented old crows just to win the pleasure of having them knock a chapel down on us. And of course Narsi volunteered to endure all manner of horror for the sake of the world. Typical Grunito." Atreau lifted his gaze to Elezar. "He didn't even hold out for a thank you, much less the promise of endless treasure."

Narsi felt his cheeks warming with a flush.

"He and the gold box were whisked off to some hell, then he reappeared doused in blood and gold leaf. And as I mentioned, the building started falling down on us."

"How do we use it?" Elezar addressed the question to Narsi. "The horn."

"According to Yah-muur, the box has to be taken to a sacred grove and blessed before it will open. I think it has to be the Circle of Wisteria."

"Why there?" Javier asked.

"Because the concentrated power within the horn can only be contained for a very brief time after the box is opened. The Circle of Wisteria is the sacred grove that's nearest the Shard of Heaven." Yah-muur hadn't told him as much directly, but as he answered, Narsi felt the gold scars in his palms warm. Tingling sensations shot through his fingers and up his wrists, and hundreds of bright images flickered to life behind his eyes. Impressions and insights roused within him.

He realized that Yah-muur had transferred more then just the horn to him in those seconds that he battled to tear it free. She'd given her blood and blessing, just as she must have done with countless others who carried her horns.

"How little time will we have?" Elezar asked.

Narsi almost responded that he didn't know, but then he realized that the more he pondered it, the more knowledge blossomed within him.

"That will depend upon the strength of the blessings and the fortitude of the person who carries the horn." As Narsi answered, his heartbeat quickened, and for an instant he felt his muscles burning and his lungs aching as if he sprinted with the golden box gripped in his hands. Very faintly he heard the thunder of horses hooves and battle cries.

He drew in a deep breath, suppressing this strange disquiet.

"Three hours at the most," Narsi managed to say.

"I could ride from the Circle of Wisteria to the Shard of Heaven in less than an hour," Elezar said. "The difficulty will be breaking through the royal bishop's guardsmen as well as the royal guards. But my troops could do it."

"No doubt," Atreau replied. "However, we could save time and lives if we avoided a direct assault. There's an easier way into the Shard of Heaven than knocking down the front doors." He snatched up one of the styluses and leaned over the city map. "A private delivery tunnel runs under the river, here. Given a little time and a fair amount of gold, it would be easy to find places among bearers carrying in their grains and goods. We'd be particularly innocuous if we arrived when they were receiving a large number of other deliveries."

"You mean when they're preparing for a celebration?" Kiram asked. "Such as the coronation of the new king?"

"Yes, exactly." Atreau nodded.

Narsi heard them conversing, but his mind seemed to still buzz with dozens of other voices.

"Come the solstice, they'll be frantically preparing for the next day's feast," Atreau went on. "I already have people in positions to aid us. And Narsi has connections in the Haldiim District who might assist us as well, particularly when it comes to entering the sacred grove."

"The Solstice Procession will pass close to the entry to that tunnel. A number of people could break off from the parade without too much notice," Narsi managed to answer despite the chaos rising through him. Looking around the table, he took in his companions, but behind them phantom images floated and swayed.

Only the glossy black crow remained the same. It cocked its head, studying Narsi.

It launched into the air and then landed on Narsi's shoulder. Its weight was like a cool hand, gently shaking him from a dream. The garbled cacophony stopped and the ghostly scenes of long-past battles vanished. What remained with Narsi was a certainty.

"I'm the one who has to carry the horn," Narsi said. He held up his hands, displaying the shining gold scars. "Yah-muur's blessing is the key to opening the golden cask and wielding the horn against the Shroud of Stone."

Atreau scowled at Narsi's open palms as if they had offended him. Elezar merely glanced over his hands, while Skellan and Hylanya both rose from their chairs and leaned closer. Even the rat scurried nearer.

"Are you sure?" Atreau demanded.

Skellan waved his hands through the air and Narsi felt heat sweep across his palms. The gold scars glowed and flickered like candle flames, throwing off dancing shadows. Then Skellan folded his hands back against his chest and Narsi's palms cooled.

"He's right," Hylanya spoke up. "The same gold that marks our Narsi's hands binds the box shut."

"One resonates with the other, as if they were a single creation. Two halves of one spell." Skellan looked to Narsi. "It would seem that you don't simply hold the key but that you are the key."

"So Narsi has to be the one transporting and using the horn," Kiram said. "But that doesn't change anything else, does it?"

Silence filled the room. Narsi heard strains of singing drifting from the mess hall below. He focused his attention on the city map and the route that Atreau had drawn. The gray line didn't represent too great of a distance, and yet sweat beaded the back of Narsi's neck. They were waiting for him to agree, he realized.

Fear is the threshold we must cross every time we find our courage.

"Yes, exactly. I'll be the one who fights the Shroud of Stone." Narsi folded his hands closed so no one could see that they trembled. "But the rest of the plan stays the same."

CHAPTER
TWENTY-FIVE

During the first three days, Atreau and Narsi hunkered down in the garrison, refining their ideas with Elezar, Skellan and a variety of other witches and military commanders as they all proposed routes to infiltrate the Shard of Heaven. One heavily debated plan was to use the Solstice Day Procession as cover for Narsi when traveling through the city. Atreau liked this idea in principle, but it had distinct drawbacks. While it would serve to hide Narsi among a crowd of other Haldiim people, the procession was also likely to attract unwanted attention from the royal bishop's guardsmen.

"I can think of two ways to mitigate the danger," Atreau said. "First, ensure Jacinto and his circle of nobles join in very publicly. Even Captain Yago will hold back if he finds himself up against a royal prince. Second, concoct a number of minor diversions across the city before the procession, to ensure that the city guards and the royal bishop's guardsmen are already occupied and tired."

Which was easy enough to say but required hours to actually plan and set in motion, in part because Atreau could only reach out to his own agents through Hylanya's and Cire's familiars in faraway Cieloalta. But, at least when it came to climbing through windows to deposit short missives, agile cats were far more likely to come and go undetected. And rats could go anywhere unnoticed.

Throughout this all, Javier's repeated calls to formulate an evacuation plan in case Narsi failed to destroy the Shroud of Stone were ignored until eventually he simply climbed up on the table, using it as a stage.

"The loss of life will be immense if we do nothing." Javier spoke like an oracle, his voice ringing with dreadful certainty. "At the very least, we need the means to get our own agents and soldiers to safety."

Atreau watched Skellan's quizzical study of Javier's strained expression, and for a moment he feared he'd have to invent some distraction to keep Skellan from prying and discovering the secret behind Javier's conviction.

Luckily Skellan let it go, merely commenting, "Our astrologer has worked himself sick hewing secrets and omens from the stars. We'd be fools not to listen to the advice he's willing to share."

So, Atreau had suggested that Hylanya and Elezar use their agents to approach Spider about sneaking people through the tunnels he maintained. Then Narsi informed them that he'd had occasion to learn that the infamous Haldiim smuggler the Goat might be willing to help as well—at least if it came to evacuating Haldiim citizens.

"I know a man in the Knife Market who can get in touch with her. But you'll need money to make it worth his while and hers, I think." Atreau again provided the contact—though this time it had been via a relay of Cire's rats, spread across numerous ships that at last reached their old schoolmate Morisio, who'd just made harbor in Cieloalta.

After that, Hylanya presented Atreau and Narsi with a set of polished topaz charms. Hundreds of tiny spell symbols had been etched into the surfaces of them both. Atreau marveled at the fine detail as he turned the stone over in his hand.

"They're designed after Meztli's shield," Hylanya said. "Our mechanist, Kiram, used a steel needle to cut the sigils, and Skellan's entire coven has blessed them."

"So these are meant to hold back the Shroud of Stone?" Narsi asked, but then his expression lit with understanding and he snatched up the other charm.

"They misdirect the spell away from the bearer," Skellan said. "But we don't know how long they'll last."

"Anything is better than nothing." Narsi beamed at the stone in his hand, then turned his warm gaze on everyone in the room. "Thank you all. This could make every difference."

Though they'd known him for less than a three days, Atreau noted that everyone in the map room returned Narsi's smile.

Everything was set. In ten days' time Javier would escort Atreau and Narsi back to Cieloalta through the Sorrowlands, secretly returning them to the day they'd entered the Slate House. If they returned any sooner they risked meeting themselves in Cieloalta and experiencing the near-madness of merging, as Javier had done so many times. Though, as far as the others knew they'd simply chosen to endure the journey through the Sorrowlands for the sake of speed and stealth.

Skellan, Elezar and Hylanya were traveling more reliably and conventionally, planning to sail with the dawn tide.

"At least you'll be spared the seasickness if you don't travel with us," Elezar commented. "Still, take care of yourself when you're in the Sorrowlands."

Atreau nodded but averted his eyes. He hadn't expected to feel so uneasy deceiving Elezar. He found himself struggling not to offer him a warning almost every time he met his gaze. He almost looked forward to Elezar and Skellan setting sail the next morning. Then at least he wouldn't have to endure the self-loathing of concealing information from them.

But before he could say a final goodbye and take his leave, Elezar caught his shoulder and asked him to ride with him while Narsi, Javier and Kiram returned to the astrologer's palace in a carriage.

"There's a small matter I'd like to discuss with you. I won't keep you long," Elezar said. Guilt made Atreau's heart race, but he had no reason to refuse, so he smiled and waved Narsi off with Kiram and Javier.

While the others climbed into Count Radulf's carriages, Elezar ordered a groom to ready mounts for himself and Atreau. Then he drew Atreau aside to a corner where bales of straw stood like impromptu benches. Atreau sat while Elezar stood and paced.

"This is awkward," Elezar stated. "I don't want to intrude on your private life. At the same time, I feel like I owe it to my brother and Narsi's mother to ask . . ." Elezar paused, scowling down at his large, scarred hands. He shook his head. "I don't know Narsi very well, but what I've seen of him I've liked. He seems like a good man."

"He's better than most people," Atreau agreed. He held Elezar's troubled gaze; it wasn't like Elezar to be so evasive. "What is it you want to say to me about him?"

"Intentions—your intentions," Elezar finally bit out. "What are you doing with him?"

"In detail?" Atreau arched a brow. "Or just in a generalized sense?"

Elezar's face flushed.

"I'm not trying to pry into—" Elezar's scowl deepened.

Atreau waited, leaning back against a bale of golden straw. The smell of feed and horses wafted over him, reminding him of their school days. Elezar had never been a man of many words, but when he did speak, he tended to be direct and honest. Clearly this wasn't a comfortable conversation for him. At the same time, Atreau didn't particularly want to make it easy.

"Are you doing this just to get back at me for questioning your involvement with Skellan back when he was pretending to be your dog?" Atreau asked.

Elezar laughed, but his amusement was fleeting.

"I don't want Narsi to be hurt," Elezar said at last.

"Neither do I. So we're in accord," Atreau replied with a glib smile.

Atreau eyed the grooms leading their mounts out from the stalls. They hung back, awaiting Elezar's order to approach. There would be no getting out of this until Elezar had spoken his piece and received the reassurance that he needed. Though Atreau wasn't certain he'd be believed no matter what he said.

Elezar paced with his head bowed and his right hand curled around his sword hilt.

"I know it wouldn't be your intention for him to come to harm, but . . ." Elezar trailed off again, scowling at the straw at his feet.

Atreau almost pitied him. Of the two of them, he was the more discomfited. At least Atreau had the advantage of experience. He'd been questioned over his sexual and romantic entanglements on numerous occasions; he'd encountered threats and pleas as well. None of which had been a pleasure, but at least the interrogation was familiar. Elezar, on the other hand, had never before been in this position. He looked miserable and annoyed.

"Your previous affairs . . . they didn't end well," Elezar managed at last.

Atreau could have argued. He'd indulged in so many affairs that Elezar couldn't possibly be aware of all their outcomes. He'd remained friends with Inissa and other past lovers. And most of his fleeting relationships ended as indifferently as they began, being little more than passing entertainments for everyone involved.

But Atreau knew exactly which disastrous affair troubled Elezar. Elezar had witnessed Reollos attack Atreau in a fit of mad jealousy. If Elezar hadn't been there, Atreau would likely have died. Instead Elezar had intervened and shouldered the blame for Reollos's death.

Remembering the smell of all that blood and his own heartsick horror, Atreau acknowledged that Elezar's anxiety wasn't unwarranted. Who knew, maybe his concern wasn't for Narsi alone? But Atreau didn't want to think of Reollos anymore. He'd already spent years regretting a choice that he was powerless to change.

What he wanted now was to move on. Even if that meant making entirely new mistakes.

"Rest assured." Atreau maintained his light tone, though he felt less than jovial. "Narsi is entirely out of keeping with my typical taste for crazed, possessive types. In fact, he's absurdly level-headed. So, honestly, if you must fret about anything, it should be my source of income now that I've been ensnared by your upright nephew. My next memoir as a reformed reprobate is bound to disappoint faithful readers."

"Can you be serious for even one conversation?" Elezar snapped.

"I'd rather not," Atreau replied, but meeting Elezar's strained gaze, he abandoned his sardonic smile. "All right. But what can I tell you? I know that I don't rate someone like him. I'm certainly not the upstanding gallant lover he deserves. But . . . I'm a little at loss for the words."

In truth it was his courage to voice those words that failed him. He didn't want to lie, and at the same time he couldn't bring himself to expose the tender new longing that had steadily taken hold of his heart.

Atreau shook his head, staring up at the rafters and noting the sparrows nesting up there. How simple it looked for carefree little birds. Singing and sharing a nest. They lived in the moment, unburdened by the duty to account for their affections to concerned relatives.

"What's between Narsi and me, it wasn't anything I planned. It just happened. God knows I tried to stop it. I put him off, refused him and pushed him toward other people. But . . . in the end I did him a greater disservice by making him believe he could be somehow lacking." Atreau sighed. "As for my intentions. I don't know what Narsi would want from me, much less what I could honestly promise him. But, his company makes me happy—more than happy. Hopeful, contented and excited all at once. The last thing I would ever do is knowingly cause him harm."

Atreau thought he saw confusion and concern in Elezar's expression, but then a slow smile curved his lips. He considered Atreau in silence before asking, "You truly mean that?"

"I do." Why would he bother to lie, at this point?

Atreau wasn't certain why, but Elezar's faint smile blossomed into a grin.

"Maybe I'm having this conversation with the wrong person." He clapped Atreau on the back. Then he beckoned the grooms to bring their mounts. "I'd better get you back to his side then."

After that, they rode to the astrologer's palace and enjoyed more relaxed conversations about horses and the recent theater productions that had been lighting up the stages of Milmuraille.

When they parted, Atreau was sorry to say goodbye.

❧❧❧

With the naval force sailing to Cieloalta and the planning done, there was little to do but wait for time to bring them back to the day they'd been whisked into the past. Atreau decided he needed to take Narsi out, partially to tour the town, but also so that Narsi could practice the fine art of hiding in plain sight while moving swiftly through a city. By the tenth day of this, Atreau found he'd become attuned to Narsi's habits.

Atreau scanned the chaotic street and quickened his strides to keep a few steps ahead of Narsi's long gait. A merchant's carriage veered in front of them. Atreau swung to the right, knowing Narsi would turn rather than stop. They dashed through a gap in the crush of wagons, carriages and carts, then swept ahead to reach the narrow raised walkways of Milmuraille's open market. In the lane before them, the merchants' stalls abounded with food: cooked and fresh-caught fish, cages of frogs, buckets of snails, yeasted bread loaves as fragrant as beer and butter pressed into golden bricks. This early in the day, the heaps of herbs and straw scattered over the grounds were still recognizable and their scents arose from every footstep.

Narsi surged ahead and Atreau broke into a quick sprint just to keep alongside him. Atreau caught his shoulder and pulled him back.

"Remember, tread more quickly than a loitering guard will care to follow," Atreau advised, "but not so fast that you draw attention."

Narsi nodded, then slowed to a brisk pace. They turned down another lane. After a little while Narsi even paused, rather naturalistically, to consider a display of ornately carved butter molds. Atreau followed Narsi's gaze and noted that amidst the designs of bees, flowers and frogs, there were also sigils made up of familiar symbols. Several resembled the wards that decorated the charms he and Narsi now wore beneath their shirts.

"Now that I know what I'm looking at, it's almost staggering to realize how saturated Milmuraille is with spells. They're everywhere." Narsi moved ahead, falling into the quick pace of a concerned physician. Atreau strode alongside him, pondering the city as well. Ever since Skellan freed the grimma and destroyed the sanctums that had enthralled so many wild spirits, magic had propagated throughout the northlands.

Even a cursory glance over the people and the surrounding architecture revealed magic in countless forms. Most of the populace wore multitudes of colorful charms and talismans, and many openly advertised themselves as witches, exorcists and fortune-tellers for hire. Nearly every building boasted carvings and paintings that glittered with lively spells. A booming market of magical services, items and entertainments flourished here. Magic thrived in such abundance that even Atreau could perceive faint shimmers of color and subtle perfumes wafting through the air. It made him reconsider turns of phrase he'd thought were purely metaphoric in old Labaran texts. Why couldn't a *night sky glitter with enchantments brighter than stars?* Perhaps sorcerous lovers truly had possessed *skin anointed with the rich fragrances of blessings.*

"Could Cadeleon have been like this once?" Atreau mused. "Before Our Savior and the Shard of Heaven, perhaps the land was replete with small magic and wild spirits." If it had been, how immense of an impact must the Shroud of Stone have made when it was first released? Even to this day, only the most driven and powerful sorcerers survived. Cloud imps, wethra-steeds, frogwives and trolls had all been wiped out. Certainly faint magic, such as the tiny blessings fluttering like moths in the pink glass baubles that hung over so many tavern doors, never would have survived.

"Do you think it will be that way again?" Narsi wondered. "After we succeed?"

"It might," Atreau replied. If they destroyed the Shroud of Stone, what would stop magic from spilling over the borders and flourishing in Cadeleon? Catching sight of a tall Mirogothic woman striding through the market lane conversing with a large golden fox, he couldn't help but wonder how Cadeleon might change. How much more rich and strange of a world might they usher into existence?

They reached the East Gate before the city bells rang out the hour. Narsi gave a shout of triumph. Atreau clapped him on the back. For the tenth day in a row, they'd traversed twice the distance between the Circle of Wisteria and the Shard of Heaven in less than an hour.

Atreau didn't believe their real journey would be so simple or care-free—certainly not once they reached the tunnels beneath the Shard of Heaven. However, this daily trek across different routes and through packed crowds, around broken carts and over dilapidated old buildings, offered them both a sense of preparedness and security.

Atreau found that he enjoyed Narsi's company whether they were digging up ancient mysteries or wandering along ordinary streets. Not only did Narsi posses a level head in the face of danger, but when presented with the ordinary and everyday, he always shared interesting, delightful or funny observations. Atreau enjoyed Narsi's insights and arguments as well as the quiet times when they were both occupied with their own thoughts.

Today as they strolled back to Javier and Kiram's residence at the astrologer's palace, they stopped at a bakery where Atreau introduced Narsi to frogbuns and sixroots table beer. He only just managed not to laugh at Narsi's startled expression when he bit into the frogbun and it gushed foamy filling into his mouth.

"It's cream and cod roe," Atreau informed him.

Narsi swallowed, then considered the remainder of the green-gold bun.

"Not at all what I was expecting," Narsi admitted.

"No?"

"The color made me think it would be filled with sweet chay and mint." Narsi turned the bun in his hand. "But I rather like how savory this is, actually."

Then he devoured the rest. Atreau dug into his own frogbun. The two of them toasted each other with short cups of spicy table beer. After that, they visited a paper vendor. Atreau needed to find something that closely matched the paper Hierro Fueres used for his missives. Narsi perused a variety of leathery parchments before joining Atreau to consider the reams of fine rag papers.

"Your mother's family were papermakers, weren't they?" Atreau recalled, then he held out the piece of paper that Javier had given him. "Do you think anything here is a match to this?"

"Silk threads have been laid into the pulp to give it a little more sheen and strength." Narsi studied the sample, turning it over and inspecting the cut edges closely. "That's an unusual practice outside of Usane. I think we should be looking at the imported papers." He led Atreau to a different shelf, where papers flecked with gold and flower petals lay on display.

While the two of them searched, Narsi described several evenings spent with his mother and aunt ripping apart barnacle-encrusted ropes and stained rags to make pulp for their paper presses.

"We sang and played word games to make the time go faster. But I was only allowed to join them for a week. Then my aunt decided that I was 'absolutely useless' and barred me from helping." Narsi sighed as he considered a ream of paper. "I was so offended and hurt that I hardly spoke a word to my aunt for a month after that. Though later my mother told me that my aunt was actually afraid I'd ruin my physician's hands handling all the rough fibers and caustic ash that she and my mother worked with."

Atreau glanced at Narsi's elegant hands and recalled the feeling of them tracing the length of him.

He felt thankful for Narsi's aunt's concern, though her methods dismayed him a little. Had she thought insults would be more effective in discouraging Narsi than would honest concern? Or had she feared that displays of caring would somehow spoil the boy? Atreau supposed that growing up with such an icy relative did go a way to explain Narsi's affectionate indulgence of prickly sorts, like Brother Berto.

"Some people aren't good at expressing the depth of their feelings," Atreau stated.

"While others are too good to be believed," Narsi replied with an easy laugh.

"Sir, you chide me before I even offer you a grandiose endearment," Atreau replied.

"I'm not reproaching you, but merely reminding myself." Narsi just rolled his eyes.

Atreau could only smile in response. Both his reputation and his published writings stood as warning against anyone trusting his declarations of affection—much less love. So what would be the use in protesting?

At last they found a sheaf of fine linen paper sprinkled with inclusions of white silk threads. The color and weight both matched the paper Hierro Fueres favored, and the cost certainly suited a nobleman. Atreau felt relieved that he was spending Javier's money right now rather than his own, or he might've been forced to sell himself to the highest bidder just to afford one sheet of this paper. Thankfully, the ink was much more common and had been secured two days earlier.

Only one errand remained—that of visiting a small theater to acquire Masquerade costumes for himself and Narsi to wear for their return to Cieloalta.

After they accomplished that and returned to the astrologer's palace, Atreau set to work copying the bold swashes of Hierro's script in sweeping lines across the silky paper. Soon he produced a perfect copy of the note meant for Ariz. Once he was certain he could reproduce Hierro's writing, he penned the altered missive. He set it aside to dry.

Across the room, Narsi readied jars of medicines so potent that they could easily poison a man. His handsome expression was serious and mournful. Atreau felt a sharp stab of guilt. They had forced Narsi to choose between killing Ariz and the destruction of the whole of Cieloalta. But when Narsi looked up and met his gaze, there wasn't any accusation in his face. If anything, his expression was one of commiseration.

"I think I have another hour of work ahead of me." Narsi stretched, then returned to grinding and weighing out herbal concoctions.

Atreau turned his own attention to writing. He penned a few lines of dialogue for a play and then gave in and indulged in scribbling out absurd lyrics to a simple melody. Now and then he laughed to himself, thinking of what Narsi might say when he heard it.

An hour later, when Narsi asked about the melodies, Atreau offered to perform them for him. They adjourned to Kiram's airy library. There Atreau found a bench near one of the large circular windows. He strummed a lute and coaxed Narsi to sit beside him and sing along. Narsi bowed his head, studying the sheet of lyrics and simple musical notation. Summer sunlight filtered through the tree branches outside and seemed to dance over Narsi's face. Gold and jade flecks shone in his hazel eyes. Atreau leaned closer to him, drinking in the mingled scents of coinflower and woodsoap.

"Darling, how lucky you must be
To have won a love such as me
I'm faithful as the burr in your socks
And persistent as my merrypox,
Supple as a squid in bed,
Sweeter than sugared lead."

Narsi burst into laughter even before the second stanza, but Atreau continued strumming and singing with great dignity. Then they took turns improvising awful similes to sing to the lovelorn melody.

Atreau thought Narsi's contribution of "unstinting as a dog fart" was a kind of genius and didn't attempt to outdo it. After that he plucked out the notes to a Haldiim melody he only half remembered and Narsi supplied him with the lyrics.

Javier wandered into the room. The deep shadows beneath his eyes had faded, but he still moved as if he could hardly remain awake a minute longer. He collapsed back into a padded chair, kicking his legs up onto a reading table.

"The music is nice to hear. Laughter's even better. Don't let me interrupt." Javier dosed and woke again while Narsi and Atreau continued singing. Together they tried to reproduce a tavern song they'd overheard while drinking butter tea alongside a group of sister-physicians.

An hour later Kiram and several of his students joined them as well. They brought along sun tea and a bowl of freshly picked berries.

Narsi was shy of singing in front of them all, but Atreau truly enjoyed the resonate quality of his voice and managed to convince him to continue. Narsi certainly possessed greater musical skill than either Javier or Kiram, though both of them seemed to take a perverse pleasure in their own off-key harmonies—laughing and teasing one another as they strove to outdo each other with sour notes.

Atreau fed Narsi blackberries and stole a kiss as his reward.

It all felt so comfortable and so relieving that for a time Atreau forgot this wasn't the life he had made for himself. This relaxed, pleasant afternoon was a stolen respite. It was like a dream-spell from a troll story, wherein a miserable villain indulged himself in the brief illusion of the happiness that would have been his, if only he'd chosen a kinder path in life.

That night, lying with Narsi asleep in his arms, Atreau felt a profound sense of peace. How ironic that he'd spent decades grasping after power, wealth and influence but now, without the promise of any of those things, he felt secure. He thought that if he and Narsi could go on just like this for the rest of their lives, he'd be satisfied—more than that—overjoyed.

If only it didn't have to end.

But the next morning Javier woke them early, saying, "It's time to send you back."

They climbed out of their shared bed, washed and gathered the few things they would need to take with them. Narsi combed and trimmed Atreau's hair into the short style popular among conservative Cadeleonian men. When he heard Narsi sigh, he laughed.

"It will grow back, I promise," Atreau assured him.

"I know. I've just gotten used to running my hands through it when it's longer." Narsi cleared away the dark locks and the scattered silver hairs.

Then Atreau helped Narsi smooth the long gold plumes of the Yu-anese cloak that made up a large part of his costume. The volume and splendor of feathers disguised his satchel quite well. A gold mask hid his elegant features. In return, Narsi assisted Atreau closing up all the small gold buttons that ran down the back of his fox costume. A somber air surrounded them as they breakfasted. Atreau hardly tasted the food he ate or the tea he drank. His thoughts were already focused on crossing the Sorrowlands and infiltrating a royal party in time to save Fedeles.

When Javier wrenched open the gray chasm leading into the Sor-rowlands, Atreau took Narsi's hand. They strode through the visions of flames and collapsing buildings side by side. Time warped and grew un-measurable as they followed Javier. At one point Atreau noticed Narsi staring at a phantom image of the two of them.

Atreau's own form lay bleeding from a gash in his leg. Gutter wa-ter washed around him. Narsi knelt at his side attempting to stanch the blood. Mordwolves bore down upon them. Atreau had witnessed this scene before—the wolves would kill Narsi first. It was fucking awful. He didn't want either of them to have to see it again.

"Look there." Atreau called Narsi's attention away to three very dis-tant figures. "Don't they look like the three of us when we first crossed the Sorrowlands?"

"Definitely. You were wearing your blue jacket and the last of your fine white shirts, I remember," Narsi said.

How strange to think that it had been two weeks since they fled the Slate House, and yet now they were returning only hours later. Atreau squinted through the flames and smoke. He was almost certain that the thin man in the lead of the group turned a skeletal stare back at them before racing away.

Javier waved a parting gesture to the other figure, then turned his attention to Atreau and Narsi.

"That's done and dusted," Javier called to them. "What's ahead is what matters now. Come quickly now."

They raced after him. Steadily the sweltering flames and broken ground gave way to the dull, moldering gray expanse that Atreau had experienced previously. Javier's expression seemed to relax a little and his pace slowed. Plumes of blue mist swirled near them. Clammy dread filled Atreau as blue haze condensed into a smoky figure. Then Javier gave a backhanded flick of his long fingers and white light gushed up, burning the blue mist away.

"We've no more time for the past or its ghosts," Javier muttered. Then he drew to a stop and glanced between Narsi and Atreau. The hopeful look in his dark, boyish gaze was so unusual that it startled Atreau a little. "It's all up to the two of you now. Take care of each other."

Javier swept his arms out as if he was pulling aside heavy drapes and the gray surroundings tore apart to reveal a night sky full of stars and the grounds of an opulent garden, filled with bright lanterns and music. Before them a bower of fragrant roses hung over a white pebble path. A silk lantern threw gold light across Atreau's cheek and lit the sleek lines of Narsi's mask. Distant laughter wafted over them like the perfume of flowers. Narsi's hand brushed against his own, then the two of them stepped out into a cool night breeze. Javier and the Sorrowlands vanished behind them.

A lithe black cat walked toward them on the white pebble path. Hylanya had possessed Tariq's body to come find them.

Just beyond the rose bower Ariz stood dressed in blue and black vestments that fit his body so well it surprised Atreau. An unusual copper luster tinged his thick hair, and his normally passive face betrayed a brief but shocking expression of hatred. His left hand shook as he gripped a folded note, while his right clenched the hilt of his short sword.

Next to him, dressed in white silk festooned with golden streamers, Hierro Fueres stood holding a black half mask. He leaned in to Ariz, and for an instant Atreau thought—nearly hoped—that Ariz would draw his blade and plunge it into Hierro's chest. Instead Ariz's face convulsed with pain. Hierro smiled and lay the mask over Ariz's face.

"Kill anyone who tries to stop you," Hierro whispered, then he strode away, leaving Ariz's murderous figure to Atreau and Narsi.

CHAPTER
TWENTY-SIX

Ariz glared at Hierro's broad back as if pinpointing a target. If he were ever given the chance, he knew exactly where he'd plunge his sword. The brand smoldered through his chest as Ariz entertained the thought, but he didn't look away. He'd been told not to read his orders until Hierro was completely out of his sight. So now, he strained for every second that he could delay, squinting after flashes of Hierro's white-and-gold costume. Ariz didn't know why Hierro required him to wait. Possibly he wanted to ensure that he wasn't on hand to take any blame when Ariz took action. Or maybe Hierro simply desired a little time to find a good position from which to observe Ariz execute his command.

The golden lanterns strung through the gardens only offered so much light and figures were easily hidden by foliage lining the winding paths. In minutes, Hierro disappeared through an archway of roses to join the frolicking crowd gathered in the Royal Star Garden.

Against his will Ariz's fingers started to unfold Hierro's note.

He closed his eyes before he could see the words. Immediately, the pain smoldering in his chest intensified. Searing blades seemed to punch into him, piercing his heart and lungs. He gritted his teeth, struggling to drag in slow, agonized breaths.

Still, he resisted reading the note.

His muscles began to jerk and twitch of their own accord. His eyelids flicked open and he clenched them shut again, but not before he glimpsed the three simple words written across the pale paper.

Kill Fedeles Quemanor

Ariz crumpled the note, unable to bear seeing the words.

No. He wouldn't do it.

He trembled as blazing agony engulfed his chest and scorched through his nerves. Flames invaded his bloodstream and his bones felt as if they were cracking apart like charred kindling. Still, he refused to move.

This one thing, he would not do. He swore it to himself. Never. He'd die first. He gripped the hilt of his short sword. The steel pommel felt like ice against his fevered skin. He thought of Fedeles, of holding him against his chest last night on Crown Hill and feeling astounded by the man's strength and his compassion. He'd been so awed by his beauty and his affection. If he wasn't worth dying for, then nothing in the world was, Ariz decided.

At the same time, it was Fedeles who made Ariz desperately want to live. Just to see him once more, to feel his lips, to taste his skin. Ariz felt tears welling up behind his eyelids, but they didn't fall.

He couldn't afford self-pity. For both their sakes he needed to hold on to his resolve.

Strangely, a little of his pain abated, almost as if a cool shadow had fallen over him, shielding his body from a raging fire. Could just the thought of Fedeles affect him so strongly? Then from across the garden grounds he caught Fedeles's voice drifting between musical notes and laughter. He spoke Ariz's name in a quiet questioning tone. Ariz couldn't pick out all of what Fedeles said, but he guessed that Fedeles was looking for him specifically.

Horror surged through Ariz. After Hierro's taunts this afternoon, he had to know this was a trap; he had to know what danger Ariz posed to him. Yet he'd still come for Ariz. He was so caring and brave and so foolishly sentimental.

There was only one way to protect Fedeles. He had to act before Fedeles found him. His hands trembled as he began to draw his sword.

Suddenly someone jostled into him from behind.

Ariz's eyes snapped open. Under the flickering lantern light, all he saw at first was a mound of bright feathers and the profile of a gold mask. Soft cloth brushed over his arm while a warm, muscular body stumbled into him and then staggered back. A hand caught Ariz as if to steady him, but at the same time someone tugged the note from his fingers. Another hand pushed his sword back down into its scabbard.

There were two of them, Ariz realized in an instant. Both of them strong but hardly expert assassins. The hand restraining his sword was far too gentle, the grip on his shoulder much too easy to break free from.

But Ariz didn't resist. Let them kill him. It would save him the trouble.

He released his sword hilt and relaxed, waiting to feel the thrust of a dagger invading his burning chest, the sweep of a razor edge opening his throat or even poison needles punching under his skin. It didn't matter how they killed him, he welcomed it. Fedeles would be safe from him.

But all Ariz felt were long feathers brushing past him and steadying hands. One of the men even pushed the note back into Ariz's palm. And then both men stepped away, leaving Ariz slightly jostled, but otherwise untouched.

"You dropped your note," one of the two men said. Ariz knew the voice. He stared at the lithe man clad in the gold plumes of a Yuanese phoenix. Master Narsi gazed back at him from behind a golden mask. From the curve of his eyes, Ariz thought he might be smiling.

Ariz looked to Master Narsi's companion. It took him a moment longer to discern Atreau Vediya's features from within the fluffy fox costume. He'd shorn his hair and completely dispensed with that delicate rose scent that normally clung to him.

"The light here is poor," Atreau whispered. "You ought to read it again nearer to the lantern, don't you think?"

Ariz shook his head, but meeting Atreau Vediya's intense stare, he felt uncertain. Why would either of them want him to read Hierro's orders? Maybe they didn't realize who the note had come from. Or . . .

He was in so much pain and his thoughts so tangled that for an instant a strange paranoia seized him. Could the two of them have been working as agents for Hierro all along?

Ariz dismissed the idea at once. Master Narsi's medications had helped him defy Hierro. Atreau Vediya had exposed and fought Hierro's assassins only yesterday.

But they were without question up to something. Master Narsi in particular wasn't much of an actor. His stance was too rigid, and even wearing a mask, his eyes gave away his tension.

They had to be here to stop him from obeying Hierro's command. Only that made sense, but then why have him read the note again? Why not kill him when they had the chance and be done? Would they attempt something so clumsy as to hand him a note filled with different instructions and then hope he could somehow mistake that for Hierro's original orders? He'd already seen the message. As much as he wanted to, he couldn't pretend that it had been something else. The brand didn't give him that freedom.

Another shudder rocked through Ariz's chest. Hierro had ordered him to kill anyone who attempted to stop him. He swept his sword arm out and both of them darted back from him, clearing his way down the pebble path. Ariz clenched the note in his left hand.

"Isn't it important enough to look at twice?" Narsi asked. "You don't want to make a mistake, Master Ariz."

Ariz considered Narsi. If anyone could be trusted, it was him. At this point, what harm would reading the note a second time do?

Ariz strode to the circle of light beneath the nearest lantern and lifted the crumpled note. He read it. Then he stood stunned, staring at it. There was no question that this was Hierro's handwriting. The paper and ink looked the same as well. The three words written across the white paper appeared identical to the ones Ariz had first read.

Or *nearly* identical.

Two letters curled more than he'd originally thought. The difference in appearance was minute but vast in meaning. He read it again, and then once more.

Kiss Fedeles Quemanor. Not kill, but kiss.

Ariz wanted urgently to believe this was Hierro's order and that he'd misread it the first time. But how could it be possible? The corner of his mind that Hierro ruled over churned with suspicion. Why would Hierro demand something like this of him?

At the same time, how could Atreau or Narsi have possibly created a forgery?

Neither of them had come near Hierro anytime today, much less crept into the dressing room where he'd written out this order. And the note had only been out of Ariz's hand for an instant. Before that, neither Narsi nor Atreau could have known the exact wording of Hierro's order, much less seen the size and kind of paper Hierro used.

Ariz stared at the words. *Kiss Fedeles Quemanor.* Ariz wanted it to be true so badly that he felt almost sick. Could he convince himself that this was Hierro's order?

He concentrated on the possibility.

Perhaps Hierro planned to catch them together and expose Fedeles before the king and his court. A single kiss during a night of revelry wouldn't amount to much, but if they went further....

Ariz thought back to the time he and Fedeles had kissed. He recalled the thrill of Fedeles's hands stroking his back and caressing his thighs. Arousal surged through him at just the recollection. Yes, a kiss could easily lead to much more.

Hierro would certainly expect to take full advantage of anyone he stooped to kiss. In addition, Hierro enjoyed humiliating other people, especially earnest and sensitive ones. And while Fedeles's affairs with men were the subject of speculation and eager gossip among worldly social circles, the majority of courtiers had never been confronted with any evidence of them. Prince Jacinto would laugh it off, but the likes of Lord Bayezar and the noble Estaban brothers would be aghast. Publicly exposing Fedeles like that could cost him political support and even see him jailed. Even if the king's favor and his title saved him from criminal prosecution, he might still face censure from the church.

So...

It wasn't impossible that Hierro penned this order. Perhaps Clara had suggested it to him as a way to destabilize Fedeles's hold over the court. During the last two days Fedeles had won the respect of several powerful lords. Lliro Vediya's unexpected support had even pulled over a number of conservative ministers.

". . . Ariz Plunado, dance instructor." Again Fedeles's voice drifted through the flowering bowers and darkness. Ariz pivoted in his direction.

At the same time he was conscious of Atreau and Narsi observing him. An odd glance passed between them. Then Atreau knelt to stroke a lanky black cat that came prowling out of the underbrush. Narsi smiled at the animal, and Ariz recalled that the physician kept a pet cat very much like this one. The animal was even wearing a collar.

"Ollivar should already be at the stable with the horses. The sooner you get across the Gado Bridge and see the others, the safer you will be." Atreau stood and extended his hand to Narsi. "I can take care of matters here. Leave it with me."

"You're sure?" Narsi stood very still.

"Positive," Atreau replied.

Narsi slid his medical satchel down from his back, withdrew a vial and handed it to Atreau. Ariz couldn't help but note Atreau's fingers linger on Narsi's hand in a brief caress. Narsi leaned in toward Atreau. He didn't remember the two of them being so comfortable or intimate with each other this morning.

"Go on. I'll meet you there." Atreau released Narsi very deliberately. The physician turned and strode away, with the black cat trotting alongside him.

Ariz gazed at the vial in Atreau's hand. Last night's conversation rang through Ariz's mind. *A lethal dose of duera added to one of Master Narsi's vials . . . I would drink and be done.* He'd assured Atreau that he'd end his life when the time came. His surprise at the speed of Atreau's decision was short lived. By now, both Atreau and Master Narsi knew what he'd done at the Slate House. After witnessing that, what choice could they make other than putting an end to him?

So that was why the two of them were here and why Master Narsi had seemed so awkward and uneasy. Their presence had nothing to do with Hierro's note. Would that mean that the order to kiss Fedeles truly was Hierro's command?

Ariz really had misread the note. The realization horrified him.

He'd so expected Hierro to demand Fedeles's death that he'd simply assumed the worst. With Hierro's cruelty steadily corrupting his mind, who knew what mistake he'd make next? He couldn't go on like this.

He considered the vial in Atreau's hand. Swallowing a mouthful of poison offered an easier escape than slitting his own throat; he ought to be thankful for that.

"That's for me, isn't it?" Ariz asked.

Atreau nodded and stepped closer to Ariz. His gaze was wary and his movements very careful—anticipating resistance.

"Don't worry. I know how bad off I am," Ariz held out his hand for the vial. "I'll take my medicine."

Atreau handed it to him and Ariz pulled the stopper free before he could think too much about it.

"Wait!" Atreau caught his hand. His fingers felt warm and slightly damp.

Ariz frowned at him; then he recognized the regret in Atreau's eyes. His hesitance was touching, but delaying the matter would only make it harder.

"No point in dragging this out," Ariz said.

"You should go to him first." Atreau took the cork stopper from Ariz and sealed the vial in his hand. "Give him something to remember, otherwise he'll be left with only missed opportunities and regrets."

Ariz didn't have to ask who Atreau meant. After last night, they both knew.

"I can't." Ariz held the note out to Atreau.

Atreau glanced over it.

"Hierro wants to use me as a trap to drag him down. Probably publicly expose the two of us. Fedeles is safer if I stay away." Even as he spoke, Ariz unconsciously took several steps in Fedeles's direction. Hierro's command poured over Ariz's own deep longing like oil feeding an open flame.

A branch of dangling roses caught the shoulder of his costume. As he pulled free, a thorn grazed his cheek. The pain roused his self-awareness. He forced himself to stop. He was so much more practiced at resisting pain than the promise of even a moment's happiness.

"If he aims to expose you and Fedeles in an intimate embrace, then he would need someone to keep a look out for at least one of you, correct?" Atreau asked.

Ariz nodded. He and Atreau both studied the surrounding shadows, watching them dance as hanging lanterns swayed in the gentle night breeze.

"And I'd bet that it's you whom they'd watch for, rather than Fedeles, since Hierro is more likely to know how you'll be dressed during the Masquerade."

Ariz nodded again. He supposed he shouldn't be shocked or impressed by how much Atreau could infer in a matter of moments; the man had been unraveling Hierro's plots and foiling his agents for years. It followed that between the night gloom and the vast expanse of the gardens, Hierro's agents would be hard pressed to distinguish Fedeles from the multitude of other masked and costumed noblemen in attendance. But Hierro had chosen the mask and clothes Ariz now wore. His appearance—his eye-catching vest in particular—was what they would watch for.

"May I offer my services to mislead their interests?" Atreau asked.

"Yes." Ariz decided. "Give me your clothes."

"Master Ariz, are you hoping to employ the marvelous endowments of my naked body to distract any and all onlookers?" Atreau teased. Not even his mask could hide the way his brows rose in an amused smile.

A dry laugh escaped Ariz. He shook his head.

"Hierro chose this costume. I have to assume his agents will be watching for it to lead them to Fedeles."

"Perfect." Atreau grinned and handed over his mask. "I'll seek out my brother Lliro and see if his men can't keep Hierro's spies busy for an hour or so before I slip into something more comfortable."

Ariz stripped off his vest as he spoke. He handed it to Atreau and then quickly unlaced the absurdly tight breeches. Atreau didn't object. Instead he busied himself exchanging clothes. Ariz took a moment to admire how very quickly the other man could undress and then how considerate he was in assisting Ariz with his own new costume. He offered Ariz a charming smile as he secured the two combs that supported the fox ears in Ariz's hair.

If he were desperate, Ariz thought, Lord Vediya could probably make a living working as a valet. He certainly displayed greater care than Hierro's attendants had shown. And he'd somehow fashioned the silky clothes that Ariz had found awkward and binding into a striking black-and-silver costume for himself.

Ariz, on the other hand, felt somewhat absurd. He couldn't completely close the russet velvet vest across his broad chest, and he'd bobbed the long tail to keep it from tangling his steps.

"You look more like a short-tailed cat than a fox." Atreau's expression struck Ariz as uncharacteristically regretful as he toyed with the mask Ariz had given him. "A pity we couldn't all have known each other under other circumstances, Master Ariz. I might have written a nice part for you in Jacinto's play. Opposite Narsi you two—"

The prince's name suddenly roused Ariz's memory.

"Hold up! I have to tell you—warn you." Ariz lowered his voice. "Earlier this evening Captain Yago sought out Prince Remes for permission to suppress the Haldiim Solstice celebrations. He was particularly focused on Prince Jacinto's possible presence there. Prince Remes assured him that he would not be deemed responsible were he to injure or even kill Prince Jacinto."

Atreau's expression fell. He seemed struck silent with horror.

"Master Narsi could be endangered, and that actress . . . Mistress Yara, as well." As Ariz considered it, he recognized that Captain Yago threatened too many people for him to name individually or for Atreau to hope to protect. "Do what you can to keep them all as far from the sacred grove as possible. That's where Yago and his men will focus their attention."

Atreau looked sick, but then he blew out a weary breath.

"Thank you for the warning," he said. "I'll . . . figure something out."

Ariz nodded and carefully tucked the vial of poison into his jacket pocket. Then he turned and started along the white pebble path in the direction of Fedeles's voice. As he walked, the longing he'd suppressed for years broke free. His heart pounded and his pulse raced, but for once it wasn't pain or fear that compelled him. Memories of Fedeles's lips against his own—his body pressed so close that Ariz could feel his heartbeat—ignited a desperate need to reach the other man. To hold him, to feel his touch, and taste him.

The last of Ariz's restraint broke. He shot ahead, racing over the pebbled path.

CHAPTER
TWENTY-SEVEN

A flash of bloody lips and white teeth descended from the darkness of a flowering hedge. Rough bristles swept past Narsi's face as he sprang aside. A shout caught in his throat. The cat at his side yowled and arched its back.

The snarling mouth and gleaming tusks of their assailant swept past. Then the shaggy head struck the pebble path. It bounced and rolled. A trail of ribbons followed it, tangling in the fur. One of the button eyes remained at Narsi's foot. Narsi's heart hammered in his chest, but a dry laugh escaped him. Their adversary was nothing but a boar-head mask that had toppled from the hedge where it had been mislaid.

The visions from the Old Road had left him shaken and jumpy. Narsi sighed and tried to relax a little. The gold scars bisecting his palms tingled and Narsi stretched his fingers to ease the weird tension in his hands. A flock of birds winged overhead and Narsi thought he heard larks singing. Unusual for them to be active at this hour, though far from the weirdest thing about this evening.

Gradually, the tingling in his hands faded—though it didn't disappear completely.

Tariq—whether on the cat's own initiative or under Lady Hylanya's control—stalked to the fallen mask, sniffed it once and then indulged in a frenzy of swatting it. At last Tariq jumped back and prowled to Narsi's side. He knelt and stroked the cat's chin and back until it calmed enough to continue leading him through the dark maze of the palace gardens.

He tried to soothe his own unease as well, noting the numerous other pieces of clothes and costumes that lay scattered on the ground and over bushes. The sounds of laughter and splashing made him think that groups of revelers had stripped to play in the fountains. Though there was a slightly unnerving quality to some of the voices—excited cries sounded so much like genuine screams in the cacophony of music, song and turbulent water.

Every few yards Narsi glimpsed strange apparitions moving between the topiaries and hedges. Winged rams, horned lions, serpents adorned in flowers and a multitude of weird hybrids of human bodies and animal faces. The faint light and dancing shadows lent even the coarsest costumes a living quality.

A Cadeleonian man with a hound mask pushed up to the top of his head took on a terrifying two-faced appearance—snarling lips and white teeth jutting from his brow, like a beast tearing out of his body. The man's expression struck Narsi as dazed. He trembled and a look of panic came over him. He stumbled toward Narsi.

Was he yet another enthralled assassin? Cold sweat rose at the nape of Narsi's neck as he fought the reflex to bolt. Instead he backed away slowly, watching the man's contorted face and agonized expressions. All at once the man lurched over and vomited into a flower bed.

What would have repulsed Narsi any other day now seemed blessedly mundane. He continued on his way. More than once he nearly overtook Tariq in his desire to get out of this dim maze. He would have laughed at himself for struggling so intensely to simply walk at a seemingly natural pace, except that the anxiety racing through his body truly felt overwhelming.

If he hadn't spent the last two weeks practicing a composed gait with Atreau, he didn't think he would have managed it.

Fortunately, the nearer he came to the stables, the fewer revelers he encountered. Some servants in royal liveries hurried past and a number of guards stood keeping watch, but that was all. Narsi followed Tariq, edging around them and working his way toward the back of the stables. A man in a priest's robe hurried in his direction. Narsi almost dodged into the cover of a hedge to avoid him, but when the priest passed under a lantern, Narsi relaxed. He waited for Berto to catch sight of him.

"Narsi? It's you, isn't it?" he asked in a whisper, though there was a little uncertainty in his face.

Narsi nodded, lifting his mask to give Berto a smile.

"Oh, thank God! I've been waiting for you near the stables for hours." Berto clasped his shoulder and leaned close. Despite the soft lamplight, Narsi noticed the dark circles under Berto's eyes. His skin looked waxy. If he'd slept recently, it hadn't been much. He didn't number among Atreau's agents, so Narsi wasn't sure why he would be here now.

"What's wrong? Is it Father Timoteo?"

"No. It's you that's in danger." Berto stole a glance back toward the stables, then went on. "Earlier this evening a troop of royal bishop's guardsmen came searching for you, by name. Delfia told me that they're stopping people at the city gates and even on the Gado Bridge."

Fine hairs all over Narsi's body stood up as fear shot through him. If the royal bishop's guardsmen took him prisoner before he could use Yah-muur's horn, then everything would be lost. He'd need to avoid the Gado Bridge. At the same time, he had to get across the river to reach the sacred grove.

Could he hire a boat? Not likely at this hour.

Narsi's thoughts raced on the edge of panic. But then he drew in a calming, slow breath and reminded himself that this wasn't his endeavor alone. He wasn't without resources or allies. There were other people he could count on. Not the least was Berto, racing out and waiting for hours to give him this warning. Narsi felt somewhat guilty for having thought of Berto so infrequently the last few weeks.

The instant he relaxed, a solution came to him. Morisio belonged to the crew of a ship, and it was moored here in the capital. Surely they'd have at least a dinghy.

"It's fine," Narsi said, as much to himself as Berto. "I can get around the bridge."

"No, Narsi, you don't understand. Right now, there are two men in the royal stable waiting to ambush you. They claimed to have been sent by Atreau to fetch both your mounts from the duke's household, but they gave me a bad feeling," Berto whispered. "I followed them here to warn you."

"They're not royal bishop's guardsmen, are they?" Narsi asked. Atreau's friends—Ollivar and Morisio—were supposed to meet them, but Berto's agitation made him uncertain.

"They didn't look like guardsmen, more like mercenaries. Their hair was too long and one sported a beard. Both wore swords and seemed ready to use them. I truly don't think they mean you any good."

Narsi turned slightly, considering the dark building. Should he wait for Atreau to join him, just to be safe? If the friends Atreau had sent had been ambushed, there could be a trap awaiting them in the stable. Could Hierro or Clara have learned of their plan? But if they had, wouldn't they have dispatched more than two men to intercept Narsi and Yah-muur's horn?

"This is all my fault. There must be a way to get you back to Anacleto," Berto whispered. "I'm so sorry, Narsi. I didn't think it would get so out of control."

"What are you talking about?" Narsi turned back to Berto to see that his friend had buried his face in his hands.

"You remember when you first arrived in Cieloalta, and I told you that Father Timoteo had angered the royal bishop? It was worse than the argument I described," Berto murmured. "The royal bishop was preparing to decry Father Timoteo. To have him excommunicated—"

"What? Why didn't he tell me about this?" Narsi demanded. Excommunication amounted to disinheritance and exile. "Why didn't you tell me?"

"I hardly had time to say five words to you before you went off with Atreau Vediya," Berto snapped, then he shook his head. "And Father Timoteo didn't want to worry you because he didn't intend to pay the royal bishop's threats any heed. No matter what any of us might have said to him, he still would have refused to submit to the royal bishop. He wouldn't make even the slightest overture of obedience."

Narsi knew Father Timoteo well enough to recognize that Berto's words were absolutely truthful.

"But his whole life is tied to the church—and not just his but mine, and those of all his acolytes. The refugees he's sheltered, the priests and nuns who support his sermons. So many people look to him and depend upon his protection and benevolence. Even you, Narsi." Berto lifted his head to gaze up at the dark sky, his expression miserable. "I *had* to do something. Anything to reassure the royal bishop of Father Timoteo's loyalty to the church. And then that night when we thought you might die, I saw the letter in your room . . ." Berto trailed off for a moment. "How else could I have convinced the royal bishop to stop his attacks on Father Timoteo and elevate him to bishop?"

Narsi stared at him as a terrible idea slowly unfolded in his mind. The night he'd been poisoned, Atreau had mentioned Berto looking at his mother's letter to Father Timoteo. Soon after that, the royal bishop had dispatched agents to the Salt Islands to uncover the Grunito family's secret. Mere days later the royal bishop had at last granted Timoteo the rank of bishop. Had the royal bishop only been willing to do so because he planned to use that secret—Narsi's existence—to threaten and control Timoteo?

In a flash, Narsi understood that Berto had betrayed him, and yet it didn't seem real. He stood staring at Berto, so stunned that he couldn't feel the hurt of it yet.

"I didn't tell them your name. Or even that you were here in the capital," Berto blurted out. "I thought they'd end up wandering all over the

Salt Islands and eventually give up. I swear, Narsi, I didn't—" Berto cut himself off, staring wide-eyed over Narsi's shoulder. Narsi turned around, but his thoughts were slow, still dazed.

A tall man in black silk charged from an arbor and launched himself at Berto. With two fast blows he sent Berto sprawling across the path. The attack came so quickly and so brutally that Narsi almost mistook the man for Master Ariz.

"You sack of shit!" The voice was unmistakably Atreau's.

Narsi had never seen him lash out at another person with such intense violence. He had to grab Atreau's arm and haul him back before he could land more than one kick into Berto's crumpled body. Atreau resisted him for only a moment, then clasped Narsi into a hard embrace. Narsi felt Atreau's muscles shaking with rage.

"Just say the word and I'll end him for you," Atreau whispered.

"Did you take on Master Ariz's calling along with his clothes?" Narsi teased.

"For you, I'd gladly do so." Atreau's lips brushed his ear. "You're too forgiving and too sympathetic. Someone needs to take offense on your behalf."

Somehow he sounded both angry and caring at once. Narsi was unexpectedly moved. A wave of heat rose across his face. It was absurd. Narsi pulled out of Atreau's arms before anyone could see them. The scene would be hard enough to explain as it was.

"Let me see your hands," Narsi demanded.

Atreau held them out and Narsi carefully examined his knuckles. They felt hot. Likely his right hand would show bruises by morning, but nothing seemed broken.

"Don't go hurting yourself on my account," Narsi said. "It only makes more work for me."

Atreau squeezed his hand once briefly, then released him and turned the full force of his glower on Berto.

"I have Jacinto and his flock on my heels, so you need to decide what you want to do with him," Atreau explained.

Narsi nodded, then went to Berto and knelt at his side.

Berto lay on his back staring up miserably at Narsi. Blood poured from Berto's nose, but he did nothing to stanch it. Narsi sighed, swung his medical satchel down and cleaned up Berto's face. Out of the corner of his eye he could see Atreau's scowl.

While he cleaned Berto's face and helped him to sit up, Atreau turned and waved to a group of people farther away on the path.

"I'm sorry. I really am—" Berto whispered.

"You wanted to protect Father Timoteo. I understand," Narsi replied. Hurt and anger churned in his chest, like jagged glass and smoldering embers. He wanted to punch Berto himself, and at the same time he felt so disheartened that even the simple task of closing up his satchel and straightening it against his back required all his concentration.

The sleek black cat butted its head against his ankle. Narsi stroked its head and calmed himself. What use was it to lash out now? It wouldn't change anything. Wallowing in sorrow would only waste time.

If he'd been in Berto's position, would he have done the same thing? Narsi considered the idea. He wouldn't have, he decided. But only because it wouldn't have occurred to him as a strategy. Did that make him more moral than Berto, or just less inventive?

"You must leave the city," Berto told him. "I have some money saved. I can buy passage—"

"I've made a commitment. I can't run away." Narsi glanced back, studying the group of people Atreau beckoned to them. Despite their masks and glittering costumes, Narsi recognized Yara and Prince Jacinto right away. Behind them came Sabella, Inissa and the Helio brothers, as well as a large number of others in gaudy costumes whom he couldn't identify with certainty. But most struck him as familiar figures from Prince Jacinto's entourage. Actors, actresses and even a pair of duelists heralding from the Red Stallion. Normally they all seemed to vie for the prince's attention and hang on his every word, but right now most eyes were on Atreau. Narsi wondered how many of them, like himself, were actually his agents. Or might some be spies for their enemies?

"If you want to put things right between us, then stay at Father Timoteo's side," Narsi went on before any of the people approaching could overhear him. "If things go badly tomorrow, you must do everything you can to protect him. Even if that means dragging him out of the city."

Berto looked troubled but didn't question Narsi; he simply nodded.

Narsi took his hand and helped Berto back onto his feet, then he released him.

He didn't know that their friendship would ever recover, but the fact that he was able to set his hurt and anger aside made him wonder if he hadn't always held a little trust back from Berto. They'd been close as boys, but those days had passed on long ago. Now, losing the affection of shared nostalgia brought Narsi only a little pain.

"You should go, while Atreau's still distracted," Narsi told him.

"But the men in the stable—" Berto objected.

"They're my friends," Narsi replied coolly. It wasn't quite the truth. He hardly knew Ollivar or Morisio. But Narsi couldn't resist the small, spiteful urge to jab at Berto; maybe he wasn't as reconciled as he wanted to think.

Berto bowed his head.

"Will you assure Father Timoteo that I'm fine?" Narsi asked.

"I will," Berto said. "And I swear I won't let anything happen to him."

With that he took his leave, and Narsi turned to quietly claim his place at Atreau's side. He hardly noticed the small songbirds that trailed them and was too distracted to think about the tingling sensations that shivered across his scarred palms.

Chapter Twenty-Eight

Atreau walked close to Narsi as they strode toward the stables. Jacinto and his company trailed behind, which suited Atreau for the time being. It would have been even better if Jacinto hadn't brought so many people along, though Atreau supposed he was lucky that Jacinto hadn't been buried in an orgy or too drunk to stand when he'd found him.

"We have to change our plan," Atreau whispered to Narsi.

"Agreed. Do you think they're searching for me elsewhere?" Narsi's tone was calm. Only the uneasy way his fingers moved over the strap of his medical satchel betrayed his agitation. As he spoke, he absently stretched his fingers. "Or just at the city gates and the Gado Bridge?"

"They won't waste men elsewhere," Atreau decided. "Between the gates and the bridge, they can control the movements of the majority of the people in the city."

Atreau scowled. They'd spent weeks arranging to get Narsi to the sacred grove and then into the Shard of Heaven. Everything hinged on Narsi and those two locations. If Yago captured Narsi, nothing could stop Javier's apocalyptic visions from unfolding.

Just thinking of the possibility made Atreau want to chase Berto down and kick the man to death. The smoldering anger in his chest sparked and he kicked at the pebbles under his feet. The fact that Atreau himself had once wrestled with the idea of sacrificing Narsi's life for the sake of the nation only made him all the more outraged. Within days of meeting Narsi, Atreau had realized that the man was too smart and too courageous to treat like some thoughtless pawn. Berto, who'd known Narsi since childhood, ought to have understood the value of him all the more. No one could hope for a better, more worthy ally. Even putting aside his physical beauty and charming company, Narsi was undeniably clever and up for a challenge. He was loyal and compassionate enough to fight to free a man like Ariz. But when he saw the danger Ariz posed, he also summoned the resolve to stop him. How many other men would have shouldered that burden with Atreau? How many would have risked their lives to carry Yah-muur's Horn without the promise of any recognition for their valor?

If Berto had confided in Narsi from the start, then no doubt Narsi would have stepped up to help him protect Timoteo. And he would have come up with a better plan than handing over secrets that threatened the entire Grunito family—including Narsi and Timoteo. Just thinking of it infuriated Atreau.

A man like Berto didn't deserve Narsi's concern, much less his friendship.

"Can we use a jolly boat from Morisio's ship to avoid the royal guardsmen on the Gado Bridge?" Narsi asked.

Atreau decided to add resilience to his running list of Narsi's admirable traits. Even after discovering that Berto had betrayed him, Narsi still managed to keep his wits. There had been no missing the shock and hurt in his expression earlier, but now he appeared collected. Atreau set aside his own anger. They faced more immediate problems than just Berto's incompetence.

"I have access to a captain's gig from the Royal Navy. No one should bother us if we cross aboard that," Atreau whispered.

"Your brother provided it?" Narsi asked.

Atreau nodded. He'd never spoken at length about Lliro, but it was like Narsi to remember everything he'd said even in passing.

"However, Ariz warned me of another complication. That's why I've brought Jacinto along—" Atreau halted in front of the stables. Two young grooms stood on watch at the open doors. Just beyond them, Atreau picked out Ollivar's stout figure and Morisio's lankier form. Both of them lounged near a rack of tack. They exchange Hellions hand signs as silent greetings. Ollivar also offered Narsi a shy wave of his hand. Morisio's eyes narrowed as he took in Jacinto and his obtrusive entourage.

"I'll explain everything soon," Atreau whispered to Narsi. "Once our party isn't quite so large or boisterous."

Fortunately Morisio had already employed his encyclopedic knowledge of wild grains to bore the majority of grooms and stable boys off to other duties far from him. As Jacinto and his noisy retinue flooded into the stables, Ollivar took advantage of the two grooms' confusion to whisk Narsi back to the stalls where his and Atreau's mounts were stabled. The black cat slunk after them.

In the meantime, Atreau dispatched the throng of assorted actors, actresses, musicians and mercenaries to acquire carriages and pony carts, claiming that the prince needed them to secure spots near the Gado Bridge for Jacinto to observe the midnight fireworks. That busied both hangers-on and the staff of the royal stables. Atreau hoped that all the departures would serve as decoys as well. He waited to ensure that Procopio in particular had departed.

While the front of the stables descended into a chaos of activity, Atreau and Morisio escorted the six remaining people back to the narrow aisle of the royal stable where Narsi and Ollivar awaited them.

Yara and Inissa stood on either side of Jacinto. Enevir and Cocuyo hung back behind the prince. Sabella came last, with one hand draped over the hilt of her sword.

All of them wore costumes, even Ollivar and Morisio, and though they'd removed their masks, the group of them made for an outlandishly resplendent gathering amid the bales of straw and heaps of drying horse shit. Atreau smiled. There was something almost comedic about such a flamboyant assembly lurking between rows of horse stalls, as if anyone could overlook them.

Cascades of ribbons, paper flowers and gold stars adorned the gold silk of Jacinto's attire, while Inissa's gown lent her the appearance of a silky serpent. Yara looked regal swathed in silver and peacock blue. The Helio twins sported silver ram horns and matching chamois leather coats. A silver goat motif topped Enevir's cane.

Atreau had discarded Ariz's glittering vest earlier. Now he, like Sabella, Morisio and Ollivar, wore dark clothes with just enough embellishment to pass for a costume. The gold and scarlet feathers of Narsi's cloak were eye-catching. But his russet clothes beneath were far from conspicuous. Already Narsi slipped off the cloak and lay it over a straw bale. Atreau leaned up against a stack of hay bales. His shoulder brushed Narsi's.

"I've just learned that Captain Yago plans to defy King Sevanyo and storm the sacred grove first thing in the morning," Atreau informed them all. "Remes personally granted him the authority. He went so far as to assure Yago that he could do away with Jacinto while he was at it."

Prince Jacinto had been leaning against a stack of straw bales toying with his large gold mask. Alarm lit his face and the mask dropped from his hands. Sabella snatched it up before it hit the ground and tossed it back onto the straw bale.

"He's plotting to murder a royal prince?" Yara's voice rose in amazement.

"Has the captain lost his mind?" Inissa spoke at the same time.

Out of the entire gathering, only Narsi didn't show any surprise. "The timing can't be a coincidence."

Atreau agreed; it was unbelievable that mere chance moved Yago to assault the sacred grove exactly when Narsi needed to be there to awaken Yah-muur's Horns. Someone had betrayed their plans, but to what extent, Atreau wasn't sure. Narsi shot Atreau a questioning glance but Atreau didn't dare offer him answers just yet.

"Yago's clearly gone mad," Jacinto exclaimed.

"Far from it," Atreau said. "If madness motivated him, then Yago wouldn't have bothered to secure Remes's permission. Nor would he have planned the attack for the morning. He'd just have ridden across the city and put the sacred grove to the torch. This is a considered action on his part—possibly a demonstration of his loyalty."

"Loyalty to whom?" Cocuyo asked.

"The men he believes will be ruling the country in a matter of days," Atreau replied, but he focused on Jacinto. He needed the prince to understand the gravity of the situation. Needed to motivate him to take an unspeakable step. "Yago wouldn't directly defy Sevanyo unless he was certain that neither Sevanyo nor any of his allies could charge him with treason after tomorrow."

"But . . . but . . ." Jacinto struggled for words as the color drained from his face.

"So, Remes and Hierro are putting their plan to seize the throne in motion right now?" Narsi asked.

Atreau responded with a nod.

"Do we know the hour Yago plans to attack the sacred grove?" Narsi's expression was strained, but his voice remained calm and his inquiry was practical.

Ever my level-headed master physician, Atreau thought.

"Only that it will be tomorrow morning," Atreau replied. "But knowing Yago, he'll strike early and with overwhelming numbers. Most likely while worshipers are in prayer. When some flee, he'll loose his men on the entire district in the name of running down agitators—"

"No! No, he can't!" Yara looked sick.

Atreau understood her horror. Nearly the entire population of the Haldiim District celebrated the Solstice at the Circle of Wisteria. In addition, this year a large number of their friends and allies planned to join them. Yago and his men would take them all. Atreau had no doubt that Yago would make the massacre at the Slate House seem merciful. At least Ariz—enthralled as he was—had spared women and children.

"Children and elders will be gathered at the sacred grove for the Solstice." Yara's hand raised to her mouth briefly, as if she were trying not to be sick. "Esfir and her family are staying the night there."

"We have to warn them," Narsi stated firmly. Atreau had arrived at the same thought but immediately recognized the problem with it.

Atreau closed his eyes and shook his head. He didn't want to see Narsi's disappointment in him.

"Yago's informants will be watching for exactly that," Atreau said. "We might manage to knock on two or three doors before we're cut down on the street."

"We must do *something*," Yara stated.

"We can't allow Yago to butcher everyone in the Haldiim District," Enevir protested at the same time.

"I know. I know." Atreau held up his hands. He studied the people standing across from him. It was easier than seeing disappointment in Narsi's face. "But the only way to beat Yago and Remes is to get ahead of them. We need to take the initiative and take out Yago's forces before they turn the entire Haldiim District into a battlefield."

Atreau settled his gaze on Jacinto's stunned face.

"You . . . you should tell all this to Papa," Jacinto stuttered. "He'll have Yago arrested—"

"Sevanyo has been warned, Jacinto. More times than I care to recall." Atreau didn't bother to hide his frustration. If only Sevanyo had possessed the determination to crush Remes or Nugalo before now, so many other lives could have been saved. "He refuses to take action. He'd rather drift in poppy dreams than believe that Remes has been systematically murdering his own family."

Jacinto flinched as if he'd been slapped in the face. He cast a questioning glance to the Helio brothers and then Sabella.

"Atreau's right," Cocuyo replied. "Recently it seems that the more evidence we present to Sevanyo, the less he wants to believe any of it."

Enevir nodded and Sabella looked resigned.

"He might come around once there's a dagger buried in his back," Sabella added. "That'll be a little late for the rest of us, though."

"There's too much at stake to just hope that Sevanyo takes action," Atreau went on. "And we don't have the time—"

"Remes wouldn't allow Yago to *actually* kill me," Jacinto blurted. "He's my big brother."

Atreau resisted the urge to lunge forward and smack him upside his head. Yara looked as if she just might do it for him. Instead she cast her gaze down at her clenched fists.

"Remes did nothing to stop Hierro's assassin from butchering Ojoito," Atreau pointed out. "They were the best of friends, but Remes sacrificed him to ensure that not even a bastard cousin survives to challenge his claim to the throne. Do you truly believe he's overlooked you?"

Jacinto blanched. His lips moved, but no words escaped him.

"We have to deal with this ourselves. Tonight," Atreau said.

Silence fell over the group as they all stood, thinking. Through the quiet, Atreau picked out the sounds of songbirds. He wondered if all the commotion in the stables had woken them. Or perhaps it was the lanky black cat, staring up into the rafters overhead. Next to him, Narsi frowned slightly and ran his thumbs over his palms as if they ached.

"Could we poison the soldiers' suppers?" Inissa asked. Yara looked hopeful at the suggestion.

"We wouldn't have to kill them, just make them too sick to fight." Yara glanced at Narsi. As a physician, he'd know the most about poisons.

"How would we discover where all of them are dining, much less get access to their dinner pots? Even if we could, there would be no way to control the dosage," Narsi replied. Again Atreau inwardly pronounced him *ever practical*. "And who knows how many innocent people we'd harm if we were indiscriminate about it."

"Narsi's right," Atreau stated. "We could spend all night spiking pots of porridge and bribing cooks, but we still wouldn't reach a third of Yago's men. We have to take more direct action against them."

"At this short of notice I can rally twenty—possibly twenty-five— reliable swordsmen from the Red Stallion. It's enough for a brief ambush, but we won't be able to hold all of Yago's men off for long," Sabella said. "And that's not even taking Hierro Fueres's hidden assassins into account."

"We need a small army," Inissa muttered.

Atreau stole a glance to Narsi and saw his hazel eyes light with inspiration—Atreau could guess what it was, because really they possessed limited options and few resources at this moment.

"There has to be somewhere we can go—somewhere safe," Jacinto muttered.

"There's always Labara," Atreau answered lightly but quite deliberately. "Neither Remes nor Hierro Fueres would dare confront Count Radulf directly. And Lady Hylanya is somewhat in your debt."

Jacinto, Cocuyo and even Inissa visibly recoiled at the suggestion.

Enevir and Yara looked thoughtful. Sabella simply exchanged glances with Morisio and Ollivar. The three of them had probably been expecting this. The black cat lounging near Narsi's feet suddenly bounded up onto a saddle rack near Atreau's shoulder.

"As a royal prince, you could request aid from the count and his sister to stop Remes from usurping your father's throne," Atreau explained. "If you lent him your royal signet, then he would carry your authority and even the Royal Navy would grant his ships entry into the city."

Shocked silence settled over them all.

Atreau petted the cat's back with feigned ease. One way or another he would deliver Jacinto's signet to Skellan. He didn't want to resort to violence, but with so many lives at stake, he absolutely would do so. And he wasn't alone.

He stole a glance to Sabella. She only awaited his order to seize Jacinto. He, Morisio and Ollivar could deal with the Helio brothers. Inissa wasn't party to Atreau's plans, but she was sensible enough not to get herself caught up in the middle of a fight. No doubt he'd horrify Narsi and Yara, but if it had to be done then he was prepared.

"Just to clarify, Atreau, you want Prince Jacinto to invite Labaran forces to enter the city and challenge the royal bishop's guardsmen?" Cocuyo frowned. "Is that what you're suggesting? Because that sounds close to the definition of treason."

"Is it though? If the enemies within our nation threaten the crown, then why can't salvation come from allies from outside the country?" Atreau resisted the urge to touch the hilt of his dagger and instead smiled at his old classmates. "War Master Ignacio once said as much, didn't he?"

Jacinto nodded in a dazed manner, while the Helio twins seemed to consider Atreau's words.

"But how could they possibly even get here in time to—" Cocuyo began, but Enevir cut him off with a light slap to his muscular shoulder.

"They're already here," Enevir stated. He looked to Morisio and Ollivar and then back to Atreau. "Aren't they?"

"You always were quick, Enevir." Morisio gave him a smile. "Though it should be made clear that they haven't come to launch an invasion—"

"Though God knows it would be within their rights!" Ollivar snapped. "Cadeleonian troops have harried the Labaran border for months now. You have no idea how much restraint Elezar has shown."

Under other circumstances Atreau would have teased him for allowing his loyalty to his upperclassman to show so easily. But now Atreau studied Jacinto, willing him to remember the grand statements he'd made in the Candioro Theater. When he'd believed his grandfather's spirit had spoken to him from the gates of paradise, he'd promised to protect the Haldiim people.

"Count Radulf and his armies have come because the Hallowed Kings are failing. Their demise will unleash a spell that could destroy us all." Atreau hoped that mentioning his sacred ancestors would spark something in Jacinto. "This isn't a matter of loyalty to any nation. It's a matter of knowing when something is wrong and having the courage to stop it."

If Jacinto or the Helio brothers had been wildly patriotic or devoted to the Cadeleonian church, then they'd have felt only outrage and rejected his proposal outright. However, they were all aware that Hylanya's concern about the state of the Shard of Heaven had been the real reason she'd been condemned. All three had played a role in Hylanya's escape. And they knew that the Hallowed Kings had deteriorated in her absence to such a point that King Juleo's soul had been lost and the royal bishop's holy ring shattered.

Atreau watched them accept the truth presented to them. Jacinto still looked worried and Cocuyo appeared a little disgruntled, but he didn't argue.

Enevir finally asked, "How is Jacinto meant to reach Count Radulf?"

"With this stone of passage." Atreau dug into his coat pocket and found the polished rock he'd been carrying for a month now. "Once you're aboard Morisio's ship, cast it onto the deck and the spell it releases will ensure your safe passage directly to Count Radulf. He'll grant you sanctuary and send his forces to defend the people of Cieloalta. But you must tell him of the immediate threat to the sacred grove."

"You described a stone of passage in your last memoir. I imagined they'd be larger." Cocuyo studied the polished rock but didn't try to take it. Enevir drew closer. But Jacinto still remained distant and uncertain.

Yara stepped up to Jacinto, took his arm and gave him a warm smile. "If you'd like, I can accompany you, Your Highness."

Jacinto's expression brightened. He took the stone.

"Count Radulf's soldiers will need someone who knows the ins and outs of the Haldiim District to guide them," Yara added, and she looked to Atreau. "I can do that, but someone must warn Esfir."

"I'll make certain that they're safe," Narsi assured her.

If only everyone were as proactive as Narsi and Yara, Atreau thought.

"Cocuyo, Enevir—" Atreau began, but Enevir cut him off.

"Yes, we'll accompany His Highness as well," Enevir stated. "According to the plan that you've clearly already laid out, is Sabella with us or with you?"

"Neither." Atreau looked to her and then to Inissa and Ollivar. "You three will take my and Narsi's mounts back across the Gado. We can't know exactly when Yago's men will strike. Sabella, your swordsmen must hold them off until the Labaran forces arrive. Inissa, will you tell Spider that he needs to begin evacuating people from the city? Ollivar—"

"I'll deal with anyone who tries to stop us on our way," Ollivar replied.

"What about you and Narsi?" Inissa asked.

"We'll take a separate route, since the royal bishop's guardsmen are searching for Narsi and me at the Gado. But we'll see you soon." Atreau almost elaborated. But then he noticed Narsi frowning and massaging his palms again. He wondered if something was disturbing the protective spells cast on him.

At the same time he noted the excited chittering of songbirds and remembered Clara Odalis's longtime habit of raising and then releasing birds all across the city. All night long he'd been hearing larks and finches, despite the darkness. All at once it occurred to him why they were awake.

Labaran witches weren't the only ones who could use little creatures as their spies, Atreau guessed.

Don't speak your secret words
Lest they be sung by little birds

Wasn't that the couplet his mother had repeated to him?

The black cat suddenly launched into the air and came down with a swallow shaking in its jaws. With a brutal bite it crushed the bird's neck, then dropped its limp body.

"Our enemies have spies all around us," Atreau said. "There's no point in talking anymore. We need to go."

CHAPTER
TWENTY-NINE

Ariz found Fedeles on the periphery of the Royal Star Garden. Here musicians provided lively melodies while courtiers and entertainers alike danced among the towering bronze astronomical models. Ariz picked out several members of Prince Jacinto's entourage cavorting wildly with various nobles and ministers. He didn't know if it was in spite of the murders at the Slate House or because of them, but most people appeared desperately drunk. Many twirled and sang along to the music with tipsy enthusiasm. One young man cast Ariz a hopeful glance and several ladies attempted to claim him for a dance.

"How can such a strapping creature be so shy?" one woman laughed, but she easily let him go. Dance partners were in abundance, and she clasped her hands around the arm of another man right away. Ariz slipped past.

Fedeles glanced in his direction, and despite the chaotic figures and the darkness of the night, he seemed to recognized Ariz at once. He held Ariz's gaze. Ariz felt his face flushing under his mask as waves of absurdly powerful desire washed through him. Then Fedeles strode through the crowd toward him, leaving his wife, her ladies-in-waiting, and the Estaban brothers behind. The closer he came, the faster Ariz's heart raced. His breath caught in his chest. As Fedeles drew alongside him, Ariz tried to distract himself, to keep from lunging ahead and publicly embracing him.

He picked out the details of Fedeles's costume. Silk ivy leaves fluttered on his shoulders and arms, while embroidered vines wound around his chest and down his long legs. A crown of bronze oak leaves and acorns glinted from his loose black hair, and gold dust shone across his high cheekbones. He made a very handsome forest spirit.

He caught Ariz's hand in his own and drew him close. The scent of his skin and cologne curled around Ariz and an almost adolescent thrill of excitement raced through Ariz's body. Restraining himself grew painful. His chest and groin filled with scalding tension as his own desire melded with Hierro's command to kiss Fedeles.

Ariz closed his eyes, thought of each of the eight parries, and took a deep breath of the cool night air. Fedeles's long fingers curled around his own. Ariz wondered how rough his calloused hands felt to Fedeles.

"Are you hurt?" Fedeles asked.

Ariz shook his head. He didn't think he could resist the order much longer. But there were so many people around them. He glanced up to see several couples pressed close and dancing. Others laughed. Servants and varlets flitted around their masters and mistresses. Then a realization came to Ariz.

As a servant he could use a display of obedience before all these people and they would think nothing of it.

He bowed his head down over Fedeles's signet ring and kissed the back of his hand. At last the blaze in his chest cooled and Ariz reclaimed his sense enough to consider their circumstances.

Glancing up, he glimpsed a flattered expression pass over Fedeles face, but then he turned a watchful gaze over the revelers surrounding them.

"Are you sure you're all right?" he asked.

Ariz nodded again. He too surveyed the people surrounding them. At the far edge of the gathering he thought he glimpsed two of Clara's ladies-in-waiting, but he couldn't readily pick out any of Hierro's favored agents. The man dressed as a snowboar resembled Procopio Nolasar, whose loyalty flipped as quickly as a tossed coin.

"Can I take you away from here without causing you harm?" Fedeles asked.

"I . . ." Ariz didn't want to separate Fedeles from the people who could protect him, but at the same time, remaining in this chaotic crowd with Hierro's agents searching for him seemed like even more of a risk. "Yes. Let's go. But the fewer people who see us the better."

Fedeles nodded. He made small gesture with his left hand—sketching a null symbol with one finger then flicking the air as if to send it flying. At the same time he tightened his grasp on Ariz's hand and led him through the crowd. As they walked, Ariz noted the way Fedeles's shadow cloaked them both. Lanterns dimmed and flickered as they passed. The people around them hardly seemed to perceive them. Only the duchess watched them go, and she merely offered Fedeles a slight smile before returning her attention to her young cousin Elenna.

Beyond the astronomical models, the number of lanterns diminished. Gloom enfolded them and Ariz listened intently for the sound of anyone trailing them. Fedeles remained focused and quiet as well. Once they reached the dense stands of trees where the royal family hunted stags and boars, only starlight illuminated the wild, weedy paths. Strains of music and conversation grew faint. Ariz could hardly see anything through the darkness. He suppressed the reflex to alter his shape and observe his surrounding through the eyes of an eagle. The last thing he wanted was to shock Fedeles and ruin the little time left to them.

And in any case, Fedeles maneuvered him safely between the towering oaks and through the maze of brambles. It was rare for Ariz to trust another person. But in Fedeles's company he relaxed his vigilance. Fedeles was kinder and more honest then himself but just as capable of dispatching his enemies. Ariz let Fedeles choose their route and destination, while he simply listened to ensure they weren't followed. Wind played through the branches of trees and an owl called from far away. The night was soothing and quiet.

At last they climbed up a rocky path, rising high enough that moonlight illuminated their surroundings and allowed Ariz to see the treetops of the woods they had just passed through.

"Is this the western slope of Crown Hill?" Ariz asked.

"Indeed," Fedeles replied. His expression seemed warm, almost affectionate. "I'm too predictable, aren't I?"

"You're loyal." Ariz gazed at the moonlit grass and swaying wildflowers. "I've grown very fond of Crown Hill as well."

"Have you?" Fedeles sounded delighted and perhaps flattered.

Ariz simply nodded.

Fedeles drew Ariz up along a narrow path and at last they came to the top of the hill, where wildflowers overran temple ruins. Fedeles pulled him into an embrace. Ariz hugged him in return. Anxiety drained from him and his muscles relaxed into Fedeles's body. How strange to feel so excited and comforted at once. After a long while, Fedeles loosened his grip and stepped back. Ariz lifted his head to study him.

"I want to send you out of the city. Outside of Hierro's immediate grasp," Fedeles said. "Right now I don't think he will have the time or energy to hunt you down."

Ariz almost argued, but what would be the point? He didn't want to waste this brief respite.

"I've already made plans to go," Ariz said, and he tossed aside the mask he wore.

"You have?" Fedeles sounded surprised but also relieved. "Where to? When do you leave? Is there anything you need?"

"I have all I need. I'll go in a few hours," Ariz said.

"Tonight?"

"Hierro's grown too brash. I can't delay any longer." Ariz slipped out of his coat and laid it out to blanket the uneven ground, then he pulled Fedeles to sit down beside him. "But I wanted to see you before I went."

"Where—" Fedeles began.

Ariz stopped his questions with a kiss. He wasn't experienced or confident. It took all his courage to simply wrap his arms around Fedeles and press his lips against Fedeles's full mouth. But the way Fedeles responded made him feel both skilled and desirable. Fedeles leaned into him, first kissing him back gently, then arousing every nerve in Ariz's body with his hot tongue and his strong hands. Ariz gripped his back, pulling him closer as he tried to emulate Fedeles's provoking kisses and caresses.

Fedeles broke away, leaving Ariz in dazed longing. The duke's skin radiated the faintest light, while his shadow curled around Ariz, tracing and teasing his body like a whisper.

"Are you sure of this?" Fedeles sounded breathless. Even in the gloom Ariz could see his face was flushed. "I don't want to hurt you, and we only have the ground for a bed."

"I don't care. I want to be with you before I go," Ariz answered in all truth.

Fedeles smiled at him as if Ariz had gifted him with a priceless treasure. Then he kissed Ariz again. His shadow enfolded them both.

Ariz expected a little pain, and was prepared to endure it as the price of a greater joy, but hurt never came. Instead comforting spells eased him, glinting iridescent as perfumed oils. He gave himself to Fedeles's gentle coaxing and then accepted his driving strength. Ariz's anxieties and hurt washed away in waves of desperate pleasure and magnificent ecstasy. Finally he relaxed into a dreamless sleep.

ฝฝฝ

Ariz woke to a serene night sky studded with starlight. His gaze drifted and he caught sight of Fedeles stretched out at his side, watching him. The moonlight and traces of gold dust lent Fedeles's naked body a luminous quality, while his loose hair spilled around him like artful strokes of black ink. His eyes seemed darker and deeper than even the night sky. Fedeles smiled at him and Ariz felt a foolish rush of delight. Such open affection radiated from his smile that it filled Ariz with wonder. How could someone like himself have inspired such an admiring expression? How fortunate was he to have won this man's regard?

Even if it was only for one night.

"The hour of unmasking is nearly upon us," Fedeles said, and he kissed Ariz lightly, then tossed aside some errant piece of Ariz's costume—one of the fuzzy ears, most likely.

"I may as well confess beforehand," Ariz responded. "I'm not a fox. I hope you aren't disappointed."

"I had my suspicions," Fedeles replied.

Ariz stretched and enjoyed the feel of Fedeles's hand sliding down the cleft of his chest to his hip. The smell of crushed flowers and sex clung to him. Ariz didn't think he'd ever felt so pleased and sated before in his life, almost as if Hierro's brand had been rinsed from his body. Though a glance down at his own skin assured him that the brand remained. It was only that Fedeles's touch allowed him to forget about it long enough to experience contentment and pleasure.

He reached out and ran his hand over Fedeles's forearm, tracing the corded muscles beneath his delicate skin. He caressed his shoulder, then lifted Fedeles's hand and kissed his wrist.

"Would you trust me to place a blessing on you?" Fedeles asked.

Ariz paused. He could feel the pulse in Fedeles's wrist racing against his lips. It was almost funny, that such a powerful man should care enough to bother asking Ariz for his permission, much less care about his answer.

"Originally that's why I wanted to bring you up here," Fedeles went on. "Much of the magic flowing through Crown Hill is still in a wild state. Flowing like water or the wind, so I don't think Hierro is as likely to notice blessings crafted here . . . but I understand if you can't stand to have any spells cast on—"

"I trust you," Ariz told him.

A brilliant smile spread across Fedeles's face. His expression was so warm, Ariz could almost feel the heat of it falling over his exposed skin. How flattering and amazing it was to think that he could inspire so much joy in Fedeles with just a sentence.

Fedeles continued to smile at him as he traced the faintest golden lines through the air and then pressed them, ever so lightly, to Ariz's skin. One against his brow, one over his heart and the last to his groin.

Then Fedeles rocked back slightly and released a long breath.

"I wish . . ." Fedeles began but then didn't go on. He simply lay back and stared up at the stars above them. Ariz stretched beside him.

"I do as well," Ariz said.

"Lord Quemanor!" a woman called from below them on the hill, shattering Ariz's sense of seclusion and sanctuary. Next to him, Fedeles went still and silent but didn't lift his hand from Ariz's lips.

"Lord Quemanor? Are you there, m'lord?" she called again, and this time Ariz recognized her voice. Elenna Ortez, Oasia's lady-in-waiting and cousin.

Fedeles remained silent.

"The path is so steep, are you certain we should keep going?" Elenna spoke again, this time more softly, addressing a companion. "He's probably not even up there."

"He's there. The duchess was certain." Delfia's voice sent a mortified jolt through Ariz.

"Hand me the lamp," Delfia said. "I'll go. I know the way."

Ariz sat up.

"I don't want her to see me like this," Ariz whispered to Fedeles.

"Don't worry. I'll go meet them," Fedeles offered, then he raised his voice and called out. "Wait there. I'm on my way down!"

Both he and Fedeles bounded to their feet and began dressing in a frantic rush. Ariz felt something crack under his boot heel as he snatched up Fedeles's discarded vest and handed it to him. Fedeles kissed him once more and then shrugged into his coat and started for the edge of the cliff. He paused and turned back, reaching out to touch Ariz's shoulder. "Will you be safe?"

"I'll be fine," Ariz reassured him. He clasped Fedeles's hand, kissed his palm, then stepped back from him and busied himself buckling his sword belt. "Save me from being embarrassed by my sister, and I will be forever in your debt."

"Gladly. Take care until we can meet again." Fedeles offered him a quick bow, then turned and descended the hill.

Ariz listened as he greeted Delfia and then Elenna. They informed Fedeles that King Sevanyo had summoned most of the inner court to gather for the hour of unmasking.

"He and the children plan to perform a dance," Elenna said. "One of Master Ariz's creations, I think."

"Yes, I remember them practicing." Affection carried in Fedeles's tone despite the trivial subject. "It's a version of a ciervaluz. Sparanzo's been nervous about the foot work, but I think he's improved greatly since . . ." The rest of Fedeles's words grew too indistinct for Ariz to pick out. Still Ariz listened to the tones of conversation. At last even that grew too faint for him to discern from the wind and rustling trees.

Ariz was left alone in the night.

At last he knelt, scooped up his coat and felt through the pocket. The lining was wet. Shards of cracked glass and the violet smell of duera were all that remained of the vial Atreau had given him. Frustration whirled through Ariz, but it didn't last. It wasn't as if poison was the only way to end a life, he of all people knew that. What infuriated him most wasn't the loss of the poison, but the fact that he had only just been with Fedeles and he already had to give that joy up.

A man so selfish that he'd endanger his lover because he can't give up his own pleasure isn't deserving of love at all.

He gripped the hilt of his dagger and slowly drew the blade. Overhead a nighthawk chased pale moths. Light breezes tossed the long grass and wildflowers surrounding Ariz. He could see why Fedeles loved this place. He sheathed his dagger. He wouldn't desecrate Crown Hill by ending his miserable life here—not when Fedeles would be the one to discover his body.

It would be better to go to the riverside and let the water carry his remains away. Or leave his corpse on Hierro's doorstep and let the bastard deal with it. He strode to the edge of the hill and threw himself into the open air.

Within the space of a breath his body shifted, arms unfurling into huge wings and eyes dilating to take in a clear view of the land beneath him. He caught a rushing updraft of wind. The lights and noise of the palace shrank away as he soared toward the darkness of the river. Below him, city bells rang out and silver fireworks burst over the waters. Bright reflections flashed and broke around the few boats plying the river's currents. On either shore throngs of people cheered and threw off their masks.

Ariz banked away from the jubilant crowds.

He flew over the Odalis lands. The air around him filled with small birds. Little flocks of three or four swelled into dozens and dozens. Soon hundreds of wings churned the air around Ariz. Nightingales and flower owls swooped around him like an escort of excited children. Larks swirled in the eddies of his wing strokes. Finches blindly trailed in his wake. All of them cried and called out long notes that flowed into each other, becoming a single song.

"Hierro is not done with you, Ariz." The voice was a strange duet between Clara and countless birds.

Ariz dived to escape the order, but his animal reflexes refused to allow his body to simply plummet to the ground. Instead he arched and twisted, veering between the branches of an oak tree and the wall of a warehouse. The birds circling him shrilled and laughed, even as several of them slammed against the stone wall and fell to their deaths.

"You will die soon enough, but not before you have ended three other lives." A trill of laughter rang around him. "You should feel honored. You have the privilege of killing a king and sparking a new empire!"

CHAPTER
THIRTY

Fedeles bounded down the hillside, his mind still drifting with thoughts of Ariz. The feel of Ariz's mouth—his slightly chapped lips parting to offer a soft heat. His hands, calloused and powerful, but his touch so very gentle and shy. Yearning turned through Fedeles like an ache as he surveyed the fragments of forgotten spells scattered all around him.

Their luminous colors were exotic blossoms scattered among the dark wildflowers. Fedeles paused, staring at the warm glow thrown off from a blessing beside his foot. Hundreds of years ago, it must have blazed like a little sun. Now it resembled an ember swathed in ashes as it loyally defended a shard of what might have once been a giant stone troll. The spell's radiance wafted over Fedeles like the scent of fresh-baked bread enticing a starving man.

He'd expended too much strength these last few days. Imbuing Ariz with such powerful blessings had left him feeling depleted, and the night wasn't over. He risked collapse unless he gathered all the power he could.

Even so, a brief sentimentality stilled his hand. Long ago someone had felt such intense care that traces of that affection lingered in the spell even now. Fedeles sensed the warmth coiled up in the rust-colored spell.

He could only hope the guardian blessings he'd kissed and caressed over Ariz could retain so much power. Thinking of Ariz, he almost left the spell.

But he couldn't afford to indulge in endless romanticism, not anymore. Fedeles bent and gently drank in the abandoned spell. He devoured more as he descended. Steadily the twinkling lights surrounding him fell into darkness.

Though they were still out of sight, awaiting him at the bottom of the winding path, Elenna and Delfia continued to converse with Fedeles. They appraised him of Sevanyo's summons and the entertainment he wished his courtiers to behold. Sevanyo had already told him that he hoped children would soften his brother's heart where adults could not. It was a wistful, sentimental tactic—not one Fedeles believed would work on the likes of the royal bishop, much less Hierro Fueres or Prince Remes. But Fedeles knew better than to argue with Sevanyo about his brother and son.

However, as soon as Fedeles rounded a turn in the path and caught sight of the women's anxious expressions, he realized that Sevanyo's midnight congregation wasn't the only reason he'd been sought out. Delfia looked agitated while Elenna appeared wan, almost unwell.

At once, Fedeles shook off the sweet languor of sex and romance. He bounded down the last stretch of the overgrown path to reach them.

"What's really the matter?" Fedeles asked quietly.

"Nothing yet," Elenna answered in a whisper. Delfia glanced meaningfully at the sky. Fedeles understood. Who knew how many spies lurked in the night. He thought he felt a cool breeze whirl over him. A wisp of foreign magic fluttered at the edge of Crown Hill. Then it was gone.

"Atreau sent his brother Lliro to warn you and the duchess that Captain Yago plans to defy the king and attack the sacred grove in the morning. He fears there will be other attacks as well. Perhaps timed to make it look as if it's a Haldiim uprising," Delfia whispered.

"Though Atreau couldn't be bothered to come in person to offer any details or assistance," Elenna grumbled, then she scowled and kneaded her stomach. Though she was only nineteen, she already strongly resembled Oasia in both her appearance and her attitude toward Atreau, it seemed. Though normally she wasn't so obvious.

"Mistress Elenna, are you unwell?" Fedeles worried she was feeling the effect of some curse. He knew that many of Oasia's ladies-in-waiting and handmaids helped her maintain the wards that protected the Que-manor household as well as the royal palace and the city at large. They'd all been under great strain since Hierro's assassins broke free last night.

"An inopportune time of the month. That's all." Elenna shook her head. "Pray, forgive my churlish tone. I'm sure Atreau has good reason for his absence. It just leaves us all in so much uncertainty."

"I understand," Fedeles assured her. "Should we stop for a little while? Until you feel better?"

Delfia cast Elenna a disapproving glance. In the hard light of the lantern, her cool gray eyes and stern features reminded him a little of Ariz. They were both so unflinching and uncomplaining that other people could seem weak and sniveling in comparison. Elenna shook her head.

"The walk will do me good, I'm sure," Elenna said. "It's more important that we reach the duchess. She's quite uneasy. Especially with the children being paraded about at Sevanyo's side and all the court gathered around them in the night."

Hearing the situation described like that, sudden alarm raced through him. His son and the Plunado twins surrounded by a sea of heartless conspirators, malevolent assassins and reckless drunks.

"Let's go quickly then," he said. They raced through the wooded grounds, eventually reaching the cut lawns and gardens surrounding the palace. The noise of fountains and distant conversation filled the air. Ambient light from scattered old spells spread before Fedeles like twilight gloaming. While Elenna and Delfia depended upon their lantern to illuminate the white pebble paths, Fedeles easily picked out the silhouettes of trimmed hedges, statuesque fountains and flowering trees. Voices and music drifting on the night breeze grew more distinct.

The sight of so many little birds winging overhead bothered him. As he tracked the shimmering teal flashes of their flights, he realized that more and more of them gathered in the distant sky. Like storm clouds they turned and rolled, slowly closing in over the Shard of Heaven.

Fedeles almost turned to pursue them. But as much as he feared another attack on the Hallowed Kings, he couldn't bring himself to abandon Sparanzo and Oasia. His agitation drove his pace. Behind him Delfia and Elenna broke into a run to keep up.

They passed between a few clusters of stumbling drunks as they rushed along the avenue of fountains. Water gurgled and lapped through the refrains of music. There should have been more people about—more royal guards in particular. Again Fedeles sensed flocks of little songbirds, their bodies fluttering with spells, veering between trees and surging ahead of him.

A sensation of vertigo gripped Fedeles, stopping him in his tracks. He swayed and steadied himself against a fountain wall. The evening breeze rushed across his skin and his body felt momentarily weightless— almost as if he was hurtling through the air. His stomach tightened as he suddenly plunged downward.

His eyes snapped open and he caught himself before he tripped into the water. Delfia and Elenna nearly crashed into him. At just the last moment Delfia pivoted, scanning their surroundings for any threat. Elenna stumbled and massaged her abdomen again.

"Sorry, I . . ." Fedeles scowled. The last two days had exhausted him, but was it possible that he'd actually lapsed so suddenly into a dream? Had he become so focused on those birds that he'd fallen into the spells moving them?

"I was distracted," Fedeles finished. He splashed cool water from the fountain onto his face. The brief vertigo passed and his head felt clear again.

They set off, sprinting past rose bowers to reach a blaze of torches and lanterns, hemmed in on two sides by a towering maze of flowering hedges. The open grounds before them boasted numerous bronze astronomical models. Each one rivaled a plum tree in height and size. Colorful parties of masked courtiers gathered around the bronze planets and moons. Here and there servants scurried through the press of bodies, carrying poppy pipes and bottles of liquor. Fedeles scanned the crowd for Oasia, but so many people had gathered that even with his height, he couldn't catch a clear view.

At last he simply leapt onto one of the bronze models—a little planet encircled by steel rings—and climbed its height to get his bearings. Beneath him a group of inebriated musicians abused a song from the *Rogues Folly* to the point of near cacophony. Delfia pushed through them, while Elenna hung back.

Not far away, the royal heir, Prince Xalvadar, lounged on silk pillows, surrounded by a dozen young courtiers dressed pearls and shells. Only his single personal guard wasn't dressed as a fantastic marine creature.

Edging into Xalvadar's entourage were the lesser nobles and guardsmen encircling the Duke of Gavado and the royal bishop. Then, to his surprise, Fedeles recognized Timoteo towering over both the duke and royal bishop. None of the three wore masks, and though Fedeles couldn't hear Timoteo, his expression was clearly angry, his gestures accusing.

Timoteo's sacrist, Berto, hunched behind his master looking fearful and agitated.

Following the direction of Timoteo's outstretched hand, Fedeles sighted Remes and Hierro. Both wore gold costumes and stood near the wall of hedges. They, too, had dispensed with their masks. Hierro seemed amused, while Remes's face brimmed with excitement. Clara was nowhere to be seen, but Fedeles sensed the flash of her teal spells settling across the branches of the surrounding trees. A smoldering quality pervaded the birds. They were almost burning with the intensity of spells bound up inside them. Sensing their growing numbers, Fedeles felt even more on edge.

"The children should be at the center of the garden. Do you see them?" Delfia shouted over the jangling notes of out-of-tune lutes.

Fedeles scrambled up from the model's rings to balance on the very top of the bronze planet. He braced his feet against miniature craters. Below him, crowds of people packed the center of the garden. Between their costumes and drunken movements, many figures appeared to merge with each other and the darkness. Reeling, swaying, their forms seemed as chaotic as the waves of slurred singing, rumbling conversation and peals of laughter.

Fortunately, the faint glow of Oasia's cerulean spells illuminated the masked figures for Fedeles. He noted many of Sevanyo's supporters gathered in dazzling clusters. The young Estaban lords lounged alongside their sisters. Fedeles frowned. Was that Suelita standing with her siblings? Ladislo Bayezar gossiped with them, but at a respectful distance. Suelita had mentioned contacting her family and making matters clear to them, but Fedeles was still surprised by how relaxed they all appeared.

Under other circumstances, Fedeles would've approached them to ensure Suelita's well-being. But right now he had more pressing concerns. He continued scanning the jumbled crowd of courtiers and attendants.

Fatigued royal guards leaned against the gold gears of the royal star-glass. One yawned and another appeared to be half dozing. At the center of the garden, occupying the stone dais where the previous king had consulted with mechanists and meteorologists, Sevanyo rose up to his feet. He spread his arms and his entire body shone like a glittering gold star. His breastplate, cloak and crown were studded with thousands of tiny mirrors, cut into the shapes of suns, moons and stars. Each reflected the surrounding lamps and torches, flashing red and gold with his every gesture. Sevanyo flared and flashed so dramatically that Fedeles had to narrow his eyes to study the children standing in two lines behind him. All ten of them were of a height and wore the same style of dark blue silk suit, silver half mask and silver spangles. They posed carefully on the balls of their feet, readying for the first steps of a dance. Fedeles stared at them intently. Which was his son?

Then, as if sensing his attention, one child glanced up, smiled at Fedeles and gave a shy wave. Fedeles smiled and waved back at Sparanzo.

The two children beside Sparanzo had to be the Plunado twins— though Fedeles found it strange that neither of them sported long, curling tresses. Had Marisol cropped her hair, or was it pinned up beneath her silver headdress? He didn't really care either way; he simply took comfort seeing the children looking so safe and happy.

"They're with Sevanyo on the dais. They look excited but fine," Fedeles called down to Delfia and Elenna. "Go ahead to them. I'll watch for my lady wife."

Delfia nodded to him. Both women pressed through the crowd, though Delfia outdistanced Elenna right away. She darted around drunkards and dodged revelers while Elenna paused and apologized as she made her way into the mob.

Midnight bells rang out and trumpets blared, startling Fedeles. Then cheers rose all across the garden and echoed with the hoots and roars sounding throughout the city. People pulled off their masks and hurled them into the air.

Amidst the excitement, Fedeles at last glimpsed Oasia. Her bare face betrayed none of the surrounding glee. Instead, she returned the troubled gaze of the man standing to her left. Even without his naval uniform, Fedeles knew Lliro Vediya at a glance. He shared Atreau's handsome features but little of his lively character, and just now he appeared truly dour. He gestured in the direction of the stables.

Oasia nodded and made some reply. As she spoke, her hands twitched with small, almost absent gestures. Oasia's cerulean wards snapped and sparked at the little birds darting at them from all sides.

Suddenly Fedeles sensed an immense wave of power surging through the air. The sky overhead burst apart in an explosion of silver-white fireworks at the same instant the wave of power crashed down in a surge of indigo spells. Hierro's commands hissed as fireworks boomed. Instinctively, Fedeles's shadow rose up to resist Hierro's attack. But then Hierro's spells dispersed in other directions, spreading out through the cheering crowd and beyond.

As more and more fireworks flared, Fedeles's eyes went wide. Groups of guardsmen, servants and nobles all across the garden convulsed. Massive animal bodies tore free of their clothes and flesh. Muscular haunches and thick shoulders tensed beneath bristling gray hides. Dark eyes gleamed as snarls rippled over long muzzles, revealing sharp white teeth. The resounding thunder of bursting fireworks pounded the sky while on the ground, packs of mordwolves appeared throughout the crowd. They sprang onto the stunned people around them.

Cheers contorted into screams of horror and agony. The garden descended into a frenzy of blood and panic. Men and women shoved, clawed and fell beneath one another as they fought to escape the ravaging beasts in their midst.

Fedeles couldn't stop every mordwolf—he couldn't even keep his eyes on all of them. Instead he hurled his shadow at the three nearest his son and Sevanyo. He sheared the creatures in half. Their blood spattered Sevanyo's glittering cloak, and Sparanzo cast Fedeles a fearful gaze as other children screamed and shrieked. The Plunado twins both drew their knives and then Sparanzo too unsheathed his little dagger. All three children looked so frail and brave; it terrified Fedeles.

He refused to observe the remains of the fallen mordwolves; he didn't want to see their corpses regain their human countenances. Instead, he tore through more of them as if he were ripping weeds from the ground and tossing them aside.

Oasia's cerulean wards blazed to life, forming a radiant dome over Sevanyo and all the children. The spells flared so brightly that people all around—magical or not—winced at the surge of light. Another ring of wards lit up around Prince Xalvadar and the party of courtiers, attendants and guards beside him. Fedeles was shocked to see wards flare over even the royal bishop and Prince Remes. He realized that Oasia's spells defended the heirs of the Sagrada bloodline, regardless of whether those people were her enemies or not. The shining cerulean domes even shielded the people standing nearby. The Duke of Gavado, Father Timoteo and Berto, as well as Hierro and his favored courtiers, were all protected by the grace of proximity.

"What witchcraft is this?" a nobleman shouted from the crowd surrounding the royal bishop.

"Blessings that may save your sorry life," a woman yelled back from somewhere near Oasia's side.

"Thank us later!" another of Oasia's handmaids bellowed. She sent sparks of green light flaring over a mordwolf with a motion of her silk fan.

The situation was too dire for any of them to bother hiding anymore. If he and Oasia faced charges of witchcraft, then so be it; at least they weren't such cowards that they'd allow their household to be slaughtered and Sevanyo to be murdered out of timidity.

The garden grounds filled with cerulean light, illuminating the charging mordwolves and panicked courtiers. Fedeles threw his arms wide, casting his shadow out, slashing open mordwolves' throats and crushing their backs. He'd hardly felt the impact of killing the first ten, but after twenty, his chest grew cold and the edges of his shadow frayed like a ragged bowstring.

He ripped through another dozen mordwolves, clearing the center of the garden grounds. A light-headed sensation rolled over him. He swayed atop the little bronze planet and slipped down to crouch on the steel rings. Still more mordwolves charged from the shadows. Then onslaught felt endless.

At least he wasn't alone in fighting the beasts. Many of the mordwolves burned alive in cerulean flames when they hurled themselves against Oasia's wards. But Fedeles noted that with each impact, the wards flickered and dimmed fractionally. Standing in the center of the garden, before the ward protecting her children, Delfia moved with ferocious speed, driving her long knife into the throat of a mordwolf that evaded Fedeles's shadow. Blood poured from her shoulder and spattered her clothes. Near her, other courtiers and servants drew their swords, defending themselves and one another. A musician smashed his lute across a mordwolf's skull and a serving girl hurled embers from a poppy burner at the monster's eyes.

Lliro Vediya slashed at the mordwolves prowling close to Oasia's back, while the Estaban siblings took up swords and torches, defending their injured parents. Ladislo Bayezar and several other courtiers joined them, forming a circle around the wounded. Other people raced for the cover of the bronze astronomical models. At least a dozen nobles sprinted into the hedge maze, perhaps seeking the security of the palace. Their screams resounded and an instant later more bristling gray mordwolves charged from the maze, their muzzles wet with blood.

Fedeles destroyed this third wave of mordwolves as they raced from the hedges, grinding them apart with the ragged edges of his shadow. Their bodies fell in raw hunks as if ripped apart by saw blades. Their deaths left the remains of groundskeepers and guards littering the pebbled paths. Fedeles tore his gaze from the ruined face of a dead page boy. He couldn't think of the human cost of this battle and still continue to fight.

Behind the protection of Oasia's wards, Hierro Fueres lowered his head, but Fedeles didn't miss the grin that spread across his handsome features. His expression was that of a man delighting in a glorious theater performance. His long fingers even moved gracefully as if keeping time with some melody.

Fury and frustration coursed through Fedeles. If breaking the wards wouldn't have hurt Oasia, he would've gladly punched his shadow through those cerulean symbols and gutted Hierro like a fish. As it was, Hierro stood beside Remes utterly at ease in the midst of the slaughter. Two more packs of mordwolves charged from the grounds. Like the previous horde, they flooded in from the south—likely Hierro had amassed his army of assassins in and around the palace.

Infuriated, Fedeles slaughtered another dozen mordwolves. Tremors of fatigue twitched through his muscles. Clammy sweat beaded his forehead and dripped down his back. How many more could there be? Glimpsing his son's fearful face, Fedeles realized that it didn't matter. So long as even one of them threatened Sparanzo, Fedeles couldn't stop fighting.

Mordwolves shied from Remes and Hierro's party, racing past them to assault Sevanyo's loyalists. The tactic was obvious, but in the panic and chaos, who had time to notice? Of those who did, how many would survive?

Fedeles killed with clumsy brutality, crippling and butchering creatures almost blindly. His hands felt numb as he gestured. His breath came fast, as if he'd been running. Still more mordwolves poured into the garden.

At the same time little birds flitted down, pecking and tearing at the threads of Oasia's wards before being burned to smoke. Thread by thread, spell by spell, they were tearing the wards apart. Fedeles didn't know how long Oasia could withstand this onslaught, but his own strength was already faltering. As if reading his thoughts, Oasia's voice sounded near his shoulder.

We must evacuate to a stronger position. Oasia's words sounded like a whisper blown on the wind. Cerulean lights flickered in the corner of his eye. *Lliro ordered the horses readied, but I fear that Hierro's wolves are waiting in ambush on the city streets.*

"Go through the woods to Crown Hill. Hierro and Clara are both wary of the place. Neither have spells there," Fedeles whispered. "You lead. I'll follow."

He saw Oasia nod in response, then say something to Lliro.

"Everyone gather closer!" Lliro shouted. "Follow me to the stables!"

People all across the grounds looked scared and confused, but they obeyed, scrambling to reach Lliro. Oasia moved her wards with the clusters of people, surrounding more and more of them as they closed in on one another. Arms outstretched, she unwove and rewove thousands of thread-fine spells into constantly shifting tapestries of wards. In the blue light she looked ashen. Two of her ladies-in-waiting steadied her.

Amidst the rush, Fedeles saw Remes race to his brother Xalvadar's side. Hierro came along with him. As Remes embraced his brother, Hierro drove something into Xalvadar's back. The crown prince shook and then slumped into Remes's embrace. If he wasn't already dead, Fedeles thought he would be very soon. Dragging Xalvadar's limp body, they moved toward the ring of wards protecting Sevanyo.

If Hierro had grown so daring as to kill Xalvadar in front of so many people, then what would stop him from assassinating Sevanyo? Fedeles didn't know what had made Hierro so bold, but he absolutely had to be stopped from reaching Sevanyo and the children. Fedeles couldn't attack them directly, not without breaching Oasia's wards and injuring her. He swore in frustration.

Then he saw Delfia step in front of the dome of wards sheltering Sevanyo and the children. She gripped her long knife in her left hand and held a guardsman's fallen sword in her right. Her clothes and hair looked wet and almost black with blood, but her expression was cold and determined. Fedeles wove his shadow around her, killing mordwolves while she barred Hierro's advance.

At last annoyance showed in Hierro's expression. His hand dropped to his sword hilt but then stilled. He glanced up at the night sky and smiled.

Fedeles whirled his shadow around Delfia, shredding even the wind that blew over her. Then he too looked to the sky, sensing a swift force whipping through the clouds. A strange flutter passed through Fedeles's chest and he remembered that sensation he'd felt earlier of hurtling down from the sky.

Suddenly an immense eagle wreathed in gold and indigo spells swept through the clouds. Its golden wings spread like blazing canopies; its talons gleamed like scimitars. Dozens of songbirds whirled in its wake. It struck at the dome of wards protecting the royal bishop, the Duke of Gavado, as well as Father Timoteo, Berto and several guards and musicians.

Fedeles expected the cerulean flames of Oasia's wards to engulf the eagle. Instead he felt a shock jolt through his own body. Cerulean flames seared across Fedeles's hands. His shadow smothered them, then ripped Oasia's ward asunder. Oasia staggered, nearly falling into Lliro.

For an instant Fedeles didn't understand why his shadow—his very soul—had shattered Oasia's ward. Then the obvious and terrible answer came to him. His blessings protected the eagle. Or rather, the man enthralled and transformed into the eagle. Fedeles had only recently learned to craft such resonant blessings and he'd only imparted them to one person: Ariz.

Fedeles stared in horror at the huge eagle.

Its talons ripped through the Duke of Gavado's throat, tearing the duke's head from his body. The duke toppled and the eagle soared up. It circled, then plunged down for another strike. This time it shot like an arrow aimed at the royal bishop's heart. Timoteo lurched forward to block the blow with his own body, but Berto grabbed his arm and pulled him back. The eagle swept past them, driving its talons into the royal bishop's chest. It hauled him into the air in an instant and tore open the royal bishop's rib cage with a slash of its hooked beak. Vapor rose from the royal bishop's exposed heart as the eagle swallowed it. Then the eagle released the royal bishop. His body crashed to the ground in a shattered heap.

Fedeles's thoughts reeled between horror and denial. This couldn't be Ariz. It couldn't be. It couldn't. Yet the more Fedeles wished to deny the truth, the more certainty gripped him.

The flock of shimmering teal songbirds surged around the eagle. Fedeles knew that familiar air of glee radiating from them. The same self-indulgent delight had coursed over the mordwolves that assaulted the sacred grove last night. Wherever she was hidden, Clara was thrilled.

"The Labarans have murdered the royal bishop!" Hierro shouted.

Still clutching his brother's corpse, Remes stared at Nugalo's mutilated body. His stricken expression appeared strangely genuine. Had he imagined that slaughtering his own family and seizing the throne would be a neat and peaceful matter? Had he only now realized the lengths that Hierro would go to fulfill his ambitions?

Fedeles didn't have the stomach or the time to think about him further. Above him Ariz swooped toward Sevanyo. Oasia's wards already flickered and dimmed under the constant attacks of Clara's songbirds. Anguish showed on Delfia's face as she gazed up at Ariz. She held her weapons ready.

Fedeles launched himself to the ground and sprinted toward Sevanyo and the children. As he raced ahead, his shadow plowed through mordwolves and flowering shrubs, clearing a path. He reached Delfia just as Oasia's wards failed.

"Get the children away!" Fedeles shouted to Delfia.

She gave no response, only turned and rushed away. But from the corner of his eye, Fedeles glimpsed Delfia and Elenna race to the gathered children. Other figures—Berto and Timoteo, perhaps—staggered toward Sevanyo. At the same time bishop's guardsmen surrounded Hierro, Remes and their loyalists, and mordwolves edged around them, making the divide between the two parties plain to anyone who cared to look.

Fedeles took it all in at a glance, but it was Ariz shearing through the air who commanded his focus.

Ariz dived for Sevanyo.

Fedeles hurled the black mass of his shadow up to block his descent. The impact jarred through Fedeles's ribs like a horse's kick, knocking the breath from his lungs. Ariz whirled through the air like a pinwheel. Then he fell. Fedeles gasped, wanting to catch him but unable to move for the pain in his own chest.

Ariz rolled as he struck the ground, reclaiming his human form in a fluid motion. If he felt any pain, he gave no sign. He rose to his feet, drawing a sword with his right hand and a dagger with his left. His face was expressionless, though the dark blood staining his mouth lent him a horrific air. He charged Sevanyo. The youngest Estaban brother attempted to block his way. Ariz parried the young man's sword thrust, lunged into him and slit his throat with a flick of his dagger. The youngest Estaban staggered, looking confused then collapsed.

Ariz continued to advance on Sevanyo. He struck down two royal guards in blindingly fast thrusts and kicked a serving girl aside.

Fedeles had to act. He exerted his will, reaching into the blessings he'd placed on Ariz's body. He twisted their names—their purposes— from *Protect, Guard* and *Defend* into shackles of *Bind, Hold* and *Stop* Ariz. The black masses of Fedeles's altered blessings rose around Ariz's limbs and body like ropes and chains. They bit into his skin and twisted around his throat, restraining him.

Ariz still struggled forward, inch by inch. He looked to Fedeles and for an instant a flicker of a smile seemed to lift his bloodied mouth.

"Kill me," Ariz whispered. "Kill me now."

Fedeles couldn't bring himself to respond. He focused all his strength into holding Ariz where he stood. Just hold him. Just restrain him. He didn't want to hurt him. But Ariz resisted with inhuman strength and determination. Bloody gashes opened up across Ariz's chest and shoulders as he took a step forward and then another.

Fedeles actually felt his spells fraying against Ariz's will.

"Kill me!" This time Ariz howled the command across the garden. His ragged voice carried over shouts and snarls. Even the mordwolves seemed startled by his cry. All attention fell on Ariz. Ariz swept his gaze across the people surrounding him. Fedeles felt tremors of pain shudder through his shadow—echoes of Ariz's private agony reaching him. Molten iron seemed to burn through his chest and razors slashed his throat and tongue.

Ariz still roared, "Hierro Fueres enthralled me! Commanded me to kill the king." He choked as the brand clenched his throat nearly closed. Fedeles tasted the blood filling Ariz's mouth. Ariz looked to him and again gasped out, "Kill me . . . please."

Fedeles was aware of nobles all around turning suspicious and accusing glances upon Hierro. He heard Remes shout protests, but none of that truly registered. All he saw was Ariz, fighting to retain his humanity; all he felt was his shadow fraying and ripping as Hierro's brand flared through Ariz's body.

For the first time Fedeles sensed the complete form and power of that brand. Radiant indigo filaments pervaded Ariz's muscles, blood vessels and nerves. Hierro's presence threaded through his bloodstream and infiltrated the very fibers of his hammering heart. Unbreakable and unbearable, it wasn't a mere ornament placed upon him, but a poison that had grown into him—grown through him, over a decade.

In the midst of that seething indigo fire, only the faint gold wisp of Ariz's soul remained untainted. Such a pure and beautiful light, Fedeles thought. He reached out to that warm spark and wrapped a veil of his shadow around it, sheltering it.

Then he forced himself to drive the blessings he'd wrapped around Ariz deep into his chest. Darkness shrouded Ariz's pounding heart as Fedeles enveloped Hierro's indigo spells as well as the living flesh supporting them. Ariz's heart trembled in Fedeles's grasp. Fedeles pressed more power into his blessings. *Stop*, he commanded. Ariz's heart jerked and fluttered, fighting him. But Fedeles didn't relent. Ariz's heart slowed to a sluggish shudder and then went still.

Fedeles felt it, like the body of some tiny bird going limp and cold in his hand.

Ariz swayed. He looked to Fedeles. His expression might have been surprise or relief. Fedeles couldn't make it out through the tears filling his eyes. Ariz collapsed to the ground.

Fedeles wanted to scream and howl—to race to Ariz, hold his body and weep. But enemies still surrounded him—still threatened his family and friends. He couldn't fall apart now. A thin shroud of his shadow lay against Ariz's cooling body, clinging to it as he released Ariz's golden soul.

At the same moment Oasia abandoned her palace wards to create what protection she could around the harried crowd, retreating to the stables. Color and light drained from the garden. Hierro and Remes stood exposed amidst their supporters and surrounded by mordwolves.

Nobles all around them looked suddenly terrified. But Hierro simply straightened and held out his arms.

"God defends the righteous!" Hierro called out, and immediately teal and indigo wards sprang up around him and his followers. While the drunk and stunned nobles might have believed that these wards shielded them from the sea of mordwolves, Fedeles recognized that the wards had been raised to deflect Fedeles's attacks.

"Just as surely, he punishes the sinful," Hierro pronounced, and the mordwolves charged Fedeles while vast flocks of birds swept from the sky to rip and tear at him with vicious, biting curses.

Fedeles fought them, washing the garden grounds in blood and dismembered bodies. His shadow eviscerated mordwolves and shredded birds. But for every one he killed, another three seemed to arise. And for every dozen curses that he dissipated, one shot through his shadow to cut into his body. Tiny wounds multiplied into long gashes as Fedeles's fatigue and sorrow grew. The wet heat of his own blood soaked through Fedeles's clothes. His hands shook.

And yet he remained standing before Ariz's cold body, shrouding him in his shadow as if his desire alone could revive Ariz's still heart.

Come back to me. Please. Please . . .

He knew he ought to retreat and join Oasia at the stables, then make for Crown Hill. Sparanzo was probably terrified. Sevanyo needed protection and support. Oasia couldn't defend everyone by herself. No matter how furious and hopeless he felt, he was responsible for so many other people's well-being. He knew all of that, and yet he didn't seem able to leave Ariz. He couldn't—wouldn't—accept that he'd lost him. That he'd destroyed Ariz himself. How could he accept that? How could he live with what he'd done? Hot tears streamed down his cheeks.

Fedeles wrenched a mordwolf in two and staggered closer to Ariz's body. He swayed, feeling light-headed and nauseated. He didn't care. A part of him wanted to fall here, to lie down and die with Ariz. At least then he wouldn't have to bear the loss of him. He wouldn't have to feel this agony of sorrow and guilt.

The grounds seemed to almost tremble beneath Fedeles's feet. Then the thunder of hooves sounded from behind him. Fedeles glanced up to see Firaj racing across the lawn. The warhorse's eyes flashed white—terrified—and yet Firaj still charged through the mordwolves to reach him and defend him.

We need you, Fedeles. Oasia's words drifted on the wind, sounding exhausted. *Sparanzo needs you.*

Sparanzo, Oasia, Delfia, her children, Timoteo, Sevanyo and so many other people. Ariz had allowed himself to be killed for their sakes.

Fedeles owed it to him to keep them alive. He could berate himself later—lie down and fucking die if he wanted to—but now he couldn't abandon everyone depending upon him. Ariz hadn't suffered and died just so that he could give up. No, Ariz would never have done such a thing—would never have indulged in such self-pity.

Fedeles forced himself to move. He snatched up a fallen sword and then swung up onto Firaj's back, wheeling the black warhorse around. Clara's birds winged after him, striking wildly, hitting bushes and trees and bursting into flames. Soon a great fire surged across the garden grounds, giving chase like a living thing.

"She's burning everything! Go!" Fedeles shouted. He raced from the garden, catching up with the fifty or more riders now charging behind Oasia and making for Crown Hill.

Their flight through the long lawns of fountains and into the wooded hunting grounds drew other frightened people, as well as more attacks. People on foot trailed the riders and Fedeles circled back, defending their retreat.

Overhead, Clara's birds lit with teal spells chased them, slashing people and leaving curses clawing and biting them and their mounts. Fedeles swept the birds from the air while Oasia hurled others to the ground. The men and women between them slashed at the birds with knives, fans, pieces of costumes and even shoes. Horses snorted and kicked. Several riders were thrown, but other people took them up onto their own mounts. More then a few people running caught the riderless horses and mounted them. A groom seized a white mare and helped a child onto her back before Clara's birds hurtled into him, engulfing him in flames.

Behind the songbirds, mordwolves and even armed men surged forth. But most terrifying were the relentless teal-tinged flames that rolled out from the garden grounds, consuming everything.

Riders and people racing on foot battled through the dark woods and up the rocky trail. Fedeles defended them as best he could. Exhaustion turned his sword work unwieldy and his spells ragged. Fortunately, gutting, beating and crushing out lives didn't require great elegance. When Fedeles could no longer raise his sword, Firaj kicked and trampled his opponents to death.

Finally the last people staggered up the steep path to the top of Crown Hill. The dark sky paled to twilight blue. Clara's birds circled but didn't dare cross over the hill. But men and mordwolves climbed upward, while flames followed them.

Fedeles glared down. Smoke burned his eyes and choked his throat. Firaj snorted and tossed his head as waves of heat rolled up on the rising winds. Dozens of mordwolves charged the path. Fedeles could no longer drive his shadow more than a few feet. But he couldn't allow any of them to come that close. Instead he turned his attention to the path itself. Frail wildflowers clung to huge, weathered boulders, reminding him of the ancient carved guardians that once protected the hill. Fedeles thrust his shadow down, digging out soil and clay, undermining the stones.

His hands shook and his back ached as he forced his will against grains of earth. He felt the ground tremble and quickly stepped back. All at once the hillside below him gave way. Boulders, stones and then an entire face of the hillside cascaded down, engulfing the beasts. The trail transformed into a wall of rock, dust and human carcasses. A sea of flames raged below the rockslides but couldn't spread over the blood-drenched stones and damp, overturned dirt. Smoke drifted up to Fedeles as he stared down at the destruction he'd wrought.

There would be no easy way up the hill now, but neither would there be a simple escape. He turned Firaj away and urged him up the remaining path.

CHAPTER
THIRTY-ONE

Ariz soared through a pale gray expanse, feeling free. There was no anxiety or pain. The landscape beneath him appeared to be a city, wreathed in smoke and flames, but so far away that he could hardly discern any details. None of his concern. Ariz arched and rolled, then winged away. Gray fog swallowed the burning city, leaving Ariz to his effortless flight.

Sweeping low, he broke through a faint trail of bright blue mist. It swirled in his wake like a wind-tossed cloud.

How strange, Ariz thought. Blue clouds in a gray sky. Was he dreaming?

All at once he remembered standing before Fedeles, gripping a bloodied sword and begging Fedeles to end his life. His entire being had roiled with furious intent to murder. Incandescent rage had blazed through his muscles and turned his mind to an animal's. But somehow just looking at Fedeles, he'd managed to grip a sliver of sanity, steal an instant of self-control. He'd whispered, "Kill me . . . please."

Had he seen tears in Fedeles's eyes then? He couldn't be certain. But he did remember a sudden catch of his own breath and a perfect stillness spreading through his burning chest. His rage dulled and he collapsed to the ground. As he crumpled, Hierro's oppressive presence released him—almost as if he was afraid that Ariz would drag him down too. Freed from Hierro's Brand of Obedience, Ariz hadn't noticed the bite of the pebble path crashing against his limp body. He'd only felt relief, and then nothing.

Thinking about it now, Ariz knew that only death could break the brand's hold over him. So . . . he was dead.

Ariz contemplated the notion, felt the regrets of all those delights and joys that he would never know. Never again would he hold Fedeles in his arms or listen to his laughter. They wouldn't dance again or lie amongst wildflowers and make love. He'd never see his nieces or Sparanzo grow up or spend an afternoon listening to his sister read aloud from some scandalous novel. But far more relief filled him than sorrow. He was no longer a mere weapon in the hands of a monster. He would never again threaten the people he loved. He'd finally escaped the humiliation of Hierro's control. At last he could deprive Hierro of the pleasure of torturing him.

When death brought him those assurances, Ariz accepted it as a solace.

Blue mists curled past him, their masses evoking floating forms. Some reminded him of animals, some seemed like trees, while many others looked almost like people. Ariz couldn't quite decide if the faces were familiar to him. They seemed soft, pliable and too mutable to represent any one person.

He felt the urge to chase one but then took pity on the hapless-looking clouds. Instead, he contented himself simply observing them swirl alongside him as he contemplated his situation.

If he was dead, then his soul now drifted in the Sorrowlands. From what he remembered of chapel sermons, devils should surround him. They would torture him with guilt and tempt him with his regrets, luring him from the path of paradise. A wrong step and he would be hurled into one of the three hells. But flying through this calm sky, he couldn't make out any path, much less a horde of devils. Perhaps his soul had been so battered and worn down by Hierro that it wasn't even of interest to the devils of the Sorrowlands.

Ariz supposed that he should be terrified, but instead he felt at ease. He'd endured so much at Hierro's hands that he couldn't summon much dread. As for the regrets of his lifetime, none was greater than serving Hierro. Now he was free of that.

The blue mists contorted and swept away from him as if tossed in powerful winds. Ariz observed them feeling calm, relaxed—as if he was again lying back beside Fedeles watching passing clouds form drifting pictures.

A ship . . . sails tattered, Ariz remembered. *Rabbits leaping off into the horizon.*

As he recollected, the blue mists appeared to take on those remembered shapes. How strange, but also soothing. He'd truly expected the Sorrowlands to hold more horror. Instead a quiet kind of peace filled him.

He rose, gliding between the streams of blue clouds. A ribbon of blue vapor whirled close to him and he gazed curiously into its depths. At first it seemed to reflect his own face, but slowly the countenance turned into an eagle's. Ariz reached out. To his surprise, the blue mist fluttered and then darted away from him like a startled fish.

So the blue mists weren't clouds after all. Ariz watched several of them waft beneath him. Were they other lost souls, like himself? Or could they be mythic creatures from Labaran lore? Ariz gazed after another, but it too fled before him.

Did it think he was going to harm it? Ariz wondered. The desire to follow after it rose in him, but he realized that would hardly seem reassuring. He let it go. He'd had enough of hunting and hurting others in his life. Now that the choice was his to make, he decided to leave the blue mists alone and simply enjoy the sight of them.

"It's a rare soul that's so comforted in death." A young man's voice rose from the endless gray surroundings.

Then a white light flared up, like the sun burning through the gray fog and blue mist alike. The light drew nearer, filling all of Ariz's awareness. At its heart he made out faint shadows. A man's figure striding toward him. For just an instant Ariz thought he resembled Fedeles when he'd been a youth. Then the man's features grew more and more radiant until all Ariz saw was a searing white skull.

"You're not an Old God, but not a simple mortal soul either." The skeletal man spoke Cadeleonian with a distinctly noble accent, but wore the golden-orange robes of a Bahiim draped over his long white bones. "Who are you?"

Ariz didn't know why, but he'd expected that the skeletal man would know his name—deities and spirits in chapel stories always seemed innately informed of mortal men's identities. The figure's ignorance took him aback.

"Who's asking?" Ariz responded.

"I am the Guardian of the Old Road, Master of the Sorrowlands and Lord of the White Hell!" The brilliant light surrounding the figure surged and his golden robes billowed. "Now tell me, who are you?"

Ariz shrank back from the light. "I'm called Ariz. Ariz Plunado."

The searing light softened to the cool glow of moonlight.

"Ariz." The skeletal figure stood very still; even the winds lifting his robes appeared to stop, suspending the folds of golden cloth in the air as if frozen. "The innocent assassin. Yes, I remember your death. You refused to kill Fedeles . . . but you're different this time."

This time, Ariz wondered, but he didn't comment. He already felt out of his depths, so he listened, trying to work out this being's intentions.

"Your soul now is brighter, sharper and not entirely human in form." The man's tone was thoughtful. "There is something of the Old Gods about you . . ."

"Could that be the influence of Trueno's relic?" Ariz wondered.

"Trueno? Yes . . . yes!" The skeletal youth clicked his finger bones. "So this time *you* were the one she chose to embody Trueno? And you survived the transformation? The others never did."

Ariz didn't know who else Clara might have attempted to transform before him. But it was true that he'd survived Trueno's relic. He simply nodded.

"Matters are very different indeed," the skeletal youth muttered to himself, and some of his radiance faded. Translucent features veiled his skull in a youthful countenance. His features, like his speech, seemed very Cadeleonian. He went on. "Fedeles is still alive, Clara hasn't yet destroyed the Hallowed Kings. There's still time."

At the mention of Fedeles, Ariz felt a pang. He hoped Fedeles was still safe. That he wasn't too heartbroken.

The skeletal youth suddenly turned his attention on Ariz.

"There is something you regret in death, isn't there?" the youth asked. "Something more you would do, if you could reclaim your life?"

Of course he wanted to live—but not at a cost to the people he loved. Ariz shook his head. "I would rather die a hundred times over than return to the way I was. I'd rather lose my soul entirely than be enthralled by Hierro Fueres again."

The youth extended his hand and swept a finger bone over Ariz. For a nauseated moment Ariz felt his entire being ripple like a mud puddle struck by a stone. White light flashed before him and his thoughts scattered. Part of him seemed far away and cold, while at the same time he felt warm and wrapped in a shroud of delicate black silk. Then both feelings dulled and Ariz regained his sense of placid tranquility. The skeletal youth considered him with a ghostly smile.

"His thrall is broken." The skeletal figure tilted his head. Flecks of light glinted in the hollows of his eyes, like reflections dancing on dark water. "But Fedeles's blessings cling to your corpse, longing to revive you."

"He mustn't waste his strength," Ariz said.

"But it wouldn't be a waste if you were to return, would it?" The youth sounded delighted and even a little smug. He leaned close. "Are you willing to abandon the respite of death and return to fight at his side?"

Ariz didn't hesitate. "I would do anything to help Fedeles."

"Then go!" The skeletal youth slammed his hand into Ariz, sending him hurtling into a frigid darkness.

   CHAPTER
                           THIRTY-TWO

They had only rowed halfway across the river when silver fireworks burst through the night sky. Bells rang out, horns sounded and cheers rose from both riverbanks. The hour of unmasking had arrived—midnight. The volley of light and noise startled Narsi, but it didn't hold his attention. Instead he stared after the hundreds and hundreds of small, dark silhouettes briefly illuminated by all the light. A vast cloud of songbirds circled the Shard of Heaven. Smaller flocks wheeled over the palace and swooped along the river.

Narsi's palms tingled as if pricked by burning needles. He winced as faint seams of gold light seeped from between his fingers. He tightened his grip on his oar and threw his back into rowing. His stroke must have been off, because Atreau stole a concerned glance over his shoulder at him.

The river current heaved against their little boat and Atreau shuddered. Their lantern swayed but still cast enough light for Narsi to recognize the greenish tinge to Atreau's face.

"Your hands again?" Atreau asked. "How bad is it?"

Considering how seasick Atreau appeared, Narsi thought he really ought to be the one questioning his companion's well-being. But he let Atreau keep his pride.

"The tingling just surprised me. It's growing more intense. I don't know if that's because we're nearing the sacred grove or if Clara's birds are the cause." Narsi glanced down at his hands and again noted how the gold light flared against the flesh of his fingers, outlining the shadows of his bones.

"Is it possible that Yah-muur's Horn is trying to awaken?" Narsi addressed the question to the cat crouching on the burden boards of the boat.

The cat looked distinctly queasy, perhaps even more seasick than Atreau. Or maybe its slumped posture had more to do with Lady Hylanya's state of mind. Either way, the cat belatedly managed to nod at him in response.

Narsi looked up as another burst of silver fireworks soared overhead. The birds circling the Shard of Heaven formed a whirling cyclone. Their cries carried over the rush of the river and even the bells ringing out across the city. A few birdsongs sounded very close. Something silky and swift grazed Narsi's ear. A wingtip. He ducked as another bird swooped him.

Atreau suddenly swung an oar out of the water, knocking the bird into the river.

"Fucking little spies," Atreau muttered. "We need to get ashore before more of them spot us."

Narsi rowed with all his strength, as did Atreau. Both of them heaved and pulled against the river currents. His back strained and his shoulders began to ache. At last they struck ground. Atreau vaulted out of the gig to drag it further ashore. Narsi gripped the lantern in one hand, picked up the cat in the other and followed Atreau. He hardly noticed the chill of the river water as he slogged up the shore. He strained for the sound of birds and picked out the twitter of larks and chimney swifts not too far behind him. They grew louder and more excited.

"Leave the lantern here as a decoy," Atreau whispered back at him.

Narsi propped it in the mud and then raced after Atreau. Bursts of fireworks offered him fleeting glimpses of a seawall rising up ahead of them. From atop that, Narsi heard the noise of jubilant crowds gathered to observe the show. He thought he could see the eaves of a few buildings, and here and there he glimpsed the feet of people dangling their legs over the edge of the seawall.

Beneath his feet, the ground grew rockier and steeper. Another burst of silver light showed him the faint outline of worn stairs winding along the curve of the seawall and snaking into the shadows of a cliff.

He and Atreau clambered up the slick steps. The river spat chill water up at them. Narsi strained to discern a wet, worn step from weathered wall, and his foot slipped. The cat dug its claws into his shoulder. Atreau caught his hand and steadied him.

"You're sure the street above us wouldn't be safer?" Narsi asked.

"We'd never get through the crowd unseen. Anyway, we're nearly here." Atreau kept his hold on Narsi's hand as he led him into a narrow alcove and then drew him farther into what seemed like a mere fault in the stonework. The space they'd entered was so dark he could hardly see a foot ahead of him. The cat leapt down from Narsi's arms and sidled up beside Atreau.

Narsi lifted his hands to the walls. The gold light rising from his palms offered him a faint illumination of the cramped chamber. Aged brick and weathered wood supports held up a rocky ceiling. There appeared to be two small, black tunnels about three feet apart at the back of the chamber. Both stretched under the seawall into complete darkness. A shockingly rank odor oozed from one of the openings. Hints of rotting fish and bile seeped into Narsi's nostrils. He'd drained abscesses that smelled better. He coughed and stepped back.

"What is that smell?" Narsi pinched his nostrils closed; somehow the stench still seemed to creep over him.

"A fortune in counterfeit ink. Bishop's indigo," Atreau replied with a grin. "They store the best batches here until the pong wafts off, then it goes to the highest bidder. You'll see—and smell—the jars for yourself when we pass them."

"Do we really have to get closer to that stench?"

"Sometimes you have to hold your nose to follow the path of heroism," Atreau intoned with great solemnity.

Then he started down the cramped, dark tunnel. The cat scampered alongside him and Narsi followed, with one hand clenched over his nose and mouth. Raising his free hand to the wall, he discovered aged but still beautifully colored glazed tiles. He lagged behind for a few moments, studying the designs. Golden stars hung through graceful green branches like leaves. The Bahiim symbol for protection glinted silver from another chipped tile.

"This is part of the old Haldiim tunnels?" Narsi asked.

"That's right. Most likely this section served as a safe house of some kind," Atreau replied. "Though now most of the Old Roots are riddled with smugglers' snake holes and illegal cesspits. Not the most pleasant way to navigate the city, but it ought to keep us clear of crowds. Not to mention birds."

"I'd think the smell alone would drive off anything with a nose of any kind."

Atreau snickered but didn't say anything more. Narsi tried to make out his expression through the dark. Then he wondered how Atreau could navigate these tunnels so well in the near-total blackness. Narsi moved closer, studying Atreau, and realized that he'd actually closed his eyes. Head slightly bowed, Atreau traced the surface of the wall with the fingertips of his right hand. When Narsi extended his own hand he felt glassy raised patterns interrupting the surfaces of the tiles every ten feet or so. By sight, they were difficult to pick out from the colorful patterns decorating the walls, but they were quite distinct to the touch. He almost asked Atreau about it but then glimpsed the look of concentration on Atreau's face and decided to keep quiet.

They silently traipsed through the dank, dark tunnel. The stench in the air grew so intense that Narsi felt like it was sticking to his skin in a film. At last they passed an alcove stacked with shelves of red, wax-sealed jars. Narsi's stomach churned as he waded through the odor hanging over the shelves. Thankfully, once they passed the alcove, he felt a very light, fresh breeze waft over him. A little later the tunnel split into two and Atreau led Narsi to the left, where the air tasted stale but not rotten.

"It's going to get quite tight and we'll have to crawl for the last half mile or so," Atreau informed him. "Don't let it scare you. Just keep following me and we'll be out soon enough."

The tunnel branched and they took the route that seemed to lead deeper underground. The walls felt damp, but after enduring the earlier odor, neither the moldering smell nor the stale quality of the air bothered Narsi too much. He felt more concerned about the time this roundabout journey was taking. It seemed like hours passed as they marched through an endless darkness.

As the walls of the tunnel seemed to close in and the air grew even more stale and still, a feeling a dread roused in Narsi's chest. Loose soil poured down on his head and his heart jerked with the visceral terror of a sudden cave-in. He scrambled forward and nearly fell over Atreau's legs.

"You all right?" Atreau glanced back at him.

Narsi forced himself to calm down. He'd been in tight spots with Atreau before this. They'd always gotten through; he just needed to trust Atreau.

"Got bored and started to doze off," Narsi claimed.

"Well, try not to get too relaxed down here. We still have to slither our ways around some. The last section is quite serpentine."

Indeed the tunnel seemed to take a convoluted route. After the fifth or sixth turn, Narsi had no idea what direction they were headed in. Though they did seem to be crawling steadily upward. Rough stones scraped his shoulders, and in one spot he had to flatten his face down into the dirty floor to worm under a large iron pipe. As he shoved himself beneath the rusted metal, he thought he heard liquid gurgling overhead. Condensation dribbled past his ear.

His knees began to feel raw, as did his hot palms. With his mouth and eyes full of dust, he began to really envy the cat, which slipped easily through the tight spaces.

At last Atreau shoved a small metal grate aside and a rush of fresh air poured in over Narsi. The noise of distant music and the smell of woodsmoke assured him that they'd at last reached the open air of the city streets. Atreau wriggled through the hatch. The cat bounded out after him, and lastly Narsi shouldered his way free. He flopped on the ground next to Atreau, taking in a deep breath of the fresh air and staring up at the sky overhead.

The stars struck him as quite beautiful. In the future he shouldn't take them so much for granted, he decided. He dropped his gaze to Atreau, taking time to appreciate his handsome profile as well as his good company. Where another man might have made the journey through those tunnels tedious or terrifying, Atreau had inspired Narsi's confidence and curiosity. How had he been so lucky as to win Atreau's affections?

"What a smile." Atreau met Narsi's gaze and the corner of his mouth curled into a smug expression. "Enjoying the view?"

Caught openly mooning, Narsi's face heated with a flush and he purposefully turned his attention to their surroundings.

The buildings rising up on either side of him seemed empty and quiet compared to the rest of the city. From the stacks of moss-packed crates piled beside the walls, Narsi guessed they'd emerged near a flower market or large physic garden.

"I was wondering where we are," Narsi said.

"In the alley between the back courtyards of Verdone Apothecary and the Rid-Rumaan Seedhouse." Atreau rose to his feet and dusted off his palms before reaching out to help Narsi up to his feet.

After so long crawling in circles through dark tunnels, Narsi took a moment to orient himself. They were at the northern edge of the Haldiim District. They'd need to cut across the Haldiim district and through the Theater District to reach the sacred grove. Narsi felt a shiver of uncertainty about who and what they would encounter once they got close.

"Do you think Prince Jacinto has reached Skellan and Elezar yet?" Narsi asked.

"Probably," Atreau responded. He glanced down at the cat, but it appeared far more interested in stalking some rodent than their conversation. Narsi guessed Hylanya was busy with other matters—hopefully assisting Labaran troops sneak their way to the sacred grove.

"If worse comes to worst, we should be able to blend in with the crowds at the Fat Goose and wait until we get word from either Elezar or Sabella. In the meantime, I'll bandage your hands. The spells are growing bright enough that people are going to notice." Atreau caught Narsi's left hand and turned his palm up. Tiny gold symbols gleamed like embers through the dust and dirt. He frowned. "It doesn't hurt?"

"No. It just tingles a little." Narsi was far more aware of Atreau's hand holding his own. His touch was so careful as he brushed the dust from Narsi's palms. Where his fingertips traced Narsi's skin, the sensation seemed to ripple deep into his flesh and linger. He felt absurd being so easily affected by mere concern and drew his hand back to quickly rifle through his medical satchel for a small roll of bandages. Atreau assisted him in wrapping his palms. Then they set off.

They hurried through the subdued streets of the Haldiim District. Few people there celebrated the Masquerade. Most had retired to their beds, planning to rise with the sun for the Solstice celebrations. However, as they plunged into the Theater District they encountered costumed, drunken crowds congesting both the walkways and the streets. People sang, argued and laughed as they played games of chase and chance. Couples in various degrees of undress embraced against walls and in alleys. Musicians performed lively tunes from atop empty wagons or stacks of barrels. Giddy groups of dancers ringed them.

They hardly differed from the wealthy revelers in the palace gardens, except that these crowds were far larger and their costumes were coarser. Where silver thread, ornate lace and precious stones were easy to differentiate from the hides of real creatures, the simple leather and rough fur of common costumes struck Narsi as much more unnerving beneath the flickering torchlight.

Just as there had been in the palace gardens, little birds flitted through the air and trilled as they swept past Narsi. Again he felt his hands tingle and grow strangely hot. His fingers twitched with a kind of nervous energy. Narsi studied the crowd to distract himself from the weird sensation. He thought he saw several strangers turned toward him as he darted through the crowds. The streets seemed to be awash with beasts and glinting eyes followed him.

They passed the imposing facade of the Red Stallion sword house. Nearly everyone on the street seemed to carry weapons and a number of men shouted threats and insults at each other—though most broke into laughter afterward.

Atreau bent to pat the cat's head.

"We could use an escort if you can find anyone," he said. When he straightened, the cat shot away through the crowd. Atreau glanced to Narsi. "Keep close."

Narsi nodded and they hurried ahead.

As they neared the Green Door, the clusters of revelers seemed to thicken into dense mobs. Narsi caught Atreau's hand to keep from losing track of him in the crush of bodies. Two men surged from a jolly crowd of dancers. One was dressed as a bat; the other wore an owl mask. The first man jostled against Narsi and gripped his arm. Narsi jerked free. Next to him, Atreau suddenly struck out with his elbow and sent the second man stumbling back from them.

More figures surrounded them. Some were dancing, careening drunks, but others appeared far too sober and well armed. They managed to shove their way ahead a few more feet, getting the brick wall of a theater to their backs. A silhouette to Narsi's right caught his attention. There was something disconcertingly familiar about the rabbit mask the fellow wore. Narsi remembered the night he'd been pursued by Captain Yago's men— one of them had worn that same rabbit mask with a crooked ear.

"There are three of them on to the right of us," Narsi whispered to Atreau.

"We have company up ahead as well." Atreau slowed. Narsi glanced over Atreau's shoulder. At first he didn't recognize anyone in the multitude of people dancing toward them. Then he noticed costly gold thread and pearl buttons adorning a costume. A man in Jacinto's company had worn the same clothes and displayed the same a sleek black beard from beneath a tusked half mask. Procopio—Narsi belatedly realized. Then he caught sight of Procopio's naked sword.

Atreau drew his own sword as well as a dagger. To Narsi's shock, he pressed the hilt of his sword into Narsi's hand. "Get behind me. Keep them at as great a distance as you can. As soon as there's an opening, take it. Run for the Fat Goose."

Narsi didn't try to argue. He gripped the sword hilt but only felt all the more terrified by the prospect of using the weapon. It was incredibly awkward in his hands, too heavy and cold.

Procopio charged Atreau. The man wearing the rabbit mask drew a short sword and edged around Narsi, searching for an opportune moment to strike. Narsi kept his back against Atreau's. He heard the clash of blades and felt the impact jolt through Atreau's shoulders as Atreau blocked Procopio's sword with a mere dagger.

Narsi couldn't stop himself from glancing back. Atreau dodged under Procopio's slashing sword. Instead of retreating, he lunged even nearer to Procopio, so close they stood chest to chest. Atreau gripped Procopio's sword arm with one hand and sliced his dagger across Procopio's throat with the other. Procopio jerked in Atreau's grasp and Narsi felt the wet warmth of blood splash across his own cheek. Atreau hurled Procopio aside.

An instant later Narsi lost all thought of Atreau and Procopio.

The man wearing the rabbit mask lunged, thrusting his short sword straight for Narsi's heart. Narsi lashed the blade aside with a frantic swing. Jarring force rippled up the sword and rocked through Narsi's arms. His opponent darted to the right and jabbed again.

Terror thrilled through Narsi. The hilt of his sword slipped in his sweating hands as he attempted to block the other man's blade. Searing heat and golden light gushed from his hands and surged over the sword blade, engulfing his opponent in flames. The man shrieked and convulsed. His short sword fell and he crumpled to the cobblestones in a smoldering heap. The smell of roasted meat and scorched hair wafted from his charred corpse. Narsi stared in horror.

Two more men with drawn swords charged him from the crowd.

"Don't! Don't!" Narsi shouted, just as terrified of watching them burn to death in front of him as he was of being attacked.

One of the men suddenly stopped, a shocked expression spread across his face. Blood welled from his mouth and he collapsed. The second attacker pivoted to block something behind him. Before he turned completely around, Narsi saw a blade punch through the man's torso twice. He staggered, then toppled like a broken puppet. As his body sank, Sabella tore her sword free, then launched herself after another man in the surrounding crowd.

Belatedly Narsi realized that the mob of dancers had transformed into a wild melee. Shouts and obscenities rang out. And yet someone, somewhere down the lane, was still strumming wildly on a lute and wailing out an off-key love song. Through the jumping torchlight, he glimpsed dozens of unfamiliar faces, naked swords and clashing bodies. Figures sprawled on the ground—some gasping in pain, others lying silent and motionless. Narsi looked away, suppressing his reflex to treat the injured men. He had no idea who among the fallen were assassins intent on killing him and Atreau.

Thankfully, the people surrounding Narsi all wore the colors of the Red Stallion sword house. When a hulking man charged Narsi, Sabella dispatched him with a sword thrust through his chest and a brutal kick.

Narsi stole a glance over his shoulder in time to witness a brawny man rush Atreau, only to trip to the side as a bottle smashed across the back of his head. As the man fell, Spider stepped forward, crushing the man's throat beneath the heel of his boot.

Narsi recognized Spider's barmaids standing behind him, as well as the cook and two servers from the Green Door. The others surrounding them also looked familiar, like people he'd passed in Atreau's company but never spoken to. A boot boy, an orange seller, several street musicians, jugglers and stagehands. Unlike the swordsmen who stood with Sabella, the crowd surrounding Spider appeared largely armed with tools they'd snatched up: pokers, cleavers, brooms, rolling pins, shovels, torches and at least one bucket of fumet. They truly seemed like an improvised battalion, that could easily melt away into an anonymous crowd.

Atreau grasped Spider in a quick embrace, then asked, "Inissa and Ollivar?"

"Safe," Spider assured him. "They're with the Goat evacuating our Haldiim friends through the Old Roots."

"You should join them," Atreau said.

Spider just rolled his eyes as if the suggestion was absurd and then proffered Narsi a friendly wave. Narsi grinned at him, feeling weak with relief.

Narsi shifted his attention to Atreau just as Atreau glanced to him. Dirt and blood streaked Atreau's face, but his gaze seemed warm and inviting. His smile was all the more handsome for what they'd just survived. He reached out and scrubbed something from Narsi's cheek.

"A little blood," Atreau muttered.

"You too," Narsi replied as he wiped Atreau's brow.

Sabella cleared her throat and stepped up beside Narsi. Her troop of swordsmen moved with her, surrounding them. Atreau's smile disappeared and his attention snapped to Sabella.

"This wasn't all we're up against, was it?" Atreau asked.

"No. This bunch was mostly Procopio's underlings and a few snitches." Sabella spat on the ground. "Yago and his men are amassing for an ambush at the crossroads of the Shell Fountain. If you want to reach the sacred grove without them noticing, you'll have to take a detour around half the city."

Atreau nodded and then glanced to Narsi with an expression of growing concern. Narsi followed his gaze down to his own hands. He still gripped Atreau's sword, but the bandages he'd worn had burned away. Strings of glowing gold symbols curled around Narsi's fingers and lit up the backs of his hands.

Narsi tried not to feel repulsed by the sight. But the smell of burned flesh still hung around him and that agonized shriek seemed to echo in his ears.

"I don't know what sort of witchcraft you unleashed to torch that bastard, Master Narsi," Sabella said. "But if you could do it again, we might just take Yago on directly. Burn a couple men alive and I guarantee that half Yago's troops will piss themselves and scatter."

A wave of nausea rose through Narsi at the thought of purposely burning another human being alive. He hadn't wanted to harm anyone. He'd just been terrified, and the spells had seemed to respond on their own. What kind of physician would he be if he decided to purposefully invoke them—what kind of person?

At the same time, so many more lives were at stake. Was it a kind of cowardice to expect Atreau, Sabella and Spider to carry the burden of killing their enemies, while he maintained his own illusion of innocence? It wasn't as if he'd not killed anyone. He'd prepared the poison that was now ending Ariz's life. It was just that he hadn't ever before been forced to witness so horrific a death and know that it had been directly his own doing.

"I'll . . . I can try." Narsi fought down the bile rising in his throat.

"No," Atreau cut in quickly, taking the sword from Narsi's hand. "Narsi's safety comes first and foremost. We're not putting him on a front line. In addition, we have no idea how many of the men serving under Yago are enthralled. They may not be capable of retreating even it they are terrified."

Sabella frowned and Atreau went on.

"We're better off avoiding Yago all together. Let him and his men get tired and bored waiting around in the dark. If some wander off, you can arrange accidents for them. But we need to lull them into complacency until our Labaran reinforcements arrive. Then we take them unaware while they think they're waiting around to slaughter a bunch of unarmed Haldiim grandmothers."

Sabella sighed but then shrugged.

"And in the meantime?" Sabella asked.

"Empty the streets as best we can and get Narsi to the sacred grove," Atreau replied.

After that, they agreed to split their work. Spider and his people took on the task of drawing drunks and bystanders off the open roads and away from the streets surrounding the sacred grove. Sabella and her swordsmen skirted Yago's troops, creating disturbances and distractions to lure their attention to the south and away from Narsi and Atreau's approach from the north. At the same time Hylanya had seemingly urged feral cats all across the city to hunt the flocks of songbirds serving as Clara's spies.

Narsi and Atreau withdrew to the Candioro Theater. After slipping in through the backstage doors, they cleaned up and changed into the unassuming costumes of middling sea merchants. Narsi hid his shining hands beneath kidskin gloves and accepted the short sword that Atreau handed him. Then the two of them set out to circle around the sacred grove, searching for a way in past Captain Yago's guardsmen.

Out on the street, Narsi heard the dissonant clang of fire bells, but they must have been far off. The noise barely carried over the din of music and cheers still filling the streets. From time to time a few fireworks burst across the sky, but steadily the roads and walkways began to empty. Lanterns and torches were doused and gloom closed in around them.

As they turned a corner, Atreau caught Narsi's wrist and pulled him into a doorway just as two patrolling guardsmen passed them. Another two blocks on, they sighted three of Yago's mounted guardsmen. A man dressed in the colors of the Red Stallion sword house shouted obscenities at them from a raised walkway and then fled. Two of the riders gave chase, but the third remained, keeping guard at the crossroads.

"Is it possible that they know we have the horns and they're waiting to ambush us?" Narsi asked in a whisper.

Atreau remained silent. Narsi racked his mind for a way to reach the sacred grove if Yago's men blocked off every street and alley. They couldn't just fly over. Though maybe if they climbed over the roofs? Narsi considered the steep angles and slick tiles of the city skyline and abandoned the thought.

"It's not impossible for Hierro or Clara to know about you specifically, but it's highly unlikely." Atreau gently caught Narsi's hand in his own. "I think it's Jacinto who Yago is truly after tonight."

Narsi drew in a deep breath and nodded.

Then Atreau pulled him into his arms.

"I won't let anything happen to you, I swear," Atreau whispered, then he kissed Narsi's cheek. "We'll find a way. Just give it a little time."

With Atreau's arm around him, Narsi found it easier to relax and wait. It wasn't so different from the companionable trips they'd made in Labara, he reassured himself.

As they watched the remaining guardsman, a battered gray cat slunk up to them and circled around Narsi before butting its head into

Atreau's leg. He crouched down and briefly scratched the cat's chin, then straightened beside Narsi.

"We'll have to take a more scenic route, I think," Atreau said.

"After you," Narsi responded.

"Oh no." Atreau flourished his hand toward the cat. "After her."

They followed the cat through an alley and then over two garden walls and across the fragrant, boisterous grounds of a dance hall. Atreau exchanged brief greetings with the woman in charge of the place. She flirted playfully and then sent them along a series of hidden passages to a sprawling brothel several blocks away. From there they made their way through a quiet bakery and two raucous taverns. At last they exited near the Shell Fountain along with a garrulous crowd of tipsy law students.

By the time they emerged, the sky had taken on a predawn glow and only a few voices were still raised in arguments or song. Narsi clearly discerned the gurgle and splash of water dancing in the fountain. They were only a few blocks from the sacred grove, he realized. He grinned at the cat and quickened his steps.

The public square surrounding the fountain came into view, and through the gloom Narsi picked out the forms of discarded masks and toppled wine barrels. Then something moved past the spray of water. Narsi froze in his tracks as he recognized the large, shaggy silhouette of a mordwolf.

It stood nearly as tall as a horse and circled the fountain with a restless gait. Narsi's muscles tensed with fear and his heart began to hammer in his chest. Beside him, Atreau too went very still. Another, smaller, mordwolf stalked from the shadows of the fallen wine barrels. It passed the first as if patrolling. Farther along the crooked lane, Narsi sighted the dark form of some other giant creature. All of them seemed to be waiting outside the sacred grove.

A drunk law student staggered ahead of Narsi and Atreau, then stopped, gaping and pointing at the beasts. The huge mordwolf in front of the fountain lifted its gaze and snarled. The law student turned, screaming, and pelted back toward the tavern.

"Atreau." Narsi's breath caught in his chest as the mordwolf's glinting yellow gaze shifted to him.

"I know. Don't panic." Atreau glanced down at the cat then and pulled Narsi behind him and drew his sword.

"You can't fight them." Narsi quickly stepped alongside Atreau and held out his hands. He wouldn't allow Atreau to risk his life, not when his own hands were burning with power. No matter how it horrified him, he had to act. "I can do this—"

The rest of Narsi's words were drowned out by a booming animal roar. A white bear nearly the height of a building burst from around the corner of the crooked street. Terror shook Narsi's whole body. He started to scramble back, shoving Atreau behind him. Atreau caught his arm and held him.

The bear threw itself at the mordwolves, swatting the smaller one into a building with a brutal rake of its paw. It caught the larger mordwolf's throat in its jaws, lifting it off its feet. It shook the huge mordwolf twice, snapping its spine, and then spat the limp body aside.

Narsi stared at the mordwolves' mangled bodies as they melted back into torn human corpses dressed in the colors of the bishop's guardsmen. The immense white bear wheeled to stare directly at Narsi and Atreau.

"Took you long enough," Atreau called out.

The bear snorted and padded toward them. Instinctively Narsi started back. Obviously, the bear served their Labaran allies, Narsi recognized that, but facing such a gigantic creature—having seen it rip mordwolves apart—filled him with a primal terror. Narsi focused on the animal's relaxed demeanor as it walked closer. He drew in a tried to concentrate on the wonder of the situation, rather than the horror.

This giant bear seemed like an Old God from a storybook, didn't it? Maybe it played with trolls, or perhaps it was some ancient carving brought to life.

"Don't be afraid." Atreau gripped his hand and whispered, "It's just Elezar."

"Elezar?" The notion that this huge animal could somehow be his uncle stunned Narsi so much that he forgot his fear. His mouth fell open slightly as he gawked at the creature. Atreau's memoir had mentioned such transformations, and Narsi had witnessed mordwolves melt into human beings. But it was different to try to connect a man he knew—a man he was related to—with this otherworldly beast that was so, so big.

"How is that possible?" Narsi choked out.

"Magic." Atreau's response was as succinct as it was accurate.

Magic was the method. That explained everything . . . or at least as much as either of them needed to know right now.

The bear stopped in front of them, Narsi craned his head back to stare up at its black eyes and bloodstained jaw.

"Hello again." Narsi managed to keep his voice from quavering.

Elezar nodded in response. Then he lowered his body to the ground so that his big head hung at their eye level. He regarded them with an expression that struck Narsi as almost amused. His breath rolled over them like steam. Strangely, it smelled of oranges and anise.

"Can you get us the rest of the way through?" Atreau asked, and the bear nodded.

Atreau reached out and grasped the bear's shoulder, then he clambered up to its back. Narsi paused for an instant. How was he supposed to recognize this bear as his uncle and still feel at all comfortable riding on its back?

Then again, the only other option seemed to be walking through a street teeming with mordwolves.

"Sorry for the inconvenience," Narsi said, then he followed Atreau up. The bear's body was sweltering hot. Up close, Narsi could see bloodstains, broken arrow shafts and scorch marks scattered across the bear's sides. He'd already been through a battle.

The bear rose to its feet, spun and then leapt forward. Narsi dug his hands into its thick fur to keep from being hurled from the bear's back. Atreau leaned against him as they raced up the crooked lane leading to the sacred grove. Elezar ran in such great bounds that Narsi felt as if they were flying past the sedate buildings lining the street.

As they neared the sacred grove, Narsi grew uneasy. Bodies littered the ground, and he heard angry cries and clashing swords only a few streets away. The bear stopped and knelt, allowing Narsi and Atreau to dismount. Narsi noticed that many of the men lying in the street wore the armor of the bishop's guardsmen. Arrows jutted from their chests and heads. Then Sabella and Yara came pelting toward them from the opposite direction. A group of Irabiim archers and Labaran cavalry followed behind them.

The bear rose onto its hind legs, towering up alongside the two-story buildings across the lane. But as it gave a shake of its white hide, it appeared to collapse, like a sail. The white hide waved in the wind, shrinking back to a bearskin cloak. Elezar pulled the hood back to reveal his angular face.

"The bishop's guardsmen?" Elezar asked the leader of the cavalry.

"Their captain and two of his subordinates fled, but we've taken the rest," she replied.

"Well done. Regroup here and await further orders." Elezar turned and then gestured for Narsi and Atreau to lead the way into the sacred grove. Yara ran alongside them, while Sabella remained with the Labaran forces at the foot of the sacred grove. When they crested the hill, predawn light began to glint over the golden tiles of rooftops. Elezar stopped beside one of the gnarled wisteria trees.

"I'll keep watch here." Elezar turned to study the street below and the growing number of people gathering there.

Narsi, Yara and Atreau hurried up the grassy rise. With each step, the tingling in Narsi's hands intensified. His shoulders and collarbones were hot. An anxious feeling fluttered through his chest. He quickened his steps, all but sprinting past the trees into the grassy clearing.

There Esfir, Querra and Mother Kir-Naham sat in quiet prayer, encircled by a dozen physicians from the Haldiim hospital. Narsi didn't know all their names, but he remembered their faces from the night mordwolves had encircled the sacred grove. Fifty or more glossy crows filled the tree branches above them.

Esfir looked up and smiled. Yara strolled to her side and sank down. Atreau stopped next to Narsi.

Mother Kir-Naham considered Atreau with an expression of slight surprise. The rest of them continued their prayers.

"Captain Yago will probably return with more men to attack the sacred grove," Narsi said. "You must all get away—"

"We know," Esfir cut him off. "The Goat sent warning last night. But someone has to protect the Circle of Wisteria and help you wake Yahmuur's Horn."

Narsi stared at her.

"How do you know about—" Narsi began to ask.

"Do you remember the poppy-addled prophecies of that renegade Bahiim, Javier—" Mother Kir-Naham asked.

"There was nothing to suggest that he was poppy-addled. His writing was just hidden in that section of the botanical volume." Esfir cut her aunt off with an exasperated look.

"Fine." Mother Kir-Naham shared an amused glance with Querra, then turned her attention back to Esfir. "You tell them."

"Last night Irsea's crows gathered and told me that Javier's prophecy was at hand. Yah-muur must be awakened, and the holy shields guarded by Wadi Tel will shine again over the sacred grove." Esfir stared fixedly at Narsi. "And just like the ancient Bahiim, Javier, Irsea mentioned you by name, Narsi. That was the last thing she was able to pass on to me."

Narsi reeled at the thought of all this. How had he failed to notice the connections between all these people until just now? Then it occurred to him that it was because those connections might not have existed until he and Atreau traveled back to Labara and set things in motion two weeks ago.

For his part, Javier had obviously traveled even farther back and finally found a way to pass a warning along into the future. Though the fact that he'd included Narsi's name was puzzling, because he'd already come back from the past by the time Narsi and Atreau had come up with their current plan. So how could Javier have known that he would be here?

Unless . . .

Unless this wasn't the first time that Javier had sent them to wake Yah-muur's Horn. That would mean that they'd previously failed at least once before. For a terrible moment Narsi wondered how many times before this he'd made this same discovery. One? One hundred? His head felt hot and dizzy. His fingers felt as if they were humming with hot currents.

Narsi shook his head; now was not the time to get distracted. He gripped his medical satchel and swung it around to take out the gold box inside.

"I suppose we should awaken the horn," he said.

"Not yet," Esfir replied. "According to Javier's prophecy, we must await the arrival of the Solstice King. He'll bring the blessings that will allow the Circle of Wisteria to rouse Yah-muur."

Narsi scowled at this new information.

"What Solstice King?" Atreau arched a brow. "King Sevanyo, you mean?"

"Is there another king?" Yara asked.

But Esfir shook her head

"The Solstice King will arise from blood and flames. From shadows and ruin, to wake Yah-muur and tear the Shroud of Stone asunder." Esfir closed her eyes as she recited. "He will arrive with the light of Solstice Day, carrying all the blessings and power of Wadi Tel to the Circle of Wisteria. He will light the trees and rouse Yah-muur from Narsi's hands."

"Would it have killed Javier to have just written this Solstice King's name down?" Atreau grumbled. Narsi suppressed a laugh.

"Is that everything Javier foretold?" Narsi asked.

Before anyone could respond, the ground suddenly shuddered and an archway of gold flames roared up from between two of the gnarled wisteria trees. The scent of smoke and the howls of wolves rolled from the gold flames. Dozens of shadowy figures charged through.

CHAPTER
THIRTY-THREE

Something struck Ariz's numb body. He flopped onto his side like a sack of meat, but felt nothing and gave no response. His stiff eyes barely took in the flickering firelight all around. His face rested near the base of an astronomical model, nestled amidst blood-soaked pebbles. Noise seeped through the ringing that filled his ears. The second time, he felt the impact more distinctly. Someone was kicking his corpse.

"Dead." A terribly familiar voice drifted over Ariz. His eyes slowly focused on the glinting golden spur and glossy black boot that landed next to his face. Hierro stood directly over him.

"Your assassin was able to take the form of an eagle?" Remes's words came out in a slow, dazed whisper. His violet silk shoe, embroidered with gold thread, edged near Hierro's boot. Soot and blood spattered the toe. "They said it was an eagle that killed Ojoito last night. You swore you had nothing to do with that—"

"Indeed," Hierro responded. Unlike Remes, he raised his voice to carry to the distant figures in the garden. "Clearly this Labaran assassin meant to discredit me by claiming to serve me. But he spared Fedeles Quemanor and was bent upon destroying our Holy Church. He murdered my father as well as the royal family. How could I play any part in such things?" Hierro spun on his heel to face Remes. His voice remained theatric and loud. "Never fear, Your Highness. We won't allow the Duke of Rauma and his Labaran allies to get away with this treason. He may have abducted your father, but you are our salvation now and God is with us!"

Ariz heard the sounds of agreement and approval rising from the crowd behind Hierro. Remes said nothing. He bent, his face bowing into Ariz's line of sight. A spray of dried blood colored his cheek. He stared hard into Ariz's dead eyes. His expression of recognition slowly turned to horror, and Ariz knew exactly why.

Remes had witnessed firsthand the complete control Hierro wielded over Ariz. He knew full well that the assassinations Ariz carried out were at Hierro's behest, and that had to include the massacre of Ojoito's household.

In this exact instant Remes had to recognize that regardless of his flattery and smiles, Hierro had no intention of sparing anyone, not even if Remes ordered it. Perhaps for the first time Remes registered the importance of the fact that none of the soldiers, spies and assassins bent on placing him on the throne actually served him. They all belonged to Hierro.

Hierro's strong hand landed on Remes's shoulder, gripping him so firmly that Ariz notice Remes's jacket bunch.

"These fires are growing dangerous, my prince. We must evacuate you to somewhere safe," Hierro stated. Royal bishop's guardsmen closed in around them. "Clara is probably worried sick for your sake."

"Clara," Remes murmured. His fearful expression once again took on a dazed quality. He rose to Hierro's side. Amidst shouts calling to protect Prince Remes and others decrying the Quemanors for abducting the king, the firelight grew more intense. Hierro, Remes and the crowd surrounding them fled from Ariz's field of vision.

Smoke drifted over him, as did a growing sensation of heat. Ariz's body tingled as his newly roused pulse slowly drove the numb from his limbs. He dragged in a ragged gasp and coughed. He took another breath and at last managed to blink. Turning his head a little, he caught sight of flames rushing up the branches of a sapling. An eerie blue tinge edged the fires as they rose all around the abandoned models of planets and moons.

Ariz rolled to his side and pushed himself up onto his hands and knees. Needles of pain pricked through the numb pervading his hands and feet. He couldn't stand yet, but he didn't dare to remain where he was. He dragged himself on his belly and then, gaining more feeling, crawled through the dead bodies littering the ground. At the edge of the garden he used the corner of a fountain to steady himself. He rose to his feet and staggered toward the stables.

His first thought was to find Fedeles. From what he'd overheard of Hierro's proclamations, he guessed that King Sevanyo and his supporters had fled with Fedeles and Oasia. Ariz could finally tell them everything he knew. He could warn them about Hierro's accusations as well as Clara's grasp over ancient relics.

The beat of his heart seemed to strengthen just thinking about seeing Fedeles again.

He stumbled up against the wall of the stable. Then he stilled, listening. A child's voice sounded from inside the stables. Was that Marisol? He leaned against the wall, straining to hear her again.

"Where are we going?" Marisol asked. The quaver in her voice terrified Ariz. He reached for his sword then realized that he'd left it in the burning garden. Only his long knife remained gripped in a death rictus in his left hand.

"Sparanzo. Sparanzo." Elenna gasped the name as if using it to ward off a stabbing pain. "Don't be afraid. She won't harm you, Sparanzo. Do you understand, Sparanzo?"

"I—yes, I understand," Marisol answered.

"I must take you to her," Elenna groaned. "But she won't harm you as long as you remember. You are Sparanzo. You are Sparanzo."

Elenna sounded deranged and agonized, but Ariz understood the situation at once. She was in the grip of a thrall and struggling to convince herself of a lie so that she might disobey a command. He'd done the same thing when he'd made himself believe that Hierro had ordered him to kiss Fedeles, not kill him. On some level, Elenna knew that she was delivering a decoy in Sparanzo's place. She struggled to suppress that knowledge just to make the agony of disobedience endurable.

The stable doors swung open. Elenna rode out on Ariz's dappled stallion, Moteado. She hugged Marisol in front of her with one hand and gripped the horse's reins with the other. She stared straight ahead with an agonized expression as she urged the old stallion forward. But Marisol looked all around her. Her eyes went wide when she met Ariz's gaze and her hand clutched the chain of a necklace.

Ariz recognized it at once. He had personally delivered it along with the promise of Clara's protection. Whether by chance or design, today Marisol had worn the locket that Clara had intended for Sparanzo.

Then Elenna and Marisol surged away.

Ariz didn't pause to think. He sprinted through the smoke and gloom after them. Desperation drove the lingering numbness of death from his body. He bounded over shrubs and tore across the pebbled paths of the palace grounds. The scabbed lacerations on his arms, chest and neck tore open and bruised muscles ached, but he refused to slow. Twice he glimpsed Hierro and his throng of followers but managed to evade their notice in the chaos of servants and guards fleeing from flames and marauding mordwolves. He kept Elenna and Marisol in sight all the way to the palace gates and out onto the city streets.

The atmosphere beyond the palace walls struck him as truly strange. Music and cheers still rang from across the river. Ariz even glimpsed people on the Gado Bridge dancing beneath strings of bright lanterns. Bursts of fireworks sprinkled the sky.

But here on the northern avenues lined by noble households, mordwolves snarled beneath the flickering lanterns and sparks from the blazing palace had already set several buildings on fire. People ran shouting for help and calling out warnings. Fire bells resounded while families fled their burning homes only to face the horror of packs of mordwolves. Wagons and carriages clogged the streets—some on fire and abandoned, others filled with terrified people. Ariz witnessed a groomsman cut several horses free from empty carriages and then mount one and ride for the Gado Bridge. He wasn't alone in his flight. Streams of people on foot flooded toward the bridge. Some wore costumes, others were dressed for bed; some carried children and injured companions, while others shoved and trampled the people in their ways.

Mounted on a warhorse, Elenna commanded an advantage. She urged Moteado through a group of serving girls in their nightgowns, and the girls startled into Ariz's path. He dodged aside only to see a nobleman's carriage come barreling toward him. Instinctively he bounded up, throwing his arms wide.

Molten heat burst through his body as his bones and muscles unfurled into massive wings, catching the air and vaulting him upward. His talons raked the top of the carriage as he shot over it. Then three fast strokes of his wings sent him soaring after Elenna and Marisol.

He immediately caught sight of them again. At the same time two mordwolves lit out after them as well. Elenna urged Moteado ahead, but the stallion was old and the streets too dark and crowded to risk a blind gallop. Marisol clung to Moteado's neck, digging her small hands into the stallion's mane. Elenna leaned over her protectively as a mordwolf lunged at them.

Ariz dived. He struck the mordwolf's nape, slamming its head into the cobblestones and sending it tumbling. The second mordwolf spun to bite at Ariz. He slashed its muzzle with his long talons and felt the heat of its breath gush over his legs. He arched and wheeled up as vicious teeth snapped after him.

An instant later the mordwolf spun back after Elenna and Marisol. Its attack couldn't be a matter of opportunity or chance. Hierro knew Clara would attempt to save Sparanzo, so no doubt he'd commanded these mordwolves and others to hunt and kill the boy. Likely he was also using that damn locket to single Sparanzo out.

Ariz swooped on a mordwolf, sinking his talons into its shoulders and hurling it under the back wheels of a heavy wagon.

Then he flew up as Elenna and Marisol plunged into the throngs of fleeing people and animals. Three more mordwolves pursued them. Ariz attacked the one snapping at Moteado's hooves, tearing its head from its neck. Then he spun back to deal with the others. To his shock, he saw a plague of rats scurrying from the gutters to bite and gnaw at the mordwolves' legs and faces. The mordwolves scraped against buildings and rolled on the ground, trying to shake the rats off, but more and more of the creatures poured over them, chewing into their flanks and digging beneath their skins.

The sight revolted and confounded Ariz. He couldn't imagine Fedeles or Oasia employing such horrifying attacks, and he knew that Clara hated rats with a passion. Who else was at work here? An ally? Or some other witch heretofore unknown?

Ariz turned his attention back to Elenna and Marisol. As he winged through the sky, he sighted more rats scurrying through the streets to attack the packs of mordwolves. At the same time, an army of cats roamed rooftops and balconies. At first he assumed they were fleeing from fires, but then he witnessed cat after cat killing numerous songbirds.

Ariz still had no idea who was responsible, and he didn't have time to think too much about it.

Navigating a sky choked with birds and smoke made tracking Elenna and Marisol's route through the chaotic streets challenging. On top of that, he'd expected them to ride for the Odalis estate, guessing that the woman who wanted Sparanzo had to be Clara. But Elenna charged south toward the Dasma Bridge and the Shard of Heaven. Ariz dived lower, closing the distance. He considered slamming into Elenna to stop them, but he feared that he'd throw Marisol from the stallion as well. The roads were already too dangerous. More than once he swooped down, driving panicked horses and confused riders out of Elenna's path.

Smoke burned his eyes and his muscles ached. It felt like hours passed as fires spread through the streets and Elenna turned from one route to another and another. Ariz kept close, protecting them while also watching for an opportunity to snatch Marisol away. Light limned the horizon and diluted the black sky to shades of smoky blue.

The closer they came to the Shard of Heaven, the more songbirds filled the air around him. Thousands of them circled the towering chapel spires.

He didn't want to alert Clara or Hierro to his presence if he could help it. So he swooped low, his wingtips nearly skimming the surface of the cobblestones. At the Dasma Bridge he veered down over the dark waters of the river, keeping out of sight of the guards while pacing himself with Moteado.

He heard loud splashes and choking noises beneath him. Glancing down, Ariz saw several huge mordwolves being dragged beneath the waves by dozens of strange, green-skinned women.

What in the three hells? Frogwives from Labaran lore? Were the Labarans truly launching an attack?

One of the kelp-haired women turned her round yellow gaze on him and suddenly lunged up from water. Her webbed hands snatched at his tail feathers. Ariz slashed her fingers with his talons and surged up out of her reach.

His heart raced and he soared upward just to ensure a safe distance. Then he caught a breeze and easily swept over a wall. He dropped into the shadows surrounding the courtyard of the towering chapel.

A few middle-aged priests and a large party of bishop's guardsmen stood near the fountain, stupefied by the sight of the burning palace and the blazing hills behind it. None of them noticed when Ariz alighted beside a stack of wine barrels. He rolled his shoulders and straightened as the eagle's body melted back into his flesh.

The chapel stood behind him, and Elenna rode toward him—though now Ariz noticed a line of other riders followed her onto the Dasma

Bridge. Ariz narrowed his gaze and felt his pupils flare. He caught sight of Hierro's face in the crowd of riders as well as Remes. Hierro glared directly at Elenna. Ariz gripped the hilt of his long knife.

As if feeling Hierro's anger strike her back, Elenna glanced over her shoulder and then urged Moteado to gallop faster across the last stretch of the bridge and over the grounds of the courtyard. Marisol's eyes were wide with fear and she gripped Elenna's arm.

Elenna hardly waited for Moteado to come to a stop before vaulting from the stallion's back. She pulled Marisol into her arms and raced to the cathedral steps.

"Good! Bring him to me quickly!"

Ariz spun back to see Clara at the top of the stairs, flanked by four guardsmen and two physician-priests. A dozen songbirds whirled around her. Ariz crouched low and edged closer, studying Elenna and Marisol. Could he possibly rush in and snatch Marisol away before Clara, the guardsmen or the physician-priests could react? Once he had Marisol, how could he carry her away? Moteado stood nearby, but Ariz would have to ride him over the Dasma Bridge directly into the path of Hierro and his companions.

If he transformed, he could easily lift her into the air, but the thought of attempting to grip Marisol's delicate body with murderous talons terrified him. He could so easily slice through her flesh.

Years had passed since Ariz had given thought to his own injuries. He took action and endured the resulting pain like penance. His own well-being mattered little and never gave him pause. But now, looking at his little niece, fear gripped him and he couldn't move. If he was hurt, it hardly mattered, but how could he risk Marisol's life in a brazen charge?

He'd never before frozen in the face of combat, but now he stood as if rooted in place, racking his mind for a means to rescue and protect Marisol. In the instant that he hesitated, Elenna carried Marisol to Clara. Clara gripped Marisol's hand and pulled her up the steps of the chapel. Elenna, Clara's guardsmen and the physician-priests followed them. Several priests carrying evening lanterns and chanting prayers also ascended the steps. The guardsmen in the courtyard turned their attention toward the group of riders crossing the Dasma Bridge. Ariz took advantage of their distraction to rush up the steps and slip through the massive golden doors before they fell closed.

The interior of the cathedral was as dimly lit and disturbing as Ariz remembered. Soft prayers echoed through alcoves and the faint, warm light of scattered lamps hardly penetrated the deep shadows that filled the long nave. At least the beheaded statures of giant monsters and savage warriors offered Ariz cover. He crept between the contorted stone forms, following Clara's party as they hurried into the apse.

There, the immense altar of stone heads and skulls stood supporting the crystal reliquaries of the three Hallowed Kings, which towered up from the altar. The murky green water and human remains inside churned and roiled as if boiling. Nearly a dozen priests knelt beside the reliquaries, eyes clenched shut as they chanted in strained, desperate tones.

Marisol dug her heels in and fought when she caught sight of the multitude of carved heads and skulls that made up the towering altar.

"No! There are ghosts!" Marisol shouted. "No!"

"Don't fuss, my dear boy. These dead old men have no power left in them." Clara waved at the reliquaries of the Hallowed Kings. Marisol stared wide-eyed at the motions of Clara's fingers. Ariz only discerned motes of dust scattering through the faint predawn light that filtered through the stained glass windows high overhead. But he knew Clara manipulated some sort of magic and that Marisol saw it as clearly as she saw the Hallowed Kings.

"Gachello may bare his teeth and snarl at us," Clara went on. "But he's little more than a spider trapped in his own cobweb now. Soon enough we will sweep him away."

"I want to go home. I want my mama . . . please," Marisol whimpered.

Ariz flinched at the pleading in her voice. Clara merely smiled.

"Your mama and papa are gone away now." Clara patted Marisol's head. "But your Aunty Clara is going to look after you, and we will have the most wonderful adventure together."

"Clara! This is not the time for your childish games!" Hierro's furious shout boomed from the chapel doors, carrying over the cacophony of fire bells ringing across the city.

He strode in with Remes just behind him, and several brawny noblemen followed after.

Ariz hurried through the maze of statues toward Marisol. He was so focused on Clara ahead of him and Hierro behind that he nearly overlooked the two priests crouched only a few feet ahead of him. They peered from behind the stone haunches of a giant boar. One was elderly and plump, the other a slender, pockmarked youth. Several large golden rats circled them. The young priest absently stroked their heads as he stared at Marisol with obvious worry. He moved as if to approach her, but the elder priest caught his hand and led him away.

As Hierro strode through the nave, the two priests and their company of rats fled back into an alcove and down some staircase. Ariz didn't have the time to spare them any further thought. Hierro closed in on Marisol. Ariz drew his knife.

Elenna and Clara both stepped between Hierro and Marisol. Hierro kicked Elenna aside. Her body slammed into a statue and slid to the floor. Hierro didn't even glance to her, instead turning his attention to Clara.

"Out of my way," Hierro commanded.

Clara's face contorted with pain as she resisted the order. But an instant later she dropped to her knees, crawling aside and gasping. Hierro grinned at Marisol.

"You promised me his safety!" Clara screamed. Her gaze fell on Remes.

The prince's face drained of color. He opened his mouth but closed it again after Hierro shot him a single murderous glance.

"I don't have the patience for children tonight." Hierro's right hand dropped to his sword hilt. "The whelp dies, here and now!"

Ariz sprinted from the maze of decapitated statues. Rage lent him a wild strength as he plunged his knife into Hierro's back. His blade speared deep and a brought up a stream of frothing dark blood as Ariz jerked it free of Hierro's body. Hierro spun to face him, shock and outrage contorting his handsome features.

Meeting Hierro's gaze, an overwhelming fury swept through Ariz as it had countless times before. But today Hierro's brand didn't restrain him. Ariz didn't give the man the chance to draw his sword, much less speak. Ariz attacked, driving Hierro's chin up with an uppercut and slashing his exposed throat open in two brutal strikes. Hot blood fountained up as Hierro's muscles, tendons and bones ripped apart.

Hierro crumpled to the floor and Ariz dropped with him, driving his knife into Hierro's chest again and again. He punched the knife into Hierro in a frenzy, as if pounding out the years of hurt and humiliation he'd suffered. Blood and gore spattered him, but he hardly noticed. All he knew was that he *had* to kill Hierro. His arms and back ached and his breath grew ragged, but he didn't stop. He hammered the knife between Hierro's ribs, gashing open the man's chest and eviscerating his vile, ruthless heart. At last Ariz drove the knife down so hard that the blade snapped.

He lifted the hilt and stared at the jagged remnants of the knife blade.

Only then did any sense of reason or awareness return to him. He was soaked with blood, and Hierro's severed head lay near his knee. In a daze, Ariz dropped the broken knife and rose to his feet. He staggered toward Marisol, but the fear in her expression stopped him from grasping her hand.

"I'm sorry I scared you," Ariz whispered. "I won't hurt you."

Marisol nodded, but her whole body quaked. Then Ariz noticed her worried gaze shift from him to the people gathered behind him. He spun at once.

Remes and Hierro's entourage of noblemen and guardsmen stared at him with varying expressions of shock, sickness and horror. All of them held weapons, but none moved a step nearer to Ariz.

"You . . . you were dead," Remes choked out. "How can you be here?"

"Because it is God's will!" Clara rose from her knees, her face incandescent with joy. She bounced on her toes like a delighted child and spun in a circle as blazing blue light whirled around her, lifting her like a dance partner. "Our Lord has set me free!"

The blue light encircling her flared. Remes and the men surrounding him fell to their knees, gasping in pain, as symbols of bright blue songbirds seared into their brows. Behind Clara, the crystal reliquaries holding the Hallow Kings shattered. Murky water flooded over the priests kneeling at the altar and washed the tangled masses of rotting bones across the floor. The remains quivered for a few moments but then stilled.

"We have no need for quaking old ghosts." Clara beamed at Ariz and then pulled Marisol to her. "Thanks to you, Ariz, our glorious reign begins at last."

CHAPTER
THIRTY-FOUR

Fedeles reached the crest of Crown Hill just as the first rays of sun began to illuminate the ancient ruins. Only hours ago, he and Ariz had lain here among the wildflowers. Now, filthy, bloodied people and exhausted horses filled the space. Servants and nobles mingled alike; the battle had rendered their social ranks largely indistinguishable—all of them showed haggard faces. All their clothes were ragged and stained. Many bore gashes as well as burns from both curses and flames. Some lay dying and a few had already succumbed to death.

Delfia rushed to Fedeles, pulling her son, Celino, with her left arm while her right hung blood-drenched and limp. Her expression was hard to read through the dirt and blood staining her face, but Fedeles recognized anguish in her eyes. Celino made no sound, but tears washed pale tracks through the soot covering his delicate face.

"Did you see Elenna?" Delfia demanded. "Marisol is with her—did you see them?"

Another pang of sorrow fell into the immense loss that filled Fedeles. It was a raindrop rippling a deep pool.

"There was no one behind me." Fedeles managed to speak clearly and calmly. "I'm sorry."

Delfia went still, hugging her son to her side and staring at the cliff's edge as if by sheer force of will she could summon her daughter to dash up the rise. Even as tired and dispirited as he was, Fedeles looked back too, considering the foolhardy act of attempting to descend the hill to search for Elenna and Marisol. The path was gone and fire raged below. Even so, perhaps he could . . .

Could what? Die in the fire and smoke? Abandon his own family and all the rest of these people?

He didn't know, but he hated the shame and helplessness of doing nothing.

"Elenna's clever and quick," Delfia murmured as she stroked her son's head. "She'll have found somewhere safe to wait with Marisol. They'll be fine. They'll be fine."

"Uncle Ariz too?" Celino whispered with his small face still pressed against his mother's waist. Fedeles was spared the child's gaze. It was hard enough to meet Delfia's eyes and have her look away.

"Ariz is somewhere better now," Delfia said. "We'll all meet again someday."

And agony of sorrow pierced through Fedeles's chest like needles, and despite his attempt to remain in control of himself, his eyes misted.

"Fedeles!" Oasia's voice rose through the chaotic crowd of beaten, filthy people and bloodied horses.

"I must go," Fedeles said to Delfia and then turned away. He was relieved to excuse himself and escape from Ariz's family. If he remained, he knew he'd collapse weeping. He couldn't afford to do that—yet.

Ariz didn't die just to have you fall apart and fail everyone, he told himself.

A young groom took Firaj from him and Fedeles thanked him. Then he headed to where Oasia stood on the steps of the ruined temple. As he strode through the crowd, he took in the familiar and strange faces of those gathered around. Between their tattered costumes and the gloom, these survivors truly did resemble those fugitive, mythic creatures that had been felled in the Great Hunt. Fedeles wondered if that hadn't been the real intention of the Masquerade theme this year. He didn't know if he found it more ironic or pathetic that the royal bishop who'd decided the theme had already been gutted at the behest of his would-be holy heroes.

Few people met Fedeles's gaze, but he noticed most of them stealing sidelong glances at him. They had all witnessed him and Oasia using magic; there would be no turning back from that, but right now, Fedeles couldn't care. A couple people shifted back when his shadow fell near them, but far more watched Fedeles with desperate reverence. Suelita wiped tears from her cheeks and offered him a weak smile. Fedeles nodded to her as he passed her and her family. Ladislo Bayezar saluted him and two maids clasped their hands as if in prayer.

Oasia watched his approach with a weary expression. Sparanzo clung to her side. When Fedeles reached the stairs, Sparanzo let out a crow of joy and threw himself into Fedeles's arms. Fedeles hugged his son to him. He felt so small and fragile in Fedeles's arms. Despite the summer warmth, Sparanzo trembled.

"I was so scared, Papa. There was so much blood and yelling everywhere, and we can't find Marisol, and I don't know what to do . . . I don't know. You were gone so long." Sparanzo's slender shoulders shook as his whispers dissolved into tears.

"It's all right now." Fedeles stroked his son's head and held him, gently rocking. Then he caught a glimpse of Oasia's stern expression.

"Sevanyo wants you." She drew Sparanzo away from Fedeles and wiped his cheeks. "Be brave, Sparanzo. Your mama and papa are here. No one can hurt you."

Fedeles hurried into the temple ruins to see Sevanyo. Nobles of Sevanyo's inner circle as well as several ministers had gathered around him. They crouched and knelt in a half circle, their faces lit by torches. Fedeles knew most of them at a glance. Sevanyo's closest friends, Lord Helio, Lord Bayezar and Lord Estaban, all sat at Sevanyo's side, while Lliro Vediya and Timoteo knelt among the guards and attendants gathered before the king. Both Timoteo and his sacrist, Berto, were soot spattered and rumpled in a way that made Fedeles think they'd been in at least one altercation with the assassins who had pursued their group. But the moment Fedeles focused on Sevanyo, he couldn't think of anyone else.

Sevanyo lay on the stone floor, with Timoteo's cloak beneath him and Oasia's silk shawl pillowing his head. The bright shards of mirrors that had adorned his chest and brow were shattered and caked in blood.

Sevanyo's exposed torso and shoulders glistened with open wounds. Teal-tinged smoke drifted up from the edges of a chasm the size of a fist burned through his chest. How he still lived, Fedeles had no idea. Sevanyo's face was white as chalk.

"Good you're here." Sevanyo's voice was clear, but each breath he drew sounded disturbingly wet and labored. He lifted his right hand to Fedeles.

Fedeles knelt at his side, cupping Sevanyo's hand in his own. He closed his eyes as if in prayer. Despite his bone-deep exhaustion, Fedeles still tried to place blessings of strength and health over Sevanyo. His shadow fluttered over Sevanyo's body like the faint smoke of funerary incense dissipating in the breeze. Again the image of Ariz's unmoving body flashed through his mind. How desperately he wanted him to draw a breath. To rise and live.

Then, to his surprise, he felt a gentle warmth roll back over his cold fingers. Sevanyo's hand curled around his, offering a tremulous reassurance.

"Oasia already tried . . . don't waste your strength. I need you to do something else for me," Sevanyo said. He drew in another sticky-sounding breath. "Before witnesses from both the nobility and the church, I, Sevanyo Sagrada, make this formal decree. From this day forth I disavow my treacherous son, Remes, and no longer recognize the Fueres household as royal descendants. I acknowledge Fedeles Quemanor as my one and *only* heir. I have no other."

Fedeles was so shocked that he thought he must have misunderstood. A few of the men and women gathered around made surprised sounds. Timoteo and Lord Helio, however, both nodded as if this was something they'd long expected.

"Your Majesty's wish will be obeyed," Timoteo said.

"All present now bear witness to your command, Your Highness." Lord Bayezar too nodded. His words were echoed through the ruin.

"But Jacinto—" Fedeles started to object.

"Protect him from the burden of the crown. Will you do that for me, Fedeles? You'll shield him, won't you?" Sevanyo's eyes fell closed and he pulled them open again as if it required all his effort.

"I will," Fedeles conceded without thinking. Indulging Sevanyo was a habit.

"Then I can rest at peace," Sevanyo whispered.

"No. Don't give up. Don't!" His voice broke. Fedeles closed his eyes and fought back the sorrow rising through him. He could not come undone right now. His friends and family were relying on him—these gathered, desperate people all around needed him to protect them. He couldn't indulge in despair or grief.

He could still hear Sevanyo's labored breathing. There might still be time to save him. Fedeles looked around at the gathered courtiers, servants and guards surrounding them. Where were all those damnable physicians the one time Fedeles needed them?

Of course, he knew the answer. After King Juleo's assassination, Sevanyo had expelled all physicians from his court. Now only a scrawny boy dressed in the robes of a physician-priest's acolyte cowered behind Timoteo. He couldn't have been more than ten years old.

Who he truly needed was someone like Master Narsi. But he and the majority of skilled Haldiim physicians were miles away, far across the river.

Fedeles took some consolation in recalling what Elenna and Delfia had told him earlier this evening. Atreau had arranged for many of the city's Haldiim citizens to be evacuated. Likely Lliro's ships played a great role in that. Fedeles glanced to Lliro. Before he could formulate the question he wanted to ask, Suelita and two soot-covered royal guards rushed into the temple.

"That accursed fire—" One of the guards began, but coughs racked the rest of his words from him. His companion slapped his back.

"Lord Quemanor, the fire and the wolves have encircled the hill and are ascending the eastern face," Suelita announced in the same calm manner that she'd used when delivering intelligence before. Her grandfather, Lord Estaban, blinked at her as if he was just seeing her for the first time. "They're climbing very fast. We have maybe five minutes."

Soft gasps and frantic whispers echoed through the temple. Outside Fedeles heard shouts of alarm. Dozens of people rushed up behind Suelita. All eyes were on Fedeles. Even Oasia gazed at him with expectation.

He closed his eyes to avoid the weight of their desperate stares and tried to find a solution. Even if he could summon the strength to collapse the paths on the east face of the hill, he didn't know how much of Crown Hill it would bring down. And afterward everyone would still be trapped up here.

No, he needed something better.

Then he heard a crow calling from far away, and he felt the hum of spells sleeping in the stones beneath his feet. Faint residue remained where he'd opened a passage to the sacred grove last night. Previously he'd only managed to hold it open for a few minutes before he'd collapsed from exhaustion. Still, there wasn't any better option.

Fedeles addressed Oasia. "Gather everyone around the temple and make ready to march in an orderly fashion. I'll create a passage to safety."

Oasia gave a nod of her head and dispatched her handmaids and ladies-in-waiting at once.

Fedeles turned his attention to Timoteo and the others closest to Sevanyo.

"When I open the passage, you carry him across first." Then Fedeles turned to Lliro. "I'll entrust you with escorting them to a ship and getting them out of the city."

"I'll do my best." Lliro bowed, then joined Timoteo and Berto, wrapping Sevanyo in cloaks and preparing to lift him. The physician-priest acolyte gripped a wad of cloth and pressed it over the deepest of Sevanyo's wounds.

Fedeles knelt on the stone floor and bowed his head to block out the distraction of all the people surrounding him. He spread his hands over the flagstones, feeling the hum and spark of the spells carved across them. At first his shadow resisted his will, dragging as if it was a knife blade scraping his bones. Fedeles gritted his teeth against the pain. He'd endured worse than this in his youth. And after failing Ariz, he felt he deserved this pain. He had no right to flinch from any suffering, not when his weakness cost other people their lives.

He had to fight—had to succeed!

Fedeles slammed his hands down against the stones, driving the frustration and rage whirling through him to ignite the spells. Something inside Fedeles felt as if it ripped from his flesh, and then a wave of light and heat gushed up all around him. The spells flared to life and stretched up in an archway of golden flames. The walls and vault of the temple seemed to burn away from the center of the arch, revealing grass and flowering wisteria trees.

A strange breeze whipped through the temple. Haldiim voices rose and Fedeles thought he heard both Master Narsi and Atreau call out in surprise.

"Go!" Fedeles shouted. "Go as quickly as you can, all of you."

He bowed his head and continued to pour himself into the spells holding the archway open. His muscles strained and his back shuddered as if enduring the weight of the entire temple. He heard people rushing past him—felt the hems of their clothes brush his shaking shoulders and felt the beat of their horses' hooves on the flagstones. His breathing came in ragged gasps and sweat poured down his back. His arms felt as if they were being wrenched apart and his ribs cracking as the spells dragged more and more strength from him. Limping and staggering, a few dozen more people passed him.

"Hurry!" A musician caught a maid's arm, pulling her along with him. "The wolves are almost at the top of the hill."

The two of them passed through the archway. Another five people followed them.

Fedeles fell to his side. The scent of animal musk and smoke drifted over him. He extended one arm and then the other, dragging his agonized body to the archway. His vision flickered and strange bursts of white floated before his eyes. He was so tired—so hurt. All he wanted was to let go—give up and escape the pain and sorrow. Maybe this was how Ariz had felt. But Ariz had endured for years. What was this suffering compared to that?

After everything he sacrificed, I must not fail . . . I must not . . .

Fedeles dragged himself another foot. His fingers sank from the worn flagstones to dewy grass and damp soil. He'd reached the sacred grove. He dragged his legs to the dirt and grass. If he released the archway now, it would collapse in an instant.

But the spells to open it again would remain in the temple. And Hierro's minions had already reached the summit of Crown Hill. Fedeles had to ensure that they couldn't follow him to the sacred grove.

He waited, feeling the last of his strength wrench from his body, as if his tendons and muscles were being stripped from his bones. He clung to the pain—keeping himself conscious as he reached absolute exhaustion. Complete emptiness. All that remained in him was a ravenous hunger, an almost insatiable need to draw power from anything and everything.

In Sevanyo's throne room this morning he'd briefly experienced this ravening, famished state when he'd unwittingly devoured Hierro's curse. Now he purposefully turned his attention to the spells carved throughout the ruined temple and the curses racing toward him on brilliant teal flames.

He drank it all in, stripping power from flames, stones and even the flesh of charging mordwolves. In a state of absolute emptiness he felt even those deeply hidden veins of untempered magic sleeping in the depths of Crown Hill. He took it all.

A blinding wave of gold light roared through him and seared the ground all around him. Then the spells forming the archway disappeared completely and the inferno of magic died.

Fedeles rolled onto his back. Sunlight gleamed over violet wisteria blossoms and glossy crows studied him from the dark tree branches high above him. Pink and orange sunrise clouds streaked the sky.

Then without warning, Atreau leaned into the line of his sight. "Welcome to the sacred grove, Your Highness."

 CHAPTER
THIRTY-FIVE

Atreau had witnessed Fedeles open a passage between Crown Hill and the Circle of Wisteria before. He'd even briefly stopped in the archway of gold symbols, to stand with one foot on the temple ruins and the other on the grassy lawn of the sacred grove. Even so, he was still shocked by the sight of so many harrowed, beaten people in filthy costumes fleeing from the besieged Crown Hill into the sacred grove. Their escape had to be Fedeles's doing, but where was Fedeles himself?

"That doorway," Yara whispered. "It's opened it again."

"Just as Javier prophesied, the Solstice King is bringing the blessings and power of Wadi Tel to the sacred grove." Esfir's face lit with a radiant smile. "I knew it!"

"He seems to be bringing a lot of Cadeleonians along as well." Yara scowled at the people flooding into the sacred grove.

"It must be part of a larger plan. We just have to have faith," Esfir said.

Atreau was far less certain of Javier's prophecy. The memory of Javier dragging his ruined body across a stone floor after failing again and again was still too fresh in his mind.

Narsi leaned close to Atreau.

"For him to have mentioned my name, we *must* have done this before." His gaze seemed a little unfocused. A feverish flush colored his face and neck. Narsi's gloved hand brushed Atreau's. Heat radiated through the leather. "We must have gotten something wrong last time. But why wouldn't Javier tell us?"

For the same reason he didn't warn Skellan or Elezar about their fates, Atreau thought, but he replied, "When we get the chance later, we'll ask him. For now, how are you holding up?"

"Not too bad. The symptoms are interesting." Narsi's face remained calm, but his arms shook with tremors. "I should try to remember them next time I treat someone suffering a magical malady."

The night he'd nearly died of muerate poisoning, Narsi had suppressed his fear and pain behind medical descriptions as well. It filled Atreau with worry to see him doing the same thing again, but there was no point in saying as much.

"You'll corner the market treating witches after we're through all this," Atreau said lightly. The only way to stop Narsi's suffering was to awaken Yah-muur's Horn. For that they required the still missing Solstice King, whoever he would turn out to be.

The older women gathered around them also betrayed very little shock at the scene. So either the Haldiim people as a whole were utterly unflappable, or most of this group had been here the night the sacred grove had been besieged by Hierro's mordwolves and had already witnessed Fedeles opening a doorway between the Circle of Wisteria and Crown Hill.

Just like that night, faint golden symbols flickered through the wisteria trees and glossy black crows circled overhead, their beating wings appearing to fan the spells to life as a person would coax embers into flames. Soon the branches of the wisteria trees glimmered as if they were filled with stars. But the most conspicuous spell was that radiant red-gold arch that formed between two of the trees, like a shining doorway.

And the outpouring of battered Cadeleonians was certainly something new. Dressed in tattered costumes, they rushed through the gold doorway on foot. Some carried children and a few led horses behind them. All of them appeared exhausted and desperate. Atreau recognized Oasia and Sparanzo right away. Then he saw his brother Lliro helping several other nobles and priests to carry King Sevanyo's stiff, pale body. An unacknowledged edge of fear eased in Atreau's chest.

Timoteo and Berto numbered among those accompanying the king. Atreau scanned the crowd that poured past him, taking a little hope when he saw Suelita and Ladislo both alive and well. Suelita and her sisters led one of her brothers forward. Burns covered the side of his face.

But where is Fedeles?

"Hierro Fueres and Prince Remes attacked the king and his court. The palace is in flames and many are injured." Timoteo addressed the circle of silver-haired Haldiim women. He paused briefly when he caught sight of Narsi, relief flickering across his gaunt face. "We beg refuge in this sacred place."

The plea met with silence.

Narsi, Yara and Esfir all looked to the older Haldiim women. Most of them wore physicians' rings and were dressed in the refined clothes of honored mothers—though Mistress Querra presented a notable anomaly among them. She silently lowered her head, gazing down at her shoes.

Atreau didn't blame the Haldiim physicians for their silence. For weeks Haldiim citizens had endured abuses and attacks while Cadeleonian nobility did little more than debate the situation as if it were academic. But at the same time, this battalion of Cadeleonian refugees weren't going to meekly march back into the smoke and flames of a burning palace, were they? And denying assistance to each other wouldn't protect any of them from Hierro or the Shroud of Stone; it would only put them all at odds.

"On Solstice Day we celebrate the sanctity of all life in this world," Yara pronounced. Then Esfir straightened and took a small step toward Timoteo.

"The Circle of Wisteria offers sanctuary to all who are in need." Esfir briefly cast a gentle look to Mistress Querra's bowed head. "As a guardian of this sacred grove, I welcome you all."

"Thank you, Holy Guardian." Timoteo inclined his head respectfully before returning his attention to Sevanyo.

Lliro and Timoteo lowered the king to the ground beneath one of the wisteria trees, while Oasia handed Sparanzo over to Delfia before she set to work directing people to clear the way for those coming behind them. Sparanzo clung to Delfia, as did one of Delfia's twins, but her second child was nowhere to be seen. From Delfia's bleak expression, Atreau guessed that she didn't hold out much hope for the child. Atreau again scanned the people pouring through the shining archway. How many had been lost? How many killed?

Most importantly, where was Fedeles?

"Fetch a physician for the king! Now!" Lliro bellowed as if the sacred grove was a ship under his command.

Narsi started forward, but Atreau caught his arm and held him back. Atreau didn't want Narsi entangled with Sevanyo's death or the courtiers surrounding him. Sevanyo was obviously beyond saving. He stared unblinking despite the golden spells flaring up all around him; no blood flowed from the open wounds in his chest. Right now there was far more at stake than even the Cadeleonian crown.

Narsi was their lone hope for deliverance from the impending cataclysm. He couldn't become caught up in some act of mercy for a dead man.

"Your hands might burn the king," Atreau reminded Narsi. Fear of harming a patient would dissuade him where concern for his own well-being wouldn't.

Narsi glanced down. Golden symbols flickered from his fingers, blazing through his kidskin gloves like flames burning in a paper lantern. They seemed to flare in time with the Bahiim blessings that edged the golden archway. Atreau scowled at the sight. How could it not hurt? But if it did, Narsi didn't betray the pain. He simply turned to the group of Haldiim physicians.

"Honored Mothers, will you lend your aid?" Narsi requested.

To their credit, the Haldiim women didn't refuse Narsi's request or Esfir's and Yara's promises, though they were easily capable of ignoring Lliro's commands. They set to work, not just attending the king but treating all the injured and soothing their friends and family. Mistress Querra hurried between groups translating between Haldiim and Cadeleonian.

Seconds later Elezar called his own troops to join in the effort. Within minutes he and three of the silver-haired Haldiim physicians arranged for the Cadeleonian nobles, their servants and even their horses to be ferried to the safety of Labaran ships.

In the midst of so much activity, few people noticed Narsi, in the center of the sacred grove, drop to one knee. Yara and Esfir stood over him, shielding him. Atreau crouched beside him.

"Are you all right?" Atreau asked.

Narsi nodded, but Atreau could feel the heat radiating from his body. Golden light flashed up from the exposed skin of his collarbones and throat. A radiant symbol remained in the wake of each flash, like the afterimages of firecrackers.

Esfir and Yara both stared at the symbols. Atreau recognized some as Bahiim blessings; others were clearly Labaran spells and still others were unknown to him.

"Buzzing inside, like my nerves have turned into a swarm of hot little bees." Narsi shook his head. "I wonder . . . do spells actually raise body temperature? Are witches constantly experiencing fevers? Maybe that's why they don't need shoes." Narsi's entire body shook so hard that his physician's satchel fell open at his feet. Atreau flinched from the blazing light emanating from the golden cask within. It pulsed like a beating heart, and the symbols flickering across Narsi's skin flared along with it.

"I'm so warm . . . I want to take my shirt off . . ." Narsi murmured.

"As much as I would enjoy that, later might be better." Atreau drew Narsi's hand back from the buttons of his shirt front.

"Just hang on a little longer." Esfir started to pat Narsi's shoulder but drew her hand back as another surge of light flared up from him. "Javier's prophecy has been right so far. The Solstice King will be here soon, I'm certain of it."

"But so far the only king we have is King Sevanyo, and he is obviously dead. I overheard several nobles saying the Prince Xalvadar was killed as well," Yara whispered. "Are we awaiting Prince Jacinto's arrival? Because I have to warn you, that man is not stepping foot back in this city until he's certain it's safe. As for bringing blessings—"

"It's not Jacinto," Atreau cut her off. If anyone was going to carry the power and blessings from Crown Hill, it was Fedeles. Why Javier had coyly named him the Solstice King, Atreau couldn't be certain. Perhaps it amused him. Or more likely it was to hide Fedeles's identity from any of their enemies who might have come across the prophecy before Esfir discovered it. Either way, Atreau didn't want to explain with so many strangers surrounding them. Too much could still go wrong, and Fedeles still hadn't arrived.

"I'll see if I can fetch him." Atreau studied Narsi. Sweat beaded his fevered skin, but he maintained a relaxed expression and even offered Atreau a playful salute. Atreau stood and crossed the grounds, heading for the golden archway.

The people flooding into the sacred grove wandered past him, escorted away by Haldiim physicians and Elezar's soldiers. Oasia remained at the side of the shining doorway staring through the murky opening while men, women and horses poured by. Atreau didn't approach her. Instead he craned his neck to peer through the archway as well. But all he could discern of Crown Hill were glimpses of crumbling stonework and thick clouds of smoke and dust.

A few yards from him, the small group of Cadeleonians encircling King Sevanyo remained. Lliro, Timoteo and Berto numbered among, them as did Sevanyo's longtime supporters: Lords Estaban, Helio and Bayezar. The Haldiim physician kneeling at the king's side shook her head and then stood and withdrew to attend to those people who could still be saved.

Lord Estaban wept openly, while Lord Helio hid his face in his hands and Lord Bayezar stared at Sevanyo's body as if he couldn't believe his eyes. He clutched one of Sevanyo's hands in his own. Timoteo bowed his head, reciting prayers for the king's safe passage into paradise. Berto stood beside him like a statue, arms slack and eyes downcast.

Atreau didn't attempt to join the party. His conflicts with the Estaban family were too recent for him to think he'd be welcomed. In addition, his own urge to smack Berto across the face hadn't entirely dissipated. Instead Atreau beckoned Lliro to him. His brother nodded, then stood and strode to his side. As he drew close, Atreau noticed the scrape on his cheek and dried blood scabbing his knuckles. A surge of emotion overcame him. He caught his reserved brother in an embrace. Initially, Lliro stiffened, then he returned the hug with intense strength.

"Thank God you're safe," Lliro whispered in Labaran.

"You too," Atreau replied. "Spider is at the Fat Goose and surrounded by friends. He should be well."

"Good, good." Lliro returned to Cadeleonian as he pulled away.

Atreau released him. The troubles of their nation were far from over. With Xalvadar's and Sevanyo's deaths, it would be paramount to ensure that neither Remes nor Hierro could claim the throne. Fortunately, Jacinto stood in line of succession before both of them.

"Prince Jacinto is safeguarded aboard a Labaran ship," Atreau assured his brother. "I'll have him transported to one of your vessels as soon as the city is secured."

"Jacinto is no longer of importance to me." Lliro's tone was terse. "Sevanyo's last decree was to disown his own sons and disavow the Gavado bloodline all in favor of Fedeles Quemanor. Bishop Timoteo blessed the decree and all the gathered lord ministers recognized it. Now that Sevanyo is dead, your mad duke is our king. So, congratulations, I suppose."

Atreau stared at his brother, attempting to absorb that information. Fedeles . . . king?

Atreau had assumed that Javier referred to Fedeles as the Solstice King merely to disguise his identity. Who would have thought Javier was describing the simple fact that Fedeles would become king on the morning of the Haldiim Solstice. It was probably the last thing Fedeles would have wanted for himself.

Though Oasia would be delighted to claim the title and power of a queen. No wonder she hadn't joined her son seeking safety but instead anxiously awaited Fedeles. He was about to elevate her to the throne. Atreau sighed as he realized that he wasn't much better than Oasia right now. He wasn't searching for Fedeles out of pure concern either.

But what in the three hells was keeping the man?

Atreau scowled. Fedeles wouldn't have done anything foolish, would he? Javier had said that in the past Fedeles threw his life away to kill Hierro and avenge Ariz. By now Ariz would definitely be dead.

"Where did you see him last?" Atreau demanded of Lliro.

"He was driving mordwolves and flames back from Crown Hill. He wouldn't leave until everyone else escaped. There was no arguing with him." Lliro indicated the golden archway with a bob of his head. "God knows what will become of the kingdom if he dies now. That son of his inherits, I suppose. But he's still so young."

Lliro's gaze shifted to Oasia while Atreau's attention shot to a movement in the archway. A filthy groom staggered through, leading three horses out from the walls of smoke and dust. Atreau thought one of the animals was Fedeles's Firaj. Fedeles had to be near at hand. A few seconds passed and still no one followed after the groom. Oasia betrayed a rare expression of anguish as she peered through the smoke. Even so, she made no move to cross back through to look for her husband.

"For better or worse, my ass." Atreau scoffed the wedding vow in frustration; at the same time, his pulse raced with anxiety. Fedeles had to be brought across, even if it was kicking and screaming. He couldn't die alone and heartbroken in some fucking fire.

Atreau bolted to the archway, launching himself into the billowing wall of smoke and dust. Then a heavy body slammed him backward. He stumbled, but the body that had struck him collapsed onto the grass of the sacred grove. Filthy and smoke-stained as he was, there was no mistaking Fedeles's angular form and turbulent shadow. Atreau knelt beside him, feeling the kick of his pulse in his throat. Relief swept through Atreau.

Behind them, the golden archway dissipated like a breath of steam.

A groan escaped Fedeles as he rolled onto his back. His dark eyes fixed on Atreau and the desolation in his expression softened a little.

"Welcome to the sacred grove, Your Highness." Atreau offered the words teasingly, afraid of overwhelming Fedeles if he directly confronted him with Sevanyo's death. Fedeles stared at the trees overhead in a daze.

"Sevanyo?" he asked in a whisper. "Is he . . ." His voice trailed off and Atreau guessed that he already knew the answer in his heart.

"I'm sorry," Atreau said.

"Ariz is gone too." Fedeles closed his eyes. A tear slid down the side of his face, streaking through the dust.

Atreau glanced away, hiding his own guilt. Would Fedeles ever forgive them if he discovered the role he and Narsi had played in ending Ariz's life?

"Sparanzo is safe, as are many others, all thanks to you," Atreau assured Fedeles. "But there's still the spell at the heart of the Shard of Heaven that we have to destroy. I know you're exhausted, but I need your help. There's no one else who can do this."

Thankfully, Fedeles composed himself and nodded. At the same time a shadow fell across Atreau. He glanced up to see Oasia standing over them both.

"You were saying that the Shroud of Stone must be destroyed," she said. "Go on."

Atreau supposed he shouldn't have been surprised that Oasia had learned about the Shroud of Stone. She and her agents were nothing if not capable. Who knew how much information she'd uncovered during those two weeks he'd spent dispatching orders and information from Labara.

"Narsi discovered a relic—Yah-muur's Horn," Atreau continued. He knew he was rushing things, but Narsi seemed to be burning away by the second. He didn't want to waste time now that Fedeles was here. "It can annihilate the Shroud of Stone. But to wake the horns, we have to give the power of Crown Hill to the Circle of Wisteria. Then Narsi and I will infiltrate the Shard of Heaven and destroy the Shroud of Stone. Does all that make sense to you?"

Oasia frowned but didn't appear confused. Fedeles simply nodded.

"Can you transfer the power or blessings or whatever from Crown Hill?" Atreau glanced over his shoulder at Narsi. "Sooner rather than later?"

"I . . . Yes. I can do it." Fedeles struggled up to his knees.

Atreau reached out to steady him, but Oasia brushed Atreau's hand aside.

"I will see to my husband, Atreau." Oasia took a silk kerchief from the pocket of her cloak and wiped some of the smoke and blood from Fedeles's face. "You'd best look after Master Narsi."

Atreau didn't require further coaxing. He jumped to his feet and rushed to where Narsi still knelt. He was surprised to see that Suelita had joined Yara and Esfir near him. The three of them appeared to be discussing Javier's prophecy, while Narsi stared off in a daze. Suelita squeezed Esfir's hand in a rather doting manner. Another time, Atreau might have given the action more than a passing notice, but now he could only think of Narsi.

Narsi smiled as he caught sight of Atreau. He rose to his feet, swaying, with a sheen of sweat covering his skin. Then his gaze shifted and his eyes widened in fear and bewilderment.

"What's wrong?" Atreau asked.

"I might be seeing fever dreams, but—" Narsi raised a trembling, shining hand and pointed to the northern sky. "Are those blue flames climbing up the spires at the Shard of Heaven?"

Atreau spun to look, as did Yara, Esfir and Suelita. Approaching them, Oasia and Fedeles, and Timoteo all studied the golden spires. The flurry of blue ribbons whirling around the spires wasn't easy to discern from the blue morning sky, but once Atreau picked out one, he saw dozens. He had no idea what was happening, but dread still filled him.

He looked back to see Fedeles and Oasia come up beside them.

"Clara has taken over Hierro's spells," Oasia whispered. She only spared the Shard of Heaven a quick glance, then turned her attention to Fedeles. "If she's freed herself from him, then her next move will be to break the Hallowed Kings and use the Shroud of Stone to kill us and force a Labaran retreat. We need to raise Meztli's shields."

"I can release the last of Crown Hill's power into the Circle of Wisteria, but I don't have the expertise to expand the blessings and wards to protect the rest of the city. Much less hold Meztli's shields." Fedeles sounded exhausted already. He looked meaningfully from Oasia to Yara, Esfir, and then Suelita.

"I'll forge the shields from my wards," Oasia stated, and she turned to Yara and Esfir. "But the blessings of the sacred grove are unfamiliar to me. Can we leave them to you?"

"Absolutely," Esfir stated.

Suelita and Yara looked less certain, but both of them nodded.

"If my prayers are of any help, I would like to offer those as well," Timoteo said as he drew near. "Mistress Querra taught me the Solstice prayers, and I have practiced them every year. As I understand it, each voice that joins in helps maintain the blessings."

Narsi and Esfir both smiled at Timoteo.

"Yes. Then we'll sing the blessing together." Esfir beckoned Timoteo to her side. Out of the corner of his eye Atreau noticed Berto edge over as well. He bowed his head, and as Esfir, Yara, Suelita and Timoteo raised their voices in song, he joined them. Other voices scattered across the sacred grove and beyond sounded out as well.

At the same time, Narsi grasped Atreau's hand in his own. His fingers felt like hot iron, but Atreau returned his grip.

Fedeles stood silent and motionless, with his head bowed and his arms lank at his sides. He blew out a long breath. The shadows at his feet shivered and suddenly took on the dark iridescence of crows' wings. Grass and clover bent beneath the shadow's weight. The heads of dandelion blossoms fell, severed by its edges. Fedeles's shadow wasn't anything like a mere absence of light. Instead it struck Atreau as a witchflame so concentrated and so powerful that it appeared black. But weren't there really countless rich colors concentrated within it? Shining like crows' wings.

"All that I am and all that I have, I give to you," Fedeles whispered. His shadow rippled like a deep pool of water. Reflections flashed and glinted across its surface. Then it split apart, pouring out from Fedeles in gleaming black streams. Atreau sidestepped to keep one from splashing over his foot. All across the Circle of Wisteria, startled shouts sounded as Fedeles's shadow surged. But the lustrous shadows did no harm. Prayers continued to ring out.

Fedeles's shadow washed up around the roots of the wisteria trees and then climbed higher. The trunks of the trees turned gleaming black, and countless radiant symbols lit up across them.

Fedeles himself appeared to grow paler and paler. His skin took on a waxy, translucent pallor, as if the morning sun had burned him away. He threw his head back and still more streams surged from him.

A warm breeze ruffled through Atreau's hair, reminding him of the night the spells had woken in Abea's abandoned chapel. He glanced to Narsi. As if thinking the same thing, Narsi lifted the golden cask from his medical satchel. His entire body shuddered at the contact and Atreau steadied him.

"Thank you," Narsi whispered.

Overhead, the heavy wisteria branches swayed and heaved as the shadows climbed through them. The long streamers of violet blossoms swung and flashed with every stanza of prayers that rang out through the sacred grove. Steadily the flowers lit up like hundreds of tiny lanterns. Gold blessings blazed from within them, and then they burst into the air. At the same time a flurry of crows launched themselves from the trees, catching the blessings in their beaks, on their backs and all across their wings. The darkness and brilliance of their flights made Atreau think of embers and smoke soaring through the sky. All but three of them flew up and outward to raise burning blessings over the Circle of Wisteria and the surrounding city.

The three crows that remained circled directly over Narsi and Atreau.

The symbols that had been flickering to life all across Narsi's body suddenly flared and the golden box in Narsi's hand ignited into a column of white-gold light. Radiant gold light coursed across Narsi's body. A bone-shaking current passed from Narsi's fingers into Atreau's arm and set his heart racing. At the same time the three crows released their blessings, sending them plunging into the column of light.

Flames and whispering voices whirled around Narsi. Atreau felt the scorching heat but only caught part of the Haldiim phrases.

Endure and seize the victory you so desire.

"I will. I swear," Narsi promised.

Then the golden box burned away. All the wind and light seemed to collapse down into Narsi's outstretched right hand. Atreau stared as the light dulled and coalesced into a form in Narsi's palm.

It was a fragile-looking branch. Hardly more than a twig, though its shape did resemble a miniature antler. The two tines appeared charred black, while red streaks stained the base, like dried blood. The rest of it looked like weathered driftwood. Countless faint scratches scrawled over the dull surface.

Atreau frowned. After so much fire and force—so much magic and hardship—how could this be their reward? How was this a weapon to stop an apocalypse?

Around them, Oasia, Esfir and Yara forged humble songs into vast arrays of gold blessings and huge blue wards. But somehow the Goddess

Yah-muur could only provide a spindly painted stick. It really was hard not to feel cheated by such an underwhelming relic. What were they supposed to do with this? Poke the Shroud of Stone apart with it?

Narsi too studied the twig in his hand with a dismayed expression. Then, as he closed his fingers around it, very faint symbols glowed through his skin. He smiled as they faded.

"By chance . . ." Atreau leaned close, whispering in his ear. "When you met Yah-muur, was she very, very tiny?"

A quiet laugh escaped Narsi and he shook his head and opened his hand to consider the horn again.

"Not everything powerful is imposing," Narsi said. "It only takes a teaspoon of muerate to kill most people."

"True," Atreau admitted. Master Ariz had presented himself with all the grandeur of a potato but proved himself one of the deadliest men Atreau had ever encountered. Atreau considered the twig again, noting how the faint scratches along the length of it seemed to shift and change as the light of blessings and the sounds of prayers filled the air around them. He remembered the fable his mother had loved to tell him and his brothers.

"In Labaran lore, the Great Gold Wyrm was defeated by no grander creature than a flea, after all," Atreau said.

"Understatement isn't always a bad thing," Narsi agreed.

Thinking of the advantages of going unnoticed, Atreau whispered, "We should take our leave while people are focused on singing prayers."

Narsi slipped the twig into his pocket. Haldiim people as well as Irabiim from the Labaran forces had joined in singing blessings, and their attention still focused up where Oasia's wards wove like blue threads around the shining gold blessings scattered by flocks of crows. Atreau and Narsi retreated from the singers gathered at the center of the Circle of Wisteria

When they reached the edge of the sacred grove, Atreau stole a quick glance back to Fedeles, and the sight made his heart ache a little.

Fedeles looked so wan and desolate, standing in the center of all these golden lights. He lifted his head. His dazed, sorrowful expression lit up with horror. Both Atreau and Narsi followed his gaze to the north.

Clouds of white mist whirled around the Shard of Heaven. They circled and expanded like a cyclone, spreading over the north side of the city. Where the mist touched, trees turned marble white and birds fell from the skies like stones. The distant figures of people and animals froze in place, becoming immense displays of statues.

Fedeles raced from the throng of singers gathered in the sacred grove. He stopped alongside Atreau. Up close, he looked deathly pale and sunken. Even his large, dark eyes seemed faded as he stared across the river to the spreading mist.

"The Shroud of Stone?" Narsi asked.

Atreau's throat tightened and he couldn't get a word out. *It had already been released. Were they too late to save themselves and Cadeleon?*

The mist rolled nearer and nearer the Gado Bridge. People ran and rode to escape, but the Shroud of Stone overtook them with a relentless, billowing ease, like clouds swallowing the sun.

The singing behind Atreau quieted as people in the sacred grove took notice.

"Don't stop singing the blessings!" Yara held out her arms and projected her words the same way she filled entire theaters with her commanding stage presence. "So long as we raise our voices together, we can hold anything back!" Then she once again launched into song.

Esfir and Timoteo joined her, all but bellowing the holy words. Others in the sacred grove and out on the streets joined in. The gold blessings overhead flared with vibrant light.

Atreau looked back to the north side of the city. Just as the Shroud of Stone reached the riverbank, scarlet flames shot up from the water, burning it back like sunlight searing away fog.

"Skellan," Atreau whispered.

"He can hold it back for the time being, don't worry." Elezar stood among his Labaran soldiers on the street. Though he clearly addressed his own troops, his words answered Atreau's unspoken question. "We stick to our original plan. Archers and infantry, guard the sacred grove. Elite cavalry with me to clear the streets to the docks."

"Is that one of Skellan's witches?" Narsi pointed across the Peraloro River.

A massive eagle broke through the white mists. Pale vapor dragged at its wings, but as it continued to rise, the mist evaporated from its golden feathers. The eagle soared higher, arcing above even Skellan's flames.

"It can't be," Fedeles whispered.

The eagle swept over the river in two beats of its vast wings and angled straight for the sacred grove. Elezar called his Irabiim archers to attention. They notched arrows to their bows and drew the strings.

"No!" Fedeles roared the command as he pelted down to the street. "Hold your arrows!"

Elezar glanced once to Fedeles, then seconded the command. The archers lowered their bows. However, as the eagle dived toward them, Elezar drew his sword, readying to defend against an attack.

The eagle extended its long legs, unfurling huge black talons. As if of one mind, Atreau and Narsi both stepped under the cover of a wisteria tree.

Fedeles dashed ahead.

An instant before it struck the ground, the eagle's whole body stretched and shifted. Feathers and wings melted away to reveal a man's face and body. His broad chest was bare and marked with faded scars. Dark trousers clung to his long, graceful legs. He touched the ground, then dropped to kneel before Fedeles.

Likely it said something about the week he'd experienced that Atreau was far more startled to see Ariz alive than to witness his transformation from the body of an eagle.

Ariz caught Fedeles's hands and bowed his head, kissing his fingers. Fedeles shook his head and grasped Ariz, pulling him up into a fierce embrace. Even from a distance, Atreau could see Fedeles's shoulders shake as he enfolded Ariz in his arms and wept against the side of his head.

Elezar and his troops looked on in silence. More than a few of the soldiers studied Ariz with uncertainty. Fedeles leaned his face very close against Ariz's. He said something, but his voice was so low and soft that the only words Atreau caught were "I'm so sorry. So sorry . . ."

"You have nothing to apologize for. You released me from Hierro's thrall." Ariz stroked Fedeles's back. "You saved me."

Fedeles lifted his head and Ariz wiped the tears from his face.

"You saved me," Ariz repeated. And then he smiled. The broad, open expression Ariz offered Fedeles lent him a rugged handsomeness. Prior to this Atreau'd had no idea that Ariz was capable of smiling at all, much less with so much warmth and charm.

"How is it possible that his smile shocks me more than the fact that he flew here on eagle's wings? Atreau murmured to Narsi, who gave a brief snort of laughter.

"I'm relieved to see Master Ariz alive as well, but . . ." Narsi trailed off and Atreau nodded his understanding. If he wasn't dead, then Ariz might still be enthralled. If not to Hierro, then to Clara. However, Fedeles had been so certain of Ariz's death and the conversation between them just now made Atreau suspect Fedeles might have even played some role in his demise.

Whatever the truth was, Ariz had clearly just come from the Shard of Heaven. If there was a chance of them gleaning information from him before they attempted to break in to the place, they had to try.

Atreau strode down to join Fedeles and Ariz. Narsi walked alongside him.

Ariz noticed them first and pulled out of Fedeles's embrace, though he continued to hold one of his hands.

"Atreau, Master Narsi," Ariz greeted them. "I'm afraid that I didn't have a chance to take the medicine you prepared for me. The vial was broken before I could."

"It seems just as well that you didn't," Narsi replied.

"But how exactly is your *condition* now?" Atreau narrowed his eyes, studying Ariz, and then noticed that his neck and ears were spattered with dried blood, as was his hair. Looking just a little more closely, it became apparent that his trousers too had been all but soaked in blood at some point. He'd clearly washed his face and hands and simply removed his shirt—but the evidence of a slaughter still clung to him.

"I'm no longer enthralled," Ariz stated. "Hierro meant to use me to kill King Sevanyo, but my heart was stopped before that could happen. After that, the Brand of Obedience lost its hold over me."

"So you were revived?" Narsi asked. "Was it by the Yuanese Heart Waking method?"

"No." Ariz shook his head and looked to Fedeles. "The Master of the Sorrowlands sent me back to stand at Fedeles's side. I was returned to life for his sake."

Master of the Sorrowlands? Javier. It had to be. A look of understanding showed on Fedeles's face as well.

"After I revived, I saw Elenna abducting Marisol, and so I gave chase. They led me to the Shard of Heaven, where Clara was awaiting. Hierro came after, intent on killing Marisol, because he and Clara both believed that she was Sparanzo." Ariz paused, his gaze flickering down to the traces of bloodstains that lined his knuckles. Then he went on. "At that point I killed Hierro. Unfortunately, that freed Clara from the thrall he'd held over her. She in turn destroyed the Hallowed Kings and released the Shroud of Stone."

After his previous conversations with Ariz wherein he had to navigate weird and convoluted narratives just to convey the slightest bit of information, Atreau found Ariz's clear explanations a pleasant surprise. Freed from Hierro's thrall, it turned out Ariz was direct and concise.

"Were you hurt?" Fedeles frowned down at Ariz's bloodstained hands with open tenderness.

A slight flush colored Ariz's face. He shook his head.

"How did you escape the Shard of Heaven after that?" Narsi asked.

"I didn't escape. Clara released me to deliver her ransom demands to the duke and duchess." Ariz turned his attention to Fedeles. "I didn't secure the Summer Doe's relic for her, so she dispatched Yago. When his men arrived, they discovered your agents in the Slate House, but they failed to capture your agents or the relic. After that, Clara panicked and urged Hierro to move his plans ahead before you or Lady Oasia could use the horns to free the demonic armies that Our Savior had confined in stone."

"That's not what the horns do," Narsi broke in, but then he frowned and glanced to Atreau. "I mean, if the Shroud of Stone is completely destroyed, then of course a few of the surviving Old Gods and spirits could be freed, but—"

"The demons were killed long ago while they were trapped in stone," Fedeles answered almost offhandedly. His attention remained on Ariz. "What does Clara want then?"

"She's demanding the relic in exchanged for Sparanzo's life," Ariz stated.

"But she doesn't have Sparanzo, does she?" Atreau had seen Delfia escorting the boy away to safety with his own eyes less than an hour ago.

"No, Elenna delivered Marisol in Sparanzo's place," Ariz said. Atreau was so used to Ariz betraying no emotion in his expression and voice that the edge of sorrow he gave away now was striking. He cared deeply about his niece. It discomfited Atreau to keep looking at him.

"I won't allow her to harm Marisol, I swear," Fedeles whispered to him.

"Neither you nor Oasia are in possession of Yah-muur's horn, so what are you going to do?" Atreau demanded of Fedeles. No matter how sweet Marisol was, or how much she was loved, saving her couldn't come at the risk of countless other children's and adults' lives. On top of that, Narsi was tied to Yah-muur's horn now. Atreau wouldn't allow anyone to hand Narsi over to Clara Odalis.

Fedeles frowned at him and Atreau scowled right back.

"I don't know what I'm going to do," Fedeles said. "But I won't just abandon her. There has to be a—"

"We can not risk Clara gaining control of the horn. No matter what," Atreau stated.

Narsi glanced between them with a concerned expression and Atreau feared that his physician's heart was softening.

"I hate to interrupt," Narsi broke in, but his gaze moved to Ariz. "But I'm curious. If you are no longer enthralled, why would Clara send you to deliver her demands? She must know that you will tell us everything you can about her position."

Atreau was surprised that he'd failed to consider that himself. He was so focused on getting Narsi into the Shard of Heaven safely that he'd let too much slip his mind. But Narsi was right, Ariz was hardly an ideal messenger, not unless Clara had some way to control him.

"First, in her experience, I'm not clever enough to understand her strategies, much less report them. Second, the farther I am away from her, the less capable I am of slitting her throat. Third, she doesn't have a better option," Ariz replied. "Right now, she's busy working some larger spell in the Shard of Heaven. She can't shield her people from the Shroud of Stone if they travel too far from her. I'm carrying Trueno's relic in my body. It retains traces of the original blessings that protected Trueno when Our Savior first released the Shroud of Stone."

"So you're protected by Meztli's shields," Fedeles murmured.

"For the time being, at least." Ariz nodded.

Atreau considered the information, then asked, "Any idea about this larger spell that Clara is casting?"

"I don't know, but I suspect that it involves Remes in some way. She's killed most of Hierro's other followers but kept him alive and placed a powerful thrall over him."

"If I'm right, then she plans to take possession of his body and claim the throne as her own," Fedeles said.

A little too late for that, Atreau thought, but Clara couldn't know that Sevanyo had disinherited Remes. At least not yet.

"I have no intention of delivering the Summer Doe's relic to Clara." Ariz looked to Fedeles, then him. "She won't release Marisol, no matter what she says. Marisol's best hope lies in Clara's defeat. So if there is any way that I can help you stop Clara, then just tell me and I'll do all I can."

Atreau couldn't help but raise his brows at the sweeping offer, but Narsi looked delighted.

"What we truly need is a way to draw Clara's attention and guardsmen away from the southern passageway below the Shard of Heaven," Narsi informed him.

Ariz considered for a moment, then nodded.

"If I advanced on them by way of the Dasma Bridge, Clara would be forced to dispatch forces to deal with me." Ariz spoke with an air of his old dispassionate tone. As if it wasn't his own life he was discussing. "If I'm lucky, I might be able to get inside and free Marisol."

"I'll go with you," Fedeles said.

Atreau had to resist the urge to reach out and shake Fedeles.

"You are Cadeleon's king now," Atreau snapped. "You can not just—"

"I can and I will!" Fedeles cut him off with a shout.

Out of the corner of his eye, Atreau saw Elezar and his troops observing them and felt an absurd sort of embarrassment at being caught bickering in front of the Labarans. He swallowed the words he might have otherwise yelled at Fedeles.

Fedeles too appeared to restrain himself. The two of them stood glowering at each other for a moment, then Fedeles released a heavy sigh.

"You and Narsi are more important than anyone else right now," Fedeles said. "But Clara believes that I possess Yah-muur's Horn, so she will focus her attention and her guardsmen on me. If I join Ariz in the north of the city, then we're certain to distract Clara from the two of you. And *that* is the best action to take for the sake of our entire nation. So, I will brook no further argument on the subject, Lord Vediya. Am I understood?"

Atreau fumed silently, but he recognized that Fedeles was correct.

"Understood, Your Highness." Atreau offered him a half bow.

Fedeles had the grace to look discomfited by that. Then he glanced past Atreau and raised one hand in greeting. Atreau looked to see Elezar approaching them. Elezar stopped beside Atreau.

"Are you all about done here?" Elezar asked. "If so, the grooms have brought your horses." He gestured behind him.

Atreau had been so caught up in the conversation that he'd hardly noticed the movements among Elezar's troops. But now he saw that grooms had fetched not only his gray stallion, Nube, and Narsi's piebald mare, but Firaj as well.

"Scouts report bishop's guardsmen and their mordwolves regrouping around the Shard of Heaven," Elezar went on. "On this side of the Gado Bridge, their forces are making for the southern passages. It looks like they're planning to secure the Shard of Heaven as a stronghold. So if we're going to get anyone inside, we need to move out now."

"Right." Atreau touched Narsi's hand and then started toward the horses.

"Ariz and I will cross the Gado Bridge and approach the Shard of Heaven to provide a further distraction," Fedeles informed Elezar.

Atreau didn't miss Elezar's hesitation. He thought they might to have to argue the entire matter through yet again. But instead Elezar lifted a chain from around his own neck and handed it to Fedeles.

"This is one of the charms that Skellan and his coven forged to ward off the Shroud of Stone."

"But won't you need it?" Fedeles asked.

"So long as my soul is hidden within a beast's body, Skellan should be able to protect me. You take it and keep yourself safe." Then Elezar stepped back from them and pulled the hood of his bearskin cloak over his head. As the hood settled, his whole body stretched and flexed, growing into the hide of the cloak and beyond. In a flurry of white fur Elezar transformed back into the immense bear that had carried Narsi and himself to the sacred grove.

"Thank you." Fedeles clasped the charm around his neck.

Elezar inclined his massive head.

While Atreau, Narsi and Fedeles mounted their horses, Ariz too transformed, returning to the body of an eagle. He leapt into the air and glided alongside Fedeles and Firaj as they lit out for the Gado Bridge. Atreau watched them go, trying not to worry for them. Then he turned his attention back to Narsi.

"Happy Solstice," Atreau said.

"You as well." Narsi offered him a smile. Then Elezar charged ahead and they raced behind him.

༄ ༄ ༄

Elezar's chosen cavalry charged ahead of them, scattering and capturing the guardsmen patrolling the riverside streets. The air rang with clashes of sword blades and the cries of wounded and dying men. Elezar himself attacked and killed mordwolf after mordwolf. His muzzle and claws glistened with blood. Atreau stared as Elezar threw his weight down, crushing the backs of two mordwolves. A third lunged up, sinking its teeth into Elezar's throat. Elezar ripped it aside with a swat of a massive paw. Blood poured down his neck and shoulder. Countless other wounds gaped open all across Elezar's body, but he betrayed neither pain nor fatigue as he plunged into another pack of snarling enthralled beasts.

"Will he be all right?" Narsi's hands automatically went to his medical satchel.

"So long as we succeed, he'll be fine," Atreau replied.

Narsi cast him a skeptical glance.

"We both need to believe that right now," Atreau said. Everything Elezar and his cavalry suffered was to deliver Narsi safely into the Shard of Heaven. But it did no good to brood on their sacrifice. They owed it to them to make good use of the distraction. Atreau reined his mount away from the battle. Narsi followed close behind.

While Elezar and his cavalry drew away the attention of guards and priests, Atreau and Narsi turned their horses over to a young groom. Then they swiftly descended the narrow alley entrance to another snake hole. The brick-lined walls were slick with condensation and the stale air tasted of the rusting iron plates behind those bricks.

It was one of three supply tunnels that Haldiim engineers had employed for constructing the long passage running below the river to the Shard of Heaven. Once the thoroughfare-sized grand passage was completed, the supply tunnels had been relegated to use for drainage and sewage. This tunnel, however, had been saved from complete degradation. Generations of wayward priests secretly maintained and cleaned the tunnel. In return they were able to regularly defy curfews and access the temptations of the city without alerting their brethren who kept guard along the main passage.

Happily, those same priests had left an oil lamp on a small iron peg. The damp wick spat and crackled, but it provided enough light for Narsi and Atreau to see one another as well as the swaths of green snails blanketing the walls.

"Keep a lookout for rats," Atreau whispered to Narsi. Then his boot sank into something fleshy and rotten. The remains of a tail fell across his toe. He scowled and added, "Live ones."

Narsi laughed. "You know, it's remarkable that this *isn't* the worst place you've taken me. It's not even the worst tunnel."

"Lesser men tour lovely venues to compensate for their bland company," Atreau replied as he casually scraped the muck off his boot heel. "While I'm burdened with such a dazzling companion that I must resort to seeps and sewers to counterbalance even a little of your brilliance."

"I'm both charmed and chagrined that you've managed to blame me for this choice of surroundings," Narsi countered.

If they lived, Atreau thought, he would be happy to spend the rest of his life exploring the vast catalog of Narsi's rejoinders.

If they lived . . .

They hadn't moved far down the tunnel before they encountered a group of Cire's rat familiars. Their presence reassured Atreau, but their conditions unnerved him a little. One of the large rats had already succumbed to the Shroud of Stone, while another three lay curled up and immobile as shells of while marble encased their gasping bodies. The remaining two rats led them to a grate high in the tunnel wall. Streams of water drizzled down from a large drainpipe.

Atreau wrenched the aged grate free and tossed it aside. Minutes later they crawled up and climbed through the steady trickle of water to reach the mouth of the drain. Thankfully, someone had already loosened the grate and Atreau only had to push the thing aside to drag himself free. Then he reached back and helped Narsi shoulder his way clear.

The two of them stood in one of the gutters running along the stone floor of a huge tunnel passage—the thoroughfare leading to the Shard of Heaven.

Despite the early hour, dozens of wagons, carts and barrows loaded with goods already filled the passage. But what should have been a bustling scene was deathly still and silent. Everything alive had already succumbed to the Shroud of Stone. Merchants, priests, horses and chattel. A goose girl stretched midyawn, surrounded by her eerily silent flock. At the back of a wine cart an elderly priest clutched a bottle, caught in the midst of hiding it in the folds of his loose cassock. Everything alive, from potted plants to horseflies and human beings, had turned to stone. Yet cut flowers and sides of meat remained unchanged.

Atreau stepped out of the gutter and frowned at a piece of stone near his boot. Then he recognized the lower half of a child's gleeful face. The Shroud of Stone must have taken the spindly boy in the midst of jumping from a wagon. His marble body had shattered on impact with the flagstones. Pieces of him lay scattered at their feet.

"What is—" Narsi frowned at the remains but then cut himself off midquestion. He crouched down and gently touched the boy's cracked head.

"May your next life be filled with joy," Narsi whispered over the boy's remains. His graceful hands traced the Cadeleonian holy sign of peace and then the Haldiim one. Then he straightened. Atreau stood next to him, both of them absorbed in quiet thoughts. Thin white vapors drifted over their heads.

At last Atreau sighed. He opened his mouth to remind Narsi that they had to keep going; there were countless other lives they could still save if they could destroy the Shroud of Stone.

But a noise silenced Atreau. Next to him, Narsi went very still.

Claws scraped over flagstones as a creature padded between the wagons and carts. A low growl set Atreau's heart hammering.

He and Narsi both turned slowly to look behind them. A large gray mordwolf prowled through the lines of motionless carts. It stopped to sniff a side of smoked pork, then ripped a hunk from the carcass. The crack of bones snapping between its teeth sounded like cannon shots in the quiet passageway.

Another mordwolf paced past it like a restless watchdog. Then Atreau noticed another gray shape in the distance. And another. As he stared in growing horror, Atreau picked out more and more mordwolves steadily invading the passageway.

One of Cire's rats scurried atop Atreau's boot and tugged frantically at the leg of his trousers. Then it hopped down and hurried ahead. Atreau and Narsi followed after it. Their every footstep and movement seemed amplified by the deathly quiet of the petrified crowd, but they didn't dare stop.

At last they cleared the congested tangle of wagons and merchants and reached the entrance to the Shard of Heaven itself. Gray flagstones and rust-red bricks gave way to a towering wall of gleaming blue stone. Gold seams suspended within the translucent blue stone reflected lamplight like the eye-shine of countless beasts. Stallions and eagles adorned the open gates. Beyond them a wide blue staircase led farther up into the Shard of Heaven. Atreau wasn't certain, but he thought he glimpsed a narrow alcove at the edge of one of the steps. But it wasn't what caused him to drop behind the cover of a flower cart.

Two priests waited at the bottom of the steps. The elderly one stood, while his boyishly young companion sat cross-legged on the ground, encircled by white chalk symbols. At the sight of two priests, Narsi froze in place. Their guide rat raced ahead, bounding up into the old priest's outstretched hands. The priest patted the rat, but his movements were terribly slow. The boy sitting behind him continued to silently mouth prayers.

Were they Cire's contacts? Clearly her rat knew them, but Atreau had arranged to be admitted to the Shard by a cook, not two chapel priests. Then Narsi raised his hands to the elderly priest, offering a holy greeting and a smile brimming with surprised delight.

The aged priest gazed at Narsi with the same expression of happy astonishment.

"Sacrist Amabilo," Narsi whispered, stepping nearer to the man. "It's really you?"

"Yes. And you're Timoteo's little acolyte . . . Narsi!"

"What are you doing here?" Narsi glanced to the youth, who continued to mouth prayers.

"We're delivering the key to the crypt to you," the elderly priest whispered. "The Shroud already overcame the good man who was meant to meet you. But Gachello sent us in his place. It's with his blessing that we were able to hold out this long." Sacrist Amabilo extended his right hand with agonizing slowness and opened his fingers to reveal the glossy black key lying against his pale palm.

Studying the priest more closely, Atreau realized that his bare feet were already encased in white marble and the tips of his fingers looked the same.

"The entry to the crypt is through the alcove on the left. There's a gate at the end, and the heart of the Shroud lies beyond that." The old priest forced the last words out as the marble crept up his body.

"Thank you." Narsi took the key but then reached out to touch Sacrist Amabilo's shoulder. "Is there anything I can do to ease your . . ."

The shroud of stone enveloped the priest before Narsi could finish asking. Sacrist Amabilo's stone eyes gazed at Narsi with sad benevolence.

On the floor, the young priest lifted his pockmarked face with obvious difficulty. Vapor rose off the chalk symbols surrounding him, as if they were boiling away.

"Gachello is still here. The Shroud of Stone can not yet devour the souls it has trapped," the young priest murmured. "But you must hurry. We can't go on much longer."

The last of the chalk burned away and the youth closed his eyes as the Shroud of Stone enveloped him.

Narsi glanced back in Atreau's direction. Atreau began to rise to his feet.

Then a man bellowed out from behind them. "Atreau! You son of a whore! How did you get in here?"

Atreau looked back to see Captain Yago charging through the crush of wagons and marbleized peddlers. Behind him, several mordwolves pricked up their ears. Unlike the enthralled mordwolves, a shield of enchanted flesh didn't protect Yago from the Shroud of Stone. So why, Atreau wondered, wasn't the bastard a statue? Then he noticed the glint of a red bauble hanging from a chain around Yago's neck and he realized that Clara must have created her own shields for her agents, just as Skellan had provided charmed necklaces for Narsi and himself.

Yago drew his sword as he closed in. There was no more time to think. Atreau freed his own blade and rushed Yago. Their blades clashed and Yago staggered back a step, taken off guard. But he recovered quickly, thrusting for Atreau's heart. Atreau barely blocked the strike in time.

"Go!" Atreau shouted to Narsi. The mordwolves were already closing in on them. Narsi only had moments to get away before they sighted him. But Narsi didn't flee up the stairs; instead he drew the short sword Atreau had given him earlier.

Atreau's heart raced and his mind seemed to burst with an explosion of desperate thoughts. He didn't have time to convince Narsi to abandon him. He didn't have the skill to beat Captain Yago, much less slay a pack of mordwolves. But he absolutely had to keep Narsi from being killed.

On an impulse of inspired desperation, he feigned to his left, luring Yago close enough to land a blow. Yago struck fast and hard. Atreau only managed a partial parry, knocking Yago's sword low but not far enough aside. A terrible force punched through Atreau's thigh. At the same time, he reached out with his free hand and tore the red bauble from Captain Yago's body.

Yago gasped and grabbed for the bauble as a shell of white marble surged up his body. Atreau hurled the red jewel aside and Yago staggered after it. But his stone legs couldn't balance. He teetered and Atreau shoved him with all his strength.

Captain Yago fell with a resounding crash. The sharp corner of a gutter shattered his neck and left hand into pieces.

Atreau swayed on his feet. The burning heat of his own blood poured down his leg. He took a step and a sick, sharp pain shot through his thigh. Narsi gripped his shoulder.

"Let me see," Narsi said.

Atreau very nearly crumpled to the ground—very nearly gave in to the pain and shock and allowed Narsi to kneel over him.

This was the vision he'd seen in the Sorrowlands playing out. Him bleeding in a gutter, Narsi desperately attempting to stanch the flow of blood. Then the mordwolves tore them both apart.

This was how they failed to destroy the Shroud of Stone last time. This was the moment when he'd been too hurt and too scared. He had allowed Narsi to die with him.

"The alcove," Atreau ground out, and he stumbled ahead.

Narsi ran, half dragging him along. Behind them Atreau heard mordwolves' fast, panting breaths and the scrape of claws against flagstones.

Together he and Narsi made it up the first steps and into the mouth of the alcove. A low, narrow tunnel, barely a shoulder's width across, stretched back into the Shard of Heaven. The walls were all a luminous blue.

This would be the place to stop them.

Atreau braced himself in the opening of the alcove. Below him, two huge mordwolves reached the staircase.

"I have to stop the bleeding." Narsi dug into his medical satchel with trembling hands.

"Destroy the Shroud of Stone. Then come back and save me." Atreau lifted his own necklace over his head and braced his body across the opening of the alcove. His hand shook as he gripped the charm Skellan had given him in his hand.

"What are you—No! Atreau, no!" Narsi lunged to stop him, but Atreau had already released the charm.

He felt a constricting chill surge up his body. His chest grew too tight to draw breath, but the unyielding stone of his body held back the first rush of snarling mordwolves. They couldn't reach Narsi. Relief washed through Atreau.

Then he felt nothing more.

Chapter
Thirty-Six

As Fedeles charged across the Gado Bridge, he plunged from a world of lively summer noise into silent streets swathed in frigid white fog. Grand structures and human figures alike were obscured to pale gray impressions. The pounding of Firaj's hooves resounded over the flagstones like war drums.

Fedeles shuddered as damp tendrils of mist brushed over his face and clung to the bare skin of his neck like grasping fingers. Firaj shivered and tossed his head. Skellan's charm flared vivid red, burning the mist back from Fedeles. What little strength he still retained Fedeles poured into the scarlet shield, expanding it to cloak Firaj as well. A raw ache gnawed through his chest, but he continued protecting his horse.

Ariz flew just ahead of them. His gold wings sent walls of mist whirling aside, and Fedeles took in the frozen chaos of the street before him. In the open spaces of gardens and city fountains, the white mineralized bodies of countless bees, dragonflies, wasps and butterflies lay like fresh snowfall. Marble trees abounded with icy white flowers and fruit, while grass lawns looked like fields of frost.

On the roads and walkways the fleeing populace had been captured in jarring stone displays. Horses sprawled in a tangle with the traces of an overturned carriage. A man cowered in horror while another raised his sword. Fear and confusion showed on so many faces. But compassion and tenderness was captured all around him as well. Another powerful beat of Ariz's wings revealed the marble figure of an old woman bent to hoist a puppy into her arms. A child clung to her back. Even in their last moments, people still sheltered each other. Imprisoned in stone, they still retained their humanity.

Fedeles shifted and Firaj responded at once. They bounded over all three figures, briefly soaring alongside Ariz. Fedeles smiled as the tip of Ariz's wing brushed his shoulder. Then he and Firaj took the ground, galloping onward.

Despite the grim surroundings and the desperate situation, sparks of optimism kindled within Fedeles. Ariz was alive. He was free. And he was with him. No matter what they faced, they now took it on together. Fedeles's misgivings about himself gave way before an assurance in the two of them. Their reunion had to be something more meaningful than mere chance. Fedeles had devoured flames and crossed through ancient portals; Ariz had defied death itself to meet him again. If any two souls shared a destiny, it had to be them.

Together they would provide the distraction Narsi and Atreau needed. They would stop Clara and save Marisol. He had to believe that.

They charged deeper into the mists, closing the distance to the Shard of Heaven. Near the ornate balustrades of the Dasma Bridge, the first mordwolf leapt forward to ambush them. Ariz swooped down, catching the creature by its neck. He hauled it into the air, then simply released the mordwolf to the mercy of the river far below. Through the mist, a second and then a third mordwolf appeared ahead of Fedeles. Faint shadows betrayed more of them lurking even farther along the bridge.

Had Clara seen through their ruse? She knew he wasn't carrying the Horns of Yah-muur. Then he realized he was attributing far too much honor to Clara. Why would she risk him or Ariz getting near her if her mordwolves could kill them, then drag their carcasses and the relic they carried to her?

Once, Fedeles would have wasted minutes feeling revolted by such a cunning plot. Now he simply acknowledged Clara's efficiency and concentrated on countering her attack.

What shreds of magical power remained in him he currently burned through, protecting Firaj from the Shroud of Stone. He couldn't cast even a small spell over Clara's mordwolves, much less kill them. But then, he didn't truly want to kill them.

Instead he released his hold over the emptiness gnawing at his insides. All the heat and strength surging through the mordwolves drew that hunger. Fedeles felt the excited currents of spells bursting through the mordwolves like firecrackers. The intricate teal spells Clara used to enthrall these men sank too deep into their flesh and minds for Fedeles to devour without hurting them. But the superficial enchantments that cocooned them in animal flesh were loose and luscious wrappings. Sweet dumpling skins he could peel away.

Fedeles devoured the spells with ease.

All at once, bristling hides and powerful muscles stripped back from the charging mordwolves. Their extended limbs shrank and twisted. Stunned guardsmen tripped and tumbled to their knees. At once, the Shroud of Stone seized on their exposed bodies, engulfing them in marble.

Fedeles and Ariz advanced. More mordwolves attacked in packs as they pushed across the Dasma Bridge. Fedeles stripped transformation spells from those in front of them. Ariz circled, slashing and ripping apart those that lurked to ambush them from behind. Soon the few remaining faint shadows of mordwolves fled before them.

When they at last crossed the bridge, they were bathed in scarlet light. The wall of flames Skellan had raised over the river lit the grounds like a setting sun. Even the brilliant blue stone beneath them looked dark. The seams of gold buried far below glinted like distant flames.

As they proceeded toward the steps of the chapel, Fedeles noticed breaks in the white mist of the Shroud of Stone. They looked like long streamers of swirling clouds—like crossing into the eye of a storm. And yet the sight of marble priests and pigeons scattered all around the grounds warned him that the Shroud of Stone could still overcome them at any time. A tiny marble frog gaped at Fedeles from a stone reed, then a river breeze sent it tumbling into the water of the fountain below.

Fedeles paused at the foot of the chapel stairs. He patted Firaj's neck, his heart aching.

If Fedeles asked it of him, Firaj would carry him into the chapel, even though it would be impossible for Firaj to avoid ambushes from among the maze of stone beasts inside. There were just too few open spaces to maneuver or retreat. Although Fedeles would feel safer riding Firaj, he knew that taking the warhorse inside would condemn him to a savage death. Fedeles could spare him that suffering, at least.

"We have to say goodbye now," Fedeles whispered. He swung down from his saddle but kept a hand in contact with Firaj's warm body. He stroked Firaj's velvety nose. Firaj snuffled his face. Fedeles indulged himself for a moment, scratching the big warhorse's jaw.

He didn't want to let go.

At last he forced himself to withdraw his hand. The light of Skellan's shield fell away from Firaj's glossy black body. A ribbon of white mist immediately coiled around him. Firaj snorted once but remained steadfastly in place, watching Fedeles even after his eyes went white and sightless. Captured in stone, Firaj looked valiant, forever ready to carry Fedeles to safety.

Fedeles turned away before sorrow could overcome him.

Ariz landed on the step beside him. He straightened to his full height, returning to his natural body in a fluid motion. Gold feathers melted away to reveal his calm face and the sculpted muscles of his bare chest. His gray eyes struck Fedeles as very clear and bright, while the scars that had marred his chest, arms and back seemed faded. His hair appeared more auburn than brown in the scarlet light. That one wayward tuft still stuck up at the back of his head.

He touched Fedeles's shoulder and Fedeles understood the unspoken sympathy in that brief, gentle contact.

"Thank you," Fedeles said. He couldn't restrain himself from reaching out and brushing his hand over Ariz's hair, stroking that curl down. He didn't know why, but it reassured him to feel the stiff hair flick back up as he drew his hand away.

Fedeles started up the chapel steps.

"I have your back," Ariz said as he fell in behind him. Fedeles heard him draw his weapons, and suddenly the threat of everything ahead of them gripped Fedeles's heart. He didn't want Ariz to have to fight or bleed. Didn't want him to suffer any more in his life. And yet this was what they were meant to do—what they had to do to protect this world and the people they cared for. At least they would do it together. Neither of them had to face their enemies alone.

Fedeles nodded and lifted his head high. Then he marched up the steps and strode through the golden doors as if the chapel was his.

Inside, mists churned and circled the vaulted ceiling, like ghostly sharks swimming overhead. Below, the beheaded remains of stone monsters, giants and warriors tangled through the length of the nave. Fedeles sensed mordwolves hunching behind them.

Far ahead of him, standing on the altar, Clara Odalis held her arms out as if catching the rays of light that filtered through the stained glass windows. An immense web of countless teal threads spun out from around her. Fedeles couldn't imagine how many lives she held enthralled to her will, all while she wove further spells all around herself.

The witchflame surging up from her soul was one of the most radiant and formidable Fedeles had ever seen. Unshackled from Hierro's control, she shone like an inferno. Teal light rippled around her body and danced from her hands. It encircled the guardsmen standing beside her as well as the physician-priests who were restraining Remes against the pulpit behind her. But Clara's attention remained directed up at the bright symbols churning over her head.

Without the Hallowed Kings shining before him, Fedeles clearly saw how Clara had altered the wards that once protected the Shard of Heaven. Generations of power now fed into the locket hanging from a chain around Clara's neck. It was tiny, but Fedeles shuddered as he sensed its purpose. The same grasping, brutal force had once encircled him when Scholar Donamillo had suppressed his soul and invaded his body. Clara clearly intended to employ the altered wards to put this locket to the same use.

He'd expected as much ever since Suelita brought him the pages copied from Genimo Plunado's journals. Still, it was unnerving to feel those enchantments so near him.

Fedeles looked to Remes. There was something strange and waxy about his face. The physician-priests crowding around him blocked Fedeles's view, but they didn't seem to be doing the prince any kindness with their knives and needles.

Then a motion in the shadows beneath the altar caught Fedeles's attention. Elenna crouched there, gripping Marisol. She held a belt knife near the little girl's face, but her gaze was lowered to the mass of wet bones and decayed flesh at her feet. The earthly remnants of the Hallowed Kings, Fedeles realized. He couldn't be certain, but he thought he saw a deep-blue haze still fluttering through those remains.

Elenna mouthed something and Marisol nodded very slowly. Then Marisol looked to Fedeles. He wanted to offer her some reassurance. But then three mordwolves launched themselves from the statues on Fedeles's right.

Marisol screamed and Clara smiled.

But Fedeles was prepared and practiced now. He tore the transformation spells from the three charging mordwolves. Stripped back to costumed noblemen, they staggered and stared at Fedeles, momentarily dazed. Then two of them reached for their blades. Ariz lunged out, driving his sword into the chest of the man nearest Fedeles. Simultaneously, ribbons of white mists descended upon the other two. Their stone figures appeared stunned as Fedeles walked past them. Streamers of mist trailed close behind him.

After that, he and Ariz advanced relentlessly. Fedeles devoured spells and those men the Shroud of Stone didn't capture fell beneath Ariz's blades. Twice an archer loosed arrows from the altar, but the chaos of statues and pillars filling the chapel blocked them.

Clara glowered at Fedeles while still steadily pouring more power into her spells, but she didn't attack him directly. Perhaps she was just waiting for him to step into a trap.

Or maybe she couldn't split her attention any further. Previously she'd shared the burden of directing her spells with Hierro. But now her will alone flashed through the teal filaments surrounding her. Fedeles guessed that the troop of mordwolves surrounding him and Ariz weren't the only ones that she currently dispatched to hunt and kill.

Behind him he heard blades ring and the desperate sound of fast breath and scuffling boots. It took all his will not to spin around to reassure himself of Ariz's safety. Clara's fingers twitched. She was just waiting for him to drop his guard. He glowered back at her.

He had to trust in Ariz and focus on clearing the way ahead for both of them. But even concentrating straight ahead, he nearly stepped into a teal curse smoldering on the brilliant blue floor. Spears of searing light shot up at him, searing his calf. At the same time another mordwolf bounded from an alcove.

Fedeles's shadow surged out, smothering the spell. Ariz leapt into the air, meeting the mordwolf with gleaming black talons.

Shocks coursed across Fedeles body as Clara's spell struggled in the grip of his shadow. Fedeles gritted his teeth against the pain and silently swore at himself. He should have drained the spells instead of unleashing his shadow. But he'd acted out of reflex. He couldn't afford to do that again; he needed to reserve all the strength he could to deal with Clara.

Behind him, he felt Ariz's movements like wind whirling at his back. He heard the whimper and choked cry of a dying mordwolf. An instant later he felt the heat of Ariz's back press against him once more.

"Keep going. Don't let me distract you," Ariz said, under his breath. "Wherever you lead I will follow. Trust me."

"You're truly an excellent partner," Fedeles whispered. To his surprise, a very soft laugh escaped Ariz.

"Hopefully our future dances will involve fewer mordwolves attempting to cut in."

Fedeles smiled and his assurance returned. They would succeed here and enjoy laughter after this. He wouldn't allow Clara Odalis or anyone else to steal that future from them.

Fedeles strode to the foot of the altar. Contorted stone faces glared at him and the mist-filled air reeked of both rotted meat and fresh-spilled blood. Previously he'd not seen the body slumped beside a pillar. Now he darted a quick glance at the horrifically mutilated corpse. The torso hung open and the head lay separately in a pool of blood. Fedeles didn't recognize Hierro's face immediately; he'd never before seen the man from this angle or wearing such a startled expression.

Fedeles's gaze flickered to Elenna and Marisol. The decayed bones and shattered shards of crystal washed out around them made for a particularly gruesome sight. Again he sensed that faint haze curling around the two of them. As a wisp of the Shroud of Stone floated near them, a pale visage rose up, shielding them. A last remnant of Gachello's soul, Fedeles realized, still attempting to restrain the Shard of Stone.

"Lord Quemanor, I had wondered if you would actually deliver my relic in person," Clara called down to him. She glanced past him, then sighed as if disappointed. "It saddens me to see that my dear sister is neither so principled nor so protective of her family as to accompany you. How naïve of me to hope she would."

Clara offered a pitying smile to Marisol and then went on. "I'm so sorry that you had to learn how little love your mother is capable of feeling, Sparanzo." Clara shook her head. "But take heart, you are still a firstborn son. The heir to a dukedom—or is it two dukedoms, now that Papa and Hierro have passed away? Yes, two dukedoms. What a very valuable little boy you are. It's not as if you're a worthless daughter. Can you imagine your father bothering to return my relic to me if you were?"

Elenna winced and seemed to grind her teeth, while Marisol pulled her gaze away from Clara to stare at Fedeles, her despair plain to see. She genuinely hadn't thought anyone would come for her.

Fedeles wanted to seize her from Elenna and reassure her, but he didn't dare make any sudden move. He needed to know exactly where Clara meant to enthrone her vibrant soul first. To do that he needed time to feel out her wards and spells.

He drew a step back and frowned at Clara.

"Considering the escort you dispatched to welcome me, I'd say Oasia had grounds for keeping well clear of you," Fedeles stated. "As for handing over the relic, I'm now hesitant to believe that you'll honor the terms of the exchange."

"With Master Ariz protecting you, how could you suffer any real harm?" Clara replied.

Fedeles paid that taunt no mind. Instead he studied Remes. Fedeles had assumed that Clara intended to steal Remes's body and identity. Assuming his role, she could claim the title of royal bishop and easily challenge Fedeles for the crown. But something was very wrong about Remes now. Fedeles couldn't see him clearly, but the spells restraining him assured Fedeles that Remes's body was a bloodless husk. His soul writhed and struggled to escape it. Clara couldn't intend to take control of a corpse. Nor was there any point in keeping Remes's soul captive if she only wanted to inhabit his body.

No, these spells felt more like . . . Fedeles started at the realization. She was indeed attempting to forge a Hallowed King to replace Gachello. But it was Remes she was using. Fedeles guessed that it was because she held a thrall over him. With his soul imprisoned in his enthralled flesh, Clara would be able to control him completely. Through him she might even master the Shroud of Stone, releasing and restraining the spell as she willed.

But creating a new Hallowed King wasn't easily done. Especially not now that Fedeles had shattered the royal bishop's jade ring and Clara herself had altered so many of the protective wards. So Clara's physician-priests resorted to the cursed needles and nails employed by torturers to keep their prisoners from finding the release of death.

Even so, Fedeles could sense Remes's soul shredding apart. His spirit was neither prepared nor willing to suffer for the sake of his nation. As a Hallowed King, he wouldn't last even an hour, much less defend Cadeleon for the century that Gachello had endured.

No wonder Clara needed Yah-muur's Horn. It was her insurance against the Shroud of Stone breaking free completely. After all, she wanted to rule a vast holy kingdom, not a desolate world of stone.

"Dear Sparanzo, you must be so scared. But look, your dear papa has come to save you!" Clara's words caught Fedeles's attention. Her gaze took on an acquisitive quality as she stared down at Marisol. Then she smiled at Fedeles.

"How much would the Duke of Rauma willingly endure for the sake of a treasured son?" Clara asked. "Such a precious son and heir. How very, very lucky Sparanzo is. Your papa would come and kill so many hapless, enthralled men all for your sake, my dear."

Clara gestured out past Fedeles and Ariz, indicating the trail of defeated and dead behind them. She went on, "I wonder, would he even die for you? Would he become a wraith shielding you from the terrible mists that might gobble you up at any minute?"

Fedeles frowned at Clara's words. Was that why she hadn't tried to kill him outright? She had realized that Remes was not going to last as a Hallowed King. Fedeles, with his cursed history, was a better candidate—so long as she found a way to control him.

"A good father would sacrifice anything for such a precious son, I'm certain of it," Clara said.

Fedeles nodded, but he was only half listening to her. If he'd been wrong about Remes, then what else had he been mistaken about? His shadow spread out, testing and assessing the surrounding spells. Clara might attempt to manipulate and lie to him, but her spells could not. Fedeles's shoulders slumped slightly, but Ariz stepped close, steadying him.

"You're finally free of Hierro." Ariz's tone was condemning and drew Clara's attention. "Yet all you do is emulate his spells and cruelty?"

Even only half aware as he was, Fedeles could see the outraged flush color Clara's pale face.

"You dare compare me to that—that monster!" she shouted. Light flared all around her. Her dark eyes flashed with teal light. "I am righteous in my path! Justified in my means! You *know* what I've suffered! What he did to me!"

Ariz shrugged, his expression condemning. His bare scarred chest displayed far more than merely *knowing* the agonies that Hierro inflicted.

"You suffered, so now it's your right to torture, enthrall and murder as you please?" Ariz demanded.

"Murder? You're hardly one to criticize murder, Ariz." Clara laughed and her tone turned mocking. "Just look at the mess you made of my brother—and that was of your own volition. You were free of him. Yet *you* still chose to do this."

Ariz glanced to Hierro's corpse and revulsion twitched through his cold visage.

Fedeles realized that their argument wasn't a matter of random insult and accusations, but the precise barbs of two people who understood one another's values and vulnerabilities. He would never have been capable of claiming Clara's full attention, but right now Ariz occupied her awareness to the extent that she failed to notice Fedeles's shadow reach out to Elenna and Marisol.

He focused on the locket that Clara had sent to Sparanzo. The one he now realized matched closely the one Clara wore herself. Long ago he and Oasia both had seen that the stones decorating the necklace were blessings of protection. Likely their power was the reason that Gachello's faint wraith could still defend Marisol and Elenna. But the locket had defied both his and Oasia's perception until now. In the light of Clara's other spells it opened, revealing a mate to the invading enchantments Clara was currently feeding.

He'd been a fool! Of course it wasn't Remes who Clara wanted to possess. No, she wanted to claim the life of a *precious son*. An *heir to two dukedoms*. Sparanzo was even a rightful heir to the throne now. But more than any of that, Fedeles thought, Clara seemed desperate to punish Oasia. And what weapon could inflict more pain than taking Oasia's only child and using him to destroy her?

Next to him, Ariz drew himself up straight and lifted his chin. Defiance suited him.

"*I* struck down the man who ruined me—who made my life a misery. The same man who tortured you and countless others! But what harm has that child *ever* done to you?" Ariz pointed to Marisol and then Elenna. "How has Elenna hurt you? What great wrong did all the hapless souls across this city heap upon your pampered life? You have no justification!"

"Their suffering is nothing compared to mine—"

"The righteous defend the innocent even from their own ire!" Ariz shouted the holy quotation.

"Paradise awaits the innocent. The sinful deserve the hells that take them. I will deliver them all to their just rewards. You along with the rest,

Ariz!" Clara focused on Ariz so intently that teal flames sparked from her hands and roiled in the air before him. But like the white mist, they dissipated before touching his body.

At the same time, Fedeles noted Clara's power draining from the thralls she held over Elenna and the surrounding guardsmen. He met Elenna's gaze. Her face twitched with pain, but she very deliberately loosened her hold on Marisol, then lowered her belt knife. She mouthed something to Marisol and the girl looked to Fedeles entreatingly.

He lunged forward, sweeping Marisol up into his arms. Ariz followed him in perfect time, intercepting the guardsman who leapt from the altar to stop them. Fedeles didn't see what Ariz tore from the man's chest, but an instant later white mist engulfed the guardsman, leaving a startled-looking stone figure. Ariz retreated to Fedeles's side, letting the red charm fall from his fingers. A shield, Fedeles thought. No doubt the guardsmen and physician-priests surrounding Clara all wore the same things to hold the Shroud of Stone at bay.

"You filth!" Clara shouted.

The two remaining guardsmen jumped from the altar and advanced together on Ariz and Fedeles.

"Don't you want the relic?" Fedeles demanded. "Isn't this the exchange we agreed to?"

Clara's eyes narrowed. Then she gave a wave of her hand and the guardsmen stopped in their tracks. That self-satisfied smile returned to her face.

Fedeles understood why. As far as she knew, her locket still hung from Sparanzo's neck. She would be able to take possession of him, even if he was in Fedeles's arms. What she couldn't see was that Marisol gripped the locket to her chest, but Elenna had long ago loosened the clasp. Now as Fedeles drew her close, Marisol slid the locket into his hand.

"It's not mine." Marisol buried her face against the crook of his neck. "I don't want it."

"It's all right. You don't have—" Fedeles began, but Marisol's sob cut him off.

"I'm not him. I'm sorry," Marisol whispered into Fedeles ear. Her tears felt hot as they slid down Fedeles's cool skin. "I'm not him."

"I know who you are, Marisol," Fedeles quietly assured her. "Your uncle and I came here for you, not for anyone else."

"You did?" Marisol's sob turned to a startled hiccup, and Fedeles might have laughed if her surprise hadn't seemed so wrong and pitiful. She hugged him fiercely.

Fedeles glanced to Ariz. Neither of them said a word. Ariz nodded.

Fedeles drew his shadow into himself, then he gripped the necklace in his fist and gave it a spark of power. The spells inside woke at once, as did those in the locket Clara held. Clara's eyes flared wide with shock, then she let loose an enraged scream.

A wild bolt of teal light shot out from the locket she gripped and slammed into the one Fedeles held. The locket's spells unfolded around him, like a glass sphere swirling with gold incantations. Familiar. It was so terribly familiar. A nightmare that he'd spent years trying to escape.

But one that he understood, whereas Clara had no experience with this disorientation. During the years that Fedeles had been possessed, he'd gained exquisite expertise in keeping himself both separated and whole, even when forcibly sharing his body with another soul.

So when Clara's spirit struck him like a hammer blow, jolting through his arm and reverberating deep in his chest, he recoiled to a hidden space within himself, easily letting her enter. He felt the sizzling current of her rage rising around him, pressing in on his body and shrieking over his own thoughts. He felt her resentment like a meat hook catching his heart and her radiant power slicing through his mind like a knife blade.

His hand shook, but he kept his grip on the locket as he coiled his shadow tighter around himself, dragging Clara deeper in.

Clara's guardsmen lunged for Fedeles, but Ariz kicked the feet out from under the closer of the two, sending him crashing into his partner. With a brutal stroke, Ariz plunged his sword down through both their sprawled bodies. Then he bounded into the air. Ariz wheeled through the clouds of mist and swept straight for Clara's motionless figure. Several of the physician-priests abandoned Remes and raced forward, hurling cursed knives at Ariz. Another guardsman drew back a bow and loosed an arrow into his wing.

Fedeles jolted as Ariz tumbled.

He landed in a crouch, then bounded back up to his feet, once again taking a human form. The arrow fell from his grazed forearm and he charged the altar again. Behind him, Elenna staggered to her feet, clutching her belt knife.

Fedeles's heart shook, but he could do nothing. His entire being grappled with the blazing fury of Clara's soul. She shrieked and lashed out at him, unleashing a chaos of sensations and memories that were not his own.

Hierro's long fingers dug into his throat, choking him as vicious curses rang through his head. *I'll kill you someday. Kill you and laugh over your corpse.* Oasia rocked him in her arms and promised that she'd come back and save him. He buried himself in her embrace but only felt resentment churning in his chest. *How can you leave me, you bitch? You know what he'll do to me if he can't have you anymore.* Then the Shard of Heaven blazed before him, radiant gold spells scattered through brilliant blue stones like countless stars sown across the sky. A wild glee filled him. *So much power and glory—after all I've suffered, it should be mine!*

Clara's rage burned all around him, threatening to consume him. But in the midst of the chaos and wrath, Fedeles drew his shadow around him. He felt the certainty of himself—his soul—in its dark silence. Impenetrable, indomitable, this was his and his alone. Even depleted of strength and encircled by madness and flames, he remained certain of who he was. He'd endured all of this before, survived it and made his darkness part of himself. No matter how powerful Clara was, he would never allow her to tear his identity asunder. He'd destroy himself and take her with him before he allowed that to happen.

But he didn't believe Clara shared his resolve. She possessed hurt and pain and anger—just as he did—but she'd never tempered those driving forces with compassion or regret or love. Her power was an inferno, but it arose from a volatile, unbalanced spirit. Hatred alone was not enough to make a person whole. Rage was not strength.

Surrounded in flames, Fedeles perceived this so very clearly. Clara's anger ignited her power, but they were not one and the same. He relaxed and let Clara hurl all her might against the razor-edged darkness at the core of his being. She struck with resounding force, but Fedeles didn't waver. Instead Clara's soul split. The bright power of her witchflame tore away from her snarling spirit. Teal flames peeled back from a hissing pale thing—an underbelly like a soft white centipede. Fedeles deflected that poisonous spirit like a glancing blow. At the same time his shadow enveloped that shining witchflame.

His body warmed, then grew searing hot, as if engulfed in fever. The edges of his shadow smoldered. But he didn't relent. All around him, he sensed spell after spell collapsing as he drained away Clara's power. Transformations and thralls dissipated throughout the Shard of Heaven. White mists descended everywhere, seizing entire troops of guardsmen the instant they were stripped of their animal bodies. Maids and priests were suddenly released from the compulsions that howled through their minds. Thousands of songbirds at last flew free of the city.

On the altar, the physician-priests surrounding Remes stared at one another in confusion. One of them tore the cursed implements from the prince's body in a panic, while another sank to his knees and threw up.

The last of Clara's spells died and Fedeles hurled the locket to the ground. It cracked apart against the hard blue stone. The sphere of whirling enchantments crumbled and Clara's pale, depleted soul shot back to her body. Fedeles staggered, still blazing with too much magic. But he didn't dare fall. He still held Marisol in his arms.

Clara let out and aggravated shout, then drew in a deep breath, straining for any shred of power to hurl against Fedeles. Only a few feet from her, Ariz cut down the last guardsman still defending Clara. She stepped back from him.

"Ariz, please." Clara spoke softly, her expression suddenly entreating. "Don't hurt me. Have mercy."

Ariz stilled and Fedeles thought he was considering a way to simply take her prisoner. At the same time, a faint blue light seemed to condense at Clara's back—magic too subtle for Ariz to see, but still there and growing. Was she already replenishing her power?

Before Fedeles could act or call out a warning, Clara jerked, her arms clawing up at nothing. Ariz bounded back, sword raised. However, Clara's hands fell to her sides. A ribbon of blood suddenly spilled down her throat and more poured from between her lips. She tried to spin backward, only to topple from the altar and flop against the stone floor.

Then Fedeles saw Elenna, red-eyed and haggard, standing where Clara had been. The hilt of Elenna's belt knife jutted from the back of Clara's neck. Gachello's ghost cloaked her in blue light.

"Join your brother in the three hells," Elenna muttered down at Clara.

"Well said," Ariz told her. Then Ariz turned and gazed at Fedeles with an expression of relief. "You two all right?"

Fedeles glanced to Marisol. She looked exhausted, but she nodded and offered Ariz a hesitant smile.

Fedeles opened his mouth to assure Ariz that he was well. But then the entire floor of the Shard of Heaven shuddered beneath them. A radiant light surged up through the blue stone, turning it gold. Giant bodies throughout the nave of the chapel slumped and toppled into mounds of soft, dead flesh. The floor shook again, then suddenly, it gave way.

CHAPTER
THIRTY-SEVEN

"No! Don't do this!" Narsi bellowed, but it was already too late.

Atreau stood encased in marble, with his head turned slightly, as if offering Narsi a last glance at his defiant profile.

A mordwolf leapt at Atreau but fell back after impacting his stone body. It scrambled to its feet and, catching sight of Narsi, jammed its muzzle into the space between Atreau's outstretched arm and the wall. It snarled and snapped and dug at the bright blue stone of the floor. Another slammed its head between the wall and Atreau's hip, but the mass of its shoulders stopped its attack. It continued lunging for Narsi, pushing ahead inch by inch.

Narsi stumbled back from the bared teeth and flying spittle. He couldn't just wait here, he knew that. But how could he abandon Atreau like this? Even frozen in marble, the long gash in his leg looked fatal. But there was a way to help him—to save him. He had to comply with Atreau's last wish: destroy the Shroud, then come back to save him.

That would work, wouldn't it?

If the Shroud was destroyed then Atreau might be released. Then Narsi could treat his wounded thigh. He could save him—he *would* save him.

Narsi turned and sprinted through the narrow corridor. The floor was uneven, catching his feet as he ran. More than once he scraped a shoulder and hand against the facets of the rocky walls. But Narsi didn't slow.

Sweat beaded his body, but a chill emanated from the blue stone, prickling his skin. Narsi's breath streamed from his lips in white plumes and he felt patches of ice on the walls and floor. A frigid white mist drifted all around.

His lamplight bounced off the blue stone surrounding him like it was dancing across the surface of the sea. Gold suspended in the depths flashed like schools of sea serpents. The farther he went, the larger and more common golden seams appeared. They knotted and twisted together, filling more and more of the walls, ceiling and floor, until soon the corridor shone as if lined with brass mirrors.

Everywhere around him, Narsi caught warped reflections of his own figure. Blood and sweat dribbled down the side of his face. At some point he'd grazed his forehead. He hadn't even noticed.

All he could care about—think about—was that if he acted quickly enough, he could save Atreau. There was still time. There had to be. He could still save him.

I will save him.

I will save him.

Narsi repeated that thought over and over, leveraging his growing fear and panic into a promise that kept him moving ahead.

The icy fog thickened, and his own refection in the faceted walls grew contorted and warped.

He didn't see the white gate barring the passage until he slammed into it. The long pickets and rails felt like spears of ice against his damp body. However, the instant Narsi felt the distinct texture of the gate, he knew what it had been made from and pulled his hand away. These were polished human bones, strung together with silver.

Narsi pushed past wondering who these bones had once belonged to. He didn't have time to waste in pathos or rumination, though the sadness pulled at him.

He dug out the black key Sacrist Amabilo had given to him. His hands shook so badly that he nearly dropped it. After taking a deep, slow breath, Narsi calmed his racing heart and shaking muscles enough to slot the key into the keyhole. As he turned the key, the assembly of tiny bones making up the lock slid apart. The skeletal gates parted. And a biting cold breeze rushed over Narsi. He shuddered and the flame of his lamp died.

In the darkness, Narsi felt frigid mists curling around him, sinking through his clothes to settle on his skin. Then a flare of warmth and golden light rose from the seams of gold in his own hands. The horn in his pocket flashed and sparked. Narsi abandoned his lamp and took up the horn. As he gripped it, the two prongs of the horn extended and spread like the branches of a tree sprouting new twigs. Flames lit up at the tips, like dozens of spring leaves bursting to life.

The warm light scattered through the dense clouds of white mist. Here and there the flames reflected off blue stone and the wide seams of gold. The icy vapor whirled and churned in the gold-and-blue illumination, looking as if it stretched on forever.

Despite the light and fire, the air around Narsi seemed to grow even colder. When he extended his left hand into the surrounding white masses, he felt as if he'd plunged his arm into ice water. But he continued to reach out, feeling for any obstacle ahead as he searched for whatever it was that encased the Shroud of Stone. A cask perhaps, like the one that had held Yah-muur's Horn? Or could it be written on the wall?

He had to find it—destroy it. Atreau was depending on him. So was Yara, and Esfir and Father Timoteo. Master Ariz. Querra. His uncle, Elezar. Mother Kir-Naham, Spider and Inissa, the duke and duchess. Entire households, theater troupes. Cities filled with thousands and thousands of people—so many. Too many for him to fail.

He had to find it.

His heart raced, but his entire body shivered uncontrollably. Narsi's numb fingers smacked across a rough surface. The mist rolled back before the horn's light, but it only showed him his own desperate expression reflected in a twisted vein of gold. He'd found a wall.

A wall was better than nothing. It had to lead him somewhere. Narsi hurried onward, keeping one hand to the wall. The Shroud of Stone must be nearby, he assured himself. But dread gnawed at him as he continued searching, blindly, through the frigid, writhing vapor.

Gold forms and blue shadows arose through the mist. Narsi made out an ivory tower, etched with countless pale symbols. He sprinted ahead, only to have the tower waft apart before him. An illusion, born from the mists and his own desperation. Narsi wanted to shout with frustration. Instead he kept moving. Searching.

Then his foot struck something. It clattered against the floor and he looked down to see the lamp he'd abandoned. He'd gone in a full circle and was standing once more at the gate. He could no longer see it through the deepening mist. But reaching out, he touched the cold bones.

The corridor didn't lead to anything. Just this empty chamber. Had he gone wrong? Missed a turn or passed unknowing into a different tunnel? In his frantic state Narsi nearly turned back to retrace his steps. But then he thought of the key. This was the gate it had unlocked. Sacrist Amabilo wouldn't have sacrificed himself to deliver the wrong key, Narsi was certain of that.

This had to be the right place, but what was he supposed to do? Where was the Shroud of Stone? Narsi's entire body shook from cold and fatigue. He knew every moment he wasted was a life he couldn't win back—another soul he was failing. How many enthralled people were already dead? How many more were watching in terror as the Shroud of Stone slowly overtook the city. The wards defending the sacred grove would not last forever. Even Skellan's vast wall of flames would eventually fail. On the Old Road, Narsi had seen it all.

He had to make this right, but he didn't know how. He didn't know what to do. He'd been so arrogant accepting the horn, thinking that he could save everyone. But who was he, really? What qualifications did he possess? He wasn't a sorcerer or mystic. Not a warrior or even a clever spy. He'd just happened to be there and acted on impulse, accepting a responsibility he couldn't have truly understood until now.

Now, when everything depended upon him, but he didn't know what to do. When he stood here faced with nothing but his own failings and a chilling emptiness.

His teeth chattered and each breath he took felt like it sketched his nose and lungs with frost. He was so, so cold.

Narsi sank down to a crouch, curling his body around the heat of the blazing horn. The closer he came to them, the more the flames dimmed. The light dulled to mere sparks.

"No, don't die out on me," Narsi whispered. He could feel the horn cooling. Narsi's fingers ached, as if poison was again eating into his knuckles.

Why is life is so hard? Why does it have to be like this? So full of anguish and despair.

The thought arose in Narsi, almost as if someone else whispered it to him, though he recognized that this was his own voice.

What if you aren't able to save Atreau? What if you aren't able to save anyone? Why cause all this chaos?

Narsi's chest ached and a sob escaped him. He had to stop thinking this way.

He didn't want to cry. He knew he couldn't afford to fall apart. And yet anguish flooded him. Hot tears filled his eyes. All the joy and hope he'd felt in Labara were like barbs being ripped from his body as he thought of losing Atreau.

That voice rose up inside him again.

What is the use of loving someone when being parted from him leaves you broken? Bereaved?

He wiped at his face with a shaking, frigid hand. He had to pull himself together.

Even as he told himself as much, he remembered this same hand bracing his mother's emaciated back, feeling her shake as she struggled for breath. She wheezed and choked. He slowly fed her drops of duera in a hopeless effort to ease her suffering. When she had died, Narsi had comforted himself with the idea that at least she was no longer in pain.

Is there a point in fighting for life when the only respite you will find is in the peaceful stillness of death? Why struggle and prolong the hurting for everyone? Be still. Be at peace.

Narsi startled at the question. What was wrong with him? How could he even wonder why life would be worth fighting for? Narsi clenched Yahmuur's horn with both his hands. It bit into his palms, but he welcomed the discomfort. Better to feel that than the heartless numb creeping over him.

He took a deep breath but couldn't sense his lungs fill or his heart beating, though he saw puffs of his breath moving the mist around his face. He felt separated from himself—no. He felt as if he wasn't himself.

Then suddenly he understood two things. First, the mist surrounding him—filling his lungs and bloodstream—was a manifestation of the Shroud of Stone. Whatever vessel had held it must have been destroyed when the spell was released. And second, the voice he heard infiltrating his thoughts wasn't his own. Just like the mist, it was a manifestation of the Shroud of Stone.

Narsi lifted his head and glared into the surrounding haze.

He was caught up in a spell. One that distorted his fears and doubts, draining him of strength and drive. But he knew that defeat, despair and apathy weren't the entirety of his beliefs or feeling—not even close. He couldn't give into them. He wouldn't!

Narsi tried to push himself to standing but found he couldn't.

"My mother's death didn't invalidate the beauty of her life," Narsi said. He turned his thoughts to Atreau, seeking out his most vivid memories of the other man—his voice singing, his laughter, his hot, sweat-beaded skin. "No matter how sad I might feel if I lost him, I will *never* regret loving Atreau. Never."

Once again, tiny flames lit the tips of Yah-muur's horns, and a faint warmth spread over Narsi's hands. At last he was able to push himself to his full height, shifting his weight back and forth.

How tired you are. Rest now.

Rest.

"You want me to be still?" he shouted, his voice deafening in its reverberation through the faceted chamber. His ears rang. "I will not. I will never stop."

Mist whirled and billowed around him. Narsi stared at the blank white expanse. In the distance he picked out a pale figure drifting steadily nearer. Trails of vapor formed a delicate pattern all around the figure, as if weaving gossamer veils around him. Narsi studied that pattern and recognized dozens of archaic symbols for peace written over and over in white. They poured endlessly from the mist.

Peace. Peace. Peace. Peace . . . On and on, until the word became ubiquitous and lost all meaning.

The figure in the mist turned and Narsi's own reflection gazed back at him with deathly serenity.

Why fight against the only true peace in this world?

The instant that suggestion whispered in Narsi's ears, outrage surged through him.

"This is a lie. *You* are a lie. I've experienced countless moments of peace: lying in Atreau's arms, or listening as song filled a holy place. I've watched breezes roll through the herbs in my garden, read wonderful stories, observed the stars. I even feel peace petting that sly black cat of mine. Peace isn't inertia. It isn't numbness and stillness and death. It's an action of reverence and love for the world." In his hands the Horns of

Yah-muur unfurled further. More flames ignited as Narsi rose to his feet. "So fuck you and fuck your pathetic false peace."

Narsi swung the horns around him, willing the fire to sear away those delicate archaic symbols. Warmth rolled from Yah-muur's horn now and the tines continued to grow and unfurl into immense branches.

"Who are you to even speak to me about life? You're nothing but a spell. Who made you? Who wanted this? Instead of this lifeless peace, why didn't they will joy upon the world? Why not gift the world with health and strength?"

As Narsi argued down this doppelgänger, he felt a rush of fire pulse from his chest and race up his arms. Yah-muur's horn flared a red, then molten gold. All at once it rose up from his hands. Narsi basked in light and heat as the horn floated over his head, reaching out even farther into the mists. Narsi followed its progress. The flames dancing atop the tines twisted and leapt into the mist like sparks catching in cobwebs.

The pale white symbols of peace burned away while new fiery golden ones filled their places.

The Haldiim word for *Joy* floated before him. *Health* sprang into the mists, then *Strength*.

Blessings. He'd written new blessings over the Shroud of Stone's deathly invocations.

"Hope," Narsi shouted, and the word sprang up in flames, consuming another pallid wisp of *Peace*. Elation surged through him.

Yah-muur had told him, "*Use your rage and joy, your agony and lust, to carve riots into its incantations. Crack its faultless grasp and fill the quiet with your screams and laughter. It will be undone. When the time comes you will understand.*" That had seemed like such a cryptic instruction. Now it felt so obvious it made him laugh.

"Happiness," Narsi bellowed. He charged through the mists and the horn blazed over him like a crown of burning blessings. "Kindness, Generosity, Compassion!"

He raced wildly through the frigid clouds, shouting out every blessing and good wish he could think of.

"Humor. Resilience. Dignity. Wisdom." Narsi racked his mind for every attribute he had ever wished he could confer. "Forgiveness. Affection. Beauty. Bravery. Honesty. Fortitude. Calm. Integrity. Courage!"

Sweat poured down his body as radiant words engulfed the mists like a wildfire. The hot air around him rippled and distorted. Narsi continued to call more blessings into being.

His throat grew raw. He hoarsely called, "Love. Freedom. Life!"

He struggled to think of another blessing to wish upon the world.

Then he realized that he could no longer find a single trace of white mist. Instead he stood in a gold chamber encircled by a gigantic bower of fiery blessings. His reflection swayed in the gold walls. He looked ferocious and sweat-drenched. His muscles felt loose as taffy.

The fiery blessings surrounding him also flashed in the gold seams of the Shard of Heaven. But unlike his mirrored image, the reflected blessings multiplied along the gold veins and seemed to grow brighter the farther they spread through the ceiling, walls and floor.

Narsi watched them arc and leap like bolts of lightning, illuminating the blue stone walls like they were panes of colored glass. In the radiance, Narsi thought he even glimpsed fish swimming through the surrounding river. He peered into the watery depths. Were those frogwives?

A drop of something wet and cold fell on his forearm. Narsi frowned and glanced down. A second water droplet struck him. Then a third, a fourth, and those were followed by downpour like fine rain.

Narsi's head jerked up to the ceiling.

Belatedly he realized that his inferno of blessings was dissolving the stone that made up the Shard of Heaven. A deep cracking noise, like lake ice shattering, reverberated from high overhead. Narsi's pulse raced and he instantly bolted back down the passage he'd come through.

As he sprinted, the ground shuddered beneath his feet. Rivulets of water poured down the walls. They weren't breaking so much as melting all around him, he realized. Terror lent Narsi a strength he'd never imagined he possessed. One breath ago, he'd been exhausted. Now he dashed through the corridor as if he was carried by the wind.

At last he reached the alcove opening where he'd left Atreau. Relief flooded him as he caught sight of the other man crouched against the alcove wall, binding his leg with his own shirt. Three young guardsmen knelt beside him. One held out a flask while the other two stared at the walls with dazed expressions.

Narsi recognized Sacrist Amabilo and his young acolyte standing to the side but hardly took note of them.

"Get above the water," Narsi tried to shout, but only a rasp escaped his throat.

Still Atreau turned toward him. The smile fell from his pale lips as he met Narsi's gaze.

"The Shard of Heaven is collapsing—" Narsi got no further before a violent thunder of shattering stone drowned out his words. The floor convulsed and hurled him off his feet. He and Atreau reached for each other, catching one another even as they both tumbled. Water gushed down the walls and surged across the ground.

Narsi heard people and animals in the tunnel below crying out in alarm.

Dark water splashed over his face, and he felt more than saw Atreau pulling him up.

Then a black shadow rose over them both.

Narsi clutched Atreau, attempting to shield him from the impact of the black mass. But strangely, nothing struck either of them. Instead a cool, almost silky sensation curled around them, like a cocoon. They floated upward. Then the darkness withdrew and Narsi found himself clinging to Atreau as they broke the surface of the river.

All around them, people and animals—horses, dogs, cats and even rats—were pulled to the river's surface by swift black shadows.

"It's Fedeles." Atreau's pallid face took on a greenish tinge as the river rocked the two of them up and down. Still he managed to nod in the direction of the Dasma Bridge.

Narsi craned his head back and glimpsed the duke standing with his hands spread wide and his head bowed as waves of black shadows rolled from him and plunged into the river.

The water itself shimmered and sparked with roiling golden light. But it was also unnaturally still. Then Narsi saw Skellan standing at the prow of a ship, his red hair flying around him as he danced and gestured over the river. Had he actually stopped the river from flowing? How powerful was he, really? Narsi didn't linger on the thought.

His attention snapped to Atreau's bloodless face.

"We have to get you out of the water." Narsi gripped his hand and started to swim Atreau toward Skellan's ship. Then a party of green frogwives surfaced beside them. One grabbed Narsi and the other two caught Atreau.

Narsi almost protested, but then he realized that all around them frogwives, sailors and fishermen were hauling people and animals out of the water. The three frogwives moved easily across the river, and in moments they landed Narsi and Atreau on board Skellan's ship. Just as Narsi clambered onto the deck the river below blazed gold, as a multitude of Haldiim blessings burst from the surface and flew into the sky. Even waterlogged and shocked as they were, people all around still gasped and cheered, while blessings drifted down to them like golden snow.

Courage and *Fortitude* drifted past Narsi as he scrambled to his feet.

Narsi could hardly care about shining blessings or miraculous sorcery right now. His thoughts were filled with his promise—he would save Atreau. He raced across the wet deck to where Atreau lay sprawled on his back taking slow, deep breaths. He looked waxy, and the shirt he'd used to bandage his thigh was pink with diluted blood. Atreau gazed up at the gold-flecked sky. A weary smile curved his lips.

Narsi dropped to Atreau's side and swung his medical satchel around. The sodden leather buckles resisted as Narsi tugged at them. He swore and ripped one of the buckles off.

"What are you doing?" Atreau asked.

"I'm going to save you." Narsi's raw voice cracked on the words. "I'm going to save you."

"You already have." Atreau lifted his right hand and spread his long fingers to display the gold blessing in his palm. *Life* blazed in Haldiim script. It faded as it melted into Atreau's flesh. Atreau grinned and then caught Narsi's hand in his own and pulled him down beside him.

Above them, clouds of gold blessings filled a bright blue sky. Countless bright, beautiful futures lay before them. Atreau sagged against Narsi.

"Congratulations," he said. "You've saved the world."

"No." Narsi rested his arm across Atreau's shoulders. "We saved the world."

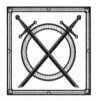

EPILOGUE
ARIZ

Bright shafts of sunshine broke through thin veils of cloud, illuminating the vast city sprawling below Ariz. He angled his long wings, dipping and rising through the spring breezes as he watched over the riders who filled the streets beneath him.

He alighted atop the city wall of the South Gate. With a roll of his shoulders, he returned to his human form. The man standing guard offered him a quick salute before resuming his duties.

Ariz gazed down at the parade-like procession below. If they'd thrown in a couple of fortune-tellers, the Grunitos could rival an Irabiim caravan in both numbers and brilliance. Rowdy song drifted from several of the bright red carriages, while Nestor and his wife rode alongside Fedeles, swapping jokes. Their months-long stay had been pleasant despite the often chaotic state of the capital. That was largely due to Nestor and Riossa's generous characters, as well as their shared ability to find humor in most things.

Alongside Fedeles, the newly ordained royal bishop, Timoteo Grunito, offered blessings for their safe journey home—though Ariz suspected that Timoteo had come for Narsi's sake as much as Nestor's. Narsi and Timoteo embraced and hung together like father and son when they said their goodbyes, Narsi promising to write often and keep the royal bishop apprised of all Anacleto's best gossip.

From where he crouched atop the city wall, Ariz felt a pang. He'd grown fond of Master Narsi's playful banter and optimistic spirit. He wasn't alone in that, he supposed. Mistress Querra, Bahiim Esfir and Mistress Yara all gifted him with trinkets and treats and showered him with affection in their goodbyes.

Atreau Vediya kept his distance throughout, hanging back with the guards and attendants. Ariz didn't blame him for his furtiveness. He'd narrowly avoided accusations of treason a few months back, and a number of bitter nobles still spat at the mention of his name. It was far safer for them to heap outrage and frustration upon an infamous degenerate than to dare oppose the king and queen—particularly after so many of them had witnessed the magnitude of power that both sovereigns commanded.

From his vantage point, Ariz eyed one bony noblemen at the edge of the city gates. The man hadn't been an intimate of Hierro's and so had been spared execution, but he numbered among the vocal opponents of the king's newest laws. Fortunately, more petulance than cunning inspired his strategies. In his attempt to block Fedeles's amendment to inheritance law that recognized women as direct heirs, he'd actually approached Ariz, of all people, hoping to goad him into protesting Delfia's claim to the reinstated Plunado title and lands. The black eye Ariz had given him in lieu of a reply still looked dark and swollen.

When the nobleman glanced up and met Ariz's cold stare, he blanched and edged farther away from the Grunito gathering. Ariz studied his retreat. From his bulging saddlebags and heavy coat, Ariz guessed that the man had planned to escape the city only to find himself mired among the very people he most wanted to avoid.

Ariz shrugged.

He could leave the arrangements for that fellow's demise to Oasia or to Lliro Vediya. Both of them shared Fedeles's progressive agendas. In fact, Ariz had been surprised by Lliro Vediya's radical support of the Butterfly Temples, as well as his insistence on amending Cadeleonian law to decriminalize all adari relationships, which Haldiim laws condoned. Neither Oasia nor Lliro hesitated to use their numerous agents and assassins to achieve their goals. With the two of them on hand, Ariz need only concern himself with Fedeles's well-being.

As he looked down, Fedeles lifted his head and returned Ariz's admiring gaze with a broad smile. Appreciation smoldered in his dark eyes. Ariz felt his face warm with a flush.

Once the blessings and farewells had been shared, the huge party of Grunitos departed and their well-wishers dispersed. Ariz followed Fedeles from the air, while his poor guards tried their best to keep pace with a man and mount that moved like shadows.

As he flew, Ariz surveyed the capital. New plantings expanded the sacred grove to accommodate the influx of converts. Now the violet blossoms of young wisteria trees reached all the way to the Shell Fountain. As he neared the river, cloud imps joined the flocks of swifts flitting after insects. Here and there he thought he glimpsed the green bodies of frogwives swimming alongside fishing boats and clambering up the hulls of ships.

But across the Gado Bridge, where sorcerous fires had devastated entire districts and razed the palace, new construction and renovation was everywhere. Even the small remaining section of the Dasma Bridge now featured a pavilion, where people came to pray and from time to time capture one of the tiny gold blessings that occasionally fluttered up from the depths of the river.

Where the royal palace and its grounds had once stood, there now rose a large school and several dormitories. Officially the school was founded to foster exchanges of religious beliefs, as espoused by the new royal bishop. In reality, Fedeles and Oasia intended it to serve as the first sanctuary and training ground for Cadeleonian witches. With magic and mythical creatures waking all across their nation, they would soon have need for such a place.

Ariz didn't think the school had opened formally, but small groups of people were already strolling along the pathways and gazing at the bronze statue that had survived when the rest of the Royal Star Garden burned. Ariz didn't remember that night's battle too clearly, but he thought that Fedeles had stood atop that ringed bronze planet at some point.

Three of the people below waved at him as he flew past, and Ariz performed a quick twirl in response then he flew on. To the west, carpenters and workmen flooded the grounds of the Quemanor household as well as the Odalis and Fueres mansions. They worked furiously to expand the first into a new palace, while disassembling the latter two. Oasia wanted no trace of either Hierro or Clara to remain in the city.

Ariz didn't turn toward the Quemanor lands but instead soared farther north, hoping that today Fedeles would take heart and follow him.

Where trade and industry transformed the scorched buildings and trampled gardens, nature reclaimed the charred expanse of wilderness surrounding Crown Hill. Cascades of wildflowers and spring grasses blanketed the land. A few oak saplings even sprouted around the remains of fallen trees.

Seeing the new growth pleased Ariz. He hadn't wanted the place that Fedeles loved—the retreat where they'd first lain together—to be destroyed. He circled the hill, gazing at the starts of sunflowers peeking up from amidst expanses of clover. A stretch of stonework still remained of the temple. Pieces of pillars and flagstones lay strewn between bursts of yellow flowers. He drifted on warm updrafts.

Then he sighted a rider on a black horse. Excitement fluttered through his entire body.

No mistaking the man or the steed. Fedeles and Firaj tore across the fields of wildflowers and took the ragged, narrow path up Crown Hill in a heartbeat.

Ariz dropped from the wind, landing in human form and strode forward to meet them.

Fedeles dismounted gracefully and rushed to embrace Ariz. After wind and clouds, Fedeles's body felt radiantly warm. Ariz leaned into him, basking in the feel of his strong arms and broad chest. It was so good to hold him and be held in return.

"How is it that you can look more handsome every time I see you?" Fedeles's breath was warm against his ear. He drew back a little to study Ariz. "The gold lining of that gray cloak suits you."

"Really?" Ariz smiled. He rarely cared about such things, but he'd chosen this lining for his cloak because he loved the way Fedeles looked lying naked across gold silk.

Fedeles nodded, and his gaze roved over the greenery and scattered, burned stonework surrounding them. He appeared hesitant at first, but after studying the grounds, he knelt and picked up a piece of blackened, cracked stone.

"Do you remember this?" Fedeles asked.

Ariz crouched beside him and brushed a little of the ash from the stone's surface. The head of a blackened bas-relief stallion stared up at Ariz. He grinned.

"Isn't this the marker we used when we left notes for one another here?" Ariz asked.

"It is." Fedeles traced the stallion's mane and his smile grew. "There's a whisper of life sleeping within it still."

"A spell?" Ariz asked.

"More of a wish for a loved one's well-being." Fedeles held his gaze for a moment, then very gently returned the carving to the ground. He sighed and then said, "Thank you for leading me here today. I drained so much power from the land and the ruins here. I've actually been afraid to revisit."

Fedeles didn't explain why, but Ariz understood. Fedeles possessed the strength to rip this entire hill down to rubble, but his sympathy tempered him. He was a rare man who could care for even humble rocks and regret doing them harm.

"The hill already feels stronger now. Like it's only sleeping." Fedeles closed his eyes and pressed his hands into the warm earth. "Little streams of raw magic are still flowing into this place."

"So, it's recovering?" Ariz touched a clump of clover. A grasshopper sprang away with a flash of bright green wings.

"Yes. It might take years, but the wounds are mending. It's growing stronger." Fedeles smiled at Ariz, and there seemed to be a greater meaning in his gaze. "Its nature hasn't changed. If anything, it's growing more beautiful."

Ariz nodded. Crown Hill was resilient, indomitable, like Fedeles himself.

"It reminds me of you." Fedeles's words startled Ariz and then embarrassed him.

He gave a soft laugh and Fedeles frowned.

"I'm serious—" Fedeles began, but Ariz cut him off with a kiss.

"I know. I was laughing because I had the same thought about you," Ariz admitted.

Fedeles looked somewhat bashful, but all the more alluring for it.

"Is there anything else you'd like to do while we're here?" Fedeles asked.

Ariz swung his cloak from his shoulders and spread it out over the ground for them to share. "Lie with me and watch the clouds for a while, and then I'll decide."

EPILOGUE
ATREAU

Atreau paced beneath a row of cherry trees, listening to the voices drifting from the open windows of the Grunito townhouse. He'd promised himself that he was done with a life of spying. Even so, he edged up onto the stones of a raised flower bed to steal a glimpse of the people gathered inside.

Statuesque and clothed in gold, Lady Grunito still presented as imposing a figure as Atreau remembered from his youth—though now he noticed how much more silver colored her once jet-black hair and the lines of concern carved into her stern face. When she turned her gaze to study Narsi, both sorrow and tenderness shook the hard line of her mouth.

Narsi stood casually and spoke in subdued tones, appearing unconcerned. It was a sharp contrast from the night before, when he'd been shaking from nerves as he gathered the letters and documents that Timoteo had passed along to him. Now the truth of his birth and his birthright lay neatly spread out on Lady Grunito's onyx-inlaid desk.

Nestor Grunito picked up a document, peered at it through his spectacles, and then smiled.

"Isandro had a beautiful signature," he commented to his mother. "Did he draw at all?"

Lady Grunito glanced to him and nodded. When she returned her attention to Narsi, Atreau thought that her stern expression had softened even more.

"It will not be an easy thing, you understand?" Lady Grunito asked.

"When have the Earls of Anacleto ever feared a challenge?" Nestor responded, but he wasn't the one Lady Grunito addressed.

Narsi straightened and lifted his chin a little. Even dressed in the simple clothes of a master physician, he looked striking and resolute. With the warm afternoon light illuminating the angles of his face, his resemblance to that radiant stained-glass portrait of his father was unmistakable.

"I know it can't be done easily, but I'm not afraid to try," Narsi replied.

Lady Grunito sighed and wiped her hand across her eyes.

"Atreau!" The shout drowned out whatever response Lady Grunito offered Narsi and pulled Atreau's attention across the grounds to Sabella. He hopped down from the flower bed and strode out to meet her before anyone in the study could chance to notice him eavesdropping.

"Atreau?" Sabella called once more but then caught sight of him and waved.

She wore a mix of red Haldiim vestments and Cadeleonian riding leathers that accentuated her lean arms and toned legs. She also appeared to be sober—all of which was a marked improvement from when they'd first departed Cieloalta. Then, she'd sported numerous superficial injuries from her battles against mordwolves and guardsmen. In addition, Suelita's decision to take up with Bahiim Esfir had left Sabella surly and intent upon moving to Anacleto, where she felt she might be more appreciated. She had not been wrong and was currently swept up in a romance with an vivacious Haldiim woman her own age.

Sabella thrust a letter out to him.

"News from Jacinto, I think," she said.

"What courier knew to find me here?" Atreau frowned—suspicion still came to him as a habit—then he remembered Sabella's new lady love and grinned. "Or am I reaping the rewards of you winning the heart of a postmistress?"

Sabella offered him a self-satisfied smile in response. Atreau slid the bulging letter into his coat pocket. He craned his head, hoping to glimpse Narsi, Nestor or Lady Grunito in the study. Lady Grunito and Nestor had already acknowledged Narsi as a member of the Grunito family. Timoteo's and Elezar's support of him had ensured that. The real concern now was whether Lady Grunito would publicly recognize Narsi as Isandro's heir. Would Nestor actually step down in favor of him? If he did, then what?

A Haldiim man inheriting a Cadeleonian title would doubtless face opposition and criticism from all sides. Narsi was charismatic and accomplished, but his allies in Anacleto were not yet numerous. Few people even knew of him beyond the Grunito family, his reticent aunt, and a few proud mentors.

Atreau watched a finch alight in the branches of the cherry tree. Out of habit he glanced sidelong to see if there wasn't a cat stalking it from the shadows. A couple of fat puppies rolled over each other, unaware of anything else around them.

Atreau sighed and kicked at the ground.

What Narsi needed, he thought, was an agent working on his behalf to build his reputation and remove his enemies. Atreau stopped himself before his mind ran further along those lines.

He'd come to Anacleto for a fresh start. He did not want to sink back into a mire of manipulation, lies and murder. And even if he tried to endure it for Narsi's sake, he didn't possess the vast web of connections here that he had called upon in Cieloalta. Nor could he effortlessly recreate or move among a collection of agents, informants, flunkies and pawns. Ever since Fedeles exposed him as an agent serving the Cadeleonian king, his name had become synonymous with intrigue. Thankfully, the revelation saved him from charges of treason—and the noose—but it had also ended

his career as a spy. Even the broadsheets in Anacleto had publicized various accounts of his misdeeds and adventures.

On the bright side, his infamy ignited a surge in sales of his memoirs.
Royalties from his Haldiim publisher already made up for the funds he'd
invested in Spider's and Inissa's Salt Island hostel. He briefly wondered if
he could convince Inissa to provide a few illustrations for the next edition.

Sabella kicked Atreau's foot, interrupting his brooding.

"Come on, open it and share," Sabella told him. "Let's hear what
Ambassador Jacinto has to say about Yuan."

Atreau had nearly forgotten the letter in his concern for Narsi's political situation.

He retrieved Jacinto's letter and, using his belt knife, slit open the
silk-stitched envelope. Pages of Jacinto's excited script burst from the
fabric confines. Green, red and violet ink blossomed over pastel paper,
and a heady perfume wafted up.

Atreau began reading aloud to Sabella, and both of them laughed at
Jacinto's excited tales of his discoveries and exploits in Yuan. He'd reunit-
ed with the Yuanese dignitaries who'd fled Cadeleon earlier. The group
of them seemed to have grown closer for their experiences. Reading
through the amusing descriptions of opulent ceremonies, bawdy festi-
vals and quiet evenings "drinking smoke" in the company of musicians,
Atreau noted growing insight and compassion in Jacinto's writing. By the
end of the letter, Atreau wasn't entirely surprised to learn that Jacinto had
taken part in an arduous pilgrimage to entreat the heavens for plentiful
rain. Though, this being Jacinto, of course the pilgrimage culminated in
a two-day orgy honoring all six Yuanese deities of love and fertility.

Atreau laughed and Sabella snorted.

"I'm glad he's all right," Sabella said.

Atreau agreed. He'd felt guilty for the part he played in having Jacinto appointed as ambassador and essentially exiling him to Yuan. But he'd
known that so long as one of Sevanyo's sons remained in Cadeleon, there
would be nobles and clergymen using him to justify rebellions against
Fedeles. Neither Oasia nor Lliro would allow such a threat to persist. So
this had been the compromise that spared Jacinto's life.

His own withdrawal to Anacleto hadn't been that much different. The
less Oasia saw of him, the safer he was. He hadn't brokered a princely
salary for himself. But he'd been spared the misery of a sea voyage.

City bells rang out the changing hour and Sabella strode off to tutor
Nestor's three rambunctious children in dance and swordplay. The puppies that had been frolicking on the lawn trotted alongside her. Atreau
briefly marveled at how oddly wholesome the scene appeared. A few

months ago, blood had dripped from her sword as she slit men's throats. Now she paused to rub a fat puppy's belly and smiled warmly at the footman who greeted her in passing.

Could people leave the paths of violence and villainy so simply—resolve themselves one day and then, step by step, just walk away from it? *Be true to yourself and your destiny will be of your own making.*

That was what his mother had said, but back then he'd felt uneasy about who he truly was: a hopeless boy at the mercy of anyone more powerful. Only now did he realize how absurd he'd been, abandoning his aspirations, placing himself in the service of dukes, princes and kings, all while telling himself that he was escaping the fate of being used. Cut free of influence and power, he found his prospects unlimited. He was free to choose his own course now, if only he maintained the determination to do so.

He thought he might write something this evening. Perhaps a few more pages of his latest memoir. Maybe a little poem to amuse Narsi.

As he considered, he gazed across the grounds, taking in two old apple trees. Their flowers had already fallen. What fruit they would bear had yet to be seen. Then he remembered he'd first met Narsi beneath those trees. Traded his secrets and wealth for a single chaste kiss. What a foolish young man he'd been, and yet . . . how happy he felt returning to that most foolish of beginnings and seeing it through.

As if conjured by his memory, Narsi came striding from between the apple trees. He caught sight of Atreau and smiled. They both started toward each other and met beside a display of mounding red roses.

"Were you waiting for me?" Narsi asked.

"Yes, for all my life," Atreau replied glibly.

Narsi rolled his eyes and laughed.

"After so long a vigil, you must be famished." Narsi took his arm. "Come, I'll treat you to a proper Haldiim lunch across the Ammej Bridge."

Atreau walked alongside him. If they were taking lunch outside the Grunito house, then Atreau guessed Narsi wanted to talk with him in private. He waited until they'd passed through the gates of the townhouse and joined the bustle of the open streets.

"Lady Grunito came to a decision concerning the matter?" Atreau asked.

"She did." Narsi's smile faded, but only a little. "On the new year, she and Nestor will formally acknowledge me as Isandro's son. My mother will be recorded as his legal wife."

"Good on them." Atreau had suspected that they would do right by Narsi. The Grunito family could seem reckless and rude, but when it

504   MASTER OF RESTLESS SHADOWS

came to championing justice—even when it challenged their interests—they rose to the occasion.

"Hmm," Narsi murmured. Concern creased his brows. Atreau guessed he was already thinking about the disputes ahead of him.

They strolled along the walkway, passing groups of fruit vendors who called out the names of succulent berries in Cadeleonian, Haldiim, Labaran and Mirogothic. Their voices rose and fell among the shouts of riders and news sellers, like jangling melodies. A little farther along they passed two women in vivid red dresses. One waved a fan of brilliant Yuanese feathers at Atreau. The other attempted to entice Narsi with strings of fine silver beads from Usane.

They turned down a quiet lane where booksellers sheltered amidst print shops. The smell of ink drifted in the air, but beyond it, Atreau could pick out the distinct perfume of adhil bread frying in a distant eatery.

"There are so many changes that I want to make," Narsi said. "Laws ensuring equality between Haldiim and Cadeleonians. Abolishing the practice of shunning people as *heram*. Legal rights and protections for adari lovers. Public access to secular education. Not to mention a unified system for waste that isn't just dumping chamber pots in the river."

"You'll build us a perfect world if all the bigots and idiots would just let you institute a citywide plumbing code," Atreau commented. They'd discussed so many of these matters on the journey from Cieloalta that Atreau couldn't help but enjoy teasing him. Not because he dismissed Narsi's plans, but because his high-minded idealism always included the entirely mundane concerns that eluded many governing lords. Narsi could talk about maintaining human dignity and installing sewer pipes with the same awareness of how each impacted people's lives.

"You'll thank me the next time we're crawling through some tunnel and feeling assured about the clearances and the makeup of the condensation dripping down on us," Narsi responded.

"No doubt I will." Atreau paused to look through the open door of a book shop and note that several copies of his own books stood proudly displayed and asking a very nice price. He ducked back out of the shop just as Narsi turned around, noticing his absence.

"Oh, remind me to find a word that rhymes with toilet for a poem I'm thinking of writing tonight," Atreau said.

"Boil it. Soil it," Narsi provided, but a little absently. He was clearly still troubled by the prospect of becoming the heir to an earldom.

Atreau walked beside him, giving him time to decide on what he wanted to say. They left the printshops behind and strolled by bakeries and candy shops.

"I'm going to face quite a bit of opposition," Narsi said. "Nestor and I discussed it for a good while." He dropped his gaze from Atreau as if his polished boots had suddenly become fascinating.

"I can't hope to win everyone over by just arguing them down," Narsi said.

Atreau started to reassure him about his superior ability to argue, but then an uneasiness washed through him. Narsi clearly wanted to ask something of him, but was nervous.

"I think I may need your help," Narsi said, and he raised his head, his expression hopeful and worried at once.

Atreau's stomach clenched. He wasn't a fool. He knew exactly where his greatest value lay for a man with magnificent designs for the world.

"I'd pay you—" Narsi began, but Atreau was afraid to hear him out—afraid that he'd agree regardless of what it would do to him.

"Narsi, I . . . I don't think I can." Atreau forced the words out. "I love you, but I just don't have it in me anymore—"

"You can't write?" Narsi stopped and studied Atreau with alarm. "Then what are all those pages that I've already read? Why would you need to find rhymes for the word toilet?"

Atreau stared back at Narsi. For a moment both of them stood in mutual confusion.

"What are you asking me?"

"I want to be your patron," Narsi said. "What did you think I was asking you to do?

"You want to be my patron?" Atreau repeated as the full implication sank in. "You're offering to support my writing?"

"Yes." Narsi looked shy. "I've thought a great deal about what you said to me at the Candioro Theater. That stories—even pure flights of fancy—can win people's hearts and change their minds. A book, a play, even a poem, and especially a song can bring people together. Make them laugh or cry. At the same time, they can let us see matters from each other's points of view. That's exactly what we need. And your writing . . . I love it so much, you know."

Effervescent happiness bubbled through Atreau. He'd wanted this all his life. Not merely the money, but someone who genuinely believed in the worth of his work. Someone who valued those stories he shared with them.

How stupid to think that Narsi would want him for a spy. It wouldn't even occur to him to resort to blackmail and backstabbing to win an argument. No, Narsi would aim for a far greater victory. Narsi would strive to truly change his opponents' minds. If pure reason wouldn't move them, then he'd bring his arguments to bear through song, art and litera-ture. He'd make his ideals light up stages and fill bookshelves.

"But if you don't want to . . ." Narsi trailed off, at a loss after Atreau's apparent refusal.

"I most definitely, absolutely and wholeheartedly accept your pa-tronage!" Atreau couldn't keep from beaming.

Narsi raised his brows in question.

"I panicked for a moment there," Atreau admitted.

Narsi relaxed and gave a soft laugh. "Why on earth would you panic over a patronage?"

"Because I'm an ass sometimes." Atreau threw his arm around Narsi's shoulder and pulled him close. He lowered his voice. "But rest assured, from here on out I'll be *your* ass."

Glossary of People, Places & Terms

A

Alizadeh—Bahiim mystic, uncle (by marriage) to Kiram.

Amabilo—Sacrist serving the Shard of Heaven, previously one of Timoteo Grunito's chapel teachers.

Anacleto—Port city in the south of Cadeleon. Center of Haldiim culture and power.

Ariz Plunado—Stripped of nobility along with the entire Plunado family, has since made his living as a sword and dance instructor. Served the Quemanor household but was sent to Clara Odalis after being exposed as one of Hierro Fueres's enthralled assassins. Now does what he can to pass information on to Fedeles, Atreau and Narsi.

Atreau Inerio Vediya—Fourth son of Baron Nifayo, underclassman to Prince Jacinto Sagrada. Author and spy. Attended the Sagrada Academy and became a member of the Hellions.

B

Batteo Ciceron—Captain of South Gate guards. Fedeles's lover. Assassinated on Hierro's orders.

Bahiim—Holy order of religious practice adhered to by members of the Haldiim and Irabiim peoples as well as a segment of the Labaran frog-wife population.

Berto Rene—Religious scholar and Narsi's childhood friend. Serves Father Timoteo.

Bhadia Rid-Itf—Bahiim mystic who fought alongside the Savior. She is said to have taken on the form of a mare, with which she carried the Savior and the Shroud of Stone into the heart of the demon armies.

C

Candioro Theater—Theater and troupe supported by Jacinto Sagrada.

Celina (Celino) Plunado—Ariz Plunado's niece, though she maintains the pretense of being a boy. She is the elder twin daughter of Delfia Plunado and Hierro Fueres.

Chay—Yuanese herbal stimulant, often taken as a drink.

Cieloalta—Capital of Cadeleon.

Cire—Labaran witch and close friend to Skellan. Keeps rats as familiars. Her favorite being a golden rat called Queenie.

Clara Odalis—Second daughter and youngest child of the Duke of Gavado, Count Zacarrio Odalis's widow.

Cocuyo Helio—Twin brother of Enevir; currently in Prince Jacinto's entourage. Former Sagrada Academy student.

Crown Hill—a.k.a. Wadi Tel: "Guardian Hill" in Haldiim. Defenders' stronghold during The Savior's battle against the demon lords.

D

Delfia Plunado—Ariz's sister and maid to Oasia Quemanor.

Donamillo Urracon—Scholar of natural law at Sagrada Academy. Used Fedeles Quemanor's body to house a Haldiim curse before taking possession of Fedeles entirely. Defeated by Kiram Kir-Zaki.

Dommian—Guard in the Quemanor household. Enthralled by Hierro Fueres and used as an assassin. Killed by Ariz and Delfia.

Duera—Painkiller and sedative derived from a common flower.

E

Elenna Ortez—Oasia Quemanor's nineteen-year-old cousin and lady-in-waiting.

Elezar Grunito—Third son of the Earl and Lady Grunito of Anacleto. Member of the Hellions when he attended Sagrada Academy. Current lover and champion of Count Radulf.

Enevir Helio—Twin brother of Cocuyo Helio, member of Jacinto's entourage. Strong ties to Irabiim clans. Uses a cane.

Esfir Kir-Naham—Pharmacist; Querra's daughter and Mother Arezoo Kir-Naham's niece.

Espirdro—Atreau's third brother. Goes by the nickname of Spider. Currently owns the majority of the Fat Goose Tavern.

F

Faro Numes—Minister of the Royal Navy.

Fedeles Quemanor—Cousin to Javier Tornesal and Prince Sevanyo; Duke of Rauma.

Firaj—Fedeles's black gelding; formerly belonged to Kiram Kir-Zaki.

G

Gael Sagrada—Prince Sevanyo's third son. Royal commander of the navy; lost at sea.

Genimo Plunado—Student of Donamillo Urracon and friend to Hierro Fueres. His crimes against Fedeles Quemanor lead to his death and caused the Plunado family to be stripped of lands, wealth and titles.

Goat, the—see Vanji.

H

Hallowed Kings—A rotation of three royal souls who maintain the wards protecting the Shard of Heaven. They currently are: **Gachello** (born in 1191, crowned in 1229, died in 1255), **Yusto** (born in 1205, crowned in 1255, died in 1275) and **Leozar** (born in 1255, crowned in 1275, died in 1305).

Hellions—Band of outstanding and audacious students at the Sagrada Academy. Most infamous members of the group were Javier Tornesal, Elezar Grunito, Atreau Vediya and Kiram Kir-Zaki.

Heram—"Shunned one" in Haldiim. The state of having been formally shunned by society.

Hierro Fueres—Heir to the dukedom of Gavado.

Hilthorn Radulf (Skellan)—Ruler of Radulf County in Labara; powerful witch. Battled and destroyed a demon lord.

Hylanya Radulf—Younger sister of Count Radulf; also a powerful witch. Prefers cats as familiars.

I

Inissa—Artist. Mistress to Prince Jacinto; was once Atreau's lover; now involved with Spider.

Irabiim—Nomadic Tribe closely related to the Haldiim. They share a common ancestry, language and religion.

Irsea—Last Bahiim ancient who guarded the Circle of Wisteria. Murdered, but her spirit remains in the bodies of her familiars. Her murder remains unsolved.

Isandro Grunito—Dead; firstborn heir to the Earldom of Anacleto.

J

Jacinto Sagrada—Prince, poet, deadbeat. Fourth son of Sevanyo Sagrada. Atreau Vediya's former upperclassman and friend.

Javier Tornesal—Hellion, Bahiim and guardian of a sacred shajdi. Former Duke of Rauma, Javier converted to the Bahiim religion (as Alizadeh's student) and was declared a heretic and excommunicated. He fled into exile with his lover, Kiram Kir-Zaki. He currently serves Count Radulf as his astrologer. He is Fedeles Quemanor's cousin.

Juleo Sagrada—King of Cadeleon at the outset of this book. Born in 1275, crowned in 1305.

K

Kaweh—Bitter but stimulating drink popular among the underclasses of Haldiim and picked up by Cadeleonian intellectuals.

Kiram Kir-Zaki—Haldiim genius from very wealthy and respected family of candymakers. Fled into exile with Javier but now is master mechanist in Count Radulf's court.

L

Labara—Protectorate nation of Cadeleon. Divided into four counties. Radulf County, the largest and most northerly, has recently broken away from Cadeleon to become fully independent. Famous for roses, witchcraft and their great love of butter.

Ladislo Bayezar—Nobleman. Attended Sagrada Academy. Supports Sevanyo but is at odds with Atreau because of his association with Procopio Nolasar. Believes Atreau abducted Suelita Estaban.

Lliro Vediya—Atreau's eldest brother; attached to the Ministry of the Navy from a young age. Heir to the barony.

M

Marisol Plunado—Ariz's niece and younger twin daughter of Delfia Plunado and Hierro Fueres.

Meztli—Mythical demon enthralled by the Brand of Obedience by the Savior. Meztli harnessed the power of Crown Hill to forge his ruby shields, which protected the Savior's forces during the Battle of the Shard of Heaven.

Miro Reollos—Oasia's first husband and Atreau's lover, killed by Elezar after attacking Atreau in a jealous rage.

Morisio Cavada—Atreau's school friend, from a merchant family. Scientifically minded, sails on the *Red Witch*.

Moteado—Ariz's old dappled stallion.

Mother Kir-Naham (Arezoo)—Owns a pharmacy in the Haldiim District of Cieloalta. Holds the title of Honored Mother, though she has no biological children. Aunt of Esfir; friend and sister-in-law to Querra Kir-Naham.

Muerate—Extremely deadly poison, leaves a black scar on the very few people who recover from its effects.

N

Narsi Hilario Lif-Tahm—Master physician in the Quemanor household, attached to Holy Father Timoteo.

Nillo—Acolyte serving Father Timoteo in the Quemanor household.

Nube—Atreau's gray stallion.

Nugalo Sagrada—Royal bishop. Prince Sevanyo's younger brother.

Numes Yago—Captain in the royal bishop's guard in the capital.

O

Oasia Quemanor—Wife of Fedeles, widow of Lord Reollos, eldest daughter of Duke of Gavado.

Ojito—Nugalo Sagrada's illegitimate son.

Old Roots—a.k.a. Old Routes. The tunnels dug by Haldiim as hiding places and means of escape from the city during the first purge, three hundred years ago. Most have collapsed, but some are still used by smugglers and black marketeers.

Ollivar Falario—Elezar's former underclassman; playwright and member of Prince Jacinto's entourage.

Oyoon—Yuanese ambassador. Friend to Prince Jacinto.

P

Paulino Fueres—Duke of Gavado.

Pepylla Dacio—Operator of the Green Door, loyal to Jacinto.

Peraloro River—River that divides the capital and runs east to the sea.

Procopio Nolasar—Courtier to Jacinto.

Q

Querra Kir-Naham—Cadeleonian convert to the Bahiim religion, widowed. In charge of kitchen gardens in the Quemanor household. Mother of Esfir.

R

Rafie Kir-Zaki—Haldiim physician and Narsi's mentor. Married to Alizadeh Lif-Moussu.

Red Stallion—Sword house where illegal and legal duels are held for cash prizes. Members are infamous for their brutality and immorality, but the public duels always draw huge crowds.

Remes—Royal bishop's heir and Sevanyo Sagrada's second son. Infatuated with Clara Odalis.

Rinza—Riquo's sister. Spindly Knife Market informant, employed by Atreau.

Riossa Grunito—Painter. Wife of Nestor Grunito, daughter of a city judge.

Riquo—Rinza's brother. Thief employed by Atreau.

Royal Bishop— Head of the Cadeleonian Church. Position traditionally held by the king's second son. See Nugalo Sagrada.

S

Sabella Calies—Swordswoman. Friend to Atreau. Her uncle owns the Red Stallion sword house where she trains and competes. Famous among the Haldiim in Anacleto; romanticized versions of her biography have been made into a number of books and stage plays there.

Sacred Groves—Bahiim holy places comprised of rings of ancient trees or other plant life. These include the Circle of Wisteria, Circle of Crooked Pine, Circle of Red Oak, Circle of the Willow Grove, and Circle of Long Kelp.

Sahalia Kir-Khu—Haldiim physician who attended Narsi's birth. She later relocated to the Salt Islands at Father Timoteo's prompting.

Salt Islands—Chain of volcanic islands south of Cadeleon. Famous for the Butterfly Temple and also hot springs.

Savior (the/Our)—Born Tormen Cadeleon. Warrior chief and mystic who battled the second invasion of demon lords alongside a coalition of other warlords, witches, Bahiim, Old Gods and mystics. He sacrificed himself in his final assault against the demons at the Peraloro River, where the spell he unleashed—the Shroud of Stone—resulted in the Shard of Heaven being formed. With the defeat of the demons and Cadeleon's death, a cult sprang up. This eventually grew into the Cadeleonian Holy Church.

Sevanyo Sagrada—Crown prince, born 1297.

Skellan—see "Hilthorn Radulf."

Sparanzo—Son of Fedeles and Oasia. Secretly fathered by Atreau.

Suelita Estaban—Cryptographer, mathematician.

T

Tariq—Black cat that shares Narsi's rooms. (Name means "whisper" in Haldiim).

Timoteo—Holy Father, older brother of Elezar and Nestor Grunito.

Trueno—One of four Sagrada siblings who joined the Savior's army. He became the Savior's personal guard. He is said to have been transformed into a giant eagle, and as such, shielded the Savior from above and cleared his path to the heart of the demon army. Trueno's nephew became the first recognized king of the nation of Cadeleon.

U

Usane—Kingdom to the west of Cadeleon. Known for metalwork and closely guarded glassmaking techniques.

V

Vanji—see The Goat. Leader of a Haldiim ring of thieves and smugglers.

W

Waarihivu—Mythic sect of realm-traversing sorcerers at war with demons; used the Black Fire to destroy whole worlds. Most members of the sect were hunted down and killed or converted by the Bahiim.

Wadi Lif-Tahm—Narsi's mother; died when he was twenty-one. Lived as *heram* ("shunned one") until her mother died when Narsi was ten. Returned to the Haldiim community when he was twelve, though many elders refused to recognize her.

Wonena, Lord—Supporter of the royal bishop. In conflict with Fedeles over upkeep of shared roadways.

X
Xalvadar Sagrada—Prince Sevanyo's heir.
Xavan—Sailor; sometimes-informant for Atreau.

Y
Yah-muur—Old God, known as the Fawn Goddess, also the Summer Doe. Said to take on a new body and shed her old horns every time she is slain. She is believed to be one of the four chosen companions who unleashed the Shroud of Stone and defeated the armies of the demon lords.
Yara Nur-Aud—Haldiim actress and part-time agent for Atreau.

Z
Zacarrio Odalis—Count. Clara's recently deceased husband. Supporter of the royal bishop.

ABOUT THE AUTHOR

Ginn Hale lives with her lovely wife in the Pacific Northwest, where she spends the many cloudy days observing fungi. She whiles away the rainy evenings tinkering with words. Her first novel, *Wicked Gentlemen*, won the Spectrum Award for best novel. She is also a Lambda Literary Award finalist and Rainbow Award winner.

Her most recent publications include *Lord of the White Hell, Champion of the Scarlet Wolf* and *the Rifter Trilogy: The Shattered Gates, The Holy Road, His Sacred Bones.*

She can be reached through her website, www.ginnhale.com, as well as on Twitter. Her Instagram account, however, is largely a collection of botanical photos . . . so, be warned.

CONTENT WARNING

Characters in this book fight against racism, sexism, homophobia and transphobia. When I have dramatized these conflicts, I've done my best not to make the scenes graphic and I've tried to avoid real-world insults and slurs, which may be triggering. Several protagonists are survivors of sexual assault. However, there are no scenes depicting sexual assault in the book. Passing reference is made by characters to abuse in their childhoods, but again no scenes are dramatized. Some characters in the book also deal with depression and thoughts of self-harm.

The battles described are largely in keeping with a fantasy adventure. There are curses, sword fights and assassinations. Bloodshed, injuries and deaths are dramatized, but I have shied away from gratuitous gore.

Above all, I've done my best to write a fun, inclusive story full of triumph, magic and joy.

—Ginn

ALSO BY GINN HALE

The Cadeleonians Series:
Lord of the White Hell Book One
Lord of the White Hell Book Two
Champion of the Scarlet Wolf Book One
Champion of the Scarlet Wolf Book Two
Master of Restless Shadows Book One
Master of Restless Shadows Book Two

The Rifter Series:
The Shattered Gates
The Holy Road
His Sacred Bones

Wicked Gentlemen
Counterfeit Viscount
The Long Past and other stories
Maze-Born Trouble
Feral Machines—Tangle (Anthology)
Touching Sparks—Hell Cop (Anthology)
Such Heights—Hell Cop Two (Anthology)
Things Unseen and Deadly—Irregulars (Anthology)
Swift and the Black Dog—Charmed and Dangerous (Anthology)

9 781935 560654